Soul Skin

By; Jan Porter

www.InspiredSoulWorks.com

Blessings on
your Journey

♡ Jan .

Soul Skin By; Jan Porter www.InspiredSoulWorks.com

Editorial Assistance: Sandra Ackerman, James aka Buster Fykes, Robert H. Porter

Cover Design: Jan Porter

Cover Photo Model: the amazing; Marthi aka 'Mu' Irene Porter-Crowley

Disclaimer: This novel is a work of spirit world fiction. If any of the characters or stories ring similar to yours and you feel offense, I ask, where would we be without those luscious life journey lessons? We are all branches of the same tree, interconnected and all of our journeys are sacred; cherish them

"I love you not because of who you are,

but because of who I am when I am with you."

Roy Croft

This story is dedicated to: Gloria Irene Porter

"I am always with you, Mom. We summer camped, magical ice storm watched and wooey woo explored. Together we walked through the shadows of life and jig danced into the light.

With loving gratitude to my family: spirit world son James, J.D., Mu and Dad. "I kiss smooch love you on left cheek, right cheek and forehead too, then fill you with loving Mom angel love, inside out, top to bottom, here and there and everywhere throughout all of time."

To all of my original Wild Women Soul Sisters both past, present and those yet to be and inspirational sisterhood spirit world muses.

"One woman is a tiny divine spark in a timeless sisterhood tapestry collective; all of us are Wild Women."

Each soul path is a divine unique fingerprint that adds to the beautiful cosmic tapestry. Life is a series of defining moments, cross roads and gateways opening. Always and in all ways follow the heartbeat of your own soul path of most light and love.

Much love and inspiration to all, who seek and find their authentic wild natures, consciously choose to forgo a traditional lifestyle for an authentic spiritual journey.

All of you continue to amaze and inspire others

"She takes my hand and leads me along paths
I would not have dared explore alone."
Maya V. Patel

"I pray you . . . your play needs no excuse."
William Shakespeare

Chapter 1 ~ Gran

Grizzly Bears!

Big, brown, fuzzy grizzly bear slippers on her feet.

Alone in the dark of midnight, Navi cocooned against harsh northern snow with computer glow and blue haunting winter's full moon illumination streaming in through the window.

Legs splayed wide open, computer keyboard between legs and computer mouse on right knee. A mouse can work just about anywhere you place it. Wind slammed snow spatters against the old cottage farm windows, rattling wooden doors and seeking entry. The flip and click of mindless hours of solitaire's no-brain semi-conscious alpha state had months ago replaced meditation and prayer: escapist Zen. Lately, OM-sleep remained elusive as frantic thoughts ran amuck, much to the profound annoyance of Stephen. Then again, pretty much everything about Navi annoyed the crap out of Stephen. Should he wake now, his burning glare would first question the ungodly hour, then upon registering just how late it was, wrinkle nose in disgust, grunt and guffaw followed with a terse, 'Jesus fucking Christ Navi, go to bed!!!'

Shrugged shoulders rolled off the imagined jab. Solitaire worked; late night alone space away from him.

Perhaps it was the onslaught of menopause, of early aging internal changes part in parcel with mood swings clashing with his random waves of hostility.

"No. You're still an Arsehole!"

Rubbing an aching wrist after long hours of click, click, click, scroll, click, click and scroll of computer mouse, Navi grinned 'Carpal Tunnel Syndrome from Solitaire could make a good work related insurance claim.'

Abruptly flipping monstrous bear slippers off with one hand then tucking feet lotus style up and inside her ratty old purple homey housecoat, 'How is it possible to have such cold feet with monstrous slippers and three pairs of forty degree below zero socks on?'

Taking visual inventory of donned sleepwear consisting of three pairs of socks, flannelette pajamas and an old tattered purple bathrobe, yet still cold. A shiver crawled up a petite frame, rattling spine that drew attention to where long wet auburn braids lay like ice packs, still wet from a bath three hours ago. 'I should go and get one of the kid's toques. I could blow dry, but then by morning I'd look like a spastic male lion that has had his tongue stuck in a light socket.' A pre-menopausal period cramp remnant jabbed then faded.

An old re-occurring childhood argument flashed in internal hearing range of Mother's stern school night directive rippling a shock wave through an already strained nervous system. 'Okay, okay, okay. Yes, Mother, I'm avoiding sleep. Well, if you were here, I would dive into your arms and sob. You would comfort me, tell me with maternal warmth and knowing that everything was, is fine.' She would not, simply not a nurturing demonstrative maternal type and the truth forged a lonely tear bulge welling up within that balled stuck mid throat then dissipated in disassociation. A religious doctrine and minister fearing soul, a life lived in anxiety of what Mother's church cronies thought. Restless chaotic thoughts cycling round and round later promised disturbing dreams. An inner haunting dark shadow skirted consciousness then faded. Stuffed away from waking mind, the predatory shadow often taunted when vulnerable.

It had been a taxing winter. Stephen's Neanderthal responses to Navi's want of communication and intimacy was; preverbal lower evolved primordial pig-male; 'you just need sex'.

'No Stephen, I don't need sex, I need to be made love to!'

Digging chilly hands into cozy old robe pockets, eyes scanned shadowy shapes of a loveless bedroom nest to the stranger in bed, called Stephen. It was hard to fathom that the sprawled out drooling stranger was wedded husband of some ten years. Marital stranger-dom. Mouth gaped open, Neanderthal Moron snored contentedly. A string of drool trickled down through a greying beard, drained downward scruffy scrawny neck and pooled below a bulging old man haired Adam's apple. Wrinkling nose in mixture of awe and aversion, Navi observed a puddle of slime forming in the pocket at the base of his throat. Odd looking at him now, as though for the first time in their long years together, only now consciously aware of an inner growing detachment from him and general house apathy. They had become strangers, roommates and distant acquaintances.

Navi swiveled the worn computer chair to comfortably fully view and observe the scrawny middle-aged old man that sprawled over the bed. 'Funny looking boy-man; still has all of his hair. Curious that it is still mostly a sandy blonde and not grey white like his beard; doesn't match, see Gran? Look! He's got those wild bushy black eye brows, a uni-brow that in no way of colour and texture matches hair or beard. Buy some hair dye mister. Gad dammed scrawny and gangly, well except for that potbelly; a bagel receptacle. Looks better with business clothes on because naked; looks Grinch.

Then there is that limp noodle. Look at it peeking out of the comforter. Hey, I do not insult under endowed men, but his is not just small, it does not want to salute me, ever! Un-circumcised, it mimics a tiny blind pudgy worm. I wonder if David Suzuki would be interested in its archaeological or biological origin. Maybe it is alien spawn. Maybe it will un-cocoon furl into an alien butterfly one day and flitter off to its own planet, to its own kind.

Some credit is due for annual lame romantic gestures, but more often than not, it feels like marital duty. 'Worse, it had occurred that he might just be giving enough to keep her in tow, committed and hoping. Long ago, at a loss of what to do to get his noodle aroused and stand at attention only to have him whimper and whine like a wounded child. What in the hell is that all about?'

Yes, there was something inherently missing, something passionate that had long disappeared, if it ever really was there. In fact, something profound had died during their wedding day. The last in synchronistic passion occurred the day before their wedding. They had known each other only two short months before marriage and blending families. What had she been thinking?

A resentment rose, 'Hmmm, yup, Marketing Art Department Head by week day, engrossed Metal Sculpture 'cum Artiste Extraordinaire' full time by evening and weekends to the exclusion of family or anything else that may divert his attention. Sigh.' So much distance had grown out of unspoken and unresolved issues into an abyss of emptiness. A chasm of unjustified too busy with work and kids pre-occupations and rationalizing excuses had grown thin.

Had she not been so naïve and blinded by the lure of want of traditional family, of value ideals, she would have a life less over worked, over loaded and Billy Holiday blues singing lonely. Not abnormal compared to other couples perhaps, but dammed empty. A wave of emotional exhaustion gave way under burdened shoulders and her gut imploded. Catching short, she consciously over ruled a forceful rising grief jab that shot into her chest cavity bulldogging throat vomit and spilled out of burning weary eyes.

'Matt has cancer', grief and fear echoed within and reverberated out into the cosmos.

Glancing at Stephen, consciously willing him to stay asleep, yet wishing a loving companion to awaken and offer comfort. Seeing no response to want and need of comfort only served to validate his disinterest of intimate relations or closeness of communication, which was on hold and would be for a long time to come. The frenzy and turmoil of normal day-to-day life with the added randomness of a cancer diagnosis just two weeks before Christmas had shoved *life* into a state of shocked paralysis. Instantly, all of his normal life attention had been abandoned, merely to collect dust on a faraway shelf and forgotten.

Choking back a mid-throat tear bundle, rivulets of anguish tears burned crimson cheeks and nostrils bubbled clear mucous. 'But it sure would be a lot easier if he would at least talk about things. It had to be at least a month maybe more. No, it had been much longer than that, before Thanksgiving.'

Hands rose to cover grieving eyes, as though Gran's photo on the bureau gazed with onlooker judging shame, mingling with inner guilt and utter loneliness. Silent sob waves ebbed, heaved and flowed followed with a deep sighing breath. Eyes and nose carelessly wiped with old robe sleeve.

Love is supposed to set your spirit and soul free. It was a waste of energy to seek intimacy where it was un-offered, she waited a miracle.

Differing paths had long become par for the course. Stephen barely speaking to his wife in over three months was common. Years of co-existing in the same house had grown his nasty mind game of subtle cruelty ruled home existence. A calm harmonious and confident mother and wife role was now consistently undermined and hearing of her latest indiscretion falling out of Stephens lips when amongst friends or family. Catching his prey off guard, smirking Neanderthal husband puffed out chest catching captive audiences off guard. Stealthily on cue, a cutting resentment filled remark about her abnormal spirit world communion, cut as a welder's torch cut into metal. A laser sharp bullet from a sniper's gun, "Oh, for Christ's sake Navi, it's just a joke!" Only joking was the usual justification empowered by both audience discomfort and Navi's vulnerabilities. Empowered and cowardice primal scathing jabs.

Occasionally a targeted audience would snicker in taking his side, catching humour while missing the powerful energetic hits. More often than not, a captive downcast audience sat quietly shifting uncomfortably waiting for tension to subside.

Had it not occurred to Stephen that rather than making Navi look as inept, odd and foolish as intended, the displays only served to demonstrate the cowardly arsehole that he had become? Hostility masked, as humorous wit was unfortunately not only a cowardice norm in his family culture, but had been a norm within her family as well. Navi quickly ascertained that traditional counselling approaches were lost upon her spouse and in taking a stand, he would lamely hand-flick a feign apology until the next time.

It was not so much a church community and public roasting, but a driving force behind those jabs in calculated intentional delivery that always rendered her impaled, and in the moment, she was unable to counter. Perhaps retaliation was too much bother; rather, she liked to think that she simply had more class. Somehow, it had to do with the topic of being different, of seeing and talking with spirits that hurt so deeply. The rationale for the hurt, aside from obvious church and public scorn, evaded her higher intelligent logic. Why should she care what others thought and said?

'Where does all of his hostility come from? Irksome shit.' A normal person might assume that he would be mature enough to talk about what is bothering him, but no! I have had moronic bosses pull that crap. They have you by the knickers; mortgaged up the gizzard and focused with putting food on the table, so acquiesce. But then again, in some families, it is just normal. Maybe he is simply daft but more than likely; he is just a primordial arsehole.' Yes, whenever family and friends visited, Stephen took on a role of jovial wonderful host, gifted artist, Picasso of our time and as a side role; martyr for putting up with Crazy Navi.

'Oh, there it is. I have that bugaboo ferreted out. That is another problem right there.' Despite all of her white-collar professional capabilities, some part of her must have actually agreed with the crazy inference and bought into it.

Navi had always felt different. How could she not? Most people have at least one inner critic and she could poke fun and mimic Mother unnervingly well. Mother had yet to come to terms with the 'wooey-woo' stuff. Navi 'saw' other worldly apparitions and Mothers responding disapproving anger flashes nailed her into silence. Often delivered so stealthily that no one else seemed to catch the exchange, yet succinct and always final. Mothers cutting looks also referenced Navi's failed relationships. Like Mother, Church community's truth was that the woman's daughter was different and Mother hated the knowing of this.

"God Navi why can't you just be a normal happily married woman? Why can you not just do what you are supposed to do?" It was Mother's exasperated Irish roots surfacing in the 'Jesus Christ Almighty' that hung in the air long after delivered, thus leaving daughter in an emotional whirlwind and wounded child shame rather than the grown honourable white-collared professional that she was. It royally pissed her off that this bugaboo was still within her making spiritual maturity a far off goal.

Navi was a dam good social worker because of this different seeing aspect of her being. She 'felt' what her clients felt, 'saw' dream like pictures or movie bits of their lives, saw ancestral and angelic images and heard their spirit people talking to them through inner ears. She often saw colours around people and places, sensing their experiences, memories and passionate emotions.

As a child, she preferred to be alone, adapted to and balanced a constant bombardment of imagery and sounds of foggy people not understood. It was here that she relaxed. Simply, it was a calm space and all around better place to be, quiet and peaceful. Away from the house when Mother was stressing over something or other and the fact that shit always rolls downhill, it was their natural order of how life was. Navi being the only daughter was more often than not, a targeted and unwitting dumping place. She had not yet grown beyond the habitual way of relating within the family dynamics or may have fortuned an a-ha moment in realizing that rather than there being something inherently wrong within, it was a family bad habit of it always landing in her soul.

What had yet to register in her adult conscious mind was the simple fact that the cause of the dumping was never actually about her at all; it was just a bad habit. It was of using another's obvious vulnerable sense of different-ness as an excuse to stress-dump. It did neither good. To anyone with common sense objectivity, let alone a spiritual master, it was an unwitting role that she and family fulfilled.

Approaching late forties, a serial monogamist rather than a one-life-time committed blissful marital partner, only further fuelled internal pressures of trying to be normal. She had to give it an absolute best shot. There were the kids to think of, so she ignored Stephen's shadow side as much as possible. In her mind's eye, during his angry and distant periods, he wore army fatigues, ignoring her. Yet beneath the surface a terrorist lurked; often-waiting months for an unsuspecting Navi target, to line up in his sites. Years of experience provided the knowing of what he was leading up to at any given point. It was a waste of time to try to avert through direct conversation and simply waited for his 'hit'.

BANG!!!!

A powerful force whacked the window above the computer, rattled then BANGED again, startling her bones. Howling north winds blasted against the old country house, she contracted her robe tighter against a cold draft. The forceful poltergeist whacked, rattled and banged on the other side of the house seeking entry. Eyes followed its sound trails, ready to take action against its unwanted intrusive demanding that her windows and doors give way. 'That is one hell of a wind; almost circular; not good.'

Unintelligent poltergeist wind whipped around the house pounding its fists on walls and windows, challenging frazzled nerves.

'There is something out there tonight, spooky, an entity, a spirit of some sort and not too bright of a boob.' Shifting into mother wolf alpha power, spine arched, attitudinally dismissing it with the flick of a hand. "On your way, whatever you are. Get your nuisance ass out of here and off to the light." It mildly zipped around the old farm cottage once again, less forceful now, from one window to the next in meek desperation. "NOW!!!" Heart pounding in annoyance, hesitating, waiting for a possible last challenge, willing to go higher into Arch Angel Michael mode, when hearing nothing more than the normal snowy wind, relaxed.

Yes, a consistent preference to be alone at home with kids, as opposed to being with others, the normal adults. The mysterious and elusive 'others' that Mother made reference to in word, body language and 'oh God have mercy on my soul for what I must endure in this woman child of mine' eye roll. Ah yes, a generational throw back to the Stepford Wives generation, the Leave it To Beaver and mother June Cleaver ideals imagery who ruined an entire generation of women's natural sense of wildness and uniqueness. Of course, in every neighbouhood, Gestapo-ish church ladies lived by the book whom were mind numbingly boring and bossy, wreaked havoc playing insidious mind games that inadvertently re-enforced male dominated with Hollywood idyllic visions.

'Ah, thank God for clients and kids. This I love.' Navi's pre-teen daughter Abby, was innately kind, loving, knew how to have fun and how to just be. She demonstrated that the apple did not fall too far from her mother's tree. Even as a babe, Abby demonstrated what she 'had'. It was their secret.

Thus it was that Navi lived in two worlds simultaneously, feeling lost in between and solely belonging in neither.

Mother, like millions of other Mom's in that era, learned a fifties' and sixties' version of parenting style that fell somewhere short of Queen Elizabeth and June Cleaver while in a pinch resorted to several glasses of sherry in stressful acquiescence to Stepford Wives ideology. Earnestly, they tried to protect their children from the social mayhem that was taking place in the outer world. Visions of a Black America rising against oppression imagery filling television screens in the fifties, terrified the woman who subsequently vowed to never step foot across the border, not even to shop in Buffalo.

'To succeed Navi, all you ought to be concerned with is marrying a good man who is job stable and a dam good provider. Your real job is to look after your man.' While the golden child academically achieved brother aimed for the corporate world, the others funneled into trades, the girl delegated to domestic care with the sole aim of being married off. Dismal failure scapegoat syndrome, Stephen was the second adult relationship and it was slipping away. Abby's father T.J. had chosen a whirlwind affluent lifestyle, T.J. was in the picture long enough to donate magical sperm and left only shadowed relationship grief. Recalling the glimpse of past was indeed a vague memory, another lifetime, 'someone else's lifetime', she dismissed following that trail of thought, too long ago and foreign to current existence.

Now, you may critically agree that Navi is a somewhat of a misfit and maybe you are cynical and summate that she is not a traditional dutiful wife by idyllic standards, with other worldly wooey-woo looming in her periphery and the relationship accomplishments or lack of and you may be right. Navi's life, it seemed, surmised an ugly duckling parable. How can one know where they do belong and with whom if they have yet to experience like soul and like mind in the physical world?

One man's nuisance junk, might just be another man's precious treasured divine twin soul mate. Living alone with escapist fantasies, clients and raising children while existing in a business world that was essentially foreign to an authentic nature fuelled a growing sense of homesickness that was yet to be understood let alone clearly articulated.

There was more.

A hibernating cocooned metaphysical nature lay dormant within her soul that impatiently awaited the light of day, for wings openly owned, embraced and shared. Aside from spirit communion with her long dead Grandmother, there were growing dreams and visions of far off magical sacred places, mystical adventures, of night journeys that left a vague elusive want and longing of more. More so, occasional images and ancient spirited shawl clad female presences whispered comfort, calling her to another worldly existence. Their essence vague, yet hinted of a timeless sisterhood network of belonging. Women through time, all cultures, appeared whispering in foreign languages, beckoning. A spirit world soul mate man slid through in sleepy guard down inhibition, giving way to heated passion. Straining to maintain foothold in this world, she willed the real world contrary dangerous fantasy apparitions away, save for the more church acceptable presence of Father Joseph, Mother Mary and Jesus.

A ghostly image of a greyish white haired man, penetrating deep blue eyes softly playing harmonious acoustic music dreamtime visited, a love unrequited, a fantasy soul mate man.

Bored with the dutiful mind and soul limiting role set for her, she imagined a higher calling of wandering through impoverished Aids stricken Africa, collecting cast off children and providing them care. During frustrating times, she imagined herself a comedic version of 'Saint Michael's Chosen One', or Merlin Medicine Woman Shaman and Conjurer powerfully wielding forces of nature to right the wrongs of the world and any manner of injustices. Yes, Joan of Arc incarnate, with magical sword in hand, righting wrongs in bloody righteous battles. There was no chosen one in reality; her path, role, Mother, church cronies and Pastor had dictated a shoes-too-small woman's lot in life long ago. Perhaps at birth or perhaps prior to landing in a physical skin it was written that her lot was just to be a skin sack for a rack of bones that ate, slept and took care of children, arsehole husband and social work clients.

For you Freudian thinkers, she is an escapist with disassociation tendencies, just another unhappy woman. Get that woman on anti-depressants and into therapy, another blight misfit, mooching off the social coffers of hard working dutiful taxpayers. Like so many spiritual wannabes, traditional expectations thrust upon since birth, programmed for church fellowship and doctrine, the workplace, marriage and child rearing where soul longings, soul mate love and finding one's true self was irrelevant. Expectations were set fresh out of toilet training to strive for at least an upper middle class existence, if absolute affluent anal class was unattainable. Striving to conform and live up to the image, the mirage was exhausting and left her feeling not only inept but wired wrong.

Certainly mother's constant directive that grace and flare was a wife's survival kit best tool, drove home the failure. Of course, one must have also honed the elegant art of cooking, entertaining and laundering dress shirts. Without giving away the dirty secret that, you were actually just making ends meet, learning the art of how to accent a thrifty blouse with just the right accessories to give the illusion of real class, good taste and elegance. A vital ideal Mother tried desperately to instill the ideal gracious wife/host gig. Oh, Navi did those things mediocre in front of Mother, yet at work conferences and Stephens's dinner parties could out skill competition, easily.

Mother left a collection of British Royal Family publications within eyesight to all who guest graced the family home. The display was a loud yet subtle message for all to align behaviour within desired aspirations. Yes, the Royals were the pen ultimate ideal, wild Irish roots squashed, denied. One must at all costs keep those embarrassing wild Celtic DNA roots at bay and strive upward in the social ladder and illusions of social graces, social decorum and grander. Heaven forbid giving in, to that wild Celtic nature that must take enormous amounts of energy to keep it at bay.

'What wildness lay dormant in your bones Mother? Heaven forbid your soul runs underwear less and bare foot wild and free, with abandon. I suppose you fear you'll end up in your own private potato famine excommunication like your father's parents.' It was in many ways a hopeless battle because Mother's authentic genetic lineage lingered under the surface of family matriarchs descended from a long line of Celtic women. Adding fuel to the hiding of the family's truer nature was the speculation, that her biological grandmother was half Celt and part Native.

Now Dad's classy British roots did not show in yearnings for royal aspirations on his part by any means, just contentedly indifferent to the constant chaos of a house with so many kids in it. All attempts of Mother's to whoop kids into idyllic good church going Protestant family aspirations were lost when teen boys ran wild and free, eventually giving way to her aspiration, married and living the Golden Child material world life. Yes, brothers were strangers, Mother bragged constantly of their achievements and acquisitions; they did everything 'right'. Ah, but during the sixty's, one long haired dope smoking brother wore army fatigues, another satisfied a wild nature in driving race cars, the others into big boobs while studiously climbing up the achievement corporate ladder. Having all of that male testosterone in the house, kept Mother busy feeding bottomless appetites. In cynical summation, a house slave who ran endless mounds of laundry through an old ringer washer to hang on backyard clotheslines no matter the weather. Upon her lap was also delegated the constant attempts of discipline to an illusion of decorum and order that diverted attention from an insignificant and problem child Navi. Mothers' contrary to true nature strivings and pre-occupation with the boys gave daughter a saving grace from rebellious opposition.

Mother's stoic anal Christian rules of decorum and propriety faded lame with a good sousing; during neighbourhood parties alcohol semi-freed her wild nature, happily dancing, near naked, with abandon. Those were the times when Navi had a warm affinity for the woman. Had Mother followed that authentic true nature, she may well have grown into a wondrous entertainer.

Gran on the other hand, satisfied with pioneering era lot in life was strong, calm, loving and all-knowing in a graceful manner, neither denying Celtic roots nor aspiring to be anything else than what was. Yet, there was more. The elder women whispered secrets with knowing looks in Navi's direction, yet never made privy to.

Thoughts drifted to housework calling her attention. While domestically busy, she travelled and explored the world against role cast laundry, cooking and entertaining for a loathsome man. 'Men can wash their own frigging dirty underwear and socks.' Cynically she imagined displaying his soiled underwear on the dining table in front of Stephen's business dinner party guests.

Ideal home life image was to be upheld. Childish urges to ruin suits; fart when presenting a dish to arrogant pretentious business guests, burping loudly, or spilling a carafe of red wine on his crouch during snotty family dinners. Of Stephen displaying his limp Alien noodle in demonstration of what she was expected to tolerate. Oh, yes, numerous passive aggressive fantasy scenes ebbed and flowed of wiping snot on a suit jacket, or wolf howling during those boring and egotistical home studio tours. 'Gad, he is an arrogant and pompous arsehole when people come to see his art work.' A facade that fed his ego as onlookers cooed in submissive adoration.

Rural life was all she had really known, except for a brief city life with Abby's father. Somewhere along life's path, having submitted, fallen in line with the womanly role set out for her, boxed into conformity of rural Christian life with a future of never ending domesticity. Community Church set the pace, tone and cultural norms and by God, there were a lot of them. Open mindedness was quickly snuffed out and occasionally, literally, driven out of town. Oh, Navi used to participate in all matters church all right, but rebelliously refused to participate in the archaic rituals with the same fear of God and sin repenting as the rest. It seemed not only archaic but conditional upon conflicting standards, off the mark given her view and experience of spirit world. Nor did she pray in subjugation, she snuggled and talked with Father Joseph, communed with Mother Mary and the real human fun loving young man and big brotherly Jesus. As a child, Jesus made funny faces to elicit her giggles during monotone sermons, covered his ears during choir and organ led hymn singing, yawned and offered quizzical looks during fire and brim stone morality sermons. His antics always brought forth fits of snort snot flying giggles much to the scorn of both Minister and congregation.

Experiences with those upstairs, meaning God, Mother Mary, Father Joseph and big brother Jesus offered an intimately private sense of communion and oneness. Contrary consternation to expectations of churchwomen and Mother's cronies, never sought church or elder counsel on any personal matter. Directly chosen by God, the Minister was an ancient mindless and harsh dinosaur who obviously did not see the bigger picture as she saw it, he did not know a loving spirit worldview as she knew it. Navi tried not to hate the man, did not begrudge nor judge; it is just that he and the rest of the congregation seemed not terribly bright. It was an unspoken danger zone, best left unvoiced, unsaid and unchallenged. She was simply, odd woman out and knew it was best to keep fantasy experiences private. The tedium gig seemed to work for them as it was. Relieve opportunity arose as her brothers discovered unbridled teenaged freedom; in testosterone mayhem, all decorum was ditched, all found freedom as family church going became a distant memory.

It seemed, through her front line social worker eyes that many people wandered aimlessly lost, messed up on medications all because of some even more messed up spirit-bogie hanging around them and wreaking havoc. Some nasty assed bogey harassed and drove unsuspecting vulnerable souls crazy, just because professionals could not see nor hear what was really going on, benevolent or otherwise. If other worldly friends made them happy and a better person, then it was no one's business to judge or label otherwise. After all, if one were to do an in depth study, throughout mankind's history, people have always communicated with spirit people, animals, plants, rocks, rivers, stars, wind and trees as a matter of course. Academics and sceptics conclude spirit world sightings as a fantasy coping mechanism for lower evolved humans where modern remedies such as lobotomies, heavy sedation and psychotherapy continue to be solutions readily available.

'Yes', mumbled Navi 'that's why depression stress is so rampant in our time. Are we any happier with all of these modern anti-depressant pill pushing medical academic norms? I think NOT! Just look at any indigenous culture, ones that are still intact that is. Lower evolved my ass. Technologically, maybe but as people living within a cooperative community and within their environment harmoniously without destroying it, absolutely, without doubt, and empathically, YES they had it right!'

Children were closer to God because they instinctively knew how to just be. They did not need to debate the reason for their existence amongst themselves, nor engage in in-depth analysis of how the cosmos works. They did not construct huge buildings, corporate systems or sophisticated rules to support it all. Children just were, of God, then eventually, academically educated and un-learned.

Navi had often considered moving elsewhere but could not fathom disrupting the kid's lives so assumed her lot, knowing that it was enough having a spirit friend or two to share strange otherworldly experiences. Occasionally an acquaintance would sense those otherworldly connections and boldly seek consultation on other worldly spiritual matters. Certainly, she never came out of the closet publicly as a deep fear of banishment from organized traditional church and psychiatric intervention kept the secret in check. They were archaic options akin to modern day versions of witch burnings and frightening mad houses.

Navi heaved a sigh, stopped clicking the mouse and rubbed computer strained eyes, then an aching wrist. Glancing over toward the wardrobe, she wondered when it was that she stopped wearing pretty things, girl clothes. 'Where did my hot and sexy black dress and Italian heels go? Ah, gave those babies away. Someone had borrowed them for a dance. A style for teens and trolling young women, slinky dresses make you cold and high heels hurt your feet. Must be a man thing; push up wire bras, shaving legs, make up and plucking eyebrows and oh God, waxing! No intelligent woman would put herself through that, or do they? Apparently we do.' Exactly when and why she had stopped, she could not recall. Was it because rural life came without want, desire, nor expectation of a different life, or was that just an excuse? Had it been a conscious choice of acquiescing to a life of mediocrity and its complete absence of magic, of passion and basic respect? Day to day life had become so busy, so routine, and so very serious; especially with Matt so sick now.

'But, oh, how divine it would be to wear a sexy black dress with my hair all done gorgeous and no underwear underneath, straddling some loving handsome man in the back seat of a limo!' Images of passion accompanied rapid heart pounding, heat flush surprised. Allowing sensuous thoughts to surface in an otherwise loyal heart, then immediately off kilter ashamed. 'Wow! Where did that come from? Be careful girlfriend, you do not want to be manifesting anything like that now. Ah, it is okay. It is just stress. Nothing's wrong, really, just need to get through Matt's treatments, then couple away with the Grinch man and all will be well again.'

Despite the private world of misfit-ism and home stressors waiting for resolution, Navi was surprisingly a people person away from home. She knew how to love, intuitively saw each person as their divine soul, trapped in a world of manmade rules that confined and often killed a human spirit. Some great unknown truth haunted vague that shadowed authentic happiness.

Attention turned to the house. All was quiet and rather than feeling typically content with the quiet space, discontentment was increasing. The kids were becoming teenagers. The quick Mom inventory in her mind did the 'who, what, where, and when inventory'; Matt was part of Stephen's package from his first marriage. Abby was basically unknown to her biological father T.J. 'It's okay, girls need their Mom's more, Dads are for emergency money and bi-annual pretentious rich extended family gatherings. Navi avoided all contact with the man, ashamed, not wanting him to see and know that she was still unfulfilled. Thankfully, too pre-occupied with his hectic affluent life and socially appropriate picture perfect wife to blatantly point out the obvious disinterest in Navi`s life. A rationale, kept her safe and unaccountable for her part in their separation.

Matt and little Abby, asleep in their rooms downstairs, all accounted for. Living with one full time kid and the other one part time made the house quiet and at times, almost too quiet. Mommy radar never leaves a Mom. 'I wonder if I'll ever get used to the noise reduction.' Quiet moments made ears ring.

Window screen rattled blizzard winds.

'God, it's so lonely in the house now. I wonder if I'm having some sort of midlife crisis. But this weird angst isn't normal, even for me.'

Eyes turned from blizzard to Gran's portrait on the bureau. The familiar warm sensation locked within heart to the old woman in the picture. Keyboard and mouse placed back on desk, nearly falling out of the swivel chair resisting sedentary achy body stumbled over to the bureau and took Gran's picture in hands.

'Hi Gran, I know you are out there, somewhere. I imagine that you are out there, floating about, watching over us silly sods down here.' The thought brought a smile. 'God, I miss you so bad, some days more than others.' A tear surfaced and throat choked. 'Boy, could I ever use one of your loving' hugs today! You know Gran I still have your picture here, watching over me on the bedroom bureau. Do you remember that picture? There you are, standing there by Granddad's snazzy new Hudson and waving at whoever took the picture. You look so happy. It almost looks like you are actually waving right at me, now. How old were you then, Gran? Geez, must have been seventy and already ancient old in childhood eyes. I bet that you never imagined that this picture would be so important to someone else, decades down the road.

I really like this image of you, the 'you' that I saw through my childhood eyes. That's how I still see you; standing over your old wood cook stove with arthritic gnarled fingers, cooking some masterpiece of a Sunday dinner. Yummy fresh baked cake or pie. I can smell roast beef, hot brown gravy and mashed potatoes. Still makes my mouth water now, just thinking about it. I cannot imagine how you managed to raise your own kids, run a farm, as well as the church, and sell home baked goods out of that kitchen. Wow, what a woman you were! I look back at you now, with my working mother's eyes, I cannot fathom how you did it all. You did it all and made it look easy, natural.

Your hugs were angel love. Your big breasts were like soft pillows. A little girl sure could get lost in your arms, lost in grandma love! Your heart was big and expansive as the night sky. Not just grandmotherly hugs, by any standard, but enveloped in warm loving light of God itself. In an era when children were to be seen and not heard, you always seemed to look right into my soul and smile, making me feel pretty darn special and I thank you for that.

When I close my eyes, I can still feel you.

Hey, come to think of it, I do not recall ever seeing or hearing scorn from you. That is kind of something you know. No bloody wonder you are still, after all of this time, special in my heart.

Hey Gran, while I think of it, thanks for ignoring my teenaged lies about those so-called days of school closures and not ratting me out. I still treasure those days of playing hooky with you, snuggled up, playing cards and eating treats.

What is it like for you now? Is Granddad with you? Is your old black and white motley dog with you? Do you miss the farm? No, do not answer that, I like to think of you all still together there, a cozy happy family, still working around the farm.

Really though, I wonder, what is it like for you now Gran, without a physical body and with no limitations of the mind or senses? I cannot imagine what it would be like, waking without middle aged aches and pains, no mind filled with fearsome earthly worries. I am sure that you had your share of aches and pains and worries, although I might have been too young to notice.

You are out there, aren't you?' Navi gently set the picture back on the bureau then stood looking out of the window into driving snow-filled wind. "Is anybody, somebody out there?"

A warm loving wave flowed through her body, reminiscent of childhood times "Yes Navi, I'm here and I'm listening. Yes, the farm, the animals, your Granddad and my grandchildren remain my fondest memories. Yes, life is very different here, yet the same in some ways. And yes my darling, I hear you, and I am with you."

"Funny, I'm just noticing now, how I can feel your presence. I never really thought about it before but once in a while, I can kind of feel your voice inside of my head, I feel you in my heart and I like that, feels so good and so soft, warm and loving; safe. I suppose it would be equally as profound, if you were nasty, like if this was actually paranoid schizophrenia and that would be awful. I really feel for those poor sods. I like to think that I was your favourite granddaughter, still am. Ha."

"I AM always with you. Every child ought to have an adult in their life that is that child's biggest fan, no matter how old that child is."

"I hope you had someone like you in your childhood. God, I miss you! Hey, I still have your rocking chair. I nursed my babe in that chair, connected to you.

You know, this talking with you in this way makes me mindful that acts of heresy are still here in some ways and are still punishable by public scrutiny and the lock up ward. Some things have not changed much in the last one hundred years. While we are not burned at the stake in quite the same manner, we are still subject to the loss of privacy and autonomy in these things. Yes, we still have to deal with academics and the pervasive Christian sceptics, not to mention Children's Aid Society, sort of quasi-colleagues of mine that might really quite enjoy intervening for the sake of my children. Do you really watch over us? Probably not, I am sure that you have your own stuff to do. I can't begin to fathom what it'd be like."

"You have a lot of questions tonight, my Little Chickadee."

"I still love it when you call me that; Little Chickadee."

"You are welcome. Heaven and Spirit realm visitation is like a good meditation, similar to being in love. I used to talk with your Great, Great Grandfather and your Great Aunt Myrtle. I am quite fond of them. I did not meet my own father in my lifetime he died in the war days before I was born. I always felt his presence, love and heard his encouraging words."

"Hmm, it would appear that I am becoming completely unglued." Perhaps mental illness is a matter of human perception. It is however, ultimately based upon what someone else thinks. Soul sickness is soul sickness; no matter what culture you happen to find yourself in. The prescribed remedy or cure differs. Yet all of the spiritual teachers say that it is assured, all souls do eventually heal."

"You are just afraid. You must find out, then stand confident in who you really are, who you know in your loving heart yourself to be. While the ideal for a marriage to be is to help each other grow and prosper, growth comes from our most challenging experiences. You must keep your thoughts as positive as possible and give gratitude often. You came into this world divine, as such, are worthy without question. Always remember this, my Chickadee."

"I'll try. I wish I could visit with you in person, have a cup of tea, play a game of cards and of course cheat. These are my fondest childhood memories, being with you. I miss Dad even though I hardly knew him. You are right, I am scared and I need someone to talk to." Navi backhand wiped away tears.

"Gees, I still feel guilty about sneaking chocolate bars when you sent me to the grocery store for errands. You probably already knew that. I think you always made sure there was an extra fifty cents in my hand, didn't you?"

"Our visits were a blessing."

"Oh my God, you did know all that time!

Maybe we were more alike than I thought. I would not care about those things with my kids. Heck, I pull Abby out of school for special time, and call it a 'sick day'. Do you still think you could beat my arse in a game of Gin Rummy? Actually, that would be kind of fun! Confidence you say, faith. It is hard to trust, when someone cannot consciously see or hear this God and so on. Well, sometimes, I think I can, when I am quiet. I guess I have to tune in to you folks out there. Why is that so hard? The older I get, the more real you become and the less normal I feel and the less hope I have of being normal."

"Aim for the highest, practice, explore and trust what comes."

"That's the hard part. They do not teach this in school. But then again, I have been getting glimpses of and speaking with spirits all of my life."

"Someday it will be taught in schools. The world needs children to be broader pioneers to explore and establish a new world order. When the world is ready, they will see and 'know'. Your children are a part of this bigger plan."

"Yes, I think I've heard that somewhere before, about the schools of the future. You know, in the daytime out there in the world of children, work and housework, well, this stuff just seems so distant and unreal. When I read about this stuff, I think that, while I am thinking about it, that maybe I am a bit of a bridge between heaven and earth. Holy Dina, it is so hard to do it with any kind of consistency let alone to practice, then to make this part of my everyday life. I live in the wrong part of the world, the wrong culture for this living moment-to-moment and loving moment-to-moment stuff. I know that I do not get to go home just because I think life on the other side will be easier. I am stuck here in this box of a life and I am supposed to be manifesting heaven on earth?" Navi plunked back into computer chair, swiveled around in a circle then back again then abruptly jumped up and began to pace.

"Ha! What was that movie? Ha! Build it and they will come? I am soooo NOT up to the task! It is kind of a tall order for me. I am no spiritual master. My life is so ordinary except for this stuff, Mother disapproves and Stephen gives me that weird flake look of his. At work, they refer to me as the hippie chick. My idiot boss calls me Jesus freak and that really pisses me off! God, sometimes I get scared just thinking about doing all I have to do to get through a day. I am no Jesus. I am sure no Gandhi and I am sure as hell no Mother Theresa! What is it that I'm missing?"

"Just be you darling. What is it that you really want?"

"God, I hate those simplistic questions! Maybe it is not a matter of what I want at all! There is a Divine plan for each of us as individuals and then another one for the world, en masse? Which is it?"

"Yes."

"Geez, just what I thought, oh that really clears up a lot for me. Thanks. Oh, are you saying that maybe it only matters what it is that I want within some higher mission or purpose? It's that something that I came here to do?"

"Yes. Do you need to change the world single handily or just your perception of it?"

"Answering a question with a question is really annoying."

"I wonder if that's how your children and clients feel when you are teaching them to think for themselves and make their own determinations."

Response gracefully accepted, rapidly followed with a flash of anger up her spine and bolt out of her mouth. "Jesus! Why is it that whenever anyone asks questions, we get more questions or trite platitudes? I do not get it! Where is the instruction manual? Where is the one eight hundred number to call? Where is the class or real life teacher, the school, for this stuff? Am I supposed to know what to do and have the courage to do it? Spiritual platitudes, or is it that I am just not sophisticated enough to get this shit?"

"You do have it."

"Well, I don't know about that, having Matt sick with cancer isn't what I have in mind for manifesting Heaven on earth! If this spiritual stuff really does work then why can't I heal him? Shit, there is a danger right there. Jesus could have done it. How am I supposed to manifest some sort of miracle on him and make it all go away?"

"That's not up to you, now is it darling? Hand those worries over to us."

"I know. Gran, it is not just the cancer, there is something else is going on, something is happening. I am so restless, I cannot eat properly and I'm having trouble sleeping. I am losing patience with my co-workers and with the stupid never-ending rules at work. There is an abyss between Stephen and me. I cannot quite put my finger on what the bigger problem is. Does that sound crazy, or am I just too self-centered, selfish and self-righteous for my own good? Seriously, I would gladly give my life for Matt to be better, without a second thought, in a heartbeat. For God's sake, he is only fourteen years old! Yes, I know that ultimately this is his deal. This is ultimately his deal spiritually, mentally, physically and emotionally with all the support, we can muster. The rest of us are going through this with him, but we are secondary to his deal. God, I am useless to him. All I have is love for him. I pray for his highest good to be the outcome.

I just cannot help feeling and that there is something else going down! I am going on about my day and then I get these hot flashes and weird sensations like the earth is groaning and shifting under my feet. Sounds foreboding, I can hear an earthquake, rumbling and vibrating through the core of the earth then up through my body. It sounds like pieces of the earth are actually shifting pieces of a giant puzzle shifting into position. The earth moans and shudders like a groggy giant, stirring from deep sleep. I can feel it shifting, like something old, heavy and slow but powerful. I am sure no one else can hear it, because nobody ever says anything. Is the earth really changing? Are the prophecies real and coming?"

"Grace, faith and love it. Nothing can stay the same. Thus is the nature of the universe. It is only change."

"But I feel anxiety gripping my stomach, yet somehow, I'm okay. Odd that. I really do not get the sense that it has much to do with Matt and his cancer. Oh and then as I am going to sleep at night I get weird sensations in my head. It feels like shards of lightening ripping through the back of my head and through the centre in my brain. Am I developing epilepsy? Do I have a tumor? Maybe I am going to die. Maybe I am going to have an embolism or stroke. If I went to the doctor, I am sure that he would send me for all kinds of tests to find nothing. He would tell me that it was psychosomatic, that with Matt being sick, it was stress and give me a prescription for anti-depressants. Worse, he might think that it is something that requires extensive probing and testing and come up with some obscure Latin medical termed syndrome that I cannot pronounce. Yes, it can only be managed by heavy medication and after a lengthy consult with Stephen and decide to reinstate electric shock therapy and failing that a full lobotomy.

I do not have time to be sick. Maybe I am becoming a brilliant Psychic. Maybe I will be a Catholic Stigmata! If I were to pass over now, that would be fine with me. I am tired and weary. I think I would like to go home, up there where you are. I am so very tired. I feel like all I have done for the past twenty years is raise kids and work. When I look back on it, I don't know how I did it. No wonder the housework slid so much. I sure would love a real vacation, warm and exotic.

Gran? Are we humans really evolving as a species? Sometimes, I wonder. It takes a lot of energy to fit in with the world. Perhaps I care too much of what others think. It is a slow process. I had better stop thinking about passing over and be careful of what I wish for. You are quiet. You're just letting me vent aren't you."

"Yes."

"I don't understand."

"Well Dear, in order to evolve, everyone must be afforded the opportunity to experience what it is like to feel as though one is not growing for a time, yet we always are. Change is inevitable. Consider Albert Einstein's concept of time, it is not linear but simultaneous. The universe has a very different sense of past, present and future than what we thought on earth. It is an interesting application. This is a clue for you, that you can journey backward and forward through your timeline, other lifetimes, others lifetimes and by intentionally changing how you feel about a situation, effectively change its ripple effect."

"Okay, now I feel like I am in a lecture hall all by myself, taking an exam that I not only have not studied for, but did not attend the class. I am confused, where was I when that class was in session? Probably out having a cig or smoking a joint! If there was an instruction booklet provided upon my birth, my lifetime here, I did not get it. If there is a direct phone line to God, I do not have it. I fear that he, she or it would not take my call anyway. Anyway, this is no class I ever heard of in public school."

"You compare public school and a tiny college experience with the infinite intelligence of the universe?"

"I know what you're going to say, this is that Shakespearean thing; there is more to this world, than meets the eye. Oh, and seek the answers within, kind of shit."

"Perhaps, it is part of the spiritual path that you yourself have chosen?"

"Everything you need to know is already within you, kind of shit."

"Keep exploring and watch your perceptions change. What you understand and know to be true today will change in time, and then change again and so on. Just do it your own way. There really are no short cuts to a magical destination darling. It is love and the journey that matters."

"I'm a New Aged Moron!" In sudden snit and snort of laughter, she held her stomach, trying hold in a tiny post child-rearing bladder from releasing. It was always like this now, whenever she sneezed, coughed or laughed, burning pressure followed with tiny dribbles. Openly blaming Abby's in womb thumb sucking bouncing on her bladder.

"It's good to be skeptical as long as you draw your own conclusions and not on what someone else thinks."

"Yes, I know that! You know I have thought about going back to church and even checking out some others but after the service, the fellowship flies buzzing around like flies on shit really irks me. They are like retail sales people in a department store. Yummy fresh meat to convert and save but really they are bored, nosey and want to know everything about you so they will have something to talk about with their gossip cronies. It makes me sick the way they pretend to be one with God so they can use this cover to critique and condemn everyone else.

I am frustrated. I want answers. When I think about the masters and mystics who have treaded the human path before, I realize that their journey was a solo endeavour. There must be a way to grow spiritually and be happy while maintaining a family and a job. Sometimes I am really jealous of all of the super moms who work their progressive and successful careers while raising the most amazing achieving children while having the best material homes, vacations, visits to the spa."

"Why must it be either? If you could only have one or the other, be poor like Jesus or Gandhi and rich in spiritual life or be materialistically rich like the Rockefellers and Trumps, which do you chose? Or perhaps these are desires that one eventually out grows."

"Well BOTH! Ha. God, of course but could not I have both and still get there? I mean that is what abundance is about, creating hearts desires. I know that spiritual abundance is more than money and material things that you think you really want. I think I am going to have to work on that one. I am still not sure that I see the difference. Although I know the adage that, it is harder for a rich man to get into heaven that it is to pass a camel through the eye of a needle. I know that there are many lonely rich people out there, but there are also many lonely poor people. I don't see the connection."

"Perhaps you could consider if when you purchase a thing, are you feeling love or agonizingly debating whether you can afford it?"

"Yeah, like I don't have enough on my mind. Matt is going to pull through, right? It is just that old sense of mortality. Sometimes I am not afraid of him dying because I know that his spirit will continue on, while other times I am terrified of even getting into a car accident and having him or Abby die that way. By the way, I know what you are trying to tell me about conscious shopping.

I feel so separate from everything, and afraid that I am crazy and that God and faith are just silly human egocentrism. That God is just a big crock of shit, this spiritual stuff is a big immature crock of shit as a path for dumb cow people to follow.

I really hate this earth place at times! Violence and asinine rules squeezing the living shit out of everyone's spirit. I ask you, what is the meaning of my life? Sigh, I guess that is for me to figure out. Ha, you are not going to tell me squat, are you? Seriously, the more I read about spirituality, the less employable I feel I become. Oh! I have a flash vision of the outcome; I am in a straightjacket autistic-ally rocking to some inner music that no one else can hear. I am kidding you, of course. When I compare my life and successes to my peers, I fall very short of the mark. I cannot even find a pair of underwear that fits right. Crazy Navi, on a direct road to the white jacket and pretty coloured pills that make you forget to even think."

"Chickadee. You can go with the flow of life gracefully allowing change or you can live the dark night of the soul. Journey the changes, soul search, re-birth, transition, grow and evolve."

"Shit. My head hurts now. Honestly Gran? I really have no fucking idea of what you are trying to tell me. I think I know, but it's just too deep, abstract and doesn't help jack shit in my life right now. This is too mind fucking deep scary unnerving and philosophical for me right now. Fuck it! I'm going to change a load of laundry. I need clean underwear and a bra for work tomorrow."

Navi grump puttered downstairs to the laundry room. Proud amazed, how easily she could sense her way around in the dark, careful not to startle a mouse jetting out in the dark. 'How was it possible that laundry grows when not in the room? It breeds and multiplies in the dark like alien mold spores; a universal Motherhood truth.' Another load in the wash and, 'damn it', wet towels in the hamper and piled on the floor were rapidly creating black spotted mildew on dry ones.

"Damn it! That really pisses me off!" Navi envisioned rudely flipping on all of the lights, waking everyone up, lining them up and grilling appropriate laundry protocol. Alas, did not, would not and worse, would forget about it until the next time.

Ambling out to the kitchen, she opened the fridge and stood waiting for inside light blindness to fade and hurting dark eyes to adjust. "AHHH! Bloody hell, that hurts! Retina burn!" Standing with fridge door wide open was an annoyance that she would have given the kids holy hell for. "God, why do they always put empty juice jugs, milk cartons and empty cheese wrappers back in the frigging fridge? God, yuck, that thing that looks like a pig's ear is actually an old twisted piece of ham that might have still been good, if someone had left it wrapped properly. Yeah, wake the little fuckers up! Get them doing housework in the middle of the night." Entertaining, but it would not be worth a grumpy Stephen wrath. Closing fridge door to unappetizing fridge contents of late night snacking, she remembered a can of Coke hidden in the tablecloth drawer. "Ha! Nobody goes in there, not even Stephen. Score! A coke no one will notice and a smoke. This is good. Life is good."

Navi stared out of the kitchen window into white speckled darkness.

"Well Gran, if you really are there, even if I am having a breakdown of sorts, or if I'm working my way through the proverbial 'dark night of the soul', please watch over Matt, the family, wild women everywhere and of course little ole me. I'm feeling really quite cynical and I want to cocoon. I want to be alone. I desperately need seclusion. I hope that my friends and extended family will be patient with me while I deny social engagements. I think I really need some time out. I am feeling weird, even by my own definition. I am becoming quite meticulous about whom and how I spend my time. My faith in the all that is has all but left me, and I am thinking that spirituality is not true growth but a crutch, a torturing joke. BULLSHIT!

It's difficult to be around people. I've been playing recluse while in a crowd, preferring my own company. This is the plaque of Western society, is it not? To be surrounded by others yet, profoundly alone. God I could use a hug! It's been one hell of a winter. PLEASE, take care of Matt. Make him want to live and live well. Please take away his suffering, no more hair down the shower drain and give him back some skin colour. He's starting to look like a prisoner of war!"

Navi bent head in hands and sobbed.

"And for God's sake, do something about the cancer treatment side effects! Fuck! The kid can't eat without puking. He should be enjoying teen social life, not fighting for life. You know girls, hard-ons and zits. He is still a boy and much too young to be faced with such adversities and certainly, too young to be facing his own mortality. I know that he has the chutzpah to master whatever it is that he's going through, with the right help that is."

Face in hands, Navi sobbed, realizing just how scared of losing Matt she really was. Always the strong one, the counsellor, the positive and carry the faith for all. That was priding her ability to transcend the adversities of the world and struggling to transcend the horror of cancer. As sobbing and tears passed, a slow warm wave washed within. A deep breath sigh, arched back then blew her nose.

"Oh, thanks to the folks who sent him the jazzy new computer, just in time for Christmas? Spirit in action and miracles come true, through complete strangers. These times require a leap of faith, a quantum leap of faith and a whole lot of GRACE. Think I am going to need help from you Gran, or anybody else who might be floating around out there. If you don't, I'm screwed!"

Her attention turned to a familiar rumbling floor underneath vibrating feet. "Bloody washing machine, sounds like a transport truck driving right through the house. Hope it doesn't bust a gear or wake up the kids. To hell with laundry, I'm going to bed."

Washing machine OFF, she ambled out to the living room's wood stove, cranked the door open and jammed in a big all-nighter log. Into the bathroom, leaving the door wide open and light off, she hiked up old robe and nightgown in one bunch and peed. Suddenly overwhelmed with fatigue, ferociously rubbing weary childlike eyes then headed back upstairs to bed without stopping to flush or wash hands. She pulled back a corner of the covers and slid in, robe, slippers and all.

"You are sensing a massive change coming, within and without. Give your anxiety to us. In the meantime, my darling, play with your children, go for long walks and stay connected to nature, there are indeed spirit path finder's as you have sensed. Your soul will take you on the right journey, trust it."

"Gran? Stop. I'm too tired and I can't deal with this existential BULLSHIT!"

After an hour of tossing and turning amidst anxious thoughts, suddenly in want of another smoke, Navi ambled over to computer, lit up a smoke. "Maybe I am just too sensitive."

Internet search; 'SENSITIVE': definition:

"A 'Sensitive' typically refers to those who are super-sensitive or use sixth sense capabilities. Higher powers of observation, information gathering and assimilation abilities, a Sensitive is reputed to able to intuitively access, ascertain, sift and sort sensation or finer frequencies, impressions, sounds and imagery. Typically a Sensitive is also known as one who is able to communicate and commune with the spirit world to access and utilize unseen powers to assist others. Unconscious awareness of or untrained Sensitive's are often reclusive, unable to cope with acute overwhelming external stimuli, frequencies or low audio waves. Trained, these people report the ability to facilitate capabilities similarly to tuning into radio stations. Many are able to scientifically prove discernment of various frequencies and vibrations as well as temperature, emotions, intentions and even light and darkness.

Archaeologists, academics and scholars determine that throughout history, various religious societies and mystics report possessing and harnessing these unseen capabilities; dream journeying to ethereal spirit worlds at will as natural spiritual enfoldment skill sets are grown, harvested and honed via metaphysical training. Without proper skill development such as reputed in shamanism, metaphysics and other holistic healing techniques, many are unable to discern, filter, block and dissipate the harsh energies of others, resulting in continual absorption which activates disease, emotional unbalances, mental illness and even fatality.

A trained and skilled 'sensitive' can actually raise negative or lower frequencies and energies conversely, such as saints and mystics or spiritual healers, and are able to invoke and access assistance from divine sources and or spirit realm.

Exhausted and cold, she closet rooted for her old shawl, its blanket embrace enfolding and cozy. The old Hudson Bay company vintage shawl enshrouded comfort when feeling lost and scared. Worn, it suddenly felt as though a connective warm familiar magical gateway to ancient women throughout history, the spiritual sisterhood network.

'Oh, God, I am exhausted.' Sliding back into bed, she strategically curled into a fetal ball avoiding physical contact with Stephen. Instantly drifting as warm calm sleep waves washed within arousing images of some loving far away spirit man. A familiar elusive loving ghost man who visited through dream states, whose personality and visible presence was obvious as it was any live person. Yet, this one was different. Striving for more of the mysterious vague image, searching for detail and seeing only a wrist, his greying hairline surrounded deep blue eyes accompanied by inaudible distant melodies and a sense of familiar recognition of like mind and soul loving.

Consciously striving for more, in a flash, *Navi embrace blended with the nameless faceless spirit entity, skin, bones as inner body parts disappeared and melded into one being, one soul, as naturally as though it was simply common, throughout many mutual life times.*

Images and intimately loving sensations drove home harsh isolation and loneliness, which made making marriage work with Stephen harder. A conclusion that soul skin man did not live in this world but was instead, purely a conjured fantasy and born out of loneliness was often dismissed. Yet this night, soul skin man came as magical comfort.

Behind sleep heavy eyes, he came to her. Aware of his graying hair and soft skin; electric as wondrous harmonies softly played. Delicious skin sensation mingled with song as Navi slid away to another time, another place.

Donning an old white cotton dress, long brown hair half tied with a ribbon gently moved under wind caresses with bare feet grounded on earthen floor. Wood smoke and satisfied with dinner slow cooking on hearth, she made her way out of their tiny log cabin, to the small farmyard, surrounding home, chicken pen, horse corral and a rough hand hewn barn where Tom leaned back in relaxation. In quiet contemplation out over a crop, maybe wheat, a golden sunlight gently bowed over and dancing lightly with a breeze, late summer evening sun is shining, streaming through trees that lined the field. Husband, Soul Skin man engrossed in reverence of awe and gratitude for all that is good and beautiful with their world.

Navi stood in awe and reverence of watching 'Tom' Soul Skin husband. 'Ah, so your name is Tom in that life time and your reddish brown and curly hair was Celt native with black mix, maybe.'

Casually lighting a pipe, he gently puffed distinct homemade blend musky aroma as smoke curls that danced and faded in the wind. Smells of his tobacco carried lightly in the wind with hints of his own smell. Nostrils flaring, taking it all in, air fresh carrying musky decaying scents of late summers evening earth and pine caressed her face and hair. Pulling out her hair ribbon to allow wind caresses to dance and flow as sun streamers warmed skin. A dog, a mutt golden lab chases a toad in and around Tom's legs. A nearby creek gurgles as water dances over rocks. Navi strolled toward Soul Skin man Tom and from behind, she wrapped loving arms around his chest. Turning slightly he whispered, "I can feel you within, so close, I don't know where your skin ends and mine begins. I can hear your heart beat inside of mine, drumming, breathing in one beat attunement. I smell your smell, of earth of love. I close my eyes as you cover your hands over mine and I am lost in you. This is heaven darling."

"There is no need for temples;
no need for complicated philosophy.
Our own brain, our own heart is our temple;
my philosophy is kindness."
Dalai Lama

Chapter 2 ~ When all else fails, go to church.

The alarm's clock rude bleating awoke Navi promptly at seven o'clock into nagging nerve-jarring annoyance into a rebellious rolling over in duress. Accustomed to waking up tired and weary akin to millions of working mothers, this day started with a rude bolt, blasting into action of tussling kids. Assist Matt to rouse enough to go to his mother's then Abby fumbling a lunch, books and backpack onto a waiting school bus only to face the drive to the office in another snowstorm.

Pulling faithful old comforter overhead and curling fetal, a childish little two-year-old monster Navi, silently screamed in defiance, 'NO, I don't want to'. Allowing serious rebellion to counter into practical adult consciousness with a quick rational calculation of vacation days owing, a management decision was confirmed; she was staying home.

Ignoring chaotic morning noise as kids battled for bathroom, breakfast, socks and cookies, Navi tossed and squirmed, knowing there would be no rest, not just yet. At Abby's ear piercing squeal, pausing only to gather velocity into crisis jangling already tenuous mother nerve endings, she whipped old comforter off allowing cold breeze to invade sweaty comfortable body letting of an irritated "ARGGHHH."

Silence ensued down below, catching short, she presumed Abby was side tracked playing with toys or dancing to some internal music that only she could hear, stalling school preparation. Guilty mother hesitated then stumbled over to desk and called in sick strategically a mere three minutes before arsehole dick head human resources Neanderthal chauvinist pig human resources manager would be in his office, then sighed in relief upon hearing an answering machine click in. Breathing heavily from mouth, nose pinched sounding fully plugged she did what any cowardly employee did to gain a day's peace; "Nime no cuming to whork today. Nime thick at home. Thee you tomorrow. Ifffin doo need andyting, do kin callded me at homa."

It was a cowardly deed perhaps, but safe.

Navi knew full well, that she would run to check the call display number and barring any child emergency drama, would certainly not answer any work related calls. It was delicious freedom, sans guilt and a bugger that mental health days were not justified absences. Employers make you lie and say that you are sick in order to have pay for time off. Desperate mental health care versus food, hydro and mortgage demands fuelled existing stress. 'Shit, even having a sick child at home is not a justified absence. Some human services organization I work for!'

Stretching off grumpy mood residue that had invaded her late night anxious space, her stomach aversion rolled in not yet coming to terms with what had become of her life and day-to-day existence. In weary awareness, in shadows of consciousness lingered a dark pervasive need to process all that was happening and not happening. A driving need for quiet space this day came as a mature adult knowing un-requiring of any further justification.

Soft mumbles of children downstairs, a spoon clinked on a bowl, smells of toast mingled with wood stove smoke and Matt's treatment craving for nippy old cheese and strawberries entailed standing with fridge door wide open while he snacked. All was well for the moment; they had found food and nourishment.

Staring out of the bedroom window into light snow drifting in wind currents, an awareness of the frumpy ensemble from the night before arose as old robe shifted with body movements allowing wisps of sleep and sweat smells from body aroma embedded nightwear. 'Yuck! I stink! Oh who gives a shit, it's not like anyone is going to get that close enough to me this morning that matters.'

Continuing conversation with Gran as though visiting for the first time in her country home, the tour began, "Here is my smoking place, my contemplation place."

Sideways tilt of head to barrier snowy wind blasting in a window partially opened, she lit a cigarette, blowing curls of white spirited smoke into moist crispy air. "How is it that aboriginals use tobacco for prayer but it is considered such a deadly sin to the rest of the world? Because of a little added formaldehyde and smidge of cyanide. God only knows what else. Because we use it to pacify ourselves and not as originally intended as a means to connect with Great Spirit, God, Creator, Divine? I guess it is the intent behind the action that ultimately counts. Too bad it's not socially acceptable for adults to just suck their thumbs." Images unfolded of impeccably dressed and coiffure white colour professionals milling about offices with pacifiers hanging on designer chains around necks, then all curling up fetal on lounge couches with teddy bears and thumb sucking for afternoon naps. "Hmm, the world would likely be a much friendlier place if people were allowed to curl fetal now and then. Just curl up, rock and thumb suck would probably mean a lot less war and hostility."

Cigarette stub butted out on windowsill sent sparks flying off into white spotted wind currents as she slammed the window closed, now mindful of the clock. "Huh, look at that; it's seven thirty eight a.m. and the moon is still out, how magical."

Attention turned to sounds of water running, Stephen was already in the shower and running late for work. No 'good morning darling' for her again today, this was a 'no talking to Navi' period. In pained rejection and abandonment, she returned to smoking window, lit up and puffed smoke into blasts of wind that now blurred the huge, brilliant, neon white ball of last night's wintry moon. Dipping over the horizon, green haloed moon cast eerie blue light shadows over snow-covered fields. Specks of magical lights sparkled in crisp snow. Blue wintry morning light shone splayed in between disappearing moon and rising sun's yellowish orange.

Jutting her head outward into crisp biting blasts, nostrils filled with fresh breath halting gasps. Eyes closed to savour sensations, cool snowflakes danced on warm eyelashes, nose and cheeks. A body shiver wave brought forth a tightening of robe and withdrawal from the blue magical bone chilling outer world. A last glance noticed subsiding winds and emerging forest lines beyond seasonal abandoned crops. Eerie misty light blues fading as Grandfather Sun assumed his light-bearing role over horizon.

A deep sigh brought a body aroma waft of self-consciousness as she hesitated at the dresser then dumped baby powder inside front of flannel nightgown. A welcome relief to olfactory senses, she smoothed it under stubbed armpits then down to nether regions. Another bigger sigh of contentment, monstrous bear slippers slid on, she puttered down the old narrow farm cottage stairs. Kids moaned and groaned as they made their way about their rooms. Out of the living room window, wind filled white specks swirled under eaves trough, blinding the driveway.

"This is the winter world where the nature spirits come alive. They dance in between the moon and sun shadows."

Abby dramatically emerged out of her bedroom with assaulted airs of an unseen force complaining; "Mommmmmm, there's only one pair of socks and they match, I wanna wear purple n' green."

The petty drama sent crippling annoyance ripples through a mothers tethered nerve network, annoyance of caring about what teachers and other more together mothers facial and gasping chastising criticisms 'Scum Mommy, can't even provide appropriate clothing for her children!' Yes, it was a thing with Abby; never wearing matched socks, which sent each new teacher into pious anal distress fits of concern. This was the kind of thing, small as it seemed, that added fuel to already imagined accusations of inappropriate care from the Children's Aid Society and snotty old lip pursed churchwomen. 'This is how we lowly types are kept in line, a culture that is inherent with fear and intimidation, ruled by it.' A woman who was old enough ought to be also mature enough to have outgrown outer critics, who in time became automatic inner critics, it was a universal conundrum and she was not alone. In fact everyone had a critic in life, albeit an inner one at least. Inner being and psyche critics came from misguided parenting, archaic religious doctrine and state systems that tried to keep order and control over its masses. A critic's job was designed thusly, to keep appropriately on track and us safe from our unruly wild natures. To whose judgment we dare wonder. Surely, this cannot be harsh judgment of an unconditionally loving God, Jesus, Buddha or other ancient spiritual master. Surely, these are all manmade rules, men with control agendas. Originally intended to be cultural guidelines for getting along in eras long gone, outdated antiquated and insufficient in today's innovative global culture.

Navi's inner critic was not wholly conjured as her own church condemnation fearing mother, but a summation of those fearful controlling unhappy mothers everywhere. No, not a bad mother by any means, just a painful striving life mission to instill the right mode of social graces and decorum, the right decision making rationales that reflected a mysterious higher authority figures in a higher all-knowing mind and social strata as dictated. The first aim is to ensure survival in a chaotic world, the next to grab life by the balls and not let go.

Wind and nature spirits playfully and joyfully jostled windows. Envying their childlike abandoned freedom, adult Navi mother must stay indoors. With radio's blaring, in house school children oblivious to the wild and free spirits, one stressfully focused on un-matching matched socks.

A heavy winter storm car driving fear lump dropped in the pit of an empty stomach, as awareness shifted to the living room window blustering and banging against driving snow. 'Snow again, God, driving in it and shoveling the dammed stuff.' Always hauling firewood and trailing bits of bark and dirt over floors and carpet, then late night, every night, stoking the frigging fire.

She contemplated why exactly it was that she did not live in Bora-Bora or Arizona. Failing any logical explanation Navi wondered if her habit of referencing their county and little country home as Snow Dump was actually in some cosmic way inadvertently manifesting and fuelling heavier snowfalls just by the power of thinking it so.

'Will it ever stop snowing? God!'

Into the kitchen, she ambled then abruptly stopped in shock and disgust. Allowing a tear laden heavy sigh out, with hunched burdened shoulders took visual inventory of the mess that awaited her and only her. 'Why can't they scrape their frigging dishes clean before they put them in the sink? Oh what's the use?'

Big bear slipper gliding over hard wooden floor to the counter window, she gazed, trying to remember what her garden looked like without heavy downy comforter mountains of snow. The breath taking awe-inspiring spring and summer beauty of colour and scented symphony of flowers escaped visual recall. Now there was only a blanket of white against black trees and grey sky.

Eyes closed, she pretended for a moment that the kids were both healthy and happy on a summer's sun filled day, playing in the pool, chasing fireflies, dragonflies and butterflies and singing to the neighbours' cows. Yet the kids were not, one would bedroom seclude himself behind a closed door with radio blaring while the other littler one hoped and prayed for school cancellations. The secluded one was sick, very sick. Wincing in protection against two different sounds piercing, contrary stereo blaring sensory chaotic overload. It was a war cry, rebellion of each having to face their day ahead. One insistent on wearing un-matched socks, the other steeped in sickness and meds. 'Ah, it was a bane of motherhood!'

Navi winced ears against assaulting pop rap-ish metal against blackboard screeching teenaged stress music to a pre-occupied window gazing Abby. If indeed there is divine intervention, the girl will go to school this day and turn it all around in a good way. 'I don't want to waste a good sick day surrounded by a bored little precious one. God, I hope Stephen does take Matt to his Moms as he said he would. I don't think I can handle looking at him so sick today.' Guilt and shame at the thought threatened a wave of tears. Arching back upon inhalation, calling on reserves of all coping mechanisms within and borrowed, she promptly turned to the tasks at hand of a sick, very sick child, a very dirty kitchen and laundry piles that consistently bred in the dark of nights while she slept.

Over to the far end of the counter, the prize invested high-end coffee maker called to morning ritual caffeine fix. Set it up before bed, then in the morning, Voila, Presto! Fresh from God and all that is good in the cosmos, wake up call. A cup poured, fridge door opened seeking cream; she reeled backward in disgust; only scientific experiments gone horribly wrong under guise of various abandoned unwanted leftovers. Odd growths of furry fuzzy greys and greens begged only her appropriate care in proper burial and safe passage to the other side. Of course, no cream and the milk jug was empty as it always was when she was in want. Children and husbands were naturally immune from seeing these things, often did without rather than rectify, lacking the basic life skill sets required in doing these complicated taxing tasks. This was mother's job. A job that mothers did very well and apparently, pride-fully enjoyed. 'Alas, if you were a good mother Navi, you would have been awake and up early preparing the first and most important meal of the day for your cherished loved ones. Let us not get started on that disgusting smoking habit of yours. Tisk. Tisk. A child sick with cancer in the house no less. You are selfishly making coffee for yourself before attending to your little girl and a very sick boy!'

Rebellious Navi stood ground. She would not acquiesce to guilt and shame.

She gently closed the fridge door and with a black cup of coffee cupped in both hands, ambled into the living room to couch curl. 'Black is better anyway, it is warmer and I need warmth. It's freezing down here!' The old dinosaur wood stove's fire had gone out again. It did not seem to matter how jammed full it was packed the night before, it always went out too soon. She dreaded starting a fire from scratch in the winter. It took so long to clean out ashes then kindling start up lighting process to a bigger log gradual build up enough to heat the old house. The draftee old farm cottage got too cold, too fast. 'Why can't Stephen tear himself away from his workshop for just enough time to either fix it or put in a new one? Even better, how about something cleaner and more energy efficient like one of those new sci-fi looking wind mills, ground source heating thingies or solar panels or something?' Noble solutions to aspire; always procured installed and satisfied on some distant far away day. Then again, initial money out lay never seemed to top their priority list of existing. With bi-weekly, four-hour Matt's treatment drives to the big city, all available money round up or borrowed was to cover those expenses. Time off work, gas, parking, Matt has to have this, needs this, somehow magically and gratefully seemed to be covered. Life would wait.

Sounds of a kid's chaotic morning rituals mixed with sleepy frustration over finding socks, books and clothes, pants, clean underwear and winter outer wear emanated outward, assuring Navi she was not only capable but was ungraciously sparing her lack of motherly attention thus averting further guilt. Simply, she was not up for the usual pre-day prep of sorting everyone out. 'No, I just can't do this morning. I cannot clean anything right now. The kids will have it all looking the same in fifteen minutes.' It was always easier to just clean like mad, when no one was around. Old training teenager as a nursing home attendant came in handy.

Navi sat at her computer desk and flicked on a solitaire game. 'God, I'm really dreading the long drive to work tomorrow. They are calling for snow squalls all week. Geez, it never used to bother me, but now, it rattles me through and through. I get all anxious looking out of the window in the morning then I am nervous all day at work, looking out windows and listening to the radio for road closures. When I do drive, I have to drive through eight different weather systems to get home. I can't see in whiteouts anymore, it's like I go into some alpha state, seeing one snow flake at a time come and drift off while trying to stay on the road and not end up in a ditch somewhere. Driving in a snow storm is like trying to not focus your eyes on those mystifying star screen savers on the computer.' Rather than give energy to the fearful thought, she tried to picture the drive in her mind's eye, as though she could by will alone, set up a safe, clear and comfortable drive.

A wind gust blasted the north side of the house in slapping defiance, 'Can't mess with Mother Nature.' The wind hurled over the roof threatening eaves trough ripping and dismantling as a nasty East wind rattled front windows. 'Jesus, looks like two different storm fronts coming in from different directions.' The old wooden front door shuddered, barely hanging on to hinges against spooky invisible poltergeists. 'Well, it had better not completely snuff out the fire.'

A cold breeze wafted by her nostrils carrying a revolting smell of rotting carcass, distinct smell of dead mouse. 'Ah, damn it.' She followed her nose sniffing back into the kitchen. She sniffed again fighting a wave of nausea. Pulling out the fridge on screeching motionless tiny wheels, floor scratches deepening into wood, she tracked that distinct unique smell of dead mouse with eyes following a tiny path of black mouse turd. 'Hmmm, there are lots of little shiny objects. Brat-Kat must have been a crow in her last life.'

Mingled with tiny black turds and not a mouse as suspected, but a rat carcass, was an extensive array of jewelry and other shiny objects. Navi sighed, what initially seemed like a simple mouse disposal job had now turned into a major rat and filthy cleaning job. Holding her nose away from offending decay, she turned debating whether to call Stephen up from his workshop to do the dastardly deed. He might raise his voice. He would definitely complain about being late for work, he might ignore her or he just might come. Either which way, it would elicit a dramatic production in front of the kids.

Their house, surrounded by farms meant seasonal house infestations of mice, occasional rats, snakes seeking rodents, gazillions of spiders and flies, clouds of bats and the annual spring winds that brought fresh manure smells into the house. Grossed out, arched back, she fought down rising waves of nausea, looked to the heavens for strength, needing to psyche up mastery for the task.

'God damn it, where in the hell is Stephen?' Her ears scanned the house, tuning into his sounds. 'Ah yes, as always in his workshop, viewing the current creation before work. Priorities understood. Do not worry about the children, Darling! Alas, there will be some wonderful sculpture for the garden to manifest itself out of that dingy workshop and it will not matter that the house and the kids go to chaos. What a man, must have got a new idea in his sleep last night. Thanks for the help, darling.

NOT!

Arsehole! Your work is so much more important than helping get the kids ready for the day, or God forbid, cleaning up.' She laughed for a moment, thinking how every once in a while, Stephen would decide to do a deep clean in the kitchen; everything would be left shoved into one corner of the counter with a thick splotchy layer white powered cleanser left on surface of counter, toaster, bread box, bread maker and sink taps. She laughed, knowing that there was actually a time early in their courtship when this was cute and had felt all warm, wanted and needed as a woman. 'ARGH, I was so stupid!' Those occasional cleaning attempts actually made him feel like a fully contributing and justifiably equal caregiver in his mind. Navi did not have illusions about equal anything anymore. 'No folks, it does not matter that we are living in the modern world. Some things just do not change. Domestic chores and childcare are a woman's lot, as career and outside interests was man's domain, lucky men.'

Would he come? Still not talking to her, rather, a wall of hostile ignoring averting silence screamed within the core of her being. It was an old pattern and sore point Achilles heel that he hooked into and played on, where squirrelly emotions ran rampant in moments when they did cross paths. It was his proverbial unspoken long-term marital oral sex scream 'Fuck You'.

This calculated ignore Navi thing pushed a shadow place magic button that was elusively bone deep. A lifetime unconscious panic button alarm that triggered normal church folk rejection and banishment away from the social norm majority of those who lived in the real world. The spirit world was a different matter of course. That was how it was. Audacious airs of superiority and calculated mind games gave him stolen power fed into some sorry dark hole in his soul, of what was lost on blind-sided Navi. Thrown off balance and despite years amassed in counselling others, she knew that it took two to tangle. Somehow, if things were going to change, it would have to begin with her. Thus it was, like billions of other un-blissfully married couples, inner pains, hurts, shames and insecurities, projected outward onto those they professed to love.

Fantasy idealistic married couple images free floated in her mind's eye, which only served to compound existing pain of not belonging and of not being truly loved, by any adult. Catching short, fully knowing that those fantasy aspiration ideals were in fact a concept acquired from media and marketing agendas. Oh yes, the great American dream, your soul mate who naturally and passionately honourably protects the other's vulnerabilities, and most certainly would not, could not fathom, intentionally, willfully manipulate and coerce the beloved. That was, after all, the higher evolved spirited picture of marriage, was it not? Had Navi known the truth about Stephen, the truth behind his projectile cruelty, she would not agonize. In fact would not have married him. Soul wings free in higher flight.

Naively determined to someday get past his strategic game playing and actually have a romantic loving relationship, kept her engaged in want of an illusion that would soon set her free.

'Ah, the dangers of counsellors: tolerant to their own detriment, and always trying to fix people, never giving up.'

Their argument issued over his proclamation of using her car to take Matt to treatment in the city. Was it normal? Did Mother and Dad or Gran have those arguments? If they did, she never saw it. Like a true matrix warrior, within his mind, the entire unresolved and subsequent conversations and strategic angles, been pondered, rehearsed and polished. Upon approach, unsuspecting daft woman, would instantly be thrown off balance. No matter what she offered up as a possible solution, he had already made up his mind that the other, would dramatically guffaw and throw his hands up, dismissing a completely unreasonable Navi. His case presented to unsuspecting Navi delivered with just the right amount of indignation showing, demonstrating that he is much angrier than daft Navi, who is stunned preoccupied, not knowing what had just hit her. This was how it was, it was always so well-rehearsed in Stephen's mind, every angle, every word tailored to guide his desired outcome and with years of successfully counselling others at work simply did not help when blindsided by him. Ah, but she would always rise to the challenge of trying to circumvent this game, take the loving, let us calmly and wisely talk it through approach. Maybe, he knew this, hence the game played on. Navi sod just keeps hoping that someday, life partner man would grow out of his need to play this game.

She turned toward the fridge, reached for disinfectant, a garbage bag, a wad of paper towels and knelt down on hands and knees. She pulled a plastic grocery bag over one hand forming a cup trying to ignore sensations of stiff furry rat in her hand. With a tail dangling out and sliding along her wrist she stood, "SHIT!!!!!!!!!!" arms outstretched and shook the contents allowing tail to drop inward and quickly tied a knot then opening the front door against pounding wind and snow, hurled the bag and contents out into a gust of wind. "SHIT!!!!!!!!!!" The wind immediately caught the bag; rat flew and plunked on top of the barbeque. "SHIT!!!!!!!!!! Yuck! SHIT!!!!!!!!!! SHIT!!!!!!!!!! Bloody hell"

Navi hesitated, picturing traumatized kids, or cat bone crunching munching on it. 'To hell with it, Stephen will see it and deal with it.'

Back toward the fridge, kneeling, she began to scrub while mouth breathing to avoid rank dead rat stench and feces.

'Stephen must have an inner critic. Probably a military battle strategist.'

Navi packaged bits of rat turds and dirt into an old plastic bread bag and tied the end of the bag in a good tight knot.

Replaying their last heated discussion, it was loud like shouting, although no one actually raised their voices. She felt it in her heart, in her body rattling bones. Typical marital buttons pushed, strings pulled then before she knew what had hit her, he fired his ultimate drama bullet; his son had cancer. Well, of course, no argument and no contest. Of course, Matt was a priority, of course, of course. Yet there was a nagging elusive insight that she could not put a finger on. Stephen's resolution was simple; leave her with the very scary Junker van.

She had sat gathering adult composure at the top of the workshop stairs, preoccupied, staring at him while he worked and trying to figure out what his punch line might be. How was it that he could spend so many long hours in this cold, damp and dusky old workshop, futzing away at sculptures and not get sick? How does he not go blind from the persistent welding sparks? I guess it is that blue glow of the torch. How did he come to conclusions about things all on his own and then become the law of the land, without her consultation? It must be some primal and Neanderthal DNA coding, that he accessed in male genetic soup. Primordial warrior man swamp and cave soup, where he accessed ancestral warring brother hood inspiration. Hunched over hairy furry dirty men sat aside campfire, ripping meat off bones with teeth, grunting, holding own penis in hand burping and farting. Life is good. Whack a female over the head, drag her by the hair, hump wildly then peacefully snore asleep. Life is awesome.

What and where was that magic piece of the puzzle, that magic motivating bug that killed their relationship? When Matt first got sick, he shaved off his traditional artist's ponytail. Deliriously happy with the dramatic shaven head cooing attention he was getting, he would respond to friends, family and acquaintances with sad eyed quivering lips and puffed chest with dramatic flair and sighing. What irked Navi was that she cynically and instinctively knew him well enough to see through bogus altruistic honour of Matt's recovery. More irritating, no one else seemed to see through the façade. Perhaps folks simply played along. After all, who would dare question his intentions, a game both enjoyed.

Is that not what people do to show their support of cancer victims while raising money for the Cancer Society? None of it would make Matt better. Surely, the hair cuttings and money went to a noble cause. Still, there was something ugly and dark about the whole thing. Cancer was like torturous rape and vile murder. It was a vicious and ugly disease that rendered victims and families weak and vulnerable and therefore, difficult to maintain one's grace despite petty resentments and outright fear. Suddenly he was of late, demonstrating a newfound undying support for the boy's comfort, no longer critically riding Matt's ass. Well thank God for small miracles! Yet Stephen was also arbitrarily disregarding everyone else. The boy was of the same genetic personality traits and characteristics as his father, but balanced and in a good way and once one of Stephen's favourite roasting targets for a change of scenery from Navi. The sparring roast was okay for a time, assuming they all had to work out guilt and other issues that came part in parcel with having a terminally ill child in the house.

'Would he have done all that for me if I was the one sick with cancer? Yes' she thought in hope, 'but not for the vast love he has for me, but because he loves the drama, shamefully so, loves the picture it presents to the world.

Yes, my husband loves to present pretty pictures of home, family and sculptures so that people could ooohhh and aaaawwww.' Navi caught herself short. It rang immature and cynical, even to her.

She wondered what cynical things he thought of her. While he never said so much to her directly, she only had to wait until her friends or family were around. Stephen thought that his suave shindig and witty manner always elicited laughter. On the surface, one would call the man a small and cruel asshole, but in Stephen's mind, done so brilliantly well, that his audience would laugh and comment on how funny and witty the man was.

What angle could she try to get him to discuss the car situation?

A tattered old bungee cord kept the ancient van's back door almost always shut. Tight bends and corners however, brought a distracting slamming-opening of back doors while sledding sideways on bald tires. No, it just could not hold up in this weather, not to mention the fact that the muffler vicariously hung on mangled wire coat hanger and duct tape. Then there was the matter of actually seeing out of the windshield; frayed wiper blades blew in the wind and left streaks of slime making her bob in search of a spot to see out of. It sounded like an army truck and bounced all over the road on a good day, let alone a snow stormy one. Stephen normally drove the thing back and forth to work seemingly unbothered and unscathed no matter the weather. She figured that he kept it as a dramatic piss off demonstration to both ex-wives; he did not have any more money to give. Yes, it was a prop to give them both a message, don't take me to court again! I have nothing! See how poor I am, see how I suffer?'

Attention turned to Abby's whining upstairs. Navi's mind and soul shot out and upstairs like a mother magnet that only a mother would understand; mommy radar. "I have to! I got the school skate-a-thon dis afternoon", she blurted to Matt, as though the event was more important than his need to pee. 'Oh dam, I forgot about that.' Navi shouted up the stairs; sorry kiddo, I am not driving you in this weather, not today. It is too much of a blizzard out there. I'll take you on Saturday and we'll have the whole afternoon and hot chocolate too." Listening for a response and hearing none, Navi envisioned the projectile nah-nah tongue in Matt's general direction. Oh yes, and pick up early to be back at a dental appointment in town, then shopping. Matt's Mom who had the luck of having a corporate lawyer for a brother-in-law, did well, very well indeed, as Dear Stephen simply could not compete with a man more eloquent and closer to his primal warrior nature than a seasoned criminal lawyer could. Unknown to Stephen, the woman was calmly stealthily brilliant; as art curator at the gallery, she offered special contracts and commissions on his work. She did very well indeed.

It was a step mommy's bugaboo budget stressor that Matt's Mom did not allow hand me downs nor second hand clothes shopping. No, shopping entailed a trip to the big city's best stores, spas and luncheons. Third wife Navi had long since felt resentment residue for how well they were doing. In resentment stead, a silent admiration, albeit an enigma, awe for her fortitude of mission to have the best and only the best. Matt could not care less, nor Abby.

Every Christmas like clockwork, the woman would mildly threaten Stephen with court action and he chicken ran. A big cash-out axe wielded at his head, desperately selling prized sculptures to accommodate. Navi mildly envied that she had the audacious smarts to do it to him. It never ceased to amaze, how Stephen acquiesced to the financial demands and legal threats. Out of love for her own, Navi never gave up hope that the extortion would end, likely when Matt had children of his own. In the interim, there would be university and a wedding.

Despite disparity issues within blended family, she maintained a fantasy of the two of them one day functioning as a happy healthy couple. It simply was not in her nature to fight for money and material possessions. Matt's Mom focused on her career. Still managing Stephen's work occasionally, quietly tolerating him from a distance knowing that he was pretty much incapable of managing his own financial affairs, made up for her dues by skimming extra off his sculpture sales. Integrity and principles have to help the abundance flow in the end.

Driving the kids to school, then commuting into the next county to the office in a snowstorm in the rotten crap box of a vehicle was on a normal day, a good hour and a half across country. Images of driving the old shit box in snow squalls, riddled her body with aversive anxiety.

Navi had sat watching, while Stephen, lost in thought wheeled a router around and around some sort of wooden base of a new sculpture, oblivious to her presence. The sculpture looked like a giant heron, graceful and majestically wing spanned in flight. It was without a doubt, simply incredible and it was shaping up to be his best yet. 'It is an amazing gift; how he makes such beautiful things out of rusty old scraps of metal. Truly, the man is gifted. Truly this man is connected with the divine.' She had always seen the divine in his work. No normal person could make such beautiful things out of other peoples garbage. Picasso; gifted, ahead of his time perhaps, but no less troubled a soul than he, and not a whole lot better at dealing with relationships than his ghostly dearly departed twisted brilliant mentor.

'Am I selfish, or just really stupid?' No, I suppose Gandhi's wife would have preferred at times that he might forget about saving Africa and India and could just take one damned moment to fix the damned well so that she could wash his damned soiled loincloth!

There had to be a better way, an easier solution than risking the lives of the kids, driving the old Junker was just not right by any standards. Navi did a mental inventory of their finances. There was no room left on her credit card to rent a van for a week; that would be at least five to six hundred dollars, minimum. She had suggested when Matt was diagnosed that they 'get another loan and buy a reliable van, balls to the budget, but we'd all be safe'. Then maybe in the spring she could buy a newer van. Stephen had responded to her brilliant solution by blurting that she was cold and inconsiderate, should gladly hand over her car if she were not such a selfish person. If she did not like the Junker, then she could rent a van and pay for it herself.

Navi was dumbfounded. Guilt. Tears. Fear. The abandonment dagger lingered and stung. Taking a deep breath, she proposed that they get him a newer van of his own. Easily done, their buddy would be glad to help, given the situation with Matt. Stephen was in a not speaking to beloved Navi period, and her words fell on muted ears. Discussion was; closed. He turned on the loud roaring router to emphasize the point.

If she could just have held ground a little rather than the normal off balance as she was in the moment, hurt and guilt would not have pervaded. The anxiety of driving the van rattled weary bones despite being accustomed to driving in snowstorms.

The router stopped for a moment, he glared at her over top of metal dust speckled glasses. Obviously giving the situation more thought, bulging angry eyes widened and lips pursed, face flesh anger red "You should have taken care of everything yourself. You should have done something, Navi! Work it out. I am busy here. I have to deal with Matt's treatments."

Discussion closed, neglecting to clarify exactly what she was supposed to do. Dumbfounded, Navi's emotions whirled pounded an already sore heart. 'That's it, drop a bomb, don't elaborate and don't discuss it.' Navi knew what was to follow; he would not speak to her, left yet alone trying to figure what to do.

Abby was always good for snuggles and thankfully, oblivious to Navi's own occasional childlike needs for comfort and affection. Childless adults had cats, dogs, birds, fish, snakes and turtles to love up and care for. A magical child, who innately loved, was intimately demonstrative, old soul wise and eager to share all, including gum scavenged from sidewalks. A blessed Navi instantly allowed waves of loving healing to flow from angel child comfort.

As per usual, Stephen had gone about his business being animated, friendly and jovial to everyone else in the frigging house and silently shooting hostile barbs into the core of her being. One day, the pendulum of power would swing back permanently. Taking a deep breath in and a relaxing somewhat, she made her way into the kitchen and began to sort dirty dishes.

"Yes Gran, I stare out of my kitchen window like millions of other women around the world trying to figure out their idiot husbands, dysfunctional families and lot in life."

A vision played before her movie screen mind's eye of some ethereal sisterhood support group. All meeting at the same time and place each day from respective kitchen realities, consulting and consoling each other. Images flashed and faded like clips from different television shows blending the not so bright materialistic June Cleaver types with the altruistic social evolutionist Oprah's, with trashy mouthed feisty bitch slapping women from reality shows who intermingled with overwhelmed grannies, family remnants lost to the Aids pandemic. The world outside was ever changing and mothers who carried the woes of world upon shoulders and within souls. They were too busy with day-to-day doings to form one massive matriarchal power revolution. Kitchens, or better yet, bathing spaces inevitably became private temples away from it all, communion with Gaia and the all that is, places of solace, contemplation, meditation and rejuvenation. Navi's external world support group beyond the wild women gang and kids were Chickadees, Raccoons and Crows that cohabitated in the back forty.

In the moment of guard down relaxation, tears burned for release behind lonesome eyes. One deep breath held it all at bay refusing unbridled spillage from weary eyes; she would not allow him to see her soul raw tears. Ashamed in the moment of her own lack of spiritual self-mastery, these exchanges hurt deeply and smacked of ineffective victim mentality. Perhaps, she simply had too high a tolerance level for his shit based on some naive notion of what being a higher evolved soul might be.

Little winged creatures flapped and flittered in feeding frenzy at the feeder while a geographically dislocated opossum whom she named Nigel fed on their discards in the snow. The scene brought forth a wide gratifying smile in adoration gaze. They were friends and extended family that kept her company, especially through the long winters of Stephen's silent hostile withdrawals.

SLAM!!! The slam of the front door sent a shock wave through her stretched nervous system, reverberating and pounding through her ears. It was a final word from Stephen that shouted, 'Fuck you, Navi. Have a nice fucking day!'

'Arse!' A deep breath in, she allowed a calming wave of silence to flow within. A fly by loving embrace from Matt brought welcome tension relief. Stephen was indeed taking Matt back to his Mom's, then off to work.

Abby in snowsuit stiffness made her way up the tall school bus steps. Snow pellets threatened entry into Navi's coat and up pajama legs, watched an adorable Abby smile and flop into her best friend's bench seat. Knowing that daughter was in good spirits brought a wave of satisfaction and smiles.

'Ah, it is a glorious thing I am officially in hibernation. No bath just yet, nubs can grow into dread locks.' Pausing, glancing at the phone, 'Nope, not answering the phone, someone else can handle any emergencies. I am a mama bear, cocooned in away from cold wind and snow, safe from the demands and noise of the world for a day.' Navi picked up a novel, curled up in her bed with layers of p-jams and slippers and all, getting up occasionally only to pee and to eat. It was indeed a deliciously glorious morning.

By noon and still not ready for bath nor house work, yet laziness of lying in bed reading done, her mind drifted to earlier days as a child in church.

Women huddled and busily prepared food in the Church basement kitchen after each service while children played with abandon under the supervision of men who sat on their duffs at the picnic table outside chatting and smoking. Gran was the family matriarch as well as for the whole of their church community. While articulated adoration was voiced, it was obvious in body language and facial expression within her interactions and other's demeanor that all looked up to her strength and wisdom. Discreetly, all sought her maternal guidance before considering consultation with their Minister. When Gran croaked, she left a quantum abyss within Navi's soul that only little Abby and Matt came close to fulfilling. Thinking on it now, Gran's parting left a profound homesickness hole in her soul.

During Gran's post funeral gathering, adolescent Navi hid childlike in the church stairway eavesdropping in on kitchen bitchy female prattle and gossip. Tension was mounting as meal preparations ensued amongst subversive politicking, rallying and jostling for positioning as to who might now assume Gran's role as congregation leader. An unofficial now highly coveted position within the Church hierarchy in the minds of all the women. For all appearances, the inner feline political rallying was executed with grace and calm, yet nasty. With un-articulated words, thoughts, intentions and body language, it was a gang assed bloody hen fight with only dismembered carcasses left by going home time.

Mother had naively entered the jostling arena, naturally assuming that she was next in line in assuming Gran's role, given the simple fact that she was the next direct descendent in line. This assumption on Mother's part was a fatal mistake and quickly snuffed out by a direct hit from Mrs. McPatterson, "Jean, did you ever get the hang of your mother's knack for making her delicious turkey stuffing?" Mrs. McPatterson cooed with confidence, chortling as thrown off balance Mother looked directly at the bitch. Crimson flushes mingling with the paleness of embarrassment, Mother's inability to feign otherwise and unable to hide her shock from the low and maiming hit. Having Mother's complete attention, pin drop silence amongst the others, all engaged waiting for follow through. Undaunted bitch crone continued, "My dear, your stuffing is soooo dry that my poor Harold nearly choked to death on it last Thanksgiving." All minds simultaneously recalled the incident as Harold choked and gasped, sputtering drool mingling with projectile bits of bread and onion until Minister Bob, Heimlich rescued.

A surreal silence reverberated in the room, as all eyes focused upon the two. Mother stood still at the counter, tea towel in hand, visibly shaking, face pallor ashen then fading slowly to blazing red of semi controlled unbridled rage. Knowing this rare flash of rage from first-hand experience, Navi held her breath as Mother fought for control of her shaking body and being. Primal fight instincts ethereally ripped the Bitch Crone to shreds. Slowly straightening her spine the anal and pious religious above it all decorum gradually took hold. From Mother's core being, Navi recognized the twitching of clenching jaw and averted the livid death gaze.

Silent for too long, fire energy dissipating, Mother was simply too livid and too hurt to respond effectively and turn it around to her way. There would be holy hell to pay at home for everyone else for a month, as Mother vented displaced wrath. Mother's inability to one up the Bitch Crone deathblow spoke of temporary defeat, yet it was not over. There would be back door gossiping, politicking and complaining for months, but eventually all would acquiesce and accept the fall out with practical conclusions. Mother would glibly report that she never wanted the position in the first place, simply too much bother.

Mrs. McPatterson Bitch Crone arched her back in superiority, puffed out her primordial monstrous bosom and smiled with narrowing shifty eyes, scanning the frozen gawking women and taking a mental tally of those in new-formed alliance.

Satisfied, "Ah Jean Dear, you know I'm only telling a joke."

Navi stared at Mother who stun-glared disbelief at Mrs. McPatterson Bitch Crone. Weaker women feigned chuckles opting for stolen alliance as others regained their own composure, trying to lighten the tension. The first hit was cruel, the second hit was indirectly aimed at all of them as a statement of fact of the power of intimidation dare anyone challenge her self-assumed position. Navi noted Mother's spirit draining and pooling under Sunday best high heels. Surreally silent, mind swirling, body vibrating, Mother shredded a carrot. Women blown away, partially ashamed at their own cowardly lack of intervention and support on Mother's behalf shifted the silence by busying themselves and chatting of the day's warm weather. Composure slowly regained, two Aunties took position on each side of Mother, a demonstration of alliance, support and comfort. It was only then that Mother was able to shift in her spot.

Although, nothing more was openly aired that particular day, the new Community Matriarch assumed control. Everything that was going to be officially stated about the decision had been said, under the watchful eyes of God and the reaping of bad karma.

Through the years, no one woman took the true Matriarchal place of Gran. Politicking and gossiping became the norm. Bickering would heat up then fade. Leadership fractions drifted depending on who was in the good books at the time. Behind closed doors, secret meetings also became the norm as to who was doing what or not doing what or who had said what to whom had to be reported and hashed. Mrs. McPatterson's ineffectiveness at maintaining harmony in a good way gradually took a toll. Out of control, petty jealousies and gossip filled community mind and spilled out of archaic petty mouths while the world at large was rapidly changing. New church comers rarely came, nor did the young demonstrate interest in archaic small-minded tradition. Occasionally newcomers to the tiny rural community would arrive with smiles in hopes of joining a happy community fellowship. Greeted by trivial gossip, failing true spiritual guidance and fellowship, each newcomer disappeared in short order.

Navi at the time was just grateful that the shit fall out rarely came her way.

Long time fire and brim stone Minister Bob finally retired followed by others who came and went with the seasons as the tiny congregation shrunk. Lastly, old Pastor Stanley, kind and seemingly loving was as is ineffectual and powerless in coping with the women as Mother had been that day. Bitch Crone and her weak gang members ran the show. They ruled without integrity and without adult maturity.

It was a living soap opera version of Lord of the Flies.

Mother never forgave Mrs. McPatterson and Navi grew a new respect for the hurt impaled on Mother, vowing to allow it to rest in peace. Her brothers less tactful, still teasingly brought it up at family gatherings with the tradition of giving thanks and blessings for her throat choking 'dry stuffing', sure to make you croak. Navi never ate stuffing after that fatal church day. Not because it was not tasty, but because stuffing, especially when made by Mother, seemed filled with primordial hostility relived in the making of it. Mother continued to make it year after year, yet also refrained from eating it, 'painful stuffing was not to be ingested'.

The analogy of *stuffing* not lost upon either of them.

Three o'clock by Navi's calculations and Abby's bus would soon be arriving, bringing odorous waves of school paper and glue with little girl prattles of the day. Followed a few short hours later by one crusty arsehole, pretentious office cloud odours trailed and hung mid-air. 'Not much time.'

She shoved an all-nighter log into old smoky wood stove then scooted upstairs to the bath, intent on a full hot bath with scented bubbles. Smelly sweaty pajamas still inside robe lazily shed beside the overflowing laundry bin and onto floor. Deliciously sliding into near to over flowing soothing warm water she sensually splayed floating while resting a weary head on tub rim. Lifting long hair braid and draping it over the back rim, allowing joyous warm water caress and swirl around small premenopausal breasts that bobbed lightly at surface edge. Alone and deliciously happy, she basked as moisture heat rising fogging window and swirled in cool air.

Alone, save for Brat Kat and Dawg. 'Where on earth were those two anyway? She had not seen nor heard from either all morning. Intuitively seeing both curled up on Abby's bed, only shifting to follow incoming bits of window sunshine streamers. Like Navi, inside house animals, in a long moment of solitude, were gloriously happy.

Crisp smell of herbal soap lather, reminiscent of summer herb harvest, slowly cleansed weary senses. Turning her head and body, eyes took in the wintry garden and forest on the other side of the foggy big bay window. Smiling, her bathroom renovation ingenious design; a wide panoramic window expanded beside the tub offering profound continued enjoyment of outdoor garden, surrounding farmland and distant forest while soaking. An old antique claw foot bathtub found at the dump one summer's day brought a mission from within to haul it home. A crafty red neck neighbour had negotiated a rather steep forty-dollar pickup and delivery fee. At the time it had irked her, yet, in hind sight it was worth the forty bucks just to watch the dumb ass and his monstrously oversized teenaged moron son lift it off of their ancient pickup truck and heave it onto her front porch. It must have weighed a ton! Yes, it was worth forty dollars just to watch two monstrously fat asses bulge out of scanty jeans as they grunted and heaved the metal load up the deck stairs.

For a year, old honking tub had sat outside where they had left it. By mid-winter, Navi had rigged up a garden hose through the kitchen window and attached it to the hot water tap with duct tape. Filled to the brim with bubbles over flowing one starry snowy night; shared with a happier then Stephen, a bottle of wine and wisps of snow in the air. The memory of a rare good loving time-shared, rapidly followed with a wave of sadness with abyss re-assumed.

Now in private slice of heaven, as though built especially for her, the tub was just the right size and had just the right slanted angle. Its thick cast iron walls maintained hot water heat for hours. Long days at work and endless in between errands survived knowing bathtub heaven waited. The window view was like a slow-paced movie that played out as garden and forest changed slightly from day to day throughout the seasons. Yes, it was a stroke of shear brilliance, especially since no one could see in because the up angle was simply too high. The view extended beyond rose gazebo, garden and into the forest. Beyond the forest, a distant farm field lay flat in white as a snow dump receptacle.

Inspired by a pile of old farmhouse pine found once at an auction sale, each plank was tenderly cut, stripped and fitted perfectly into puzzle place wainscoting surrounding tub and window. It was all a beautiful stroke of inspired genius born and birthed of her eclectic country cottage style. Like the kitchen window and the old ancient sisterhood shawl, this was Navi's sacred place. These spaces she shared with millions of other working mothers who found solace in the bathtub.

Sanctuary.

Comparatively, Navi did not consider herself a nature nut, yet had to have trees and water, far away from mingling people crowds and cement.

Over the years, she had intimately come to know each tree in the yard and every inch of the acreage.

A white wash world outside, of blanketed snow covered forms. Frost growing fern like, on window indicated an obvious drop in temperature. The world outside was a sparkling blanket of tinkling white starry lights. Sparkling late afternoon sunshine dancing and flashing diamonds. Northern winds began to pick up with circulating gusts forcing white powder air born, making the outside world invisible.

The Crows Mabel and Clifford jockeyed for position at the compost bin with bits of old bread in beaks. The old black-feathered conjuror couple had long assumed the top of the compost bin food chain order of command and pecking order. Chickadee family flitted back and forth from cedars to feeder. Navi had come to recognize all eight of them. Standing at the feeder with seed in hand outstretched, they flittered and landed on outstretched gloved hands to peck tiny Niger bits and black sunflower treats.

Lone possum lovingly named Nigel, sat on her rose garden gazebo wall, contentedly munching on an old crust of bread as drool dripped out the side of his mouth, whilst strategically keeping watchful eye on the compost bin and front porch. His delectable treat of preference, was cat and dog kibble. Safe here for now, but sooner or later, local farmers would catch wind or sight of his ass and do him in. The Ministry of Natural Resources would hoot and turn a blind eye in farmer favour, whose horses would be spared his fatally poisonous possum urine. Eventually Nigel would have to go, and secretly, she hoped that he and his relatives would conclude their own inevitable demise, and head back to the southern states from whence their ancestors came, of their own accord. Better yet, scientists will discover and proclaim that possum pee is not fatal after all, just another rural myth.

The two hundred year old Grandmother and Grandfather Maple trees stoically stood guard along the forest fence line. Grandmother Maple consisted of a huge V split mid trunk, like a monstrous vagina where honeybees hived and swarmed each spring until late fall. Tall Grandfather Maple was solid and donned one large frontal phallic like branch that extended outward and upward. With unabated pride, his constant hard on boldly spoke of masculine passion that remained an unknown experience in Navi's life. The image and example obviously lost on Stephen.

A circle of white pines called Stone Hedge was home and playground to a raccoon family. While only the biggest, the fat daddy Patriarch named Buddha, ever ventured close to the house and the shed. His calm pudgy demeanor foraged for garbage and pet food leftovers to feed his motley little

Stone Hedge gang. They contentedly lived, played and entertained on the periphery of the garden, her heart skipping in reverence at the beauty of it all.

The only disruption to the slice of heaven, where all animals seemingly lived in harmony, sharing space and compost and feeder, was Tree Rat. Nasty and vicious, red squirrel was quick to anger, faster and more agile that an angry hornet, it often chased after Brat Kat where Dawg had simply learned early on to give it a wide birth. Navi loved this place. Sanctuary.

A bolt of noise rattled her reverie as the back door slammed shut, rudely entering the sanctity of her deliciously private space.

"Mom? Mom? Hi Mom. I'm gonna watch TV now, k?"

Where had the time gone? Sanctuary was over for the day. Elated Navi acknowledged foresight in having stayed home was now ready once again to cope with life.

As Stephen with Matt in tow bolted through the front door the wind seized opportunity and blew in snow and cold, cold air. Assuming his early home arrival was due to bad weather she then gave way to feigned annoyance, "Why does everyone have to slam that door?"

A peanut butter and jam faced Abby met Navi mid hallway and blurted "Hi Mom. What'd ya do today?"

"Hi darling."

Navi scooped Abby up in loving warm mom arms and pulled Matt in with a hair ruffle and shoulder squeeze in place of a full hug. "Um, I went to church." Stephen sharply and quizzically glanced at Navi then dismissed any questions in his mind and made a beeline for his workshop, letting the door slam behind him.

"Wonderful to see you too, Darling" the sarcastic blurt a little more audible to younger ears than she had intended.

"There are two ways you can live life,
as if nothing is a miracle,
as if everything is a miracle."
Albert Einstein

Chapter 3 ~ Auschwitz!

Saturday.

Abby, back from upscale city slicker shopping, donned a shiny new designer ski suit with matching toque, mittens and boots. Abby's stepmother, had graced her with a once in a life time visit. Navi dismissed a petty envy jealousy jab of the woman's affluence at Abby's father's hands. Feeling abandoned left out of that financial and caring loop rapidly dissipated as the Barbie doll Sue emerged from the BMW. Her fur coat openly demonstrated a pink stylish bosom enhanced cashmere sweater in perfect tasteful harmony with manicured nails, coiffure hair and Hollywood sunglasses. Expensive perfume hung in nippy air. Dawg jumped up and down on designer jeans, wildly sharing excitement, as glamour woman bobbed in avoidance of perceived filthy, flea infested, undisciplined mutt. Normally, Navi would easily divert Dawg's exuberance but in the moment immaturely enjoyed the waltz.

"A young girl needs to be current with snow suit fashion trends for country toboggan hill extravaganzas, even when one resides in farm country where most of the kids wear hand me down farm coveralls." Navi cynically mused.

Oblivious to maintaining fine keeping of new snowsuit with price tag still dangling from back collar, Navi smiled and watched on as streams of snot mucous formed and slithered down Abby's nose only to be backhand sleeved wiped enroute outside in the snow with Dawg bouncing behind. Abby otherwise in second hand, was oblivious to fashion trends and just happy to be out of school, out of the house and hanging with Dawg in the snow. New snot streams formed lines dangling out of little girl nose. Feeling the tickle of it, she quickly wiped using the back of a fancy new mitten. Now mats of hair mingling with drying snot stuck to her cheek and forehead. It was divine retribution; her daughter's affection could not be respectfully bought. Dawg's attention was diverted with a found delicious morsel of Kat turd, and then dove into a downed Abby for a kiss lick. "Ewwww", "Ewwwww", whined a snot crust-faced girl. Disgusted, awkward with the slumming exchange, Sue queen waved to an oblivious snow emerged Abby.

Matt's mom pulled up to the snow banked porch, grey boy gingerly emerging, home from another round of chemo treatments and wearily headed for bed. Navi intimately knowing the routine, he would only be capable of giving into and awake only for meds the following day. It was odd that, Matt's mother did not seem to be caught up in the 'Matt's sick drama campaign'. Navi figured that like her, most mothers would lock up and dote on their child if they were that sick. Not Matt's mom, she did not skip a beat. She knew that everything that could be done; was being done. Status quo was the best route, which included allowing Stephen his dramas. Navi had a growing deeper level of respect for the woman and gratitude of all that she was.

Sounds of crappy old rock and roll screeched from down in the workshop mingling with power tools and welder's torch.

Matt in bed, Abby snow tunneled in drifts. Why do mothers always inventory? A mother goose counting little chicks, yes, okay, all accounted for, now I can actually relax for a bit. An embarrassing long litany in response to a simple question always ensued; 'How old are your kids?' She would have to pause and look up at the sky as if accessing some mysterious database, or the Akashi Records themselves or some other higher intelligent source. Then pause to calculate, well Matt is first in line, yes he is um, sixteen almost seventeen, I think, or is he only almost fifteen and Stephen's only child from his first wife. Then, um, Abby, um, is six, no, seven years younger than Matt is, yes. No, wait. Eleven? I know if you do the math they are a little too far away in age for friendship, so that would make her, hmm, yes, nine or not quite because she has a birthday coming up, so ten save a week or two, bringing up the rear, yes, Abby is twelve I think. Sigh. No, please do not ask me what grades. What makes it all worse is that they go to different schools in different counties. I don't know why, it's just the way it all worked out." The feigned gaze of interest ignored by inventory Navi, who in these moments simply could not help the blithering litany, it simply flowed unabated from her mouth only stopping in exasperated embarrassment upon noticing the preverbal audience's glazed over eyes.

Stoic in the face of a childhood illness and trips for treatment, the waiting, praying and normal doings of life, continued. Bills paid, work went on, the care of all things not Matt's chemo treatments and Stephens's art career, fell to Navi with day-to-day happenings looming overhead with commuting to work, little Abby, pets, work, errands and chores.

Navi glanced at the kitchen calendar. "Damn. I took Friday off and now I have to take Monday morning as well. Why in the hell can I not get a damn dentist appointment on a weekend? I hate wasting precious vacation time on a kid's dental appointment.' She would inevitably have to take a whole day off to accommodate one child's appointment. Abby's Dad T.J. lived far away in Florida with Barbie doll Sue wife and the task of which Navi had previously and happily agreed to taking care of, of having early jaw aligning for too many big teeth bracing apparatus gizmos glued and retro-fitted, now felt daunting and overwhelming. Sizing up the possibility of rescheduling, she considered its importance. Abby's teeth had long outgrown her small jaw to which an opportunist affluent seeking orthodontist spared rare missed appointments. Young for the treatment, necessity turned crisis with one root canal after another until weak enamel had left fragile teeth that could crack at first crunch into a taco chip. No, it was the last one and it had to be done right away. Simply terrified of the entire dental visits now, little girl toad would require wailing drama and heavy sedation.

Winter is, and should be a mass cocoon time for everyone, a waiting time until spring. You could not make concrete plans for anything, because you never know when it will snow squall and blizzard. It was a holding time, a time of waiting for the world to come alive again, come alive with colour, sunshine, sounds of tiny wildlife and the fresh deep smells of the soil and the earth.

February dread was closing in. It was a short and dark pervading month like November, long, dark and dreary. Dreary days brought sad unsettling dreams out of the shadows like evil haunting spirits.

Consciously calling in Soul Skin apparition fantasy man, she allowed sensual warm bath water to caress skin and hair. A glimpse of his hand, head shaped with greying hair and blazing blue eyes bringing forth a wave of soul longing, a calling. Feeling a loving ghostly hand caress hair and touch hand on hand, she drifted away enveloped in angelic twin soul arms. Skin disappeared, a blending of pure soul and spirit into intimate oneness.

As quickly as the moment arose, it faded. A luxurious bath bringing no real solace, she slid down into hot water, sending a mass of fresh scented bubbles air born, only to snap and disappear. Braids hanging over back of tub rim, eyes closed seeking harmony.

Instantly, Navi found herself in spirit form, hurling out into space, transporting far away.

Surreal time slowed to a stop.

Where am I?

Auschwitz?

No!

Yes!

Back in the tub, slinking chin deep in hot water and bubbles that crackled and tickled inside of her nose, acutely aware of how unusually calm and contented she now was. Noting it had indeed been a long time in coming. Eyes slightly opened to halo glow of candle flickering, casting strands of orange and yellow light beams splaying prism shadows on the fogged bathtub window. Allowing the warmth and calm to sink deep into bones and tissue a growing awareness of another strange tingling sensation rippled within her skin. Eyes closed, she consciously aimed for OM, withdrawing into space world of nothingness, Om and contented 'all that is' space.

In a flash, Navi's body disappeared. Aware of her physical body left in the tub, her spirit transported yet again up toward the ceiling. For a moment, hovering conscious aware mind still with both as body in the tub, spirit body floated above. A grasp of slight panic shifted into a natural desire to maintain equilibrium that instantly vanished as a warm wave of calm and lightness pervaded her being.

Watching from above, her body motioned to cry, heave and wail leaving her faint.

Waves of dizziness and nausea flowed, calmed then mingled with foreboding then finally, stillness. Split awareness of body in the tub and hovering above, distinct in two places simultaneously, yet one simultaneously.

Physical eyes winced as a flash of light almost blinded her, while hovering spirit eyes gazed into the fullness of light. Instantly, flew up through ceiling, attic and roof. Hovering, spirit eyes turned to glance back, seeing through roof, attic and ceiling onto physical body safe in tub.

Assuming full spirit body consciousness and its spiritual power and newfound freedom, she sped, aiming directly into the blinding light. At impact, an explosion of smaller rainbow lights fire worked the starry night sky mingling with strange muffled harmonic sounds and soft loving voices. Basking in the joyful array of lights and angelic music, her thinking mind was distinctly aware of them as separate outside of her physical body yet, as one. Gradually soft comforting voices and harmonics faded as a harsher greyer lower one grew in volume as though one was turning down a radio while turning up a television set.

Abruptly, she found herself standing in someone's apartment. Knowing familiarity and instinct told her that this was her home, yet in this lifetime, she had never seen the place before. A stab of anxiety arose in the pit of her stomach, a slight panic of wanting to bolt. How could she be here in this strange ominous place? How could she be here and where exactly was she?

Aware that she was somehow accompanied by an angelic presence and 'observing', as people mingled about and around her invisible presence, a child scurried right through her body.

Navi felt herself split consciousness again; aware of her encased in a physical body in this apartment kitchen, doing dishes as spirit mind hovered, observing the fading invisible field.

Navi or 'Anna' could hear her soul skin husband chatting at the doorway, friendly and familiar with an old lady neighbour while their two children tussled about in the living room, snickering and giggling at a private joke. Slightly annoyed that they were ignoring duty of music lessons at hand, Anna relaxed upon hearing little violins squeal, wrenching on anxious nerves. How odd, this was normally such a joyful time. Moving to the hallway to find out who and why there was a knock at the door, Navi hesitated, glancing down at the body of the woman she was in. Fuller breasts bounced slightly under a soft pink cashmere sweater. Aware of being several inches taller with thicker legs covered by grey woolen stockings under a darker grey woolen skirt that rested well below her knees onto calves. Black old woman nurse shoes donned her feet that reminded her of footwear that her own great grandmother wore.

BANG!!!! Anna jumped out of nervous skin as their apartment door banged open wide slamming husband aside to a wall. Uniformed men were instantly inside of their apartment. With alarmed heart pounding, she instinctively bolted to gather children. Mind racing, a small boy and a smaller girl gathered into her bosom, hiding fearful faces into her neck. Heart pounding within her ears mingled with harsh voices of two men in black uniforms. One stood with a pistol aimed directly at her while the other pushed husband out of the doorway at rifle point. Her dreamlike head swirled and she swiftly found herself ushered out of the door with babes in arms herded down the front stairway.

A voice blared into mind soul and bones, 'Nazi special forces soldiers'.

"ANNA! ANNA!" Husband was shouting, wailing, calling from down the street. Two more green uniformed soldiers met them at the stairway landing, wrenching daughter first, and then son from her tight grip and harshly into their own arms. Tiny arms outstretched to her, "Mama! Mama!" screamed tiny red faces wet with terror. Wide eyes, tears and mucous intermingled with traumatized pleading. Her mouth opened, screams emitted outward from within, lost in chaotic air and falling onto deaf ears.

It was happening all so fast, yet in the moment she struggled against gripping arms in maternal force to bolt after babes. Shuffled roughly then barely using her own feet, she was fumblingly dragged down lobby steps and out into the open street. Ears perked searching, listening intently for direction of her babes that only murmured amongst harsh voices, shouting, scuffling, crying and wailing of others in the backs of large canvassed trucks lining the street. Children wailed, dogs barked, babies cried. Primal instincts took awareness to babes somewhere far behind her.

Anna strained against firm body grip of the uniforms that bound her. Frantic eyes and ears searched the street and trucks for her babes and husband. Pushed and shuffled inside the back of a truck her eyes scanned for her babes, who were nowhere in sight and no longer heard. Husband was nowhere to be seen, no longer heard; just barking dogs and soldiers everywhere. Wobbly, taking an open spot on a side wooden bench, her body began to shake only now, threatening a wave of terrified tears. Glancing around at the silent sobbing of others, a shared raw fear within eyes and ears also strained for glimpses of loved ones out of the truck's back tarp window. A family friend, a neighbour roughly pushed by in front of her, blocking any view of the street. Strong musky smell of old canvass, of fear on the breath of those sitting too close for comfort filled her nostrils. The truck sputtered and bolted to life and with each heaving shifted gear, gathered speed. Tarp flapped and snapped loudly in the wind affording glimpses out into the street as the same surreal scene played out door to door.

Several familiar women whimpered in fear, while others strained necks in vain, to peer out through the flapping for view of loved ones and to ascertain what was happening. Unspoken, unbridled, silent panic, Anna opened her mouth, audibly screeching, "Little Baby Anna! Little Jacob! Husband!"

A long hot stuffy drive to what by her calculations felt about an hour or so, the truck slowly down, shifted and heaved abruptly to a stop, then jerked into reverse. Sounds of heavy metal gears then shifted and jarred in lurching synchronicity as the truck heaved forward in accommodation. Shouting voices in another language that was somewhat familiar yet instinctively understood gave way to doing whatever the forcing tone dictated, yet not daring to query why. The Tarp flap opened into a large metal like container, brought conscious realization of a train container, an open cattle car? Soldiers slammed downed the tailgate then at rifle point, motioned and ushered the truck riders into the boxcar.

Strangers in various forms of silent shock and fear stood all around her. Women huddled with older children as old men grasped empty sidewalls. Darting panic eyes brought no sign of little Baby Anna, little Jacob or her beloved Husband. A jolt sent all whirling, no room to sit, barely room to stand. No one dared to speak, nor make a sound. Some whimpered eyes darting in fear while others blank, stared distant, shaking. Panic washed through her body, heart pounding in her ears then the box car spun and swirled as her body crumpled to the floor while hot urine leaked through underwear, skirt and down one leg.

Screeching squeal of metal train brakes pierced through head pounding dizziness. The train jarred once again, sending people scrambling for something solid to hold onto. Through pounding brain and fighting dizziness, she made out words that she understood. An old man helped her to her feet, gesturing that kind people had accommodated her fall. Quiet murmurs within the boxcar now became audible. A young adolescent woman quietly asked of an older well-dressed woman; "Where are they taking us?"

Faces and ears turned to the old woman who glanced at her, and then gazing straight ahead into nothingness replied; "Stop over point. I heard one say that we are going to Oswiecim Work Camp. We are Prisoners of War now."

A tiny old man leaning on a cane in the back spoke up, "No my Dear. That is what they tell us, so we go with little resistance." Anna stood on tip toe to look at the old man's face, his terse expression and tone gave confident power of knowing of some terrifying truth shared with the old woman also knew truth within her soul. "Endolsung der Judenfrage" he blurted. "What does that mean?" demanded a young woman. "Oh my Dear, it is the Nazi's final solution to the Jewish problem. Some will go to work camp and the rest of us will become soap. They will take the fat of our bodies and make soap of it. Kaderu. Jewish soap!"

A numbing silence fell upon the riders, each to their own fear filled thoughts.

Anna recalled rumours growing within the community of people in other places going off to work camps and never returning. Her faith had chosen to forgo giving audience to the ripples of negativity and fear, heart sad now, knowing ignorance seemed naïve at best.

With a squealing jar, the door slid open. Eyes adjusting to the afternoon light, it looked like some sort of industrial compound, surrounded by a high metal fence with barbed wire lining top edges. Soldiers milled about everywhere, some with dogs barking and pulling on tight leads.

Rudely hurdled into straight lines that stretched forward and backward as far as eyes could see, hundreds, maybe even thousands ambled along to an unknown fate. Inside a drab industrial building, women waited in line. The old woman from the boxcar urinated where she stood in the line ahead. A tall heavyset burly soldier barked orders at the old woman using words that Anna could not understand.

Inside, what looked like a simple large empty room, save for large bins that lined one wall, were what were she assumed to be Nazi women in white laboratory coats, barking orders. Not understanding their words, she scanned others for comprehension. Women began stripping; clothes off, jewelry off, even hairpins and tossing all into large bins. Compassionless white jacket Nazi women were rough with the old in a manner that defied innate respect for elder experience. About to rescue the old boxcar woman; a younger woman had ventured to aide, then was immediately struck by a white coat woman wielding a brick, in raised hand.

Soldiers entered, women scrambled to cover themselves and each other of nakedness, as the bins wheeled out of the room carrying the remaining life belongings.

Compassionless white jacket Nazi women barked more orders, motioning a line formation with faces to the wall. Each head was quickly and roughly shaved then all ushered back into line and out into another long narrow hallway. Shuffling, covering nakedness as best they could, into yet another room that looked like a large public communal shower. A blasting spray pelted into the huddled line from a long hose nozzle held by compassionless Nazi women. A foul nostril stinging white chemical dust engulfed the room and hug in stale air.

Alone now, naked women huddled in the foul dreary shower. Women stood looking for direction from old boxcar woman, who whispered, "Delouse! They think we have insects, parasites." Old woman gazed off into some unshared knowing as a single tear slid out of an eye corner, spilled down a white dusted cheek, and pooled in the nap of her neck.

"No Work Camp; Death camp; our final Synagogue." She calmly added.

Anna huddled herself in a corner, arms wrapped around her knees whimpered 'Little Baby Anna, Little Jacob, Husband?" Women huddled in aloneness, some holding small children, each to their own quiet paralyzed shock, panic and disbelief. Quiet sobbing of the younger, while older ashen faces with glazed dissociated eyes starred off into memories and what if's. A stream of light shone through a tiny window in the metal door, dust particles twinkled like first snow, dancing freely.

'Grandmother used to say that those sun streamers were Gods love touching the earth.

'Where are you my husband? Are you still alive? I am here husband in this terrible place. Will I see you again? Where are our babies, dear one? A numbing sensation washed through her body sending ripples through tiny skin hairs. 'Where are my children?' Straightening spine in defiant refusal to allow terror and darkness to envelope her soul and mind 'Must carry on. Must find babies.

Anna focused on God sun streams and dancing snow dust particles, defying terror that awaited conscious thought. Deafening silence mingling with ear ringing, as distant soldiers shouted and dogs growl barked, then gradually faded, leaving the only real audible sound, water dripping.

Awareness shifted to outside in the distance; the muffled sound of trucks moving about. Closer now, a dog barked wildly, growled, and then silence once again. Women huddled alone where they were, then shuddered in unison as a loud SNAP of a gunshot rang through the air close by, followed by a piercing BANG that vibrated through cold naked bodies. Somewhere off in the distance, a baby wailed, shattering maternal nerve endings that yearned to respond to its urgency cry.

SLAM! Jolting in unison as the large metal door opened. A large burley woman entered their shower room, pushing ahead a weeping fat woman. Flung onto the hard floor, the fat woman wailed dramatically in abandoned nakedness, while others watched quietly, too helpless in shock to respond. White smelly snow dust fresh on her skin congealed with tears. Mammoth breasts flopped as she gained her footing "BBABY! My BABBYY!" Primal maternal rescue passion slammed on the closed metal door. Huddled bodies remained where they were, hearts and souls responded in the ethers, tentacles around her. Waves of shock shared and washed through her, life force sliding away and huddling to the floor like the rest.

Time and place became surreal, stench of chemicals, damp mold and cold mingled with a deep, dark sense of foreboding. Anna turned awareness back to the fading sun stream; mind dissociating away from the dark terror at hand. Conscious mind raced to retrace the events of the day, trying in vain against heart pounding in her head to make sense of it all. 'Where are my babies? Where is husband? Are you alive?

A calm prayer emitted begging they be sparred terror and suffering. 'I pray that this just be a nightmare. I will awake and everything is as it should be.'

The only light was growing dimmer now, as the sun stream faded. Judging by the ache in the back of her eyes, she knew that it was now early evening. Her babies would be hungry.

Two mid aged women in a far corner began to whisper. Recalling, as she had herself heard, rumours of entire families and acquaintances that had been taken away by Nazi's and were never seen again. Elders had been gathering in the square each morning to debate and argue the merits and validity of each rumour.

"Yes, they were taken away and never seen again! We should leave, now!"

"No they don't! It is just fear propaganda spread by the Nazi's themselves!"

Anna's attention drew back to fat maternal woman. Mammoth breasts spilled over folds of fat as swollen nipples trickled rivulets of milk, a nursing mother whose heavy breasts demanded nourishing a baby. Anna's own nipples tingling rippled in maternal response, in sisterhood memory of not so long ago.

Without fresh air, the shower room echoed with emptiness and post delousing chemicals that clung and stung the inside of nostrils stirring gag reflex. Sun stream gone, she imagined floating in a tropical cave grotto where ancient healing waters flowed. Seekers floated in divine timeless unison with some distant ancient loving Goddess.

At what seemed like midnight, the metal door bolted open once again. All eyes watched as two soldiers entered, hesitated then hauled two women, younger women, away. Hearts pounded, waves of fatigue washed over exhausted bodies aching with fear and tension. Some women barely audible in prayer, turned thoughts upward in care of women taken, for loved ones and for themselves. Others lay motionless, too afraid to pray. Time surreal, thoughts unable to ascertain how long she had been there, or what time it might be. Thoughts searched for God's miraculous intervention and soul want of legions of interceding angels to come. Pray to open eyes from a night terror, of escaping with family intact. Seeing only from her own dark empty grief, profound loss pervaded her being.

Anna's thoughts angrily turned to God and faith. She searched demanding guidance from synagogue, comforting words contained within cherished Kabala. Desperately wishing for higher knowledge, her mind searched sacred knowledge for secret mysteries and pathways shown by elders and ancients. Knowledge lost upon her, fatigue brought only longing for home, for loved ones. Grief from want of being able to summon divine magic to will it all away, left empty, as a bad dream.

BANG! The metal door banged open again. Shaken out of thoughts, all eyes watched, as two soldiers boldly entered and walked directly over to and hauled one attractive young woman to her feet. One soldier locked emotionless eyes on Anna. Instantly standing as a gruff hand pulled on her arm, following soldiers and the young woman out of the room, down a dimly lit hallway and out into the cold night. Cold night air hit her bare skin, eliciting spine rattling shivers as body hair rose tall in search of warmth. Smells of burning garbage assaulted her senses, 'sulfur? no.' Cold night and a new kind of fear shuddered within her naked body. The young woman ahead veered sideways under tight grip as soldiers approached and opened the tailgate of a nearby truck, taking Anna to a small officious looking building close by. Inside, blinding lights assaulted tired eyes. Heart pounding eyes adjusting, made out images of four soldiers casually drinking, while light American jazz music played on an old phonograph. She had recently enjoyed dancing to that tune at a community party. Eyes adjusting more focused and startled into the cold soulless gaze of one soldier. Quickly, she bowed her head averting eye contact without losing awareness of danger that lurked behind his disconcerting stare. Acutely vulnerable in nakedness against calm masked madness, cruelty and pure evil. Senses alert, intuition alarm bells rang from within, rattling bones and nerve endings. For the first time, insight behind the Nazi mind showed images of another perspective of the condition of which she had found herself in. Seeing self through his eyes, she was dirty filthily Jew garbage. Propaganda untruths steeped into his psyche. All rational normal emotions long gone from childhood initiation into harsh military regime, his own wife and children lived in perpetual fear of his existence and presence when home. She now understood that all of the community rumours and of the old man and old woman; were true. The soldier did not 'see' her, long incapable, did not know, did not truly understand what was happening, nor his contributory role within it all. He only knew what had he been repeatedly told and what had been bred into his soul. Brainwashed. Fear masked as disgust; deep dark fears of people just like her.

Yet, she could not fathom how anyone would be afraid of her, of people like her. Business profits were available to everyone and not exclusive to a select few. The mysteries of faith and worship were available in every culture and not to a select few. Natural selection was not annihilating others in war and genocide; it was the natural evolution of differing species. She saw the history of her people since time began, most often in exodus, feared and hated by others. The result of one's actions enforced and used by state leaders as an excuse to steal murder and rape in assumption of unearned fortunes.

RAPE hung in the air.

Did they not know that part of her synagogue prayers were for them? Mind swirled with images of the seeming never-ending cyclical wars perpetuated by greed and the tyrannical warmongers that continued to breed like some strange theatrical play time after time and era after era. While costumes and customs changed to the era, the same game re-played itself repeatedly. Did they not see this?

Anna saw it all in the flash of a glance. Catching a knowing or sensing inclination of divinity, higher, above normal human fear, glimpsed within. Curtly he turned away, dismissing the audacity of her directness with an arrogant shrug. Invisible as she was to the others, she fixed on him knowing the danger that rang in her solar plexus, as a cornered rabbit waiting for rabid wolf to make its move. Casually, while considering his position, he filled a glass with unlabeled alcohol, and then downed it all. A loud guttural burp brought a round of laughter as he slammed the glass upside down on the table, sending an ashtray air borne then to the wall.

As though summoning a dark force magical force on command, his confidence invoked and interceding on his behalf, he grinned and watched as Anna slumped to the floor then gathered her exposed nakedness. Huddling in, arms wrapped around knees her eyes focused on a speck of dried blood on the floor. Shudders and violent shivers of shock rocked her body and soul in offensive defiance of knowing what was about to take place.

Blood spec expanded and contracted. After a time, she gathered the courage to scan the room around her. It occurred to her now, that it was some kind of sorting room. Along the far wall, on a long table, were piles of what looked like human teeth with gold fillings in them with mounds of watches, rings, wallets and papers. She remembered having to strip, then a compassionless Nazi white jacket probed a finger into her mouth and for the first time in her adult life, her wedding necklace was gone. It occurred to her now in the periphery of memory that as she had sat in the truck frantically searching for children and husband that soldiers were ripping apart their apartment, their home. Out of the window flew their clothing and furniture. At the time, Anna could not fathom what they had been looking for, barely giving it any thought at all. Now, the comprehension was clear. Imagery of stolen belongs amidst camaraderie elicited shuddering waves of shock and revulsion.

Another shudder wave rattled her core with foreboding danger. His calm assured patience as captive cognitively registered the gravity and cruelty of the situation. Her nakedness, her physical body knowing that it was now a commodity of commerce like sifting through a rummage sale for items that can be re-used or garbage to be tossed away.

One soldier stood up rattling the table, stretched, farted and let out a loud inebriated bellowing laugh. He turned toward her and in the blink of an eye, she felt herself reeling backwards into the wall. She had not seen the move coming. The impact was hard and powerful, cracking bones within. He had power kicked her on the right side of her head. A sharp pain blasted within her head, up her spine then ripped through her body. Sounds became faint as a loud buzzing sound pervaded her hearing. The room reeled and spun around. The form of the soldier standing over, hands on hips. Pant buttons and belt undone, yelling something at her that she strained to make sense of but could not understand. What did he want? His voice faded as the loud buzzing rose once again. Still yelling as though she were simply stupid and disgusting, others still at the table casually laughed. Then two other soldiers stood up, butted their cigarettes in the ashtray in the centre of the table. They ambled slowly, jovially surrounding her, their pant buttons and belts loosening. Her hair was clenched from behind and she was yanked backward, exposed breasts and open legs. Rough hands squeezed both breasts hard and tight, faintly resisting against exploding from gripped pressure. An arm surrounded her belly from behind as another hand groped in between her thighs. From the front, something hard ripped its way and jammed in and out of her vagina. Ripped inside and out as distorted raucous laughter mingled with an ear piercing high-pitched ringing, she held onto consciousness. Anna felt her soul bolt and want to take leave of its physical body. She felt herself reel like a rag doll, grasping for hold and finding nothing to hold onto, and then abruptly flipped over like a dog in heat about to take in its breeding mate. Her hands slid and skidded along the floor as another entered, slamming in and out of her vagina. A submissive dog callously humped by a wild rabid alpha dog. A mare savagely bitten on the neck, a tooth and jaw hold in place while being humped wildly from behind. Primal and devoid of human compassionate thought. A whimper emitted from somewhere inside of her being. Humping subsided then began again. Navi waited for it all to stop, sliding in and out of consciousness as a boot slammed into her ribs and then her chin, sending her reeling sideways. Another crack into her jaw and *streams of blood and saliva drooled aimlessly in strings. Grasping for stability she swirled off her knees, dizzy, and hit the floor. The floor spun in circles under her form. The room whipped around as a wave of vomit catapulted up and out, burning her nostrils and sinuses. Throat dry, taste of blood on her lips, blood, vomit and drool mingled together. Then everything went black.*

When Anna awoke, gradually gaining awareness of surroundings, she first felt cold soft things touching her bare skin; cold, very, very cold. A horrible stench assaulted the inside of crisp blood dried nostrils; a toxic chemical smell mixed with rotting animal carcass. Gradually, puffy swollen eyes began to clear, adjusting to dawn's early light. She began to make out a form about two feet away. Striking brown eyes stared unblinking straight at her. A bald man lay motionless blankly staring at her. Oddly ashen white, sickly white, his naked body covered in what looked like a greyish powder of some kind. Eyes glazed and unmoving, her comprehension slowly registered that she was looking at a man, a dead man. Panic bolted backward from within, slamming an invisible wall of painful resistance, which in fact met no movement at all. Her body remained against will and the man's body remained equally as still, his gaze fixed on her. A new awareness of something heavy lying on top of her, someone's skin on hers; as if the weight of another body. As she filled with panic, the man simply unaware of her plight blindly starred straight at her, still and quite dead. His body powder smelled and now occurring to her, looked like poorly done theatrical or opera paint.

She screamed, but made no sound. She bolted again, but could not move. Panting wildly, understanding that there were simply too many broken bones. Eyes scanned beyond the dead man. Mounds and piles of like white powdered bodies lay still, strewn and heaped everywhere, all sides. She was one among many, in a deep earth pit. White naked bodies heaped in piles lay discarded one on top of another.

Heart raced, she willed herself to move, but could not move. Her eyes stretched in their sockets to scan the outside of the pit, beyond the bodies, for help, for a way out. The pit was as big as their synagogue. It struck her odd this thought, this comparison.

Everywhere, was blinding powdered greyish white stench, they were all white.

'Snow? No.'

Dead, with still eyes open, staring into the air. 'All dead.'

'White Death'.

Tears spilled out over eyes, as a heaving and shuddering sigh brought a wave of otherworldly calm.

Her awareness returned to the eyes of the dead. It struck her then, that their eyes were amazingly calm.

Calm, all calm eyes as if they had seen the face of God.

Navi/Anna left in this horrid place of the dead was not yet dead. Callously the soldiers had neglected to finish the job. Barely alive, and still alive, did not want to die, not here, not now. She wanted to run, run fast and far away.

She wanted to go home.

She wanted to be safe in soul skin husband's arms.

She wanted her babies enfolded within and safe, as they should be. Tears of maternal love comfort longing trickled and stung dry cheeks.

A strange wave of calmness slowly washed within, overtaking body, heart, and mind. Images and moving pictures played before her eyes, only now comprehending that children and husband had already passed over into the heavens, home with God. Smiling, happy they hovered before her softly calling "Come", "Come Mama", "Come Anna". A force from within shifted and moved in effort to run into their arms, yet her spirit body resisted still, not yet wholly released.

Awareness turned to a loud buzzing ringing that came from within the top of her spine at the back of her head as body cells tingled and vibrated. A pulling sensation from the top of her head, her crown as though instinctively, the childbirth of her own essence, her own soul knew the natural rhythm of exiting in its physical body. She relaxed, allowing the rhythmic drawing sensations lift higher and higher until her spirit soul became free of its broken paralyzed body. A hesitating resistance, then conscious allowing, brought the calm of instinctual inner knowing that she was indeed going home.

Navi could no longer feel any sense of her physical body, shifting awareness away from surrounding forms of decaying bodies. Smokey images of spirit people hovered over the bodies. Tonal sounds like some distant harmonic music entered her mind and swirled throughout. She noted how good, how wonderful and joyous she felt. All natural inclination to resist was now gone. With a final calming out breath sigh, she let go.

A blinding light grew above in intensity and enveloped her in the bosom of a grand loving presence. For the first time in her life, she felt a wondrous new kind of relaxation and comfort. Any sense of physical pain and emotional discomfort had quickly become a distant memory. A bright light was now growing all around her, then ever so slowly, enveloping her. Focusing on the light above her head, another light extended outward meeting with one that shot out of her heart then washed within as well as all around her body.

Smiling now and marveling at the glorious sensations. Time had somehow suspended itself. The magnificent light pulsated as though a heartbeat or breath rhythmically vibrated, as specks of rainbow danced indescribably and joyously alive. Growing bigger than the sun on a warm afternoon, enfolded and enmeshed with babes and husband, Anna was home.

Gloriously warm, comfortable and slowly drifting loved as Navi lingered within Anna, aware of the oneness of all of life, God, it, herself. Her soul longed to follow, to go and to stay there in that final divine place, forever home.

Home.

Images of her own life inter mingled with Anna's then faded. As a child laughing and playing with Gran, then studying music as a young Anna, and the joyous competence it gave. The first youthful love meeting of soul skin husband at synagogue faded as Navi met Stephen at an art gallery, in love with his gifted art works. Babies born, first Jacob, little Anna then Abby, joy in the miracle of birth. Toddlers played happily in a park. Anna's children finally mastered their violins enough to play in perfect unison. Anna delicately ran fingers through soul skin husband's beard then made slow intimate love while children slept contentedly in their beds. A romantic sunset beach stroll, soul skin mates held hands, tenderly snuggling. Joyful onlooker reverenced the cat giving birth to tiny mouse like kittens. Tea with best friend Catharine in the soul sisterly sharing of bonded friendship.

This was Love. Navi and Anna had both known Love, been loved and loved others, as well as self. Slower now, the images of Anna appeared, as the music teacher that she was born to be, floated from the shower.

It was now that Navi was still one with Anna that insightful understanding arose with absolute clarity; she was to use her gift of music and song to enhance faith, to enhance spiritual growth, her own as well as the others she taught. She understood with profound clarity that she had had that opportunity with the women in the shower. Through music, heart, soul, intention, it was not to avert the travesty but to aid in the transition or ascension with song. Sing of the joy of life, of all life, of sacredness and divine love, high above the ignorance of limited human understanding. Raise spirits through love and sound. Sing of faith, of God until bodies 'vibrated' higher and higher into true peace, joy and love of God everlasting. Sing in unison, becoming 'one', one with each other, and one with God as natural transition in birthing wholly back into the light of God.

Home.

Back to the pit, as though viewing the final scene as a bystander, objectively she stood looking on and seeing the process of Anna's death and all the others. Soldiers and compassionless white jacket Nazi women, gathered life belongings tossed into the street and loaded onto trucks. People were stripped under gunpoint and left naked to die in toxic showers. Nazi eyes gaze directly at her, the one that had looked into her eyes prior to rape. Looking into his eyes and into his heart now, somewhere within *was* a good man who was otherwise honourable yet unwaveringly dedicated to his career. Fatal was his youthful unquestioning faith in the directives of superiors in simply doing his loyal 'duty'. The Nuremberg defense does not alleviate one from personal and moral responsibility in the eyes of God. He worked his abilities as he was trained and as he believed it to be; duty with grace within the truth of his God of understanding, he was programmed and trained to not think, just follow orders.

No blame.

In the blink of an eye, Navi understood it all, compassion for all of life. As Anna, there was no lingering residue of fear or remorse for the soldier's actions. Power over one person's will by another is still coercion by using the energy of fear. Trained to fear authorities as student solders, in turn used primal will to incite fear in those perceived as below them. Justified as fulfilling a God delegated mission, albeit, fuelled by fear, as so many wars and other atrocities had been throughout time. A higher truth lay hidden behind blind duty honourably proposed as ridding the world of diseased dirty rodents lay an authoritative driving greed quest for power absolute, money and resources.

In this higher divine mind space, Navi instantly forgave them their ignorance, and herself of the 'singing' mission lost in the shower. In the moment, forgiveness was not so much about forgetting and allowing atrocities to continue or a matter of disallowing appropriate accountably, but rather, in making a conscious choice to un-engage from the darkness. She in turn set her soul, spirit free.

It was to be a pinnacle life lesson. Had she fully comprehended the gravity of the teaching experience, Navi may have altered her choices in the months and years to come.

Navi could still hear, in this surreal semi-awake space, Anna softly singing as though time no longer held relevance as toxic shower terrors dissipated. Singing, the women moved to a higher place through the vibrations of joy in song. Huddled together, hands held, each moved in spirit unison as one mass ascension shift into blazing divine light. Fading images lingered as each woman, man and babe was met by beloved family and friends who had already arrived on the other side; loving embraces, joy and laughter. Anna had reunited with babes and soul skin husband as earthy cares of the world vanished. In a flash, all were gone and none looked back.

Still in the bathtub feeling quite stunned at how real the experience had been, Navi could still smell, hear and feel aspects via a simple thought. She felt and heard trails of singing, songs of love, unity and joy. Songs foreign to English ears, yet somehow understood.

Navi's trail off vision showed Anna in the toxic shower women through media eyes, reported as an oddity to the Nazi's, and to the world at large where news trickled; known as the 'Singing Jews', the day that Jews sang to their death.

'OH! You can partially affect the outcome of an event. Hmm. It did not change or alter the fact that the deaths occurred; it merely changed its emotional impact and residue energies. By singing, it made it a glorious reunion into the spirit world. I think I get it. You can change how you feel about a thing, which changes its long term lasting effect. Somewhat. Maybe. Hmm. I will have to think on this more.'

Attention shifted to sounds of laughter in Navi's own house. Familiar sounds of children, her own children. Distinct smell of Stephen's cologne, home in bathtub and looking out at a snow covered garden.

Stephen hammered again on the bathroom door, "Going into town for munchies and movies", he blurted. Navi's heart pounded and shook from reverence interrupted and made no effort to respond. Still in the bath, skin wrinkling and lingering smells of chemicals and death, the essence of another world dissipated. The gist of physical pain of broken bones and torn vaginal flesh lingered, interspersed with elation and joy. The divine dichotomy of pain versus profound joy of physical death and transition home into the spirit world was nothing short of amazing.

'This is what it is like to die. Enveloped in divine love and loved ones. If of course, you have the awareness to see and think it that way, then yes it is possible.'

Navi reached a foot out and with splayed toes, gripped the hot water tap handle; curling around metal spokes and slowly turned it. 'It is a skill', she grinned, having always prided herself on her ability to do this, an ancient primal gift of dexterity. Grinning, recalling entertaining kids by crossing her eyes and sticking tongue out and up into a nostril, which always brought fits of giggles.

Warm tub water filled nearly to the brim, cozy and soothing, she made the transition to life in the now.

Finally out, dried off and long heavy wet hair twisted up into a towel, fatigued and chilled, she rooted through the closet for her old shawl, its blanket embrace enfolding and cozy. Old Hudson Bay shawl brought forth ancient spiritual sisterhood communion. Still in silent awe, sang the beautiful enchanting ascension song, first quietly and slowly, then with more exuberance. Closed eyes carried away to some joyful other worldly sphere then suddenly stopped; allowing reverberating tones to ring through body, stillness, silence, time and other life times. Harmonics vibrated rippling through every cell in Navi's body as images of foreign candelabra like symbols exuding violet flames whispering Elohim and Ein Soph.

"I love you Anna, thanks for sharing your journey with me."

Navi curled up in Gran's old rocking chair drawing the obvious visual connection of how chemo made Matt look like the dead in the pit and that distinct smell of cancer, chemotherapy drugs on breath; decay, death and toxic chemicals. Everyone smelled it, yet no one dared say a word to Matt. Unsure of the relevant connection yet, it had more to do with her. Was this a past life with soul skin man or just a bad dream? Does this have anything to do with Stephen, Matt or anything?

Feeling Gran's presence, she shifted her inner ear to altered awareness.

"My darling Chickadee, it has been said many times before, that we are not human beings having occasional spiritual experiences but spiritual beings having human experiences. Despite atrocities, be assured that being on this earth plane is a 'gift'. Sometimes dreams, especially unsettling ones, are the best way to get through to you. This too is a gift. There are many lessons and many gifts within a journey."

"I know God will not give me anything I can't handle.
I just wish that He didn't trust me so much."
Mother Teresa

Chapter 4 ~ Home Alone

Clenched hands gripped the car's steering wheel, a grinding toothed Navi slowly inched, navigated a snowstorm white out. Radio weather dude had neglected to mention a blinding snowstorm. Driving back roads from North Cape First Nations Reserve seemed much safer than chancing main road highways, the adage of tall trees intermittently lining roadsides as guidelines. Winter driving on the way home from work often meant any number of different weather and road conditions. Sunny and clear at the office, black iced roads by Brownsville and white out by Greentown.

'Shit! Where am I?' Navi panicked, slowing to a halt and striving to stay focused on the road. Looking in all directions and glimpsing a stop sign, she edged a little closer. Opening the window to make out a snow covered road sign. Four way flashes blinking, head jutted out into blinding wind and snow. Failing clarity, she emerged and trudged over a snow bank. Reaching up on tiptoes to wipe off the snow packed road sign brought another panic wave. 'Shit! Shit! Shit! What in the hell am I doing on County Road Eleven?' Back in car warmth and looking at a quarter tank of gas needlepoint on the gage sent heart racing and pounding.

'Shit! Shit! Shit!

Oh God, I am going to have to make my way back to Brownsville and get gas. Better stick to main roads.' A slow precise six-point turn with all flashers on full, praying and hoping any unseen car, might see her and be able to stop in time. Heart pounding in ears, calming safe, she gingerly headed back in the direction she had just come from.

No debit card to be found, she rummaged through coffee stash coins, pockets, floor, nooks and crannies for a measly sum of ten dollars for gas, a squeeze of much needed crappy cup of gas station coffee, little bag of native smokes, sale bag of chocolate covered almonds and of course, a pee.

Taking a few deep breaths in, and an Angel protection invocation prayer, she headed south once again.

Around the first bend, a transport truck showed the way with all flashers on. It was getting dark behind the sea of hell bent white flurries and Navi was grateful for the trucker's guidance. Following slow behind, she began to relax a little and lit a smoke, feeling a tad cocky remembering that she was 'safe' with new top of the line snow tires and grateful to be in her own car and not the Junker. The trucker began to slow and gear down its wheels then SPLAT, a wave of slush sprayed onto her windshield followed by a metallic screeching sound. Nerves jangling and heart pounding, she gasped as the driver's side windshield wiper wind gust flew off and disappeared.

Seconds turtled by in surreal time space. That space where life slows down and movements are slow motion exaggerated; foot slowly off of the gas pedal and hovered over the brake pedal with the other foot. Four-way flasher button shakily pressed on while slowly gearing down to a crawl, strained eyes searched out of the passenger window for a safe place to pull over.

'Shit! Where is that truck? Am I even on the road? Is someone going to plough into me? Oh God please do not let me hit anyone; do not let me run over anybody. Oh God, oh god, oh god…. Please help!'

Calming waves washed within, bringing a conscious knowing that all was good, as other worldly whispers of coaxing and inaudible directions guided her; a loving presence, loving like Gran.

Strained eyes focused through slush-crusted windshield against sleepy mesmerizing snowflakes and intermittent red taillights of the truck still ahead. Grabbing the focal point opportunity in alignment, she kept pace. Approaching the highway and county road crossing recalling where even on the clearest of days the 'town' was not much more than a stop light, coffee shop and gas station. Gently pulling right toward the shoulder, she prayed that there were no people or small children out walking in the storm. Steering wheel gripped hands held steady, erect straight back leaned head far left and over to view through the passenger window.

Coming to a full stop, stick shift in park she laid forehead on steering wheel as heart and head pounded and stress tears rolled down cheeks. Another breaking point of heart pounded through chest, threatening to break wide open with months of stress filled with Matt sickness and Stephen's anger. Finally, allowing weariness and loneliness to feel what it wanted.

As sobbing lessened, white squall dissipated.

Shaken, she stoically blew her mucous filled nose and wiped weary eyes.

Wiper blade.

Emerging gingerly out of the car against pelting wind and slipping over slush, she abruptly slammed the car door catching coat edge that sent her sliding down onto knees as hard ice slammed her bottom.

"SHIT!"

Another wave of tears welled then, stoically choked back on hold. Gloves jammed in pockets, hands and fingers exposed and red in freezing wind, she stiffly removed the passenger side wiper. Cold red numbed hands turned it over in hand, bringing realization that its screws were gone. She saw in her mind's eye, the screws flying through the storm to be with its wiper.

"Now what am I going to do?"

Hands wet, freezing and stiff, Navi scrounged under car seats then trunk for something, anything to secure the wiper blade on. Finding an old twist tie, she gingerly fed it through the eyes of where the screw and bolt should be, then twisted ends around and around, secure as it could be. Standing in blinding biting wind, squinting in all directions for a lay of the land and seeing only flecks of snow in driving wind, she turned her face into it and bellow screamed a primal scream.

"ARRRRRGGGGHHHHH!!!! Is that all you have? Is that it? What in the bloody hell do you want from me? Fuck! Fucker Fuck!" A toddler's hissy fit with hands clenched and stamping feet set free yet another albeit weaker scream.

Throat resisted, choking on a cluster of snowflakes sucked in on the edge of another holler sent her coughing and hacking. Snot and tears froze, mingled with wind gusts, taking breath away. "Fuck, I can't even fucking scream right!" she whined in defeat.

Calmly allowing Mother Nature to wind blast stress out of hair, pores and cells, she stood fast. She jig danced, swirling around in circles, boots, scarf, hair and coat flapping wildly, a mad woman gone winter strange 'oh ya, uh huh, uh huh, uh huh, if they don't find ya rich and Barbie doll pretty, they find ya handy. Who rules? Uh huh, uh huh, I do! Oh yes, ah am da crazy woman.'

If she had any duct tape, she was sure that she would have used it too, somehow.

Driving in a white out is like watching an old computer mystifying stars screen saver. The challenge now was in trying to maintain focus on the road. Eyes inevitably caught a snow speck and followed it, wandering off. Like a hypnotic magnet, eyes had a mind of their own and want only to follow individual snowflakes drift gently off into the netherworld.

Navi hated driving in white outs and it did not get any easier with time. When young, one is not consciously mortality aware. Now it just scares the living shit out of some. Yes, maybe that is reality, just a universal computer screen saver; simulated mystifying stars coming right out, randomly and making our fucking eyes lose focus until jolted back after nailing another car's ass, or off the road into a ditch or worse, driving over a child!

Two grueling hours, a full pack of cigarettes, an entire bag of chocolate covered almonds and an extra-large coffee and finally, Navi arrived home, drained, exhausted and rattled.

No one seemed to notice that she was home so late except Abby. Navi was grateful to be home safe and shifted attention from snowstorm driving to home life. Still shaky and now a tad faint, a sudden craving for an entire bottle of Mexican Tequila with worm intact pervaded her thoughts, so she searched for alcohol. Finding nothing, she turned the kettle on. Smelling no dinner cooking, took off coat, boots and hat, noting that Stephen had yet to come up from the workshop to greet her. Hearing the usual radio talk show blurting in between spits and snaps of sparks flying from his torch, she bypassed the kitchen and went upstairs to shed work clothes. A little prattling Abby shadow trailed behind as Navi shed the days coverings, suddenly self-consciously aware of armpits stink from too many coffees, too many cigarettes and way too much stress.

There were sounds of Matt rummaging downstairs in the kitchen cupboards and fridge, obviously looking for food that he could keep down indicated that he was rallying around the latest chemo treatment. Automatic 'Mom on Duty' grace deep breath, she slid on old purple robe, swiped deodorant under arms then playfully under Abby's arms, then headed down stairs.

Candidly grateful that Primal Asshole was still in the workshop, she wrapped Matt and Abby in her arms, "Yum, Yum, Yum, Gawd Lord Love a Duck! How I love these boogers! Want to smell my new deodorant? It's called fresh stress opium."

"Ewwwa, Mom."

Turning Matt's face to meet hers in hand, "How is my main man today?" Matt grinned and turned, feigning annoyance while swooning yet allowing the loving embrace.

"Ah Navi, not so bad and not so good."

"Manage to keep anything down today?"

"Yup. Ate a lot of cheese and strawberries."

"Good stuff kiddo. What should I prepare for the young Prince of Princes? Cat turd on toast? Road kill a la Possum? How about Aardvark n' Lizard Gizzard Gumbo again? Ah wait, no, sorry, geez, kiddo and we are fresh out of Lizard gizzard."

"Ahhh, dam. N' that's my favourite."

Abby added, "Ahh Matty, Mommmm, I hate that stuff", pretending to pout.

"Alllll right, both of you scram out of my kitchen or I'll put you to hard sweaty slave kitchen'ish labour."

She stared into an empty fridge, empty aside from mounds of cheese and strawberries specifically set aside for Matt. 'Thank God.'

She scanned a mail pile on the counter; taxes over due, hydro adjustment bill, her week late pay stub now useless, pay amount rarely changed. She tossed the mail back onto the counter and sighed, knowing without looking at them where they stood. Stephen's pay went to child support, alimony, driving back and forth to the city, hospital parking lot fees, gas and meals away. Her pay cheque could not possibly cover all what needed to be covered. She did not know how long they could keep going like this and in the moment's weariness; there seemed no end in sight. The world could not seem to give her a break, a tiny reprieve just because Matt was sick. Closing her eyes and taking a deep breath, she weary sighed, 'God', the world just seemed to keep coming at her like the mystifying snowstorm stars.

Navi opened the big freezer and picked out a no name brand casserole. 'Yuk, why do I even buy this crap? Oh yes, because it's cheap and it fills the gullet'. She threw it in the oven and cranked the heat up to four hundred degrees, excessively high 'Still tastes crappy no matter what you do to it but at least this way, it'll be done sooner.'

Eyeing smelly dirty dishes piled and overflowing in the sink followed a sudden beer craving, no not a beer, six of them. She opted for a hot cup of tea then slid up stairs for a quick tub soak, time to gather wits and energy for the evening and shake off the day stress residue and hellish drive. Bathtub sanctuary brought drifts of sleep, sliding into water then waking alert.

Navi maintained a tuck in routine, no matter how old the kids grew, instinctively knowing that they thrived and coped better. A good night chat and snuggle routine, sure to tell them how precious they were and that she loved them, inside and out. A day's highlight kept them bond connected to each other. Life was fragile, unpredictable, and when it was time to go, to pass over, these would be the moments that would matter.

"Hey Matt, can't believe you actually ate Crap Casserole!" A grinning Navi step mom stroked scanty bits of hair on his head and rubbed his thinning frame back until he slid into a sound and peaceful sleep. "I love you Matt. Keep on kicking that Cancer arse. I am so proud of you."

Navi Mom pulled mandatory Little Mermaid comforter away and sharing old sisterhood shawl forming a tent, its blanket embrace enfolding the cozy two. "Daughter, imagine that this old shawl's wrapping, connects us to ancient women throughout history, a spiritual sisterhood. Curling up on her side, she watched precious daughter who undressed a bald Barbie.

"Abby why are your Barbie's bald and naked?"

"They're not Barbie's, Mom, I'm too old for that stuff and Dahhhhh! They are Amazon Women. They been through cancer n' they are going to cremate Richard Davidson. They are going to put his ashes in the volcano. Then they are going to have a big party 'n celebrate."

"Had a rough day with Richard again, huh?"

"Yeah Mom! N' he's such an Asshole!"

"Abby!"

"Well, Mommmm, he said that Matt was just faking so he didn't have to go to school every day like everyone else. Then he started dancing around, faking he was all hurt and wounded, pretending to be Matt or something. Then on the bus, he told me that Matt was going to die."

Navi thought, 'fry the little fucking Bastard! I'll help you do it!'

Abby stopped, hung her head, sniffed, wiped spilling tears with the back of one hand then a string of clear mucous snot with the other. She gathered Abby up in her arms and onto the mermaid covered bed wiping a wounded little girl face with old shawl. Mother love was enfolding her little girl baby ball. Rocking gently back and forth, she quietly sang every childhood song that she could recall. Abby, who had not sucked her thumb since kindergarten, sucked away unabashed. Navi's heart ached. 'No, the world does not stop for those who are vulnerable.' Long after Abby had fallen asleep, mother gingerly kissed precious little girl's soft silky forehead and turned on the princess night light.

The house quiet now, Stephen had stoked the fire, turned out the lights and obviously gone to bed. Exhausted, mustering a smidge of energy, she slowly climbed up the stairs. Arsehole Primal Man snored rhythmically on his side fetal, a pool of drool forming on pillow with comforter covering body cocooned, except for a protruding hairy bum.

'Gawd, look at that. Warrior man does have a softer childlike side. I wonder where that part of his soul goes upon daylight waking.'

Window pulled slightly open allowing gusts of wind carrying flecks of snow to blow in, she lit up a smoke. Squinting against tiny pelts of snow, a final quiet alone moment brought warm contentment mingling with anxiety of the long winter's stuck record; driving in snow storms, coping with Stephen and Matt's illness fall out. Allowing a truth to surface into consciousness, the weather reflected into her emotions leaving anxious fear, rejection and abandonment.

The storm was not letting up.

Navi groggily slammed a spastic hand down on the rudely beating alarm clock, rolled and snuggled back into comforter, robe, grizzly bear slippers, and shawl unable to recall crawling into bed and falling asleep. Stephen, already in the workshop, squealed power tools; rudely ignoring others wishes for more sleep. A pulled pillow over her head in protest, she stealthily reached for the old MP3 player, long discarded from Matt, and cranked the volume blaring of mediation into weary brain cells. Eyes closed, she saw only snow blizzard and howling wind making the normally soothing meditation voice further annoying the crap out of her tethered nerves. Remembering that it was Stephen's turn to take Abby into school and her turn to stay home with Matt, she relaxed and lightly dozed.

Matt asleep, wake him up for meds and food around ten o'clock, see if he might keep something down. Mother inventory; ample supply of Matt food and left over Crap Casserole, double check his meds, line them up in order on the kitchen counter, one more treatment then wait for surgery day, careful to not to bring a cold or flu home and trying to keep busy, to not think about Matt's cancer and pending surgery. Waiting was brutal, it was hard to face being alone with his post treatment side effects. A conundrum; it was harder to not be with him.

A humble love seeking Abby hesitated then sensing open invitation, crawled into her bosom, "Hey! I thought you went to school."

"Nope. Hee, heee, it's a snow day Mom."

"Ahhh. Muuuhaha. A little slave child for the day!"

Weary moms who found time and space to lay or sit down, magnetically attracted children, pets and husbands who sought maternal primate clinging attention. Two legged Mothers are perpetually busy tending to food, laundry and refilling toilet paper rolls or must boldly venture forth into Black Holes to find and retrieve socks. Relaxation is simply not allowed.

Abby fetal ball snuggled, drawing Navi closer, blending body and soul.

"Mom?" whined a little girl's voice.

"Yes, Abby."

"This is all so weird, Mom. People are in the house, but it is lonesome at the same time. Everyone seems so far away, even when he or she are in the same room together, n' scared, n' scared that something awful is going to happen. No one says it, but everyone is afraid that Matt will die. I think the Angels say he won't die, and won't always be sick, and that no one should get used to this kind of sick, whatever that means. And Mom? Matt smells gross. N' he told me he wishes that everyone would stop being afraid and get back to life. Mom, it sucks bum being at home n' school sucks bum 'cause of Matt. So how about that Mom? I don't think Matt will die."

Silent tears, Navi contemplated her young daughter's astute and wise observations. Mutt Dawg sensing emotional upset, nuzzled in between, seeking affection, 'if you love me up you will feel better'. While family and friends did seem almost aloof and indifferent lately, she surmised that it was a self-preserving disassociation, consciously far away from the fatal gravity of the situation. Abby, normally easy going and young enough to be closer to God than the rest, was living within the situation mix as the barometer for how things really were.

Stephen however, was difficult to read. Being a man of few words and whether intentional or not, often sounded prophetic when he did speak. Perhaps it was not so much a matter of not caring about her any more, he just could not align himself with guilt and fear. Either way it was confusing, the distance was killing her and oddly harder to face than Matt's prognosis.

Thinking on it now, early in their relationship, his happy go lucky, easy-going wise manner had been a refreshing delight, home was insensitive aloof isolation. To the outside world, he remained the happy go lucky charming gifted artist, his shadow side saved for brief and cutting exchanges with his wife. It was a cruel dichotomy, his saintly public image that naturally mingled with wit, saving nasty stress ventilation for her in private. It took phenomenal energy to uphold the charming public persona and pent up stress had to come out somewhere and Navi was a safe dumping ground target.

Mother's adolescent programming, a role set out early on in life, Motherly ineptitude and stress of not having achieved the great American dream ideals of raising successful children into successful adults, dumped continuously on the vulnerable misfit daughter. Years of college education and social work did little to aid outgrowing the misfit role. Compounded with religious teachings about the evils of those who communed with otherworldly spirit beings, all soothsayers, seers, and conjurers, and of course, sinfully demonically possessed. Traditional medical society still shared the religious view somewhat, where rather than delving into ancient traditions and harvesting the spirit world gifts, sought to institutionalize and medicate the demons into submission. Images of religious priestly persecution and excommunication flittered and mingled with strait jackets and mad houses.

Historical accounts of religious medical world cruel attempts to deal with those 'gifts' and still, admittance of such meant devastating and frightening outcomes. Yet, the bible and other religious texts were full of opposing accounts where those utilizing their gifts were deemed saints and prophets. Aboriginal cultures around the world all believed that if one did not commune with dead ancestors and spirits, there was something wrong with the individual and healing ensued.

Navi consciously shook off the controversial imagery, knowing that in time, some day, when Matt was well again, both children grown; understanding and inner peace would come.

Family and friends had further distanced themselves, and in turn, her avoidance of others was simply a matter of self-preservation. Simply, there was more going on than she was able to articulate, and she could not think of a living soul to talk with about the spirit world aspect of life.

Occasionally, Abby's eyes flickered, showing resentment of the extra money that Stephen was openly spending on Matt, then feeling guilty, she quickly adjusted. Navi had heard Abby mumble "Asshole" under her breath just last Thursday after Stephen had picked her up from school. Fed up with the adult stress at home, she simply and wisely just wanted to be with her step grandmother for the night. A good evening of grandparent spoiling was desperately wanted and Stephen had flat out refused. Thankfully, he did not hear her slight, lost in his own thoughts as per usual, but Navi felt it. Quickly he had gone from jovial to livid, voice raised and forceful, face flushed red, he one way bellow argued at her. No, she must stay at home with Matt. There would be no mid-week spoiling at her grandmother's house. Navi, livid with the pissy dumping of stress on her daughter yelled, "STOP! The girl needs some time out and grandparent spoiling, a sign of maturity and good coping skills that you wouldn't know anything about."

Perhaps Asshole Step Dad Stephen may just have simply needed his stepdaughter around but was not mature enough, or too stressed, too articulate his want of her company at home in a good way, a mature adult way. Glancing at daughter, she stoically glared out of the car window, steadfast. Navi smiled in pride of the little girl old wise woman for standing up for herself, while acquiescing to his command, refusing to give into the ultimate battle. A day would soon come, where Step Dad Stephen would unwittingly give way to wiser alpha dog stepdaughter. Teen-age hood was coming and Abby, lacking Navi's insecurities, lay a wise warrior woman waiting to blossom.

Being a Step Mommy means that you are to be on hand when needed yet, delegated to second or third or fourth place behind biological parents, family and close friends. Navi looked at the newly highlighted areas on the kitchen calendar. There was no question that she loved Matt as her own child, he already had a Mom who part time lived with a Step Dad and numerous other grandparents, cousins, family friends and another life at their house. Now, the summation of her current role was the pink highlighted sections as alternate Friday's home with Matt. Without respectful discussion and asking, Stephen had delegated her participation in assumption that she would naturally abide.

'Thanks for chatting with me about this Arsehole! I don't know if my boss will approve that, it's short notice and with what I've already taken off for Matt, I know he will be pissed, it's an awful lot of time off when I'm not his biological mother. I don't know if I even have any more vacation days left.' Pressure and stress piling onto weary shoulders; she wiped a tear and turned away. Housework was merely a way to process problems and maternal pride in a well-kept home had long gone.

Last Friday when gathering laundry, she had heard the shower running and Matt softly whimpering from within the bathroom. Private man-child by nature that he was, all instinctively gave him space. His way of coping consisted of occasional mini breakdowns in private, emerging in short order, magically in good humour once again. Maternal instincts and pride concluded that he was actually coping better than most adults would have. Stephen had initially insisted that he stay at the hospital under social worker supervision, to which Matt scoffed off with a tisk and the flip of a hand. Thrown off balance by Matt's obvious adjustment, Stephen reeled in aversion as the Clinical Social Worker turned, strongly suggesting that he himself begin private one on one counselling. Catching Navi's grin, Arsehole adjusted his spine and shoulders and turning on a dime, retorted, "I don't have any problems, Matt does" and pointing at Navi, "She sure as shit does."

Stephen averting eyes away from the women in his son's hospital room, turned on heel to glare out of the window, staring into soulless city landscape. No, he would most certainly not abide. The plain professional white-coated clinical Social Worker remained where she stood and began scribbling notes onto her clipboard.

Ceasing Social Worker audience, Navi shifted into professional masked drama of her own, "What has happened to our family Stephen? We are all waiting for this thing to pass, for spring to come and for life to get back to normal. I feel as though this thing of Matt's has dispersed our family. Matt has cancer. Our family has cancer. We all have cancer. We are all going through this thing and it is eating away at the very fiber of us."

Turning slightly to address her directly, Stephen's burning glaring eyes caught her like a laser beam. Catching himself short, he shifted his spine and shoulders, anger stuffed and shelved for private home time, Stephen regained masked composure then pretentiously dismissed the Social Worker. Abruptly, he turned his gaze back out the window. Navi caught a glimpse of another Stephen she had not seen before, a tearful sad gaze that faded as quickly as it had manifested, stoically buried. Feeling the authentic yet brief agony, she also knew that while this honest side of her husband existed, it would be a cold day in hell before he would share it with her. Habit, a dirty bad habit of dissing her instead, was too ingrained. Dauntingly, she shifted her own spine and shoulders, determined to stay supportive, patiently intent on finding a way to the inner core of her man, sharing and bonding in intimacy in the kind of love that she longed for.

By late afternoon, Arsehole bolted in through the door, allowing blasts of cold air in. "Snows finally letting up, roads and stores all open and in good shape. I'm taking Matt back to his Moms and doing errands." It was the first time in ages that he had been civil to her.

Navi accepted a long overdue invitation to meet friends at a diner in town, daughter in tow. Abby had become a natural addition to the eclectic group and rather than shopping, husbands, retirement savings plans and children, conversations entailed philosophy, mysteries of the universe, aging quirks and menopausal body functions. Laughter and creativity while nurturing each other inevitably healed wounds, and hinted sisterhood bond.

The dullness of winter sunk into souls making moods somber with grey sky threatening yet another heavy snowfall. The visit would be short as all had long country drives home to venture. Catharine, particularly anxious and unable to relax, could not shake an adrenaline tizzy. "Got to get yesterday's stats in before five o'clock, got to get to the bank machine before four o'clock to cover the rent, got to pick up the dog at the vet's before four-thirty, got to practice my theatre lines for rehearsal at seven, and then got to be at the Gallery to emcee the new art showing by eight." Full of mounting inner pressure to be all, Catherine abruptly bolted out of her chair and SMACK, slammed head first into a partition in the middle of the diner. Reeling backward, struggling for balance and rubbing a dozed head, felt for welts and bruising. Looking back to where and what head rudely encountered, dangled a picture frame on the partition. Gingerly standing, squinting against throbbing pain, all eyes followed hers as Catharine read aloud the words on the picture,

"MIRACLES HAPPEN HERE."

Raucous laughter broke as the literal and impacted message registered. Catharine sat back down gingerly rubbing the rude wisdom insult away then ordered a double hot chocolate with extra whipped cream. Navi hugged her like her own child as old woman maternal server scurried out with an ice pack in hand.

Wounded noggin and spirit, a little chocolate, loving hugs and sympathy doth miracles make unto themselves.

April

Navi lazily leaned out of the bedroom window smoking, absorbing sun light streams. Cigarette smoke curled up and away into the first warm air current in six months. Wintry, light deprived eyes squinted against bright spring sunshine, igniting spring inspiration passions from within. The last snowstorm had officially passed as mounds of dirty snow residue began their annual melting descent. Smells of spring life would follow the now exposed musky earth dirt scents. This was the most exciting time of year, as long hard country winter brought spring's rapid bursts of new life.

She had confidently thought that she was ready for this day but now that it had arrived, struggled to face it despite spring reverence. This day was inevitable and following the added stress of cancer treatments and unknown outcomes, now the complicated and unproven surgery loomed. Matt could die on the operating table this day, and yet the smells and imagery outdoors was breathtakingly glorious.

Life was forever a strange dichotomy of joys and problems.

A moment of averting procrastination, Navi lingered, watching crows gather in a cluster of maples. Noisy and vying a massive variety of other newly arriving bird species, still in semblance of flying order, waved to upper branch positions as lower pecking orders acquiesced downward and off to other trees. Three ground hogs emerged from holes, representing the animal kingdoms affirmation that spring had sprung in the country. Crows, typically inhabiting territories in pairs, now gathered in massive conference. Clustering on back roads, favouring Conservation Areas, they gathered each spring in murders of hundreds at a time, eerily reminiscent of some Alfred Hitchcock or Edgar Allan Poe story. Chickadees delightfully round tabled at the bird feeder and below, picking up discards of seeds peeking out of old snow.

Crows loud bellowing caw was a reminder that there was a higher order of what is right, higher and far above human laws and thinking.

'I guess that's my message from the universe for today.'

Thunderous squawking bombarded ears and senses as the sky filled with Canadian Geese. Sticking her head further out of the window in wondrous awe, then slightly ducking as incoming waves flew directly over the roof, one after another, driven to find last year's grass and new root shoots in the swampy fields. In gaggles of at least a hundred or more at a time, with wings outstretched, they announced joy while descending and skidding across thin iced covered fields. Squawking and honking like a cheering crowd in a soccer stadium, they settled and began foraging.

Spring was literally exploding. In awe and reverence for life, she could not fathom living anywhere else. Abby leaned into her side, "Look Abby Girl, spring is exploding!" Picking up the growing primate girl for a full outside view, "Listen to the ruckus of the Canadian Geese out in the field."

Abby wide eyed grinned, "N' lot's a goose poop Mom."

"Right you are daughter. The Crows are spring conferencing and the Chickadees will soon abandon this winter home for summer feeding grounds. Look around Abby girl, the world is in our back yard. Oh geez, look at the time! Onward!"

"Mom? Is Dawg n' Brat Kat coming with us?"

"No darling', Catharine will drop by and care for them."

"Is Matt's Mom coming?"

"Yes, of course. Now kindly un-cling yourself young wench." A grinning daughter gripped harder. "Ah Jesus n' Murphy, can I get ready now? We can't be late."

"Hee, hee, hee." Abby crawled onto her mother's back.

"Oh, I see, I am mother primate and must pack my bundles with you attached?" Pausing in front of the dresser mirror, "Hmmm, we look like Quazi Motto."

"Who?"

"Never mind. Do you have your toothbrush packed?"

"Ya Mom."

"Is Matt all set to go?"

"Ya Mom, he's ready."

Navi quickly unhinged daughter, dressed, finished packing and slid downstairs.

Abby, lazily sat at the dining room table eating frozen waffles directly out of the box and watching cartoons. "Yeeeuck!" retorted Navi.

"How can you eat crap like that?"

"They taste really good, just like fudge popsicles or something. Ya Mom, der really good. Dad wouldn't probably like it, but who cares?"

"True."

Into the kitchen and overlooking the mess, eyes caught a hint of green grass outside of the window and lingering a moment, was struck by a cluster of crocus buds pushing up through snow residue. A thrilled smile crept through bones in a way that she had not felt for in over a year. Garden girl. Country girl. Nature girl. Tree hugger.

Lingering, Brat Kat and Dawg gingerly made their way through bits of snow, seeking out the perfect defecating spot. Snow in mounds and patches had Dawg in an anxious tizzy looking for a spot. Born during November snow, he now searched for familiar snow spots to poop. Sadistic joy in watching the frantic search gave way to compassion; she strategically located some old turds on the grass to ease his pooping transition to spring grass, the rest was up to him to figure out.

Taking an armload of luggage out to the car, a task that could have waited for Stephen, a step mother's opportunity to sense how Matt was holding up emotionally. He was already in and waiting. Navi relaxed somewhat eyeing the mound of blankets, pillows and magazines he had amassed. Nose into an old comic book, Navi worked unnoticed around him.

Emptying the trunk of wintry bits, Abby's snowboard peeked out through a pile of discarded fancy stepmother Barbie Doll Sue purchases of dirty snowsuit gear. 'Likely snot encrusted too', she thought. Matt's travel bag to and from last treatment, still there, neatly folded and relatively clean, spoke volumes of their opposing personal habits. Grabbing the overflowing pile, she turned toward the garage, wondering when it was that they ran out of room in there for a car, and then headed out to the shed. In a strange moment, perhaps a glimpse of Abby's wooden cradle that Father had made resting up above in rafters, she had barely time to grieve his passing a year ago. They had hardly seen her parents since that last Christmas together before he retired. Mother and Father had found new life, travelling to their Florida trailer each Thanksgiving. Mother had hardly been since February, opting to stay in the new house, perpetually busy with women pals and the last vestiges of a shrinking church community.

Thoughts turned to Stephen. Unlike her parent's seemingly content couple existence, his family coped oddly with life, she thought. While there were consistent family gatherings, there was an array of aloneness and isolation from each other, a role-playing of idealist family functions.

Still, that one restless night back in February, that strange sense of foreboding had never really left her. There was still something very wrong that lurked in the periphery of consciousness awareness. The kids were coping. Work was fine. Home was lonely and empty; abyss distance had actually begun shortly after they were married. With a bolt, it occurred to her now that they had not made love in over a year. 'Good God!"

Her mind flashed images of Christmas holidays and being half in the bag, Stephen grunting rutting pig, groped her breast and crotch. The frustration of trying to maintain an erection where she had finally allowed herself to respond almost to orgasm, he came abruptly, whimpered and panting, rolled off, snoring immediately. Left in arousal, left wanting, the longing dissolved, faded and shelved. Before that night, she had tried and tried again to arrange romantic evenings with candles and massage only to find his member a limp noodle without ever having an erection. Even a submissive donning of a lacy bra, undies and oral sex could not arouse an immovable limp noodle. Concluding that she simply was not doing it for him, at least right now, she stopped trying and awaited his approach. She waited for Stephen to find his way back to her.

Staring out into goose filled open farm field, surreal space whirled and waved within. A space where in the fraction of a second, defining moments and lifetime journeys occur, *Navi suddenly found herself on a mountaintop surrounded in misty brilliant orange and magenta sunset. Aware of soul skin man standing on her right, his image a foggy apparition, yet within semblance of form, his familiar loving warmth recognized. Comforted, stirred satisfied joy as awareness turned to an ancient aboriginal casually sitting upon a rock ledge. Ebony leather skin highlighted his penetrating deep brown eyes, striking contrast to a long grey white bushy beard. Bald under a twine headband, a black and white feather casually danced in a slight breeze. A wooden staff held firm his gangly scrawny posture. Eyes calmly stared, giving way to glimpses of a universe of knowledge and other worldly journey's that bid untold secrets of the cosmos and spirit world.*

With staff outstretched toward the sun, as it dipped below horizon pulling brilliant streams of mauves, reds, yellows and oranges through dissolving mist. Night stars filled a darkening blue-black sky and surrounded a brilliant white orange full moon. Moon glowed larger as its misty white and jade green auric ring pulsed in heart beat rhythm.

Staff pointed downward over the mountain precipice and following the lead, Navi and soul skin man crouched, moving closer while mindful of the magnificent height. Mist dissipated bringing forth a vast canyon of pottery clay reds and oranges. Long dried riverbed, rock and pebbles left where once water rushed beyond to its unknown sea destination.

A firefly danced inches away, hovering, wobbling, hesitating, showing it's twisted and bent wing, yet still able to take flight and bleat its flashing greenish white light outward. Acknowledged, firefly disappeared into the dark of night.

A vibrant white light, seemingly as a shining star, the size of a baseball, animated and very much alive, a live being, scooted into view and hovered a foot in front of them. Its handicapped child like personality of pitiless joy emitted its higher wise connection with the divine. Followed by a beach ball sized light, moving slower, emitting a low hum as though a manly middle aged fat man, bouncing slightly as it ambled along the river bed below. Three basketball-sized lights rapidly appeared, interchanging positions, playfully zigzagging, zipping and laughing along the former lights path. A larger darker light abruptly gave wide birth around the three viewers, emitting a crusty grumbling sound followed by a more greyish blue light ball, which gracefully passed in view. A saintly Mother Mary presence gently bowed in introduction. Finally, a car sized brilliant clear violet light ball hummed and pulsated into view, its magnificent ancient personality emitting knowledge of the cosmos while favouring aging arthritic bones.

Old ebony leather skinned man retreated his staff, his calm wise words heard from within Navi's own body, "All of life on this earth and beyond exists, has purpose and contribution to the all that is. There are not, crippled, handicapped useless creatures and beings, nor are they misfits and unwanted by the Creator. Everything exists and is as it is, for higher reason, higher divine agenda. In ignorance and lack of knowing this higher mind, are misunderstandings and mysterious miracles unrevealed to humankind.

All is spiritual. All is energy existing and operating within cosmic law and the Divine Creator. Nothing can die, be destroyed, or cease to exist. Yet nothing shall forever stay the same. Physical form changes, inner mind and being changes and all eventually evolves back into full consciousness of the one higher mind.

The essence of who you really are has always existed, in all ways and shall ever be so. You cannot know all that is, simply take comfort in knowing that spirit exists, the One exists, that you too will grow and know. This time of trials too shall pass before another begins."

"In the night of death, hope sees a star,
and listening love can hear the rustle of a wing."
Robert Ingersoll

Chapter 5 ~ Pieces Missing

After loading up the car, they set out for big city hospital surgery. Matt seemed to have adapted very well to the waves of physical symptoms following chemo treatments and finding his own inner strength. Navi's thoughts turned to re-check, mother mind, if she had remembered to pack his meds, and underwear. Sadly, only one pair of underwear was all the change of clothing he was going to need.

After a long drive and numerous pee stops from Navi's tiny post child birthing bladder, and growing apprehensive procrastination, they arrived. Approaching the massive hospital foyer doors, Matt stopped abruptly, "Navi? Dad? Stop! I don't want to go in there!"

No matter the outcome, his life would never be the same. Stephen arched his back, preparing for what appeared to be one of his alpha dog coercive arguments. Cutting him short, Navi intervened, "Matt, if there was any way I could trade places with you, I would, in a flash. If there was any other place on the face of the planet I would choose to be right now, it certainly isn't here, doing this."

Adjusting his own approach, Stephen added, "Tell you what son, we check in, let the nurses do the blood work, then I'll treat everyone to a feast of steak and seafood." Navi was first elated then pissed; knowing exactly whose already stretched credit card would be picking up the tab.

Inside and ushered into a sterile institutional bland room, on floor duty Head Nurse and assistant argued with Stephen and Matt. They were reluctant to let him go out anywhere; did Stephen and his wife not know the gravity of the situation? Undaunted parents in hand with a little girl and sick boy's pleading eyes, pious nurses glanced at each other in acquiescence followed by a terse string of thou shall and shall not do commandments.

Avoiding looking at the grand total, Navi silently paid the bill.

Navi with Abby in tow checked into a motel room close to Stephen's city relatives, booked a connecting room for Stephen so he could come and go as needed. Matt's biological mother opted to stay with friends in town, closer to the hospital. Abby had already settled in to watching four seconds of everything on television, remote control extended in front of her, engrossed in the vast novelty and variety of channels. Navi, seizing the opportunity, retreated to the bathtub allowing anxiety waves to surface and fade.

"Be strong, Navi."

Mind wandering, David co-worker and coffee friend from work had strongly advised her the day before to take her own car, in case Stephen decided to stay. 'Maybe I should have listened to him, feeling kind of out of place here.' Feeling weirdly trapped in noise, crowds and cement, and alone in a strange land, 'I don't belong here, I should not be here.' Shrugging the fleeting rush of rural tranquility homesickness, 'I want to be here for Matt'.

The next evening with a store bought coffee and smoke in hand, Navi sat on the outside steps of the motel deck, smoking and reviewing the day. The sun long down, night stars appearing through solid light of the city, cigarette smoke seemingly mingled with two airplane white smoke trails as they crisscrossed the sky leaving a giant white X. City noises and smells assaulted the senses. She picked apart a dandelion, while cigarette smoke curled up and into stinging squinting eyes stimulating tear ducts. She hand waved the smoke away, unwilling to allow stress tears to flow, not yet, not here, not now.

This morning Matt had a complete bone structure and internal organs. Tonight he has not. Tonight he lay in semi-conscious post-surgery shock and fever. Diseased, bone, muscle tissue and tumours scraped away. His natural mom and Stephen remained watch vigil by his side. The best surgical team available, a rare form of cancer had drawn the attention of oncologist specialists from near and far.

It is surreal space watching a love child retching vomit, losing hair and healthy glow. You cannot single handily fix it. You cannot cure it. You cannot ignore it. You cannot simply give them a magic boo-boo kiss then grieve in private. Love him and pray.

The power of a mother's love seemed capable of amazing power solutions to life's challenges. In alone, one on one time, Navi comforted and empowered, giving the matter to Matt to sort out in his own way with what was plaguing his body. She had approached with what faith and belief system he did have. Matt and his sense of God were previously un-chartered territory, now sharing tears, pain and discomfort. She was grateful that Matt had support from oodles of people he did not know, and then some.

Before surgery, family gathered in his room, joking, chatting and generally avoiding the reality of what was to occur. Matt quietly plucked away at lottery tickets while giant dinosaur balloons danced in the ceiling fan breeze.

Hours went by until; breaking the stilled silence, Matt's mother impatient gruffly opened a trashy woman's magazine. Wittingly enticing Stephen into answering quiz questions on relationships, specifically, how good their sex lives were. Playful banter turned sour as Stephen fired a biting crack, "Navi does not like sex." The stab of this remark hung in the air, the direct surprise hit instantly embedding burning embarrassment. No, a livid Navi caught off guard, scanned the room for family reactions and caught a knowing look in both Matt and his mother's eyes. Navi found her composure and looking squarely at Stephen retorted, "Oh, I like sex Stephen, just not with you."

Navi knew instantly that she had taken a huge step over an invisible and indefinable boundary with Stephen as well as their family social protocol. Roasting targets were not to retaliate, an unspoken family rule. Historically, she dutifully kept her vulnerable and hurting feelings to herself but now, the blatant truth of their lack of coupling was now, openly displayed. Stephen had baited and she had not only bitten back but had quickly found composure. While this was hardly the time or place for airing personal gripes and complaints, she felt relief. Out it had blurted and there it was, still hanging in the air of family discomfort. In the grander scheme of life, she knew well enough not take Stephen's jabs personally. A private unspoken truth hung in the air and one could cut the room tension with a knife.

Navi grinned, feigned composure and left the room under guise of getting snacks for everyone. In the hallway, Stephen's pious mother stood huddling in a corner, talking into her cell phone "Stephen and his wife aren't sleeping together". A flash of anger rose up Navi's spine as she retreated down the hallway, livid with the woman's childish and inappropriate gossip timing.

Earlier, when it had finally come time for Matt to go to pre-op, an entourage of nurses and orderlies arrived, quickly moving people around and dressing him, or undressing him and into one of those, 'see everything from behind' gowns then handed over his boxer shorts. Navi felt his embarrassment as orderlies then proceeded to argue over which gurney to use. Pre-occupied with union protocol rather than Matt's comfort, had it not been such a dramatic and serious occasion, it could have been a hilarious slapstick comedy skit.

At pre-op, a cantankerous nurse approached Matt, picked up his chart and callously asked, "What body part is to be removed today?" Matt nearly bounding off the gurney as she patronizingly and calmly patted his shoulder, "There now. I have to ask that, to make sure I have the right patient." Matt's gurney brakes released, she held up her hand to his family entourage, "STOP" waving off loved ones. A hundred loving tendrils trailed out after him and followed into the surgical unit.

Surgery doors flapped as Matt's adults stood stupid and lost. Unable to go with him, unable to change what had to be done and utterly, helpless. All consciously struggling with the urge to run after him to comfort and spare him this terrible deed.

Navi's mind raced, it was not too late, there had to be a healer, a shaman or medicine man that could intervene. She knew of no one and in the moment, took it as a personal failing on her part, her spiritual mastery a farce.

Matt's mom quietly gathered her coat and shoulders dropped, walked away alone. Navi's heart followed its attention to Stephen. Motioning forward, intent to hug embrace, he reeled backward, body recoil resistance and face cringing in offended rejection. Navi, reeling in hurtful, off balance rejection, tried to recover, blithering words of hope, "Somehow everything is going to be all right Stephen."

Suddenly, it occurred that the words were sincere, a sense that Matt was going to be okay. He had turned his back, opting to share the moment wrapped in his mother's arms. Navi could not help but feel out of place, had dutiful wife failed Stephen, insufficiently playing her wife and stepmother role and unwelcome outsider. It was not the time for taking silly emotional reactions personally, yet heart sunk emptily watching Stephen and his mother stride down the long corridor, arm in arm.

Navi navigated hallways and corridors outside to power smoke. Wandering aimlessly until confronted in a dead end corridor by the chapels bold wooden entrance door. Completely alone, calming, she admired artistic seventies style religious icons; a traditional cross with Jesus impaled on a cross bleeding and a crude painting of a Caucasian Hollywood Mother Mary donning Hollywood make up holding a haloed baby. Head hung in hands; she sobbed then prayed. Grateful to be alone in the chapel with God and Spirit, glad that Abby was in the good care of Stephen's sister for the day.

As whirling mind chatter slowed, recall took form from months earlier when first aware of something seriously wrong with Matt. He had complained about a small bump on a middle right rib. She had looked at it, no obvious visual cause for concern. Then acting upon the concern jabbing alarm in her solar plexus, noticed magenta discoloration edging the small mound. "Hmm', not wanting to alarm the boy, "Matt let your mom know when you get home tonight. If it starts to hurt or changes colour, or if it's still there tomorrow, one of us will take you to the Doctor." The strange sensation of touching it, stayed with her into the next morning. She had tried to shrug off the quick nagging pangs of fear and not wanting to be dramatically off, scuffed his head "Ah, poor baby has a boo-boo".

By four o'clock, Matt phoned her office to complain, the bump on his stomach was really starting to hurt. In the hectic business of work, fear rattled bones. Abruptly leaving work and flying home, she lifted his shirt then holding back a gasp, saw that the bump had grown twice the size with deep black blue angry colours surrounded by a ring of bright red. "Oh Matt, call your mom right now and ask her to make a Doctor's appointment today." Into the Doctor's office by four thirty, whisked into radiology then directly to the Oncology Clinic in the big city for further testing by seven. The Doctor monotoned gravity, "Expect to stay for a few days possibly even a few weeks."

It shocked how fast a parent could go from kissing a seemingly innocent bump to oncology. The reality of the fragility of life, mind spun. 'Kind of makes you understand why Moms worry the way they do.'

Navi blew wiped tears and nose shifting thoughts, searched the chapel for snotty tear filled tissue disposal. Seeing none, she stuffed them into her purse and made her way back to the waiting lounge. Stephen sat snuggled into his mother's bosom, oblivious to his wife as a doctor approached, "It's all over. Matt is in the recovery unit."

Hours later, the darkness of night descended, bringing a swaddled Matt back to his room. Lights dimmed as all gathered around his bed as medical computers beeped and tiny lights flashed. A barely conscious Matt groggily accepted a line of hugs. A somber grieving wake line of tearful family members came and went, leaving Navi candidly wondering whether or not to shout, "Ah for God's sake, he's not dead, this is not a funeral procession".

At last, Navi took a turn, bent over for a gentle hug when he grabbed and pulled her into a tight embrace then whispered, "Navi, when you guys left me at pre-op and they took me into the surgical unit, I was terrified! Then this warm, light feeling came over me and I just knew that I was going to be okay, everything is going to be okay. I have been to the pits of hell. There is only one way to go now, Navi. I thought you should know. I know what you always talk about, but now I get it."

"You're right Matt. You have done this thing. You are on your way now. I really love you. Good night sweetheart."

Navi bade his family goodnight and in a flash was out of the hospital and into the night hailing a taxi. Abby picked up, they quietly headed back to the motel. Daughter tucked in asleep, Navi curled up in her old ancient sisterhood shawl on their bed.

Little girl roused semi-awake, snuggled inside shawl and into mother, "Mom, I sense that he's okay and in good hands and sides, I'd have probably just got in the way. I'd rather see him and hang out when he's better tomorrow." Abby, fully awake now, reached directly for the remote control and fixated on an Oprah re-run.

Navi retreated to the motel deck wondering why it was that Stephen and she were staying in separate rooms this way. Close yet so very far away. How did this happen?

Navi assuming that Stephen would be joining her when he got back from the hospital, at least to confer left the door unlocked. He did not. When Navi awoke the next morning, she knocked on his door and upon hearing silence in return, realized that he had already gone directly to the hospital.

Stephen had rebuffed at pre-op, had not sought her out post op or come in the night and did not come to her before leaving again. Yet she would rather have stayed with Matt in the hospital but that was not her place. Navi wanted to go home, now. Go home rather than be here, unwanted. Chastising, countering that she could have gotten her own ass up during the night and gone to Stephen at any point and time. A guilt ping of a child full of cancer, with disease removed, a husband struggled for a sense of control over the uncontrollable. The analysis left sadness and needing. Throughout the day, Navi floated, seen but not heard from, attentive social graces while avoiding disapproving in-law eyes and gestures.

Abby asked for a bedtime snuggles, Navi seeking to shift mood, became a sumo wrestler pretend body slams, grunts, groans and chest thumping that brought fits of laughter and giggles. Short lived play, she was simply too tired and the exertion of body slamming exhausting, lay quietly singing a made up a rappy blues song.

"Eating broccoli is cruel, oh soooo cruel, 'cause they're really miniature mutant Christmas trees and meant to be displayed and admired with lights and tinsel, not eaten. So Darlinggg, pllleeasseee don't eat your broccoli."

Abby giggle rolled her eyes. Navi relaxed. It felt good to play. Being with the kids was after all, something she knew how to do.

"Pay attention to the faith and go with the flow attitude of the young."

At the hospital, with Abby in tow, Stephen stood with his back to her surrounded family, crying. Matt's mother had sunglasses on, quietly chatting with a priest. Navi reeled around to see Matt's bed empty then bolted into the hallway looking for her stepson. A dream, it was just a bad dream.

She rolled over sobbing then drifted back to sleep. The haunting dream picked up where it left off, surreal. *People mingled about, and seeing what looked like it might have been Matt; she dutifully graciously attended to guests and children while wandering among people offering food on platters. For all other intents and purposes, Navi did not exist, invisible, surrounded by families and friends. A ghost.*

Awake once again, Navi wandered out onto motel garden deck as a ghostly version of Matt approached. As clearly as any other real life person, Matt stood smiling. Not only just on the mend, but elated and happy.

Matt was back.

An early release and homeward bound, he proudly announced that it was a time for celebration, hooking up with pals and relieving him of his virgin hood.

"Gran, why did I not see Matt's illness coming?"

"Your job is not to foresee all and avert all challenges, but to find out who you really are and strive for grace in all situations. There is always a higher agenda, a higher plan. If those in crisis cross your path, you are there to assist and to observe. To be aware on all levels is how a true master gains confidence."

"Poverty is the worst form of violence."
Gandhi

Chapter 6 ~ LIFE

Daily life took on a new zest as spring burst forth, bringing a welcomed sense of normalcy and life. Matt had survived, overcome and transcended his brush with death, assuming remission held. It would be a long time, perhaps years, if ever, before Navi could share Matt's pre-op spiritual experience with Stephen. Sadly, rather than allowing it to be of comfort, dismissing it, further closing the door alone.

As the days flew by, he retreated further into his workshop, coming out of his shell only to dramatically reiterate to inquiring friends the traumatic events of the past months. Yet Navi waited to connect with Stephen as attention turned back to kids, school work and catching up with email.

Dear Catharine;

It's been awhile, so I have some updates for you. I AM FREE! Free I say! What a beautiful day!

It's Matt's birthday, seventeen today and apparently not speaking to Stephen for some reason. Not overtly angry, just seems indifferent. I just figure, that if they have issues with each other, they will work it out. I hope. I have decided to enjoy the freedom too now that Abby's Dad has moved back to the city. She is staying with him one weekend a month now. It's good because Stephen is not there for her, emotionally anyway. I miss her kitchen futzing, pet snuggling and chatter, plotting the next exciting second hand store haunting and candy feeding frenzy we will have.

We are still getting well wishes and gifts from people and I figured that Matt was on nine different prayer group lists, including some on the Internet! People just keep sending prayers, amazing! Wow, definitely something to this stuff.

Hope to see you soon

Love and hugs

Navi

Navi turned off the computer and attention shifted to Stephen, concluding that everyone was just waiting patiently for him to realize that he still has a life, family and to realize that this had happened to all of them. The only recourse was to give him ample space to work it out for himself. Matt had not shared Stephen's concern about the cancer, moreover, had already moved beyond the drama of it all. Driving motivation, chattering, trying to find a way to get poor unsuspecting feel sorry for his plight person or non-profit group to buy him an even better new computer, a new car, a hot girlfriend with big boobs who he could give away his virginity to, new clothes and score a dream all expensive paid tropical vacation. Growing into a monster greed and grab, he busily internet searched exotic island resorts in the South Pacific pressuring anyone who might listen with a healthy wallet. The pitch being, that he had been a fatally 'sick kid' and a 'modern medical miracle'. Much more than a kid with a terminal illness, he was really a budding crafty business mogul. He had drafted proposal specs highlighting a rationale as to how it would make the giver look good in media for sending him to a tropical island vacation, how media coverage would bring more fund raising groups raising even more capital in the next year. All of the angles covered, it was a sure thing.

Fuelling his purpose, he reminded Navi of just how cool it was that her friends had pooled their resources at Christmas and bought him a fancy lap top computer so he could do his homework, cruise the internet, watch movies and play games while in treatment. He did not. When not in treatment, he busily drafted a power point presentation, hogging her printer, leaving trails of spread sheets, graphs, marketing pictures and slogans strewn on the bedroom floor.

Navi, excited for the first time in a year, freedom from treatment stress had given a burst of new energy. Packed in a record twenty minutes and Toronto work conference bound. The Big Smoke, all-alone, with the sun shining and funky new sunglasses. Feeling good, pretending that she stayed in Motels as a matter of course, with celebrity pretensions, and secretly donning new underwear, sexy and impractical. It had been an agonizing forty minutes in Wal-Mart the day before unable to fathom why there were thousands of pairs of woman's underwear. What was one to do, try them all on? Do other women just know which ones will fit and be comfortable? None seemed remotely comfortable at first glance. Eyes lingered and halted on lacy black ensembles; forty dollars separately seemed steep, especially for Wal-Mart.

Adjusting a boob poking wire that insisted on impaling her motherhood and dislodging a G-string elastic wedge jammed into her crouch, Navi city navigated.

Around three entire city blocks during rush hour, weaving in and out of stopped cars, pulling out cars, cyclists and taxi hailers, she finally caught a wave of traffic that veered into a lane, which veered into the Hotel entrance. Avoiding tuxedoed Hotel parking lot attendant's eyes, bad acting, she pretended to be engrossed in important papers lying on the passenger seat. Truth being of course, that the shock of finding herself in a foreign ostentatious parking area stultified her.

"Tuxedoed car attendants? What in the hell am I supposed to do? Am I supposed to toss them my keys, luggage and a fifty-dollar bill and just waltz on in? Shit! I don't know what in the hell to do. Maybe they are looking at my dusty old crap car and are going to tell me that deliveries go in the back. Shit! Dam it!"

Glancing in the rear view mirror, a line up quickly formed behind. She quickly searched for a sign or someone's example to follow when eyes locked onto the sign,

Welcome to Hotel Casablanca.

Please leave your car keys and luggage with attendants.

No public or hotel guests allowed in parking garage due to security measures.

No Gratuities.

Enjoy your stay!

"Oh thank God!" Quickly grabbing purse, out of the car, an attendant magically appeared with outstretched hands taking keys then jumped into her car and squeal disappeared under an opening that led into a dark underground tunnel. A red uniformed door attendant motioned and escorted through revolving doors motioning her to a waiting fashion model masking as a lobby reception desk clerk. Peering over low-nosed hovering celebrity sunglasses, Navi hoped no one would laugh at her obvious country bumpkin being and request her leave. Feigning celeb status, a Very Important Person, she signed on the X marked lines.

Navigating to the dimly lit eighth floor, she sunglass blindly fondled the door keyhole. No, not a key, but what looked like a credit card. In a moment of panic, she glanced both ways down the length of hallway, pleased that no one was watching the fumbling six swipes of the card to get the swipe action in sync with the flashing green light versus the flashing red light to open the door.

Big busy city culture shock traumatized, she quickly spread worldly belongings out on the bed, perused the mini bar, clicked on the monstrous thin wide screened television then undressed. Lacy black bra and crouch jammed elastic thong undies flung across the room and thwacked against the far wall. A designer had been paid big bucks to select the gaudy floral and trendy wallpaper, sure to coordinate curtains, bedspread and carpet. Into the bathroom, clicked on the light and then squinted from fluorescent light's blinding glare off of white everything; tiles, towels, floor, counter, "Wooohoah" Navi backed, clicking off the light.

On the edge of the bed, eyes scanned to foreign scenery imagining furious clients and irate taxpayers storming parliament at that audacious waste of money having to pay for a government front line workers conference in higher end hotels. Her clients back home would be shocked and horrified. The irony of working with the poor and consistent tax payer's irate injustice of having to put food on a low life's plate, while the government was spending millions upon millions on consultants, fancy high tech new computer systems and now fully paid conference vacations in the big city in upscale motels.

Priorities and values skewed.

Outside, a ruckus of sirens and squealing cars blasted from down in the street below. Gingerly peering through curtains as not to be accidently shot by gang punk, Navi watched as two Police cars arrived from opposite directions, their lights and sirens blaring and tires squealing to a dramatic stop. Side walkers scrambled in doorways, down side streets, as a group of well-dressed students jumped out of a sports car and ran off in all different directions. Two bulletproof vested police officers pinned another trapped motorist on the hood of his BMW. Navi's country senses rattled and for a brief moment, panicked. 'Oh My God, what have I gotten myself into?' Within minutes, more police arrived, blocking both sides of the unfolding drama. A live movie or television show version played out of inner city happenings. Except this drama consisted of upscale sports cars and BMW's. Physically scrambling with two men then splaying them out over the car hood, pinned by a uniformed elbow, necks to windshield wipers, they were quickly hand cuffed. Then in a flash, all were back in assigned cars and disappeared. The street below was magically returning to the normal clutter of traffic and mingling pedestrians, as though nothing unusual had occurred.

Navi called home to Stephen, to check in, who actually sounded tender and reassuring! 'He's the way he used to be. He's back.' Navi felt strangely reassured with new hope. Giggling, she settled in to a Prime Rib dinner brought on a lovely silver tray by another tuxedoed room service attendant. 'God I love room service!' It was a magnificent treat from the universe and she was profoundly grateful to have it.

The conference, dismally boring, mind numbing, sleep inducing by mid-morning had brought on involuntary Attention Deficit Disorder. Guest speakers, formal with dry monotone voices made a comatose onset headache worse. Shifting, trying to stay sitting straight, then propping up forehead feigning intent listening of stimulatingly engrossed speeches that rather sounded more like Welfare reform politicking and cut backs than training of any kind. A growing annoyance and concern sifted through blah blah blah's. 'Why are they trying to gain front line support for these new legislative changes? Is that why they brought us all down here and put us all up in a fancy hotel? Ah yes, we are all being sold, marketed to, politicked. There was something ominously wrong. Front line worker opinions never mattered now. Rotten money hungry political apples, each one infecting baskets of bigger apples. Blah, blah, blah. The rah, rah, rah, blah, blah, blah of ministry reps, yes, selling the new hard arsed legislation.

'Propaganda Bull Shit!'

Navi's mind wandered and drifted off to wondering if Adolf Hitler were actually still alive and an old fart now, but very much alive, like Elvis Prestley. Alive and doing dirty deeds; secretly and subversively. 'Social Services is haunted. Did the citizens of Austria, whom voted Hitler into power before the Nazi regime emergence, foresee any hint of holocaust coming?' No, she supposed they did not. It was their great depression and hunger that saw only heroic promises of abundance, economic development, food for all and personal wealth. Sure, they did not mind his work for welfare program, after all a community is a community, meant to work together and for each other. There was pride in work and taking care of one's own. Except of course had you been a single mother in that day, husband lost to war.

By late afternoon, she slid into a dark and reclusive mood. Nauseous aversion, listening to propaganda crap in a luxurious conference centre while so many back home were struggling to feed their children, pay their bills and already doing without the basic necessities of life. The event of the past year, in hand with a naturally easy going country altruistic and humanistic manner, was creating an increasingly cynical awareness of a doom wave to which the oblivious general public was not made privy to.

The continuous big city noise of people, voices and sirens was maddeningly loud. From her window, Navi could not see a tree anywhere.

Lights cement and people milling about. 'Yuk, the city smells really bad!' Television channel cruising just made more noise, with commercials sounding like people yelling at her to buy their products that she did not know that she desperately wanted and needed. She turned it off.

Out into the strange city alone at night, she browsed eclectic shops stopping only to enjoy overpriced iced tea on a cafe patio. Overlooking the busy street life, she sipped, as evening herds of multi-cultural two-legged beings of all different colours, shapes and sizes soothed her sheltered existence. Bright lights, music blasted from cars, ghetto blasters and music buskers on corners creating a sound explosion overload.

Lighting a smoke, she adjusted her chair to make way for a family to sit at the table behind and noting that the young man was wearing a ball cap. A ball cap, no discernible hair. The tell-tale signs of cancer and treatments. Matt was still anxious about going out in public and his ball cap never left his head, he had slept with it on. The teenagers she knew would not go out if they found a zit on their face, could not imagine what courage it took for Matt to venture forth. Familiar distinct smells of cancer and treatment wafted through her nostrils. In her mind's eye, she enfolded the family in divine angel love.

Navi home and back into the daily work grind contentedly settled into routine. She loved work this time of year, clients were happy in finding paid work for the summer tourist season. Some would be lucky to get enough time in to qualify for unemployment insurance later in the year when the tourist season ended. The rest would be back on the system for the duration of the winter. It was exciting and they were excited. The world was alive again and none of the conference's propaganda bullshit had come down the corporate pipes to piss her off, yet she braced for ominous matters to come.

Distance from Stephen ensued; the brief caring phone interchange in Toronto had been an anomaly.

Restless sleep, old sisterhood shawl embraced, she journeyed.

Standing in misty jade green light, feeling taller than normal, and a wisp of silky material body covered her leathery brown lizard like skin. Holding a hand out in front, three elongated fingers and a short thumb moved in response to her will. Attention caught large long feet at the base of elongated legs. Three large toes protruded outward curving around a large thumb-like toe. Sounds of laughter, children laughing and giggling sounded within her mind and body. Strained eyes peered through mist in search of the glorious laughter only to rest upon a silver-balled sun surrounded by two smaller moons in the horizon. As though naturally gravitating toward the children's laughter, Navi abruptly stopped, confronted by a massive glass building that animated life shimmering.

An open doorway led to an inner cathedral where rather than seeing religious icon artwork, vague images of books floated, moved, pulsed and breathed in a tapestry covering the ceiling and walls.

Taking her assigned sitting spot, the marbled flooring felt oddly soft, cushioned as the material adjusted to her physical body. On each side, in front and behind, sat close friends who looked similar yet each emitting their own unique personality and attributes. Male and female alike, wore Frisbee shaped hats that vicariously balanced over long flowing straight black hair, same light jade coloured silky robes. Openly, consciously aware that earthly Navi had come to occupy the body and visit for the day, knowing instantly that she was recognized and welcomed brought her a wave of familiar home sense and belonging. This home was, the People of the Jade, the White Brotherhood.

A pudgy old Native woman, wearing a pottery clay red sari earthly type dress adorned with an eagle feather in two long braids gracefully stood in the centre of the group, introducing herself then smoothly and confidently beginning a talk.

"Natural Law is Universal Law is Creation Law, yes or no?

"Ay" responded the group in unison.

"We need only know, all that really matters is Love. There is a golden core or similar philosophy in all religions, all peoples, everywhere, throughout time. 'Love and goodwill'. Love is the creative source and power of all life. Focusing on and harnessing divine love must be the primary intent behind every higher action and thought. Love keeps us free from otherworldly fear, hate, jealousy and anger. Love has the highest energetic vibration.

The core principle is the ability to heal, just as a small child comes to its Mother, who automatically responds with loving magical kisses, as do we love others and ourselves. Love them and they feel better, we feel better. Adults in other cultures and worlds are no different in basic needs. We are all toddlers. Imagine what health care systems would be like, if everyone who got diseased and soul sick were loved, how much healthier and happy we would all be? This is why it feels so good. You feel loved as worldly and personal concerns vanish, you are inspired, whole and very much alive. Behaving in loving a way does not mean that we would not get angry, ever, but as if it is coming from a place of love, from within our hearts and delivered in a loving way, in grace.

There is no lack of food, shelter and material goods in other worlds that you will journey to and inhabit with, remember that there is only a lack of sharing. Be patient with those who are still in infancy, yet ever evolving, for they too will grow into knowing the higher universal laws of creation and know Love."

Navi awake, turned attention to the glorious magical sunrise splay through morning warm mist.

Cleaning Matt's room and still deliciously lost in Jade Brotherhood thoughts while matching socks, eyeing more poking out from under bed, Stephen came up from the workshop to pee. Usually he would simply open the workshop door and whizz outside. Stephen poked his head in the door; "WHAT THE FUCK ARE YOU DOING?" Startled, she turned to look at him, stammering explanation and catching herself, stopped short. Primal eyes blazing into her being, she shuddered. Straightening her back, she began again.

"I'm just sorting socks and doing a bit of cleaning."

"Well who in the fuck said you could do anything in here? Who the fuck said you could touch anything?"

Navi was stunned, heart pounding, mind reeling then instantly livid.

"Oh for fucks sake Stephen, Matt's not dead! It is filthy in here and it stinks. What in the hell is your problem?" Vibrating from months of pent up stress, resentment of receiving his constant bullshit attacks. The mystery phone Stephen while in Toronto had disappeared as quickly as it came. Random. Gone.

She turned, dismissing him thus ending the heated exchange. Navi hesitated, waiting for rebuttal to his nerve jarring front door slam. Stephen was already outside. She dropped socks and closed the door, pausing to catch composure breath. He revved the Junker van's engine and squealed out of the driveway. 'Exactly why do you have so much hostility? Why are we not talking? Why do we not touch and make love? I miss the, in the beginning you Stephen, dating, when you actually liked me.'

Navi retreated to the sanctity of her garden, fighting runaway tears, far and fast. There was nowhere else to go. Memoires of that strange restless night in the winter, when she could not sleep and of a bone rattling foreboding that still shadowed. Home care was still sliding and spring, usually Zen chores busy, could not elicit motivation. Annual spring garden and yard clean up beckoned of what had managed to survive the long harsh winter.

Catharine poured tea and Navi was grateful for the visit.

"Hey Catherine, I don't think I ever thanked you properly for looking after the critters and all of the house work you did while we were away with Matt in Toronto. Just want you to know, that we really do appreciate it."

"Ah, think nothing of it."

"Sorry about the mess in the house. I just can't seem to get into cleaning."

Catharine laughed as Navi showed the strange fluorescent orange and yellow coral like spore clusters growing behind the toilet. "Ah, they are so cool looking."

"Yes, I just can't seem to bring myself to take them away, to clean it. I kind of like looking at them. Besides, it pisses Stephen off."

"How are you guys doing anyway?"

"The days just seem to pass one into the other. I have become a guest in my own house. Ah sorry Catharine, don't mean to be a downer, just getting the sense that something big is going to go down and that it's out of my control. Weird, like I've just got to wait and ride it out."

"So, tell me what's been happening. Maybe we can shed some light on it."

"Well, you pretty much know what's up with Matt. Life is quiet, save for my time with Matt and for the most part, it is just Abby's puttering in creative messes. Stephen lives in his workshop, ever creating masterpiece sculptures now. Maybe all of his sexual energy is going into those masterpieces. Could be that Artist Libido thing, but I think it is more than that. I reckon that he is still trying to cope with Matt's illness."

"Pretty stressful times you've been through huh?"

"A mad man and I mean mad as in angry. I just give him space. Hurts too much trying all of the time, he is so ornery. There is no 'nice' access point. He is Fort Knox. His work has become unique and beautiful though. Soon, very soon, he will be ready for another showing, some gallery in Toronto. I can picture him in his element on opening night, networking the crowd. I can see him milling about and schmoosing crowds of elitists. Except, I cannot see myself there, but I am sure that I am. I must be. Stop me now with the agonizing already! I need the beach. I need to take a real vacation somewhere. I need to revel bask in sunshine and soothing waves. It's been a very long hard year and I'm just tired."

"Well darling, it's been a long and busy some odd years and yes, you ought to be very tired. Personally, I am looking forward to empty nest and visits by grandchildren, delicious lazy leisure time, travelling to follow spiritual aspirations and a hot man. But damn, what is the point of working and building up a home full of ambiance if you don't slow down, or enjoy it?"

"I guess. It is awesome to be futzing in the garden again. I did go to that conference in Toronto, although it was creepy propaganda bullshit. Great to be hoteling it, but there sure was a lot of woo-ha propaganda crap of new legislation coming down the pipe. I fear layoffs and severe cut backs."

"Ah yes, I gather from the news that holy hell is coming down the political pipe and all to do is ride it out. I feel for you, don't need that added stress."

"So, where have you been? I tried to find you a few days ago."

"Hee hee, well that's actually what I came to tell you about. I took a couple of sick days and went for a little road trip."

"Ha. So where did you go?"

"I went to see the White Buffalo."

"No shit?"

"Ah yup, sure did. The family that have the little gaffer are really quite lovely. Was not sure how receptive they would be to an old white woman, but they were wonderfully warm and kind. Anyway, the little gaffer's name is Rainbow Spirit and she is indeed white with blue eyes instead of normal albino pink eyes. So the differentiation in eye colour is pretty much what makes her one of several sacred indications, confirmation of prophecies, onset of new world order coming. All of that foretold coming of one thousand years of peace stuff, you know when the calendar ends at 2012.

As far as I can figure, do not quote me on it, but I think much of what is happening now, based on White Buffalo Calf Woman's teachings, those that honour that inner calling, must refrain from swearing, drinking alcohol and fighting, which is a tall order for me. It is a process of qualifying the called and a different way of life, of being and higher strengths, skills and fortitude. To forget the mind gunk and operate from within the heart, which is where the higher mind is.

Many people contribute in many ways: to protect sacred sites, share knowledge and make drastic changes in the education system so that we are growing happy well-balanced individuals. Of course, there are those who come to harness eco-friendly technology. From what I gather, there is also a heads up that we absolutely have to start working together and getting along as one global community and take care of Mother Earth. Clearly, it is time to take control away from those greedy materialistic mongers. It is time to bring in peace, harmony and balance to Mother Earth and her inhabitants.

I have always wanted to go see the white buffalos that came before her, and then when I found out about her, I just had to go. I felt as though I was one of the Magi, visiting little Jesus. I did get to pat her, lovely little personality. Oh and there is a growing movement to make June 21 an annual Peace Prayer Day. I'd like to go to those."

"That's way cool. I didn't know you were into that stuff."

"Well, I research and study a lot of spiritual goings on. Actually, I am really quite fascinated. Sure as shit, it is more interesting than just going to work every day and watching the boob tube at night. There isn't enough merry-wanna in the world to cure that boredom."

"Well I guess this conversation was meant to be then. I am having those journey dreams quite regularly now. I don't know if they are past lives or whether I am losing my mind. Don't know about the teachings either, too deep for me, although I suppose they are in my brain and soul now. Just got to allow them to do what they're going to do."

"Oh, look at the time. I have to toddle now, but we will talk more soon. Oh and by the way, if it helps you in any way, it is not lost on me that Stephen can be a real prick at times; I've seen glimpses of it. Honestly, I do not know how you can stand him.

Oh and while I am boldly blurting on the subject, I ran into your Mother a few days ago, she invited me out for tea. I got the impression that she was looking for an ally, to get you to come back into the church fold. Hee hee, I hope you don't mind, but I rather gave her what for. Gave me insight on you though, always wondered why you did not have a bigger ego, you are a humble gal you know, got so much love to give, your kids are amazing, especially Abby and your clients absolutely love you. You're their saving grace."

"Ah shucks. Thanks Cath. You are the best. I am anxious about empty nest. Matt is already good to go to university early, this fall in fact. Abby is seeing her Dad more. That leaves Stephen and me with each other. Wish I could say that I was looking forward to it more, but honestly, I'm worried."

"Ah, worry not my friend. Been there and done that. Just walk through it with as much grace as you can. It will be what it will be and if that door closes then rest assured that another one will open. Always does. Ah, but you already know this stuff. There is so much more to you than what you show people, all of those journeys are maybe leading you to better opportunities. I am happy to share this path with you and look forward to watching you blossom. And you know what? Fuck your Mother and fuck Stephen, and fuck work. I think you are really onto to something exciting with those soul journeys. Go with it, some day it shall all make sense. I have to toddle. See you soon."

Kitchen window gazing, warm May weather brought annual delicious happy reverent moments. Despite garden and yard neglect, flowers were popping up in abundance. Strange contentment, knowing windows remained unclean since last fall provided a dirt film that kept in-flight birds from seeing their own reflections of sky and trees thus sparing numerous winged lives. There was a positive spin to every problem.

'What is wrong with a little grunge anyway? If visitors come solely for in-ground pool and do not like the mess, then they can damn well clean it themselves. They may have a differing opinion of the giant orange and yellow spore farm growing out from behind the toilet.

None, not one of the church folks had come to visit with Matt sick. 'Come to think of it, I have not seen Mother since Christmas, having too much fun with gal pals since Father passed over, years ago. I have not seen much of Stephens's family since Matt's surgery either. There were oodles of cards and flowers, but normal visitors had shrunk in numbers and faded into the periphery of life. Ah but, church folks are all getting old. Their kids are adults and pretty much all of them have moved away, educated and found life beyond the county. The ones that remained were simply uninterested in church and its culture. Even Pastor Stanley is an old fart now and home visiting congregation less and less. Yes, it had been years since she had gone to church and none of them bothered to call on her. No one asked for explanations, Navi was free! 'Ah, that's what you call evolution of the species, dinosaurs do die off eventually!'

Navi, opting out of an evening at home of housework, splayed out alone on the hood of her car in the driveway, smoking cigs, drinking lube oil and filter store bought takeout coffee. Shit coffee from variety stores, lovingly referred to as 'Joe'. Beginnings of sunset colours streamed brilliant pinks, purples and blues across horizon treetops. Dragonflies' cloud hovered over garden fauna.

Office coffee buddy David and Navi sat on their rural satellite office front steps, smoking and chatting before toddling off to respective lives for the weekend. Quiet and happy to be with one another, content. It had been almost a year since they had been able to lounge about like this, like the old days. Too much had happened in the past year with Matt's illness. David had been away in Ottawa on a management-training sabbatical. They had always gravitated, being the only smokers, it was still socially rural acceptable to just hang out and smoke. Giddy and excited in being able to share that the worst had passed, survived Matt's illness and surgery. David expounded on courting his wife, a mission to re-vitalize intimacy and connectedness.

"She is a lucky woman to have a spouse that actually wants that. It takes two. I hope it all works out the way that you want." They sat quietly for a while, each enjoying the warm breeze of spring. Out of nowhere David softly said, "I hear you are going away to another conference, Darling, I miss you, just sitting beside you!"

Rattled, unsure what it meant, opted to make light of it, "Wow, what a gentle soul and good friend you are! You are so full of shit, you schmoozer!"

Eight years of working in close proximity of each other, there was not much they did not talk of. Today they parted ways to respective private lives, as they always did, like wolf and sheep dog in cartoons, punching a time clock.

"Goodnight Fred."

"Goodnight George."

Navi sat in her car reeling and stunned for twenty minutes after David had left, unable to move, unable to drive. 'What in the hell or heaven was that all about?' Waves of light and excitement rocked from within, hit by a light stun gun of strange wondrous energy followed by foreboding. Life was about to 'ka-boom'.

Navi's glorious garden bloomed despite continued neglect, carrying on without her fingers in its dirt. Even the pond thrived, alive with gold fish. Who could not love this time of year? It was the space between snow, dreary long nights and annoying bugs. Mother Earth had come alive with colour and activity. Butterflies abounded and a new crow couple had taken ownership of the compost bin. Navi named them 'Ethel and George', whose self-imposed alpha dog authority ruled over what animals fed where and when. Brat-Kat was Stephens, a neglected and cantankerous old mangy companion. Dawg's alpha dog maleness clipped at six months testicles had gone to alpha dog heaven. Both Dawg and Brat-Kat ate outside in nice weather, often waiting for crows, possums and raccoons to finish eating out of their bowls first.

Naming critters and trees gave Navi a sense of community and extension of loved ones, a little less alone. Naming car 'Buddha Mobile' gave commune for travelling and set a spiritual tone and ambiance with its dash as alter of eclectic beach treasures, crow feather and quartz crystals.

Two century old maple trees stoically stood along the back cedar rail fence line; Grandmother Maple, her 'V' shape and the honey bees that swarmed in the V each summer. Grandfather Maple, a protruding huge phallic branch front protrusion. Side by side they stood, same in age and obvious soul mates. Longevity entitling them respect, they are lucky to have each other as endearing soul mates.

Fireflies danced for her eyes only this evening as a spring Peeper Frog mind blowing deafening chorus sang brilliantly like a symphony for her ears, for her soul. 'What more could anyone ask for?'

Stephen had taken to staying away from home, his whereabouts when not on Matt time, a mystery. Abby away with her Dad, the house rang and echoed emptiness. Before settling in for the night, Navi checked her email, needing to talk to someone, safe David.

Hey David;

Did you ever notice how profoundly guilty a person can get over the silliest of things? Like when I pile my groceries in the back of the car. I am so lazy and fed up with shopping traffic that I do not want to make the trek back to the designated shopping cart return area? Yes, I quickly scan the parking lot, to see if anyone is looking, then move the cart to the other parking spot. Yes, as if someone else had left it there, and then I drive away rationalizing (unconvincingly) that they hire help to retrieve them.

Navi of the woods

Hey Navi, conjuror of the woods,

Was it worth it?

David, husband to the wife who thinks he doth be a total asshole.

Navi woke bolt upright. Residue skidding waves, her body a duck coming in for a landing, skidding across lake's surface, wings outstretched until plunk, followed by waffling waves rippling around her being. Soaked in menopause sweat, pajamas and hair clinging wet to hot prickly skin, she ripped off clothes, allowing them to fall into a puddle on the floor. Window opened wide allowing cooling night air to extinguish internal inferno. Striving for already forgotten essence of where she had been this time, living a completely different life, happy and content.

Soul skin man?

Reality of waking in a dark empty husbandless bed alone, contrasted rudely with dream. The burning need to pee emerged into consciousness as sleepy spastic legs lunged up and out of bed.

Stephen *was* there, in bed. When had he come home? Where was he? His back turned away, gently snoring, feet unconsciously and tenderly finding the back of her legs. A cruel reminder of love held during dating, lost days after the marriage. Essence of the dream escaped, save wisps of sunshine and happiness.

Confused and frustrated, Navi turned to Gran "What do they mean? Are they premonitions or past lives? What are they trying to tell me? Am I going insane?"

"*BE STRONG*, my little Chickadee."

"Geez. That almost felt like someone yelling. I'm not going to get into a car accident, or someone is going to die, or what?"

A calm wave of warm lovingness washed within, soothing, followed by a hint odour of roses, followed by harmonious music, a spirit world calling card. One more trip to the bathroom, "I always have to pee. Maybe I should invest in some adult diapers, soon. When I am old and if I am to be infirm, I shall write nasty and crude notes in colourful magic markers on my diapers for my caring staff and Abby to read. HA! Nah!" Abby had giggled with the joke once, threatening that she will write BITE ME on the back ends to piss off the nursing home care workers.

"Be strong, Navi."

"For everything you have missed,
you have gained something else,
and for everything you gain,
you lose something else."
Ralph Waldo Emerson

Chapter 7 ~ Vision Quest

Navi happily dressed with good-bye kisses well planted on a snoozing girl child forehead then out of the house in under ten minutes. An alone road trip away was magic motivation. Everything had been packed and laid out the night before.

Conference bound, headed towards Thunder Bay for a glorious long drive, with three days and nights of motel solitude. No other co-workers wanting to do the trip added bonus enjoyment; it was to be a vacation away from work and family demands. So much had happened this year and since the Toronto trip lacked full refresh, she still desperately needed time to recoup. A long road trip offers mind space, time to think a thought and feel a feeling without interruption. Once the brain blithering babble slows down, objectivity comes.

Navi had a good hour's drive before the ferry dock. Her mind raced in open chaotic forum, running wildly here and there and everywhere.

There was dear, sweet, Abby who was now proudly bragging Native heritage on her father's side. Tiny frame, impish smile and love of nature, Navi sales pitch rationalized that it was genetically provable that she was actually half Elf; Native-Elfin. While most adults seemed to struggle with two very different and seemingly opposing mind sets and cultures, Abby did not, just one of those children, born of mixed cultures, proudly belonging solely to all, embracing all. Daughter was a child who walked between cultures in alignment with the spirit world.

She had the confidence and inner drive that comes from surviving instability in life, which offered more mother guilt than that Abby demanded. A loving bond, like a soul little sister, a sister and magical mentorship.

Approaching adolescence, boldly and confidently announced to whoever inquired, that she was a Medicine Woman.

While Catharine was on a personal quest to find and explore obscure spiritual sites, Navi too had unwittingly embarked.

After exploring for weeks on the internet, Abby scanned various government records, genealogical sites, the archives at the local library and was getting nowhere. Navi decided to ask Ole River. Local Native Elder, or hippie chick, River was a Medicine Woman acquaintance from the reserve and as an elder commanded gentle respect from most. She eluded the air of mystery Shaman presence, yet at the same time, simply human with a blundered series of bad marriages and estranged children like the rest of the world, which made her more normal than exulted. Respectful, yet Navi kept a watchful boundary, the woman often reeked of marijuana.

River had a way of showing up in the office or crossing paths just when Navi had been thinking of her. One pack of smokes given, meant; I would like to ask your advice currency equated one full casual consultation.

"So Abby wants to get more native eh?"

"Well I think she is very astute with understanding teenager feelings and thoughts, and has a good solid grasp on which she is right now. I figure that in another year or so, when she knows who she is as a woman, she can actually go and find them to explore what they were all about and where they came from. She seems to naturally flow with growing into her innate medicine woman abilities. It will be interesting to see from her mature adult perspective when she finds out what it also means to be Celtic and hint of native, white, a woman, a person, a spirit, a soul, a part of the universe, part of creation. It is a life long journey and I suppose the rest will fall into place when the time is right."

River thoughtful, "You know that the two of you are far more in touch with your spirit than many of my people. Good contract, good road."

Those quiet yet mighty words may have been intended for Abby in her quest, but touched and haunted Navi. It was a form of validating advice intended for both mother and daughter.

David. Navi's mind drifted back to David. An enigma and coffee pal, she had first noticed his charm at a boring office Christmas luncheon. Cool, tall dark and handsome, a little aloof, but smoked, the two being the only smokers. A year later, she became one of his staff. Instant friends, great team, intelligent conversation, witty, wise, and the best team manager she ever had. Easy going yet, wise and understanding with clients, casually taking a client in crisis out for coffee chat, shoot the breeze. He was always respectful. Often, tough loving clients, in a good way. They, openly showing him adoring respect in return.

David was the bane of the county council boys. Those old boys were notoriously tight with money except if it had to do with ensuring regional golf and fishing projects; of course, days spent golfing or fishing were the norm. Notoriously adept at swindling money out of budgets to help someone with hydro bills, a cord of wood and maybe get a truckers license, he always made management decisions in favour of Navi's intuitive opinion. Respect beyond the office as a dedicated family man of over thirty years. Sure, they had problems as every couple does. Unsure what the attraction to his wife was, given her fondness for social climbing, material gain and snotty condescending manner with front line staff, which rippled tension throughout the office whenever she waltzed in. She respected their marital dedication and tenacity none the less. David was handsome, charming and so very well husband trained, their lives intertwined through crisscrossing careers, extended family and mutual acquaintances. A trusted friendship had grown over the years.

Navi's mind drifted to her children, wondering if she had done okay by them. Matt was always off to a party now, intent on losing his virginity before university, not wanting to step foot in the halls of higher learning as a virgin. Of course there were the lectures about 'if you can't be good, be safe talks, condoms now readily available in the medicine cabinet, boldly and guiltily placed despite images of mother and old bag church women huffing and cringing. Declaring playtime, he strange slimy balloon blew them up and with Abby in tow, covered each banana in the basket.

David's kids shared Matt's friends, as it is in small rural communities. When the boys and their friends were becoming teenagers and talk was turning horn dog, Navi quickly countered with the respect for girls and dating etiquette lecture; 'No means no' and don't have sex until you are one hundred per cent sure that you want to.' Diseases and emotional ramifications openly discussed and debated. If you are feeling sexy, relieve yourself before you go out on a date. Keep brain clear.

Matt horn dog could barely wait to explore sex, a blatant passion for boobs and all things mammary gland related, the bigger the better. Cancer and surgery ran through her mind again, like chaotic clips from a movie, playing at random and without control as the art of traumatic experiences went; a thing is relived, played out over in one's mind until it was accepted and emotional impact dissipated.

David was great at giving advice, though honourably she had never talked about her own marital intimacy concerns. Until now, Navi had never offered it up for discussion out of respect for Stephen, but now David was generous in giving the male perspective, offered; "Well Navi, basically, men are pigs. From a guy's point of view, either he wants intimacy or he does not. There is a big difference between cannot and will not. There is a difference between sex and making love and guys know it."

"Ah ha."

Enjoying their witty email exchanges, Navi had tried emailing Stephen weeks prior in attempt to transfer the fun and open communication. "What the fuck Navi? Why are you emailing me? We live in the same fucking house for Christ Sake. Save it for home."

A teenaged Navi had run away from home; back packing through the Rocky Mountains. Mountains and trees, wandering Kitsilano and Vancouver, then ferried to the Island. Banff explored, followed by the dry arid flat lands of Alberta, dinosaur canyon country. It had been a glorious summer, Mother and church cronies a solar system away. At summers end, she flew to Montreal during the time of the French politician Rene Leveque's quest for French rule and economic autonomy within the Party Quebecois. Quebec was a cultural shock for the back woods naive young woman. Amidst political passion that often resulted in violence, she simply could not blend nor assimilate within the contemporary cosmopolitan culture. A fish out of water, insecure in strange surroundings, she managed to find a caregiver job in a nursing home.

Mean old Monsieur Desjardin, the nastiest cantankerous miserable man that ever graced the planet, ruled both staff and nurses with a violent temper. His constant yelling and swearing in French was lost on the young girl who did not understand the language; she was assigned to his personal hygiene care. On her days off, his care fell to newer girls until his cursing drove them to find work elsewhere. His bellows fell on deaf ears, over time he made it his mission to take her out, to see her youthful health aliveness and vigor, destroyed as his had been. Navi's first day back after a holiday began with his motioning insistence that she tend to his 'hard on' first, her choice either by mouth or cunt. Instantly appalled, his bathing time offered opportunity. Naked, exposed and therefore at her mercy, she quietly ran cold water over the washcloth while he continued his lewd gestures and remarks. As the frigid cold cloth gently came into contact on the decrepit male genitalia, he profanely curse screamed at the top of his lungs, sending nursing staff and security into chaos "TABERNAC! TABERWIT!"

That was the last care session with Monsieur Desjardin. He would not have it, insisting that she was trying to kill him. Other residents, she grew to love, listening to their stories and sensing when ready to pass over. Typically, eyes glazed and stared far away, dreams became more lucid and they talked openly with friends and relatives already long passed. They slept more, ate less, growing calmer and content. The transition process was a re-birthing in action from physical death to spirit world life. Navi understood. They were never afraid, in fact, seemed to look forward to the transition. When passed over, usually in the night, there followed a cool crispness in the air and a strange gentle breeze. She could feel it, a re-birth canal, a gateway to joyful other side reunions.

Enter T.J., quickly romanced, pregnant, they moved in together, nested and baby born. Alas, a year in the suburbs of Montreal made Abby's Father no more ready to settle down to a mundane family life, a man on a get rich mission. At first, it was easy, she could take baby Abby anywhere in a backpack, hiking through Vermont Mountains with friends and travelling the underground city of Montreal via subway. Born in Montreal's biggest and oldest hospital on a full moon, a poking little head popped out just in time for a huge centipede to crawl across the wall behind the Doctor's head. Clueless on how to work the bidet left it in the bathroom and too embarrassed to ask for help. The generic French label on the tube of cream provided wonderful relief to her outer vaginal stitches and nipples. She had proceeded to cake it on liberally all over her body. When the wonder cream ran out, she humbly approached the nurse's station with empty tube in hand to ask for more. A surprised nurse looked at her, the tube, then back at her, "Mon Dieu! If your hemorrhoids are dat bad, maybe you should see your Docteur!"

Born jaundiced yellow, a kind of special glow, baby Abby too, talked and played with people no one else could see. At naptime, fits of giggles from a toddler, standing in crib, smile staring up in the air as spirits entertained. Abby's Dad, seemed to have had an aversion to their family life, happy when on the go and out in the world of wealth, miserable and unbearable to be home. 'But damn, the sex was good.'

Recalling the body memories sensations of passionate love making, she slid into fantasy. *Navi stood waiting for an attendant at an empty big city parking lot pay booth. David from work casually approached her from behind. Ever so expertly, slides strong loving hands down the length of her body. Ever so slowly and skillfully in his task that she is frozen, unable to move except heated breaths in response to electric touch, arousing each body cell making skin dance with light until gasps for air exploded in orgasm.*

'The sum of my spiritual search over the past ten to fifteen years has brought me to this point. Yep, studying the spiritual pursuits the healing arts, of whom all teach the path of mastery over the physical, to find that I am having sexual fantasies, rather than real life sex with my husband and no Nirvana. St. Francis of Assisi tried to get rid of his raging hard on by burying his gonads in snow.'

"A true soul mate matches you physically, emotionally, mentally and spiritually, all levels."

"Hi Gran. Why do our bodies betray us? Why or how is it that we can think about something logically then have our physical body do something else? Why do incest and rape survivor's orgasm in the most inhospitable of circumstances? How can the physical body orgasm while the heart and mind are crying? How can one be generally content within a marriage and yet feel yearning for another? What is this powerful passion that goes to sleep when there is no apparent outlet within the immediate relationship, only to be awakened by another?"

"So many questions."

"Analysis Paralysis, notice how the world 'anal' precedes the word analysis?"

"One needs to think of the emotional, mental, physical and spiritual parts as distinctly separate parts or bodies of ourselves, like four different people with four different agendas all sitting at a table discussing one issue. The different parts, mind consciousness or bodies are all really part of the individual, the whole consciousness. Each seek to have their needs met and are part of the God higher mind, spirit and soul. The physical part or body gathers information from its environment to the soul and to the universe. The divine will or universe and the soul speak to the physical body through sensations and yearnings to experience certain things. Each has its own intelligence, if we would only listen. It can be equally as intelligent a source of communication from the soul through the physical as your spiritual and mental states, provided they are connected or in line so to speak."

"Uh huh, sure, hmm, I think I actually understand."

"If you are unsure of a thing mentally and emotionally, then the answer is somewhere in your body, usually on the physical. Just be aware of your bodily sensations."

"Hmm. So, if the higher love, that higher place of operation that I have been asking for and yearning for to awaken this sleeping passion is through physical love with another human, how does this fit in with the idea of celibacy as a master grows out of the need for human love and channels it into divinity?"

"Kundalini or mysticism, one needs to experience and acknowledge physical yearnings first then choose where the energy will be channeled. Perhaps there is more than one way to achieve nirvana other than celibacy."

"What a quantum leap of faith and wisdom this would entail, as we make choices, we are responsible for how these choices in turn ripple effect outward. Okay, so how does this fit with me? I don't get it. This is what the masters tried to attain, when they referred to transcendence of the physical world? They face nemesis challenges finding their own inner guidance, stand strong in grace, transcending human thoughts and human sense of what is right. It took those old masters phenomenal inner strength and fortitude to follow inner guidance. I suspect that, things like that are still happening. I feel deep sorrow for every heretic that ever lived."

Images flashed of facing a witch tribunal, burning at the stake, tossed off ship, hung, stoned and buried alive. A myriad of lifetimes, of having been there and done all of that, heated in ferocity then trailed off to dissipate.

"Be careful Chickadee, it's good to take ideas, explore and incorporate them, do not assume to know the bigger picture for others."

Navi wondered if maybe breast enhancements, a vaginal tuck, have crone hairs laser removed or take lovemaking courses might save her marriage. "I ask you Gran, or whoever is out there, please help me make changes in my life for a better way of being, a happier day to day life! So be it, as is above, so is below- so they say. Let the chips fall where they may." As soon as Navi had said this, she immediately got a sinking feeling that her words were going to haunt her, to come back to bite her in the arse.

David stood waiting at the ferry dock, casually leaning against his car.

"Hey, what are you doing here?"

"I had a client, knew you would be passing through, so I hung around to bid you a good journey."

"Ah, that's nice. Good to see you."

Quiet, smoothly casual handsome, he lit two cigarettes and handed her one. Suddenly acutely sensual, she wondered for the first time, what it would be like to kiss him, an adolescent girl smoking a first cigarette. Astounded by marital boundaries crossed, mixed with an incredible drawing sensation, filled with light, suddenly longed to kiss him.

"Hey, can I kiss you, no strings attached? I just want to know what it'd be like."

"Sure."

David stood by his car, reached forward then gently and warmly kissed her. So tall, she reached up on tiptoes; he bent down to meet her. It was a nervous kiss yet warm, gentle, kind followed by a rush of heat making heads whirl. Pulling back, he smiled. He scooped Navi up in his arms and wheeled her around as if she were a small child then set her gently down, holding her shoulders gazing into her eyes.

"Oh, my God!" His face had turned bright red. "Oh my God Navi, I'm so embarrassed."

"Why?"

Downcast, searching his shoes he mumbled, "I am aroused."

Navi relief grinned, "Lovely".

Standing apart, the reality sunk into their collective consciousness in shock, joy and discomfort. Navi broke nervous tension, "Thank you. That was awesome! Sure never felt anything like that before!"

A grinning schoolboy gazed into her eyes. The ferry whistle blasted, rattling them back to the day and real life at hand

"I have to go."

"Navi Conjurer, Voodoo Woman."

"Yes right. So I've been told by someone once, but just don't know who said it."

Alone in the car, unable to move let alone drive, emotions swirled in surreal shock and joy. Elated and astounded of how right and just A-Okay this felt in her childish heart. Navi searched the inner Mother critic, for the emotional moral principles fallout of guilt and remorse and came up empty, floating. The last of the passenger cars had ferry boarded and the hatch was closing without her. Acutely aware that of crossing some omnipotent yet invisible boundary, waited for the emotional backlash hit. Joy.

"Thanks Spirit friends. I shall treasure this moment!"

The small rendezvous meant waiting for the next ferry. Alone, she wandered the harbour in reverence, water gazing deep alive and filling all of senses then in her mind's eye, sent it to him; an ethereal photograph taken and sent to a friend. Was he blown away by the intimate meeting or had already sloughed it off? It was just a moment, just a small and lovely gift from spirit.

Off the ferry, onto the Island then onto the north mainland, hours rolled by meandering the greater lake's majestic and scenic coastline. Around every bend awaited yet another astonishing view of open water, islands, rough rocky shorelines and silhouette evergreens. Finally, beginning to relax and enjoy the scenery, thoughts turned to gratitude for the time out and entered a non-thinking space.

Navi splayed out personal belongings on the massive king sized bed then took herself out to the dining room for a late dinner, alone. Sometime past one o'clock and still wide awake, she donned old sisterhood shawl and ventured to the outdoor garden hot tub, alone. Enclosed in a beautiful lush tropical garden with built in rocky waterfall, in darkness, save for the hot tub lights, she floated holding head toward the sky as rain face pelted. Tickled and pleased with such a treasure and alone to ecstatic sensations. How nice it would be to share this with someone special, perhaps in some other lifetime, she pondered.

"Thank you Spirit!"

The vision flashed lightning bolt.

Massive outstretched winged bird creature, much larger than a bald eagle, swooped down and hovered in front of her, its expansive wings obscuring garden view, its talons flexing, feathered wings tilting hovering as deep black eyes penetrated into soul and mind. Like watching a movie, full colour pictures lashed, moved and breathed before her. Stephen turned their house into an art studio contentedly focused solely on his creations. Then he was happily networking with the art market. Fast-forward now: the following year he meets a woman, young well dressed and petite. This woman acts as though she has died and gone to heaven, being in their glorious home. Navi was happy for him, very happy indeed at his newfound life and success.

She returned to her room/cave and curled up in bed, wet and alone, intuitively knowing that nothing was ever going to be the same. Eagle messenger from Spirit realm was a rite of passage that entailed facing fear with warrior bravery. People who achieved honourable courage, were often gifted a prized Eagle feather. She felt more like a deer, eyes laser locked caught in transport truck headlights.

Maybe, I will be a bag lady when I grow up. After the kids have grown and long gone, I shall take to wondering and wandering, living my life in dreamtime space, the world between the world of human and spirit. The only thing that I will have from my former life is a nametag on a dirty coat. Maybe Abby will bring me a new toque and mittens for Christmas. "Come home with me, Mom", she will shamefully beg. "NNNNah, you go happy."

A conference is work away from work, no matter what anyone says. Navi tenderly applied makeup and up-tied hair in attempt to feel comfortable inside of immoral skin, realizing it was impossible; discomfort nagged from the inside.

She flipped into work mode, grateful as discussion evolved around the table regarding trends for the new economy. Someone proposed a resolution, ". . . in order to woo industry into rural areas, we need to have a skilled labour market to offer industry scouts." Get them upgraded, get them work experience equates to get a fucking job, then off the taxpayers dole.

Rural folks dance slower and to quieter music, do not trust anything new or fancy that comes with bells n' whistles. Most city people saw country folk as archaic, Mayberry-ish and not too bright. In the quiet wisdom of rural folks, existence for the most part was content, just the way it is, a wait and see attitude. For the most part, they are just simply not interested in a big new hustling bustling local economy, liking things the way they are. She too had once thought the same, a result of growing up in her cloistered church culture and community. When a young adult Navi set out on her own into the big world, she came to understand and respect much of this mentality. She liked her most remote rural clients the best, they have a gentle stubborn and polite manner that told you the new and improved social policies are absurd. You just could not sell new and improved social politics to an old and established community. Why fix something that is not broken. Why get new and flashy when the old one works just fine. Why waste hard-earned money on flash that will fall apart later on.

Opting out of the second conference session to walk down the main drag, she meandered down franchise mall alley. Suddenly standing in the middle of the road as cars rushed by in both directions 'Today would be a good day to die, passed a thought, free and in the moment completely ready to go, to pass over.'

As soon as the thought passed, *Mother Mary appeared directly right in front of her. Real, like looking at anyone else alive except this woman wore a soft light greyish robe, Navi felt that it was Mary. Loving arms outstretched, without a word, coaxing her forward. She obediently followed her, as a child would follow its mother.*

Horns blared as a truck squealed brakes tires and slammed into an empty city bus. Once safely crossed the busy road, jangled, she sat down on the curb, gathering herself. Mother Mary had stopped, and then re-directed her out of harm's way.

Evening Oprah had guest Dr. Phil, the marriage therapist who was pointing to an enlarged picture of a sad women. "Buddy", he said to the husband, "take a good look at your wife. She is not, okay. Your marriage is not as happy as the picture you paint. You may have already lost her." Navi felt the hit from the inside out, doubled over as tears flowed. 'Oh, my God! I'm relating to the Dr. Phil Show!'

Navi called home, to Stephen, they needed to talk when she got home.

Homesick and seeking familiarity of the office and needing a reality check, Navi called David at the office. "David, I'm so sorry about the other day. I am so sorry about my indiscretion. If it's caused you problems, let me know."

"Nah, forget it Navi. All is well. Not to worry. Hey, you'll be happy to know that I've been trying to convince our new receptionist that our office is located in the middle of a Vortex and that it requires a Virgin Sacrifice; her! She's trying to convince me that I'm El Diablo, that I am the dark vortex."

Feeling somewhat relieved, Navi ventured back out to conference, networked with guest speakers, ministry reps and managers from other municipalities.

Bored and pre-occupied, doodling palm trees, beach and water in a notebook, her mind drifted to youthful adventure. In her first second hand jalopy, solo, she drove with hands soldered to steering wheel, a woman on a mission to the Florida Keys. Through torrential downpour in the Tennessee Mountains then in Marathon, another storm blasted wild and furious open ocean winds over insignificant highway. The arduous narrow highway stripped out into the ocean, with the Gulf of Mexico on the right and Atlantic on the left. A stunning panoramic view. On a deserted stretch, she pulled over to pee. Squatting, watering sand and stones, she bent, leaned sideways to pick up some funky grey sponge like rocks. On closer look, they pulsated gliding moving about in puddles. Not rocks, jellyfish! The sign across the road said, "Key West to Cuba, one hundred miles.

Key West; where same-sexed couples experienced freedom of walking hand in hand, a space where one was free to love the one they loved. This is something that would not happen back home in rural church community. Love is love. Who were we to judge where, how and in what manner love was manifest? To loved and be loved.

Home bound, across-country via Alligator Alley, where logs piled along roadside were actually live alligators, "Do Not leave pets unattended."

Navi loved a good journey. Half home body, half journey warrior.

"There are times when a battle decides everything,
and there are times when the most insignificant thing
can decide the outcome of a battle."
Napoleon Bonaparte

Chapter 8 ~ Home

It was a beautiful sunshiny day and a good day for a long drive and Navi was on a mission. Stephen's anger in its raw and primal form now matched her resolve, a habit of acquiescing coming to a close. In her mind flashed the memory of Mother's take down by Mrs. McPatterson's nasty, 'Your turkey stuffing is not fit for human consumption'.

On ferry deck, basking in sunshine, she rolled to panoramic expanse of spring sky and side view of old couple wandering the deck. They huddled against the railing arm in arm, watching ferry waves, tight together against wind. Lovely old long good love. Seagulls dipped in and out of ship's wake, healthier morsels than fast food dumpsters. From the side, waves rocked, curled and spilled against ship metal. Scenery appeared then disappeared.

Old couple sat beside her, arm in arm, close with obvious tenderness. Surely, a match approved by the heavens above, affirmation display of what we all search and yearn for. A glimpse of a bright flash of light and her attention turned to the railing as the ferry hit several large waves sending water sprays up mid-air catching bits of sun light and splaying rainbow.

Trekking, spiraling downward into ship bowels, Navi ungraciously navigated her way with borrowed drunken balance as waves rocked and rolled. Dark tiny corridor led to a hovel, echoes of water churning, she hovered over a tiny bowl while circus performer hands gripped sidebars. Legs splayed wide-open, lunch projectile launched into the bowl, splattering inside thighs.

Home emotionally and physically exhausted, a stranger in her own driveway. Sunshine late afternoon streamers splayed through trees and across pond surface. Alive with dancing dragonflies, goldfish skirted to warmer corners while invasive defiant cattails stood tall, "We shall inherit this earth". Garden's explosion of colour blooms promised a lush year. The pool open surrounded by wooden decking and sculptures, and beckoning, to whom? What beauty and ambiance had she created? Adding a plant or two each year with nature assuming the rest and presto, heaven on earth made manifest. Sanctuary, empty of couple love, echoed.

A deep breath and making her way up front steps, Brat-Kat, Dawg and Abby scurried into Mom love greeting arms. Navi dropped luggage and caught Stephen washing filthy dirty workshop hands in the kitchen sink, mindlessly spraying specks of dirt over the white counter and washboard. Navi wanting only answers and solutions, "Stephen, I'll meet you upstairs at nine, we need to talk."

Cold edge sternness in her voice startled, Abby took the cue and headed off to resume bedroom play. Stephen side head nodded and headed back down to his workshop. She riffled through the stack of mail on the kitchen counter; phone bill, credit card bill, hydro bill, another snow removal adjustment bill, internet bill, her car repair bill, grocery store flyers, a metal sculpture art magazine; same old, same old, same old. She tossed them back on the counter, to dutifully sort, prioritize and pay later. Today, she just did not care.

Tucking Abby in, she snuggled and kissed the child woman love ball. "God, how I love your clinging body hugs, little arms and legs wrapped around me. You are my little primate! My little God sent angel." Navi kissed a puckered little mouth, dropped her onto the bed then turned out the light. "I adore you little woman."

"Ga night Mom. Welcome home. Thanks for the smelly little motel soaps."

Stephen was waiting on their bed. Splayed out in opposite direction, arms folded under the back of his head, staring up to ceiling, avoiding wife eyes, avoiding physical contact. His body language confident and calm. Working blind with absolutely no idea what had been going on in his mind, in his heart, suddenly afraid, not so brave of hearing that he no longer loved her or worse; lame patronizing platitudes without meaningful exchange. Boldly Navi stood on cliff edge, ready to fly or fall to demise, summoned inner calm and resolve.

"Stephen, I miss you and I miss us. Do you remember how nice it was when we were dating? Whatever happened to those feelings, that fun? You must get sick of always dealing with stuff alone. Don't you ever just want to be wild and free, play?"

"I don't know." Now visibly annoyed and defensive.

"Why was it that so many men hate intimacy talks? Stephen, something is wrong with us. Can we please talk about it?"

Shifting body discomfort, Stephen folded hands and arms across his solar plexus, eyes closed and head tilted back against headboard, pursed lips pissy. Navi knew from years of experience that he was pissed and somehow, conversation had already gone into danger zone. 'DO NOT GO THERE' Stephen's body language screamed.

She paused searching for another angle, a different approach so chattered of kids, school projects, changes in work legislation and restructuring; lighter conversation, safe topics, allowing calm then shared the Eagle hot tub vision journey. Suddenly realizing that she was chattering alone, stopped mid-sentence.

"Jesus Stephen! Can we please just talk and sort through a few things?"

Stephen remained solidly cold and defensive. "Jesus, Stephen, would you relax, for Christ sake!"

He shifted up right, his head resting alpha dog above hers, chest puffed and pursed lips, glared into her. He moved closer, red-hot angry as foamy white spittle slowly formed around tight lips.

"You're just using that stupid eagle dream as an excuse to get out of marriage because I don't like sex!" he spat.

"WHAT? How long have you been aware that you don't like sex?" Navi's head reeled. Stephen was quiet and avoiding spouse eyes. Navi felt a wave of calm wash through her being. That was that, merely a pursuit of further detail.

"And how long have you been aware that you've had a problem with sex?"

"Well, all my life."

Stephen was being honest for the first time and ceasing the roll, pushed further, wanting details and missing pieces to make sense of their marriage and figure out where exactly she stood.

"Are you saying that you don't like sex with me? Or, are you saying that you don't like sex with anyone, with women, what Stephen?"

"Yes."

"Was it like this for you when we got married?" Stephen nodded yes.

"You had this when we got married?"

"Yes."

"Was it like this when you were married to your ex-wife?"

"Yes, ever since I can remember."

Navi was on a livid yet calm and strong roll. "You mean to tell me, that you married me and that you sat there in our first year of marriage and allowed that marriage counsellor to tell us that our intimacy problems were my fault, that I had issues? You sat there on your dysfunctional ass and let him and me think that it was my fault and that I was the problem one who needed professional help?"

Silent downcast Stephen did not answer, telling all. Slowly, casually and confidently he replied; "Oh, I always thought that was two different issues, my sexual preferences and yours."

"WHAT?!?! What are you talking about?"

"Oh, I always thought that was two different issues Navi, my dysfunction sexually and yours."

"WHAT?!?!" Navi searched her brain for a reference point and came up empty. She could not for the life of her, understand what he was referring to as *her* sexual dysfunction.

"Navi, you are so fucking stupid! Christ! Do I have to fucking spell it out for you?" Stephen turned to face her, confidently calm.

Navi began to shake, waiting.

"I prefer to masturbate! I always have preferred my own two hands. Well, except for that time with Debbie. I could get it up for her. It was alright with her, we weren't married." He said proudly and causally as though chatting with a friend.

"What??? I thought you told me that was just a passing attraction with her. You told me that you never did anything with her?"

"What difference does it make? What is it to you anyway? I know what you really are."

"WHAT??? What are you talking about? Know what about me?"

"Well DAHH! I know you are a closet lesbian. And, well then there's that Gandhi witch road thing of yours."

"WHAT?!!"

"Oh Navi, do you think I'm an Idiot? I have seen the way you hug your friends. And Gandhi witches don't have real sex."

Absurdity, madness rang and rippled cutting silent screams. Suddenly, anger drained into a strange calm.

"Is this what you actually tell yourself?"

A smile broke as Stephen with newfound unbridled freedom, prattled on about how hard it has been, how he could not bring himself to be sexually interested in his ex-wife after she had the baby.

"It's like fucking your own mother", she heard him blurt.

A wave of hysterical laughter flushed within, the kind of moment where if you look around the room for the audience, a camera in your face with some stupid smirking guy 'smile, you're on Candid Camera'.

"This is a joke right? You are pulling my leg. You think you're being witty and funny."

Stephen remained quiet, starring out the bedroom window somewhere.

"Oh My God! You are serious! This is your story and a made up one about me."

Navi's head reeled in replay, trying to grasp the reality of what he had said. 'Oh my God, the man is fucking mentally retarded. The man is THICK! Yes, he is as thick as a brick. Hmm, that's a Jethro Tull song', she mused. A slow deep breath sighed as a warm clear light of higher truth allowing inner freedom washed through her being. Now that she had heard what it was, it had yet to fully sink in, she wanted more. She wanted pieces of the comprehension puzzle of what was their marriage.

"Just out of curiosity, just who is it that I hug, that makes you tell yourself that I'm a lesbian?"

"Well, Catharine, all of them."

"Hmmm, so I hug your Mom too, does that mean that I'm having sex with her too?"

Stephen, mouth twisting, shut tight, eyes wincing, thinking. She knew from experience, that even he did not buy the lame crap load of bullshit spilling from his twisted mouth, though he would never admit it to her. It was an easier bad habit to make her out to be something so bizarre and so shocking for his mom, his family, and his friends that they would gasp drama and pity for him and not ever ask for any more details. It was the perfect church audience shut up; case closed. Old church cronies and elders disgusted. Sodom and excommunication assured.

The aftermath scene played out in her mind; gasping, huffing and shaking horror shocked heads.

"What a brilliant story you've come up with."

With Matt sick, it was a masterpiece of deception. He was right in that no one would pursue questioning the separation further. Yes, Stephen knew just the right drama to present that would divert attention and fall out to someone else. A good drama with just the right facial expressions, the right body language, coy charm, holding up okay in the face of profound adversity victim feel so sorry for me wit, the oh so awful things that have fallen upon poor Stephen. No, they could not help but fall for it. Now the story could change and adjust depending on whom. When referencing his ex-wives had fallen in love with other men, one just up and left one day without a word. Navi understood it all now, neglected for years on end.

'I wish she would've told me.' Stephen's mom had yet to recover from the first scandalous affair, she-ex-wife-abandoner who shall remain nameless, she who left husband and child for days at a time with another man, out of congregation. Smarter, she systematically cleaned his clock of every cent he had and then some; dismantling his business from under foot, maintaining insurance beneficiary and pensions then emptied his prized safe deposit box.

The pieces of the puzzle were finally falling into place. Stephen knew exactly how to play people, how to play Navi, what hot buttons to push and working them over, inside and out according to his desired outcome.

Navi saw dramatic pitied responses, truly an amazing skill, a dramatic smoking mirror and a master at the game. She was a dragonfly, trapped and tangled in his spider's web.

'The truth may set you free, but the people who are blinded by lies will burn you at the stake.' Navi shook her head in disbelief, all too bizarre to be true, and searched his face for truths. Stephen calmly pre-occupied, pulling balls of fluff from the comforter.

"Stephen, did it not ever occur to you, to take any responsibility for what happened with you and your ex-wife?"

"No. I told you, they fell in love with other men."

"And what do you think you may have, or not have done, that contributed to their leaving?"

"Nothing, they left ME!"

"Don't you think it's about time you got some help with this, before the next woman comes into your life?"

"No, I like it fine this way. There is nothing wrong with masturbating. It's easier and better."

Clearly comfortable with life choices, having long ago convinced himself that he did not in any way have a problem.

"God Navi, you're so fucking stupid. I have seen the way you always hug your friends, I figure that your spiritual women's retreats, that you were getting all the sex you needed, doing all your wooey-woo shit. I see it in your eyes; you are a lesbian witch. So see, it works for us."

"Ah yes, we must divert back on to me. Oh my God, Stephen, there it is. It is over! This is so broke it can't be fixed."

Navi heard a huge metallic door of higher truth SLAM shut, then body relax as a wonderful warm light calmed. How and when did it all happen, without her conscious knowing? Why she did not see what was really going on. Navi, suddenly felt quite stupid and very alone, abandoned.

Then out of shear morbid curiosity, "So, how often, would say that you masturbate?"

Stephen now visibly comfortable and relaxed replied, "Oh, usually three and four times a day. Sometimes, even as much as eight even ten times a day."

"But you always made out like it was me, that I didn't like sex, joked about it in front of other people."

"Well, DAH Navi, you're a Lesbian, so what difference does it make? "Does this mean that you're throwing in the towel already?"

Ignoring the lesbian dig, Navi simply said, "Yes, oh yes. Of course I am done, so done."

"Why? Like that hurts your feelings?"

"No sweetheart, you made up your mind about how our marriage was going to be or not be, a long time ago. And you just put me in the position where I had no other choice than to call you on it."

Navi flipped into professional counsellor mode and ponder searched her memory for the topic of addiction from abnormal psych class, 'Ah yes, perpetual masturbation; addiction.'

Stephen always seemed to care more of what other people thought than what was actually going on. Paint a pretty and impressive picture to others, a house built on pretty sand, ooh's and ah's of his sculptures, landscaped gardens, that poor, poor man with that sick child and wicked wife.

Shakespeare, home and family was his stage and the world outside was his audience. Navi glanced over to Stephen who was now happy, almost giddy as he jumped up off the bed.

"Got to get back to the workshop, I want that weld on the bird done before bed."

Curled inside the sisterhood shawl, Navi slept contentedly; exhausted clothes and all.

"It may never be mine,
the loaf or kiss or the kingdom because of beseeching;
but I know that my hand is an arm's length
nearer the sky for reaching"
Edwin Quarles; Petition

Chapter 9 ~ Fall Out

Waking Navi eyes opened to assaulting replay of the Stephen exchange, a stuck record playing until the need to pee became intolerable. Out right bitchily descending downstairs, mood-shifted light, free and happier with each step, strangely free, giddy yet numb. Abby happily sang in her room busy, dressed in an old silver gown with metallic gold shoes from some garage sale the summer before and salon Dawg. Licking lip, soaking up attention as coiffure designer girl, stylishly clipped barrettes on shaggy ears in between floral and Barbie hair ties, multi coloured nail polish sparkling on tiny claw toenails and donning a doll's dress. Canine fashion model contentedly sat within an ingenious homemade space ship of toilet paper rolls, paper towels rolls, cereal boxes, tin foil, old Christmas wrapping paper and tiny toy space men. His space travel company included; a teddy bear with underwear hat and fuzzy ears poking through leg holes while a disco light flashed bleating red, on what looked like ships hood. In amazement and utter joy, Navi crouched laughing inside and out until tears and mucous formed in nostrils pressuring bladder burst to bathroom. 'God bless the child.'

The impact and far reaching effects of his candid sharing was slowly sinking in. Alone in empty kitchen, hoisted up onto the counter she curled up in the window.

Sleepy eyed Dawg wandered out and scanned empty food bowl. Navi grinned, taking inventory of barrettes, hair ties and sparkling rainbow toenails. She picked him up cooing snuggles, "Dawg, some days, some moments, just feel like they stand out as the first day of the rest of your life, know what I mean?" Dawg snorted agreement, lovingly burring furry face into her neck.

Longevity in marriage equates to the other's push button predictable actions and reactions until one does not want to play the game anymore. The new game would now consist of Stephen dramatically alpha dog demonstrating that he was more upset, angrier than she was, except she no longer cared. Disbelief of what he had audaciously confided mingled with gall and the stupidity of idiotic rationalizations.

Navi met Catharine for lunch at a lakeshore day park. Park bench seagull swirling picnicking matched her emotional rendition of the bizarre sharing. Reiterating, she searched for insight to make sense of it all. Catharine did not seem surprised, "Shit Navi, I'm not stupid, I can tell when someone is not happy and Baby, you do need to get laid!"

She had managed to avoid David all morning, feigning busyness with files spread out over her desk. David would not be deterred "Time to talk Navi."

Nervous and still reeling from Stephen's exchange, "I honestly don't want to talk about anything personal right now."

"Something is wrong! I want to know what's bothering you!" Floodgates erupted and spilled.

"Wow, you are serious about this."

"Yes. I don't have any other choice. He has forced my hand into a decision so I have to respond. Do I stay and take my time sorting my life out? Staying, even for a while, would have to be on his terms. I would lose my spirit. Would it be any less traumatic for the kids?"

"Wow. Tough call, I do not envy your decision-making. If there is anything you need, just let me know. If you just need to talk, let me know, I'm there."

"Thanks David, but I really have to work this one out on my own."

New computer programs arrived containing all new software and legislation. Shiny new computers lined HQ hallways accompanied by Men in Black whom wandered about preparing for a training session. Government does not spend that kind of money on clients and family basic needs yet was spending billions in consult fees, software design, fiber optics, computers, software and training to beef up control over the poorest of the poor. A fed up cynical Navi snorted at the obvious absurd disparity in priorities, wondering if other front line was thinking the same. Lay off fear-ridden co-workers feigned interest, eagerly digesting massive new manuals.

As the training session progressed, Navi struggled to rationalize how the expensive brilliantly complicated process equated to food and housing needy people. Only a government could create and subject rocket science technology as cost savings to tax payers in basic human service provision and monitoring. How any of it remotely reflected what poor people actually needed, was simply mind-boggling. The system design identified positive statistical outcomes.

Slouched in sheer exhaustion, she hung bloodshot eyes on man in black suit speaker so as not to drift off to sleep. When the suit glanced in disapproval, she openly apologized, explaining that she had just returned from a conference, an eleven-hour drive, just last night. She was exhausted and had heard more than enough of things she did not want to hear in the past twenty-four hours. It just kept coming.

Graphs splayed out on the projector screen, 'That set up software and design cost could feed an entire county of families for ten years or more.' Suit's brand new top of the line laptop flickered, 'that little baby could pay for several low-income home winter fuel needs'. Suit continued his monotone itemization of new legislative changes. "We now begin enforcing automatic leans on home and property, reduction in benefits to sole support parents regardless of the number of children under the age of eighteen, elimination of monies for baby formula and disposable diapers, mandatory drug testing, mandatory literacy with mandatory upgrading, mandatory volunteer work, increased accountability, and child tax credits re-allocated to early learning centres."

The Adams on her caseload, were those whom had long ago, checked out of mainstream society. Who lived almost completely self-sufficient deep in the bush, home sweet home was a lean to, shack, or cabin. One with nature and far away from intrusive city people, they were her favourites instinctively understood; brilliant minds, kind and gentle by nature, and selective on who they acknowledged and spoke to. They occasionally ventured into town for supplies, a store bought coffee and maybe a store bought cigarette. Invisible to throngs of tourists and white-collar locals, only came in a crisis once a year, once every couple of years for a month or two. They always brought gifts to share of handmade artwork, smoked fish, deer meat, tomatoes and zucchinis when they could, as exchange, barter.

Elitist politicians and business moguls who ported to financially support them, who have only ever known affluence, generation after generation of money beyond wildest dreams and who were all considered to be scholars, calculated the lives of millions of poor and fringe people they knew absolutely nothing about.

Farmers with gout in every part of their bodies bartered and did under the table jobs to buy sanity morphine. Women with cancer and unsupportive doctors still had to participate and raise children on their own. Women with small children who were plagued by nasty ex-husbands and Children's Aid workers made daily life a living hell, simply because they were poor, were judged as scamming the system therefore also suspect in ability to parent and provide for children.

Cloak of Competency parents were those who seemed presentable and employable, deemed lazy and rarely made it past grade school. Falling through the systems cracks, never properly diagnosed as being developmentally borderline handicapped or challenged. Pleasant and agreeable to everything asked of them while clueless of what they were consenting to or comprehend what was truly expected.

Navi was tired, so very tired. Cancer had spread through her family, marriage and was now spreading into her job; out into the community and into the clients she so loved.

For a moment, she entertained contacting media, people should know what is happening, but concluded that nobody really gave a shit about poor people. Taxpayers were too stress preoccupied with their personal worries to be overly concerned about what terrorism George Bush was doing in the States. Worried more about pension contributions, layoffs, kids and family health care, the politics of education and electric power systems, military presence in third world countries and horrid new viruses and diseases fell to less oppressed elites. Navi knew from experience that when people found out about what she did for a living, responses always passionately leaned toward erroneous propaganda, 'get the drug addict alcoholic bums off welfare, and stop drinking beer and playing bingo instead of feeding their children'. The hard truth of poverty was, never experienced first-hand nor seen from a higher perspective. Gandhi said, "Poverty is the worst form of violence."

Caffeine jazzed Navi drove straight to the beach. Beyond exhausted wired, she sat in the car for hours watching seagulls play and dip in waves. Breath slowing in sync with calm evening waves, sky unfolding in brilliant oranges, reds and magentas as silvery moon crested. Still, unable to think another thought.

Spirit sapped, naked in front of the bathroom mirror as bath water filled, rejected wife eyes rested on tiny yet thick black hairs, ever so boldly growing out of nipple brown rings. A once majestic thirty-eight C bosom was shrinking to a whooping thirty-six A. Tiny brown skin moles mingled with blatant red and blue varicose veins around knee backs and down calves. Stretch marks crisscrossed over cottage cheese thighs and buttocks. Once natural blonde highlights were now, distinctively silver. Navi had suddenly aged. Long gone youthful maiden of natural beauty had morphed into an old crone hag. Ugly inside and out, unwanted, unattractive, unlovable and alone, yet on the verge of some great elusive truth illumination that cast shadows. Weary abandoned exhaustion soothed into sleepiness by Peeper Frog chorus from a distant pond, she was mildly envious of their mating frenzy. Oh to stay, perfectly still, listening to natural world order of spring frog mating frenzy and dream of Soul Skin spirit man, wishing she could miracle make him manifest now. A sleepy in between deep sleep and dream world, a loving hand caressed her face accompanied by a bare audible whisper. *"I wait for you, my darling soul skin woman."*

Helen, her visibly agitated former co-worker now boss, averted her eyes away from captive Navi audience, glancing at her watch without registering the time. Helen's natural tendency was to only venture away from HQ to the North satellite office for annual supervision reviews or when needing to cry on Navi's shoulder. The other only time that Helen came was bearing bad news and it was obvious from her body language which time this was. Today, Helen was all business, authority and enjoying the role as reporter of dramatic news, loving drama, politicking, status and power over employee underlings, illusions, Helen lacked both wisdom and strength of character to lead a large organization that dealt with vulnerable people. This was not generally a problem with Navi because it gave her autonomy in the old small rural satellite office and freedom to exercise judgment without a looming boss.

Curt, clear and to the point, an excited Helen tried not to smile. "Effective this coming Monday, David is to go to the records department in Head Office, part time and maintain the rest of the time." It was common knowledge that the records department was the basement, the file storage room was dark, moldy and dusty. The commute would be awful.

"David, you will also assume Margaret's maternity leave position and you will be based out of Head Office as well starting tomorrow, so pack up your stuff. The North satellite office is, officially dismantled. Cut backs you know. Wrap things up folks."

David, instantly livid, arched his back, wanting to alpha dog and hold Helen accountable. Ignoring, Helen began packing papers and put her coat on. Case Closed. Solemn silenced, David was too livid too talk. Navi in shock, vibrating, turned on heel then stormed back to her office and stood window gazing expecting to see Bitch Boss Helen driving away. Helen knocked on Navi's door then hesitating, entered without invitation. Plunking casually in the client chair, "I need to heads you up about something else."

Unsure of how much more she could take. Bitch Boss took her time, shuffling papers. Navi, a dumb founded deer stood on some lonesome highway in the dark of night, frozen in transport truck headlights. Bitch Boss cleared her throat, "Hey Navi, just a heads up, you are not welcome in the new office."

"What? Why not? I've worked with most of them before?"

"Don't know for sure, I think they all prefer to have Suzie Martin."

"Then why are you making me go there?"

"Got no other choice. The deal's done. Out of my hands. Only other choice for you is; lay off. I was kind of hoping you'd make a go of it."

The sheer terror of losing her job with everything that had just happened with Stephen, core rattled weary bones, suddenly a single mom with a dicey job. Bitch Boss forced a frown, hiding a smirk, lingering, waiting for dutiful acquiescing nicely, affirmation that Navi would rise to the challenge, that everything was kosher between them. Eyes fixed out the window, Navi struggled to maintain control of threatening tears, refusing to have Helen privy to her personal life, vulnerable and scared.

"Hey, okay then, Navi. We will catch you next week at staff meeting. Have a really great weekend, eh."

Helen popped her head back in the door and said, "Oh by the way, I know it's hard with Matt and everything, you can't take any more time off. People are talking and starting to complain. After all, you're not his real Mom."

Startled out of shock by the ringing of a phone, Navi listened in vain to a woman on the other end, "Oh, I'm sorry Brenda, what did you say?"

"I'm just calling to say, that my Doctor said, that I can't be at work this weekend. My wrist hurts. The Doctor thinks I might have 'car pool syndrome'."

Navi chuckled, 'God I love this job!'

"I'm pretty sure that the Doctor meant 'Carpal Tunnel Syndrome'."

"Abby, we have to move soon." Abby sat in the passenger seat, quiet for a moment, considering, optimism fading and began to cry, "But I'll miss the pool and Matt."

"Ah, Abby honey, you can visit the house, Stephen and Matt any time you like. We have to move, not today, but soon. We can do this together in a positive and healthy way if we choose to" suddenly not so sure, not so strong, inner knowing and inner resolve knew it was a done deal. Stephen would never let her have the house. He was rooted there, entrenched and immovable, an unspoken understanding that ultimately it was his house.

"It's okay if you need to be angry, for a bit."

Abby sat quiet for a bit, then smiling, reached out comfort loving arms in hug.

"Okay Mom, we'll do it together."

Primal Man Stephen had obviously been analyzing their marital situation throughout the day and drawn battle lines over finances. Presenting her with a file of itemized debts with inflated chest, announced that there was no equity in the house and no assets. Navi's coping abilities beyond over loaded, cynically fantasized that she had come home to flowers, candle lit intensive loving resolution.

"I'm going away to Toronto with Matt to get away for a vacation, shopping, visiting. Maybe a week, maybe more."

Stephen, who was now waving a bill in front of her nose, "And take care of that eleven dollars and eighty cents you owe me as soon as possible!"

All composure and grace lost, "What? Are you serious? Who bought your cat food? It is your cat. Who pays the bills? Who paid the overdraft? Who's been helping to pay your debts that I inherited from your first wife when we got married, that you neglected to tell me about?"

Stephen shifting into a show of vibrating anger, focused on regaining order and control. Knowing that she hated hostile displays, he amped up to primal anger. It was a dichotomy of emotions and thoughts swirling within. She shifted, regaining composure posture, spine erect. Should Stephen try to hit her, she knew without a doubt that somewhere deep inside of her she would fight. Rise to the occasion and clean his clock.

There was a hidden secret wellspring of ferocity, of pent up defensive anger from years of taking other people's shit. She knew that the anger welling up inside of her was not her natural nature manner but rather a compilation of other peoples shit she had assimilated all of her life. 'This is not mine!'

She could summon the strength of ten thousand warrior women and pummel the living snot out of him. It was not about size or muscle power. It was something bigger, a power that came from the cosmos and flowed ready to pounce.

Yes, hostility scared her, but not the way Stephen thought. Not out of vulnerability and fear of getting hurt, but of releasing that primal monster that resided within every two legged and four legged. An animating force that even while livid, knew that there was a better way to navigate the situation.

"Grace."

"What? What the fuck are you talking about?"

"Grace of Angels and Saints."

"God, you are such a fucking flake. You need serious help, psycho."

It was taking all of her self-control to remain. Normally she would not hurt a spider, now saw herself beating the living crap out of him and Helen.

"Go fuck yourself Stephen. You're good at that, you coward arsehole."

Navi caught herself short, took a deep breath and maintaining composer and grace, refusing to let him get the better of her dignity this way, not now and not ever.

Primal Man furious slammed his list of debts versus credits on the table in front of her face, holding focus of scathing hostility. Pursed lips and red face for emphasis then turned abruptly and stomped over to the workshop door, slammed for final emphasis, "FUCK YOU NAVI."

Rising to stand, a wave of swirling dizziness washed over her. Catching dining table in hand, she sat back down holding pounding head in hands and breathing deep. As mind swirls subsided, she took another deep breath regaining some composure and released aching teeth and jaw from clenching restraint. Stephen knew her hot button vulnerabilities, strategic gladiator taunting threats of physical, mental and emotional intimidation, banishment and now withholding money. It was sad that he would intentionally do this and there was Abby to consider. 'Well, that is that.'

She could not stay. If work were stable, maybe she could cope for a while. Needing to be far away from him, she turned thoughts to practical matters at hand. Packing, Navi piled clothes in arms and just as she turned to leave the closet, bumped Stephen's jacket and handful of receipts spilled onto the floor. Bending down, shoving clothes under one arm and picking up receipts with the other, her eye caught numerous tallies of five thousand dollar cash deposits and withdrawals.

The pieces of the puzzle were coming together; Stephen's family had been giving him loads of money. 'Why didn't I see this before? I see everything about my clients as soon as they walk into my office. It is like watching movie clips in my head while they talk, so I know what is really going on. Why am I not seeing what has been really going on with Stephen all these years? Wow, I must be really frigging stupid!'

Gran's presence felt immediately, "No Darling Chickadee, we are not always given a view of the road ahead, a heads up sensing that challenge and adversity lay before you. The challenge is not to necessarily avert a situation, but opportunity to adjust your sails, mind your thoughts and emotions; change how you feel about it all. You cannot always change a situation, but you can change how you best want to walk through it. Mind what you are taking too personally. The insights will come in time. For now, allow the past to bow away as gracefully as possible and know that you are guided and loved."

Navi went to throw her clothes on Matt's bed and was shocked to find him asleep. She had thought that he would be at his mother's; as posted on the calendar agenda. Gently stirring, sensing her presence, she sat down beside him on the bed and ran maternal fingers around his once hairline. Scars had healed rapidly, snoozing contentedly, semi awake, aware and clearly comfortable with her maternal loving.

"Wow Darling, your hair is coming back already. Just think, one more treatment and then done forever. Matt, you were always an intuitive one and you know that you are finished with this thing. You have won! You did it. It is home stretch now, kiddo. You'll have grand adventures and a wonderful life time ahead of you."

"Yup, I know. Navi, I have been through the pits of hell. But I've got plans now, big plans."

"Do you have any idea how proud of you, I am? You are really on your way, you have had the most awesome medical care, family support, and of course, the Mojo on your side." Matt grinned and schmoozed under the touch of her hand.

"I love you Matt, like you were my own, child. Do you know that?"

"Yep, I know that."

"Good, you do know that you are going to have to look after your Dad now. He is going to need your help."

"Yup, I do know that. I will."

Matt rolled over and instantly fell back asleep, seemingly quite content. He had known long before she did, that she was going to marry his father. Navi recalled asking him at the time, "Hmmm. . . .I don't know about that Matt, how do you feel about it?" Matt had responded by shrugging his shoulders and said casually, "It is okay with me. I needed a mom when I come here and Dad needed someone to look after him, because he doesn't know how to look after little kids."

"Yes, now I think I understand how it was. God bless your loving heart and soul."

The truth of what another thinks and says to you can hurt. Matt's summation of Stephen's original interest rang true. Snowed over in courtship, intimacy and romantic promises, she had envisioned stability, normalcy and continuity of courtship. Words can carry potency that takes grace and mastery to dissolve. A word delivered with angry emotion and intent, has as much power to maim as any weapon. A skilled master holds no receptacles, no receiving points of guilt or shame. 'A lesbian witch huh.' A gauntlet tossed to the ground by some higher master unseen spirit in challenge upon her soul to deny his unkind words, deeds and twisted thinking personally. Yet she felt the pain, the hurt; his twisted pain mingling with her own.

Navi continued packing for both moving and camping. Having difficulty focusing on exactly what to take, sitting on the pool deck facing wide-open field, she smoked. The neighbour's cows were making their annual sojourn out to field, meandering and grazing on the first of spring grass. A brief time of heaven before relentlessly haunting warm weather flies and insects emerged in droves and lingered throughout summer. Each spring the bovines broke through the cedar rail fence line wandering, nearly falling into the pool. The beautiful scenery surrounding her lay barely appreciated and felt strangely detached. North rose garden was enclosed in a gazebo style structure that housed her collection of roses. A painted Gran quote, 'Even thorns have roses my dear', read apropos now.

"Gosh, I wish you were alive and here. Roses, chickadees and I remember you, feel close to you, feel watched over and loved by you." Aware that she was saying goodbye to the place, life of its trees, plants and essence of that had become a part of her being. The in-ground pool, addition, patio, pond, gardens were all of her, her hard work and love would stay to the delight of Stephen's next unsuspecting woman. Navi no longer existed here, rejected, dismissed, banished and fucked right off. Muted years of heart and soul had gone into sanctuary home and family, a little piece of heaven on earth. 'Oh my God, I'm going to miss this place soooo much.'

Stephen joined her on the deck, quietly picking at dandelion heads. Navi's heart pounding, hoping he would be friendly and had had a heart change. Apologize and court her.

"You know Navi, that no one will ever love you like I do."

'Eh?" Navi was flabbergasted.

It translated in her brain as, 'Navi, no one will tolerate you, like I do.' She sat quietly, waiting for more, something more soulfully loving and convincing. He remained downcast, avoiding eye contact, causally picking apart a dandelion head. Beautiful tiny yellow petals surfaced contrasting green grass, King randomly beheading a beautiful spirit being.

Navi back arch braced for more. Queasy nauseous stomach rolled as images replayed of their conversation of a few nights earlier then back to their wedding day. Christmas mornings, thrilled little children reveled post Santa's visit. An empty and useless marriage counselling series to hear nothing of Stephens preferred sexual habits. There were too many nights alone, evenings alone, and mornings waking alone in loneliness. Incredible sculptured creations and her sanctuary gardens. Money given then not shared where necessity dictated otherwise. Family and friends, who knew nothing of their inner world, gossiped. Imagining him wildly masturbating in the office bathroom as work mates went on about their tasks. Then finally, images faded to the here and now with his downcast eyes casually picking dandelions. She saw him masturbating all over the house. Her mind reeled and searched for words. Empty abyss, the bank of Navi love for Stephen was overdrawn. Too much had been said, and gone too far, to wish Stephen to 'fight for her'. King Stephen casually picking off dandelion heads, his mind had already moved on to something else.

"That's it? If this is your idea of what love really is then I don't want any part of it."

Marital love non-existent, none, nodda, zilch and as that realization anchored, Stephen and the house were already gone, leaving only emptiness and nausea. Closed.

Compassionless now, she continued. "Stephen, I thought that I did love you once. Where was this professing love ten years ago? Where was it during marriage counselling? Can we not help each other through this? I feel as though that is what we should and need to do, help each other, as friends."

He livid silent brick wall slammed her, an emotional hostile bolt that validated in silent primal rage.

Ignoring his anger, she continued, "I want out. I don't like you right now. You've lied to me and blamed me for your own shit. That's small and cruel."

Stephen switched emotional gears, wiped a tear away and sniffled.

She wanted desperately to hear something that would make sense, that would click, that would make everything all right. It was as though life itself hung in balance. "I needed you and to know that I was worth fighting for, not with. I am worth fighting for. I need and want a good honourable man. Can you not see any of that? How can you sit there and tell me that you love me after everything that you said to me the other night?"

Stephen stood avoiding eye contact, hesitated then sauntered away and into his workshop.

Dismissed.

Her eyes fixated on the door of the workshop, feeling a dark cloud of anger emanate from Stephen, heavy and thick with loathing. She felt it lodge into her soul like knives embedding in bones. Navi quietly said in his direction, "Please let me go in peace."

Stephen resurfaced and stood in front of her, hands on hips. Angry eyes cut into her heart and soul with spittle edged lips, "You have a choice, you can either leave with nothing or you can leave with half the debt load."

"Ah, there it is; primal man! You are only worried about money. You shit! You do not want me, never really did, did you! You figure if I stay then I will keep looking after yours, Matt's basic needs, and the house and that way I will not clean you out financially. Wow. You are such a prick."

She imagined him standing in a gladiator arena dressed in formal regalia garb, sword in hand. Grasping for strategy, adrenaline warrior fought a dicey battle to victory. Blood dripped over a cracked lip, teeth stained red after biting his opponent's ear off, sword dripping red from multiple stabbings and trophy opponent head stashed in his bundle. Then Stephen morphed into a bull, stood hunched, fight ready, in a field, sights set on the Navi target, scraping hooves in dirt, preparing to rush his victim. Red, seething blood red, turned abruptly and returned to workshop.

'King hits and takes Queen of Hearts.'

She was Saint Michael and Joan of Arc, 'Thou shall bow down before me thy heathen Gladiator! Bow unto the higher forces of might.' Navi imagined wielding casting off into the archangel realm where nature forces adjusted to her will and gathered power, thunder rumbled and lightening gained momentum.

Navi is she-Moses on the Mount.

Navi is she-Jesus about to ascend.

Navi is she-Abraham, freeing the people from the Pharaoh.
Navi is she-Merlin working beyond time and space.
Navi is a Shaman summoning the ancients!
Navi is Saint Michael herself, Archangel.

Navi could not sleep. She slid into old purple robe and flipped on the computer, listening to an evening chorus of Peeper Frogs in the pond. Restless midnight, she fridge raided chocolate ice cream with just the container and a large spoon.

The raucous commotion out on the deck was the doings of the fattest raccoon she had ever seen. Brown black pudgy fur ball with bandit eyes, sat in lotus position with a jar of Cheese Whiz resting on a round belly. He glanced at her with irrelevance and continued to dip paws deep into the bottom of the jar, licking orange slimy cheese off tiny fingers. Navi bowed like royalty and with ice cream spoon, made the sign of the Holy Cross over his head,

"I shall name thee; Buddha." she proclaimed. "Oh my God, I'm going to miss this place!"

Fridays were wonderful freedom and grateful to be at work, such as it was, it felt relatively normal. The office felt familiar and competent despite pending changes. Their usual un-professional banter at breaks and in between appointments consisted of throwing paper balls, paper clips, candy and erasers at each other became a necessity bond, children out of control in a class without teacher. David's personal favourite was to sit in her office pretending to be a client with Turrets, "My name? Camel's Butt Stink Alien Zygote Mold Spore and my last job was Nuclear Waste disposal worker. Why is there a problem? Oh yes, I am looking for a change and thinking about Sales, or public relations or a customer service satisfaction rep."

David won, as always, the Hang Man Mystery Phrase Game challenge, Mongolian Cluster Fuck. The challenger conjured a slang crude or phrase to stump the opponent. There was an unspoken knowing and understanding of working in the front lines with its depth of human adversity, crisis, desperation, sadness, poverty and lost spirit that the dark humour gave light in an insane world.

As the office day closed, Navi's pending adventurous weekend excitement grew and rapidly lost interest in file updating, she locked the office and headed out to beach camp. David had arbitrarily decided to accompany in his own car, "Going to make sure that you have everything you need." Navi entered with trusty little campsite map as he followed behind.

Parked, camping equipment contents emptied out of the trunk and onto the ground, David surveyed the site like a protective father.

"Okay, looks fine. I am going to head home. If you get into trouble, don't hesitate to phone me."

"Ya, uh huh. Thanks, but I don't think I'll need anything." He hesitated.

"Good Bye David." He did not move.

"Go home David."

A glorious weekend on her own was simply; peace and bliss. A chilly bay breeze had her setting up her windbreak, a good fire, then a picnic of cheese and apples. Newspaper read from one end-to-end, then damp old firewood grew with added bits of cedar into tiny orange flames. Ancient and childlike fire watching ensued as trance sparks flew into early evening air. Deep breaths savored aromatic burning cedar, wonderful.

As the sun sank into tree top horizon, Peeper Frogs began evening chorus in a distant swamp. Fresh air elicited a smile and long braid set free allowed evening breeze and smoke to caress hair. Fire brightened evening as more cedar branches, comforting smells cleansing a weary spirit. Ancestral DNA surfaced out of Irish mix and activated connection to spirit and the all that is.

A pinch of tobacco sprinkled into flames sent sparkles shooting up into the heavens. "If what they say is true, that to love someone is to wish them well and that to hate someone is to wish them death, then I wish you well Stephen. I ask angel friends, Gran and the all that is, that I carry no regrets, no remorse, no ill will, no anger and bad karma. I wish us harmony, grace and the winds of divine love to wash within and between us. I hope that you find inner peace with yourself Stephen."

Satisfied, Navi sat cross-legged tossing bits of cedar into flames, pondering her Adam clients and how this was their way of life. For those that could see it and not many did, there was a radiating divine joy in their eyes. A radiant light akin to the religious artwork and imagery of saints, mystics, masters and shamans, bush clients were intimate with nature and the divine forces. Alone, authentic without social pretense, they communed with their environment knowing with certainty, a sense of God. To the rest of society, all were riff raff bush bums, misfits, mentally ill and rejects. "This is really so wonderful, no wonder some just up and leave former lives to simply disappear without a trace."

Curled up cozy in a sleeping bag beside an ancestral fire; a happy and content lazily watched as David arrived. Fresh hot store bought coffees in hand, pleasantly happy for his easy company. "I was worried about you being alone and out in the cold", he grinned.

They walked the protected wetland swamp then sat a bog, chatting. Navi began to feel the familiar wooey-woo sensation rising within. "Wow Navi, I keep getting these flash pictures that I am here but in another time, in another world and I'm with you. How weird is that?"

"It's France. Turn of the sixteenth century."

"Wow. This is awesome. It feels like a memory or some kind of kindred vision, or past life. France you say. I can see old toddy roads, with gigantic ruts seemingly impassable to travelers. Bumpy, very bumpy horse and wagon rides into the countryside, a small crude stone bridge."

"Yep, that old stone bridge - we've crossed a gazillion times. Look, there goes our horse and cart now."

Vision shared, connected, they sat quietly listening to Peeper and Bull Frogs evening crescendo. Evening mist grew and hung over bog water surface.

"Magic."

Boldly stepping into a new comfort level, "I've always been able to see things, see spirit people, see other life times or realities. I see these things in clients to help them. I do not often get this view in my personal life though. Funny that."

David smiled into the fire. The two now knowing that they had known each other throughout time.

"Believe it or not, we were married in that life, in old France. You were an Officer and we had two small children. You liked to paint, even then and made a good side living. But one day, you went off to battle and never came back."

"Hmm. I can see that. I've always had an affinity for Monet."

"I know, your wife showed me one of your paintings once, really quite gifted you know."

"Surprising, she tossed most of my work and all of art materials when we married."

"Now that is a God awful shame."

After a time of silence and of gazing into the fire, David turned, took her chin in his hand, gently turned her face and looked deep into her eyes. Suddenly drawn in a powerful magnetic attraction, he gently cupped a hand under her wild hair, tilted his head to one side then gently kissed her lips. Drawn warm into his soul, a sense of oneness, youthful and kindred free.

Reality check came with a bolt and she reeled backward. Thoughts and pictures swirled in her mind. Shocked and alarmed, Navi backed away and stared into the fire, pulling thoughts and emotions together content to leave the evening's intimate experience as a gift.

"This night is a gift and I feel blessed. That is all, married and just beginning separation. Too much too soon, yet this all somehow feels right, but it couldn't possibly be."

David's smile drained, struggling inner conflict. He casually stood, cleared throat, turned to Navi, took her hand and picked up the sleeping bag with the other then charismatically led her into tent darkness.

Navi, powerless to oppose, was lost in a joy space, surreal as outer world ceased to exist. Gentle, tender and moving as one, came gently, quickly and powerfully. While they lay intertwined in each other's arms and legs, she thanked Spirit for the gift. Stephen did not want her and somehow through the course of the past few days, a miracle occurred; wanted and loved. A dichotomy of emotions swirled as outer world marital indiscretion guilt and remorse, yet spirit gift of profound joy. 'How can this be?'

David stood, scrambled for clothes, dressed and paused in loving gaze at his lover who curled contentedly in the sleeping bag. "Thank you Navi." Pausing, he leaned over and gently kissed her forehead, tucked blankets over then left.

Lover gone, bladder sounded alarm. Scrambling a few yards behind tent, blue jean overall straps tangled in a heavy woolen sweater, her legs anchored and splayed wide to avoid peeing on clothing, she hovered in chilly late night air.

Awake and ravenous, she curled up with a campfire picnic. She could think of no living soul who would understand, but many, especially church community who would powerfully disapprove. The telling of it would blast through community, hot on judging gossiping lips like wild fire, hurting feelings and needlessly destroying ones loved as well as David's. It was unfathomable and despite all curtness and tensions with Stephen, she could not bear the thought of intentionally hurting anyone, yet here it was. Small rural community, church fringe and families were all just too interconnected. Controversy, drama, hurt spinning untruths and using opportunities to vent their own unhappiness and stress.

Dream space brought a journey. *Navi sat attending a lecture and reading of Lord Byron in a small parlour, with stuffy air sat an audience of well-dressed socialites listening intensively in rapture with the mysterious* charismatic man. There were well-dressed many who delved into the mysteries, magic and adulation of romantic loves. A dark hair curl slides sensuously on forehead, adding dramatic contrast to velvet blood red jacket over navy blue trousers highlighting freshly shined black patent leather boots. He casually unhinges a shiny silver yellow jeweled talisman amulet brooch, unleashing a white satin neck scarf, its tails softly dangle revealing Adam's apple rippling a disturbing and sexual attraction heat wave throughout audience and evening matron hostess. Unbeknownst to his listeners, his incestuous love, cousin and scarlet woman sat hooded and veiled in the chair beside Navi. Laced gloved dabbed a lace handkerchief under veil at a tear, masking profound taboo pain of forbidden love.

"What kind of man, what kind of soul and mind ponders such matters as these?" whispered a well-dressed man. Oddly charismatic indeed, an air of entitlement in all aspects of life, save for mature love. Adolescent passion, Eros, agape love, lust unfulfilled, and longing. Yet within lay the a-typical sensitivities and brilliance of a master artisan. Vain, anorexic, undisciplined mood swings shone through a mask of sensual charisma. From politics to war, he avoids murmurings of scandalous affairs, stealthily steers attention to social reform, of right animal care, of love and true religion. "I have a great mind to believe in Christianity for the mere pleasure of fancying I may be damned."

He rambled and changes subject abruptly, quoting from an epic rendition of a character named Don Juan, yet to put pen to paper. An adult man with a petulant spoiled child's soul speaks of loves lost misery, of inner pain and grief of which is obviously beginning to soul manifest in unkempt wavy hair, bloodshot eyes and mild strain of quivering lips. Soon his madness inherited family dysfunction of genes and character, would grow, descending into public mayhem as his forbidden love affair goes public. Slowly, he turned wincing slightly in pain from a childhood foot deformity and then looking directly at the lace-veiled woman, spoke, "For pleasures past I do not grieve, nor perils gathering near. My greatest grief is that I leave nothing that claims a tear. Ah! Sure some stronger impulse vibrates here, which whispers friendship will be doubly dear to on, who thus for kindred hearts must roam, and seek abroad, the love denied at home."

"I have been all things unholy,
if God can work through me,
he can work through anyone."
Saint Francis of Assisi

Chapter 10 ~ Business begins

Navi slept fitfully, *her life mingled with Lord Byron and his loves; all tormented by passion, public and church controversy as accusing faces appeared, then dissolved. Shocked church elders frowned and gasped as hurt family faces curtly appeared. At times, the roaring campfire shot out and engulfed the tent with her in it. A massive angry wind picked up and pummeled the tent then swept it out into the lake. Peeper Frogs peeped their deafening crescendos.*

Navi woke briefly and lay still as residue dream pieces dissolved. Her attention turned to soothing rhythmic gentle wind caressing trees. Leaning over, she flipped the tent's flap door and watched fire embers glowing pulse then spark up to the night stars.

She drove the car right onto the beach and snug to water's edge. Dozing through dawn then meditating through sunrise, a surreal day of dreaming unfolded, soothed by waves, afternoon sunshine, seagulls and then sunset. Exhausted and too comfortable to seek out a frigid unheated public bathroom, she peed into a paper cup, emptied it outside and watched it disappear into sand. Scrambling for hand sanitizer while grappling ringing cell phone, she balanced it using chin and a knuckle hit the speaker button. Caught awkward, relieved to hear Catharine's voice.

"Oh Hi Navi, can you please come on over? But don't expect too much from me today, I had a rabies shot this morning."

"Oh my God, what happened?"

"Well I went into to town to get smokes and on the way back I hit and stunned a raccoon. I jumped out of the car and picked it up in my arms. At which point it promptly bit me then toddled off into the woods."

This was not Catharine's first round of rabies shots, nor was it her first raccoon bite. Puttering about in her kitchen one warm summer day she heard whimpers, so followed sad sounds to a wall and placing an ear, quickly assembled children. Large chunks of drywall removed, revealed several tiny baby raccoons. Mama had strategically placed babes high in rafters, safe, only to lose them down inside the wall. Ungracious rescued, promptly screeched and nipped. Undeterred, Catharine began phone searching for rescue assistance, the Animal Control hotline. To Catharine's disgust, uninterested receptionist advised calling pest control. Intent on saving little furry lives, she kept and carried those tiny fur balls in a basket for days, even to the office. The basket of fur babes accompanied her everywhere with hope and sheer will of finding a good welcome home. It took four days to convince the farmer to assume their care. To Catharine's joy, several lived and when of age released, the growing fur balls were competently able to fend for themselves.

"Catharine, dear Catharine, you are a magnet for animals. They are attracted to you as moths are to flame. God Bless the woman who emulates Saint Francis, patron saint of animals and all things critter like!"

Navi drove Catharine and dogs to the bluff for a hike. The trail wound upward for eight kilometers, winding open bay escarpment. At the top overlooking panoramic expanse of rocky shoreline bay, open water and islands, they splayed out at cliffs edge and picnicked; watching seagulls and hawks dip and glide in air currents.

"Breath-taking!"

"Absolutely breath-taking!"

Stephen was still away and Navi was grateful for the space to think and finish packing. Opening the financial file, uncomfortable in unwanted guest solitude, the house yelled, "GET OUT!"

Dearest Navi;

I have been wondering how you are doing. Your Mom told me you where splitting up with Stephen, yes he jumped the gun and beat you to the punch. Just thought you ought to know. Your Mom said that she did not blame you and not really Stephen either. I think she felt the situation with Matt had a lot to do with it. I cannot imagine the strain you have all been under through this. As to you, you said it all a few years ago when we last chatted that when you commit to following the higher spirit of God, you go in some very interesting [to say the least] directions. I have found that people in general think I am crazy. It's genetic you know; your Grandmother, well, if she wasn't such a strong, tough old bird, she'd have made a great soothsayer in another culture, but in community and at church, she was our spiritual leader. The ministers came and went, but it was your Grandmother who ruled, and with grace and wisdom and humour. I never really ever talked to you about this, figured you would have figured out the family secrets. I can see that you have the gift too. Your mother was always afraid for you.

I thought you ought to know now that I know who you are and what you are about, because we carry the same genes. I am a different person around family, your mother and church community. That is how I found balance. My other outside friends, my real friends accept me as I am, even though they often think I am nuts. The rest of the world eventually gives up and goes away or probably from their point of view just avoid me. I like it that way.

All I can suggest, and I wish I had learned this one earlier, is just turn everything over to spirit and listen and follow your intuition, instincts whatever you want to call it. I think it is a good time to put you on the distant healing network if that is okay with you. Do not worry about Abby and Matt, they will not be too upset with this, they have you and know that they are loved and lucky to have you. They are very intuitive and great kids from what I have seen of them.

Sometimes I think some of us chose to live several different lives in one. It seems that our lives change completely periodically. Keep in touch. Keep your chin up kiddo.

Love - Aunt Diane

Dear Aunt Diane;

Thank you for the message. It figures that Stephen would blab to Mother. Your kind words mean more than you could ever imagine and yes, coming especially from you, it helps immensely.

Love Navi

Navi had crossed a moral marital boundary with David and would have to find a way to make peace in her mind, heart and soul. People do not allow extra-marital affairs unless there is something missing and wrong, either with spouse or within the seeker. David was beside himself in agony and trying desperately to sort it all out. She felt it all and felt for him. His friendship, wisdom and seeming tenacity for remaining friends had become a lifeline. No matter what was going on in his life, he always managed to seek her out.

Navi was well aware her choices with David had gone astray, crossed boundaries and subsequent confusion and compassion with David, his wife and family was smoldering. She had made the first move with a simply friendly kiss then allowed more to follow. 'How could love and intimacy feel soooo right and yet be so wrong and hurtful to others?' Moral integrity was an innate prided attribute. Yet, here she was, moral no more. Knowing that emotional hurt was also now beginning to ripple through David's house filled her with a dichotomy of self-loathing and higher justification.

Old sisterhood shawl enfolded, visions flittered of what her real home planet might be like. Playfully she slapped her chest, "Beam me up Scotty". *Home was a wonderful place, where everyone was naturally nice to each other simply because they had evolved further than lowly two legged humans had. Each exalted by legions of angels. Home had three moons and a light jade green hue. Everyone was taller there; dark brown almond eyes with lizard like brown skin and elongated hands. Community culture had evolved to the point where fear and aggression was an unknown distant memory, a concept of antiquity that still played out on lower evolved planets. People naturally loved their neighbours unconditionally, had grown so high in ability to work universe forces and energies, and so could manifest what they wanted or needed just by thinking it. They spoke to each other, with each other collectively or individually not by words, but by thoughts. Time was not linear but rather simultaneously spent playing, loving, exploring and learning via the great hall of universal knowledge. Those who were morally as evolved as any are all heard and felt others; thoughts and emotions. Home planet was the one place where everything made sense. An individual's inner light of higher mind, compassion and wisdom openly displayed as badges of honour, hallmarks of divinity.*

"While you are discovering your own divine being-ness, the divine is discovering you."

"HI Gran."

"It is not supposed to hurt or make you cry my darling Chickadee, or feel too overwhelmed and vulnerable. Stay strong in grace, observe and be confident."

As Navi cleaned, sorted and packed, to her dismay, the sum total of functional household items solely hers, were a handful of garage sale antiques and assorted nick-knacks. Eyeing over an accumulation of children's crafts, art and assorted memorabilia and family archives was the material summation of ten years of marriage. She scanned a pile of mail on the kitchen counter, a parcel without postage, from Mother.

Dearest Daughter;

Stephen came by two days ago on his way to Toronto to say goodbye and I suppose to jump the gun. I know that you will come and chat when it is your time to do so. I hope you do not mind but I chatted with your Aunt Diane, so if she mentions anything, at least you will know where it came from.

I saw an article in a Toronto newspaper about this school. I thought of you immediately. It maybe not the type of thing Pastor or other Elders may approve of, but what they do not know will not upset their knickers. I think if you are making changes dear, you might give some serious consideration of entering their Seminary. I do not mean to sound negative, but marriage just does not agree with you.

Aunt Diane, I, and some of the women are heading out first thing in the morning, a last minute gallivanting trip down south to a time-share in Miami. I will be in contact, when I return. I might just make a winter go of it, so it may be next spring dear. At any rate, I shall give you a dingle when we arrive to exchange contact phone numbers. Love to the children. Do give the Seminary a thought dear.

Mother

Inter-Faith Spiritual Seminary College, New York State

Dear Potential Student:

Thank you for your inquiry and interest in our Seminary College programs. At this time, the majority of our courses are available through our Distant Education program as well as in class sessions. Please peruse the programs and return application and choice of study along with appropriate transcripts, references and letter of intent. We also require a minimum of five personal and employment related references to determine Ministry suitability.

Please be advised, that some of the first year course curriculum are pending updated changes. I include a copy of the Canadian Ministry of Education approval of our new standardized formats and tuition rates. Feel free to contact us at the enclosed phone number should you have any questions.

Sincerely; Registrar, Rev. Joe Cox

'Well, I'll be dammed!" Dawg sat curious, tail wagging, watching and waiting. "Seminary? New York State?" Navi set the letter down and looked at the envelope again. In exasperated overwhelmed with stress moment, her mind simply unable to wrap itself around anything more, tossed it onto empty computer desk. As the envelope hit the desk, it slowly slid off and splattered onto the floor, as another paper slid counter sideways landing beside her foot, another from Mother. Navi hesitated opening it, preparing for bad news, ripped it open, a newspaper article fell out and onto the floor. Picking it up and unfolding read its bold headline: **Local Bethany Woman in Her Sixties Graduates From Spiritual Seminary College.**

"Shazam, this is just too weird!" She sat down and read the entire article, lit up a cig and then read it again. Mind whirled with curiosity of this mysterious school in New York and older woman who was now an Ordained Minister from this same place. From a rural Ontario community, an Ordained Minister, inter-faith and spiritual. "Holy crap in a basket Mother, this is most intriguing. Good on you."

Navi flipped on her computer, sensing that she was about to stumble upon some great truth.

'Our Seminary College is one hundred and fifty years old. Most students who take the courses are working towards becoming non-denominational, inter-faith or inter-denominational licensed Ordained Ministers. "Me? A minister? Geez, I don't go to church anymore. I loathed church. And heck, it isn't like I am morally qualified anyway."

Idea dismissed, she sat back in her chair scanning rental unit classifieds and just as she picked up the phone to make a call, it alarm rang through sensitive nerves. Stephen's Mother was beside herself livid with Navi.

"I demand an explanation from you young Lady!"

Navi had never actually heard the woman angry before and the fact that it was directly targeting her, threw balance off. She would have to talk with her at some point but the woman was so completely out of the loop with what had been really going on with her own son and so far out that it simply was not Navi's place to blab it to her.

"I understand how you might think you know your son, but obviously you do not. If your son is not man enough to be honest with you, I can do nothing except gracefully decline any explanations at this time and say goodbye."

Indignant, not waiting for a reply, she hung up. "Anger *is* fear turned weapon."

'If I close my eyes for a moment, I can awaken from this nightmare. And everything will be normal again. For all of my days, I have just been trying to find a place in this world that makes sense. I have to find balance like Gran did, if only for Abby. What inner knowing truth and inner guidance system gave her such solid fortitude to be who she was? I must somehow find this confident grace, if only for Abby.'

Navi slept fitfully, conscious thoughts battled subconscious survival fear emotions. Inner yearnings and wishes vied for survival with worst fears. Dreams strung in a myriad of smaller dreams lingering in between waking abruptly to fall back asleep and resume, begging Navi to understand relevance and messages.

Awake, standing low on four legs as mist clears. Navi She Wolf. I am Canis Lupus. I am Teacher, Guide and Way Shower.

Stretching, strong legs out front, toes splay and furl spine over long slender body as I flex powerful muscles against a short metal chain. My eyes follow the chain embedded around a tree, my neck rolled in sore response against my tight tethered collar, worn from weeks of binding restraint. From where I sit, I carefully watch man master's cabin and wait for slop food. At night, I "will" a field mouse and squirrel to come close, for my nourishment. Little bones easily crunched under strong teeth. Man master is convinced that I would replace his dead German shepherd canine as his guardian, companion and servant. He does know the mystical creature, which craves sensory and mental stimulation of wilderness, earth and cosmic mastery. Curious by nature, I work in higher mind, heightened senses and am agilely able to synthesize information rapidly. Wolf's howl is the spirit world messenger. I am La Loba, Wolf Woman.

I watch and sense Man Master's body, facial expressions and voice for patterns. Often angry bordering on cruel, I know when to submit, then occasionally, friendly and jovial giving a pat or playful or rubbing oil into my ears keeping biting flies at bay. Never fully knowing what to expect of man master beast, I summate is of rabid unpredictable madness. Yet, I am tied captive. Beyond chain is a gate and I watch man master each day as he flips its trigger, coming in and going out.

Alone, I urinate at chains end, leaving my scent as a calling card for Raven who visits bringing news of forest and wilderness beckoning. Raven magic and adviser of change, shape-shifter beckons the courage and stamina of my soul. A long journey about to unfold, I acknowledge and wait. Alone, out of man masters hearing range, my mouth forms a 'U', head tilts to the sky, a deep breath in and I howl, calling to distant wolf pack that echoes in rally cry. Cellular memory vibrates familiar in unison with Pack's higher community mind. Fur stands erect, ears twitch and turn, tuning in. Soul longing soon answered as first heavy snow begins, offering a surprise opportunity. I wait for snow to build. Unsuspecting rabbit meanders by, confused by snow laden covered tracks and scents, I have my first full meal in many months and I am fortified for a long journey. I consciously adjust my blood, slowing down to conserve energy and heat against cold winter's night and ripping wind.

Man masters evening fire, asleep in cabin warmth as winter wind blows colder and darkness descends. An eye to cabin, neck muscles expand and suddenly, worn neck tether finally gives way. Stealthily I approach the gate, nose nudging upward and gate swings open.

Nose to the ground for man track scents then to the air for open wilderness direction, I bolt into the night.

I am navigating forest, peaking thirty miles an hour. I run straight toward pack's rally cries, knowing that at dawn man master will hunt my trail with gun and hound dog. He will not abide my absence and wish my return to his cabin as a rug beside another wolf's long dead carcass.

Too soon, I reach a precipice and stop abruptly. Eyes and ears scanning back path and forward horizon. My energy gathering, I'm calmly panting, with adrenaline pumping through my wild blood.

Snow clouds part slightly and a full moon appears, showing a trail zigzagging around precipice and down into valley below. Fresh running water scent wafted in air, I know I can follow its course, losing my tracks and scent among its flow. Breathing slows as I descend, careful of footholds, I hear pack distant rally cry out in the night. Closer now, my voice and body responds. I must make my way to where they are, to home and freedom. Sensing man master's early morning tracking, I am mindful and focus on my tracks and scent. I put my spirit into the moon for safekeeping, he may win the hunt and have my body to do with as he pleases, but he will not have my spirit.

At that moment, soul skin male mate advances from forest shadow into open space below cliff along river water's edge. Out into the open upon, he carefully approaches. I drop my head in submission and roll as he nuzzles my neck, then smells my scent. We play, dance, nuzzle and share sent as I allow my hind end to rub against him.

Pack's rally cry bellows closer as we scamper off zigzagging toward them. Gathered, we begin a long wintry night's journey ahead to new territory, far from hunter's willingness to hunt. New territory, adjustments to unknown packs domains we must go.

Navi understood the relevancy of she-wolf; teacher who empowers cubs, family mind, loyal and fiercely protective, mating for life.

It was the last day of life in the rural satellite office and its lonely walls echoed emptiness where once an abundance of life and activity flowed. Packing, sorting, reminiscing; and then startled with a knock on her door as one of her clients sat down in front of her desk.

"Navi, I got to tell you what happened to me."

"Sure, let's hear it," grateful for distraction.

The tall handsome bright blue-eyed gentle former Marine Engineer unzipped his ragged coat with nature stained hands. An aroma of wood smoke and fresh earth air emitted from his essence.

"Well, I was riding my bicycle home from town last night. I come upon a deer, dead at the side of the road. It looked fresh and I figured it was a gift, if you know what I mean. Better for me to take home and eat than the Ministry of Natural Resources. So I went home to get my machete and my backpack n' some bungee cord. I quartered that beautiful baby right there on the road. The head, the chest and the front legs I saddled on my handlebars. The hind end I rested on the seat behind me, those legs just a dangling. The two large chunks of meat I squished into my backpack, dripping blood all over the frigging place. I thought I was nearly a goner, when this woman driving a car caught me, and the sight of me n' my gift in her headlights. That woman did a perfect 360 at 80 kilometers an hour and went back from whence she came. I made it home unscathed, but I got to tell you, I was some shitting my pants scared that she was going to go home and call the Ministry of Natural Resources on me."

"Well more likely she was thinking about calling the Police."

"Oh, maybe, I never thought of that. I just did not want the Resources people confiscating my gift because road kill is supposed to be turned in. Anyways, I put the chunks into my well out in the yard behind the cabin. You know my fridge. You know I do not have electricity or refrigeration of any kind. Anyway, I figured it would be cool and safe in there for the night. Nevertheless, when I woke up this morning and went to check on it, that maybe I might have some deer meat to cook up for breakfast and it was gone! There was nothing' left in the well. The bears had come in the night and got my deer bits. Still, got to watch for those Natural Resources folks, they are always confiscating fish, hunting equipment and even pickup trucks."

'God bless them all.'

How odd for the garden to be finally maturing, so prolific and abundant now that Navi was saying goodbye. Sweet sorrow, she let her braid out in reverence of wonderful sunshine on skin, gentle warm breeze caressing hair as fingers dug into soil and jammed up finger nails. A dichotomy of emotions swirled and settled in alignment in rapid adjustment to change.

Shirt off allowing warm breezes and sunshine to caress naked skin, breasts freely danced. Each mammary exhibited a distinct personality; one extroverted and wild in nature while the right was an introverted wallflower, 'Goddess Sisters', she mused.

A Chickadee family flittered in and out of evergreens.

"Mom?"

"Yes honey bunny."

"Mom, the after school baby sitter said that she was very concerned over your marital separation and how that might affect me. I told her that I am choosing to remain positive about the whole thing. Did I say that okay?"

"HA! Wow. Really? Wow! You go girlfriend! So what did the babysitter say to that?"

"She laughed. Hey Mom?"

"Yep?"

"It's my birthday."

"I did not know that. When did that happen? How come nobody told me?"

"Ah Mom, cut it out. So, well did you get me a new shaving kit? Huh? Huh? Huh?"

"Gaze upon thou Mother Dearest eyes young maiden daughter. Nope. I refuse to be bamboozled by a budding teeny bopper."

"Ah, dam, I thought as much. Can I have a veggie burger and birthday cake then?"

"Yep, that's what I was thinking. By the way, it is not lost on me how grown up you have become. Guess I ought to double up your school work huh?"

It was their last night at the old country home. Armed with pillows, blankets and all lights out, outside, they splayed onto the deck. In darkness of night, a distant late evening storm flickered and rumbled, approaching the open field to the east as Fireflies danced over the pool.

"Magic!"

"Mom?"

"Yes Babe."

"Do you remember when we lived in India?"

"Yes Babe." instantly startled with the imagery and calm confidence.

"You were my big brother and I was a little girl. Our parents had died or gone off and we were dirt poor living in a garbage dump."

Not wanting to dissuade or influence her one way or the other, "I can see that."

"I got real sick and you took me to a mission. The old woman in the robe with white hair took me in. You saved my life, but you did not come too. No boys allowed, I guess. I did not see you for a long time after that. I missed you something awful. I became a teacher and you worked on wagons and stuff. We got a little shack together until we got married. Nobody wanted to marry me when I was still at the mission, too sickly and weak. Nobody wanted to marry me when I came and lived with you again, not for a long time, 'because you didn't have any dowry money or a goat and chickens to give away."

Abby dozed, snuggled in, basking in Peeper frog symphony. A stark revelation; they were two peas in a pod, a genetic fluke. A hidden aspect that she would have to protect and keep an eye on. Waking slightly, Abby wrapped around Navi, a loving parasite, chattering that she wanted a shaving kit for her birthday, to shave her legs. Weary of the lame sales pitch, Navi tossed her into bed and covered her up in mermaid blankets, pretending to yell and swat, "Bed Bug! Bed Bug, Get the Bed Bug!"

Abby squealed with laughter. "Ahhhhh Mom, I want a shaving kit for my birthday, I want to shave my legs."

"Sigh; ask me when you're sixteen kiddo. Consider yourself tucked in, young woman. And hey little one, while I have you captive here, please be careful who you tell and share those stories with. You can come to me any time, but please do not just blab to anyone. Not many people are going to understand."

"Ah, I already know that Mom."

Navi searched for information on Spiritualism and Shamanism, searching for answers on why her life was in chaos, why she was so different from other women and hoping that Mother's lead would take to where she would feel wanted, needed and to belong somewhere with someone. Finding little insight and solace from Google or Wikipedia; she clicked into e-mail to find a message from David.

Dear Navi;

I have ascertained that you are the best friend that I have ever had. Please be good to yourself and know that I care.

Yours, David

Navi was grateful for the lifeline and friendship.

Office packed, Navi sat waiting for moving truck and once loaded, sat in the empty chamber alone. With Abby away visiting a gal pal from school, she seized solace opportunity and drove along the long winding beach road. Down a dirt side road to a secret place known only to late night teenager's party weekending, she built a small bonfire. The cosy riverside cove hid a small sand dune surrounded by evergreens overlooking calm meandering water. The ambiance and serenity of gurgling river water brought instant, quiet, peacefulness. Gentle surround sounds of nature and river water winding its way inland, meditation. Navi fed a wasp a sweet cherry, watching with close up fascination, its straw like gizmo sucking up juice.

Saturday morning brought yet another moving day into their new tiny beach community cottage. Amidst boxes, bags and assorted chaos of over flowing household goods, Mom and daughter feasted on macaroni and cheese out of its cooking pot then chocolate ice cream in its container.

Late afternoon coffee chat with David brought more revelation. Casually and confidently, he reiterated a late night discussion with his wife about mutual separation. Surprised yet not surprised, the news rang right and true in her own soul, yet wanting to believe the outcome was for the highest good.

"I am officially available."

"Well, maybe you think you are but buddy, you are still married and you both have to take time to process, make sure you are both doing the right thing. Talk and take care of each other. Be good to her. I proclaim thee 'Magus'. Thou art a magician, and worker universal forces. Go forth and heal thy family!"

"In the interim, I shall paint a nude of thee."

With the honourable boundary shift, old sisterhood shawl enveloped Navi and daughter, relaxed into sleep and to each to dream their dreams with joyous abandon.

"Spirit of the water, flow through me, to me. Come to me She-wolf. I call upon you. Allow me to feel your wildness, your child-ness, your love."

The world distant and far away, behind a magical ocean cottage, laid wilderness sanctuary. Kindred spirits, soul skin wolf mates enjoying the beautiful divine spring day, free. Butterflies flittered in off shore breezes as otters slid down mud inclines at river mouth. Wolf tag, splashing and dancing in snow fed stream. At peace and grateful, nuzzling, a love mating gift shared, human adult life time of loneliness dissolved in a moment, unspoken and new awareness of manifesting heaven on earth. Surrounded in magnificent light, a sense of once in a lifetime soul communion.

Shhh, Darling'. You cannot see tree roots growing nor wind, only know its results. Faith will carry you forward for the many journeys ahead until we meet in physical once again. I love to see the morning sun, shining on your breasts. Warm breezes dancing through your hair, feel your fingers, combing through the hair on my chest. Arms around you, feel your skin so soft and bare.

Until then, remember when you were a child and remember me. I wrap my love around you, and shelter you from the cold winds. I blow my warm breath against your skin to relax you. Then I shall watch over you, as you gently drift off into sleep, always watching you."

"Hello there, darling soul skin man. Thank you for that gift. Whoever, and wherever you are."

"Being deeply loved by someone
gives you strength, while
loving someone deeply
gives you courage."
Lao Tzu

Chapter 11 ~ A New Chapter

Summer hit with a blasting heat wave and what better healing space than the beach? Soothing two lost grieving gals of old life in the old farm country home with its pond, garden, in-ground pool, forests and creatures to lazy days wandering and lounging at the beach.

With boxes left unpacked, a disoriented Navi ventured into the new office. Wrapping a weary mind around unfamiliar territory with dicey office politics, she jumped in with both feet fighting a flight instinct to run back to the old, familiar and safe rural office. Bolt and run far away. Intuition bells rang foreboding danger, yet seeing no other option settled in with hesitation and resistance.

It took less than one hour for Navi to comprehend that she was beyond unwelcome within established inner office sanctum. She tried dismissing rude innuendoes and signals, intent on making the best of it. The other option was unemployment. Tensions and alpha she-dog control games were foreign to her nature. Off balance and vulnerable, pecking order agenda clearly set, get in line quickly or die gaming began in full force.

By noon, she had ascertained that the clients where much more city-like; with resentment of anyone who managed to score 'the big job' in the next county south at the car manufacturing plant, which meant union rates, on-the-job training, benefit plans, retirement plans, shares in the plant and most of all, a huge salary. The rest tried to eke livings at Mac Donald's, Wal-Mart, cutting grass, resort housekeeping and other seasonal jobs. All in all both new office mates and clients were a miserable bunch.

When she flipped her computer on, a new and complicated software program rudely awoke, pulsed, begging attention, a learning curve. It contained a bureaucratic series of new guidelines and welfare legislation.

Bottom line, clients would increasingly be squeezed like insects until they simply gave up. The new computer system was also obviously making powerful accountability of its front line workers, not just clients. An inner tug-of-war between trying to empower and find resources for clients and that of making the client fit into the program and its strict categories. Bitchy co-workers too were struggling to assimilate and make sense of the changes. Her altruistic nature grieved a philosophy of helping the poor and vulnerable. It could not possibly last long, too inhumane.

It seemed as though all had to rapidly adjust to higher up pressures of making the shift while being expected to simply trust, without question, the judgment and will of the powers that be. Legislation was not as simple as policy or business practice, it was law and there was nothing that could immediately be done to change what lay ahead. Billions of taxpayers' dollars had already been pissed away on high-end computers, software, fiber optic phone lines and training consultations. Consultations or propagandizing at every level of government and it was here to stay for a long time to come. Perhaps out of fear of their own pay cheques all seemed to be rationalizing away the changes, just doing their jobs.

Images flowed through her mind of how post war crime tribunal Nazi lawyers proposed and argued the Nuremberg Defense; a soldier was not to be held accountable for dirty deeds because they were merely following orders. In the end, the defense was overruled, setting precedence for individual accountability.

The mood was rapidly growing thick with fear. Restructuring and downsizing was imminent. Formerly a cohesive supportive and caring work environment turned into subjugation and competition, a dark sinister slithering snake. A cancerous virus web spread throughout the organization. It was a silent atrocity, shown only to the public as a revolutionary way of delivering social services with unprecedented cost savings to hard working taxpayers.

It was an illusion that perfectly fed into angry middle-income mass mentality. Yet taxes went up. Municipalities are assuming the brunt of the program set up, and operational cost. The ingenious design had grown out of consultations with California and Texas. Prior to that, Navi saw, the model arose out of Austria, following Hitler's democratic rule during a time of great depression and oppression. A mentally ill monster had arrived in savior's clothing.

Smug Bitch Boss Helen and her indifferent old boy higher ups did nothing to alleviate growing fear and tension among staff. A detached 'let them squirm' attitude rapidly replaced friendship, camaraderie and dedication. Now management was providing information and responding to speculations on a need to know basis only. Cruelly, front line staff angst over feeding their own families and paying mortgages out of the great unknown fear; job loss. David had been demoted to basement grunt duties while maintaining regular caseloads. What could happen to them? Fear bred fear upon fear. They gossiped in shadow corners, surmising personality flaws that led to his eminent demise as an office golden child.

Navi avoided back corner discussions, as if a plague. Dangerous dark places. She had priorities and problems that had nothing to do with work. Choosing to stay positive, that there had to be a positive aspect, good to come of it all that remained yet unknown and that would make sense later.

When Navi went to sleep at night, she could see the computer screen, rather than client faces. She was psyching herself up for another wave of legislative changes and trying to remain positive. Status quo and positivity was not working under pressure to use manipulation, coercion and force, as directed in the demanding demeanour welfare cops.

Without doubt, the new system was haunted. It was consistently either not spitting out client's meagre cheques at all or mistakenly reducing them. A bombardment of client phone calls ensued, of those desperate to pay rent and feed children, sending a volume of clients to the food bank and other community supports. She drafted detailed information sheets to help navigate the systems, including the pro bono legal clinic. All T's crossed, all I's dotted, requirements, expectations, options checked and the cruel spirit entity of the software system failed to cut cheques.

New clients smiled and nodded heads, signed mandatory contractual agreements without discussion or question without understanding a word of the legal jargon. They just wanted food and rent paid so they could get through another month. A new level of oppression and fear was growing in the community lower ranks. When people are this afraid, they should not sign anything, especially a legal document that they did not understand. It did not seem legal and surely, it was unethical. It was common sense that given any other legal situation, one could not bind nor expect anyone to sign a legal document under duress and have it hold up in a court of law. On the other hand, could they? The new government was enforcing changes and cutbacks in every non-profit and government sector.

Thus, amidst a changing chaotic external world, the two cocooned. Sanctuary at home, work and school. Seeking fresh air and solace, she took to meandering second hand stores during lunch away from established cliques that neither extended invitation nor involved her. On the outside, she maintained an air of balanced objective professionalism, yet on the inside, strained and vulnerable.

Out of the corner of her eye, a youthful young man caught her eye, his long pony tail, beard, weathered leather jacket and happy go lucky manner brought back a flood of memories of life with Abby's father T.J. Freely van meandering across Quebec and mountainous Vermont, carefree and in love. Vague imagery of their time together was all that remained, save for rare occasions when she avoided direct contact in daughter visitation exchanges. Their carefree lifestyle long abandoned as daughter came into being, his path abruptly diverted to living a life of affluence and materialism, hers to single parenting and social causes. It seemed as though neither had looked back. He had long been living the great American dream, free to pursue his earthly desires, she to muddle along alone. Her marriage to Stephen added to a growing sense of relationship and employment ineptitude, mingling and building upon each other in a manner of validating her failure to conform to normal social standards of acceptance. Yes, T.J. had the Midas touch, was obviously thriving and happy. The thought pained in comparison. At least there had never been a terse word or thought during their time together or their departure from one another that she could recall. Thinking on it now, she could not recall one single argument, not even in parting, simply lingering indefinable soul sadness. She was happy for him, glad that their parting had allowed him to follow his dreams unencumbered.

"Where on earth am I going Gran? Where is the one eight hundred number to call for directions?" Navi searched for an idea or inclination that she could grasp, to hang onto. 'Ha, I know, I'll finish those spiritual seminary courses, become an ordained minister and then the 'piece da la resistance', be publicly stoned and burned at the stake by own church cronies!"

Her mind drifted, looking for a focus point that showed the pathway to stability and familiarity. Stephen had taken her by surprise. An initial attraction based in mutual interest of an art exhibit and their children, courted and married within months. Wed under an umbrella of old maple trees by the pond in their own backyard. Kids entertained by a clown, piñatas bashed, faces painted while guests mingled in lush country gardens. Lovely and dreamy, a day filled with happy memories, a Brady Bunch, raising children together that turned two short days later.

"What in the hell happened?"

Navi sat in her favourite Adirondack chair, left behind on the deck of the old country house. It felt strange to be at the old farmhouse. Stephen had readily agreed on meeting there with a private mediator rather than going down greedy lawyer highway. She had thought it premature with Matt still recuperating, but Stephen insisted. Acquiescing, she agreed, worried about his tendency to procrastinate on loans and credit cards. He still had yet to transfer the house, banking and utilities into his own name. Her name was still on joint legal agreements and as such, in a fall out, would be held financially responsible. He was notorious for forgetting to pay bills. If they could just put some preliminary financial and legal issues on paper then they could sort the rest out later.

Business suit mediator man slowly pulled into the driveway and she was suddenly nervous. Intuitively unnerved, sensing that something was amiss. Something was wrong. Too late now to step back, shook off the feeling. The large man presented a hard all business manner. Both Navi and Stephen had met him before, seemingly friendly. Eventually everyone crosses your path. Hiring him to do the job had seemed an obvious choice.

Sitting on the deck waiting for Stephen, she offered tea, shaking off discomfort and foreboding. He seemed grumpy, annoyed to be kept waiting. She bolted ahead, giving him the gist of their situation and finances. After twenty more minutes of tense silent waiting, he looked at his watch, "I can't wait much longer."

Stephen did not show up. Stephen did not call. Then the realization hit her, a whacking two by four realization across her head.

"Oh my God! I think I know where he is. He has traded places with Matt's mom and taken him for his last treatment" a wave of burning humiliation swept through, embarrassment then spine-rippled anger.

"Oh, my God! Don't I look like a crass and greedy bitch!"

Business suit mediation man guffawed shock and appall, then turned and glared intently as she shifted body in uncomfortable repulsion then began re-packing his briefcase.

"Yes Ma'am. You surely do!"

Navi's mind reeled, searching for where and how life had gone so off kilter.

Still burning with naive humiliation, she pulled out of the driveway. Stephen had worked Matt's illness once again. It was clearly, a masterpiece maneuver. Navi was an IDIOT clear and simple. 'How I must look to the rest of the world! I AM totally screwed!' Outwit, one up, direct hit, adversary down, flattened. 'King takes Queen of Hearts' once again.

The new beach home felt empty of tree, critter life and suddenly felt foreign and unfamiliar. Lights off, out on the deck, she curled up in a blanket on a lounge chair and stared up at the starry night sky.

"All we need to do to receive help is to ask."

Navi saw and understood suffering of those souls in purgatory as visions of hell fire engulfed its victims. Hell; not a place but a state of mind, where in the throes of suffering, moaning and crying, agonizing those who could not yet ask for help. Mother Mary cried gently with those lost souls, patiently waiting of them to ask for help. A soft voice spoke, "Life has a way of bringing us to our knees and demanding that we hand over our lives to something higher."

"Hi Gran, I can feel you there."

"Often things don't go how we want and yes darling there is always a higher agenda behind what human eyes perceive. No one is garbage, not ever. Everyone is of the Divine plan, no matter how things may appear to be. Find joy and appreciate it. Live your life every day, every moment, no matter what! If you slip into fear and negativity, pull your thoughts and focus back towards God and us. And my little Chickadee, love the one that is hardest to love."

'I have come to my healing place.'

Navi woke up at midnight, trails of a dream *wandering someone else's house, a funeral wake. Who had died, and who the people were, in her house, not her home, but her house? Elegantly dressed in a classic black dress and heels, hair styled up in glorious class against a pearl necklace lying across lower neck, she gracefully mingled. A perfect wife, serving appetizers and offering glasses of wine then retreated to the kitchen privacy. He had been a social climbing charming business mogul on the outside and on the inside, a twisted bastard. Community and family now sung his praise. A wonderfully gifted talented man not yet in his prime, a real community man and who was generous to the core. Not a drinker by nature, she discreetly slung back whiskey shots.*

From behind, strong sure hands embraced and slid upward, cupping her left breast. His other hand caressed inside a thigh, sliding upward under her skirt, then up over and in stockings and panties. Instantly wet, her body submitted to his touch as she managed to reach out and grasp the counter to steady her in orgasm. David had come in quietly through a back kitchen door, unknowingly to guests and left as quietly as entered without saying a word.

"Do not grieve my loss. Grieve for the dead man who did not know his higher self."

William, an old gout crippled client and his cancer ridden wife travelled over two hours in a broken down old duct taped bungee corded pickup truck to deliver a large Emu hind leg and a giant zucchini for Navi's birthday. Their luck was consistent bad luck as chickens disappeared at the nipping jaws of fishers. The furry little beasties would slowly peck at each chicken until they dropped from blood loss. Easy to haul, in the dead of night carried off. Nature could seem cruel. Their hobby farmland laid barren save for waves of seagulls, who ate seeds as fast as William could plant. The optical illusion fun house tilted left with entry stairs slanting right in opposition. It was sweet home to the couple, which eked out a meagre existence. Their sparkling joy, despite all odds, kept them under the Natural Resources wire with the local reserve that supplied them with fish in trade of zucchini and emu. It was the best gift imaginable, touched by its soulful purity.

Arriving home, hundreds of balloons welcomed her. Cottage inside and out and even Dawg trailed streamers. Catharine Guardian Angel had been there.

Abby produced a found kitten, discovered at the school bus stop, "Happy Birthday Mom!"

Unsure of what to do with the obvious feral barn cat, she graciously and cautiously accepted it as 'Kat', a medical experiment gone astray, immediately took to climbing curtains and shredding furniture. It hung, legs splayed out, claws embedded on window screen.

Abby smiled, "Isn't he adorable?"

Dawg and Kat established immediate alliance; Kat dismantled everything above waist; food on the counter, car keys, important papers, cigarette packages and plants onto the floor and madly shredded them.

"I don't know daughter, I've only been home twenty minutes and already Thing One and Thing Two have managed to turn this place upside down. I think he's feral. He looks like he has been slam hit in the back of his head with a two by four. God Abby, that's a misnomer, he's really plotting to take over the household and systematically destroy it!"

"Ah Mom, you just need to bond with it."

"Ah darlin', I know that you're partial to him, but outside is bred into his soul. You know that he needs to live outdoors and a farm or barn is where he's going to feel at home."

"Ah, I know Mom. I was just hoping."

She took one in each arm and squeezed them tight and kissed foreheads.

Tent pitched haphazardly in the yard, hands scooping munchies and campfire ignited. Catharine arrived and as she zipped into the cottage to pee, Abby snuck feral Kat into her car. When Catharine returned to look for her smokes, a spastic fur ball awaited. Wild chase ensued as Catharine's dreaded pincher fingers snapped after Abby's behind. Squeals, giggles and grass-stained knees followed Emu roasting with sweet potato spuds on campfire grill. Navi, repulsed by Emu covered in black with chunks of coal and wood bits, gladly ingested by Abby.

"Not bad, but Emu meat smells like dog bum and tastes like old rubber."

"Oh? You've had those have you?"

"Hey Mom, I had a dream last night. I was dream travelling and I zoomed right in on Stephen, he couldn't see me, but I could see him. There's definitely something really wrong with his mind and soul. Yes, it is good that we got out of there. Oh he can be a conniving prick, can't he?"

"I suppose." Uncomfortable with daughter being this far advanced, too much information, embarrassed and ashamed that she had put her girl in the situation in the first place.

"Ah, and Mom, don't worry about his Matt. The Angels showed me that he is gooder than good, has immediate families and his own life to lead as an adult now. He's fine and loves us and even though he may never tell you, he does understand and is okay with the fact that you had to leave his dad."

"Tell that to me every day would you? Oh and tell my Mother and the rest of the world while you're at it. Hmmmm, you're a very astute daughter. Yes, Stephen has darkness hidden in his soul that he must face, and face alone, if he is to have inner peace. No matter what, we must not go there with him. This is his personal journey and not yours to rectify. When it all comes about, you will have to make a choice, one way or another. Everyone comes and goes in our life for a reason. Few have soul mates for a lifetime."

"Ya, I can see that now. Oh, and Mom, I also saw that when you are menopausal, in a few years you will spiritual cocoon for at least four some odd years then emerge, re-born anew, come into the fullness of your true divine power. Until then, go in grace. Oddly, your true destiny will unfold later in life. Hmmm. I am also getting you in school of some kind, something to do with spiritual work. You have a triple cross over your heart. You have been saint, healer, teacher, shaman, medicine woman and seer in all of your past lives."

"Ha, who are you? It's funny you should say that."

Navi explained the strange letter and article.

"Oh, I've heard of that place. I saw it in a dream."

"NO WAY!"

"Oh ya, wonderful place, nice people and very open to exploring things ethereal if you know what I mean."

"So you don't get that it's a bunch of wacky flaky idiots skittering about doing silly wooey woo stuff?"

"No, not like at all, but I got that it is quite old and respectable. There were people from all over the world who came to visit, Tibetan Monks, shamans, healers, celebrities and interesting. I think it's a wakeup call for you, and me."

"Well then, I will check it out Darling. It is time to come home to who we really are and do what we came here to do. Let's not waste time or energy agonizing over what is past. Allow those doors to close as gracefully as we can and strive to not take other people's crap too personally. When there's a lot of shit going on around, we shall do what the master's do, tend to what needs tending to, then go have some fun."

Abby asleep, Navi curled up with Ugly Kitty Kat and Dawg on the deck in dark evening anonymity. Gazing and melding into the stars, into the universe, she sensed Gran's presence. "Hi Gran. I'm looking at your old deck chair here and thinking; if you find an antique, well an old piece of furniture or jewelry say in an antique shop, and you recognize it as yours from a previous lifetime, shouldn't you get to re-claim it and at no cost? I wonder what the shopkeeper would say to that idea. Or how about driving by one day and see a house you lived in, you know worked hard all of that life time to buy, only to have to work hard in another lifetime to buy it or another again. It does not make sense why you we have to keep buying furniture and houses every life time. How about a famous writer or painter, you should collect your royalties. Oh what proof do I have you skeptical people you, well just pull up the Akashi Records on the computer, you'll see."

Gran giggled and soothingly caressed her granddaughter's hair and face.

"I know that you will but darling Chickadee, do not look back."

Navi had been phoning and leaving messages for Stephen once a week. "How is Matt? Abby wants to see you." Stephen finally responded to her weekly calls by sending her an email earlier in the day.

Navi;

When are you going to come and get your shit out of my house? Do not phone me anymore, if you have to, send me an email. If Abby wants to see me, give her my email address.

Stephen

Not one word about how Matt was. That was ten years of marriage. 'Fuck you very much, for everything, Arsehole!'

The following day Navi, Abby and Catharine borrowed a farm work beaten pickup truck and headed out for the house under overcast pregnant clouds and mild thunder. Abby busied herself outside with ancient house Brat Kat as the moving gang browsed throughout her glorious garden. Boldly walking in the front door, Navi heard Stephen in the shower, so sat waiting at the kitchen table. Obviously not seeing nor hearing Navi, he rudely dried himself as he walked. Navi giggled, wondering how she could gently announce her presence.

Directly into Matt's room where she had been sleeping weeks before and left a number of boxes, he slammed dresser drawers and ripped open her boxes. She leaned over to one side to see what he was doing. From her vantage point, she saw only his Grinch full moon.

Navi snickered, 'What on earth could he possibly be looking for?' She was about to quietly go back outside to wait when Stephen suddenly came out into the living room and froze upon seeing Navi standing there.

"OOOPS!" she said quietly under her breath.

Startled and slowly registering that she was there, he reeled slightly backward catching his balance. She had startled him, white face red as a hand groped to towel cover his noodle.

"What the fuck are you doing here?' He burned.

"We've come to get the rest of our fucking shit out of your fucking house. Didn't you get the email?"

"No I didn't get your fucking email. Thanks for letting me know."

"Oh you are most welcome."

"Well good then. Get the fuck out! Get your fucking shit and get the fuck out of my house!"

Stephen turned on heel and stomped upstairs to their/his bedroom. Professing his love not so long ago, she fantasized how that welcome could have been, Stephen down on one knee, her hand in his as he lovingly gazed up into her eyes pleading, 'Oh Navi, I have missed so badly. Please stay, darling. No Navi, do not go. I need you. I love you. We'll work this out.'

Stephen, beyond ballistic, strained against self-control knowing Navi's daughter and friends waited outside. Habitual macho temper tantrums now ineffective, stumbled zipping up pants, open shirt flung haphazardly over shoulders as droplets of water dripped off uncombed bangs and onto his nose. Striving to maintain a dramatic display of anger through pursed lips and glaring, huffed and catching her smirk, tumbled over dangling shoelaces, too off balance to play his dramatic exit scene.

'Ah ha! Queen of Hearts takes King. Or maybe King is caught with knickers down so forfeits to Queen!'

Overcast sky cracked and split open as a torrential down pour ensued. Stephen, squealing tires, peeled out of the driveway. A thief in the night, taking only clothes, knick-knacks, antiques and bare essentials, she paused to scan the house, and its presiding spirit guardian now screamed GET OUT! Nearing the end of the driveway, a small furry critter moved in the car's rear view mirror "Oops! Open your door Abby, we forgot Dawg."

The loaded Beverly Hillbilly pickup truck drove off in downpour with its heaped pile of junk. The truck swayed and lurched as it turned onto the county road.

"Hey Abby, when I first came in Stephen was rifling through my packed boxes, I can't think of anything of his that I might have packed. I wonder what he was looking for."

"I don't know Mom, maybe a pair of your underwear to keep?"

"Bless the child for comic relief. You are a nut."

It was a pivotal moment; daughter was obviously okay, everything was going to be okay.

It was time to grow. She had to do something about David, if she were to have any peace of mind, peace of heart. The other part now was vocation, the job, but decided to start with David. She e-mailed him, pleading him to talk to his wife and sort things out. She did not want to be anyone's 'other woman' and had to let him go. His wife's feelings haunted and David was torn, increasingly distraught. While a loveless existence of many years, they still had couple history, survived inevitable adversities and good times.

Hi Navi;

I am going camping for the weekend. I desperately need to get away from everything. Have a wicked assed cold, running nose, cough, sore throat, maybe fever and the works. Still, I must go and do this. Hope this does not deter thee from visiting with me. If thou art a grain of sand upon the beach, then thou art the most beautiful of them all. The Magus seeks thee on his hands and knees. I miss thee darling.

David the mucus Magus

'Work out your own shit David.'

No sooner had Navi set up on the deck with iced tea, sunglasses, sunscreen and delicious sun shining down when the phone rang. It was David, sick and trapped at the campground without car.

"PLEASEEEE come Navi."

She hesitated then went off to rescue David.

"Why don't you just call your wife and go home David?"

"I don't want to go home. I want to be here. Look even Gill says I should stay." David pointed to a seagull that had taken residence on a picnic table, quietly supervising their every move.

"Oh my God, someone else names the wild life. Okay fine, have it your way. Nevertheless, if you get sicker, call your wife or me I don't care. You shouldn't be out like this when you're sick."

"Yes Mother" David grinned glossy feverish eyes.

City stressed campers set up sites, promptly blasting their own particular taste, a cacophony outdoor rock concert. Praise for the Park Rangers who turned all down at sunset. An air mattress yanked out of tent and under stars, campfire, picnicking and stars gazing. Silent sharing companionship, solace in an uncertain future thrust upon them.

"Stay the night."

"I am too tired to drive home. No hanky-panky though."

"No worry, I am way too sick to contemplate such activity."

David, snorting a back of throat snore was fevering. She brushed his silky bangs from his eyes and he grinned, deep in sleep. A moment to put in the memory banks for posterity, wanting to remember this moment as a happy and loving time. As she floated in between sleep levels, a voice whispered, *"It takes practice in following the path of most light and love, not always a logical choice; it will someday be automatic reflex. Follow the light always, all ways, even when you think it runs contrary to social consciousness. In the beginning, the hardest thing that you can do is to follow what is right in your heart and soul. Your logical mind dictates pursuit of safety and status quo in attempt to keep you safe, hence the urge to conform. For you, this is especially* true when you know that to make a one choice for yourself will hurt others. Remember that they have a choice in how they wish to respond to the changes in life and life's challenges.

There is always a higher order of what is right and what is wrong; that's man's laws and rules for conduct. You cannot be a follower of others paths and evolve. Carve your own path for others to follow in you. You can sense their intent, but cannot always know what the divine plan is for another. You see glimpses, but you do not truly know the whole picture.

The strength of every great master is developing this wisdom, for self and for community. This is how we evolve. Allow those things that no longer serve your higher good to fade away gracefully. It requires great personal responsibility to sift through choices then stand by those decisions and navigate consequences. What is it that you really want Navi? The choice is yours. In time, you will know the divine will is your will, no separation. There are only two things that motivate a choice; love and fear."

At dawn with David sleeping soundly, she slid out of tent and drove home.

Hi Navi:

Alas, this is still very much a mucous Magus. Shortly after you left, I broke into a monstrous sweat, dripping off my forehead and nose and soaking my clothes. I had a hell of a time lighting the fire because every time I bent over to light the paper and kindling, my sweat dripped off my forehead and put out what I'd lit. I gave up trying to light the fire and decided I would go for a walk to the store. I was walking along the campground road and could not but help notice that people walking towards me stepped way off to the side looking at me weird. Of course, I knew I was kind of sweaty and dirty looking so I went to the washroom and had a good look at myself in the mirror there. I think I would have stepped away from myself too. I looked like I had the freaking bubonic plague. I kept on walking to the store, very dreamlike, bought some ruby red grapefruit juice and drank it.

I had a weird feeling that I was hovering in between worlds, could not cross over. Missed you beyond words and worlds and so wanted you to come back, so bad. Gill my surrogate seagull companion, did not come back either. Maybe you did come back, though. A dragonfly paid me a visit. She let me rub her back and wings with my finger before she took off again. Mostly I sat by the fire reading the Peaceful Warrior Woman novel.

I am a peaceful warrior man, breathing properly, tapping into other realms, aligning with physical, mental, emotional and spiritual bodies, what you have been talking about in your spiritual pursuits. So, I read until dark, lit a candle, read until the candle guttered out. I found your other sock and your blanket still there. Sounds weird, but I went to sleep clutching your sock and still had it in my hand in the morning. Kept wishing you were still with me. I really did feel weird spatially. I had a hell of a time sleeping. I was a lot sicker than I thought. I used your camp blanket because it felt like you around me and when I closed my eyes then I would see your face.

I am alone, with the exception of your sock. I am very tired and not feeling too good. I am not sure that I believe in 'them', like you. Do you think less of me? I love you with my being.

Doubting David (the mad Magus who has lost his mojo if he ever had any)

A nothing resolved dilemma and no indication of conversing with his wife. Resolution, bold and succinct was what would ring her yahoo bells. At work, he procrastinated but always managed to pull off brilliance just in time. Always avoided gossip and when in cross fire, would wait until the right moment to have a say and when he did, spoke cuttingly truthful from some place higher that would make Gandhi proud.

Dear Doubtful David;

It does not matter whether you believe in them or not! They believe in you. Seek only the ones that are of light. They never leave you. Simply ask, allow and be aware of their presence.

Navi

Hey Navi

I have been thinking about you and Abby quite a bit lately. Are you Okay? I am fine about everything, so stop worrying.

Am sure you remember that strange light experience that I had pre-op. Well been thinking more and more about that, figured it was a wakeup call to go in that direction. Anyway, I will do summer school, starts on Monday, but I have changed my mind all the way around. I am going to go for my Masters in Divinity, your Aunt Diane has pulled some strings. Guess she used to date the Dean, go figure. Anyway, it is Acadian in Nova Scotia, so I'm going there for the beginning of September. I will not be able to see you both for a while. Oh and Dad is pretty pissed about it but then brags in front of other people. Some things just do not change.

Hey, I am growing my hair out. I figure that by the time I am in school, they will love me so much they will not care about the dread locks and beard that I am going to grow!

Give that Abby monster a big squishy hug, a belly berry and a head noogey for me. Tell her that she is the absolute best little sister that a guy could wish for.

Your favourite stepson Matt

Hi Darling;

I miss you immensely. I am honestly floored with your decision, yet once sinking in a bit, I totally get it and I support your path one 100 gazillion percent. Can't wait to see your new do, so send lots of pictures and write when you can. I am glad, very glad that you are keeping in touch.

Love, hugs and squeezes.

Step Momster xoxoxoxo

Matt and Abby were both Indigo Children; born spiritual warriors who were destined to aid generations to come into the prophesied thousand years of peace. Mature and wise beyond their years, intuitive and innately able to perceive the world from a higher point of view. All Indigos had a wired in, tuned in powerful inner guidance system. Looking at the globe around them and disgusted, they strive to carve out their own paths and way of thinking. There was hope for a very different, evolved global community and unique future.

Abby's natural intuitive abilities were public school academia disapproved. Why was it so difficult for school staff to understand kids and empower them? They were Attention Deficit Hyperactive Disordered problem kids. An Indigo Child's struggle for autonomy apposed conformity thus, were the bane of the education system. Abby's old soul uniqueness and easy-going manner was a constant source of irritation to teachers. A C average kid, she did not feel the same academic pressure, just peaceful and content no matter what.

A natural medicine woman even as a toddler, created her own concoctions. Whenever anyone seemed sad or out of sorts, would just gently put a hand on their shoulder and love them, or share a funny story. Nurturer by nature, often the first to get the medicine box and tend to hurts and bruises.

"Abby, what worries you the most about everything that is going on?"

"Nothing, I know that you love me."

"Of course, Stephen will find someone else somewhere down the road."

"I don't care what he does or doesn't do any more. I have not been there in weeks. He's such an asshole!"

"Ah Abby. Don't be too hard on him. He has never had a budding teen daughter before. You might have to tell him how to be there for you, stand up for yourself and negotiate with him."

"Why do I have to? He doesn't give a shit about me or you."

"You don't have to. Keep in mind that he has had a son with cancer. There is a different kind of love and bond between parents than there is between the majorities of couples. He cannot make sense of it, so he tries to control it and shuts out what he cannot. Use the time to figure out how you would like your own life to be. Wish him all good things.

Sending him anger only keeps you hooked in to that side of him that you don't like, the stuff that doesn't feel so good. We sometimes get angry and scared when we don't understand why a person does what they do or says what they do. Sometimes that anger and frustration that we are feeling about them, is actually what you are sensing or picking up about how they are feeling inside. It is not even yours. There is always a higher view than human thinking.

If you are ever unsure Abby, just stop and ask yourself 'what is the most loving thing I need to know about this person, this situation', then allow your angels to give you insight. Sometimes it takes a while and could be something that you hear on television, see in a movie or read in a book or dream. The Angels have their mysterious ways of getting you the information that you really need.

The biggest trap of all, and this is something that I want you to remember for the rest of your life, there will always be people along the path that for some strange reason, do not like you and take issue with you. You might feel hurt and think that they are right in giving you the message that you are bad. This is wrong. You came from a long line of good women, and before that, you were a spirit floating around the heavens. You came from divine God essence, you are God divine essence and even when you make mistakes or have crappy days, this cannot change. You are God, Goddess in action. This doesn't mean that you now have to be super-duper goodie two shoes or pull miracles out of you knickers, it just means that you are good God Goddess just exactly the way you are.

Do not allow anyone to insinuate, tell you or make you feel otherwise. Your responsibility is to learn how to navigate life your own way, in a good way, following your own heart and soul in balance with the rest of the world and use your gifts only for good."

Head hanging, staring at the floor, daughter mind processing, Navi continued, "Besides, if you think of this stuff with your step dad as practice for when you start dating, you're ahead of the game. And I'd sure feel a lot better about you dating, knowing that you can sort out relationship stuff and hold your own when you need to."

"Did you ever love him?"

"Yes, I think I did, in the very beginning."

"He blew it, didn't he?"

"We both blew it. Some things just became bad habits. I am I telling you this now because you are heading into your own relationship years. I will always be available to you. I carry you and Matt in my heart always in all ways. That's a promise."

Catharine was sitting on the deck when they arrived home. "Where have you been lady?"

"Oh, on the spur of the moment I decided to go to Arizona. Sorry I did not tell you, did not tell anyone, I just went. I went to a casino to set up a healing grid and altar for all of those people who are hopelessly addicted, losing everything they own and families. When these people reach the point when they are reduced soul wrenching asking God for help, Spirit intervenes.

I hiked out into the desert by myself. I spent the entire night standing in a circle of stones, for protection. I just stood there all night. I read somewhere that this was a shaman or medicine woman's initiation, to be completely alone in the wilderness, you know, face and confront your own fears. I've always wanted to do this, and so I woke up a couple of weeks ago thinking about it again, so seized the opportunity."

"God, weren't you scared?"

"Ha, no. Towards dawn, I saw a shooting star. That means that another good soul is being born you know. The colours of the sun coming up over the desert were, magnificent."

A beach afternoon amidst a zoo of vacationers as little indigo medicine woman Abby, bodysurfed shoreline waves in joyful abandon while Catharine prattled about airports and customs officials. Rather than being afraid of Homeland Security, she made new friends, referring to each on a first name basis and parting with invitations on return trip to drop by for dinner and meet the family. Catharine was a 'free spirit', happy and alive. Navi spilled work David happenings.

"Ha, Ha, ha." She stood up stretched and looked Navi squarely in the eyes, "It's about time. You were asleep. Live your life Navi."

Bodysurfing waves with Abby, baking in the sun and eating chocolate, while fresh air and glorious sun permeated their cells. Wading fresh great lake water, holding hands, then catching a good wave, they dove under. Eyes open, breath held, sun streams cascading and illuminating under lake sand, minnows and tiny seaweed tendrils. Mermaid goddesses, as sensuous long hair moved with waves caressing their skin. As heads surfaced, their eyes greeted bright sunlight sparkling on water the surface and bodies bouncing on gentle surface waves. Young woman child mermaid swimming under water, grabbed first at her ankles then pulled down her bathing suit bottom. Little hands in hers, she swung her around and around over the water surface, into squeals of delight. They floated on top of the water, seeing only sky, wide-open sky; hearing nothing of tourists, feeling only the gentle rocking movement of water. Senses danced in celebration, arms raised to bold sun and expansive sky in gratitude, free, alive and happy.

"Guilt is the tension we feel to change
to accommodate to
what someone else wants and expects."
Richard Bach

Chapter 12 ~ Some Vacation!

An alien at work, neutrality and altruism translated as aloofness. Residue guilt at simply being a woman, a mother, a daughter and an ex-wife; a burden carried universally, a generational acquired bugaboo that kept most women in tow, compounded with adultery, made her excessively vulnerable. A logical and unfair attraction target for gossip, guilt and vulnerability attracts attack from those who are weak within. We do not like seeing in others what we do not like what resides within. The rare times when someone approached, was to engage in ally hating of some poor unsuspecting client or co-worker. Sigh in refusing to feed hate and become an ally of destruction, fence sitting was dangerous positioning. Self-preservation and explaining higher view perspectives, were unceremoniously met with sullen faces and deaf ears. Navi acquiesced to allowing the hits, there was nowhere else to go, a sponge rock in a hard place.

Gran's presence felt instantly warm.

"There are times in life when tolerance for a crappy situation continues to exist. It is not because we feel we are deserving, penance, a core lesson that has yet to heal in the higher truth and light of objectivity and spiritual maturity."

Navi contemplated hearing once that masters, mystics and shamans would intentionally seek out adversaries, nemesis and atrocities in order to test their own capabilities. To raise above shoes too small and petty human role limitations is a signpost of a true master.

"Guilt and shame are rotting seeds within that while universally human, are learned behaviours based on what another dictates and expects that run contrary to what our souls long for. There is nowhere else in nature or cosmos where guilt exists. A bird does not shame another, it may alpha dog for feeding position but it does not shame nor does a bird feel guilt. Shaming and using guilt are abusive control mechanisms used over someone perceived by both, as weaker or vulnerable, herding into submission and conformity.

Ah but my little Chickadee, more importantly in your case, it is not so much about guilt attracting attack, you are outgrowing shoes that no longer serve you. New workers will become a different breed. Fear not and take comfort that the way will be shown. Often, situations arise not because there is a thing wrong with you that attract problems, but because you can help in some way or it is there in your face, simply to tell you that that path, that door, is now closing.

So cry if you need to, but do not hide your face in your hands for too long. Listen for spirit whispers of love and know that this life is a gift."

Navi lay out on the deck lounging, reading a bit, soaking up the sun and grateful to be home and not at work. Attention drawn to a neighbour's tree, she suddenly 'saw' it, as if it where human, thoughts and feelings. This was how all the ancient cultures connected with nature; everything had a spirit, a personality, and life. It seemed to be calling.

"Hey, You, psssst"

"Hey you're a tree, talking!"

"No shit!"

"Hmm, a tree with attitude."

"I want to tell you that I was perfectly happy with the original owners of the house. As a seedling and young tree, I loved when the children played around me and the owners put a bird feeder in my branches, the birds would come. I had lots of attention and companionship. Now no one pays any attention to me and I have a growing aversion to the current inhabitants. You not only ignore me, but you do not feed the bird friends and the house exudes unhappiness at times. You can see why I bend so far over toward the house, trying to get your attention. If I could but pick up my roots and run, I surely would. I like you."

"Ah, shucks, thank you."

"Hey, but I'm okay, I'm going to outlive them all, ha."

"So now I am talking to a tree with a sense of humour!"

Old Fart Gangsta retirement neighbourhood members dressed in upscale city clothes and sunscreen took turns with their lawn care using power tools in synchronized cutting grass and lawn vacuuming. Here they were living in the country, manicuring lawns with chemicals, pesticides and fossil fuel guzzling equipment, spending gobs of money and effort, distinctly city people mentality. City people migrated, originally attracted to the beach and surrounding wilderness and took retirement root in the northern areas. Uncomfortable terse glares of disapproval directed at Navi and her dismally unkempt lawn only fuelled her resolve to continue its complete lack of manicuring care.

Dramatic show of casing her cottage, a blatant lack of adhering to community standards, they evening walked with pedigree doggies in tow. Various wild flowers of amazing hues, shapes and fragrances grew amidst dandelions and thistles despite Old Fart Gangsta expectation to conform. Resenting the noise of continual lawn mowing, hedge trimming and lawn vacuuming, there was the added bonus of synchronized doggie walking, gangs. Three times a day, on cue, they gathered and in assigned formation traversed the hood morning, late afternoon and evening. Dawg's unleashed bladder and bowel excursions amplified Navi's clear and utter civil disobedience. Dawg who managed maybe three tiny rabbit sized pellets was used to scooping out his own poop spots in his own territory on the lawn. A leash was for long walks, hiking or city.

Despite her want of a little nature peace, quiet and sunshine on deck or lawn garden, Gangsta activities and noise drove her indoors. A bucket of chocolate ice cream and a large serving spoon soothed her opposing nature soul, settled to check e-mail.

Hey ho Navi Girl.

I really think that this is a good thing for you and Dad both. I am buffering the rest of the family as well. They do not know Dad, as we do.

The university is hotter than the country on days like this; I guess the concrete soaks it up & stores it. We should all have the same schedule as our members of parliament, ha, ha. Here is hot sunny weather deep golden tans & lounging @ the beach during your time off from work.

So anyway I am done all of my treatments, Yahoo! Phantom pains are really pissing me off this week. It feels like my guts are twisted and going right through the bed, sometimes. I stand up in the morning to go to the bathroom, & for a minute, it feels like a big empty hole in my belly. Weird, but they have me on some new meds that seem to be doing the trick! Thank God! The nurses told me about Therapeutic Touch; kind of like that flaky weird Navi shit stuff is everywhere.

HA! I got over $5,000.00 bucks for my birthday. I guess there is some sort of payoff for being a sick kid; of course, it helps a bit if you know how to work it, ha. Uh huh, we will see how far that goes towards Divinity classes. I chuckle. Ah well, it will help me set up my new crib.

The new roommates are going to take me to a pub party this weekend, they say I have to get out and socialize. So much for being laid, guess with my new path that might have to wait awhile, okay, a long time.

Anyway, tell Abby I said Hi, aggravate her in some way, and tell her it is from me.

From the stupendously and stunningly handsome teenager known as Matt"

My Dearest Matt;

It is great to hear from you again so soon! Absolutely, I think you will find that alternative healing stuff fascinating and wonderful, enjoy!

I am so unbelievably proud of whom you are and what you have single handily graced yourself through! You are without a doubt, truly awesome! Knock their socks off kiddo!

I knew you were on your way, I said that you have special mojo, but you have surpassed my visions and prayers of beating it! Wow!

Take it easy on the partying, pace yourself; you still have a lot of drug residue in your body. That is my mom thing for today. I do sure miss you.

Love from your favourite Navi person who loves you immensely! Xoxoxo"

David

I am going to put out a petition that sets up a bylaw stating that everyone must cut his or her grass etc., only on certain days of the year. Yes, synchronized lawn cutting, an annual event, it will be beautiful, akin to water ballet, master piece theatre, a symphonic harmonic convergent epic musical and object de art! Power tools substituted with goats, inappropriate attire only, and fresh farm manure in lieu of toxic chemicals.

I am that hippie chick nature loving anarchist neighbour who defiantly allows tiny sandy grass bits and tiny wild flowers to nourish. Had Gangstas seen the vast glorious array of corral like fungus growing behind the toilet in my last home, they would hold me in war crimes court.

No, I do not trim hedges and I do not walk Dawg in the evening. Dawg is used to seeing only cows and small wildlife, unaccustomed he is, to taunting Gangstas. I boldly encourage the canine lad, I tell him often; Dawg, you are the MAN! Assertively protecting your human girls and in gratitude we honour and applaud. We do feel so much safer with you around, even when you cower between our legs! Dawg complains that he might be ferocious if testicles were still intact, oh so much more powerful.

Do vasectomized men feel this as well? I am not sure that women feel any less powerful without child creating organs. Post child-rearing women of course and menopausal women whose body chemicals rage in transition do.

I resort to deck lounging, beaching or Old Fart Gangsta watching. No one else seems to have campfires here in their yards, what is that all about? Are they too messy, or too dirty?

Navi of beach hood, is dreading Office Bitches Den of unrequited joys.

A flashy top of the line brand new beige minivan gingerly pulled into the driveway. Abby emerged home from a camping trip early, her backpack half-slung over one shoulder. Friend's little brother, in the hospital, laced with poison ivy from head to toe. They snuggled and wrestled.

"Hey Mom, guess what?"

"What?"

"I swam with a water snake, ate roasted marshmallows and a lot of hot dogs."

"Snakes? Ewwww but Cool. You ate a hot dog?"

"Yes, veggie dogs. Not bad with lemon juice squeezed on them."

"YUK!

"I love you mom. You are not a neat freak. Mom? Why do grownups always think that kids like hot dogs? I like veggie hot dogs, just not the regular kind and not all of the time."

"Don't know lovey. I am glad you are home. I missed you. Dawg missed you. Ugly Kat missed you."

Navi grabbed a box of Fruit Loops, a blanket and made a small campfire. Primate mother and child curled fetal snuggled together on lounge chair, starry night sky gazing.

"What is your home planet like? How it is different from earth Abby?"

"The people there all get along and they like it so much better there, than here. And my home planet banned hot dogs, because it makes kids puke."

Hi Navi;

think i'll dispense with capitals, a little easier. old farts are bad enough in ones let alone droves of them. i shall sic david suzuki on them, in your behalf. of course, must video said synchronized lawn care event. thou hath instigated a wave of new thought; thou shall proclaim a national holiday for subsequent events in thy honour. i am missing you greatly i do i do i do wish i could be there with you.

David

David Magus;

Abby's Dad had taken her to a Football game and bought a small teddy bear team mascot. Dawg is smitten. Thunder struck head over heels in love, is shamelessly humping it. In fact, he is doing this now, while I write, sigh. Ambiance, eh? Impresses guests too! Hey, I want my tent back.

Chow for now Mermaid of the beach

Hey, mermaid non grass and weed cutting anarchist;
I close my eyes and paint a mermaid drifting in the sea.
Your one and only magus

Sleep stunned and spastically stumbling out into the living room, Navi eyed Abby, whom had obviously long been watching cartoons amidst a pile of blankets, pillows and blankets, cereal, crackers, cookies, juice boxes, peanut butter, an apple and a loaf of bread all splayed smorgasbord around her. Tired, cranky and unable to deal with girl's private party mess, she nuked a cup of last night's coffee and went out to the deck donning grizzly bear slippers and old purple robe to cigarette smoke signal powers above, into a manifesting jovial mood.

"Ah Crap!" An SUV pulled into the driveway. "Mother."

It had been ages since she had visited let alone a full conversation. Mother hugged gingerly scanning first Navi then living room. "Well, I've never seen you like this before!"

Abby promptly took to the table; kid radar zooming in on eating homemade grandma pie. Abby stoically arched her back in strong, grown up impatience and in divine innocence, calmly and playfully muttered, "Oh Grandma, get over it, we have."

Shocked gasp, "tisk", she continued, heated, "Oh for God's sake, I see that the apple doesn't fall too far from the tree! And you," pointing to Navi, "You're just like your grandmother!" Intended as an insult, Navi grinned from ear to ear, relishing the glorious notion. "Really Mother? How so?"

"Well! You're just like her, an embarrassment to the church. When she began menopause she was no longer respectable. Those dam hot flashes turned her into a blatant shameless Seer."

"Oh really? I don't recall anyone ever having a difficulty with her. Seems to me, she was more of a community leader than any Ministers or Pastors we've had. What are you talking about?" Navi had flipped into counsellor mode, enjoying the switch in relationship, an upper hand as Mother verged on the edge of spilling more matriarchal truths.

"Well that's my point!"

"Eh? Spill Mother."

Abby's body language poised with gripping curiosity, she dared not make a move, so as not to be sent to her bedroom and out of earshot.

"It's true what everyone hints at, your grandmother talked to spirits, animals and plants. Everyone knew that she was a seer; no one dared say anything 'cause they knew that at some point, they'd all either been to her for help or would at some point. She did not give a dam what anyone thought about it, but was sly about how she gave messages, so as the elders and Ministers could not nail her on a damn thing. I used to be so damn embarrassed about her when I was growing up. Why could she not just be normal like everyone else? People were always calling on her at ungodly hours."

Navi and Abby were coming into calm alignment with an aspect of who they really were. It was genetic and not a mutation nor of demonic possession or mental illness. "How come you never told me any of this before?"

"Someone had to protect you from the world. I shut mine down when I was a girl, so that I could have a normal life. Like your Aunt Diane did. I don't think any of your brothers had it, a problem with the girls in this family."

"Oh, I see Mother! Did Dad know?"

"No. I certainly never dared share this, although I have often thought he had inklings. If he did, he was kind enough not to mention it."

"Have you had a happy life?"

"Enough said. Protect your daughter."

Evening glorious sunshine streamed through trees as distant waves, while masses of beach partiers car stereo blasted different tunes, simultaneously. Figures, given that Old Fart Gangstas have unofficially declared a day of rest. David arrived bearing schmoosing bribery gifts of iced cafe grande' mochas with whipped cream, sprinkles and flowers. Off balance with uninvited boundary crossing from a still married man, she cautiously invited him as far as the deck lounge chair.

"Ah, Hi David. Abby, this is David, you remember, my friend from work?"

"Yep" Sizing him up and over, she took his hand and led him into the sanctity her bedroom hovel cave, catching Navi even more off guard. Abby never allowed anyone into her room.

Single mother, uncomfortable and burning confusion of wanting to protect daughter from unrealized relationship unannounced drop by visit and camaraderie, wolf rose and graciously cued his leave.

Hi Navi;

Sorry about dropping by earlier without calling, I sensed your discomfort with Abby and I. Did you forget? Friends? However, if you do not want me there with her, let me know, I can respect that. Hey, she is a neat kid, although somewhat messy.

I just want to paint again, I long to paint.

Worked all day getting house ready for real estate appraisal re: separation process. She who once loved me without end now looks at my handiwork and notes that my work is off by 1/8"- AAARRRGGGHHHH! This house is old, crooked, fucked. Yours truly no longer gives a shit. I will just let her keep the fucking house rather than try to sell it off.

But dragonfly mermaid, my dear, the Magus just cannot handle this shit much longer. Interesting, I realize that I do not like who I have been all of these years when with her. I guess the past 26 years were always off by about a 1/8th of an inch. No wonder it does not bear the stress. Sorry for the diatribe

Disenfranchised in Hooterville—Magus

Navi did not respond. Was David looking for some kind of validation? Sharing the processing of his marriage with her felt wrong, it was none of her business. She curled up in bed, reading herself to sleep. The phone rang, startling her out of peaceful mind space. David. Soused and slurring, she listened without saying a word, wondering where it was going.

"Navi? I needed to hear your voice, delightfully sleepy as it is. You had told me once that I have control over where I go, both in this and other worlds. Learning and growing can be painful. I know that I have life decisions to make, with every fiber of this humble being of mine. Darling I want to, yearn to grow spiritually. I want to share myself with you, heart, mind, body and spirit. Someday we will go, you and I, to the land of the Hopi. Ah, a silent Navi. You are Always in my thoughts. Good night."

Speechless, she hung up. David had been drinking, so she disregarded it all. She did not want to be the reason for issues in their home.

Early the next morning at his insistence, she broke down and met for coffee, him begging, distraught and verging on tears.

"David, when are you going to talk to her, I mean really talk to her? Tell her what you need to, from your heart. Talk to her as you talk to me. Allow her opportunity to hear and see how it is for you, how it is for her. If you love her as much as you have always said that you did, then she deserves to know your heart. It's up to her to decide if she wants to carve out a new path with you."

"Where do I begin? How do I say what I want, what I need, without hurting her or getting into the same old unresolved issues?"

"I know this first hand. We all want to be loved just as we are. Sometimes the loneliest place to be is in a house with people who do not really know you, do not get you, or don't like you. Life is a Shakespearean stage play, where cast members have been thrown all together to play peculiar roles, except no one really knows that it's not real, that it's just a play. Nor do they know ahead of time what the plot is or where the story is going to go. At some point, the roles become wearily tiring and you want to stop, re-do or change the entire script, except it seems as though no one will let you. Those roles are set in years of ritual, habit, familiarity and social expectation.

If you attempt to make a change for yourself within or without, others yank your chains so hard that you run like hell, or they yank you back into line, into status quo. They know your vulnerabilities and hot buttons. They use all the cons; plant seeds of doubt into you because they are scared of you wising up to their insecurities and leaving. Oh and of course the cons that yank your chains are super nice rah rah rah, tally ho. Most of us launch pad in via our physical mother's womb, dumb as stumps and then spend the rest of our lives in religious, cultural or family doctrines of thou shall and shalt not moral codes. There are hidden agendas and unwritten rules embedded in the role, subtly developed over years. You have a part to play and you must play and damn it, smile whilst doing it. Be that: the picture perfect home and family, which has the stamp of approval from church, family and society. For gad's sake, hide your dysfunctions.

With a little awareness and strength, you begin to awaken to your own authentic and natural way of being and growing. As you do so, it becomes simply too painful not to start picking and pulling away the weeds, the things that no longer grow corn for you. It all takes phenomenal courage and tenacity at first, but ever so slowly you grow into knowing that it cannot be any other way, so thus becomes your natural state of being and growing.

Oh and be forewarned, guaranteed, they will test and you will test, life will test your resolve to re-discover your true self. Then somewhere, sometime, another crossroad appears; you will submit yourself to status quo, or you will find inner strength to carry on with a new and different life, with or without them and their stamp of approval and support.

Shit, I am no expert, far from it, still navigating my own shitty shadows. That is just what came to me, through me. I suppose that little lecture was meant for both of us."

"Sometimes you think and talk way above my head Navi. I will think on it."

"My weird and wonderful friend Gary left a miserable marriage and moved far into the northern tundra, seeking a quest and journey of the great unknown. A natural psychic yearning synonymous, he was a shaman. For years, with church condemnation in mind, I shamefully avoided him. Now I'm delighted to find that that friendship door is still open. Once in a while I get to hear from him and hear all about his wild journeys."

Reserve counsellor role suited Gary's natural affinity of indigenous culture. The reserve was still reeling to find emotional, spiritual and economic stability following generations of government, religious and sexual abuse at the hands of Catholic and Protestant missionaries and other white intervention intruders. Much healing unfolded despite continued welding of authority and intervention, sadly, missing the whole picture mark. It was common for reserve folks to get so web tangled in red tape, lifetimes wasted with filling out more forms simply waiting for permission to possess or build their own home. The process would not exist in a white community. While government preached propaganda through media of valiantly settling old land claims and treaties, providing bail out cash to hard hit communities, it was a strangle hold spiders web of government bureaucracy. A gift of empowerment and autonomy could go a long way to rebuilding a community harvesting its own innate skills, abilities and resources into a strong and healthy autonomous viable economic unique entity.

Now in mid-forties he was pursuing Chaplain-ship as well as Shaman apprenticing. Always learning, exploring new ideas and taking courses, he had studied the healing arts, mysticism and Celtic Shamanism, hot on the trail, hungry to learn and grow.

There was a tiny beacon of light on the horizon, of a different life and different world. Inner vision and physical eyes were beginning to see the world as rapidly changing. It was left over from the hippie revolution, its peoples becoming more independent in thought and action. Gary and Catharine's walk outside of normal traditions was now inspired. Both Catharine and Gary exuded an inner light and happiness that socially did not reflect their personal adversities. He had the courage to follow his own path and in making his way even further into Nunavut, taking a step further, a new chapter, a mission calling to work with Inuit. Catharine seemed oblivious to what other people thought of her lifestyle and travels.

Their example offered hope and inspiration, of the stepping out of norms and of following their own curiosity rather than traditional status quo.

Mother's email had been a wakeup call that haunted thoughts throughout the day. Imagining what it would be like at the spiritual school and what it might feel like to be ordained, a Rubik's cube shifting and sliding into new alignments, ponderings were slowly giving way to change. When she tried the minister's role on, in her mind and body, bursts of laughter in the absurdity of the concept opposed who she had always known herself to be within the world. Yet the light beacon called her forward. Navi flipped through the web site again then emailed a registration package request.

Dawg and Kat wrestled incessantly, interrupting train of thought, "Has no one ever told you two that you are not supposed to get along this well?" As soon as animals settled, the phone rang and in hearing David's voice, left it to the answering machine.

"Navi? Navi? Damn you are not home. Where are you Navi? Think I will keep it simple. Love you darling. Hey, thinking of you at your beach sanctuary and the endless rolling of waves over sandy beaches. Let the soothing white noise and motion heal you. Catch you later. Oh by the way, it's David."

No sooner had Navi finished filling out forms online, a persistent David dropped by with takeout coffee and a humble demeanour. Navi cautiously acquiesced. Looking directly in her eyes, taking her hand in his and without hesitation in front of Abby blithered, "Navi, this is the summer romance I never had, but always dreamed of. I never thought it would happen. Too bad it's taboo!"

Navi burned brilliant shades of red glancing at a grinning Abby. Livid and delighted, uncomfortable and unaccustomed with such niceties, his words fell and hung mid-air. Neither was eligible. Seeing her discomfort, he picked her up and swung her around and around. Abby giggled. She pushed him away and busied herself at the kitchen sink. David picked up Abby and swung her and then carried her under one arm as if she were merely a bag of potatoes, her heartily laughing and squirming.

Navi kept her detachment, just a family friend as they sat on the deck amidst swirling dancing dragonflies that fluttered and hovered before one landed on her nose. She crossed her eyes in an effort to view it up so close.

"Mom, what does dragonfly mean?"

"Hmm, well the dragonfly is about illusions. When you forfeit who you are or what you think inside of you is right, because someone else says otherwise then you give away your power. Dragonfly reminds us to see through the illusions that other people present and keep your own power. When Dragonfly comes to you it means that they will guide you if you are willing."

"That's cool. I love dragonflies. They're magical."

"Yes, they are at that."

She looked at David to read his reaction of her indigenous spirit nature exposure. Smiling, as he picked up Dawg and held him in front of Abby as though he were a puppet.

"Abby and Navi, I have retained David here as my legal counsel and representation. The matter at hand, and of serious nature, is that I require a daily serving of gravy on my kibble. Also of paramount concern to me at this time, is the fact that you have been neglecting to purchase the good stuff. We shall not have any more of the no name brand crap. You, masters of mine, the stuff clogs up my bowels, leaving me unsatisfied in flavour as well as enjoyable bowel movements. So starting tomorrow, you shall comply, or I shall be seeking the aid of Ugly Kat here, and we will have no other option than to file a class action suit against the both of you."

Abby rolled in fits of laughter. Navi looked at Dawg, pondering canine demands.

"And what, Mr. Dawg, have you been doing, are you doing, to contribute to the general wellbeing of this household that entitles you to first make demands of any kind and second to expect daily gravy compliance?"

David turned Dawg around in hands, looked deeply in his eyes, "Dawg I think you're busted. Cannot argue that."

Dawg replied, "David, you're fired!"

"Mom, I like David. He's funny."

"Yes well, don't get your knickers too excited. He's probably not like that all the time."

"I am so!" noticing Navi's glance that bellowed bullshit "Well, I'd like to be."

She went to the deck to have a smoke before bed. It annoyed her that Abby liked him, yet delighted her, which was alarming. There would be that inevitable getting hurt part that was coming, and coming soon. She butted out her smoke and stood looking hard at old purple robe as though for the first time. It was part of an old life, a different chapter and no longer wanted. Grizzly bear slippers would have to go too, eyeing ensemble over; bottoms worn thin and they no longer kept feet warm. She got out a garbage bag from the kitchen and tossed them in. She put on a camisole and undies, free and mildly sensuous.

Navi;

Impression of the day:

Today, I stole a piece of melon from heaven. In my mouth, it was cold clean and green. I do not believe the angels minded. I received pillars of wisdom from a friend, about dragonflies. Sadly, I left the gist of it behind. I left the dragonfly behind.

Yet even still, I smell the evening air and it smells fresh, alive, like my friend. I shared cherries with an angel. I watched Dragonflies dance. I sat on the deck like a lifelong friend talking of wind and spirits. I shared an embrace. I see her toes touch the earth, while she climbs the backs of the seven dragons to heaven. I would see through her eyes if I could. Thinking her thoughts with her and knowing her knowledge. Feel her sensations knock at the doors of the world. Eat again heaven's melons and not offend the angels.

So, Navi, my thoughts as always be with thee, I'm not so sure it is a good thing right now that I visit often when Abby is home, only because I fear it disturbs you. Old David could be wrong, I often am, but the last thing I would want to do is cause you or yours any needless discomfort.

Yes, the young one 'sees', how she interprets I know not, but you are so right when you say that she sees. You are a lovely mom. I maintain thou art a woman of great gifts, how I wish you could see them yourself.

With you as always - David

David did not belong to her. As magical as life seemed when with him, some inner dark shadow haunted, elusive beyond anxiety of church condemnation of her mystical nature and failed relationships with Stephen and Abby`s father.

In the moment, she strived to recall life with T.J., Abby's father and could not, save for a vague image and heart pounding departure, differing lifestyles. There had been no abuse, no argument. He strived to live the great materialistic American dream, while her nature ran quiet and mystical. It had been a teenage romance and despite their many young years together, Navi, for the life of her could not recall more. No magical mature objective insight surfaced to illuminate why exactly it was that she was serial relationship handicapped. An emotional psychic block that surmised and validated that there was, had always been something inherently wrong with her, born with the curse of spirit world visioning and communing. Vacillating between longings for more of it fed inability to balance both worlds.

Abby who had run from her own bedroom and landed on Navi's back, a gripping primate, dropped to the floor rolling and wrestling with animated karate moves.

"I must say that children benefit from random body slamming. AAIIIAAAYYEEEE!"

Abby, squealing and giggling added, "Hey mom, we're kind of like Calvin and Hobbes."

"Yes, except better, because you got to catch a kid when they least expect it and give their belly's a good raspberry blow. . . blllliiiirrtttt. EWE Abby! Your belly needs to go to the bathroom! That is it; show the kid who is boss, I say, master of the house. If only you could show some kind of fear and not giggle so. Why are you not in bed, young munchkin?"

"I'm thirsty."

"Well then, get yee butt into thine kitchen for a drinketh. And make surest that thousest pees before thy crawlest backeth into thy bed chamber young maiden."

Navi let the phone call go onto the answering machine, audio on and loud enough for both to hear David's voice.

"Dragonfly lady- where art thou?"

Gals looked at each other and grinned, still entangled in a knot of bodies.

"Old Magus is feeling somehow out of touch. Is dragonfly truly only illusion? Nah, says the wise and sagely Magus."

They looked at each other and giggled. David continued, assuming privacy with the answering machine.

"Poor sod, Magus, so self-absorbed, for the true dragonfly is in the bath, cursing the Magus, for in his knowing mind's eye he sees the youthful dragonfly naked and wet. The Magus slaps himself silly for feeling mortal thoughts, for surely the Magus has not had such stirrings in years and how sinful it is to envision the demure dragonfly gleaming with beads of water coursing down her torso. Magus is getting himself hot. Call or write the Magus before he descends fully into madness. Oops, too late."

As the answering machine clicked off, Abby resumed her attack on Navi, intent on returning vengeful belly berries. She did not call or email David. The more they attached to David, the harder it would be to let him go when the time came.

"Abby, why can't I find underwear that fit? It is not that I am large or grotesquely disfigured?"

"Well Mom, you're not grotesque, you're more like a dwarf."

"Oh you little rat! Let's go shop the beach tomorrow for new beach toys, jump trampolines and body surf some beach waves."

"Hi Gran, I feel you there. Hey, I got my first course in the mail today. Remind me why. I do not have any affinity for organized religion and I have an aversion to orthodoxy. I am not much of a joiner; groups end up politicizing everything to death. They become cliquey and go off side tracking, making up more rules rather than living, exploring as individuals, changing, growing as a group, as the individuals grow. Having a place to go to, to be one with God, Creator, Universal Forces and rituals steeped in tradition have been good and stabilizing for mankind. Every human war had to do with differing interpretations of belief systems in certain governments, states or economic powers. It is too bad that the philosophies the great masters tried to teach of love and brother hood have and continue to be lost on us.

"They say that when people sincerely wish for help, it will be there. It comes appropriate to their own unique need, not necessarily, what they want, or to someone else's ideals. A person attracts help in a way that reflects their soul's desires and for the highest good of their evolution."

"I prefer my temple to be nature, a glorious bath tub soak, sunshine, sunsets, gardens, snuggling and loving my loved ones and such. It seems as though the more I learn and read and go through, the less I know."

Mother and daughter lay curled up on Abby's bed with Dawg and Ugly Kat, reading the 'The Call of the Wild' novel. Later, just dozing off to sleep, a THUMP on the roof brought her instantly to her feet, heart pounding. Out cautiously onto the deck, afraid that an animal was going to jump down on her at any moment, she heard a loud and shrieking "Aaauuuuooooh". She jumped back, heart pounded eyes strained adjusted to the dark of night to make out the form of a small person then recognized the red sock on one foot and black sock on the other.

"Abby! What in the hell are you doing up there?"

"Oh, hi Mom. I am Buck, you know, the dog gone wolf wild from the Call of the Wild book you read me. I'm a she wolf dog calling for my mates."

"Oh God! Get down here and into bed, you little beggar!"

Abby tucked in, Navi slipped into a soothing dream: *The magical ancient healing grotto, salt buoyant Navi floated naked, arms outstretched, breath echoed back from stone, a hidden sacred space. Gentle waves bounced water, long hair caressed skin. Sisterhood women came during Moon time cycles, taking turns, alone and in oneness divine, emerging anew.*

"Confusion heard his voice, and wild uproar stood ruled,
stood vast infinite confined;
till at his second bidding darkness fled,
light shone, and order from disorder sprung."
John Milton

Chapter 13 ~ Storm waters brew

Turning off the dirt pot ridden road and in through a cedar rail gate, mother and daughter ventured into summer camp at the stable. Abby strained over the dashboard taking in a chaotic view of the farm, as annoyed chickens flapped wings, vying for road occupation. A goat trotted along the passenger side, splattering a litter of kittens. Old black lab lifted an eyebrow, holding sunspot basks resting in a warm grassy place. Boss, business owner, cowgirl woman and former youth worker stood waving a warm welcome from the old farmhouse porch.

A side turn into the parking area, she navigated, inching and looking for a spot amidst motley dogs, cats, horses, chickens and a big grey pig roaming around her car. The only parking spot semi-available, was old brown quarter horse occupied, which casually stood ground swish-tail eyeing her. Hesitating and instantly annoyed, Navi waited for it to wander off. Abby poked her head out of the window and clicked her tongue. The old horse twitched and perked ears, whinnied, bounced his head then toddled off making way.

"Ha, that's how that is done Mom."

"How did you know to do that?"

"Ha. Just did, Mom."

Four mutts of varying breeds and sizes surrounded Abby, jumping, rubbing legs, squirming for position and greeting, seeking attention. 'The child is an animal magnet.' The woman had a pile of kids of her own that intermingled with those signed up for camp, trailing off with towels in hand and assorted beach toys to an in ground pool in the back yard. A happy, calm good feeling atmosphere was miracle relief, knowing that her daughter is in good caring hands.

The quiet office sanctuary, she dug in, sorting and prioritizing files and messages piled on her desk, beckoning. She pushed papers aside glancing in distaste, as the pettiness registered. A pang of subordinate rebellion crawled up her spine. A co-worker had seized Navi's vacation time to devise a multitude of make work projects. Now Navi was pissed and flat-out work weary tired. Spinning her chair around childlike in petulant circles, slamming to an embarrassed stop, upon seeing that Old Betty had trundled into her office and sat down.

"Uh, Hi Betty. What's up?"

Old Betty, catching Navi's childish moment, grinned in approval. The native elder smelled of wood smoke and herbs. Wild shoulder length black hair held one tiny braid with a grouse feather attached to a sinew tie. A poster model for all things native woman, save for the purple Hawaiian printed skirt over top of bright white running shoes and red sports socks. Old Betty had been her first client, an instant bond upon sizing each other up, of mutual respect and intuitive knowing. Nomadic Betty knew no borders or pegged category. She freely went where, when and with whom Creator and Ancestors directed. On government paper, she resided on a First Nation's Reserve, yet like many of the old rural folk would go on the welfare system just long enough to cover what emergency money they needed to keep going.

Betty, hardly employable by traditional white standards, was yet respected. Never a thought for personal gain, she constantly took in lost troubled youth, much to her own detriment. She and her brood had recently lost their house at the hands of one troubled Alcohol Syndrome fifteen-year-old boy, the fire trap house burnt to the ground. His new marijuana bong design experiment had gone terribly wrong.

Always in a state of calm grace, no matter what bizarre drama and events were taking place. She was, in Navi's eyes an amazing example of divine grace, all wrapped up in an old native woman's crooked old body. A by-product of Catholic institutional boarding school hell, she left the safety of mother's bosom at the tender age of four to assimilate into unimaginable abuse. Yet through it all, she managed to embody the state of non-attachment, grace and forgiveness. As an elder, occasionally came to the office under the guise of free coffee and chats, yet seeking side assistance for one of her troubled brood. Her power and wisdom noticed, respected and consulted on all matters reserve by Band members, community and extending far beyond south of the border by those who had the eyes to 'see' her.

"Oh, okay Navi, I see dat yer busy ta day." It was an obvious contrary observation made with a straight face delivered with humour that Navi understood immediately and laughed.

"Ah not so much Betty. Help yourself to a coffee and have a seat. It's good to see you."

"Ah ya, tink I will. Jis wonderin if I could get some money to fix my car for Tuesday. Gotta take young Jessica n' her baby to Toronto fur a custody and access hearin'."

"Ah Betty. You are not on our system right now, you would have to re-apply first with one of our workers, go through the process. Could take a week, then I would have to find some loophole to get it covered. I cannot even pretend that it is for job search. With this stupid new computer system, there is no getting around it. I'll give Mary a call at the Sally Ann, she'll find you some travel money and anything else you need."

It was an odd play, this go around thing with Native folks when they already knew how the off reserve system worked. They knew how to access money for the things they needed through the system at the reserve band office, unless they were currently on the reserve 'shit' list for whatever stupid reason that comes from living in a small cloistered community. Assuming it was one of those times, likely Jessica was on the shit list too.

Old Betty, nodded in agreement, both smiled in mutual knowing, both master's at advocating for others and finding ways to get things done. Quietly reflective, both noting that neither rarely did this magical resourcing for self, it was always to help some poor sod out of a jam. Both, selflessly accepting whatever came.

This play blatantly demonstrated how useless the system had actually become in meeting day-to-day needs of the people it should be serving. Navi had observed a different kind of role-play with the city front lines in the social support systems. Too many ignorant well-intentioned white people, educated from a different world and culture, just never understood it. A sad knowing that the pendulum of helping people had already shifted in opposition. It was an altruistic wakeup call, this would be the last time she would see Old Betty from behind the government desk.

"Ah, yes. Just thought things might have changed ere. No eh?"

"No, all legislation now. I'm afraid it will be this way for a long time my friend."

"Ah well den, I guess I jus sit ere n wait fur da bus den."

"Sure. Where are you going?"

"Ah. Me and da girls are goin to da Casino. Dem promo companies give ya a free bus ride, dere n back agin, a free pass, tirty dollars worth in casino chips, an all ya kin eat buffet vouchure n a free pass fur da nightly entertainment. Ta night is da Elvis impersonators. So we go once a month, get outta town on a bus ride, see da country, eat and see some celebrities do dere stuff, cash in da casino chips fur cash n come ome wit tirty dollars in r pockets. Bedder n bingo."

Navi laughed, "Ahhh, good on you. Have a blast."

After she prioritized her work, she returned a pile of make work projects to her co-workers desk, turned her computer over to e-mail.

Navi Darling;

I fear that it will remain difficult for some time to come. I guess it was not as over as I thought it was. Talking about it and actually doing it can be two different things. Confusing, she had brought up separation a lot over the years and now that it is here on the table, it is wild madness. There is little difference between a significant death and a family breakdown, there is grieving. She wants me to stay. The spirits guides are silent.

Would love a hug with thee.

David

Dear David;

Take good care of her David, walk in grace.

Navi

David door closed, she sought solace by diving into a dismal sandy garden. Navi called in sick. Gutless immature and childish perhaps, yet it was simply delicious. Soul soothing sun shining outdoors with hands in garden dirt massaging earth mother, warm wind caressing her hair, sun kisses upon her skin as a robin family flittered and chirping amongst evergreens. A sole mission to take on reluctant garden spirits and bring it to life, she needed a garden fix, ambiance, and a connection to the world of things natural and spiritual. Puttering in sandy soil, planting flowers with compost and water soaking, Abby followed behind prattling about her day. Names of all the summer camp animals and children recited, chores, duties and first riding lesson explained followed by her tale of afternoon swimming. Abby was indeed in good hands at camp and Navi's body relaxed for the first time that day, good to have her hands and fingers in the sandy soil, warm evening breezes through hair and skin.

'Why is it that the phone always seems to ring when I'm indisposed?' Toenail polish splayed, stumbling on heels, she aimed for the ringing phone down the hall. Home phone blurted a happy sales pitch into annoyed ears. Worse than a computer generated auto voice, a chirpy telemarketer read from script, a horsefly like plague. Abby bolted through the front door, panting from a cycling swimming trip, just in time to head her mother off at the pass and answer the phone. Abby grinned from ear to ear, and listened. A Cheshire grin crept over her face, body contortioned, in developmentally handicapped pretension.

"Hi. Do you like pizza?"

Navi broke into hysterics, sidling up close, ear listening close to phone. The woman repeated her marketing pitch speech.

"I want to know, do you like pizza?"

"What? Is your mother home?"

"Aw, you married? Would you take me out for ice cream?"

"What? Is there a grown up at home?"

"Do you have big boobies?"

"Mom! She hung up!" They fell onto the floor rolling in hysterics.

Navi declared war! Beach sand carried in wind, covered floors like icing sugar. On and in everything including the sofa, it fine sandpaper ground into sensitive skin. Sand was embedded in nostrils. When she breathed, her nose wheezed. It embedded itself into scalps, in between toes and unsuspecting buttocks. She tersely swept sand muttering obscenities in analogy of office work revulsion. An inner battle of donning and keeping up a brave face while stomach churned and bowels howled for intervention. She knew not what other option to follow. Sliding into the office parking lot, the other women's cars were already there. A stray cat sat by the back door staff entrance. At closer look, a skunk stood nibbling pavement titbits. It did not look like it was going to leave any time soon, so she turned the car off, lit a smoke, and sipped coffee. Slowly munching on an old apple core, it spoke softly and gently.

"Two legged woman, you need to connect with and spend more time with those who are of like kind, like scent, like mind. When you do not, the scent or mind and nature of others that are not akin to you, they actually repel against you. Take heed of those that you are currently attracting and what kind of medicine they are bringing." Skunk hesitated, acknowledged her presence then ambled away.

Office prattle abruptly silenced as she strode inside, trying to ignore the obvious silence and lack of 'good mornings'.

"Good morning folks."

"Good morning", someone inaudibly grumble replied.

Little yellow sticky notes concerning clients and files, filled open spaces on her desk. Ignoring, she flipped computer on, scanning priority file updates and critical legislation changes then sighed and went to personal email. Elated, the first one was from the Gary traveler man.

Dear Navi;

You came to me last night in a vision. I was sitting out on the tundra, watching the northern lights dance, when I saw you.

The facts of your life right now are thus: Only time is capable of understanding how great Love is. People love you so much they would die for you. The only reason anyone hates you or thinks they hate you, is because they want to be like you. A smile from you brings happiness to others, even if they do not like you. Every night, SOMEONE thinks about you before sleep. You mean the world to your friends and family, even if they do not tell you. Without you, your friends would not be truly living. You are truly special and unique, in your own way. Forget about rude remarks and try to remember only compliments. Continue to believe in yourself and you will receive more than you thought was possible.

I saw you last night, so sad at work and kind of had a feeling that you needed to hear this today! Just be grateful for the reminders you get from the spirit realm and feel confident that all IS well. Just hang in there while spirit does the work. Spirit will look after you and show you the power of that faith. Navi, talk to your guides and do not be afraid.

Hey, guess what, while I am writing this, I am actually en-route to Igloolik, via the Hydro boys who are allowing me to use their laptop, cool eh? We have kids very sick from sniffing petro fuel. The bears are sick from eating oil out of open drums and spills. I will see what I can do for them. I feel as though someone is going to be on my path up there, specifically, that I am to help in some way. Well, will see what happens. Fear and doubt are ever so close to me also! Hint, hint!

I know it is all there and I am sending love ahead of me. This human 'doing' stuff really challenges the energy of being! Hey, if you do not hear from me for a while, it's because my path has been re-directed further north or there is no available Internet. Must go for now. Stay in the light! By the way, I sense that Matt is doing wonderfully. I am glad that you are in his life!

P.S. Hey, what can I say, it is a long drive, time on my hands. Thinking about you, spirit just will not let go. I forgot to tell you that I hooked up with your friend, River in Wawa a few weeks ago, and didntcha know that would happen! She was doing some kind of elder speech with the Ministry of Culture, the dumb twits. I do not know how she has the patience for the anal assholes! We spoke today and have made a plan to get together for coffee. She is flying in to help the elders here, lead a community healing ceremony, probably a sweat lodge. Hey, I can relate to processing! These people are taking me on the milk run; I am on a grand tour. Each moment is part of my letting go to go.

I started with three duffle bags, down to two and will probably let go of a bit more that is the past before I get on the plane. I am feeling an inner peace that has a quality I have not experienced before! Some reporter from a magazine in the states wants to do a story on me and he pays cash up front. This sure is interesting. I am in it for the WHOLE enchilada and it feels great! I will write you, when spirit allows. Enjoy this day my friend!

In Love and Light ----- Gary

"Hey, Gran, I can feel you. How does this abundance attraction thing work? How do, how come, I find myself in an office where I'm not welcome, with no other prospects?"

"Well Chickadee, people consistently accept second or third best, they are programming poverty and lack mentality. You can choose to believe that no matter what, you are a part of the divine, a part of the universe and as such, are a magnet to divine abundance. More importantly, those in service go where they are directed and when."

"Hmm, I'll have to think about that."

Dawg waited sprawled on the couch, glaring as she entered the house. Scanning the entryway then beyond, a trail of kitty litter on the floor led into the hallway then into her bedroom. From bedroom to closet were Kat turds mingled with kitty litter, shredded tissue and partially chewed underwear. Muttering away at Dawg she folded up the floor mat and dumped the spoils into the wastebasket. Passing the bathroom door her eyes caught mounds of shredded toilet paper heaped inside, outside of the toilet bowl and piled on the floor. By the bathtub lay four pair of underwear, each with the crotch shredded out. Gritting irritation teeth, she picked up shredded undies and tossed them into the garbage. At the garbage bin, spread out over the floor laid an array of compost remnants; eggshells, coffee grinds, potato peelings and old salad bits.

"ARRGGHH!" Hands on hips, eye narrowed and teeth gritting "WHERE ARE YOU, YOU MANGY MUTT?" Scanning the expanse of the kitchen, living room and down the hallway, Dawg was stealth hiding. She took a deep breath, temper flaring.

"DAWG, where are you?"

Dawg appeared from behind, he had been following close, proud of his achievements of the day and unwavering in his declaration of demand for attention. She looked down at him in a standoff; hands on hips, dramatic displeasure display opposing a curled and wagging tail of audacious I am so loveable that you cannot be angry eyes. Navi alpha mother wolf growled barring teeth as Dawg slowly, backed away, turned and scrambling for solid footing, ran down the hall and into Abby's room, then plunged under her bed. She chased to a standstill as eyes registered Abby's room mess. Young girl socks and underwear shredded piles.

"ARRRGGGHHH! That is it little boy. You are on time out for the rest of the evening!"

Dawg slowly, tail under tucked, crept to his bed and curled in submission ball, eyes focused on her.

Evening Navi;

It seems that I am at loose ends without you.

Dog is spilling water hang on, sorry, back again. The damn dog is autistic.

Oops, now he is chewing up old dog's food dish, hang on. Back again. Now he is busy chasing the cat.

Darling, like you darling, I see you as a dear friend first and foremost and before all else. I miss you.

Love Magus, who is battling with an idiot dog

Dear David;

Idiot dog problem is a universal theme tonight. It must be a canine consciousness revolt wave.

I have a quest of sorts for you; Close your eyes and imagine that you are in a cave. It is completely dark. Get a sense of your surroundings by using your senses, spatial awareness. Explore and gain a sense of the perimeters of the inside of the cave. When you are feeling comfortable and safe, find the light and turn it up so that it expands completely, filling yourself, then the cave, then beyond.

Let me know how it goes.
Navi

Dear Navi;
I tried the cave thing, could not find the light. I freaked out claustrophobic and panicked. What am I missing? I look forward to seeing thee.
David the Mighty

David;
I sigh. The light sought in cave is the light within you, tune into and crank it up. It will show you the way.
Navi

There was but one drive through coffee shop. Too lazy to get out and go in, she whipped around the corner of the building, met by a long line of nice newer cars, tourists.

"Abby, get out your pad of paper and a pen, you're going to take notes."

"Sure Mom."

"I do believe that there should be rules of drive through etiquette posted at all drive through coffee shops. I shall hereby and forthwith decree, the following rules for posting at all the franchise outlets, for a small fee of course:

Number one; if you do not know what you want before you drive up to the speaker, park and go in. The women waiting on you and the people behind you do not want to wait while you explore the menu.

Number two; you are not allowed to itemize forty-five individual flavours of a party package of donuts. Either order them mixed or all of one flavour. Long line-ups are the curse of others who only want one item and are in a hurry. Park and go in for extensive lists.

Number three; If you are the driver of a vehicle full of children or otherwise generally fussy car guests, use your fine dining hostess etiquette and carte blanche choose and order for them. Because, you see the women inside cannot handle lists beyond three items, they will get it wrong, so park and go in anyway.

Number four; it is quite all right to tell the cashier at the window that the guy behind is your husband and that he is paying for yours."

Hi Navi;

Yes, we shall maintain a friendship that shall transcend all adversity. I get the sense that something is going to be wrong. Please dream of me.

Magus

Sliding into old shawl embraced sleep; a mumbled foreign language audibly rose, and then dissipated.

Standing on deck with a young daughter snug against a blinding late night rain storm, holding onto wooden railing, long early eighteen hundred's dress and robe pulled in tight, a whipping flag in blasting rain filled wind. Lightning flashed showing David standing in a small wooden boat, as waves heaved and hurled, inching further away. "DAVIDE! DAVIDE! Mon Deau, Mon Beau, vien ici, vien ici." Lightning flashed, the wooden boat further away, David turned to grab an oar and return it to the oarsman. He was actively paddling toward shore, not her. David appeared then disappeared in lightning flashes further and further away. Allowing the distance, not fighting to return, save her and child. "DAVIDE aide moi, aide moi!"

The ship heaved as another wave rolled and dipped it the into water's surface, sending daughter sliding on slippery deck. Fierce motherly grip on daughter retracted, safe aside. A larger swell elicited the ship's groan, slowly rising and then a complete roll. Into cold water they spilled, head knocking on wooden barrel, a thick rope slapping her face. Mother's grip firm on child, legs kicking off water sodden boots, they rose gasping air and splattering water filled lungs. Floating and bobbing, eyes adjusted to the dark rain. Lightning flashed, showing a floating skid just a few feet away. Turning onto her back, child turned onto back aside, she kicked legs, pacing, breathing carefully in reach of the skid.

Safe for now, huddled back against wind, her child embedded within mother's embrace. Ship rose and broke the water's surface, groaned, then slid down, disappearing into dark watery abyss below. Lightning flashed, the horizon in all directions empty, save for heaving waves and rain. No ship in sight and no David, daughter disappeared far below water surface. Drifting in darkness, she heard an angelic voice "Fear not, thou art home bound." Heart exploding then calming, Navi let go to join her daughter.

Squinting for recognition, a beat-up rusted and blowing black smoke two-toned brown Honda coughed to a stop. Catharine waved out of the window as the little beast shook and shuddered its last breath. It belched out a final puff of black, quivered, and then stilled.

"Isn't she cool? I call her the Goddess Mobile. Well I do not know if she will live up to her namesake, but I made it here. What a steal though, I bought her for forty dollars."

Abby tore out of the house and flew into Catharine's arms who promptly Mosquito Monster pincher fingers chased her in and out of the back shed, in and out of the house, around and over the deck with pincher fingers, threatening little buttocks. Amidst chaos, the phone rang. David.

"Hi Sweetie, hope you don't mind my calling, but I got to tell you what happened today."

She stuck a finger in the open ear, blocking outside noise, pulled up a chair and sat down. Dawg had joined the ruckus, barking and yipping wildly in excitement. Ugly Kat hid in between Navi's legs in terror. She held the phone tighter to ear.

"Sorry I can hardly hear you, speak up. I am listening. What's up?"

"I won't take long. I saw your Polly friend today, pleasant person.

She explained that she communes with light, God's consciousness or cosmic thoughts, and hears from entities of the light. The rest my love appears to have been an affirmation of my love for you, your love for me. She said that there is a connection between you and I, that my marriage ending was inevitable. It is A-Okay, and is as it should be.

Then she gave me specific directions; sort out financial affairs fairly with a lawyer, do not tell my wife about you because our marital issues have nothing to do with you and there is no need to hurt either of you, have an honest talk with my wife which will ease the way. That supports what you have been saying, then to go in peace.

Are you there? You are quiet. Oh God, I am feeling terribly exposed now, I have to go. It sounds like a zoo at your place. Good night, sorry I could not block 'us' out, evidently I wear my heart and thee on my sleeve.

She stammered to find something to say, mind reeling. "Wow, I don't know what to say. I'd like to talk when it's not so crazy around here."

"Ok, wait, I want you to know that I shall always love you, no matter what life brings. Bye."

Catharine set about nuking hot dogs while Abby pretended to pick bugs out of her hair. Catharine yelled, from behind, "Gourmet hotdogs are ready."

"Ah God" said Abby, wrinkling face, "Gross! I do not want a hot dog. I'll puke!"

"Chill out baby girl, I made you a tuna sandwich with squeezed lemon as a topper; just how you like it."

"Cool!"

"Hey Catharine old buddy, I just realized that I haven't had a period since last February. I think I am going into Menopause, a baby Crone.

Catharine shouted, "Yahoooey! Welcome to my world. Isn't there some old wisdom and ritual we ought to know about?"

"God gave us a body in perfect condition and it can do the changes on its own. We just must go with it and ride the heat waves, like a surfer. Our blood and energy is moving in new ways now. If we resist, it will make us depressed. The change is bone deep and it is fighting it that brings osteoporosis. We will need some extra weight to go through the changes, dieting in transition is bad medicine. We will need lots of time out, alone. Re-arrange our boundaries. If we resist too much, it will not only depress, but manifest sickness."

"Wow, how do you know all of this stuff?"

"I could tell you that I have no idea. I don't access it or use it all the time. I shut most of it out when I was a kid. But once in a while a question pops up and the answer flows out of my mouth or into my mind. Some wise otherworldly spirit person talks or shows me pictures, through me."

"That's a gift Navi."

"Maybe curses, just ask the church cronies, or mother. It doesn't exactly make me super employable or marriage material. In this case, there is an old medicine woman in a tattered dress like robe with an old shawl wrapped around her head and shoulders standing beside us. She is warm, familiar and wonderful motherly flows love through us. Oh wait, if you are interested, there is more."

"God yes, please! Let 'er rip!"

"Are you aware of changes in your sexual desire? We are becoming a maiden again, sexual, that is menopause. It brings the freedom of not having monthly cycles and thus changes the flow of our energy, Kundalini. If we let go, we will find that it is a wonderful and freeing thing. We're older and wiser than when we were young maidens, so it's only logical that our sex life will be profoundly better."

Crimson face Navi, embarrassed eyes cast down in contemplation of the spirit world exposure. Seeing Catharine and Abby both gripped in attention, continued.

"Oh and just watch how the change in Kundalini enhances your spiritual growth."

Navi turned off in house lights then ventured out onto the deck and resumed blanket curl on the lounge chair. She lit a cigarette and watched smoke trails spiral up into the stars. Catharine joined beside her, curling in her own blanket, while Abby, eating a candy apple, slid under mother's blanket.

"You belong to the world. The world needs more, like you."

"I would like that Mom", whispered a sleepy daughter.

Navi felt a ripple of anger rise up her spine. "I do not want you heading down this road, until you are old enough and mature enough to make those choices in a good way."

Navi reflected on Mother's last visit; revealing family secrets of their lineage. Mother's misguided assertion of secret in protection of her daughter was now, more understandable. Life comes full circle; insight illuminated a different kind of protected maternal love.

She woke to the smell of delicious fresh perked coffee and French toast. A silence pervaded the room as Catharine burned sage and sweet grass.

"You have heard about the American military doing experiments in the earth with radio waves. There are a number of military bases in the far north, away from the eyes of the general public. They have sunk pipes deep into the earth and are playing with lasers, frequencies and vibrations. They are collecting data with interest in its applications for weather control and earth climatic changes. They do not have any idea how dangerous this is.

The native elders have been aware of this project for quite some time and are keeping a close eye on them. I do not want you to worry. I am telling you, because I need your help. One of the symptoms of this project is that it throws magnetic fields off, not down here yet, but certainly up there. That is why there is so much soul sickness. I will be joining Gary and Old River, in Igloolik tonight. I will be attending a weeklong fast, prayer and healing ceremony with the elders. I want you gals to tune in and send healing light and prayers."

A shift in Catharine had appeared overnight, an edge of authority that radiated from her heart, love, egoless. She took her leave in stealth silence, so unusual. Normally it took an hour of hugs, chatter and chaos to say goodbye after a visit. A sense of foreboding lingered after her.

Just as she had curled up on the deck chair with an iced tea, the phone rang, Old River.

"Navi, I've made arrangements for Abby to come with me to Arizona next summer. She will stay with some friends of mine. It's time for training."

"What?" Instantly livid.

"It's all arranged and it's time, Navi. Get a grip. She is a medicine woman and belongs to the world."

Navi felt the familiar rise of alpha she wolf energy crawl up spine and heart pounding in ears, LIVID.

"Now you listen to me River! There is no God dammed way you are taking my daughter anywhere, anytime! She is still a child! I do not give a rat's ass shit who or what you think you are or who or what you think my daughter is! There is NO way you are taking my daughter anywhere anytime!"

"Navi that is just your insecure ego talking."

"I don't give a fuck what you think of me! Just who do you think you are?"

Navi vibrated mother's wrath; Joan of Arc, Arch Angel Michael, Wolf Mother crossed and stood powerful in protection of threatened child. Phone silence pounded in ears and ripple reverberated throughout the cosmos. Catching her composure, she took a deep breath, invoking grace.

"Look River, it is time that we parted ways. Thank you for all of the good things you have done for me over the years, in many ways you have been a good friend. You have crossed the line here. I do not want to see you anymore. I do not want you to come here and I do not want you to ever, contact Abby. That door is closed and if you do not have the decency to respect this, I will make sure that you regret it. And don't bother me on the etheric either!"

Navi slammed the phone down on the receiver as a wave washed and shuddered. "Oh my God, I just told River to go fuck herself. Ego that, Baby!"

Navi was proud, clear and strong, and on a roll.

David was next. She had to let go.

Out on the back county road, sitting on a large rock, back-to-back, they reverently watched dragonflies dance and glitter in sunshine streamers through trees. Looking out over fields of corn, butterflies flittered amidst wild flowers and tall grasses. Logical resolve was wavering.

"You have to work out your marriage."

David sat head bowed in defeated silence, pondering, taking it in. Neither could choose abstinence. That was that.

Navi drove to the beach alone missing his soft voice, loving touch and wit while her mind yelled 'do not touch' and her soul longed for his company. There was no getting around it; she was falling for David. Into a glorious setting sun, she prayed from her soul for all involved; Stephen, kids, family, David and his wife, Abby and herself.

"God, please watch over us, show us the right way for the highest good of all, and validate our choices."

David was certainly an illogical path, wreaking emotional havoc and in the light of day and human perceptions, an affair with him certainly did not respect man's rules for righteous living. In trusting intuition and how good it felt being in David's company, there had to be a higher agenda at hand. The inner battle for right thought and action ensued. The fact that they both pursued intimate relations while he was still married, he was still in his matrimonial home, left her feeling small, knowing that it was wrong. Sensing that pertinent information and insight was missing, in time, all was going to be right.

She lit a cigarette, propped feet on the dash, leaned head back and watched the unfolding sunset sky blaze in glory. 'Thou shalt not covet thy neighbour's wife'. Extra-marital affairs were tawdry, sleazy, cheap and without moral responsibility. Certainly, it was a sin worthy of fiery hell, a scarlet woman, now loathing orthodoxy more than ever.

She loved the legends of Saints. Who decided who was worthy and who was not, were men, such as church authorities. Her vision and experience of God was more individualized and omnipotent. God, in her experience, was intimately personal. Experiencing God within an organized religious group or persona without formal structure was one's own spiritual fingerprint within the all that is. Perhaps, marriage was utilitarian, for survival only. People used to not live as long as they do today. Love pursuits were the unique crux of the human condition. Every story told of elusive loves and want of being someone's special and one and only.

How many married women curl up to romance novels and movies each week, hungry, needy, then repent sinful thoughts on Sunday, remaining unfulfilled? How many people tried to change each other into that which they were not? All while seeking something bigger, something more intimate, more passionate. Was it the ultimate union with God or the creator that people sought, somehow trying to experience Nirvana through another person? It is through relationships with others that people learned the most and grew.

'So how do I, one who had considered herself morally responsible, honourable and spiritual find myself in this predicament?' She had no clear answer.

Home to an empty house, dog and cat fed and watered, she soaked in a bubble bath with soothing candle flickering light, standing on an abyss. The phone rang; she did not budge. David.

"Hi Navi; You are either out or in the tub. On a dark night, the flame of love burned in my heart, by the dark of night and secrecy, your inner light was my guide. To join my love as one, transcending the world, hands caresses skin in lover's embrace. In my life, I have kissed the lips of the angel who challenged me so long ago to manifest heaven on earth. Okay, then, that is all. Good night. Oh, this is David by the way, just in case I forgot to say."

When Navi finally pulled herself out of the tub, with lighter, she grabbed a coke, cig and turned computer on.

Dear David;

I do not know why, for the life of me, our paths have crossed. I do know that somewhere there is a higher order of what is right and what is wrong. You are married and as such, your histories together and those years of bonding must take priority. This is respect. This does not mean that you mean anything less to me. It would seem that we are at a crossroad. Go into your heart and be one with however you perceive your higher power. Be gentle and kind to your Beloved. She is a lucky woman to have you.

Navi

Out onto the deck and into the late evening darkness, feeling freer, she swirled, hair spinning, looking upward towards the stars spinning in the night sky. Bats zigzagged and flittered about, eating an evening dinner of gnats, mosquitoes and black flies. Picking up frenzied speed, the bats circled and dive-bombed her head. Panicking, waved arms, madly and wildly as terror visions of them tangling up in her long hair and biting into her jugular, sucking blood.

"River! I can feel you! FUCK OFF!"

Night sky stilled, bats retreated and sensing River had also retreated, her shoulders, fists and jaws relaxed.

"Yes spirit friends, I get the message too. Bats are messengers signifying a rebirth, shaman's birth. Bring it on! Give me all you've got. I need a life.

Dear David;

I am sorry; I will not be answering the phone. I need time out.

Navi

Navi and daughter, were barely out of the car at the campsite, as the in your face nosey church crone friend of Mothers greeting assaulted. With hands on hips audaciously blurted, "So! How is Stephen?"

Abby folded herself into her mother's side, sensing a she-battle.

"I really wouldn't know." Abruptly turning her back on the woman, striving for composure and avoidance of direct conflict, she motioned to daughter to empty the car and scanned the site for Aunt Diane. She really had not been prepared for public inquiry yet, nor pending disapproval of church crones, as she had thought. A glimpse of the woman standing still in her spot with mouth gaping, shock gawking huffed, the old crone turned pursed lipped to approach Aunt Diane for explanation. Abby cowered behind Navi as Aunt Diane boldly approached.

Sensing the situation in a flash, she straightened her spine and announced, "Navi and Stephen are no longer a couple. Matt is doing fine. I'm glad that Navi and Abby could join us for the weekend."

Dismissing further questions, and taking a stand to support Navi, whilst another woman stood gawking in alliance with old church crone; obviously the first time she had heard the news. Navi squirmed crimson, face flush with discomfort of public display, when clearly it was no one's business. The rest of the campers dismissed themselves from the heated interchange to their respective sites and continued their own tent set up. Choking dry stuffing, Navi burned angry, hurt.

The woman unaccustomed to being alpha dogged and not easily rebuffed, intent on holding a higher pious ground, continued, "Well! I think it is awful. I mean your timing Navi. After all, isn't Matt still in treatment?"

Church decorum in community had long held audacious bitch rights following Gran's death. As a child, Navi recalled Mother's deadly stuffing incident, not fit for human consumption. She took in a deep breath of composure and grace, then turned, fighting grief tears, struggling and straining to bare up against the seeming constant barrage of judgments, disapprovals, job on the rocks, losing the house, kids, yes, worried about the kids and having Abby exposed to this crap. The only apparent way out was to explain the intimate details of the past ten years, but it was simply none of anyone's business. It was certainly none of this woman's business. A ripple of anger and humiliation ran up her spine, and glancing at Abby, was followed by a wave of resolve and grace.

"I'm sure that you feel you have reason to ask but you don't. I'm sure that you feel justified displaying your rude nosey questions in front of my daughter but she does not need to hear this from you. I cannot and will not talk about what happened, that is between Stephen and me. However, if Stephen wishes to discuss it with you, that is his prerogative. I will not. Just as I will not discuss your personal life nor pass judgment on your private life, that I obviously don't know anything about, nor do I care to know."

A dramatic standoff; Navi stood ground on behalf of absent Mother, wise to have opted out for Florida, warrior ready, as deadly stuffing memories re-surfaced. She would not submit to the same nosey church crone judgment and annihilation. The assertion that some of those women felt, to judge and jury then piously decimate, was mind blowing. On behalf of Mother, her daughter and all scorned women throughout time, Navi pulled Abby into her side in reassuring embrace, safe, protected against primal attack, against ignorance, she stood her energetic ground. Standing solid, grounded, powerfully ten feet tall, daring retaliation.

Sensing escalating volatile tension, Aunt Diane gracefully made her way in between the two, making light and jovial remarks, pulling in and holding both women and Abby in her arms. Livid, she allowed the semi conciliation hug out of respect for Aunt Diane, but Navi was pissed, fed up and scared. Refusing to allow the bitch crone to see rising fear tears, she turned away and set about unpacking the car.

A stress whopper of a headache settling in as the last bits were arranged, Navi could not settle down, nor settle in. Abby was unusually quiet and out of sorts. After trying to make the best of it for an hour and still fighting tears, she turned and packed gear, then spent two minutes explaining that they both just wanted to go home. As soon as they left the campground, the weighty burdens of the world dissipated, shoulders relaxed in freedom. Magically, Abby perked up, content. Navi was proud. Too much had happened and Navi knew that they both simply needed time and space to process it all. They stopped at a general store and bought bags of junk food, chocolate, ice cream and chips for a driving picnic dinner.

Cancer and other major illnesses are a community rallying hot happening events list, unless of course, you have AIDS, syphilis or affairs, then no one wants to rally, let alone hear truth details. Cancer and houses burning down are acceptable crisis, thus; people will rally to your side. If you are addicted to gossip and drama then a willing participant can easily be found to exchange. If you happen to be a smoker, drinker or are a bingo maniac or some other addiction then suddenly, it is everybody's free reign business. One must simply, stand still and accept audacious berating judgment while jurors expound on your evils deeds. Pious cowardice behind pretense of God and misguided church doctrine, ignorance kills vulnerable souls.

"Abby, I want you to remember this day. Remember that the bottom line to every hissy fit judging rant you may find yourself in is that you never really know someone else's story and you certainly don't know the higher agenda or divine plan of another person's life and actions."

"I know that Mom. Sometimes I get so angry, that it scares me. But then I stop and think, as to if it's important or not, and if the other person is too stupid to get it anyway or not."

"Wise young one you are. Oh God Abby, wait until they find out about the David saga!"

Once home and phone unplugged, they curled up to watch movies; allies in the face of public inquiry. She grabbed a handful of popcorn and stuffed it into Abby's pants, up shirt and in pockets. They scrambled as if wild beasts to munch up the bits before the other one could get to it, much to Dawg's pleasure. Ugly Kat oblivious to the war preoccupied herself exploring the inside a plastic shopping bag that lay on the floor.

Sometime around midnight she carried a sleeping Abby into bed. She grabbed a cold coke, slid into nice silky new jams, content to be home, alone with daughter. The more she strove to understand and resolve the polarities of spiritual path and opposing social expectations, the less she understood. Making peace within was not going to be simple.

How I miss you Navi!

We are apart and I am at loose ends. David is lonely. Blessed is he who has a dragonfly who glows like a firefly. I marvel that you listen to me. I tell you things I tell no one else, I could paint with you.

Tonight I walked before the heavens had settled in, not yet dark but past the light. I saw one star, one very bright star in the southwest and I thought of you staring up into the stars and wondered if you were thinking of me, I wish to share firmament with you. The stars that shine on thee my love also shine on me.

Magus - alone at home

On Monday morning, Navi began gathering up advocacy power and re-created the easy to understand tip sheets on how to navigate the system for clients. She envisioned public attorneys petitioning a class action suit against the government, human rights violations, navigating bitchiness from all directions. The phone rang, startling, Helen blurted, "Navi what is this entry note about?"

"I don't remember."

"Why have you not closed this file?"

"I'm not sure, I'd have to review that file and get back to you?"

"Navi where were you on such and such a date?"

"I don't remember, I'd have to go back in my agenda and look. Why do you need to know this stuff?"

Helen's tone was dismissive and condescending. "I don't have time to talk. I have had to attend a fund raising golf tournament with the county boys." Boss woman was in and moving with the old boys, securing some sort of position and status. In the beginning, Navi had been the golden child of the team. Rattled, she searched for the something unsaid in Helen's voice, unnerving and empty. The work door was closing soon.

"Mom, the babysitter has an extra horse and we can board it there, it wouldn't cost much at all."

"No."

"Ah Mom, think on it. It would be good for you too. You can ride with me any time you want. Just imagine how much fun that would be. You'd have to get us some riding pants, riding boots and our own grooming stuff, though."

"No."

"Ah Mom, I know, don't ask you anything when you just walk in the door, later right?"

Navi

I really, really want to paint again. I have to resort to exploring snoring, sleeplessness remedies. We shall begin this quest for the antidote in the documents of the Middle Ages; I understand that bloodletting was popular for many afflictions. On the other hand, perhaps your desire for kinship with the nature elements, say, maybe a poultice of frog or newt, or sheep's bladder.

What sayeth thou, oh, masterful all-knowing Navi

David

David;

I have a more historically effective remedy for sleepless ails and snore filled nights. Troublesome husbands were dealt with a batch of 'special' jam; one jar with black slimy stuff on top, otherwise known as 'botulin spores' will suffice. A little on problem sod's morning toast, a stroke by mid-afternoon, a lovely sociable wake a few days later. Voila! Relief!

Now if you have an aversion to hag hairs on women, we will have to quest remedies for those as well, sneaky and elusive beggars that they are! You would be surprised how many women, post childbirth, menopausal, must contend with the affliction. Estrogen stabilizes, while testosterone rears its androgynous head of hairs. The Holy Grail of youth is alive, and money in the pursuit of youthful appearance is well in advertising America. Balls to wellbeing and forget about your insides. In short, snits, snorts, and crone hairs are keeping us humble.

Changing the topic, Abby likes it when I tuck her in and fart in her bed. Do not bother asking her, she may deny it.

Dragonfly Navi Goddess Lady

Some days start out just as any other, not. Navi awoke to a screaming headache. They are defining days and she arrived at work with an urgent email from David.

Oh, Navi;

My wife knows about us, about you. I assumed that she knew, or saw us, or someone she knows saw us together.

I told her that I was in love with you. She went ballistic. As it turns out, she did not really know, just a wild guess. Women's intuition I suppose.

I am so sorry for everything.

David

Navi shut her computer down, shoved files into a drawer then called into head office. HQ Human Resources still in out of town, politicking his job security schmoozing, she left a message; "something has come up, I have to go". She drove in surreal time and space and decided to leave Abby at the sitters for the time being. She needed to think, needed help, chain-smoking, stomach splitting in two. 'Transcend this, BABY!'

As the sun went down in a glow of oranges, reds and violets, the bandstand went up. Floodlights lit the main street and the main beach area. Tourists filled the street, mingling in and out of gift shops. Cotton candy, candy apples, fudge, popcorn, roasted peanuts, balloons and firecrackers, suddenly seemed to be everywhere. It was a street dance fundraiser for a farm couple who had lost six head of cattle in a fire last weekend. All proceeds to replace the barn and cattle. Rural small towns are a great place to live if your barn burns down, but not if you left your husband while his child was sick and had an affair. There were acceptable, community minded approved tragedies and then there were the ones that were not. The community had more churches, fellowships and bible study happenings than anywhere in the county. Yes, fires and cancerous children were great community rallying events. What Navi was up to was still cause for banishment, stoning and hanging.

Boldly, they sat on a curb, snuggled together watching tourists gather for the dance and watching locals, who were visibly distinct in appearance. Locals really did not go out of their way to keep up with current fashion trends. Many middle aged and older women still had the same seventies and fifties hairdo's respectively. Why buy new clothes when summer was so short, the same going out outfit was good and fit thirty years ago. Men proudly wore a redneck dinner tuxedo; rural signature red plaid flannel shirts, work boots and the much-coveted John Deer deluxe ball caps. In direct contrast were the tourists, whom looked like television ads for Gap and Eddie Bauer. They sported the hottest runners, khaki pants, sweatshirts tied around necks and even though it was evening, celeb sunglasses. As though stepping out of a magazine ad, freshly showered, scrubbed, manicured and perfumed, black fly and mosquito heaven. City women wearing stiletto high heels gingerly navigated the beach. From nearby reserve, native teenagers arrogantly strode midway, boldly challenging all to make way. A Mennonite family hung in periphery, curious, wanting to stay and watch. It was a strange mixture indeed.

Tourists thought that locals were daft and all inbred. Locals in turn, thought that all of the tourists were stressed, rude and bitchy creatures, with no respect for the environment. There was always a joyful welcome for tourists in the spring and early summer, it meant work for the seasonal workers and a boost for the local economy. By the end of July and beginning of August, locals were simply too burnt out from all of the stress and mess that city people brought with them.

Abby danced to some corny Rod Stewart rendition of Maggie Mae, a joy to watch, as city children mingled and danced among local children. Children danced freely. They moved to their own inner beat and rhythm, oblivious to all else. Some moved only a leg or two, some moved with little butts propelled, jutting here and there. All had a joy, a shine in their eyes. Tacky coloured strobe lights flashed amidst sunset colours. Crowd freedom moved to the beat. 'When I pass over, I would like to remember this.'

Jangled out of reverie with a shoulder tap, Navi turned to see one of Stephen's neighbours. Same age, but this one looked a dumpy twenty years older from years of hard farm labour and raising children. A kind woman, but very set in church community ways and beliefs from generations of being raised in farm country.

"Condolences about Matt."

Navi's spine instantly rippled bitchy, "He's not dead, he's very much alive, but thank you very much."

"Did you hear about the Johnston's farm, terrible shame all of those cows, that barn was only twenty years old."

"Yep, rough go," replied Navi, cynically thinking that between the insurance and the fundraiser the couple would come out far ahead. Likely already procured a double herd of cattle and larger modern barn.

"Why haven't we seen you around at church or the general store lately? Come to think of it, we didn't see you at the Strawberry Shortcake Festival or fireworks on Canada Day."

Navi could see the lie, her eyes told the truth that she knew exactly why; word gets around fast in a small town. Wild fire.

"Oh, I've been busy", dismissing the woman's disrespectful lie, curtly advising that discussion was firmly closed. The woman showed no effort in moving on. She stood pious and stoic, holding ground waiting for Navi to spill, confess, demonstrate drama and due remorse for gossip milling later.

Annoyed with the audacious gossip fly hanging in for more, "Hey, is your hubby still on the wagon? How is that going? I heard he did a little lock up for drinking and driving and giving you shiners."

Hesitating, the woman stood unabashed, balancing arguments. They still considered themselves to be fine Christians, went to church every Sunday, helped out at fellowships and socials, so no matter what, they were still in. The church members would not give up on hubby until he stopped going to meetings. As long as those church folks see that you are attending meetings, there is hope that the good lord will catch and heal his sins.

Redneck Church Baby Crone Woman reeled around, knowing, nodding in, Touché. She pretended to catch sight of a friend and toddled off into the crowd.

Navi heading to the bath, stopped abruptly in exasperation as the phone rang. She hesitated, debating about answering or allowing it to go to answering machine. David's tone was serious, a terse edge rippled through her body that jangled her heart.

"I'm just calling to tell you that my wife and I are trying to work things out. I really wanted to talk to you in person, but I think this is best. I want space from you Navi. I have assured my wife that I have ended things with you and that I shall no longer associate with you. I'm sorry."

David did not wait for response, dial tone. The phone hit and run cut was deep, surprising Navi with just how much it hurt. While logically expecting the moment to come at some point, the heart and soul hearing of it, hurt deeply.

Awake, tossing and turning, trying to process, Navi curled up with the computer inbox.

Hi Navi;

I just had the sense that you might need this today; those that choose to follow the souls will, play with desire, often finding nirvana in another's arms, ultimately becoming their own master, true. But they wander the worlds at personal will rather than divine will, and will be accountable to someone, somewhere, sometime. Life is going to shovel shit on you. Shake it off Navi and step up! SHAKE off what does not belong to you, stay focused on what makes your soul sing and live! Enjoy Your Week.

Gary

Navi;

The following is true, what it means I do not know. Last night my wife and I went for a walk, to talk. It did not go well.

Walking up hill back to the house, a large black butterfly or moth, I think a moth, soared out of some bushes to my right and hit me right on my heart chakra, then flew off. It was almost violent, with panic and doom.

She said that if I still loved you, nothing would work. I said nothing, could not say anything.

I let the dog out the front door and I stepped out into the night. From my right, a large white moth flew racing towards and struck me, again hard, right centre on my heart chakra, then flew off. I shuddered. I did not know what it meant. I just know that I have never been struck by kamikaze type moths in the heart and even if I had, never in such close time sequences and never in black and white.

My feelings for you have not changed. I have much to deal with here right now. I need some time to be.

Magus

In dark of night aloneness, Navi submitted to God, Creator and Spirit realm. Unsure if the attraction with David was of personal will or divine will, she handed over the dilemma.

Drifting in and out and in between worlds, as mist dissipated, she stood overlooking the healing grotto. A chilly wind gripped old sisterhood shawl tighter in, as massive flocks of seagulls dived cave entrance waves for evening dinner. Spirit Navi, ruffled wings, launched and took flight, flying free and was soaring higher and higher away from the human condition.

Following shoreline due south, then to the inland lake system, a rocky ledge offered rest. Upon landing, she re-assumed human form yet was still not of her own physical body or lifetime.

Midwest, eighteen hundreds wilderness, with their makeshift lean-to solid for the night, Soul Skin man took her hand. Buckskin in contrast to golden brown skin, long dark hair tied with braided sinew. The sunset was a brilliant array of colours: oranges, pinks, mauves, purples, reds and yellows. Grandfather sun dipped and slid in and out of clouds that had taken on sunset colours, summer blossom clouds. From the Southwest, the sky grew dark and foreboding. A summer storm was building up strength and speed, aggressing in from the greater bay water. Blasting wind picked up carrying the smell of lake rain in the air, fresh, cool and crisp. Heavy clouds rumbled and gurgled, picking up power and speed. Lightning flashed within, an ominous storytelling setting. Lightning shards flashed and shot across the early evening sky. Storm winds picked up greater speed. Holding steadfast, in thrill of the moment, wincing against its power, their hair danced wildly in the wind.

Navi's senses attuned to hair caresses tickling her face. The scent of him hung and swirled in the air amidst the warmth of his being. She breathed the moment sensations in, of his being-ness, and sighed. A sacred joy moment with Creation, she thanked Creator, Spirit, Ancestors. The rain and gales descended upon them quickly, as they jumped into the makeshift lean-to and embraced in silence.

The next morning's aftermath of the storm left a sense of calm in its wake, with a tail wind bringing in tall powerful waves. Navi curled up against a large boulder, eyes greeting Grandfather Sun, then watched water birds surf wind currents over the waves. It was a good fishing day. She covered herself in a blanket shawl, fighting goose bumps, while Soul Skin husband waded out into the chilly water. Quickly feeling his body temperature drop, he ran shaking, as Navi wrapped a blanket around his shivering frame. Embracing a shaking teeth chattering man, warmed in love, he slowed still, warmth emanating.

"If you shall pass this day, before me husband, how would I know that you are still with me?"

"I shall never leave you."

"This journey is one day, yet many, many seasons shall pass before we find a new home. Many white people in between. I am glad that we do not make the journey alone. I fear that many will die along the way. Children, the old and sick, cannot travel far. I fear that many spirits will die along the way."

"Woman, follow heart always, do what needs to be done, share of your faith and love."

Part Two ~ David

"Many of us spend our whole lives running
from feeling with the mistaken belief
that you cannot bear the pain.
But you have already borne the pain.
What you have not done is feel
all you are beyond the pain."
Saint Bartholomew

Chapter 14 ~ Penance

"Mom? Mom? Mom?"

Abby's voice cut through dream soul skin space and rudely into awakening. Turning over slightly, embracing daughter, drawing her near, smells of girl sleep sweat breathed in and anchored into memory.

"Mom?"

"Yes Darling."

"Mom, if you die before me, how will I know that you are there with me, in Spirit?"

"Daughter, I shall be with as long you want me or need me. I shall always be with you and there for you, even when you are sure that I am not. I shall be with you at your boyfriend's first kiss, school graduation, difficulties, ins and outs of your career, wedding day, when your baby arrives and postpartum despair. I shall give you strength and courage to follow your dreams despite adversities. I shall make my presence known to you when you notice the sunshine on your face, scent of roses, white feathers - an angel calling card, a baby's sigh, jokes shared with a friend. Believe me daughter; I shall be here for you always and in all ways. I love you, and that's bigger than anything."

Bathing suit donned, at the river's edge, perched overlooking waterfalls, several tourists jumped and dove deep into a rocky foaming pool below.

Gathering nerve, Navi and Abby watched on as several children cannon balled with complete abandon. Eyeing each other, they shed sundresses and sandals, untied long braids and walked hand in hand. Wading current water to precipice, they hesitated as frantic water rushed in and around feet, cascading far below into a foaming pool.

"Are you sure it's deep enough Mom?"

"Well just aim for the centre of the white spot, that's the deepest part."

They glanced at each other as kids; climbed giggling and laughing.

Abby, still holding Navi's hand said, "Ready Mom?"

"God, I'll never be ready, not in a million years."

"GO!"

Time slowed surreal, as they splashed deep into foaming swirling water. Scrambling for Abby with one hand and releasing bathing suit crouch wedge with the other. Jammed inside her nether regions with force that followed by magically removing top bathing suit, now surface floating around her neck. Water flushed into her sinuses and out again, freeing residue mucous. She looked up and saw above, an Abby, flailing arms and legs, already surfaced. She glanced below seeing cutting rocky edge four feet behind. Safe, a kick of legs and surface aimed, she broke water to the crushing roar of waterfalls and the swirling current. Abby bobbed giggling, laughed hysterically spitting water, wiping at a string of snot.

Up onto a rocky ledge panting and giggling, pausing to breath and allow a rush of exhausted elation.

"Let's do it again, Mom." She grabbed Navi's hand, as a teen flew from the top of the falls and into the foam below. The girl surfaced, crying. Navi was ready to jump in, just as the girl's father dove in. Navi and Abby looked at each other and without a word, they concluded "enough".

Lunch was at an outdoor cafe amidst throngs of tourists of every different shape, size, and colour imaginable. City women clothed in fancy sundresses and celebrity sunglasses lounged under umbrellas, sipping iced tea. In the winter, you could not get anywhere near the beach because the snow piled mountain high and the ice faults made it impassable. Stores boarded up, as blustering gusts and snow devils made it as a ghost town, a scene from a movie. Today it was all exotic sun and sand.

Country people venture out occasionally just to see city people antics, circus ants. When late August tourists came, it was multi-national families; they splayed out of several vans and cars with dining tents, portable tables, coolers, barbeques and comfortable chairs. Cosmopolitan global, every nationality represented and inter-mingled without incident. Summer at the beach also meant that locals blended in with the immigration global melting pot, a futuristic glimpse of the new cultural norms. The world was rapidly changing.

Startled awake by the ringing phone, light still on and a new textbook sliding off her chest, Navi's heart raced. Glancing at the bedside clock, the bleating bright red 11:30 did not register. Then spastically, she bolted out into the kitchen, tripping over Dawg and Abby's schoolbooks, to the phone.

David was hysterical. "I have nowhere to go!"

"What?"

"I hhaavvee nnoo wwhheerree ttoo ggoo!!"

Struggling to regain waking consciousness, unable to grasp what in the hell he was talking about or what he was asking of her, impatient annoyance responded with a curt, "Wwhhaatt?"

"I need a place to sleep! I can't stay here!"

"Uh? Oh, of course."

Slowly composing, a pot of tea on, Navi psyched for an intense visit. David arrived, visibly shaken; hair disheveled; eyes red and wild. She poured cups of tea, motioning to the kitchen table.

"Glad you felt you could come here."

A spirit snuffed David downcast his eyes, then began. The gist, she already knew; he and his wife had a terrible argument. Of course, not a new occurrence, but this time, she was central.

"We'd been tidying up after a nice late night dinner with my wife's parents. After they left, we sat at the kitchen table chatting with brandy and then a bottle of wine. It didn't take long until inhibitions were lost. It seemed as though she was over the initial shock of finding out about us and was now building up a rage. She proceeded to set boundaries and demands on how our life was going to be. Oh my God, she was angry, fuelled by alcohol, she stood up and in my face, raged. She said that from here on in, I would require her permission as to where I went, with whom, and when. I am not to tell another living soul about my affair with you.

I will be sleeping in the den from now on. I am to go on Monday and buy her a new car. I am also to go and put the line of credit and all debts in my own name and the house, deed and the insurance policies in her name. I also have to forsake my indiscretion, explain to her what really had happened in a way that shows her how much I love her and how I was seduced by the 'witch slut'.

I just sat there, frozen in silence, while she spewed wrath. I pretty much felt like she had every right to do so and was prepared to do penance. My mind reeled when she demanded to know the details of my sexual experiences with the 'slut'. God, it was painful to see her like this. I felt as though my head and heart were going to explode. When I did not respond, did not speak, she went upstairs to the bedroom and began throwing my clothes and personal items out of the window and into the yard. She threw a crystal vase that I had given her on our tenth anniversary against the wall, shattering it in pieces. She was angry and empowered, a warrior princess, an Amazon woman. At one point, she fired at me that I was never to expect to touch her again, that my days of having sex with anyone were over. I figured that she would exhaust herself so I just let her go.

I did not interfere. I thought that she had every right to be livid. She even hurled my antique art box and easel that my Dad gave me as a kid out of the window. She grabbed my clothes, my paintings, and briefcase and even tossed out my winter coat. She came and stood in front of me with her hands on her hips and said, this house and everything else in it is mine!

She slugged back a quarter bottle of brandy while taunting me, demanding that I 'fuck her', like I 'fucked my slut'.

I refused.

My heart was breaking in two.

I figured that she just wanted to erase all traces of you, make everything normal like nothing had ever happened."

"Or maybe, she just wanted you to love her fully."

David sat still taking his tea mug in both hands, sipped then gingerly placed it back down on the table.

"She took her clothes off right in front of me, something she never does. I followed her to the bed. She just lay there. I was crying. I tried to make love to her, to heal her. I wanted her pain to go away, to make the hurting stop. It was sickening, the way she just laid there. It was surreal and I felt nausea. I came abruptly, mildly, and withdrew immediately. I just sat on the edge of the bed beside her, weeping. She said nothing and made no effort to move.

I wept, feeling like I had just raped my wife and had not made love. The room swirled and I jumped off the bed and ran into the bathroom, just in time to projectile vomit into the toilet. While I was in the bathroom, she got up, threw the rest of my things out of the bedroom window and locked the door behind. I was still naked. I went to the bedroom door, begging her to open it, I wanted to talk, talk it through.

"Get out of my house!" was all she said. I stood at the bedroom door for a long time, begging her to open it, to talk. My pleas met with loathing silence. It was a profound loathing, angry and distant silence and I felt it in the core of my being.

I grabbed some of my dirty clothes from the laundry basket downstairs and sat in the kitchen for some time, eyeing the strewn household items. I sat down on the floor picking up broken crystal, and then I just sat there crying. I cried for our years together, for her pain, years long lost intimacy, and sharing.

All of those years with her, I was trying to do more. It has been such a god-awful lonely time. Funny, how you can love someone so much and be so profoundly lonely at the same time. There was no way I could make her happy, give her the things she wanted, the riches, the good life, be the suave Sugar Daddy. I could never quite measure up. I always fell short of the mark, inept.

I grabbed a large garbage bag, gathered up my belongings off the lawn and threw them in the back of my car. I drove backs roads for over an hour, wandering, lost. Then I called you from a pay phone. I don't know where I'm going."

Navi said nothing, frozen, numb mind reeling, stood up and kitchen busied, avoiding face and eye contact. Shaking hands re-filled the teapot; her mind swirled, and then she instantly felt the depths of his wife's pain. She had had no idea that they had actually still cared for each other that much, that his wife cared, yet picked up the dejected look on David's face, telling a different truth. Obviously, she had not been privy to the fact that he had been confiding at work for years, a different story. His story over the years spoke of their marriage as estranged without intimacy, common goals and wants. No, his sharing, confiding to Navi, did not match the story of the scorned response this night. Obviously, she still cared a great deal, for whatever her reasons might be.

She arched her back, took a deep breath, and with tea pot in hand, turned back to the table and sat down carefully, trying to hide her hands shaking. He head buried into an arm. Sunk into the depths of sorrow, of the pain he had caused his wife. Navi poured more tea, unable to hide her shaking as he sobbed. Stoic, she sat waiting, waiting for a cue of what to do next, or for the sobbing to subside.

David looked up, tears still streaming, his back straightened and continued talking. She was only partially listening now, searching for answers, whilst reliving it all again. Then she had a vision. Like watching a movie with colour and sound in front of her eyes, his wife in time, finding independent feet without him. In time, happy with her new found freedom. Then within a respectful time, she meets and marries an older man. Yes, she could 'see' that he is good for her, bright, successful, affluent, wise and loving. He sees through the family drama and bullshit behaviours that are of separation and divorce residue. Beautiful and happy, with a large tastefully decorated home, she, occasionally testing him with mini-dramas.

Navi remained silently listening, not the time to share a vision, nor was it her place to.

"Maybe you should go home and talk to her."

David replied by shaking his head adamantly, "NO."

"Well, in the morning you must go to her."

Navi slid away from the table and formed a make shift bed on the couch.

"I wonder if I should call my wife to see if she's okay. I don't deserve to be comfortable, when I am sure that she is not."

Navi knelt watching as he fetal curled, wondering what it would be like to have someone love her as much as this, to actually have someone give a shit, to care so deeply, to be concerned after everything that they have been through. He fell asleep quickly, emotionally and mentally exhausted, deep into the sleep place where one was simply too tired to dream, a void, a nothingness.

"This too shall pass, David. Things will be better than you now think."

Standing, turning, she drifted down the hall, turned lights out and curled up in her own bed. Unable to sleep, nor separate or detach, swamped in powerful wife emotions. 'Instant karma', Navi thought, power striving to re-direct both to calming soothing distant waves, while sharing the shedding of silent tears.

"Gran, can things possibly get any worse?"

"Life gives us adversity, affliction. These are the teachers of life. Let your faith in the light of your path lead you. You have chosen to follow the light of your soul and you must now have the courage to walk your actions. Insights will come. New skills and wisdoms will grow in time."

David was gone, blankets folded neatly on the sofa, a pot of fresh coffee and gone without a word. Navi was relieved, appropriate that he had left this way. After all, what was there to say? She assumed that David had returned home to assess and smooth damage and to try to make things right with his wife. Strangely calm, she had unwittingly become their scapegoat and an integral part in the events that had caused harm to another and for that, she was profoundly remorseful. There seemed no undoing of it.

Shifting awareness to motherhood, she strived to regain balance, if only for her daughter's sake, and set about making chocolate chip pancakes.

"Mom? Mom? Mommm???"

"What?"

"I'm hungry."

"How do you know this? Are your fingers tingling?"

"Nooooo."

"Are your legs and arms numb?"

"Nooooo."

"Do you have tunnel vision with a bright light at the end?"

"No, hee hee "

"Are you hearing voices? Are they calling from the nether world?"

"No, hee hee hee."

"I guess you can wait for breakfast."

"Okay."

Just as Navi was leaving for work, David called.

"Hi Navi. I just wanted you to know that I did as you said. I went home and tried to talk to the wife, to no avail." His voice was sad and weary.

"Good. I am glad you did that."

"I've moved into a friend's guest room for the time being."

Navi remained respectfully detached; he would need time and space to recover from the emotional drama and time to figure out what to do. As she hung up, she prayed for someone to watch over him and his family.

Sometime during the night, a strange yet powerful dream awoke her. *The White Brotherhood had come to her, surrounding her bed, vague images of clear white mist that felt familiar, safe and loving. They displayed images of a mystical city that hovered over the Sahara desert and then of another over Mount Shasta. They were beckoning her, calling her. Navi then willingly followed them into a city; she knew not, which one. It was warm, peaceful, loving and friendly.*

People spoke only with minds and hearts. She understood this to mean that you must truly function as a master here. There were no secrets. You could not absently minded think to yourself that so and so is fat or ugly. Thoughts like those were loud and extremely hurtful to all. This rarely occurred, but when it did, one was quickly challenged and accountable. The pain and sorrow felt by one affects all. One must see only the divine in each other.

She was then directed to a large crystal building, a friendly and welcoming learning temple. She looked up and could not ascertain nor fathom where the ceiling ended. In this place of knowledge, she understood instinctively that one could merely sit and focus attention on a query and receive information in the mind. Like tuning into a radio station, one must concentrate and focus their intent or else the mind will be bombarded with many voices at once, all noise and chatter.

Learning was not so much a conscious knowing, but more, a sensation, a feeling within her body, internalizing something important, relevant. Outside in sunshine and fresh air, joyous children laughed in play. The thought lingered that the sounds were heard with her mind and not with physical ears.

David sat nervously upon the deck steps, humble and lovely.

"I understand that you love me. I can see that. I thank you for giving me the space I need. I think of little else."

"Well, make yourself at home. I need a shower. I need some time to process the fact that you are here. What does this mean?"

"May I use your shower? I desperately need one. I will fill you in when I am done."

Inside, Abby set about making cucumber sandwiches and juice, with a smile she whispered, "We have a late dinner guest." Abby loved company, it was reason enough for parties.

"Hey Abby, here I am, in your house and you're making me dinner-wow!"

Abby giggled wrestling with Dawg.

Late hour and increasingly uncomfortable with the growing camaraderie between the man and her daughter, during a commercial break and with clenched teeth she blurted, "Go home now. It's late."

A little shaken, obvious that he had been hoping to stay the night, stay for good, he cast his eyes downward, kissed her forehead then left. Abby quizzically side glanced at her Mom.

"You can't fall in love with someone else's dog and just take him home. If it is meant to be, it shall be in a natural good way."

Understanding the analogy, daughter pulled blanket tight, clicked the remote's power button then curled into her mother's embrace. Comfortable on couch in primate oneness, they fell into contented bonded love sleep.

Soft angelic harmonies caught her attention as a man's southern drawl sang. Ears perked, wondering if the television was on or a radio. As awareness tuned in, she realized that it was coming from within, from spirit world, no from another reality, someone somewhere, alive.

"I am calling woman, I want to fly you away with me to be my own one love. If I could, I would fly to you. I would hold you in my arms and never let you go. I would take you to my world and gently make love to you until you fell asleep. And I would watch you as you dream. I would nurture your soul back to its rightful state and guard over you. I would walk with you into my garden where our love grows. I would carry you, listening to your every word and would love you for all eternity."

Conscious awake "Who are you?" query fell silent in response. "Whoever you are, you are romantic but you are scaring me. Go away. I don't need any more complications. If you are real and are my true soul mate then show yourself in the real world."

Silence rang echoed in response.

"Every new beginning comes from some other beginning's end. I think that is an old Seneca quote, although don't quote me on it. Like you, figure out in your heart what makes you happy, gives you joy, excites and even scares the living shit out of you. That is what you said, that is how you know you are on the right path. Do not let anyone talk you out of it, grab your happy dreams by the balls and do not let go, do not let anyone dismiss it, talk you out of it or snatch it from your spirit. Crazy and dismissed at first, then argue its lack of practicality and merit then eventually it is accepted as fact, reality and assimilated as a new norm. You just must focus on what makes your heart sing and do not let them side track you, no way and no how."

"I said that?"

"Yep, Navi Darling, you did indeed."

"Wow, I don't know what to say David Magus man. Well, I really wish now I hadn't encouraged you to follow your dreams."

"Ah, be happy for me. Everything will work out as it is supposed to, right?"

"Ah, give me some time to adjust. I'm kind of blown away at the moment."

Nosey Abby poked in the fridge, more listening than perusing.

"Look I am happy for you. I can see that it is a done deal. It excites, you are happy about your decision. It just scares the living shit out of me. Just give me some time here."

"I'll be fine, no matter what. You told me once that no matter what, you just got to live your life and do what has got to be done."

"I said that?"

"Yes, you did. Knowing you, you're so much more than being just married, toiling at a meaningless job and journey dreaming other worlds and realities."

"Then you should maybe not have listened. I'm really quite irresponsible."

"Naw, you were right. You are the best. You free my soul and spirit."

"Ah shit David, what about income and home stability? How will we make ends meet while you are painting?"

"Look, I've got a year with my severance package and unemployment insurance. I just need a year to get the first painting series out of me. I will pick up a job somewhere, even if I have to pump gas. But I've got to tell you, I can't ever go back to being a drone in some office and not painting."

"Am I in that picture of your grand Artiste future David?"

Catharine bolted to the door, shoved Abby playfully outside then slammed the door shut behind her, holding it so Abby could not come in. Suddenly giving way and standing aside, girl Abby tumbled in and thumped onto the floor. In retaliation, she scrambled and primate clung on to a leg, while Catharine hobbled over to the table and sat down, girl still clinging.

Cueing tension, she waited for an indication to stay or go then relaxed, as David excitedly reiterated his solemn vow to make a go of painting, full time. Navi's mind reeled imagining his charm, wit and easy going manner a smash hit in the snotty art world, but there was something about the solo steadfast focus that took her by surprise. Suddenly she felt left out, abandoned without rational explanation for the opposing emotional response. Left out, left behind, as Stephen had done.

"Look, it's what I want to do. We have talked about this and you have encouraged me, inspired me. I don't get your reaction."

Third wheel in the party, Catharine scooped up Abby and headed for the deck.

"Ya, I can see in your eyes that you've made up your mind. Just give me some time to adjust to process this." Spirit panicked, heart pounded and for a brief moment, her heart ripped, broken as though she may never see him again. The stormy dream replayed with ship sinking, him in the small wooden boat, lost at sea.

"What? Well, you knew that I got a grant in university and I can do it again."

"Yes. No. Well, yes, I know. I just did not know it would be full throttle so soon. God, you are still in the throes of separation and have just walked away from any financial claim to your house and pensions, everything. You have agreed to pay off all debts and continue spousal support. It is admirable but with my work so dicey, the thought of it all, well, honestly, the whole scenario scares the shit out of me. I only got twenty grand from the fall out with Stephen and that will not last long."

It was Déjà Vu, left out of financial equation again, second woman's second best with nothing but debt and a hardship Stephen story again, except that he worked but both of their first wives worked them.

Sensing her mothers' upset, Abby danced and bounced in distraction then hung clung off of Catharine, whining.

"Look, we'll work it out. I have got to go but we'll chat about it more, later."

She turned to Catharine, lost.

"Hop in gals, we're going on a little road trip!"

Grateful for distraction, they drove back roads into wilderness core as the Quaker journey experience unfolded.

"Rather, as it turns out, a vision quest. I thought I was setting out just seeking the off the beaten path of spiritual knowledge and away from all of those new aged morons, but it was really all so much more. I really wanted to know what makes them tick.

Ask and it is given, I found myself with an elder leader hanging out in the mid forest canyon. He had a large cloistered family who lived in an immaculate old cabin beside a tiny community church. Community extensions lived closer to town. Oddly, or in synchronicities of divine flow, I began inquiring in town, to chat to someone who might know the Quakers history and culture. The town librarian led me to an outskirt community, which in turn led me to Old William.

Community, sizing me up and once or twice over, provided a list of instructions and minor supplies. Map in hand at dawn, I hiked into the forest. It soon began to rain, list and map quickly washing into a watercolour painting, unreadable. I took a deep breath. Unsure of where to go, I stay put, built a circle of protection containing an inner circle. Darkness descended, as did torrential downpour. I stood there all night like that, silly sod that I am, did not make the circle big enough to lie down in. Ha. Anyway, somewhere in the wee hours of daybreak, I heard footsteps approaching quietly, ambling pitter-pat, closer and closer. Surrounded by dozens of little yellow eyes, I squatted and squinted; trying to decide, to what kind of creatures those eyes belonged. Oddly unafraid, what looked like wild dogs at first, I then realized they were more like huskies. Staying outside of circle, they sniffed and skirted around the circle, sniffed the air, sniffed me and then scooted off into the trees."

Engrossed Navi and Abby smiled as Catharine casually continued.

"It is always an afterthought that one considers an important thought; FEAR. Unknown to me prior, I was into a confrontation, facing darkness and the great unknown, lost in the forest did not really sink in until afterward.

I did a lot of thinking and processing that night. Oddly, the majority of thoughts arose about not belonging anywhere, an epic marital failure and social misfit. As soon as my mind exhausted itself, I began to hear wilderness night sounds. That is when I realized that I am who I am, as I shall always be, in this lifetime. Simply, I cannot be otherwise. So lone she wolf, I journey on, calmly and assuredly knowing that while misfit I may be, I am of God and a part of the all that is, just being me."

"Wow. She wolf woman Catharine and Saint Francis of Assisi."

"Ha. Maybe. It was not long after those huskies left, that an old man appeared and motioned for me to follow him. I packed up my backpack and dutifully followed for about two kilometers. I was so close. At his cabin, he spoke little, opting for facial expressions and body motion as direction. Chores; I peeled wild apples, snuggled and wrestled dogs, split and stacked fire wood, as the old man tended to other chores. Late afternoon, sitting on a stump, old arthritic hands agilely whittling, he calmly began to speak.

He said that he was just a wee boy when it all happened. He must have been very old. Ancient in fact, because most of the big shit that went down, occurred mid to late eighteen hundreds. Either that or he was just full of shit. Anyway, what folks out there know is pretty much true, those old Puritan worshipers all being so devoutly religious, almost fanatical. Well it began with one woman and then spread out into the community, then, to other communities.

Ghostly Red Indians overcame all, via possession. First one, then two, then four, then twenty, then more and more, all possessed by Native American Indians. There they were, all worshiping a God that they knew to be righteous and in the knowing of that selective piety, slid into channeling an entire clan and speaking native tongue. One woman was making a scene in church, rocking and rolling to the divine glory of the Creator. Community and ministers sent in a tailspin that would not be contained nor eradicated. Within days, the majority were all possessed, speaking in a native tongue and a rocking and a rolling, hooping and a hooting. William used the term possessed cynically, interjecting that this is what all sceptics and society use to describe things that they are too ignorant to fathom.

Legend has it that the dead Indians came to them because they were the closest of white people to God, creation and nature. Those old Puritans made a habit of following the light of God, not so much of manmade rules and such. In time they calmed, realizing those spirit Indians simply wanted to teach and share warnings of global events to come. Rather, news travels fast, and out into the world, their condition spread like wild fire. Priests, scientists, media and curiosity seekers arrived in droves from all over hells half acre, to aid and watch a mass exorcism. A frenzy of all different faiths, trying to cast the demons out of them, unfulfilled. Media had a field day circus. Academics, scientists, medical practitioners alike sought legal intervention to do their thing.

Old William figured that while the benevolent communion was actually good for the community folks, it scared be-Jesus out of the rest of the world. It is a wonder that they were not burned at the stake, or gallows hung. Had it occurred in back home England, they likely would have eventually been put to death or institutionalized.

Anyway, that is how the Shakers and Quakers got their name. Names that described what the possessions looked like; shaking and quaking, possessed.

Old William thought that most are still missing the point. The messages were important validations in following one's own inner sense of God and of living the spiritual life. That is why the Indians came in the first place; they were already so close to God. I think that they are lucky to have experienced that kind of phenomena, yet it is so sad to have had ignorant multitudes and probing sceptics swarming."

"Wow, what an adventure you have had. So world adventurer, what's next for you, stigmata?"

Catharine glanced sideways then chuckled, "Maybe."

"David, are you up for a small road trip?"

It was a large piece of undeveloped property off an old county road. They hiked in by trail for a couple of kilometers until they came to a small winding river. It had an ancient wooden walk bridge over it that led in to a grove of cedars. They sat on a bridge overlooking the riverbank below. Old willow and spruce trees hung over the river, giving it an enclosed feeling. Wild ferns and flowers gave it a magical garden look. Sitting back to back, the sun streamed diagonally through trees as warm breezes caressed their hair.

Silent nature, save for the trickling of water over a stony shoreline. At points, the overgrown river boldly showcased cattails and old cedars; long fallen, that splayed out across the water's surface, serving as a critter's step bridge.

A dragonfly courting and mating frenzy surrounded them in a swirling warm air dance. A magical other worldly volley of nature spirits and fairies advanced, acknowledged and retreated into shadows. Tiny wings sparkled in sunshine, a whispering spirit world on wings, tickling.

"Transcendent magic, I thank you Navi. I really needed this. I could never have imagined such bliss." David opened his backpack, a red cherry and cheese picnic. "Navi, you show me what living in the light means. This is what it is really all about, is it not? Sitting here like this, in this special place, is being in the light, right?"

"Yes. I figure that when I pass over to the other side, this is the kind of thing that I will recall and be ever so grateful for. I will be so glad that I took time out from world doings and had these wonderful experiences. I hope so anyway."

"So, if people do this sort of thing, even for a second, even just once, they can actually remember it all of their life and into the next, do you think?"

"Such a tiny experience in the shit storm of life, yet so powerful, so overwhelming that simply to have had the experience is enough. Not only will you remember always but also, the cosmos remembers. Everything can remember. It is and shall always be imprinted."

"I think I understand, a tiny moment in time can be enough of an experience of Nirvana, to help you centre when you need to draw on it. It's what we all work so hard for day in day out, yet remains so elusive to most of us, almost all of our lives."

"A key is like prayer, music, art and meditation; transcendence. The masters said that this is what life is supposed to be like, all of the time. That this is what life is like on the higher planes, as we evolve."

"It does leave a mark on a soul. I'll never forget this place, this afternoon."

"Anchor that feeling and expand it out to your wife, work, your painting, it is a natural healing balm."

August brought the distinct cooling of lake breezes, as Navi deck dived into spiritual courses, research lap splayed, sipping tea, as mind expanding new concepts that ran contrary to religious history sifted and sorted themselves out. Daughter squatted aside, a bundle variety of nail polish and hair care supplies. Girl manicurist quietly set about painting toenails purple.

"Sexy Momma!"

"Oh, I am all set for the Phil show!"

Somehow, some way, eventually, everything would be all right.

"Hi Gran."

"Darling Chickadee, the love that we all seek is of a higher realm, a higher vibration. When you accept anything less, you separate yourself from God, spirit. Anything less, is 'you' separating yourself from divine source, within and without. With practice, you grow and evolve until it is automatic and natural. Then you will find that you no longer attract these opposing experiences unless of course, to be of assistance to another. You will eventually operate solely in light. Practice. When you find that fear, anger and resentment crop up; face them. Learn to separate those emotions with simultaneous awareness of a higher objectivity. Love those shadow places, bring them out into the light of day; give love. What is a more loving thing to think, what is a more loving way to feel? It does not negate authentic emotion, it simply shifts shadow fears into love, rather than weakness."

"Thanks Gran."

"You feel it because you are both sensitive and intuitive, but also because there is still a part of you that buys into what they are saying, thinking or feeling. Dissolve those feeling beliefs from within and the thoughts words and deeds of others cannot harm you, emotionally, mentally, physically or spiritually, all parts of a whole."

"If I fall, will you catch me?"

"Assuredly."

Helen Bitch Boss woman always had a twofold agenda, a smoke and mirrors presentation on the table, her own subversive positioning. A manicured glow worthy of a spa weekend, fresh and empowered with aloof superiority, Helen slid her annual performance review across the table. Navi arched offensive back, sensing its contents and judging by the alarm bells blasting within solar plexus, knew she was going to be pissed off. Skimming pages of Satisfactory and Needs Improvement, she glared "What the..?" Shifting in untruths within her seat, Helen straightened spine and excused herself to the bathroom. 'Ah, drop a bomb then go psych yourself up for more.'

Helen returned stoic, immovable, empowered with defensive arms chest folded, daring debate and rebuttal. Ceasing a hesitated pause, woman on a mission continued, "Well I'll get right to the point. Quite frankly there are growing concerns about your work performance."

"What, since when? Ah, that's bullshit and you know it."

"There is no need to get hostile. And honestly Navi, we've been getting a lot of complaints."

"What complaints? I have not heard any complaints from any clients. Bullshit! Ohhhhh, I get it! It's my fine co-workers in the south office isn't it?"

Nailed, Helen's face blazed red and shifted attention to a menu, opening it and covering her face. "I wonder what the special is today."

Navi rippled warrior anger; she would be going home, jobless. "Since when do you listen to negative gossip and not talk with me? You used to always have my back covered. What happened to you that made you sell out someone that used to listen to your problems?"

Ignoring the personal jab, regaining focus on follow through added, "Well, Navi, quite frankly, your attitude towards your work and co-workers, has deteriorated."

"Oh right. Whose perception? Yours? When was the last time you were ever involved in my work with clients or came to the office just to hang out and see how things were going?"

Helen firmly closed the menu and slapped it down on the table. "Look, I'm not going to debate this with you ad nauseam. It is what it is. I expect you to shape up and make a go of things at the new office. Get along."

Undaunted and controlled, "You're the one that told me that I wasn't welcome there. I cannot help what they want or what they think. I am just trying to do my job in an impossible situation. I haven't changed how I work, I'm still the best dammed worker you have. It's you that has changed."

Reconciliation lost, Helen had long ago chosen her stance. "Well, I'm hearing that you're unapproachable and arrogant."

"What? That is utter bullshit and you know it!"

"No need for hostility."

"What do you expect? Where is my support? I am going through hell with the separation from Stephen and out there working front line bitches den, alone. Good manager you've turned into."

"Oh for God's sake Navi, don't be so melodramatic. Maybe you are too much of an altruist for the job. The new legislation dictates a different breed of worker. Maybe you're no longer cut out for the work."

Livid, an ousted and disposable employee sucked in a deep breath as a weary mind reeled trying to take it all in, find objectivity and the upper hand.

"Wow!"

Helen distracted with the server; discussing each special of the day and variations to her particular taste and diet of the month. Navi picked up a menu and saw only a foreign language before her, strange nonsensical glyphs that blurred in and out of vision, knowing that protest was futile.

"Helen, why are you waiting until now to address this stuff with me?"

"Well, maybe you should have responded to my memos. I have sent you at least four that you did not bother to respond to. Not one call, not a written response. Nothing!"

"When? I haven't received any such memos. I haven't received anything from you since the spring."

"Maybe if you were paying more attention to your job and a little less with your personal life, you might have noticed them, huh?"

Navi pushed the menu aside and striving to hold temper in check, picked at a coffee stain on the placemat. Helen calmly wolfed down a salad; white creamy salad dressing forming a clown's circle around lips; red liner blurred, leaving a big bulbous white chin drop. Disposed employee and betrayed gal pal watched, grinning, 'what an idiot'. Still, something else was amiss that she could not quite wrap her mind around. She stuffed the performance review papers back into the envelope and pushed it aside. "I'm not signing this right now. I need to think about it."

"Suit yourself. Just be sure it's on my desk by Monday."

Alone in the office, door closed, stacks of files waited to be entered into the computer, stat sheets to be filled, letters to be written to clients and phone calls to return. She could not concentrate, and searched the front desk for the referenced memos. Nothing. Inbox email, nothing. Glancing around first, she then began swinging back and forth in swivel chair then spinning around in circles using a foot to push off the desk for velocity force. 'What to do, what to do?'

Stopped mid spin, turned and went back into main internal email. Helen's password, a secret only Navi and HQ computer geek knew about and she was in. Scrolled and scrolled, searching for the memos, scrolled way back to the beginning of summer, opening ones with her name indicated on them.

A gasp, then reeling back into her chair, an enclosed memo of Helen's had been forwarded to the CEO; an itemized list of Navi wrong doings with specific client names and referenced file entries. "Navi had cancelled appointments without just cause or explanation to other staff concerned. Out on the road such and such a date, whereabouts; unascertainable and neglected to leave explicit contact instructions and itinerary. Navi did not call in."

"What? When? Where? Who is saying this shit?"

An e-file folder appeared with her name on it, a shaking hand opened it as heart pounded and teeth clenched.

"Jesus, why Helen, would you keep this stuff on an internet file where anyone could get into it if they really wanted to? It is not safe. It's stupid." She scanned a long list of private meeting reports that Helen had written about with Navi. "....she cried again today.... Is stressed and verbalized disgruntled profanities regarding upper management...."

"What? That's total Bullshit!"

She went back into each email message each report associated with her name then printed them all off, boxed them and locked it in the trunk of her car. All computer programs shut down, she crossed legs casual home-style comfortable and played solitaire for the rest of the afternoon. She had to think.

On a brave whim, she called Catharine who readily agreed to come and care for Abby and pets.

David arrived as she pulled out of parking lot.

"Jump in."

"I'm game."

Onto the ferry, heading to the northern outer lake system, and then sitting on deck, Navi flashed back to angst over Stephen day last May. She had wished that she had someone special to share the view and voyage with. Here was David now, arms wrapped around her, snuggled, feeling good and grateful for his presence. This time, it was her job loss and she was scared.

The Bear's Den Resort resembled a highway motor hotel adjacent to a rustic log building entitled The Trading Post.

"Navi, the term trading post is a misnomer. I'll bet you five dollars that if I came in here with a dead muskrat or something and asked to trade for some flour, sugar or some pots and pans, they'd throw me out."

"David, you were born in the wrong era." basking in anonymous casual comfort and local friendliness.

In the dark of midnight, they walked to the outskirts of town. An old cedar bush trail led into a grove of massive colourful toadstools within an ancient cedar tree cove. Shadows of nature spirits giggled, darting fairies and nymphs, they stood in another world of glorious peace and tranquility. In breathing unison, fresh forest and rain moisture aromas, communion with all that is.

"Navi, how on earth do you find these places?"

"Don't know, it seems that they find me."

Dark thunder rolled as the tree canopy lit with shards of lightening, followed by torrential downpour. Embracing warm rain with wide-open arms, fresh rainwater pelted her face and she open mouth drank of the water goddess. Each drop had been recycled millions of times through oceans, seas, lakes and puddles. Each carried the history of the ancients and of mother earth.

"Magic. Nirvana" David sighed in awe.

"Thank you Spirit world."

"Transcendent and indeed you are reverence for life and beyond woman."

"Glad you see it that way. Hope you always do."

Abby slammed the front door in a huff into her bedroom and plunged her face into pillow.

"Well, what happened?"

Face buried in pillow, "I went to see Old Polly, she's an angel Seer you know. I guess I am supposed to go to that new school Mom. Shit! Oops, sorry Mom."

"That's okay Abby, you can say it."

"You know I have new friends waiting for me and that's okay, because my old friends have changed anyway. They wouldn't be there for me the way that I need now. But I don't have to like it!!!!"

"No Ab, you don't have to like it right now, not one little bit."

David arrived and promptly fell asleep on the deck lounge chair in cool late summer's breeze, wrapped in Abby's long outgrown Little Mermaid blanket with head embraced in a purple furry Barney pillow.

"Mom? Can we keep him?"

"He's not a dog or kitten. We have had this conversation already. He's just finding his way."

Navi kept Helens printed memos and reports in the car trunk. She would figure out what to do with them, if anything when the time arose, hornets' nest caution. Swarms of angry hornets buzzed, occasionally quiet while other times, dramatically all fired up, stirring the masters' hive.

Navi confidently faxed her signed annual supervision report down to Helen at office headquarters. She had struggled signing it all morning and then in a rebellious and cynical move, signed it S.U.D.; 'signed under duress', hesitating, added 'and without prejudice' then in the comment section; 'Perhaps increased communication and accessibility on the part of management would alleviate any work performance related concerns regarding this worker'. A stroke of genius that bought a little more time yet sealed her exit, it would travel through the chairman of the board, commissioner, county boys and human resources before it lay in Helen's lap, a personnel file in archive bowels. A fate sealed, she walked out without a word, wanting to be home for Abby after school.

A stunning first day reiterated of new friends and teachers and how it smells so different from the last school.

"Except, God Mom, Cory is such an immature asshole."

"Why? What happened?"

"Well my teacher was introducing the new kids and she told the whole class about what we've been through the past year, Matt's being really sick with cancer and about us moving. She wanted the whole class to pitch in and make me and the other new kids feel welcome and comfortable. Mom, Cory teased me all day. He said that I thought that I was special because I had a sick brother with guts, his balls and hair missing. Well whoop tee do! The other kids seem really scared of him. It's not fair that I should have to deal with the asshole."

Grateful for the teachers' efforts, but she had in the end, screwed it up. Navi wrestled Abby to the floor in mock beatings of Cory and anyone else who dared take on the Wild Women Amazon Sisterhood.

"Abby, sometimes when you are going through big and tough changes, it is the Cory's of the world that add insult to injury. Just try not to let them get to you honey." She could retaliate, full unabashed venting of her own nasty stress build up.

David bantered back and forth with Abby who was in bed, supposedly asleep.

"Good night puke face."

"Good night booger breath."

"Good night camel stench."

"Good night twisted bee's knees."

"Good night brain drained."

"Good night mucous membrane."

"Good night radioactive slime."

"Good night alien spawn."

"Good night scientific experiment gone bad."

"All right!" shouted Navi. "All right you two, stop and go to sleep."

She woke to the smell of fresh coffee and following its aromatic trail, he handed her a cup and a lit cigarette.

"Oh, wow. Thank you", wondering how she looked. "You'd better be careful, you're really starting to spoil us."

"That's my game plan. Weird night; I woke up at four o'clock, just could not sleep. Paced and smoked. I just kept feeling like something big is about to go down. Weird."

"I can sense it too. Hey Magus Man; shall we take a break from everything and go to the north end of the Lake and hike the rim?"

"Well, I don't know. I've never been there."

"David, how can you live in this area for twenty years and not have gone there?"

Backpack secure, en-route toward bay's north end, following winding wood trails through rocky terrain, David grumbled and whined. "This terrain is too rough and way too many people. It's too cold!" Abby played on David's feigned discomfort; agilely zigzagging in and out of bushes and over boulders. Abruptly at trails end and out into open view of the sandy Lake, David froze in his tracks.

"Stunning, magnificent, I had no idea that this was like this. This is amazing! I'm impressed; it is truly a power place."

Cliff's edge looking down, waves crashed against rocks, slashing and bouncing. The cave entrance faced sideways out into open water. Water rushed in and out of the cave as a diver surface bobbed. Navi led David scaling around the cliff precipice and down into the cave. Once inside, a cloud of alarmed Swallows bombarded and frantically zipped in and out of their cave home. Deeply further into the cave, she took David by the hand, slowly gliding him along the rocky interior.

"Make sure your footing is solid then look down. You look down deep into the depths of the water and you can see the large hole in the bottom that seems illuminated. The hole, if swam, takes you out into the open bay. I have always wanted to swim it, but for now, will leave that to the scuba divers."

"Wow!"

Back onto the trail, seeking a shorter route, Chickadees assaulted in frenzy. Airborne circling and diving, they squawked alarm. Navi reached into her pack and pulled out a bag of trail mix. David and Abby took handfuls, holding handfuls out to the Chickadees. First one, then two, came to feed out of their hands, while Navi sat in reverence.

"How the Chickadees came to befriend humans. Once upon a time, two women sat side by side upon the grass attending to chores. One was busy washing, the other batting out carpet dust. A Chickadee came and sat upon a rock beside washerwoman. Staring, trying to get her attention, little wings flapped, squawking wildly. Washerwoman was annoyed and swung at it, scolding it to go away and stop pestering. Carpet woman came to the rescue of the little Chickadee and held it in her hands, cooing, then asked why it pestered so. Little Chickadee replied. I am merely a warning messenger. She is going to die, cross over into spirit world, tomorrow. She needs to use the remainder of her time wisely and make peace with loved ones and prepare for the other side journey."

Abby asked, "So what happened? Did the washer woman die?"

"Yes, she did."

"God, this cottage is cold. I am so fed up with living in cold houses."

"Christ yes Navi, it is cold in here!"

"I know. I haven't got a fire going yet."

David strode over to the wall and with one flick of a switch, turned on electric wallboard heaters and within minutes, it was toasty and warm. Navi was ecstatic. She had tried turning on the heaters at the floorboards but had not thought of the main switch on the wall.

"I had just assumed that they didn't work, just like at home, you know, fireplace only."

David rolled his eyes, "Where have you two been? How did you survive?"

Abby and happy mother danced madly, wild faeries, with newfound warmth. Both playing with the master wall switch as a game show host; introducing a new product up for prize, teasing contestants.

"How on earth will you manage without seeing your breath every morning?"

"David, thank you. Now, if you could just figure out how to set the microwave clock, and Abby's television, we'd truly be living in the new millennia!"

Howdy Navi,

I am back from Igloolik and at one of my new places of employment, with the Justice Department in Iqaluit. Things move to a much slower pace here and seem to change only when the wind direction changes.

The Americans sell one faction this or that to help control another faction. Someone else's regime changes hands then wow and pow, the Americans have to declare war, go in and occupy that country; does not make any sense at all.

However, there is a growing concern for the HARRP project. God only knows what the American Army is doing with this. They are tapping into and testing for air/energy/radio waves and frequencies in the atmosphere and deep into the earth. Cannot be right, cannot be good for the earth. The elders are tense. Of course, I would feel a lot better if there was a general sense of trust with the people who are running the project. It is army compound surrounded and barricaded, which is not a good sign. Of course, history with the government most certainly does not elicit feelings of wisdom or confidence that it will all be done and in a good way. They have a pretty shitty and embarrassing record of accomplishment. When are they going to stop messing with people's lives and natural resources? Oh well.

The folks here are aware of that project and have people strategically placed and on the lookout, some of them shaman. Take comfort knowing that the powerful forces of the earth and nature are no match for the elites or anyone else with ill intent. It goes too far away from higher divine forces. Mother Nature is old, wise and much more powerful than they are. If they get too close or have negative intent, the operation is slam shut down by the very forces they are playing with. It is like a toddler sticking things into an electrical outlet with wet feet!

It is comforting to know that these people know what is happening and are sure that the forces and the ancients are keeping an eye on things. I am also doing a temporary contract at the Baffin correctional centre as a corrections officer liaison and at the young offender facility as a youth officer/worker. Famine to feast!

I have been working literally every day since September eighth but I hope to have some days off next year some time! I really want to go back to the barrens and work with the old fellow, things were just beginning to happen when he was called away and I got work here.

We have a couple inches of snow on the ground and winter has officially arrived in the north.

I love it here. I feel like I am a part of the Northern Lights somehow. I love and respect their magical mysterious power. When I listen with my senses, I can hear the melodious music, tones vibrate my body as though I am sitting on a loud speaker, cool!

I have been sensing your presence recently and wonder if you are okay. I am sensing struggle again for you and a new man in your life. My prayers and light are with you and I know you will be okay soon. I do however feel quite strongly that something else may need changing; get out of the office environment???!!! Anyway, stay with spirit and know that you are loved, in abundance!

From the north to you, my friend

Gary

Thanksgiving announced its arrival as colourful leaves floated, danced in chilly winds and crunched under foot. Suitcase carrying David met with a questioning Navi gaze.

"Just for the weekend, is that okay?"

"David, it's hard on me and hard on Abby. Do not get me wrong; it is nice having you here, maybe too nice. But you're not anywhere near relationship ready and neither am I."

Lip curled in pout, shoulders slumped, "Oh okay fine but just for the weekend."

"My darling Chickadee; Unsatisfying relationships arise to show you that you have yet to succeed in communicating by ordinary means. Ask God to lovingly take care of these things, and then wisely listen to your own soul. Darling, do not give it another thought. Know that divine spirit is in there. God is in control and everything will eventually work out for the highest good of everyone."

"Thank you, Gran."

"Mom? Not only is David calm, gentle and very funny, but also he is good for you. I think we should keep him."

Navi's face flushed crimson.

"Well, Mom, since everyone likes him in the house including the pets. He should move in."

Navi's mind reeled, still battling martial turmoil; she had not found peace, frowned.

"Look Mom, he's going to be here eventually. Then it goes all black, can't see what then."

Life suddenly felt too big, too fast and too different. Peaceful David, immersed in a Monet biography, was quietly re-claiming his earlier art life, comfortable in her bed.

"Look she's not saying anything that I hadn't already thought of. Haven't you?"

"No. I haven't allowed myself to think that way."

"Hey, David" yelled Abby.

"What?"

"Good night butt wipe."

"Good night little mold spore."

Aware of his skin; soft, electric as wondrous harmonies softly played. Delicious skin sensation mingled with song as Navi was carried away to another time, another place. Visitation Soul Skin man and woman, engrossed in reverence of awe and gratitude for all that is good and beautiful with their world.

"Navi?"

"Yes David?"

"Are you awake?"

"Wasn't. Am now."

"Navi, marry me."

"Hmmm. Maybe, Maybe not. David?"

"Yes goddess."

"I'll be leaving work soon."

"Oh? Okay, well do what you think is best."

"Yup."

"Navi?"

"What?"

"Navi means 'Seer' or 'Prophet'."

"I've heard that. So does David, means the same."

"Navi? I am going to paint the great Canadian masterpiece."

"I know."

"Navi? Where did go you last night?"

"To the Grotto, the sacred healing cave, that jutties out into the greater bay. David, I have to go to sleep now, work in the morning. Good night."

"Don't you want to intimately celebrate my presence?"

"Good night David."

Soul skin man, spirit man's presence approached as Navi slid into sleep.

A spiritual embrace, skin and bones disappeared, world around faded, time stood still, one thousands lives, one soul, one kin, dancing oneness and soaring with the all that is. He whispered "Shhh... sleep sound Darling. After you roll over, I shall caress your hair and draw images on your back with my fingers while I tell you the story of a portal in time that I saw appear.

I shall tell you of us who came through that portal clothed in long jade iridescent hooded robes, floating in unison then disappearing on the other side. Then I will show you as Wolf Mates the softness of lying on moss spring warmed after a wintry journey apart and how we can always have something to sing about. I sing of a little southern gal who challenged a feral pig. We can transcend war and human atrocities with divine harmonies. To worlds where animals and trees are equal to two legged humans, one mind.

Oh my darling Soul Skin Woman, I shall tell you this and more. As you finally drift off deeper into sleep, I wrap my arms around you and thank everything on earth and heaven; that I found you."

"Tom?"

"Living under a cloud of black.
Utter a single word and watch the lightning
strike.. feel the roar of the thunder.
Periods of calm are like tears
dripping from a rainbow
and life goes on."
Donna A. Favors

Chapter 15 ~ Surfacing

As work ending in social services seemed eminent, an affair with co-worker David unfolded into a committed relationship. Dramatic inner change of consciousness was also unfolding as a lifetime of rigid church mentality dissipated and new like-minded spiritual seeker friendships formed. Sifting and sorting old church crony interpretations and beliefs bought into since childhood, of judgment and sin, a new path was emerging. Seminary courses were nondenominational and inclusive of world religions and philosophies, an authentic life waited to blossom. Plagued by other worldly journeys, menopause, an affair with David, Navi struggled for balance.

Thanksgiving had announced its arrival as colourful leaves floated, danced in chilly winds and crunched under foot. As did suitcases carrying David, met by Navi's questioning gaze.

"Just for the weekend, is that okay?"

"Again? David, you're not ready, it's only been a few months since your exit saga with your soon to be ex-wife. I'm not ready."

His lip feigned a pout curl.

"Okay, fine. But just for the weekend."

"Mom?"

"Ya babe."

"Did you like sex with Stephen?"

"Whatttt? That's kind of personal don't you think?"

"Hmmm, well I'm heading into that age Mom, hmm and judging by your reaction, well, makes me even more curious."

"Sigh, not so much if you must know. Does that satisfy your inquisitive mind?"

"No. I kind of gathered that, but why?"

"Hmm, well, um, his thingy didn't work so good for me, but worked fine for him, with his own self. Is that enough on that?"

"No, Come on Mom, give it over. I don't want to fall in love and then find out we aren't sexually compatible."

"Oh God. Fine, if you really must know, it was actually an alien caterpillar worm. I think it got tired of being yanked on all day and flew off to its own home planet."

"What? God Mom!" In laughing hysterics furthered, "You are a lunatic!"

"I know and since you are born of that lunatic gene pool that makes you one too.

Truthfully, daughter, I think you are mature enough to handle this information, just pocket it away for when dating begins. I heard somewhere that you ought to be fussy about whom you share physical intimacy. Not just because it messes you up emotionally and mentally but there is also some unseen spiritual or energy imprinting mixing that occurs. Ask God, Angels, to assist in clearing out physical, emotional, mental and spiritual bodies, leave no karmic ties, no harmful residue of guilt, shame, resentment, hurt or anything else that might pop into up your mind."

Morning coffee and smoke, curled in the beach cottage window, Navi greeted dawn, a new day. Mist lay, still hovering hip high amidst pre-winter giant evergreens. Hard massive jutting red and grey granite added striking bold colour to the backdrop of the majestic lake's greying aqua. October passed quickly and quietly saluting November and still no snow. Usually bombarded by several storms by now, only a frost blanket coated the trees, plants and grass in an icing sugar layer of ice.

In vain, she attempted to create a soul connection with the spirit of all that is; of nature ambiance with familiar trees and animals. A connection of re-awakening that she was sadly missing, old loving images spilled forth in a moment of homesickness for Stephen's old farm cottage; Chickadees, Mabel and Clifford Crow, Nigel Possum, Buddha Raccoon and Grandmother and Grandfather Maples. There had been multitudes of goldfish sparkling in pond sunshine, a roaring chorus of the Peeper Frogs mating in the spring, and warm summer nights as a Matt pre-cancer and Abby danced among swarms of fireflies; then to warm afternoons standing amidst swarms of dragonflies. Memory smells filled olfactory senses of a vast blooming garden, the warmth of summer sun breezes caressing hair and face. A heavy sigh opened eyes to the grey reality of the day and the drama that had followed life without Stephen; attention had turned to the want of a home of their own. There is valuable information to be gained in finding out who we authentically really are, through our most intimate of relations, work activities and how we came to be where we are.

Abby was unusually quiet, lost in thoughts of school politics, and why Cory Taylor-Anderson was such an asshole. The persistent little ratter had seemed relentless in pestering and insulting her. Cory was smitten with her daughter. Rather than finding it cute, she, like Abby, would like to take a round out of the munch-kin and plotted to duct tape him to a telephone pole naked, covered in honey as army ant bait. His older brother Rory Taylor-Anderson was worse, also smitten with Abby. The mean wired wrong adolescent neighbourhood skulked with a dark scowl, pensive and ready to beat the crap out of vulnerable kids. Navi's short lifetime in Montreal with Abby's father inadvertently offered a side drop kick solution. A few short French slang phrases and matrix energy warrior training, daughter was an armed warrior woman.

The next morning's school bus ride changed the tyranny for Abby. It rippled out onto the schoolyard and into the community in one fell swoop, young warrior girl alpha dogged. Barely sitting down on the bench seat, Cory began his cruel taunt. An empowered Abby casually opened her mouth and allowed each phrase to nail its target. Energetic tendrils flowed out of her being, nailing him where he stood. A stunned Anderson boy froze in confusion, dumfounded as anxious little faces watched the drama unfold.

"Back off, you little asshole shit for brains."

Angrier at her audacious stand, Cory grimaced livid, stumbled, then holding a fist to her nose waited for the normal backing down that he was accustomed to. Warrior empowered, she casually looked him straight in the eye, slid his fist away then said "Mange la merde Bovine Faeces!!!!!"

Confused, Cory's mind scrambled to understand the bizarre words and the alpha power shift and came up empty. The usual bully life force drained, he plopped defeated back onto his bench seat, face ashen in shock and humiliation. A moment of still registration to all broke into raucous laughter and cheers for Abby warrior woman.

Mexico bound, paid for from readings all summer with tourists and a manifested dream of exploring Mayan temples. Polly arrived for tea, offering a spirit reading for Navi. She lit a candle, pulled out a deck of tarot cards, shuffled them, and then slowly laid them out in a series.

"Don't get yourself tangled up in the legalities of corporate problems, just stay in grace and follow Spirit. I see David will leave work very soon, galleried within the year. I see that you absolutely must continue your spiritual pursuits, ordained."

"What do you mean, ordained?"

"Sorry kiddo, it's what I see, destiny. Only a beginning, you are an initiate, triple cross like saints, mystery schools, shamanism, mysticism and metaphysics. Seems like you grow so fast through so many chapters, with many life times all jam packed into one."

Sloughing off the reading, politely refilling tea, obviously Polly was a new aged flake and full of shit.

"Mom?"

"Yes, darling'"

"What's for dinner?"

"Road kill."

"Yummy. What kind?"

"Well, let's see what I picked up today. Hmm, it's black and white and kitty cat kind of furry, oh and a bit stinky, so it must be skunk."

"Oh yummy. How will you cook it?"

"Well first understand that you will be ingesting like mind and like soul medicine, you know how only a skunk can hang out with another skunk, only a skunk loves the smells of another skunk, well people are like that too. We need our own kind to live happy and contentedly. And judging by the way it was trampled by what appears to be a school bus, I guess I'm going to have to roll it up, tie it with a bungee cord and bake it on an old Chevy pickup truck engine like a pot roast."

"What are we having with it?"

"Well let's see. We have tails of cat, bee's knees, spider eggs and thistle thorns. Sound good?"

"Yummy."

Saturday morning adolescent Abby sprawled out in front of cartoons, Navi lingered in bed trying to recall the dream. A symbol of a spiral sun, she pulled out a sketchpad and roughed it in with colour.

Greeted at the tattoo parlour by a black streaked red haired Goth girl, pierced face and hands begged another era opera talent. Another girl appeared carrying a tiny drill in hand, black silk from head to toe, everything was black, eye shadow, lipstick, military boots and crew cut hair. Navi tried not to stare, but between the two, pierced eyebrows, noses, lips and ears, there begged the question of how either would make it through airport security. Counter girl slouched, gawking out of the window lost in thought, chewing gum with mouth open, playing with it, rolling it around her bulbous metal tongue ring. A moment of panic, thinking that maybe she should not have come and certainly should not have brought Abby quickly faded as a familiar well-dressed young man appeared. An old school dropout client had given up trying to fit into the academic system and who now was making more money in a day than she made in a month. He pulled out a sketchpad, adding touches to her design.

"It belongs on the top of your spine. This is your morning star and the sun in the afternoon before sunset, an ascension symbol. An Ishtar, Mayan."

"How do you know about those things?"

"I have learned many things in life. Like how to follow your dreams, no matter what anyone else says or thinks. Shit, if it wasn't for you, I wouldn't have a wife, a baby girl, this business and a BMW in the parking lot."

"No kidding! Wow! You have done really well for yourself. I really said those things to you?"

"It's a code I live by."

"Gees, maybe one of these days I will listen to my own advice, ha."

Abby perched on a stool to watch, eyeing the dental office like room equipment. His sketch photocopied with henna ink, wet sponge matted on top of her spine and the drilling began. Searing pain; eyes popped, mouth wide open, venting a silent scream. Wild fire ripping skin, 'one *must* come stoned for tattooing'. She braced, and hunched, with her arms tightly wrapped around her knees, "If I can survive natural childbirth without painkillers then this too can and shall be transcended". Focusing on a specific point of the floor and breathing deeply, the pain numbed. Jesus appeared, looked up grinning from where he squatted before her. Mother Mary appeared with arms outstretched, happy and giddy.

"A symbol to meld the physical, emotional and mental bodies into one spiritual body but, how to activate it?" muttered the tattoo artist prodigy.

Navi glanced at grinning Abby. "What?"

"Grandma Is Going To Kill You, Mom!"

David chuckled, peeling back her tattoo gauze patch "Wow, that's really cool almost Mayan. If I remember my university ancient history symbol-ology correctly, it has to do with transcendence and ascension. I think you are my Yoko Ono."

"Yes, that's what the kid that did it thought."

Waiting until Abby was safely in bed out and out of listening range, to catch up on the day, he whispered, "I went to work this morning and found the file auditor going through my files. I had not released them to him. I was pretty pissed that the jerk was going through my files without my consent. I know its shitty timing, but I can't work for an organization that allows the basic human right of privacy to be jeopardized by un-consented file audits. Everybody has fucked up in that organization and turned into monster bullies who think they can do whatever the fuck they want. They have interpreted the legislation as means of enforcing control and authority over poor people. I'm really sick of it."

"I think, I had better make a pot of tea."

"Yes, God war mongers. The new government legislation affects poor people in abhorrent ways. It really boils down to a miss allocation of power and authority. Power gives staff a false sense of omnipotence. Honestly, power allocation breeds corruption. I'm really worried, the auditor picked out one file in particular; a single mom with three small children. Off of her graphic designer job under Doctors orders for six months, because of the stress that her abusive ex-husband is doing, stalking and tormenting her to break down; Post Traumatic Stress Disordered. The auditor wants accountability on why I am allowing her to be off work and on welfare. I am beyond pissed. He would not let it go. Why in the fuck can they not leave these people alone? I mean surely to God, no one would knowingly choose to leave a good job to live on five hundred dollars a month?"

"I know. Helen told me I was too much of an altruist, that the new system requires a different breed of front line workers. I see that now. They are taking the human services out of human services. With the new computer system, all they really need are by the book clerical workers who won't question what they're doing."

Every rural county has at least one Bermuda triangle vortex intersection made cautiously and notoriously famous due to its sheer volume of accidents. Approaching the four way stop, Navi's eyes locked onto a clothesline full of laundry at the side of the old country house. A long line of men's underwear danced and waved hello in wintry breeze. Each pair was bowel stained dark brown. Slamming brakes sliding mid-intersection, an oncoming transport truck blasted its horn, wind whipping, rocking the car in passing, mere inches directly in front of her. Truck full circle swerved in wind wake, its trailer skid rocking the car in its opposite direction, vicariously spinning. Surreal time, hands gripped the steering wheel as the transport truck screeched and snake swerved to a stop, its ass end bouncing in back lash missing her driver's side by inches. A red family van screeched braking wheeled around her, blaring horn, followed by a man's arm extending far out of its window, its man driver producing a 'finger'.

Waiting for transport trucker to step out and altercate, she scared waited, blood pounding in her ears. Hands violently shaking, heart-thumping, shifting into gear, she slowly navigated through the intersection and pulled over onto the shoulder, then glanced back. Over sunglasses he glanced at her, hesitated, seeing that all was safe, nodded goodbye, shifted gears and gathered speed, disappearing out of sight.

Deep breathing adrenaline subsided, eyes catching dirty undies happily dancing in the wind. "Jesus! God! No wonder there are so many frigging accidents here!" White knuckles still locked on steering wheel, her head bowed and allowed a tear to trickle, then giggled relief. Giggles erupted in raucous laughter, picturing the man who belonged to clothes lined soiled delicates. Images played of his homecoming to the scenery, then promptly chastising the wife for publicly displaying his bowel problem. Cynical wife grinning pleasant revenge over some misdemeanor, "Oh, I am sorry darling."

'Time for new ones friend, those old soiled things are deadly, literally! Maybe comfortable underwear is hard to find, I get that.'

A beaten rusted red neck pickup truck turtled alongside, slowing as a quizzical neighbourly glance from an old outdoorsy handsome native man with big bushy side burns and aviator sunglasses hovered on a large pocked nose. A handmade dream catcher dancing from the rear view mirror, his old straw cowboy hat finger tilted back, revealing joyful sparkling black eyes under bushy thick brows. A nod indicating that she was indeed okay, he wave saluted, and then cranked up the music full volume. Elvis Presley's 'Suspicious Minds' blasted as an old hound dog sat steady in the back, floppy ears and drool string swinging in the wind.

"We're caught in a trap. I can't walk out, because I love you too much baby. Why can't you see what you're doing to me, when you don't believe a word I say? We can't go on together with suspicious minds and we can't build our dreams on suspicious minds..."

The bumper sticker boldly advised: TAKE THE ROAD LESS TRAVELLED.

"Aunt Diane used to bring me here, every summer." With David lagging behind along a luxurious wood chip path, Navi prattled. "This place was once a childhood wilderness, now, it's a government manicured tourist park. The aboriginal glyphs had lain safely hidden under its perfect moss protection against weather elements and away from dumb assed white people for eons.

As a child, Aunt Diane would wander off alone while I freely roamed trails, sitting upon its rocky mound communing with its ancient spirit artists. The outcrop over there, once served seasonal back bush hikers and hydro line workers as a lunch bench rest stop. Safely hidden, long before white world official discovery seeing another museum way to incorporate cement and buildings, I can remember that as a young girl, often sitting contentedly tenderly running fingers over the chiseled indentations, touching and sensing, images flowed of generations of indigenous peoples who portaged, a myriad of uncharted canoe routes inland then hiked through deep bush. In my child mind's eye, another massive network of rock underneath all of this, still secretly lays in silent waiting, still hidden under soil and moss. Further underneath that network, I can see an array of tiny caves and caverns. Even at a young age, I sensed and knew of its sacredness, I instinctively gave due respect. I remember once, approaching adolescence where I spirit attended as an observer of mysterious sacred ceremonies and teachings, still secret to modern world. The teachings, ceremonies occurred according to astrological and prophesied where select native children learned the mysteries of Creation, healing, philosophy, astronomy, and the history of the earth, universe and cosmos. While seeing only glimpses and listening in, I still felt privy to just a smidge of their meanings and understandings despite the language barrier. Now, the glyphs encased in that big assed airtight glass building structure complete with hovering uniformed staff and security cameras just seems like another sacred site in the hands of dumb assed white people."

The twenty-six dollar entrance fee seemed absurd given its preferred natural preferences. Gigantic architectural structure of glass and cement displayed a fraction of the carvings; a gift shop offered archaeological history, scientific data on the materials used and academic scholars misguided interpretations.

"See the sweet grass remnants there? Local First Nation peoples come to burn the cleansing herb mixture in ceremony to keep the area clean of white people ignorance and maintain respect of the ancestors, I suppose. If it is true that those glyphs were teaching tools, where with the strictest permission and invitation of elders, novices could learn the history of the peoples and its inner mystical mysteries then it kind of makes me one wonder and question whether or not just any old white person should be allowed in, let alone be 'owned and operated by a white government as a tourist attraction. Ah, I sound cynical, but it is still a cool place to visit.

If you focus on one carving that attracts your attention, then close your eyes, the ancestors might just allow you magical dreams of far away and ancient places or a message."

"This is beyond cool Navi. I am attracted to that one, it looks like a Great Ship with star or sun people on it; makes me think of Lemuria or Atlantis, magical. God damn I love you."

"I love you too. I honestly don't know for certain if that one is original or not. There is speculation that people have added carvings to make a bigger impression. I am always drawn to the one that looks like a naked woman with her vaginal area exposed; I get the sense that one is the root of creation."

"I wonder if the spirit of the place is asleep, tolerating public display, maybe even humouring us ignorant white folks while our tiny brains scramble and ponder their meanings."

"Look, this is the glyph I picked out. I looked it up in the book, its Storyteller. I'm a storyteller through my painting, I suppose."

"I am glad you got some sort of connection. Let's go, I want to take you somewhere else and I'm not going to tell you where."

Hours later, they pulled into Mother's driveway. The country house stood majestic beside a beautiful river that ran zigzagging north and south. Evergreens and rock surrounded the river bend, affecting a mural view.

"Jesus, you grew up here? This place is gorgeous, incredible!"

"No, I didn't. Mother came here after father died; I always figured she would go to the city. I'm surprised that she chose rural. I personally do not like it, something about the place that just does not sit right. I've only been here a couple of times actually and when I do, I can't wait to leave. It feel like death."

David's demeanor was instantly sullen and visibly nervous. Mother's eyes widened in skeptical inventory, while Aunt Diane casually, cautiously, silently, intuitively read him. Under scrutiny, he shrunk painfully shy. Navi announced "Bar open!" He accepted a tall scotch, straight up, while Mother and Aunt waited with blank faces for the change in her daughter's life to assimilate. To cut tension and divert tension, she showed off her new tattoo, as he mumbled something about being forty-eight years old and meeting his girlfriend's Mother for the first time. Sensitive Seer Aunt Diane grabbed the bottle of old scotch and led him out onto the deck.

Navi kitchen table sat with aging gaunt mother and a pot of tea, and highlighted all that had transpired over the past year. Information on a need to know basis, screened and filtered in adjustment to accommodate Mother's now fragile coping ability. She would not be long for this world, homesick, lovesick for Father. Information must be processed and translated as a positive, in daughter's favour; then in turn disseminated throughout the nosy church crony network and slightly adjusted as needed elsewhere. While she had rarely seen her brothers since high school, it was important for Mother to keep a constant inventory tab on who was doing what, and where. It was her way of staying involved and active in everyone's lives. She prattled on about which brother was making the most money, had purchased what, and had what adult boy toy and what genius child was achieving what award. It was an ambivalent relationship; being the only girl and odd, there was no commonality with the male entourage. Chatter and prattle would be short and matter of fact, with uninteresting information. Achievements were focal points in carrying on brotherly competition.

Mother never spoke of Father, even now. Moving here was a dramatic life change. Immediately after his passing, and while putting on a brave social activity face including random mini-road trips with Aunt Diane, her grief lived on. A lifetime of living the idyllic wife role, denied her authentic Celtic wild woman within. Unspoken regrets, a life lived to societal ideals, a clock that could not be turned back to a very different lifestyle. He had contentedly assumed a role subjugated to wallflower, loyally working and providing all of his adult life; silently leaving all matters household and child rearing to his wife. Devoid of hobbies, interests and passion, he dutifully worked, slept and ate without ever having really lived. Thinking on it now, he did never indicate that he had missed out on anything in life. Now, his life seemed content.

At peace, lingering hugs, teary eyes and tender face caresses spoke a lifetime of now realized daughter love. "Wow Mother, I love you. Thank you for trying your best to protect me."

Mother fatigue peered into her soul then smiled.

"I do love you daughter, more than you'll ever know. Look, just don't settle for second best in a man. I wish you'd wait to settle down again, wait for the one who will take care of you, the one you can count on to allow you to live in anyway your little heart desires. This is true love and true freedom, to be who you want to be, even if who you are trying to be is a crock. You know what I mean, the one who financially and morally supports you just as you are. Mother and daughter tear filled hug embraced, soul blending mother love. A lifetime of missed relationship dissipated, the magical love moment holding throughout time. Instantly sensing her spirit parting, Navi whispered into her ear, "Mom, I am always with you. We walk together through this lifetime and beyond. We shall meet on the other side and dance into the divine light."

Mother chuckled, "Suddenly I am not afraid to go anymore. I think I will just toddle off in my sleep. Please don't make a fuss, absolutely no funeral service or church visitations. Your Aunt Diane knows what I want, and has the church end and your brothers covered, I miss your father. I want to go home."

The feel of aging skin, decaying breath imprint lingered in a maternal kiss, bond sealed forevermore, Mother and Daughter at peace with each other.

"I'm really disappointed in you. I am really quite upset about this. How dare you just drop me into the pool of your Mother and Aunt without any preparation, at least ten years of preparation?"

"Ah, it's good for you."

"No, no. You are not getting it. I am really quite upset, traumatized."

"You're snookered on scotch, is more like it."

"So what was up with the private chin wag with Aunt Diane?"

"Basically, if I hurt either you or Abby, she will hunt me down and rip out my entrails through the tiny eye of my penis. There is nowhere to run, nor hide where she won't find me and that she and your Mother will haunt my ass. What do you think she meant by that? "

Navi grinned, the explanation would be lost upon him at this time, and it would take lifetimes.

The Monday morning debate ensued as to whether or not Abby had to go to school, if not sick. She had been crying, up late, overwhelmed and worried about the new and improved curriculum and mountain of homework. Young girl had reached her inner max of coping and adjusting, now burnt out, was tired and grumpy.

David prattled about his fender bender car accident "I was trying to get the feel of the change in snow with stupid honking assed winter boots on, and shit, I think I caused it. The other car was fine but out of it came an old woman who screeched obscenities. I suddenly felt like a terrorist. I am officially putting off driving for the time being. I am tired of work, separation wars with the Ex and I have moved in with a house full of gorgeous women. I guess life isn't too shitty after all."

David turned to pounding out a computer letter of resignation, intent on giving Helen and HQ notice in the morning.

"Oh God help me! Okay, I can only deal with one thing at a time, so first things, first."

It seemed that Abby had more homework than she had in college.

The hefty and stoic young bland pudgy teacher was instantly defensive, reminiscent of Stephen; that hook repelled Navi into an unnerved ill at ease. Straightening her spine, she adjusted a shit detector knot in her solar plexus and searching for grace positive, began, "First, I'd like to thank you for your time. I'd like to remind you of all that Abby has been through in the past year, so surely you can cut some slack with the homework load?"

The matronly teacher woman pursed lips, defensively crossed arms over her chest and waited. Alpha dog silence ensued as both energetically stood hierarchy ground. Matron teacher turned and pulled out a folder of charts and splayed them out on the desk, turning them so that the not very bright parent could see. Matron teacher straightened her spine, and then piously explained, "Your daughter's homework must be managed at home, under parental supervision."

Navi, tension building, glanced at the chart then switched to a temporary diversion by changing the subject, "Oh and thank you for the winter nature class trip, Abby had a much needed really good time."

Matron woman nodded, dabbing a tissue to a leaking nostril, then continued where she left off, slower and louder. Obviously, the student's mother was a rebellious sort, of no class significance and obviously slow. A mother wolf crossed, an anger ripple rose up her spine and then a low growl slid out of her mouth "I could be wrong, but you seem to want to organize our home time around Abby's homework. Frankly, I resent your audacity to even entertain scheduling our family time."

Matron teacher woman was immovably livid. Navi, battle weary, was pissed and ready to take her on. Matching matron teachers condescending tone one level up, she wolf alpha dogged.

"A child needs to be a child, needs to have quiet family and creative time. I would not want to work all day, then come home and do the same kind of work all evening, it's not healthy."

Abby cued that war had been declared and that her mother was losing temper, interjected, "It's okay Mom, I can work with the scheduling of homework charts if she wants me to. I will try harder."

Matron teacher woman cracked a superiority grin.

Navi was livid, not wanting her daughter to be a peacemaker at her own expense. Visions flashed of an exhausted Abby stress slept hunched over the dining table, homework unfinished each night.

"Abby, this is not okay. I do not believe it appropriate or healthy for a university student to do six hours of homework every night. This is public school. Special projects are exceptions, unless of course you are inferring that my daughter is lagging behind, in which case provide the assessment report that identifies that this is the case. No? I thought not. So then, send the absolute essential minimum and the rest of this crap you have been sending home can stay at school. You cannot dictate what happens in my home."

Matron crusty teacher woman strived to contain an inner temper explosion as she placed her hard work mound of paper work back into its folder. Standing, retaliation eyes widened, "We shall see. I have no other recourse than to take this matter up with our Principle."

Standing, Navi stood facing Matron Temper Tantrum Teacher woman, an alpha dog professionalism standoff, "I would be happy to discuss this matter with him at his earliest convenience."

In the car, Navi shakily lit a cigarette, calming.

"Mom, you seemed so angry, you were vibrating, pissed. I hope I never piss you off like that!"

"Ah, darlin' watch your language. I have been through enough judgmental and condescending shit to last several lifetimes. I am sure that I am black listed in the board of education files somewhere for navigating Matt through school crap when he got so sick. I'll bet there are notes in your files that say, 'watch out for the mother'."

It was an inner contradiction; in relationships a naive and compliant wall flower child, in advocacy moments came surges of Joan of Arc she-wolf alpha dogging that scared her. Was the majority of the world blind? Did no one else see that crap higher ups were always trying to shove down the throats of already stressed working class parents and children? It seemed as though every system strived to keep those that it fed off of, in line, in tow and with zombified complaints. Beyond, stupid government puppets, string held by billionaire elites who dictated and ruled out of greed. Follow the money trail of the ills that plague human kind and you will find an entrepreneur who sees capitalist golden opportunities, just give the masses smoke and mirrors, put a positive spin on it and they will toil their lives away supporting someone else's greed and hoarding.

On a cynical mind rant roll, the teacher reminded her of an all-around generalized catch all group who were ignorant of higher child whole needs and who based their strategy on trendy expert propaganda. Public school curriculum designed to raise subordinate labourers to fill lifeless manufacturing plants and service sector fast food franchises without regard to a child's natural inclinations and interests. Pressured to stuff and pack growing minds with meaningless activities and information day after day, to suit a marginalized materialistic culture. Some cartels under the guise of academia, political and business mogul groups get together and devise research and statistics to suit their own agenda. Who finances elections and lobbies for legislation? Who owns the media?

It was no wonder that parenting was so exhausting. There was so much expectation to live up to, when most parents were preoccupied just trying to survive and keep going. Most, just wanted to put food on the table, all else is neglected on the someday soon shelf with car, house, computer repairs and sacred time for oneself. Navi's mind was on a fed up roll. Jaguar driving Vampire Dentists suck all of your hard-earned money and hold you soap box lecture captive. The main priority in life must be teeth and gums. Family pets are taken to the Hummer driving Veterinarian who refuses to hand over a smidge of flea treatment until your pet has had a full medical, manicure groom and sixty dollar bag of dog food with chicken flavoured toothpaste to follow while really, they just want to eat table scraps, road kill and cat turds. Then in the sanctity of your own home, you turn on the corporate owned television to learn what ones materialistic priorities are amidst stark contrast to the horrors of the world. Collectively, these self-appointed authorities sucked the spirit and joy out of life.

White-collar professionals exist far removed from the realities of working class and poverty unable to see the bigger picture of their own role, misguidedly feeding some corporate greed monger under the guise of a career. Buying into propaganda bullshit that raved shaking fists, the problems of society lay upon the welfare parasites of the world. A flash of Nazi mentality arose.

The great American dream pursuits for material wealth kept billions of people in line, studiously striving, struggling to taste unattainable goals, left stressed and unfulfilled. Television's morals were a sorry unfulfilled pain in the ass to the working poor and underemployed.

Everyone was an authoritative expert in his or her field. Dental Hygienists displayed graphic posters of horrifying gum and tooth diseases while reciting tartar control, flossing, brushing techniques. Their Jaguars, BMW's and tropical suntans were ravenous bottomless money pits that ensuring regular visits beyond what any normal person could possibly afford. God forbid you spare yourself and your child scheduled visits, children's services would be knocking on your door. Oh but one must submit, trapped in the luxurious lounge chair staring at horrific images of various rotting mouth diseases, was dutifully expected. Veterinarians gave lectures on top quality sixty dollars a bag, dog and cat food, while in actuality dogs and cats preferred rotting dead animal carcasses and raccoon poop.

Olivia, a single mom neighbour worked three jobs and spent more in a month on children's tutoring and recreational activities than on mortgage, utilities and groceries combined. A summation of mounting pressure to ensure children would be successfully rich. North Americans were hot on the trail of upraising a stressed generation of human doings rather than human beings. Super Mom guilt complexes, mothers who endure and suffer until old age, when in hindsight would rather have grabbed their more natural wild nature by the bosom and make love, dance and create massive social change. 'Someday that shift will come.'

The kitchen table displayed Abby's school to do and must do charts amongst piles of supposed overdue homework. Daughter, visibly stressed, squirmed wearily in seat, rubbed forehead longing to slide off and create art, anything else. Mother surveyed the mess and concluded herself as useless, new curriculum was beyond her and attempts would only validate schoolteacher matron bitch woman's inference; stupid.

"No homework. I am taking the phone off the hook and putting my pajamas back on. We have to figure out a way to make this comfortable and manageable, but first, movie rental store. We will settle in for an afternoon of funny movies, candy, cola and snuggles. Don't worry Darling, we'll figure it all out."

"Yahoo!"

Unsure of what exactly she was teaching Abby shifted in affirmation of a stress day off, "I need a bucket of Triple Decadent Death by Chocolate ice cream."

"Mom, it's a P.M.S. day!"

"Yer funny kid. I like that. So shall it be declared and proclaimed."

"Mom, I think you'd make a great Minister, a real one, not like the fake ones you see in robes, pretending to know anything about real life or consoling someone with scripture readings that not many people can relate to. Sometimes people need a kick ass person in their corner, not to just sit and pray with, but somebody who will actually call shit 'BULLSHIT' and kick some bully ass."

"God, your language girl. Huh, so that's what you think eh?"

"Mom, have I ever told you that you are a lunatic?"

"Yes, but we is peas in a pod, poor kid."

"Well I guess it's alright being your daughter this time around. Although most of our other lives, I was your mother. I think I liked that better."

"Oh really?"

"You're a good Mom; you just suck at the real world stuff."

"What do you mean by that?"

"Ha, don't get all offended Mom, just saying that I'd rather be rich, is all."

"Get a job!"

"Right, I will get right on that. Think I will go to the beach bar and hook. Those hookers that hang out at the beach yacht club make a lot of money off of business tourists."

"I am sure that is a fitting livelihood for a medicine woman healing. Ha, just don't be bringing any stray's home."

"Mom, imagine if my teacher actually heard us talking and joking around? I'd be in a foster home wouldn't I?"

"Maybe a rich one."

"Mom!"

"You little lunatic."

"I love you, really love you."

"I love you too, really, really, really. Inside and out."

"Mom?"

"Ya Babe."

"We're not really lunatics; it's the rest of the world. Somewhere in some other era or time space continuum, we're normal."

"God I love you!"

David arrived just in time for dinner, blithering of the office, "Strange, something coming down the wire. I figured that today isn't the right time to resign, better wait and see what happens."

THUNK the window bounce waffled as a startled Chickadee bounced, striving to maintain air borne balance. Now quiet, Abby glanced at them both, Chickadee messengers, someone was dying or going to die. David uncomfortable shifted and averted attention, "Abby I'm going to go and beat the snot out of your teacher and Cory." Abby giggled edging him on then presented a colour coded, prioritized with accompanying catalogue of pictures, Christmas wish list.

"Well, you've been very busy. Now I think I know why your homework is overdue. Thanks Abby, for getting me in trouble with your teacher."

"Hee, hee. Naw, Mom, I did homework, I just worked on this after it."

"Uh, huh. Well let's see what you've got here. A computer with a scanner, a video camera set up, a stereo and a gold necklace with diamond inlay. And let's see, hmm, horse cowboy bed sheets, curtains, bed spread, carpet, socks, shower curtain, towels, phone and horse cowboy everything!"

"Well, that's not everything. That is just my first draft. I thought it would get you started on my shopping." Mother gently body slammed daughter into bed, Dawg and Kat suddenly alive and present, yelped and danced.

"In your dreams kiddo, maybe you should get a job. Good to know my medicine woman daughter hasn't succumbed to mass marketing and materialism."

"No, Mom. What's the point of you working, if I can't have things that I want?"

"Who are you woman child? Where did you come from?"

"Hee, hee. I am your daughter and I came from you, before that I came from the Arch Angel realm and mystical sisterhood."

"Oh, God! You are my daughter. Ha, sucks to be you!"

The cold weather brought the first wave of seasonal workers unable to get enough unemployment insurance money to sustain through the winter. Many were hanging on by threads and they were coming in tidal waves. Worried about getting through the winter, firewood scarce and cost per load had shot up as the Ministry of Natural Resources clamped down tighter and tighter on brush cutting. Barter fish supplies were scarce, typically bountiful as the Ministry also clamped down tighter on Native fisheries and hunting. Meat and fish normally gathered and bartered underground within community networks were in shortage. No one on her caseload could afford to shop at the local grocery stores at tourist prices.

Service jobs were closed early for the winter as cottagers vacated in droves. Land claims were hot on community minds as leased land cottage owners naively took issues to big city courts. Their ninety-nine year lease was up, as was their prime water front vacation dreams. An antiquated lease, a steal by today's standards at fair market price was no longer acceptable. County council boys battled with higher up government officials over downloading budgets, directives over fishing water rights, new hunting legislation and quotas, all still in dispute. Red necks feeling an audacious grip over a way of life retaliated by continuing to hunt and fish at will. A new fundamentalist evangelist church had arrived adding zealous to drama and local media. People were scared, winter was coming and the local economy looked grim. Fear and tempers were building as native fishing boats mysteriously caught on fire, red neck pickup trucks were turning up trashed and burned.

Off reserve, natives came home from big cities in to access welfare as extending programs and reserve housing slammed shut. Culture shocked and disgusted with legislation changes, simply refused the program and its spider web choking strings. The 'mandatory volunteer work for welfare program', a ludicrous oxymoron that was consistently and adamantly refused on reserve. First Nations simply rejected and refused to participate, thus Band Councils took huge funding allocation hits. The numerous cuts in offshore fishing and off-season work benefits were hitting the community hard. Navi struggled trying to explain the program as it was now, openly sharing their concern with government directives.

Hard core criminals sat across her desk, lost as half way houses closed abruptly. One client had come home from a pre-wedding stag to find a murdered prostitute in the trunk of his car. Mentally ill wandered in and out the outer office, helping selves to coffee, warmth and homeless lost without caseworkers. Middle-aged university suits sat ship wrecked in debt as businesses closed shop, heading for big city or abroad for slave labour. One large medical equipment supply depot, bought out by a Texan company, simply locked its doors without warning or directive on settlements. Another hockey jersey sewing business had outsourced to Vietnam. A call centre abruptly relocated to Mumbai India. It was all keeping her awake at night, unsure how much longer she could keep going in the job unless something changed.

Regi arrived smelly fresh of wilderness and bush, as he did every winter. He lived in a make shift shack deep in the bush. As always, today he was here with a giddy smile, a welcome reprieve.

"Happy to be out and about, are you Reg?" Aroma of wood smoke and fresh air wafted around her office. His old clothes, circa early seventies, carried years of stained effort in wilderness survival, surviving in the woods.

"Ah ya. This morning I chased a coyote that had stolen a rabbit outta one of my traps. I nailed that sucker with my bare hands. I was kinda pissed, no coyote's gonna to steal my dinner. Ha, I got both rabbit and coyote to look forward to for dinner tonight."

'God, I love my bush clients.'

Evenings turned to wild wrapping bagging and name tagging gifts in between random body slams. Closer to Christmas Navi and Abby would gift what extra they could spare to target hard hit homes. She knew very well just how needy some of her clients were and knew that it was a Band-Aid solution to huge gaping holes. In Navi's mind, there is no lack of abundance in the world, no lack of food and no lack of money. There was a lack of love and sharing the goods. Having one's basic needs met; food, shelter, warmth, money and belonging to love ones, ought not lie solely in the hands of God. Everyone supposedly had a spark of God or something divine within. It was supposed to be a personal choice, moment to moment of how one chose to share love and abundance with others. It seemed as though she was expending copious amounts of energy trying to fill and plug tiny holes where the big dam was unstoppable. Resentment of middle class buying and donating goods from the very corporate elites, who fed off all below them, was absurd. The cynical view smacked of elitist conspiracy. Yet, looking higher at the bigger picture it was obvious how fear of lack thoughts and economic depression bred like fungus in the dark of night.

"My Darling Chickadee, fear hinders the flow of sharing and abundance. Do only what you can, when you can then let it go. Do not carry the judgments or the suffering of others within you. It is not for you to assume and carry. Allow another to come into their own life lessons in their own time. For some this is the role that they signed up for, is why they are here. Adversity and crisis has opportunity for those with closed hearts to learn of compassion and sharing."

Tucking Abby in, Catharine phoned. "I have to tell you about what is happening, I don't have long because it's long distance, so I'll be quick."

"What?"

"Anyway, when I got up this morning, I called my mom, to find a neighbour answering the phone. My mother had just, died. The ambulance had just come to get her, but it was too late. You know that mother was in her late ninety's so it wasn't totally unexpected."

"I'm so sorry."

"Oh, actually I feel quite reassured, by the premonition. Well, the funeral will be in Rome, in two days. My mother apparently had tucked away a bundle and made prior arrangements to have her service at the Sistine Chapel, go figure."

"No Way!"

"Way. I will scoot to Rome for a few days. Her body is being prepared for shipping as we speak."

"Wow."

"Got to run now, I will catch up with you in a few days."

Navi awoke to a warm summer's day donning heavy mesh like armour. Adjusting its weight and centering its jock strap protector, she realized she was a young man, 'Aaron'.

As the mist dissipated, a white mottled horse stood a few feet away, grass grazing. Stroking mane in greeting, he tossed a saddle over its mid-section and secured leather laces. Left hand winding a hold on adorned leather sheathe, his sword adjusted as feet felt for stirrups. Right hand ran long dark hair back, making way for metal helmet. Casually trotting out for perimeter rounds, the Catholic Bishop Estate was the most bountiful in the region, rich with deer and agriculture. It was an important prideful job for such a young man. Indeed lucky that it came with cottage home to house his soul skin pudgy wife 'Peach' and two young children. Thinking on her lusciousness, his manhood stood erect, cutting short his rounds, he turned back toward home.

Peach giggled a rotund bouncing body, attending to evening meal preparations while children sat at morning meal. Navi-Aaron sat in between the two playing with a wooden toy with movable parts upon table's surface. With pure intent of mind, hands free, the toy man stood, bowed to each child then danced in entertainment. Fit of giggles and laughter as he turned Peach around enfolding her in arms. Children busily amused with dancing toy man, he abruptly lifted her work gown, spread her legs and inserted manhood. Wet, luscious and allowing with minimal gyration he came, flooding his being into her. A squeeze of her bosom and a slap in her ass, "Get to work woman!"

Giggling and wiping herself with kitchen towel, she turned back to workspace. Uncovering a bowl, he took a chunk of bread and cheese, then left.

A click of tongue and horse strode aside for mounting. Basking in post orgasm glow, he casually strode rounds. The estate employment posting had been pre-arranged by uncle upon reaching manhood, eleven. Uncle had come for him as a boy, parents and sister murdered in a land and lord dispute. Educated in academics, fencing and metaphysics, Aaron's lot in life had become a living heaven on earth. Life was bountiful and safe in the estate world, his work simple, as no one dared to trespass or steal from a man chosen by God to rule. Although, local uprisings were building in fever, taxes were ever increasing, tithing took more than they could spare, a childhood life style that Aaron had known intimately. Yet as fate would have it, heaven included soul skin Peach wife, luscious and moist, always available for manhood flow. He knew little of her, what was there to know? Willing and always readily at beck and command, was sufficient.

Still basking in post orgasm glow, manhood standing erect in sensory awareness of her, hand fondled his manhood then finger tipped to nose as the aroma of her being aroused yet again. Vaguely aware of an approaching rider, thoughts still making love, the hood-cloaked man casually drew nearer. Registering the stranger, sensing friend or foe, unrecognized, Aaron shifted attention.

"Ho! Who goes there?"

The rider remained silent, yet casual. Almost horse nose-to-nose, cloaked rider shifted in saddle branding sword in hand, aimed.

In an instant, sword stealthily entered mid stomach greeted by surprise and burning pain. Rider held Aaron's reigns in hand and with the other, sword shifted deeper inward and upward, catching lungs.

Mind leaving body, he hesitated, searching for assailant's eyes and seeing none, rather an image of soul skin wife Peach and children left to fend on the streets powered a rage up spine and out of mouth with last breath let out a gurgle "NOOOOOO!" Will summoned, the body crumpled to the ground, mind focused intent; a torturing wailing disease curse flew into the man's being.

Awareness shifted to a blinding light ahead. Magnetically drawing closer, his short life flashed in mind's eye followed by vows broken; karmic retribution futile, as an eye for an eye does not hold in the love of God, arrogant mindless attention to his post left wife and children to a life of hardship. A mindless arrogant existence, void of fully knowing wife and a higher love followed by ample missed opportunities to share bounty with hungry masses.

"You can close your eyes to
the things you do not want to see,
but you cannot close your heart to
the things you do not want to feel."
Anonymous

Chapter 16 ~ Winter

Engrossed, Abby sat, legs splayed open on the bedroom floor with streams of paper and coloured markers; drawing a map of Canada.

"How's the home work going?"

"Oh, it's not home work."

"What are you doing?"

"I'm mapping out my territory. I am redefining Canada. Look, there's a section here for bad assholes, it's an island called Montreal."

"Hmmm. Sounds like early Australia and America or Alcatraz, I feel sorry for the aborigines."

"No, that's archaic Mom. Seriously, this could work. I re-map the country then it will be easier to change the laws."

"What laws?"

"Well the first thing I'm going to do as Prime Minister Queen is, take away the American Presidents military weapons, then of those old dinosaur Dictators, corporate banking cartels, religious crazies who kill and oppress in the name of God and gangsters. There will not be any more war, poverty or sadness."

"Prime Minister Queen? With a title like that, your grandmother would be proud; she always strived to emulate royalty. That reallocation of unwanted citizens sounds simple enough, though it has been tried before, and not wholly successfully. What else will you do to actually replace those evils?"

"I'll send money to hospitals and construction guys; just so that poor people can get help when they get sick and have somewhere to live. Then I'll make it against the law for politicians and mega corporations to own or even advertise on radio, television and the Internet. Then I will buy up all of the old malls and turn them into cool places for street people to live and take care of each other. Then I'd set up a factory school, so they make really useful stuff out of discarded junk and sell it."

"You got my vote kiddo."

"Oh Mom, sorry, it's not a democratic situation, you can't vote. I assume the position by will and my subjects bow unto me."

"Sounds like dictatorship and that's been done before and not very successfully either. Hitler, except he was democratically voted into power in Austria, came to save the masses from poverty and hunger, then he moved on up within Germany and well you know the gist of the rest; of how that reign of tyranny turned out."

"Ah Mom, no worries, I have higher connections. Besides, my lunatic mother will keep me in line."

"You are adorable, crazy scary daughter of mine."

David still power processing pacing stopped abruptly and faced her. "Navi, I'm here full time. I shall make it financially so as of January, but I have more responsibilities with the Ex and her household that I have to take care of."

"I'm not sure what you're telling me or asking of me."

"I want to be here with you and Abby, officially. I want to marry you but I don't have much to offer you money wise."

"Story of my life, I want to think it over, just too fast and you haven't finished processing your last marriage. We shouldn't even be living together, really."

"Sorry if I am laying a lot on you, I am with you, "100 percent", I just need to know where I stand."

While it was honourable that David was taking care of ex-wife financial crap, it left a myriad of questions. As a creative soul, he had seen the opportunity to shift focus away from household responsibilities and whittled the day away wildly wielding pastel paints as twenty-five years of pent up untold image stories flowed onto canvass. While his moving-in process had begun under questionable circumstances and timing, there was no question that she felt as though in many ways, she was in love for the first time. In consciously weighing concerns and intuitions, then choosing the most positive attitude, choose to have faith in their shared ultimate success and rallied his support. 'When in doubt, wait it out. You just know when you know.'

Navi woke to the alarm clock bleating 4:44, shaken, groggy and embarrassed. David had made a pot of tea then led her out to the kitchen. "Hey, if you're dreaming is that disturbing then you need to talk about it, I'm all ears."

"Okay. Someone, rather a haunting shadow was following me, I ran."

"Uh huh, that's all you're going to tell me?"

"Yup, just a silly fear dream that often haunts me. I don't want to bring it alive by sharing and thinking any more about it. It's better just to acknowledge that it was a silly little fear dream, grace it and think of something better, more soothing, happier and nice."

"Huh, that's it? No gory details and drama?"

"Yup, that's it.

David?"

"Yes Navi?"

"If I were being herded by a pack of wild Lemmings toward a cliff, would you try and save me?"

"Yes Navi. Navi?"

"Yes, David?"

"If I were a sailor, stranded on a sinking ship and couldn't swim and you were a mermaid watching me, would you save a mere mortal like me?"

"Yes David. I would turn you into a merman. I would show you the forbidden, the secret city under the sea which is my home. I would show you the mountains of coral in rainbow colours. I would show you how the light from the sun and the heavens shining down through the water and splays itself out in bands across the ocean floor. You would swim the seas into eternity."

"Navi, you are a natural born shaman."

"I don't know what that is."

"Well, let's Google and see."

"A shaman uses innate skills and abilities of higher powers and energies, often acting as an intermediary bridge or guide between spirit worlds and the earth world. He or she has an understanding and working knowledge of the interconnectedness of all life, spirit world and the universe. They are generally well respected for their community dedication in benevolence. The term shaman originating in Russia, are universally reported throughout history in most cultures. Notable, are legends of death and re-birth process whereby; shaman enters the physical death process into the void darkness and underworld, typically through a fatal illness or life-defining trauma. Navigating through the darkness they then explore the benevolent spirit world, see higher truths, affirm commitment to their work. They then re-emerge possessing super human skills, information and healing capabilities, dedicating their life to the care and wellbeing of others."

"I get the spirit world journeying thing a bit. Saints went through similar training. I wonder if it's all really the same thing that they are talking about except I am no Saint."

"Thank Christ for that!"

"DAVID!"

Thus, it was that the three settled into their new lives as one, comfortable with each other's presence, routines, moods and quirks.

Navi curled up by the fireplace, warm and cozy. Winter blizzard raged, making up for lost time. Memories of kids on Christmas Eve, preparing for Santa, Santa letters sent and received. Snowshoeing through dense bush to find a perfect tree, then once home, Abby decorated. Homemade decorations and tinsel in bunches, ornaments clumped heavy, tree threatening to keel over. While most women took pride in designing a luxurious tree, it gave Abby and Matt pure pleasure; the joy in their eyes was well worth the eyesore. Stockings hung by the fireplace, straw and carrots left on the deck for reindeer; then cookies and milk for Santa. Christmas morning children delved into stockings, and checked to see what Santa had eaten; then out to the deck to see reindeer hoof prints. By seven the frenzy of opening presents ensued, a turkey in the oven, then a day of tobogganing and building snow forts.

It was Christmas Eve once again; Navi left work early and shopped for unique food items. Contrary to both nature and tradition, this day included a bottle of Mescal Tequila. A magic agave elixir with the added bonus of containing a little white maguey worm who would turn to butterfly only in spirit.

The late afternoon mail pick up was a mistake, a letter from Stephen's lawyer begged curiosity. "Hmm, and a very Merry Christmas to me", she mimicked in Scrooge's housekeeper's voice. After reading it over four times and translating the legal confab, she was pissed. Stephen was accusing her of removing important legal and financial documents from the house, which must be submitted in person to his lawyer's office within forty-eight hours.

"Uh huh, it's Christmas Eve. Thank you very much."

Obviously, this lawyer did not know Stephen. The letter went on to address specific concerns regarding the outstanding mortgage, line of credit and credit cards. Stephen did not know how to balance his cheque book let alone take care of utilities. As typical in marriage dissolutions, he neglected to acknowledge the thirty thousand in debt that she helped clear when they married. Their financial situation as presented appeared as though she had left Stephen in a 'mess'. There was no indication of bills and debts paid off before she had left or house and content equity and of which he was now in sole possession of. It was confirmation that a good lawyer was an oxymoron, Stephen a moron. 'Sorry Stephen, I have other plans, but thanks for remembering me at Christmas.'

David had gone home to drop off gifts for his family and unwelcome, uninvited past the front door, humbly gave gifts, none received. Grief tears backhand wiped, she opened the Tequila bottle as he slouch dining table sat. Drinking down emotional pain hard and fast then stumbling, he spastically slid half on socked feet into winter boots, left them undone.

"Where are you going?"

"Out onto da deck" he slurred, over exaggerating a mitten wave direction to outdoors.

She grabbed a coat and boots to find David standing on the snow covered lawn by the campfire pit, arms dramatically outstretched toward the sky. Fat fluffy snowflakes sparkled as they passed through porch lights, and then gently fell upon his face, eyebrows, eyelashes, nose and cheeks.

"AAARRgghhhhh", he shouted to the sky. "I ATE THE WORM! I ATE THE FUCKING WORM! IT'S CHRISTMAS AND I ATE THE FUCKING TEQUILA WORM! I AM ALIVE AND AT ONE WITH THE UNIVERSE AND THE ALL THAT IS! I AM THE MIGHTY MAGUS! I WIELD THE ENERGIES OF THE UNIVERSE, BEYOND SPACE AND TIME! I AM MIGHTIER THAN MERLIN! I AM HE WHO DARES TO INGEST THE MIGHTY SPIRIT WORM! THE WORM OF MAGICAL PROPERTIES! I MOVE MOUNTAINS! I MANIFEST HEAVEN ON EARTH! I AM ALL MIGHTY! FEAR ME!

Exhausted and losing balance, he plunked down on a snow covered lounge chair, shoulders heaved laughter, wrought with tears. Navi stood on the deck watching, allowing large chunky snowflakes to flit and tickle her eyelashes and cheeks. Squinting, gazing upward, tongue protruded straight out catching flakes on the tip, cooling tickling senses. Magical, yet a concern lingered, of if he would be able to make peace with his former life and find inner balance in his current one.

The New Year brought a new start as David informed Human Resources manager that they were cohabitating. While exposed, it was certainly better despite the rumours that flew entertainment and bordered on large-scale scandal. One concluded that David had seduced Navi away from her husband

and his sick son and as a result, Stephen, bordering on shock and grief insanity, had sought out David and tried to beat the crap out of him. Slut Navi had actually seduced David ten years prior, the two, in an affair all of this time. She had used witch magic to entice him away from his wife who was now devastated and impoverished. The immoral couple had a corporate agenda, consorting and scheming to undermine the entire organization.

"Oh God Gran, how on earth do I navigate all of this, make decisions, and yet remain sane?"

"The first principle is one that you already know but don't always use; learning to discern intent behind each decision. If you close your eyes and think of a decision, one option will have light around it, other options will have less or none at all. If you do not see an option with light, it means that either it is not the right time to make that decision or that you do not have enough information. It takes practice before it becomes natural. There are two emotions that motivate, fear or love. The option with the light around it is the option that is motivated by love. That is the highest good for all involved. The next part is experimenting with it and learning to trust it."

She left David warming by the fireplace, eyeing where his dirty clothes, art materials and important paper work files were now spilling out of what was once her closet. Man things spilled out over the laundry basket and onto the floor. Her eyes trailed under the bed, where Dawg had chewed the crotch out of her new underwear, each precious one. "AAArrrggghhhh!"

Navi crawled under the bed gathering chunks of chewed underwear. Messy underwear brought to mind her teenaged nursing home job in Quebec. Old Mrs. Matthews, batty, sought out some poor unsuspecting resident's toilet to have a crap in. Often found in someone else's room with her panties and stockings dangling from ankles, feces smeared on toilet, tub, sink as well as her. It always smelled like cow manure, no matter what it was on the menu that day. The smell made the mess that much more disgusting to clean up. One day, on a shared elevator ride with a business suit man holding a bouquet of flowers, the door suddenly flew open on the fourth floor to expose Mrs. Mathews standing with stockings and panties around ankles and holding her dress high in the air, screaming, "WEEEEE!" As the elevator door closed, Navi smiled in gratitude that she did not have the fourth floor that day. She glanced at the man whose eyes bugged, skin pallor and flowers tilted in front like a limp penis. 'God, how I loved Mrs. Mathews!'

It was a life lesson that would take years to assimilate.

Restless sleep, David contentedly snored beside her.

"Talk to me Gran!"

"You must keep your mind focused on grace; going with the flow and what really gives you joy. Give up thinking you are anything less than perfect, despite what others may think. Surround yourself with only those who honour and empower you."

"I know that, but I am still confused."

"Change the way you assume being a scapegoat. Is it yours? Stop, close your eyes and ask yourself how much of what you are feeling is actually yours. You then muster courage to stand by it, you are not responsible for the choices others make, only your own. Standing by decisions made with love and light despite adversity takes courage and tenacity. It breeds more courage and tenacity to see through decisions yet to come."

"I regret the way David and I began and the way things fell out, but it's not all mine. Wow, I wouldn't have thought that."

"Now, you see how it works. When you make a decision in love and light that affects others in such a way, it forces them to re-evaluate their own paths and decisions. They then have a choice to follow the light of their own path, or they may choose not to. Most often when people resist following the light of their path, it is merely because they are afraid of the unknown and of going against logic, the social norm."

"I think I get what you're saying, just all easier said than done."

"Mom?"

"Yes, Abby."

"Did you and Stephen, like *never* have sex?"

"God Abby, why do you ask about that again?"

"Well, I know what you told me about him yanking on his alien worm thingy. But I never heard you guys making sex noises, not like when you and David do it."

Navi sighed, "I know that there are things about relationships that you don't understand right now, and honestly I don't either. The insights you need, that I need, will come in good time and right time. Okay?"

"Fine! Don't share, and don't spill. Just an observation, is all."

"God don't you have anything else to think about and ponder? Like your own life and where you want to go and what you want to do?"

"Sure, that takes all of about four seconds."

Catharine arrived fresh from Rome, "I really don't have any words to describe the place and the people. Beautiful, peaceful and wonderful, it was surreal and I will never be the same. Michelangelo's work was so amazing. Maybe someday I will be able to articulate what a wonderful, magical place it is."

"I'm not sure that Catholic Church would condone the term magical", Navi chuckled.

Eyes rolling, Catharine agreed, "Fine. Holy then. Anyway, my mother's funeral was not in the Sistine Chapel, but in a tiny off site chapel. I thought that the Sistine Chapel would be cleaner and more ornate than it was. They are still restoring some of the wall paintings, so we had to navigate around scaffolding. The paintings are nothing short of breath taking, even the dirty ones, where plaster is falling off.

My favourite is the one where God is touching the hand of another. That Michelangelo was some kind of special man. Talk about being light years ahead of his time. I was grateful that the nuns allowed time to view her body before service. I was able to say good-bye and felt sure that my father and her father greeted her with open loving arms on the other side. It was really quite a wonderful experience actually. All is as it should be. Mother would be proud.

It was a very tiny service. The most stunning choir, Gregorian chanting in Latin that left us all lit unto the heavens. The acoustics in that place were out of this world. The amazing thing is that the choir did not stand huddled together in one group. They stood alone, strategically I suppose, in corners, on balcony and other areas of the chapel. This gave their singing unbelievable sound that actually made the cells in my body vibrate. It gave me the sense that I was lifted, Jesus ascending into heaven.

Do you remember that day, when you had the dream about Auschwitz and you sang? Kind of like that. Amazing.

I just wanted to be sure that I had taken the time and space to say goodbye to my mother and remember what needed to be remembered, let go of sad thoughts and let go of guilt over mistakes."

"Wow Catharine, that's amazing. She must have been some kind of woman to think of a funeral like that, sounds strangely similar to my last visit with Mother. She gave you the gift of experiencing the Sistine Chapel as maybe Michelangelo intended it to be. Hey, think about his name, Michel-Angelo, it is Michael-Angel. Hmm, do you suppose that his parents knew something?"

"Well, I think you could be right."

"Catharine, you really are something else."

"Hey, I have some other news. This is merely a pit stop."

"Where are you going?"

"Off to Mexico."

"Make sure you get some authentic Mescal Tequila, with a worm."

David had put on another pot of coffee, a man on a mission to spill out a masterpiece onto canvas; his easel and supplies now occupying the entire living room. Curling up cozy exhausted, she rapidly slid into a deep sleep. *"Pssst! Pssst! Soul Skin Woman! A blessed love thought for you darling; what is a greater sin; taking a lover, or putting your lover in a position where they need to take another?"*

"Who is that?"

"Guilt is the tension that we feel, to accommodate what others want and expect from us."

Stretching semi midnight awake, removing an earplug, it registered that David was still easel hunched madly wielding vibrant colours on canvas, magically growing an artist's goatee. Since Dawg had taken to yipping and barking at every dog walker that went by the house. In solitude quest, Navi began puttering about the house with earplugs in. At night, David's rafter rattling snoring forced the use of earplugs. Puttering out to him, she leaned against him, a loving hand caressing his wild hair. Leaning back, head upon bosom, red weary eyes gazed as he slid his hand into hers, grinning upon finding the waxy ear contractors foam plug in her hand. "Don't you think it's just a bit odd that you're using ear plugs during the day and sleeping with them every night?"

"But, how can I describe the incredible inner sanctum they provide? You have no idea about the inner quiet and peace that I get with them. Geez, for a dollar a pair, I am getting quiet that I just cannot find anywhere else. I am a seeker of the quiet. While I have your full and undivided attention, I think it's about time that I told you that I love you. I think I might even love you without definition." Wrapping arms around her, he drew her into his chest, into his being. She felt his warmth and heart beating and in the moment, closeness.

"Oh, I forgot to tell you earlier, my lawyer called and said; just thought you should know that Stephen is stating that he is just too distraught to negotiate a separation agreement at this time. I said, Oh well. I have a daughter to think of. Do it anyway. Tell Stephen and his lawyer that perhaps it would be prudent at this time to access counselling for his personal issues."

"I don't understand how you can be so calm and objective with him. Doesn't it make you angry? Don't you just want to freak out even a little?"

"No. I wasted too many years in that space, wasted half of my adult life, trying to work things out. I don't want to play those hurtful games anymore, it does no one good."

"Well then, you're a better man than I am."

"I suppose that's why they call chicks like us; wo-men."

Navi arrived at the office to files haphazardly stack piled on her desk. Hesitating, sure that she had locked them away, yet here they were. Settling in, Helen phoned, summoning her to head office, immediately. In aversive yet polite beg off, "I have a full day scheduled, we can chat now over the phone though." She really did not relish an hour's drive in snow blizzard only to hear of another stupid made up issue, she-boss could damn well come to her.

"Well fine. You will notice that some files of yours have been set aside. Do not put them away. A ministry file auditor is coming this afternoon to go through them." There was a hint in she-boss's tone that spine tingled defensive, a hint of threat.

"Why? Is he looking for something in particular? I have clients booked this afternoon."

"I'm not at liberty to discuss with you what our, I mean what his intentions are at this time. Suffice it to say, that it is to be considered a standard system operations check."

Solar plexus alarm tightened scared, angry and wavering, "What? Do you have a particular concern about my work performance again?"

"Well, just a standard check."

Her mind reeled back to the day she read Helen's memos, and to the box of the printed copies in her trunk.

"Why wasn't it addressed in team meeting?"

"Umm, it just came up."

"Who else is having theirs done?"

"Oh, just random, um, just yours to start, but we are considering having the rest of your team done at a later point."

Masked charm hid a lie that rattled. Navi wondered, 'why is she lying to me?' A voice in the background on Helen's end murmured; someone was with her. Empowerment crumpled.

"Who is there with you? I can hear someone in your office."

"Oh, umm, that's the CEO. Why is there a problem?" Helen was on the defense.

"Well I guess that's what I'm trying to ascertain from you."

CEO whispered in background then curtly, "Well that's all for now, I'll be in touch."

She sat in her chair, stunned for the moment, then got up and closed the office door. She flipped through files, recognizing client's names, as if some mystery clue might reveal itself, just as David called from head office.

"Navi, are you sitting down?"

"Why? What's up?"

"Well it seems as though the ministry file auditor has been through my files again. This time he has gone directly to Helen and the CEO, rather than talking to me. The target file is that man from the north end who I have been trying to approve for disability pension. Remember the one that was raised on the reserve and molested by the Catholic priest for fifteen years and can't even spell his own full name because he's so screwed up?"

"Oh yes. What could possibly be the problem with him?"

"Don't know exactly, but they called him and his wife in, had a meeting and removed him from the pay benefits."

"WHAT? Why?"

"Don't know."

"Geez, what's going on?"

"Well, I have to tell you something."

"What?"

"Please don't get mad at me. I resigned. I figured that this was the second file they targeted. I obviously do not have Helen's or the CEO's support any more. I don't know what's going on, really, except that no one else's files are being audited this way. I'm concerned about my clients being singled out for something, when someone may have an issue with me personally."

"Shit!"

"I'm fine, just packing up my personal stuff out of my office. I will see you at home. I will make dinner and make sure the house is tidy for you when you come home."

"He is coming here this afternoon to go through my files."

"What? God damn it! What is their problem?"

"No, don't sweat it. I can't imagine that they'd find anything remotely out of whack, so let them look."

"You know, I don't think that the CEO should have ever have promoted Helen to program coordinator, which is beyond her competency. It was okay when she was team leader and did not have legislative authority. They created a monster. Helen seems to have developed a taste for politicking. She does not know that they put her there so they could yank her chain, do their dirty work, a puppet. Look, be discreet on what you say and to whom, from here on out."

"What do you think is behind it? If they wanted to down size why don't they just lay off people?"

"Nah, it's cheaper to make people so uncomfortable that they resign, less severance package. It's easy to make anyone look like they have work performance problems, dirty."

"I don't get it."

"Well, it's a matter of corporate survival of the fittest, best survival game player. I don't want to play those games anymore, not with poor people at risk."

"I don't either."

"Look, got to go. Helen is taking me out for lunch. So hold onto your hat, I may be joining you."

"Wow, that's creepy."

"Ah, it's okay. I have a few things I need to get off my chest before I go, I'll likely be ignored but I've got to try. See you at home."

The newfound confidence of the day before vanished, replaced with a whopping headache.

Deep in e-files, a shoulder tap alarmed. The woman was livid. "What are you going to do about this new legislation? How can you possibly sleep at night, knowing what you have done to my family? You are a God dammed Nazi, carrying out orders of the third Reich. If you had any common decency, any moral backbone at all, you would stand up to your superiors and do the right thing!"

Navi flashed back to the Auschwitz dream last year, Jew not a Nazi. Suddenly, winter cold thoroughly chilled, spine shivers. The woman back straightened, eyed from head to toe, then with contempt disdain, smirk turned about heel and marched away. She fought back tears burning up into sinuses threatening eyes, walked to the office parking lot and sat with engine on and the heater blasting. She lit a smoke and leaned back in the seat scared, crying.

Pulled together enough to go back, she noticed that the files were gone. Scanning the outer office, a distinct rich man's cologne hung mid-air; in the back room sat the engrossed auditor, her files splayed wide open.

'Shit!' A deep breath then 'Oh, Shit! Mary was a positive and motivated single mom who was in the throes of upgrading for college while volunteering and raising two special needs children. "Navi, guess what? I have been hired full time, started night school and loving it. Oh, and the kids have a new teacher's assistant now, full time."

Navi's head reeled, not wanting work related distraction, not right now. Feigning a smile, "That's wonderful Mary. I am happy for you. You must be very proud of yourself." While her eyes scanned out into main office and into the back room. She stood up to photocopy Mary's college application, "Excuse me for a minute would you?" suddenly lost.

Mary stood up and with gloved hands, shoulder grabbing embraced, "Oh, I just wanted to thank you for everything that you have done for me. I was really in a rut. School is going great and the kids think it is neat that I do homework. I have registered for college, full time, beginning in the fall, and I can't wait. I could not have done any of this without you! Thanks!"

She allowed a bear hug. Humbled, elated.

Softening, "Mary, you would have gotten there without my help. You look great. Don't ever look back and don't ever give up."

Mary left, leaving office door open. Capturing the opening, Black Suit Fancy Smelling File Auditor Man had come to discuss file issues. With second thoughts, he turned on heel, shuffled files into his briefcase and slid into his coat. Briefcase under one arm, car keys in the other, he left without a word. Co-workers immediately huddled in the back office behind closed doors. Helen appeared at the front desk, face morphed serious and closing the door behind them, then stood, making no move to remove coat or sit.

"I need to talk to you."

"Sure. What's up?" trying to sound calm and indifferent while spine straightened defensive and angry over mysterious work performance insinuations.

"Look, you've got to stop asking so many questions about files and the audits. You have to stop asking questions about your personnel file. Just stop it."

"You know Helen? I really have no idea of what you are inferring. There have been a number of insinuations about my work performance lately, but you have given me nothing tangible that I can address. You have never had concerns about my work before, this is utter bullshit and you know it, so just cut the crap and tell me what is going down.

Irritated with the authoritative challenge, "I'm not going to get into why we have re-structured the way we did. I do not have to answer to you in that regard. Maybe your personal life is interfering with your professionalism. I expect you to do your job as directed."

"I really don't appreciate all the insinuations. If you have a specific problem with me, then make it clear, to the point and on the table. If you are just responding to petty gossip, well then maybe you have some house cleaning of your own to do."

Helen hands on hips deadpan and pulling rank, "I really don't like the tone you're giving me, do as I say or you can go elsewhere.'

Stance a fraction of an inch away from firing, Navi suddenly panicked job loss, clients, of losing pay cheques. There was her Abby and a profound lack of available employment options. David had just resigned and things were going to be tight enough. There was nowhere else to go. She knew nothing of coffee shop waitressing or electronic cash register and debit card functions, rationalizing the unemployable fact of not being able to keep up the physically demanding pace. Nailed and humiliated, squeezed out without tangibly knowing why, she humbled submissively.

"I don't know what to say to you." immediately regretting having acquiesced and giving her power away.

"Well how about you start following directives as they are given to you"?

Heading north, home, humiliated and scared, the winds blasted and swirled in evening darkness, the year's worst winter white out blizzard. Hands, white-knuckle gripped to the steering wheel, searched shoulder markings to indicate that she was still on the road, "Oh God Gran, Angels, help me get home safely."

Mystifying snowflakes swirled, eyes wandering. Afraid to let go, carried off with snowflakes, to dance and spiral out and into space. She inched forward, slowly but surely, plugging on and on, an endless road of white ahead.

Finally pulling up to the grocery store, she slid into a handicapped spot. No one in his or her right mind would be out in a wheel chair on an evening like this. When she stood up and out, head whirled and suddenly blood drained down and into boots. No other customers, lost, she stood in front of the bread section. It seemed as though the bread shelf had risen and expanded into a mountain of breads and bread choices. Her mind searched for some clue as to what kind she was supposed to get, there were so many, oh so many, too many. Angst stomach churned and roared, tears crawled up her spine threatening to spill out. 'No, not here, not now.' The store lights dimmed as a loudspeaker voice blurted, "The store will be closing in five minutes. Please direct your purchases to the check out. Thank you and good evening."

A wave of panic rushed, 'what am I doing here? Oh, bread, what kind? I can't remember.' A vision of all the store lights out, locked in, alone all night and into the days ahead; the staff had all gone home, storm raging, closing the entire town for a week or more. She grabbed a loaf of bread then stuck it back on the shelf; unable to face the cashier, she would cry. She looked for the exit sign, unable to remember her way around the store. Guided by some unseen force, she glided the expanse of the store then out into the snowy night.

Winds gathered velocity, belting ice pellets on face and inside office coat then down neck. She aimed for the car, searching pockets for keys, stopped, turned back against wind and searched purse for keys. Searching parking lot, then it registered, keys were still in the ignition. Door handle, locked. Around to passenger door, locked. Standing still, wind wavering weakness, scanning empty parking lot, save one car, the last staff. Back into the store, the last cashier was an old client. 'Oh shit!'

"I'm sorry. We're closed." The woman recognizing her, wanted only to go home.

Navi searched, trying to remember if she had been generous with time and good service. The single mom had been slammed with a twelve thousand dollar over payment, was trying to put herself through computer night school at the community college. 'Oh my God' she connected and instantly mortified at being associated with a system that allowed this to happen. Out of front line worker hands without recourse, she had grimly suggested that the girl fight it, legally. She searched the woman's face, looking to see if she was holding her personally responsible for it. "Yes, I know you're closing. I am sorry. But I locked my keys in the car."

"Well, I guess you could use the phone, as long as it's not long distance."

She searched the girls face, looking for some kind of clue that would indicate who exactly it was that she was supposed to call. 'David.' Then hesitated stupid, receiver in hand, trying to recall her own phone number. 'Concentrate. I know I know it.'

"Stay right there, the voice on the other end said, I'll come and get you."

Gingerly, phone back. 'Funny, I don't remember dialing the number.'

Financially buggered old client cashier furthered, "You can wait inside here, where it's warm, if you like, I've got a few things I can do, until someone comes to get you."

"No that's okay, I won't keep you. I am sure that you have a family to get home to. You'd better go now, before it gets any worse."

The woman's kindness was not lost upon her, a dammed sight nicer in crisis than social worker colleagues were. It was rural country wisdom; most instinctively separated intentional callous cruelty from community mindedness and looking out for ones neighbour. She stood leaning against the car, took a deep breath and looked up to the sky, exhaustedly seeking God, an angel, and direction, whilst wincing from tickling falling snowflakes. Another few deep breaths, then she relaxed, David was coming.

"Jump in. I am taking you and Abby out for dinner. We can deal with your car later or in the morning." David was in good humour; Abby bundled in the back seat.

"Jesus, are you all right? Why didn't you use your cell phone to call home?"

"Sure, I guess I'm okay, better now. I don't know why I didn't use my own phone, didn't even think of it. Thanks for coming to get me."

David grinned, "Oh well. My pleasure. I see that you didn't get milk or bread."

"Sorry."

"We can grab some at the general store on the way home; and chocolate too."

David pulled into the mini mall parking lot amongst assorted snowmobiles parked in front of the diner. The lights on, warm friendly smells of diner style home cooked food greeted her empty stomach. When one of their tougher bitchier female clients eye connected, her heart dropped. Bleached, yellowy blond hair tied up in a bun and covered in a hair net stood stark against mottled greyish pale skin and heavyset body. Disapproving glare registered, the audacious old woman was a neighbour of David's now ex-wife. Connections filtered, David and Navi exchanged glances.

"We have nothing to be ashamed of. We came here to eat and unwind, so let's just order and have a good dinner."

She had had more than enough and rather felt like crawling under the table. Catching her emotional state, he joked, "Hey, are you aware that we are systematically becoming banished from our own home town. There are only two restaurants and one local grocery store. Each of them seems to have either angry clients working in them or previous life acquaintances who frequent these places. It seems that everywhere we go, is a disgruntled client, co-worker, former family or acquaintance of our ex's."

"Yes, I am. Life in a small community can be both a blessing and a curse! Seems like daily, we are running into people who disapprove of something or other, or are visibly stunned to see us together. It does not matter' there is no privacy. A small rural community can be a blessing when your house burns down, but a curse when everyone knows of your business and disapproves. Clients either have a bone to pick with you about the new legislation, or they just simply want to know what's happening with their cheque."

"What they don't know to be fact, they make up, to fill in the blank spots, or just to make the story even better, juicier. Hey, do you think those two there in the back kitchen putting hate into our food?"

"Probably, I hope just hate. Hate you can clear out by blessing your food, saying a little prayer. Well you can try and transmute poison, but you need to have pretty powerful wooey-woo to do that."

"Or snot, or spit, or dog doo-doo, or mouse turds", mused Abby, joining in.

"Well, thanks Abby, I'm sure that we've all worked up a good appetite now. You know, I was feeling particularly cynical about work today, especially on the way home from work. I had Mary in earlier, and that was nice. Then the girl who let me use the phone at the grocery store, was the one that got hit with that huge overpayment."

"Ah, don't you worry about a thing. I have a feeling that everything will work out, better than we think."

It was a preferable outcome to believe, the other option was unthinkable. Perhaps acquiescing earlier, would at least buy time with Helen. She simply was not ready to face another huge door closing, without somewhere else to go. Somehow, some way, everything was going to be all right.

Navi was exhausted and asleep by eight thirty, Abby put herself to bed. She awoke to the dark of midnight and jumped out of bed to pee. Suddenly wide awake, she grabbed a coke and went into the living room, curled squat aside fire place in illuminated shadow fire's gentle light and warmth. She lit a smoke, allowing thoughts to flow.

Cold, grey and dreary days; a depressing lack of sunlight and warmth. A year ago, Matt's prognosis was still unknown. They had been prepared for his death and still had held hope for her and Stephen. Who would have known, that in short of a year, life would have changed so dramatically? David. What was to become of her and daughter? A chill crept up spine tingling under her skin. Finished, smoke butted, climbed back into bed, as David's sleepy demeanour welcomed open arms. She curled up tight, head on chest, feeling his breathing.

"Carpe Diem." He muttered.

Navi woke to room spinning and a blinding headache. Stomach splitting in two, racing to the bathroom just in time as a horrible liquid and stench exploded out from her bowels. It assaulted sense of smell and anus burned as it raged outward. Her head swirled. Another wave rippled up her spine, tiny body hair stood straight up and out as another wave of liquid burned its way out of her being. She hunched forward, bending over knees, holding stomach, and then holding her solar plexus. Fan on, incense taper lit, a cold wash cloth cooled her flushed skin. Stabilized, she ventured out, senses met with the wonderful aroma and sounds of coffee brewing. 'God bless the man who makes coffee in the morning.'

She glanced out of the kitchen window; 'Ahh, the snow has let up. I have to go to work today.' David's finances were ex-wife tangled in debts and litigation, who knew when he was going to get work again.

She arched a must carry on spine, put on coat, boots and slipped out of the back door and into the car. Steppenwolf's greatest hits blasting, emotions vacillated and shifted, she drove until anguish subsided and burnt anus calmed. No longer caring of office Bitch Den antics, of condescending deceitful boss woman and of judging ignorant small community minds, a wave of calm assumed her soul and body. Zen of Steppenwolf was the freedom of letting go of all that was uncontrollable. She was not going in to work, turned around to home.

Old ancient sisterhood shawl enfolded the weary soul. Curtains' closed, phone switched to answering machine, Dawg at bed end, Navi slid back into comfortable sleep.

As the mist cleared, Navi found herself standing short, in a little girls frame, late eighteen hundreds smock dress, bare foot pitter-patting on cool fine finished wood planked floor, worn cloth doll in hand, dragging along beside her. The other hand ran a hand over a weary fevered face, rubbing tired dry eyes, red and swollen, then pushed damp bangs back; fingers sliding through long brown wavy hair. Mucous bubbles formed and popped on out-breath, nose wiped on dress arm sleeve. A drowning sensation within tight chest, phlegm coughed up; then swallowed.

Elegant Mother Abby sat at bedside table, taper lit to illuminate an overcast day. Her dressing gown splayed outward, while her quill pen focused on letter writing. Scented rose oil dripped over taper to mask bed chamber pot odours. Fine hand embroidery fringed Mother's sleeves, dragging along after her busy hand. Lace fringe tailed curtains, lampshades and bedding, against hand painted wall borders of roses and vines. Hesitating, she stops to wipe tears and then sensing daughter's spirit presence, turns feigning jovial smile.

"How lucky was I to have such a devoted Mother care taker companion?"

Mother smiled in earnest, sharing the love warmth.

Navi understood that she had died and Mother, Abby still steeped in grief gracefully responded to condolences in writing. Whispering, heart and soul love pouring outward in comfort, "Mama, beloved Mama. I know of your pain."

"Forgive me dear child."

"Worry not Mother, there is no need for forgiveness, there is only need of understanding the divine will; love. Do not grieve Mama. You could not save me from sickness. I am fine, truly. I am with loved ones, Grand Mamas and Auntie too. I come to you often beloved Mama. How I long for my thoughts, words and joy to touch you, heal you. I can feel your warmth, I long for you to know the Angel comfort from this side of heaven's veil.

How I long for your sadness to pass, to allow sunshine into your grief shadowed soul. I shall always love you, beloved Mama."

March brought milder weather and a final settlement with Stephen. Time was a powerful healer, as was having someone at hand who cared; and having companion David and Abby at hand, paved a smoother transition. In shifting financial focus, knowing that she must maintain work, she decided to buy the beach cottage, a mortgaged homeowner once again. In strategy to stay sane and survive the office, she habitually splayed files and piles of paperwork across her desk, her door closed and worked all day on spiritual courses. On breaks, she imagined working a crusade to eradicate AIDs from Africa. Casually having coffee with Maya Angelou and in sisterly companionship; travelling the world while unveiling the mysteries of the universe. Daily, communing and candidly debating quantum physics with spirit Albert Einstein, his witty demeanour a breath of life and insight. Her spiritual courses were steadfastly steering thoughts away from daily stressors.

Yet, in workday reality, she felt more like Helen Duncan. British Helen had intuitively *seen* the sinking of two British ships during the Second World War and tried to tell the public and government. Helen often spoke with dead spirit sailors and exacted provable confirmation. Navy Intelligence Officers had been keeping the accident a secret. She had comforted the dead sailor's family members by sharing what she saw and heard. Helen investigated, tried, and convicted as a spy, then sentenced under the old Witchcraft act of the seventeen hundreds. Helen was the last person convicted before the law was dissolved under the directive of Sir Winston Churchill.

Though Navi was still getting constant memos from Helen, waves of legislative propaganda bullshit, she was air traffic control, funneling people into slots and categories. 'And damn it, thou shalt smile whilst thou is doing it.' Poor people rarely ever voted, if they did, there would be a very different government.

David turned down a job after struggling with a resume for hours then tore it up. "Fuck it! I don't want a shit assed job. I just want to be left alone to paint!" Shaken to the core, unable to find words that matched the inner pressure and terror of holding the financial load, mortgage papers were signed. Frustrated, she shifted focus away from fear nipping ankles in shadows. They were surely but slowly shifting to their own futures with magical successful outcomes.

"Mom?"

"Yes Abby."

"All the girls at school are talking about the diets they're on; like grapefruit and stuff."

"What do you think of that? You're not thinking of going on a diet?"

"Are you kidding? I don't want to look like a stray dog with worms!"

"Oh, I've taught you so well!"

Catharine arrived fresh from Mexico, hair in cornrows, tanned, eyes fresh and clear, and radiant.

"How was your trip?"

"Well, I really didn't have any yearning to explore any temples. I wanted a quiet time to say good-bye to my mom. I just lounged on the beach with a shot of tequila each evening, once with a worm. Everything is made of black beans and brown beans. I am afraid that beans tend to make me rather anti-social, if you get my drift.

Oh, I did do one small temple tour on the second day with a guide and thirty other tourists. It was illegal to remove stones but I took one. The tour was all quite bland and commercial, the guides mumbled memorized script. The locals tell more about the culture and don't think that their Mayan heritage is a big deal, just resentment residue of the Spanish. I can imagine that it would take many generations to rid a society of its former occupied tyrants. I didn't bring the stone home; afraid I was going to be in trouble at airport customs, so left it at the hacienda. Boy I am glad to be home. It feels like I've been away for a year."

"You look amazing. I'm glad that you had the opportunity to go."

"It wasn't just an opportunity. I manifested it."

"Right, you are a master of the universe."

"I kid you not. This working and magnetizing abundance stuff really works, once you get the hang of it."

"Catharine, you are amazing!"

"Well, some people just seem to live many life times in one. I think that they design it this way before they come into this lifetime, to complete and process many. You are just one of those people who do many different lifetimes in one. Simply because you are strong and are sharp enough, so as to not have it all do you under. Not many people can go through everything you have been through and still carry on. Always dust yourself off, carry on and shed that job. The system is sick. Maybe that is their karmic ball to carry from here on out. Allow yourself the knowing, that you are done. Something better will come."

"It sounds so easy, we have one pay cheque; mine. At least until David gets an art gallery contract."

"Well, maybe there is a reason why you are still there. Look, you can put a lot of energy into it and do all of the healing prayers you want, set up light around the place and yourself. You can't stop their karma, or their life lessons. Everything will work out better than you could ever have imagined possible. I am sure of it. Remember, aim higher above the mundane and ignorance of our fellow passengers. That's where happiness lies."

The Ides of March brought forty degree below zero weather, which quickly turned to ice storm. Just when winter was finally over, it would clear, turn balmy mild, then another blast would hit. Navi looked out the window watching the blizzard while listening to the news; there were consistent power outages and record cold temperatures. Working poor would have run out of firewood for heat, spring tallied electric bills exceeded anything they could possibly dream of paying. Into her office, desperate for help, any help, to ease the pressured costs from a hard long winter. Seasonal work start-up was late due to bad weather and no one had been called back to work yet.

Danny, a northern bush client, graced the other side of her desk. A breath of light and sunshine, a natural connection to Biblical Daniel played in her mind. A prophet, except this one usually came in once a year to get a cheque for Christmas; a necessity cheque, supplies for the year. There was need of; flour, sugar, kerosene and warm clothes from the thrift store. He had waited too long and found a much more intensive and lengthy application process before food could appear. True to the uniqueness of Danny, rather than completing the mandatory literacy-screening test as required, he used the form to calculate in finite math how he was going to take a generator out of a John Deere tractor found in the bush, strategizing and re-designing it for his old Massey Ferguson tractor.

Navi joyfully listened, wishing that the Ministry Black Suit Sweet Smelling File Auditor Man could see this and then wondered if the Danny's of the world would be lost on him. Amused and happy for the diversion from the seriousness of legislative changes, she sat back and grinned from ear to ear. Somehow, by being in the bush alone all year, he had somehow missed changes in legislation and political excitement. She laughed heartily inside; his visit was doing more for her heart than it was likely doing for him. It was a gift.

The bush lifestyle for Danny, like many others, was A Chosen One. Not because they emulated great masters such as Jesus, Gandhi or Buddha per say, but because they lived simply and were at one with nature. Most no longer had marketable skills to offer the labour market; had walked away from mainstream society. All consciously chose this way of life and lived off of the land. To see them around town was rare, quiet, polite and social when they had to be. They were stealth, graceful and selective on how and when they interacted with others, incredibly in tune with their environment.

"Did I ever tell you that my son was raised by his rich mother, somewhere in London? Well I got a letter from him and he's just been accepted into York University, a Doctorate of Philosophy program."

"Yes, I remember you telling me about your son. That is wonderful philosophy, must run in the family."

Danny scratched his head eyes cast down, beaming with pride. "I guess so, never thought of it that way. Maybe I did have some good effect on them after all."

"I think maybe you did."

Alone in the office, she casually drifted outside, opened the trunk and rifled through the photocopied Helen memos. Back into the office, computer on, she checked to see if Helen had changed her password yet. She had not. With the theme from Mission Impossible boldly playing in inner ear amidst a pounding heart, she scanned the list of recent email memos and entries. Why Helen would keep these online was a mystery, perhaps working from home. Similar to those that referenced Navi and David, other worker personal dirt files appeared.

'Well, hot Damn! Sell-Out Bitch Boss is keeping dirt on everybody!' She then flipped out of Helen's email box and played solitaire for the remainder of the afternoon, into alpha state; a semi busy body allowing the free mind to go higher. 'So that's the way it is. Keep notes and shit on everyone. Just in case things get tight, make sure that you secure your own position; make everyone look suspect, as bad apples. Make yourself appear angelic then play dumb, as someone else's job goes for a shit. God, not just me, but imagine how the witches would feel about seeing this when they have been helping Helen and the CEO, worried about their own jobs, false security. Hmm, what they do not know is that Helen has shit on all of them. It must take an awful lot of energy, time and strategy to keep this game going.

The reality of tangibly knowing that it was not really about her, was freeing. Just current scapegoats vulnerable from personal life dramas make easy targets.

"Shit Navi. You have enough here for a class action suit! Son of a bitch, what a dirty beggar! Hey, what are you intending to do with all of this?"

"Nothing at the moment, if I get a sense from Spirit that I am supposed to take some sort of action, I will. Otherwise I'll just take it as a gifted piece of information for my own personal wellbeing. Besides, if I played the game on their level, that would make me just like them and I don't want to go and hang out in that shit space."

"Boy, you are something else. I don't know how anyone can be so calm about all of this."

"Oh, don't let the calm exterior fool you. My stomach and bowels are not calm. I think I am still a bit in shock, guess I am officially no longer the Chosen One. I just have to figure how and when I am leaving. I cannot take on the old boys of the county, the new legislation, and Helen, on top of everything else, with no energy. I need time to figure it all out."

Abby blurted into the room, interrupting the flow of conversation, "I am going to clean my room!" Navi was astounded.

"Hey, Abby what did you do during the ice storm? Why, I have matured", she'll say to her friends."

"Aw Mom, don't ruin it. I might just change my mind."

David quiet, added, "You know, what Helen has done is called Constructive Dismissal. That's illegal."

"Well more importantly, I was not raised with that kind of thinking. I have never had any other experiences from people, except maybe from Stephen and some of the old church cronies, whom operated that way. My mind does not work that way. Actually it kind of blows my mind that there are people out there that think this is the only way to get ahead and survive."

"Oh dear poor sheltered Yoko Ono. Every organization I have ever worked for operated that way to some degree, more or less. It is just human nature. After people have worked in the same job for a while, it gets boring."

"Oh I agree to an extent, they don't move on because they're afraid. My parents taught us to stay in the job once you find a good one, so people stay when they should not. It was a different era of loyalty. Today's reality is dicey, temporary and scary. Scared that this is all there is, they try to keep something they've outgrown and really don't want anymore, at all costs."

"If you think about it, it seems like the ones that are causing the problems are the ones that hate their jobs, hate their life."

"You know, at some point, people need to be made accountable. Maybe you should call your lawyer and ask about it."

"I'm not going to do anything, at least for a while, going to sit on it and see what comes. It helps to know it is not personal, yet that doesn't make leaving any less scary."

"Hi Gran. I know you are there. I can feel your presence."

"Hello darling."

"Did you notice that I sent you the Chickadees today?"

"Is someone going to die?"

"Not someone, something."

"You're talking about work?"

"Know that I love you my little Chickadee."

April brought spring rains, earth alive and musky aromas filled the air; dirt and trees, fresh with life bursting through stale darkness of winter. Given that it was a full moon, she should not have been surprised that clients were irritable. Frustrated with extended winter, cabin fevered and just wanting to get back to work.

Pulling into their little beach community, Navi spotted a cranky old man walking his dog. Waving hello as usual, he in turn only scowled, wildly waving her to slow down. Already in low gear, his dog wandered middle road as he shook a fist. "Nice, very nice" she muttered. The old man followed into her driveway. 'Oh, great, just what I need', took a deep breath calling in divine grace and bracing herself for a possible altercation.

"Hey, YOU!" he yelled, shaking fist and marching closer. His dog happily ran off to play with Dawg, romping and tails wagging butt sniffing. Abby flew out of the door in greeting and seeing the angry old man, shyly stood aside. A few feet away, still yelling, his red face blazed and rant spewed without stopping to breathe.

"You idiot crazy woman, I am going to call the Police! They are going to arrest you for careless and reckless driving! You and your 'friend' both speed through the neighbourhood all of the time, someone will be killed! Reckless driving maniac, you are a menace! God Damn it, I'm going to put a stop to it right now!" Advancing closer, inches away from her face, she leaned gently backward firmly ushering Abby safely behind. He was out of control volatile; it would take little more to be provoked into hitting her, even in front of Abby.

Stress overload summarized in a flash: a day of full moon clients at the new office with rude and condescending co-workers, Helen and the CEO kept dirty files, acquaintances and church cronies passed judgment, driving in snow storms all winter, expressionless unfeeling ministry file auditors then in a mille second, a bitch slap snapped in her back and unleashed itself. It rose up her spine and projected out of her mouth, without conscious thought or self-control. She stood straight, arched her spine and dismissed him, "Kiss my arse, old man!"

Alpha she wolf dog empowered, she turned abruptly to go into the house, glancing behind, expecting to see him walking away, but he was following her, advancing, visibly livid, yelling and waving his fists in the air and ranting incoherently. He shook his fist toward her face, just missing her nose. She backed up, took Abby by the arm and turned away, missing the blow. He still followed; she had to do something quick, he was following her inside and might take a swing at her from behind. She reeled around and with forces of God all-powerful she wolf alpha dog bellowed,

"Have a nice fucking day, Sir! Now get off my property and go home or I will call the police. You are out of control and need to calm your ass down. Come back another time to apologize. For the love of God, why don't you do something constructive with your time and go volunteer somewhere? Come on Dawg."

She quickly locked the door behind her pride.

"Wow, Mom you are really angry. Look, you're shaking!"

"I know Abby, I'm sorry."

"No Mom, don't apologize. That was great! Awesome!"

"No Abby. He is just a lonely and bitter old man. We don't know what has gone on in his life. Maybe I should've just given him a big hug and a kiss."

"Hee, hee. That would've been something to see!"

Navi's altruistic nature ran trail off fantasy thoughts of inviting him over for dinner, leaving a flower on his doorstep. A mouse skirted across the floor in front of her, carrying a piece of moldy bread from a plate lying on the floor amongst Abby's dirty clothes, various forms of creative messes and an array of egg scientific experiments lined up on her dresser amidst papers and dirty dishes. Hesitating, taking in the stunning array, she contemplated each one. One glass held an egg covered in toothpaste, the next clouded in vinegar, then liquid cleanser, one covered in an unidentifiable black slime, another had been coloured, marked, and painted, another smelled like toilet bowl cleaner, another bobbed in blue window cleaner liquid, the rest laid broken splat spilled on the floor.

Anger rippled spine. Her own personal items had been missing, now scattered amidst health hazard, mouse turd, dirty dishes and salmonella egg mess in various states of rot.

A deep breath in, searching for calm; while livid mess monsters bred in the dark and grew multiplying while she was sleeping. Creative messes spilled out into the hallway, living room, spread into the kitchen, deck and yard. Artwork made from re-cycled cardboard boxes, pieces of metal and old broken furniture. The good kitchen scissors were crust covered with glue and paint, stuck permanently to a pair of girls' underwear. Unused tampons floated in coffee mugs, in various forms of absorption of unidentifiable liquids, experiments gone amiss. Christmas box of wrapping paper and ribbon laid scattered and mingled with glue, paints, tin foil and sticks that grew up the side of a wall. What looked like every sock owned, tied end to end from bedpost to light fixture mid ceiling. A bright sparkling smooth and pink liquid river spilled over the family heirloom tongue and groove antique dresser and ran down the front of its delicate drawers. A gifted grandmother china ornamental jewelry box lay in pieces on the bed. The family photo album lay open on the floor; pictures removed and cut up, bits spilling out and under a bedside table. Magazines, books, school papers, twisted coat hangers, dirty clothes, muddy shoes, dirty dishes and cat turds spilled out from under the bed. Teenage boy celebrity posters covered the ceiling, behind a tree branch mobile dangling liquor bottles and recyclables. Strands of Navi's wedding dress satin, silk and taffeta spanned glued to the walls.

Navi stood still with clenched teeth, shaking. Eyes closed and breath held, just a bad dream. With still eyes closed, she searched for grace. When eyes opened, a tear ran and trickled down a cheek. Unbridled, turning about face, door slammed closed behind and from somewhere within a primal warrior woman, yelled, "ABBY!!!!!!!!!"

Navi unhinged behind clenched teeth, it had been a silent fight, until Abby in tears and unable to endure the silent mother rage, gave way. "Why doesn't Stephen ever call me Mom or ask to see me? Why is he so angry? Doesn't he know how much this hurts?"

"Oh God Ab, I get it!" tensions immediately shifting to resolution. "For the love of God, you have got to talk to me more." Eleven garbage bags of garbage and five bags to the second hand depot followed, fresh wall paint, carpet and furniture cleaning with a relaxing luxurious candle lit bubble bath.

Abby's nuclear bowel movements had recently become synchronized with Navi's baths, the toilet was a mere four inches away from the tub, daughter's bottom loomed lethal a mere eight inches away from her head.

"Abby?"

"Ya Mom?"

"Your bowel movements are nuclear."

"I know, that's why I save them for you."

"Oh my Godddddddddddddd! I'm beginning to mutate!"

"Hee, hee, they're good for you Mom."

"I'm DNA mutating, aaaaaaahhhhhhhhhhhh!"

"Hey, Mom? Remember this one? In days of old when knights were bold, and toilets weren't invented, they laid their load on the side of the road and walked away contented. Or public bathroom graffiti; Here I sit broken hearted, paid a dime and only farted. Hee, hee, hee."

Navi, better for resolutions and drying off, heard a knock on the door. She grabbed some clothes and threw them on quick, met at the door with a man in uniform.

"Good day ma'am. We have a complaint regarding your lawn care, or lack of it, ma'am. You should know that you're being advised to address the situation appropriately within twenty four hours or you will be fined three hundred and twenty five dollars and the county will charge you one hundred and twenty five dollars per week following for its maintenance."

"What?" Glancing, the lawn was a tiny sea of a variety of beautiful wild flowers of blue, purple, yellow and white. Butterflies and dragonflies flitted about.

"What are you talking about? I see wild flowers. I don't see any noxious weeds or tall grass."

"Ma'am I'm not here to argue the merits or particular issues in regards to your lawn, I'm just here to advise you of the pending notice of fine. I think I'm being quite liberal in giving you twenty four hours advance notice." With that, he turned on heel and walked away then hesitating at his car he turned, "Ma'am, I surely hope that these pets of yours have been properly licensed and are kept under the control of a leash." He did not wait for a reply, an important Law Enforcement Official, who took the law seriously and loved wielding the authority of it.

Navi stood at the door and watched his car pull away and then safely out of view, stuck her tongue out. She did not own a lawnmower. They lived at the beach, in cottage country amongst patches of crab grass and an array of tiny wild flowers.

Out to the local hardware store went reluctant and community anarchist David. Four hundred dollars set aside for groceries and gas to work, the man of their house MAD muttered assembling a fossil fuel guzzling lawn mower. Beyond the audible David Turrets, a sea of glorious rainbow coloured butterfly dancing wild flowers lost their precious little heads. The beauty of nature was once again devastated, under the guise of municipal bylaw enforcement. Out of respect for nature, Navi scrambled to dig-rescue flowers and carefully transferred them to a dismal sandy soiled garden. The naked sight waved homesickness for beautiful country home, pool, gardens and more so, privacy.

She tied her hair up in a bun and donned sunglasses, regretting the mortgage now and unsure if they could survive another year, her job was ending. The little community, dominated by retired city people who brought city mentality, was an unhappy lot. There were definite codes of appropriate conduct; you must walk your dog on a leash, with a no-bark zapping collar. You must manicure your dog and lawn using whatever power tools and toxic chemical as appropriate to get the job done right. You must chemically treat your lawn weekly, posting toxic symbols and vacuum it promptly after cutting grass. Yes, they were a street gang of miserable old gangster city mentality farts who walked their dogs in sync, a powerhouse to match any inner city ghetto youth gang.

Sweat pouring off bangs, David slid indoors for a cold drink rest break. Grumpy Old Man Gangsta Fart casually walked by with dog meandering unleashed then threw something into the driveway. Grumpy Old Man Gangsta Fart obviously did not see Navi sitting on the deck. David came out lemonade glass in hand, wiping sweated brow "Did I just see him throw something on the driveway?"

"Yes."

David walked out to the end of the driveway, held a plastic grocery bag up in the air, turning it around in his hand. He walked back and said, "This is fucking war! That old grumpy bastard just threw a bag of dog shit on our driveway."

Livid, he marched inside, grabbed the phone book and dialed then professionally asked for the By Law Enforcement Officer Supervisor then ranted of bullying old people using the by law enforcement office purely as a means in which to harass and annoy other community occupants. It all just defies normal sense of logic for living in the country, let alone a beach and cottage area. It defies logic how people could go out of their way to make others miserable.

Navi sat in the dismal garden, picking weeds and doing inventory of what flowers had survived as Catharine pulled up. Still deeply Mexican sun tanned and corn rowed hair, gorgeous, "You know, watching you there in that shitty little garden made me think. You look so sad. I don't know what your situation is with money and all, but maybe you ought to think about getting another house."

"Well hi to you too. I can't afford it right now. Got time for a coffee or a nice cold iced tea?"

"Well darling, that's what I came here for. Hey are you not listening in to the Spirit realm these days?"

"I thought I was, why?"

"Well you've been on my mind so much lately. I have a friend that is retiring and doing a big garden give-away, want to go look?"

"Sure!"

Within days, Gran and the spirit world smiled as she stood in their doorway. The cottage had magically morphed; old-field stone nestled along the foundation, cedar rails formed a privacy fence, flowers, plants and shrubs flourished with abandon, everywhere. Privacy, snippets of grass designed ornamental, as though no one had cut the grass in years or needed. Navi was in love and street Gangsta old farts could go to hell.

David said, "Wow."

Abby said, "Awesome."

That evening shortly after dinner, Grumpy Old Fart Gangsta Man walked his dog in front of their house and stood at the end of the driveway looking toward the cottage, red faced and shoulders slouched. David stood at the living room window looking back, "I'll accept that as an official apology. It sure looks to me like he got a call from the local by law enforcement office. A lame apology is not enough to make me want to stay."

"What do you mean, not enough to stay?"

"Oh, just thinking that we ought to move to Toronto, get some city fix, get a life, get a real artist's life."

"No!"

"Ah, I know Nav, no worries, 'twas just a passing thought."

On Monday, Navi drove to work chanting into a positive attitude in hopes of turning the looming unemployment tide, 'I love my beach cottage house, my clients and my pay cheque. I am Mother Theresa in the bowels of Calcutta, working with the poor and the dying. Those that are the poorest of the poor and closest to death are closest to God.'

The first call of the day was Helen who had obviously slid into a bad habit of speaking in a condescending tone that she now pay cheque tolerated while thoughts drifted to a cared mind space, of renovating and decorating the cottage.

"From now on, I want you to report your daily agenda directly to me. Another ministry file audit is to be expected in the next couple of weeks or so."

"Why would you want more paper work?" Navi was on to her, but Helen did not yet know it. She still had a trunked box of printed memos, enough information to sink her good. Now, more concerned about pay cheque continuity and leaving in a good way when she was ready.

"Oh I'd be grateful for the feedback; maybe I can pick the guys brains a bit." She knew perfectly well it was not the response expected, nor was there nearly enough intimidation and fear in her voice.

Adam sat down, comfortable and uninvited. He knew that she would not mind the liberty; they had a special understanding of how things were. Adam lived a little further in the bush than the others and while she had never actually been to his place, heard legends about it. He lived in an old trailer in a thicket of mature trees, dense forest. No one was ever sure just how he had gotten it back in the bush, or whether someone else put it there and he just assumed it. His long black scraggly hair not only went unwashed, even for going into town, he used smelly animal fat to grease it back. Adam always took his time settling in and warming up to speak, never wasting words or energy on anything or anyone. While to the rest of the town's people, unkempt and dirty, he had dressed up for the occasion. The only job was as a fourteen-year-old mink farmer and furrier. Illiterate, possessed neither bank account, nor phone. He did not have family nearby, nor did he ever desire to speak of them. Adam was of special intrigue; over the years a number of Mental Health Workers had tried in vain to entice him into a psychiatric assessment and moving into a group home in town. What the workers did not understand was that this Adam was happy and loved his lifestyle. It was a conscious choice made from heart, not because he lacked in IQ and ability to reason. He did not want a place in town and could not survive marketable skill development programs. What was lost on the mental health workers was that he was intelligent in ways that also worked for him just fine. Unable, uninterested in trying to fit in anywhere else, he had made a conscious choice long ago of opting out of mainstream society.

"So, what on earth brings you in here, this time of year?"

"Oh, was just hopin' to get some indoor plumbing. Don't need supplies this year. Did real good on cedar lumber. Good and proper plumbin' isn't somethin' I can rightly barter for. It's got ta be good and right."

She looked at him sideways, scanning and taking it all in. She envisioned a woman with scraggly black hair, large bosom flopping about, without a bra to contain them, rubber boots and a twinkle in her eye for this man.

"Hey, Adam, you got yourself a woman?"

He grinned from ear to ear, "Yep".

"Well, I'll be darned. You can drop by the Salvation Army Community Centre. They might be able to help, with Habitat for Humanity, or one of the service clubs. I will call ahead and let them know you will be coming. Make sure that when you get there, you tell them I sent you. They will help you get what you need. They may already have some bits you can have, or they will set you up at the hardware store, on their chit. If they can't help you, they'll set you up with some other church folks that would be happy to help you out."

He grinned wider, pleased.

"Hey Adam."

"Yep?"

"I hear they're giving out multi coloured condoms at the food bank today."

Adam threw his head back and roared with abandon. He laughed so hard that he wiped tears from his eyes with his dirty coat sleeve."

"Navi, you're one in a million. I'm awful glad you're here."

"Adam, you're one in a million. And I'm awful glad to know you."

'Just goes to show you, there is somebody for everybody', Navi sadly pondered, 'I am really going to miss these people.

Navi arrived home met at the door by David and Abby.

"You're not going to believe this."

David dangled a special delivery envelope and she ripped it open. There it was in black and white, legal mumble jumble, bottom line, grinning from ear to ear. "My first series has officially been accepted by a gallery."

"Oh my God, yahoo! NO, no way?"

"Way! And a showing in thirty days."

"NO, no way!"

"Way!"

Work completion loomed in the air; the last vestiges hung onto by fingertips, afraid to let go and free fall into the unemployment abyss waiting for David's art to sell. 'What to do, what to do?' She needed time away from everything. With Abby away with her Dad for the weekend, she quickly packed.

Navi backpacked alone with Dawg into the provincial park semi-wilderness. Mind flurried with activity and worry, deaf to nature's ambiance. Off trail deep into bush, she aimed for a small opening rocky shoreline. Mindful to stay close enough to have others safely handy, yet far enough away for ensured aloneness, set tent and lit a campfire. Sitting on a granite boulder, sun set colour gazing, evening air chilling. Chicken wrapped tin foil into red-hot coals, an old camp pot set atop grate for coffee. A tiny furry guest scrambled in coffee pot's bottom, striving to climb jump out then sliding down, wet little deer mouse, shivering. A spare woolen sock gingerly wrapped around him, dried with headscarf then tucked him into her sweater, suspended over her heart to warm him. Tiny melody peeps from within sweater sent Dawg into fits of dancing and bouncing excitement; a new tiny friend at hand, exuberant canine ready to play. Antibacterial goop cleansed coffee pot then fresh cool lake water re-filled and set over grate fire. A cup of camp coffee in hand, a dollop of peanut butter on a finger, warmed little deer mouse was fed then curled back into sock soundly sleeping.

"Ah, cute little wilderness mouse, I wonder where your family is? I shall name you 'Wildebeest'."

Dark rumbling clouds rolled over the majestic tree top horizon, wind picking up, Navi quickly spread out coals then tarp covered the tent then bundled into sleeping bag, assuring that the lantern was readily close. As soon as the door flap closed, gale winds swirled bouncing the tent. Safe within, tail tucked Dawg slid inside bed bundle, aside sock wrapped Wildebeest, shivering and whining with each lightening flash strike and ground shaking thunder roll.

Lying awake, cleansing rain filled tent awning, a steady drip against dissipating winds as light flashes and bowling alley booms made their way north east. Mind still, body calming, finally Navi was aware of her surroundings, her home world gazillions of miles away and out of thought, she dozed.

"Navi Woman; awake."

Stirring semi awake, allowing familiar warmth of a soul spirit presence to whisper soothe.

"I am with you, one with you as always."

A white wispy body outline hovered indistinct, radiating, pulsating, sparkling and sparks dancing, a feminine power beyond all imaginings.

"Wow, you are beautiful."

"I, like you my Darling do not push nor rush change. There is a natural flow of time and changes. This visit is but a tiny seed of what wonders await you. Remember this in your darkest of nights."

Squinting, the form of a large white wolf shifted into a woman then back again.

"Your thoughts are that we are worlds apart, I am always at one with you. This daybreak I silently climb the hill beside you as wolf, moss beneath my pads. By the light of many full moons to come, I shall listen for your call. Listen, Hoot Owl alerts danger in the woods. Your dark valley will seem to know no depths, yet I stand at your side in protection. In time, your golden white coat will stir and move within the cocoon of healing. As Grandmother Moon beams sparkles upon late night water's surface and soul ripples as a Loon call, I wait. Through many a dark night, moons and seasons until crisp autumn wind blows through my coat, I lick night air in wait for you to come home. Navi Darling, open your soul eyes and see, let go and allow."

In stillness, behind wolf woman laid a northern wilderness majestic lake, full moon behind, splays water surface sparkles, and a Loon drifts by forlorn, calling of its mates. Bullfrogs answer each other's late night call, for evening's descent is communal nesting time. Wolf pack howls on distance ridge, her cellular memory answers, consoling song across the cosmos."

"Who are you?"

"Many life times with many names and many adventures of various outcomes, in another lifetime it shall be so known to you."

Daybreak awake, spirit wolf woman's essence lingered amidst after rainstorm mist. Stretching into fresh earth aroma's white mist breath hung in moist laden air, she licked her tongue at the dew, bare feet feeling moss, loons call in the distance, followed by bullfrogs then spirit wolf pack call. Not knowing what it meant, wanting to remember the experience, not wanting to go home, to work, and to uncertain life with David, she slid back into the sleeping bag and dosed.

Hiking the granite rock ridge to waterfall, crashing water danced over ancient rock, washing spirit and soul carried in the whispering cool breeze. Sweater spread out, cheese and cut apple shared by Dawg and Wildebeest. Finally, calm within and without, a deep cleansing sigh brought inhalation aroma of musky cedar, fresh lake water and cool moist air.

Rescued Tiny Wildebeest Wilderness Mouse, now well dried, warmed, rested and fed, stirred alive, ready to nuzzle and play. In joyous abandon, he perked ears, twitched whiskers and began to play, running up and down an old crocked Tamarac tree, coming back to glance at her, then away again.

Thoughts turned to where a myriad of life changes were rapidly assuming form, outcome unknown. Comfortably at home with Abby, nature, clients and spirit world, lost in comprehending her role within the stressful day world of making a living. Frustrated with a blank screened future, images and information flowed easily for others.

Navi turned around to pack away picnic, pausing, smiling in reverence to watch Wildebeest and Dawg play. Dawg in exuberance promptly pounced on his tiny mouse head. Rescued Tiny Wildebeest Wilderness Mouse was gone in a flash to the other side. Over exuberant Dawg tilted his head from side to side, waiting for playing dead Wildebeest Wilderness Mouse to jump up and resume play. Sniffing, nudging with nose, then gently batting, willing his little friend to revive.

Wrapped in his sock, with an air hole just in case, a dollop of peanut butter in a fold, Navi cooed little mouse. Dawg slunk head low to ground and whined, knowing little mouse spirit had left. By the ancient Tamarac tree, a hole deep enough not to be re-dug by Dawg, but not so deep, just in case, little Wildebeest Wilderness Mouse's carcass was lain to final rest.

"Short magical and adventurous life, untamed yet tame as can be. Spirit once in tiny body, now ran wild and free. Scamper, run and join your ancestors little one. The land of spirit world; plenty of seeds and tender shoots, May you be prey to none.

Little mouse spirit, I stop and look at life through your eyes, I see details in the world around me that I would not see otherwise. Ah, I have developed insolence for those in authority in my work and have been procrastinating what must be done. Surely, in the bigger picture of life, those clients will find other ways to get where they are going. Closing doors always take us to grander opportunities. In spirit world, you now see cosmos, star nations and galaxies, petty matters of the earth world forgotten."

Distant Crow caw shifted attention. Sensing Gran's presence, Navi sat lotus snuggling sad Dawg, contemplating the passing of little mouse into spirit world.

"Sometimes my Darling Chickadee, hanging on too tight to a person or routine, too long, causes emotional pain of resistance than going with the natural flow of change. Your journey is just beginning."

Navi had left work in soul, now strained to attend to the small framed, half-breed middle-aged woman sitting across the desk, a new client. The woman was in dire need of emergency funds yet preoccupied with finding her native ancestral connections. She had asked her boss for a short leave of absence and was promptly fired. Open birth records were revealing much longed for information and hot on its trail, relations seemed to be coming out of the woodwork. Letters sent and received, photos exchanged. Spirit intervention was well at hand.

Coincidentally, the woman's biological mother had lived only a few blocks away; her mother had stayed close, as a cashier at the corner variety store. The woman had always been keeping tabs, until abusively lonely adopted family life gravitated her to street life. A communal eclectic entourage of First Nations runaways, who eked out survival living in a rundown old warehouse, lost in an underground world of drugs and prostitution. It was at this time that biological mother lost track of her. Had she known of the woman's existence, connection, life would have been profoundly different

Maternal love was finally found through an aunt spent many years in search, despite a police report that advised of her death; a hostel worker had confused her with another runaway girl. Government birth records led to other government records, which led to identification that in turn led to an online lost persons search group. It was odd that society was still segregating into colours and cultures; a person still could not be half of this or half of that. It had to be either or.

Navi's compassion arose, while she knew of her own family and lineage, she too longed for belonging and acceptance.

Waves of tourists melded with retirees migrating with the Canadian Geese from Florida, Arizona and Mexico to the beach cottages. Peeper Frogs in mating frenzy, chorused from nearby wetlands. Tiny beach winter ghost town had come alive with new shops and flurry.

City life folded into rural beach community life, evening ritual cafe lounging at the new funky outdoor espresso bar. Black Forest Mocha, Cafe Lattés with rum liqueur and a candy store array of Italian ice creams. Nightlife entertained watching tourists, hot new city fashions and soul renewal. Amazing hair dos, ample make up, layers of shiny bangle jewelry, all accented string bikinis atop stiletto heels. All, trying in vain to sensuously walk in sand while navigating dive-bombing seagulls. Targets in sight, gorgeous city women balanced a veggie wrap or diet ice cream, to stealthy have snack snaffled by squawking white and black air divers, leaving a splat of oozing bird bowel slime in its stead. Warm days, sunsets, cafe lounging and ice cream at the beach; life was good.

Church in external world fading into distant memory, doctrine remained in inner battle. Given Aunt Diane and Mother's candid revelations of Gran, not fully integrated in a younger Navi childhood churchgoing soul. Knowing of this obvious genetic lineage of otherworldly capabilities and finding a way to balance it in the day-to-day world, offered clues and a focal point

Delving deeper into her schoolwork offered food for thought, yet offered no inner peace. History was full of Saints, healers, sages and visionaries. Sunday school bible teachings and doctrine still ran contrary to who she thought she naturally was; soothsayer, conjurer, seductress and sinner. Unless demonstrating a minimum of three miracles, proven and sanctioned by an appointed God delegate, be it a priest, bishop or she-nun, all else fell into evil category.

"Joy and anger, sorrow and happiness,
caution and remorse come upon us by turns,
with ever changing mood.
They come like music from hollows,
like wood when played by the wind,
or how mushrooms grow from the damp.
Daily and nightly they alternate within
but we cannot tell whence they spring.
Without these emotions I should not be.
Without me, they would have no instrument."
Chuang Tzu

Chapter 17 ~ Lessons from the Spirit Realm

July brought Abby's party. Carload after carload of budding teenagers, dropped off by parents who scooted off without getting out of their cars. Abby had invited her class as well as old school friends. Dawg and Ugly Kat took cover under her bed. "THIS IS THE FIRST AND VERY LAST PARTY. You can bloody well wait until university" she muttered within ear shot of Abby, who returned an ear to ear grin.

By one o'clock in the morning, the last had left. Splayed out on the deck stargazing, afraid to go back inside and face house mess post party wrath, her life in weary analogy, seemed an unfathomable mess.

Separation and divorce are part of the bigger nasty family squabbles that ought to remain behind closed doors. When people croaked, died, passed over, there were the funeral arrangements made, rituals involving clergy and loved ones who surrounded and supported you while you adjusted to life without the loved one in it. When a relationship or marriage died, there were no quick divorce arrangements made, in most cases, it took years. Those who did not attend church regularly or belong to any specific fellowship struggled along, facing their grief alone, without support, while friends and family rallied to take sides and form unusual allies. With most separations and divorces, there are no quick resolutions, no clergy or ritual to help couples go their separate ways in peace and blessings. She knew of no ritual or ceremony process to aid in spiritual psychological transition. Friends and families scattered, parting ways like the parting of the Red Sea or cockroaches to lights turned on.

A loss that was bigger than just losing a spouse; but also of dreams of the future, extended family and family identity, solidarity, sense of belonging, being needed and loved, all gone. Shared sacred vows and expectations of a higher love that would transcend and surmount all adversities, against all odds; gone at the blink of an eye, the snap of a finger. One moment, a person thinks that they are loved and supported and then, the next moment, nothing. Banished and amputated from a life known and familiar; gone.

Navi snatched Abby in arms spinning her around in circles,

"Good morning you little party animal! What a frigging mess, little warrior woman!"

"Grandma's going to die soon, isn't she?"

"Yes, love."

"Grandpa was handsome, wasn't he?"

"You see him too huh? Yes, he was."

"I'm glad that he has come for her."

"Me too. Clean up this mess. I shall meet you out at the campfire at dusk."

"Tonight we are going to initiate you into Sacred Sisterhood. There will come a time, when you will be teaching others the old ways. I want to plant a seed in you for the future because many will come to you for healings and teachings. Many will have an inner drive to learn the old ways and integrate the new. The world is changing and you are to show paths."

Abby quiet, truth rang true.

Daughter watched as Navi lit a smoke, "Tobacco is sacred, an ancient prayer herb and a way of communicating with Spirit. You give tobacco when you want to give thanks; thoughts, gratitude's and prayers go up into the heavens with the smoke. Then you pinch the left over tobacco and sprinkle it on the ground, it becomes one again with the Earth Mother."

"Yes, I know all of this stuff."

Navi sat and quietly waited, smoke curling up toward the heavens, then continued, "There are those who believe that you chose your own path before you came into this world. You wrote your own script, chose your own parents and lessons. You came into this world with innate skills and abilities that are unique and yours alone. The gifts that you have in this lifetime, the lessons you experience and chose to learn are also unique. They are different from mine, from anyone else's. Even as a child, you spent most of your time alone, playing in the light of spirit. You have always had difficulty asserting the game rules, you have a lifetime and beyond to find your balance in both worlds. This is how it is; you can read others thoughts, fears and desires."

"I know Mom."

Undaunted, Navi throat cleared "This teaching must be heard, so bear with me sweetheart, it is to ensure that you will always remember.

We may look to others for our own identity, to see how we measure up. This is a powerful urge to conform; yet our soul longs for authentic natural self and autonomy. In comparing, we never measure up and never ever fit in, smoke, mirrors and illusions. What we see in the reflection of others eyes, and their behaviour, is our own doubts, our own fears. There is no one, no such a nemesis that exists that we must concede to, other than our own divinity. Love yourself unconditionally, just the way you are.

When you see and feel the reflection of other people's judgment and disapproval, remember that they are not authorities and they are not God. The authority, the only God that you have to answer to is right there in your heart, in your own soul. When you can look a nemesis square in the eyes, face your jury of persecution with dignity and self-unconditional love and stand in the light, you have found your nirvana. Remember that you must experience this growth on all levels; mental, emotional, physical and spiritual. When you have mastered this point, you graduate to a new level.

Abby thoughtful, truth curled around burning cedar smoke.

"I'm working on it Mom."

The campfire burning, the smoldering embers crackled and danced upward into a dark starry sky. Navi stood, grounded and strong, as though upon hearing invitation opened a portal of remembering, of officiating ancient rituals. Born to assist people with life transitions and sanctioned by a higher authority, sacred images of many lifetimes shared as shamans, priestesses and medicine women flashed by.

Winging it, "We ask God and all that is divine, to assist us in aligning who we came here to be. We are here tonight to welcome Abby into the sisterhood. We ask Mother of all women, cultures, everywhere and the presence of all appropriate spirit guides, to join us this evening. We ask for guidance, and for love to surround us, enfold us, protect and nourish us, today and always. We expand this love and divinity, to all men and women everywhere. As is above, so is below."

Navi paused, gazing deep into daughter's ancient wise eyes.

"Since the dawn of time, women have been blessed with the power of menstruation, then motherhood, then menopause, which leads to, old crone. These are natural transitional passage rites that have been celebrated by women throughout time.

All cultures have migrated, assumed control of others, mixed and assimilated. Occupying foreign countries assimilated some of the original cultural values, harvested natural resources and technology. In the name of some God or other, for economic development, from a positive angle they were also philanthropists. However, economic gain and power of the masses was most often the underlying intent. Back in those times, religions and state were the same. Understand that the Romans were not Christian by heritage. With rapid growth of Christianity, they quickly saw potential and so adapted fundamentals into policies of state. All grabbed the concepts based with sole intent of higher love, but as a strategic way to rule the masses and economy. Some of the old ways managed to continue in secret.

Winter Solstice was replaced by Jesus' birthday, yet other timelines place his birthday in May, astrologically Taurus. In the British Isles, it was the work of women themselves who did much to lose the old ways, it became in vogue to fashion themselves after royalty. During Queen Victoria's reign, Roman Christian dogma diversified into factions and sects, splitting away. Laws gradually created new infrastructures, eliminating the old ways.

From a cynical point of view, it was a brilliant way to control the masses, opposition of teaching authentic autonomy as found in other aboriginal teachings. Autonomy and individuality was suspect and any deviation endangered you and loved ones lives. The Witch Craft Acts and the Heresy trials were powerful ways to set conforming controls; by propagandizing fear. Yet it was an age of profound economic gain for the select ruling few. A time of significant emerging contrary thought followed through science, away from free thought, reason, and diversity. So, the old ways still lay sleeping, quietly evolving and waiting your generation's time to come, when old ways can be integrated into the new, birthing a new world order.

This is why you are here, why we are here. Mensa and menopause brings feminine intuitive power to the surface. It has the power to conceive, to manifest life, to give birth, depending upon your intent. It is essentially the story of all Creation, to think a thought, give life to it and then manifest it in the physical, a time of cleansing, renewal. In times of old, women left their community during Moon time for regenerative solitude time out. The moon cycles bring a re-connection to nature, our own inner cycles, to the Earth Mother, the Universe, God, Great Spirit and all of Creation.

You are always surrounded by at least Four Spirit Guide women, always there for you because your journey is a master's journey."

"I love you, a lot Mom. I wish that you could have had people like you in your life when you were my age; maybe your life would have been better, easier. Thanks. Mom." Tossing a pinch of powder in the fire, sweet aromatic crackling incense sparks flew upward into night air.

Navi squatted beside her thoughtful daughter, "So medicine girl, want to talk about tonight?"

"Nope."

"Well, I do. How do you feel about it?"

"I used to do ceremonies like that too you know."

"That's it?"

"Yes, it's all good and righteous."

"Ah, a new era emerges."

The day brought a heat wave, thick stagnant heavy air challenged breathing and energy levels. Despite fans and skimpy clothing, sweat rolled down their under arms. Dawg vacillated between curl up panting under the bed and lying inside bathtubs cool porcelain, licking tap drips.

By midnight, a meagre eclectic pile of accumulated life belongings and household goods were sorted and moved outside to her new shed. Exhausted, Navi was deliriously happy to assume the sacred space. Sinking the last of her savings into renovating had been a stroke of sheer brilliance. Tacky faded and worn white and black linoleum kitchen floor, now hardwood flooring served as first meal, take-out pizza picnic spot. Warped floors, tilting ceiling beams, dirty green shag carpeting, gone. Living room expanded in wrap around bay windows; open concept old stone fireplace shone potential ambiance amidst a mass of new rattan furniture. Gone were the night dim and fiber bare tawdry floral curtains and forty years' worth of window scum. Above, old warped pine paneling walls that had hidden layers of dust now glowed clean, from fresh drywall and paint. In ceiling corners where webbed dust strands menaced outwards, hanging and dancing in mid-air, now garden lights twinkled magic. Crooked mix matching oak trim lined crocked ceiling edges now gave way to clean lines. Ornate un-matching garage sale accent lights that had dimmed under layers of scummy slime now gave way to showcased cast iron lanterns. Each ceiling distinctly differing from room to room, depending upon era and materials at hand; sprayed plaster, drywall and fragile off white ceiling panels, now flowed evenly and swam with joyous energy and fairy nature spirits.

"OM home ravenous for cash and man power influx renovations, I must be out of my tiny frigging mind."

Then it appeared; a house mouse. Grey Chubby House Mouse audaciously skittered out from inside the kitchen cupboards and scooted inches away from David sock feet, then out into the living room in under and over boxes then down the hallway, into the master bedroom and back down the hallway to disappear in the bathroom. He jumped, deliciously declaring "BATTLE!!!!" Primal warrior released, he grabbed a broom, banged on the bathroom door chasing frantic mouse through kitchen, living room, bathroom, bedroom, Abby's room, laundry room and down the hallway, to no avail. Crafty Grey Chubby House Mouse outwitted, outran and outsmarted primal man at every turn. Abby preoccupied herself with re-decorating bedroom with Christmas tree lights.

David Primal man was undeterred, calculating and waiting for evening appearance of Nemesis House Mouse, archenemy. He strategized Nemesis Mouse hunts, set up traps, including the ultimately deadly weapon, Warfarin. Sure that the colourless anticoagulant rodenticide was the way out, Navi worried about his growing obsession. House Mouse undeterred; feasted freely on dog food resourcefully nudging nose under breadbox door to bread, muffins and cookies.

"I don't know David. I think you are out-matched. This was his house long before you intruded and squat your arse here and since he is alpha dog and here to stay, can leave. Honestly? I really don't like using that stuff, it's a cruel way to die and I am concerned that the pets might get into it or that it will get into us." Dejected David frowned in submission. When they curled up to watch movies, Nemesis Mouse boldly scooted across the floor and paused in front of the television. David leapt off the couch and grabbed a broom, stealth armed and dangerous.

"That sassy little beggar knows all of the escape routes that I can't penetrate!"

"Actually David, I am really starting to get grossed out cooking food in the kitchen, not knowing what the house mouse had been into or not." Turning, grounded and other worldly omnipotent, she alpha dog called out to mouse, "Okay my little friend, it's been a blast and a thrill but you have to go now or David will be the death of you. Your choice, but make it right now."

"Ah ya Navi Darlin', that'll work."

"Maybe."

The phone rang and Navi sensing in her solar plexus that it was for her and it was not good, hesitantly answered.

"Is this Navi?"

"Yes?"

"This is your electrical company calling. We have completed a recent meter reading and re-calculated your bill. Our records indicate that you are in arrears of two thousand four hundred and forty-four dollars and forty-five cents. This must be paid in full by September fifth, or we will forward your account to a collection agency and your current electricity will be cut off. Do you understand?"

"What? That's insane! There must be some mistake! I always pay my bills on time each month."

"I can assure you that it is not a mistake. I too thought it looked unusually high, but I checked it twice and even had my supervisor look into it. You owe us over your credit limit and it must be paid immediately."

"No way, it's got to be wrong! That can't be right! Besides there is no way that I can come up with that kind of money, no way, it's got to be a mistake."

"I have your entire account up in front of me from the time you took occupancy in your last residence. It would appear that you neglected to identify yourself at the time of hook up to this service, that you were a permanent resident. Your bills were not meter read, calculated according to the previous occupant's seasonal account. So our records indicate that the meter has been read and your current balance is correct."

"No way, I'm sure that I told the person when I moved there that it was year round and I am quite sure that it is a mistake!"

"I can assure you Madam that it is indeed correct and you have to rectify the situation. Good day to you Madam!"

She hung the phone, dizzy, her spiritual training and experience and inner knowing of how abundance worked was gone, retreated back into the yucky bathroom and locked the door.

"Oh God Gran, what am I supposed to do?"

"Hello my darling. Did you notice the Chickadees that came with the house?"

"What?"

"Did you notice all of the beautiful mature garden plants, just waiting for you?"

"What? What are you talking about? I'm in crisis and you're asking me about Chickadees and plants?!!!"

"If you would only go to your new garden, put your hands in the earth, feel the sun on your lovely face and allow warm breeze to caress your hair."

"What?"

"That is all for now."

Smoldering on the toilet in an all-out hissy fit, she swore at the electric company and cursed masturbating maniac Stephen, Nazi ministry reps, conniving co-workers and friendship betraying sell out Helen, flaky other worldly spirit people who offered complex babble.

Dutifully out on to the deck, she suddenly became aware of the sun touching skin and breeze caressing hair; she closed her eyes, and with a deep breath, relaxed. Eyes opened to see a beautiful purple wild flower in full blossom. Chickadees sang for the first time since she had moved in, flittering overhead, in and out of a massive pine tree at the edge of the drive way. A loving spirit hand had tenderly caressed hair as Nature spirits giggled, dancing happily in acknowledgement. Gran touched alive and present. With spirit lightness once again, she called the electric company and arranged to make instalments and life seemed more manageable, once again. 'If only navigating work was that easy.'

Hungry, fearful and vulnerable, clients would sign anything to put food on the table for a few weeks. They did not know how to navigate the new legislation and system and had no idea what was expected, so they simply could not constitute 'informed consent', coercion.

Scratchy music sound blasted from inside of the house, jangling her nerves, so she ventured inward to its source. David proudly displayed a garage sale record player with several records, as old screeching bagpipe military favourites then Perry Como's Greatest Hits played. Abby had never seen one before and eagerly set about figuring out how it worked.

"Mom?"

"Yes daughter."

"How do you put these things in?"

"Choose a side you want and line up the hole in the record with the little knob in the centre, then lift the needle arm and set it down at the beginning of the record."

"Well which side has the music on it?"

"Oh I get it. You think it works like a CD or DVD player!"

Navi shook off the antiquated emotional reaction pang and clicked computer on.

Dear monster old Step Mommy Dearest;

Tis I, your awesome post cancer, weight gained, hair; darker and thicker, skin and eyes; healthy, clear and shining, healthier handsome adult man and more alive than he had ever looked before former Stepson.

Just thought I would drop you a quick note, 'cause I'll be up to my wazoo in higher learning. Ha, I finally got it. I finally finished university prep last week. Ha, do you know what this means? I am free. FREE I say! Well, free of the grunt beginning, now into the really heavy holy shit.

Dad is fine. I never see him much anymore. Well you know, sad, hurt, messed up when family and friends are around and just fine when alone. Debbie from Dad's office has moved in already, wink-wink nudge-nudge, got a little kid. The kids a frigging brat, temper tantrums and stuff that drive me nuts. I think *it* drives dad nuts too. But hey, I think he likes that she is so weird, every time I see her, her hair is either a different colour and I don't mean just colour, I mean bright green or blue tint or bright red, weird or it's cut crocked or standing straight up. Hey, whatever turns his crank, I guess.

Ciao for now and don't forget my birthday and Christmas

Your fabulously handsome former Stepson.

Navi busied making a light dinner trying to ignore the fact that Abby had been wearing a cabbage leaf on her head all afternoon. She tried not to bite, not to ask her, waiting for Abby to spill what it was all about, David looked at the two quizzically, "Okay, I'll bite. Who or what are you?"

"I'm Mr. LaPorte, the French supply teacher. Must be a drag, you know, being named after something as boring as a door. Must be a drag being so bald on the top of your head."

"Hmmmm. I suppose. French doors are renowned for their beauty and some women find balding men quite hot, a solar panel for a sex machine."

"Oh, that's so gross!"

"What exactly constitutes old?"

"Ah, you know, over forty."

"Wow, Abby, that's a direct hit!"

"The toad man smells like road kill, doesn't love himself, full of cancer and going to croak in a year."

Catching the bizarre exchange, David interceded, "What an awful thing to say. Why would you say that? How in the hell would you know that he is sick? Did he tell you?"

"I can see it! I tried sending him healing energy, but it doesn't do much. It is just his time to go soon, so I just pray for him. Besides, his angel buddies are hanging around waiting and they'll look after him."

Catharine dropped by for coffee with her ancient hound dog whimpering; splayed amongst old blankets. "I don't know what to do. It seems he has caught his leg on a barbed wire fence. It's really quite a deep cut. Look, it's still bleeding profusely. He's been licking the cut then vomiting blood. I still owe the vet money from last week's face full of porcupine quills. God Navi. I don't want to go by myself, mind if I take Abby along?"

"Geez Catharine, that leg is mangled up pretty good. Be my guest; sure, take Abby. Maybe the experience would be good for the little medicine woman to be."

They had finally snuggled down on the couch for the evening under blankets with Dawg curled comfortably on top of them when Catharine arrived with Abby and hound dog in arms, visibly worried.

"We sat in that waiting room for over two hours, terrified and wondering if he was about to die any minute. Well my dumb dog is going to be fine."

"That's good news, what did the vet say?"

"Ha, he said, Madam, your dog is intoxicated! I said; oh, my, I wonder how on earth that might have happened? Then he looked me square in the eyes, kind of sizing me up. I gasped, like the good actress that I am, and said "what"? As though I was shocked and offended! Well, I must confess, that I made some special brownies last night then left them on top of the stove to cool. When I came back, some were missing; the little bastard ate four of the fucking things! The cut on his leg would have been fine with a simple bandage."

Navi laughed, holding her bladder.

Catharine then carried him onto the deck. "Watch this." Catharine set the dog down holding onto his lead. Old hound dog tried to co-ordinate two legs to step forward but rather each went in a separate and opposing direction simultaneously.

"Look at him, poor bastard is still stoned out of his gourd!"

"Oh, Catharine, what would we do without you?"

"I don't know, but the little bastard has cost me fifteen hundred dollars this month! God, can you believe this?"

"You know Catharine; life with you is an adventure. Ah, you are the only living entity on the planet that would put up with that dog."

David was dog inspired, so brought home a Siberian husky with expressionless eyes, a strange mix of bright blue with hints of yellow sparkled yet spiritless eyes and unreadable gaze that instantly unnerved.

"Her name is Roxy. Isn't she beautiful?"

Navi glanced at the dog "I don't know, I can't read her. You'd better tie her up outside until we are sure that she's going to get along with everyone."

He lovingly took Roxy for a tour of the lawn and inside of the house, hand fed kibbles and water and snuggled while Dawg hid in the bedroom closet. Abby arrived from school, dashed to bond with Roxy. Within seconds, a ferocious growling sent tiny hairs erect then Abby screamed. Navi flew outdoors to see a lunging growling swirling dog chaos tangle with Abby in the middle. Surreal slow motion, Navi stood in between, dog wildly swirling to get free as Abby bum slowly backed away. Navi scooped her up and turned back on Roxy who wildly yelped, swirled and barked. Onto the deck, quiet tears streamed down daughters crimson face gingerly holding one arm.

"What in God's name happened?"

"Mom, I just got down on my knees to pat Roxy and she went for me."

"Oh, my God! Are you all right? Let me look at that arm. Did she bite you anywhere else?"

"Well, just my arm and my lip."

"Come on in. I want to have a better look and clean them up. Put something on those bites."

"Mom, I think Roxy thinks that I am an intruder. I love dogs, why do you think she hates me?"

"No honey, it's not your fault, it just means that she has some behaviour problems. This one is closer to her wild nature, I think. Maybe that's why her previous owners were getting rid of her. We can't keep her."

David crushed, took Roxy back.

Navi turned to Abby, looked her squarely in the eyes and said, "Listen, we simply cannot keep a dog that bites any one. We cannot have anyone in the house that hurts anyone else. It is a rule. I am sorry that this happened to you. Okay, I can see that something is bothering you. What is it?"

"Mom, I am sad for David, because he wanted a dog of his own so badly and Roxy really seemed to love him. But.. That's not everything." Abby sat down at the kitchen table, eyes focused on shoes.

"Mom, will David get mad at me for drifting Roxy?"

"What? I don't know what you mean?"

"Well when Roxy came after me, I got really mad for a minute. She scared me and that made me mad, so I really gave her one. I drifted her hard, a right upper cut, blasted her jaw and right fisted her in the head. She reeled backward. I think I might have hurt her."

"Oh Abby, I am so proud of you. I love you so much. And no, I don't think that you have to be nice to a dog that's trying to hurt you, just because someone might get mad at you. Honey you did the right thing. I'm glad to know that you can stand up for yourself when you feel that you need to.

Hmmm.. Maybe Roxy will think twice the next time she wants to bite someone. Maybe you just saved this from happening to some other kid or worse, a baby."

"I never thought of it that way. I'm pretty strong eh?"

"You sure as heck are. It is always wise to keep your distance and be respectful of strange animals and trust your instincts. I didn't, sorry about that."

"HELLLOOOO.... It's Catharine, the magnificent!"

"Hi, you sound excited, what's up?"

"Do you remember when I got back from Mexico and said I had met an old medicine woman?"

"Hold on, let me get comfortable and grab a smoke."

"Well, it seems to be all coming together, now, you know, my quest to explore different cultures, different religions and well, I think I'm on to something now. Anyway, I tracked her down and I am going to the International Medicine Woman Gathering in Arizona."

"Wow!"

"Oh there's some big shit that's been developing down there in Northern Arizona, between the Hopi and the Dinah. The fucking coal oil companies and the Senator, not to mention the last several Presidents, have managed to fuck up the land treaties so badly, that now they've got the two, historically, peaceful groups fighting against each other, rather than working together as allies, to deal with the government collectively. She's working with the Elders to do a peace and healing ceremony, should be back in about a week or so."

"Tell me about your insights."

"Oh, the woman's real name is; Maya. It just clicked that it was no accident that her name was Maya. You see she lived in the Oaxaca Valley. Most of the people there are devout Catholics, but with a spin. They seemed to have adapted the Spanish missionary's influence of doctrine, but also integrated many of the old ways. There were churches and crosses everywhere down there. There are old Zapata or Mayan influences evident in the Catholic festivals, weird actually.

I could not put my finger on it at the time, but I think I know what was bugging me about it. Do you remember hearing about how the old Jaguar Mayan Priests worked with dark powers, back in the days before the demise of the Mayan culture as we knew it?"

"I remember hearing about that."

"Well, when the Spanish invaded and occupied the area, there was a Holy war between the Jaguar Priests and the White Priests. When the Spanish came and stayed, the war became only worse. The Jaguars used fear as a means of controlling the masses. When I thought about the things that Maya had told me about and the prevalent superstitions melded into the Catholic rituals, I think that the one core thing that has pervaded all of this time is fear.

Nevertheless, what is really bothering me about this, is that I had dismissed her beliefs as crap, superstition you know. When I went to see her, a young woman brought a little girl who had been diagnosed terminal by a local medical clinic. It makes me think that maybe the power of thought and the power of belief is actually more than most people think. You know, like the concept of self-fulfilling prophecy. Someone gave that little girl a dirty look, maybe even wished her unwell, then presto. Because the kid, the community believes in this shit, the kid gets so sick she nearly dies. Weird, like manifesting abundance in reverse; believe it is possible and inevitable."

"Wow."

"I'm thinking I'll scoot off to the Nile and see what those old temples are about. I want to find out if there is one simple ritual or mantra system that actually works."

"Wow! Call me or come over when you get back.'

"You got it."

David jumped to answer then immediately slammed a kitchen cupboard door. He was livid pacing, she had not seen this side of him in all of their years working together nor since living together.

"Okay! I take it back. Un-fuck you! You say I am a prick like it's a bad thing. Well I am living happily ever after. What do you mean you were happy before Navi? Your discontent was there years before Navi. No way! What? No! I do not have any more fucking money! What? No. You already have the house and everything in it! Shit! No, I do not have another job yet. What do you care as long as your bills and child support are paid? Wait, I am trying to imagine you as a human with a personality. No, not all men are annoying assholes; some are dead. You are telling me that I look like shit? Isn't that the style you were going for, for me? Oh, that's very funny; a hard on does not count as personal growth. Ha, ha, Oh, very nice. I am depriving some village of an idiot, thank you very much. Are you finished? Don't tell me that I'm ambivalent about the kids and the pets. Well yes and no, well maybe a little. I'm very happy to hear that you've moved into the angry stage. No! That is none of your business."

David slammed the phone down. "Ah shit! What the bloody hell! I could have done without the validation as to why my marriage didn't work."

"Feel better now?"

"No."

"David, do me and the world a favour; go away for a couple of days. Call a buddy and go do something away from here and out of routine."

"Am I getting on your nerves?"

"Yes. I don't like the way you are talking to her, about her. That could be me."

"Ah shit, I am so fed up! I am fed up working for scratch, living someone else's idea of life and paying out my asshole for house, mortgage and bills of shit that I do not want!"

Startled, pretending to be engrossed in a textbook, she wondered what other rebound carry over waited. "Magus Man I am serious, go away and play with the guys, you need time out."

Pondering, thinking on it, fingers twisting goatee hair, "You know what? I am going to take you up on that, I think I'll got to Toronto and see if I can find some of my old university buddies, maybe tour some gallery and see if my old Dean is still haunting the halls of higher learning academia. Are you okay with that?"

"GO!!!"

With David gone, mother and daughter snuggled within a double sleeping bag aside a crackling campfire under brilliant stars amidst dancing twinkling fireflies at a pebbled shoreline. Early night's mist hung over the lake surface that snaked open bay, river mouth and adjoining muskeg alive amidst magical crescendo of Loon's lonesome calls. In the distance, two soused touristy men paddled their canoe out into open bay hooting, laughing and giggling with beer in hand and a huge box of fireworks.

Gunfire BOOM... PISST... ZIZZZ... booms blasted sideways straight across the lake surface into open water. In each moment of brilliant firework ignition, the canoe illuminated glowing neon colours, the men laid flat backwards, cigars pointing sky ward. They giggled, scrambling, and cursed as stray fire sparks spit sent tiny smoldering flames on pants and gear. Joy rush; a moment to treasure.

"Mom. Don't just say no to thong undies, look at them. They are really comfortable. Go and get some."

"No, way! Besides, they look like they'd give you a permanent wedge."

"Ah mom, I'm trying to be comfortable. Besides, I am not shitting you, they are amazingly comfy cozy, here try a pair on."

"Ah God Abby, maybe you haven't noticed, but I'm into menopause, and not so hot anymore."

Abby screwed a half smile.

"God Abby, go take a good look in the mirror! You have blossomed into a regular knock out over the summer. Your bloody breasts are bigger than mine. Look, wearing sexy clothes at your age is not just a question of age appropriate because of what other people might think. I'm concerned about attracting some guy who might think you're older than you are and getting into a situation where he may want to take something from you that you're not emotionally, mentally, physically or spiritually prepared to deal with."

"Ah, Mom. It is just underwear."

"No it's not. It is the beginning of a slippery slope down the road of dangerous conformity."

"Mom, I promise no matter how drug fucked up I get, how many years I might get doing jail time, drug rehabilitations and how many out of wed babies I birth, I'll still love you."

"Thanks for the reassurance, you little shit! If you really must, it is your body. I won't worry too much. Wherever you journey, be your amazing natural self. Just promise you will stay mindfully focused staying true to who you want to be. Bold, audacious, unique, lovely medicine woman."

"When can I Shaman apprentice?"

"You already are one. Tell me what you remember from other life times."

"Almost all of it, telling you would take a life time, how about I share my art journal with you; I can show you what I'm working on. By the way Aunt Diane is going to pass over soon."

"I know."

"And you're going to be out of work soon."

"I know. What will I be doing?"

"Finish your courses, be a minister. Ha, ha."

"Then what?"

"Rocky road ahead momma, helping a shit load of people along the way, crash and burn then shaman re-birth."

"How do you know this stuff?"

"I am remembering, feels awesome. How do you know this stuff Momzy?"

"Must be genetic. Would have made life a lot easier had I known growing up. Apparently we come from a long line of Sensitive's."

"So I gather."

"Have you ever morphed into an animal?"

"Yes Mom."

"Have you ever seen the energy exchange between people when they interact?"

"Yes, all the time. Just getting the hang of tuning it out when I don't want to know their scary emotional shit."

"Wow, you really are motoring along. I honestly don't see you needing a formal shaman structure, ask your angels for the right teacher."

"I already have one. Thanks Mom."

"Ah, you charmer you. This stays between you and me for now, okay? Promise?"

"You got it Momzy. By the way, just so you know, when shit hits the fan, I'll stay with you."

"That sounds ominous. I see that my Gran is one of your guides too."

"Yes, always has been, except now I recognise her. I used to just think she was some old lady."

"Abby? I adore you."

"I love you too Mom."

> "Every time you don't follow your inner guidance,
> you feel a loss of energy, loss of power,
> a sense of spiritual deadness."
> Shakti Gawain

Chapter 18 ~ Sanctuary

Unkempt, unshaven David contentedly sleep sprawled across the bed, mouth gaping wide, a trickle of saliva spilled over chin. Sisterhood shawl wrapped, back against warm affectionate man, cold toes slid down his muscular thighs then fuzzy calves enfolding his toes. Warmth of sleepy bed skin sharing brought intimate comfort, he stirred, and stretch shifted, enfolding her within arms, skin disappearing into his skin, into his soul dismissing dark shadow and unknown future.

As sleep enveloped, *in the blink of an eye, surroundings shifted in thick smoky fog that gently wavered in surreal time, while Navi shifted conscious awareness. Journeying was picking up speed in its transitioning, the snap of fingers, poof! Aware mind held steady, physical spirit body lagging stumbling behind. Catching up and aligning as one whole unit, heavy fog gradually dissipated.*

'Sanctuary' a man whispered in her mind's ear. Bare feet on warm soft rounded pebbles as a gentle off shore lake breeze billows long white cotton dress and caressed long brown hair. Soothing sounds of tiny waves washed onto pebbled beach in the dark of a full moon lit night. Stars bright, so close, reaching up on tiptoes a hand touched one; alive it giggled, childlike bouncing against the tickle. Smiling, each star responds in twinkling smiles. Turning toward north shoreline a short distance, a boulder wall precipice ended beach, similarly, the south shore. Dark night water ending at horizon, rippling waves alive, moving in and out and breathing in oneness of the earth mother spirit essence stilling.

Beyond, a massive ancient solo olive tree, guardian to a dense forest further behind. A flutter of wings slightly broke stillness, taking perch high above olive tree. Adjusting wings, tilting head, eyeing his guest, acknowledging her visit as arranged, expected. Crow now visible, his essence spoke of a higher intelligence. A sentient being, an obvious old friend felt familiar and loving. With the tip of an outstretched wing, in circling motion, she twirled around in circles under its waltzing direction. Giggling, she allowed the joy dance, feet light and barely upon the ground, her cotton dress swirling, long hair trailing.

Standing once again, gazing into Crow's eyes, heart and soul, smiling, knowing, "Hello Soul Skin animal mate."

"Good day to you my friend" he cawed in a deep wise man's voice. Cocking head to one side eyeing her, he then continued; "In your work, you began wanting to change the world. Do not dismay; you have done your part. Do not grieve apparent losses, adjust your vision of what is and see the difference you have already made. Breathe freely, stand tall and know this, remain mindful that there is always a higher order of what is right, beyond man's thinking, man's laws. Keep your graceful awareness. You are immortal and carry many badges of honour and divinity within your spirit being. Despite your sense of ineptitude, your higher inner light always has and always will illumine the down trodden and broken spirits. Know that I shall be with you in the days to come though you must walk the path alone. One day we shall visit in spirit world and revel in oceans of joyous kindred spirit reunion. I bow to your divine being-ness."

"Thank you my friend."

Navigating the car toward the tight outer fringe parking spot, she stopped abruptly to find that someone had assumed her assigned spot. Swerving, she boldly slid into the only other spot left, handicapped. 'Replaced already' muttering, stepping out gathering purse and lunch. Suddenly, aware of being watched, she turned, expecting to see someone standing directly and seeing no one, looked up. A group of crows perched on the carport roof, squawked, gazing directly at her. Sensing coincidence of last night's journey, she recalled crow spirit's words; a higher order of what is right and what is wrong than man's laws.

Larger alpha Crow ruffled wing feathers, tilted head sideways, black eye pulsing, whispering into her inner mind "call it, caw it like you see it."

Navi nodded head in acceptance, grabbed her take out coffee, and then lifted her brief case out of the trunk. Hesitating, eyes lingered on the photocopied memos box. A deep swallowing sigh; it all came flooding back in an instant, inciting a fear ripple up her spine, cresting overhead, ripping through solar plexus and into a gut stabbing pain. Eyes closed, then another deep breath. "God, am I really supposed to be here today? Like this? I wish I had somewhere else to go; it would make this day so much easier. A warm loving light bathed, feeling her body calmed, she thought, "I take it that is yes."

Immediately noticing the large brown envelope on her desk, she ripped it open. A work performance review; completed in cooperation with Black Suit Ministry Sweet Smelling File Auditor man who had been rifling through her client files. Before turning on the computer and taking her bulky sweater off, she sat to read. 'Kind of a glowing report on my work performance over the past year and hey, a pay increase approved.' She muttered, 'a glowing report and a pay increase too? Then, how in the hell would either one of them know if I had done a good job or not? Shit. Kind of figured I would be getting the boot this morning. I wonder what happened. I don't get it. This is all too confusing.'

Crow's voice mingled with Gran's, speaking in unison, "Stay in grace and follow your inner light, moment to moment and in each decision. Do only what you can; in light, in grace."

Suzie, the morning's first client held the presence of a classy and elegant fashion model.

"I might as well start from the beginning. You see, in order for you to understand where I'm at and what I need to do, you need to understand what happened."

"Sure, take your time. By the way, anything you say will be strictly off record unless you want me to document it."

"No. Please, this is for your ears only."

"Agreed."

Suzie slid off her coat and relaxed into the client chair.

"You see, up until about one year ago, I lived with my two baby daughters in northern Newfoundland. I had always dreamed of becoming a model and making it big. I worked in the grocery store there and saved my money to have my photo portfolio done just right. My mother helped me to scout agents. I had done some local modelling, nothing big, but I wanted something to prove that I did it, could do it and do it well.

An agent came one afternoon to the local community centre from Montreal, scouting local and rural talent. So stupid, I and about sixty other women and teens spent two days competing for one spot. A chance to go to the fashion Mecca of Montreal, all expenses paid, for the big cosmetic and clothing contracts. I won! So I packed up some things, left my baby girls with my mom and off I went by limo to Montreal. I figured that I'd take a couple of months, make some big bucks, find a place to live and then send for my girls and my mom."

Suzie paused for a moment and took a tissue and dabbed tears.

"Geez, Suzie, that all sounds very exciting. What happened that brought you here?"

"Well, that's where my story went bad. Oh, I got to Montreal all right. The man put me up in a fancy motel downtown. He said that there were about thirty other women there as well. We were to share rooms, two a piece with room service. My new roommate would be arriving later at night.

I thought I had died and gone to heaven. I remember throwing my suitcase on the bed and having a luxury shower, using those fancy bath soaps and stuff. I got to order room service, had myself a very fine steak dinner then watched cable television for a while. I decided to call home, talk to my mom and my babies and let them know that I got there safe. I could not figure out how to work the phone, I kept dialing out and getting a dead signal. I called down to the front desk. A man told me that there was a block on my phone, to all outgoing calls. He said that I could call in-rooms, room service and the front desk only. I asked him why and he said, "That was the service order given to him by my agent". Well, that unnerved me a bit, so I got dressed to head out to use a pay phone. I needed to hear my mom's voice and check on my babes. God Navi." Suzie's tears streamed down cheeks and chin, pushing tears away, took a deep breath, sighed and then gingerly blew her nose.

"That's okay, only tell me what you want to. Take your time."

"Well, the door wouldn't open. I thought maybe I had done something wrong when I closed it, you know those fancy motel door locks, like a little computer debit machine. I tried and tried and tried, but it would not open. I freaked out, so I called the man at the front desk again, he said that also was part of the service order in the contract with my agent.

I got really scared after that and didn't know what to do. There was no balcony or window to climb out of, I also realized that it was about twelve stories up. I just sat on the bed, trying to think. Then my agent came in with another girl; my new roommate. I tried not to look scared or freaked. I tried to look calm and in control. I wanted an explanation for the phone and door block. The other girl eyes went wide open. He said that I could review the details of my contract in the morning. In the meantime, we were to make ourselves comfortable for the evening. Someone would be by later in the evening, a guest. He said that the guest was a big famous promoter and we were to look our best and put our happy faces on.

This new girl and I thought it was weird. Why would a big famous promoter want to see us in our hotel room? Anyway, around nine pm this old man opens the door, in a suit and smoking a cigar. He just walked right in, without knocking. He was one of those stand-too-close-to-you-touchy-feely people. He kept running his hand through my hair and rubbing the other girls back. Man did she look scared, downright freaked. Anyway, he did a lot of blah, blah, blah shit about what you had to do to become a big star. He told us that we had to be like chaperones, accompany big important executives out to dinners and stuff, like I was born yesterday, this was really starting to stink criminal.

The next morning the agent came back with contracts in his hands. He did not bother to knock either, just came right in. He says, if we have changed our minds and do not want to make two hundred and fifty thousand in our first year, we can walk out now, with no hard feelings. Just a matter of settling the bill first and then he could tear up the contract. I asked to see the bill, I did not know that there was one, I was sure that it was all expenses paid. He said no, all the modelling administration fees were free. A limousine ride from the airport for two thousand and eight hundred dollars, the hotel room at four hundred and eighty dollars a night, room service at a hundred and twenty five dollars, cable television costs thirty-four ninety-five plus tax, and his initial service contract consultation fee at one thousand and five hundred dollars. In my mind; that was about six thousand dollars that I did not know that I owed. I thought this stuff was all covered.

Then he said that if I did not have the money to cover the bill, he could set me up with other work, I could accompany a promoter this evening and that a photography shoot would cover my bill. Then we would be square.

I was scared. I wished I could talk to my mom. My new roommate and I talked after he left. We decided that we would stick it out for a day or two, get our pay then get the fuck out of there. That night the big promoter man came back, another man took away the other girl, I guess to another room. He slapped me around a bit for hearing that I wanted to ditch him and his contract after he had already paid out big bucks to set things up and all. I really got scared and started to cry. He calmed down a bit, gave me a drink of hard liquor then... then he raped me."

"Jesus Suzie! I am so sorry that happened to you! How on earth did you get out of there?"

"Well, the next morning I showered and scrubbed trying to get the smell of his stench cologne and sweat off of me, then I realized that I didn't have any clothes, just my underwear and a bra. Someone had taken my clothes. I was sure it was room service when I was in the shower the night before. I turned on the shower and locked the bathroom door from the inside so the housekeeping wouldn't or couldn't get into the bathroom and then I hid in the closest. When she had her back turned, trying to open the bathroom door, I hid right inside of her cart. I hid there, curled up into a tiny ball. It's funny, then I had this warm feeling come over me. I wasn't scared anymore. It was starting to feel like freedom, like an adventure.

Anyways, it took a long time, but then when we got to the laundry room, the woman said, 'you can come out now. It's safe'. I crawled out; scared she was going to turn me in, but she just threw me some old clothes, gave me three twenty dollar bills and told me to go out the back door. I asked her how she knew and why she was being so nice to me. And you know what she said?"

"No. What?"

"I've got a daughter about your age, honey and you're not the first girl from up there on that floor to hide in my cart. I don't know what those guys are up to up there with all of them girls, but the girls I see usually look pretty scared. Now if I were you young lady, I'd change my hairstyle pretty quick and get lost far away and as fast as you can. I've seen them go after the prettier girls like they wanted to kill them. Well, gees, I felt like I was in some bad movie, or an awful dream. I just wanted to wake up and be at home with my babes and my mom.

So there I was, walking down the street in an oversized pantsuit hanging and floppy, too big for me shoes, my new fancy bra and thong undies they gave me. Hey they are superbly comfortable by the way and you should try them.

I couldn't understand the French signs, but I found a bus terminal. I took the first ticket, didn't matter where it went. I was just coming out of the public bathroom there when I saw those two men, you know, the agent and the promoter. I ducked back in the bathroom, locked myself in one of the stalls and stood on the toilet, so they couldn't see my feet. They came right in the bathroom checked all of the doors and looked underneath. After while I heard that the bus was boarding, so I went out and hid in the crowd, then made my way to the bus.

That's how I ended up in Toronto. As soon as I got there, I called my mom collect. She said she had been worriedly sick about me and that the agent man had called and said he was going to kill me if I did not get back to work. She told me not to come home. A friend from down the street was a cop, she would get him to help. I wandered around downtown for a while. I hid in a soup kitchen and stayed there until it closed. A nice woman asked me if I was in trouble. I felt like I could trust her, so I told her the story. She made some calls to the Women's Shelter and the next thing I knew, I was giving statements while being driven to Ottawa where they put me up in the Women's Shelter lock up protection.

Then a few days later, they took me to Elliott Lake Women's Centre. Well that's where I've been, in hiding and now here. My mom gave me the phone number at the phone booth in the mall and I call her every week to check in. The Police had gone to the hotel room, a few days after I had left but didn't find anything. Apparently, there had been other reports that sounded like the same two men. Someone had been making inquiries as to my whereabouts in Elliott Lake, so here I am and I haven't heard that they've found them yet. I haven't seen my babies in over a year. I can't stand it anymore, I'm not afraid anymore either. I just want to head back home. I've got to get some of my own money together and head back home where I belong. So can you fix me up, with something that doesn't require identification or references?"

"Jesus Suzie. Give me a minute here. I've heard some pretty wild stories, but this one is, wow, something."

"Ya I know, most people don't believe me until they start getting strange phone calls and stuff."

Navi made a few phone calls then sent Suzie over to the Salvation Army knowing that the Envoy there had connections. Though, certainly not an organization mandated service, the woman would know who and how, an underground network with a bit of cash in hand, new name identification, a new look as well as a way home to relocate with her girls.

Helen casually hovered out at the front desk then followed a tardy Navi directly into her office and sat down, serious.

"I want to discuss the ministry rep's review of your files. Specifically, I want to ensure that you are tagging all of the appropriate stats funding and of course, address certain screw ups."

Calm, strong, and unabated, she gathered strength knowing that the bullshit visit was confirmation of the end of days and casually allowing it to play out.

"Hmm... I thought the report was good considering he has never actually seen my work nor spoken with any of my clients. Actually, come to think of it, neither have you. I'd feel better by querying him in person."

"Sorry, not going to happen. You'll have to deal with me."

"Well okay, I do have a few concerns of my own, if you don't mind?"

Helen sat back, defensive, arms folded across her chest. "Go ahead."

Navi knew it was over and altruistic principles were mute. Yet, there was always hope that one day it might touch the woman, sink in, like a dandelion seedpod sticking to her jacket, to find fertile ground, seed, take root and flourish. Calm and strong in counsellor mode, she folded hands on top of the file-cluttered desk, leaned forward, a composure breath then felt a Joan of Arc warrior rush crawl up her spine and out of her mouth. With purpose and control, passing the gauntlet of a higher morality while underlying and once friendship now in blatant betrayal. A white channel of light streamed from above, aware of some higher, wiser, compassionate presence assuming direction of ensuing conversation.

"Mostly my old friend, do you remember how nice it was to work here before all of this shit started? You became a supervisor on paper but I was your counsellor and confidante. Sucks to be you, thinking you are safe as one of the good ole county boys. Don't be too comfortable; middle management is where the shit rolls downhill. You might also want to take some time and think about the issue of informed consent and how you're telling your front line workers to coerce clients into signing those contractual papers."

Helen remembering their old friendship received the wake up hit, a shaking hand and tearing eye "Why would that be a concern to me? It's legislation."

"Don't tell me that you are so far gone that it doesn't bother you knowing that the people you are being paid to serve are fucking hungry, starving, their children going without decent food? You know damn well that they don't understand what they are signing. Hell, how could they, when I'm not even sure what it's really all about. From where I sit, it looks like the makings of a class action suit against a government worker at some point. It's an abuse of power; they're hungry and scared and yet they sign it, got kids to feed and rent to pay. Hoping like hell that they find decent work before whatever it was that they signed doesn't come back to bite them in the ass, which it always does. Why did you sell out? Your husband covers home expenses just fine. My, how fast things can change. You know it's no longer a service designed to help people grow to become financially independent. If you can find your balance and guide your staff, somehow maintain a basic humanitarian philosophy; then you can navigate the new system and still help people. Ah, I see you smirking. Well think about it. The whole thing makes me sick when we don't even give new mothers enough money for formula and diapers anymore!"

Helen's eyes widened, reeling in truths, and Navi's audacious assumption of taking the old counselling role with her. Reeling eyes widened and contracted, processing truth and fear, entangled in barbed wire fence sitting, then scrambled for alpha she-wolf position of authority.

"Yes you do sound dramatic. I also have worried about the issue of informed consent, but you know what Navi? That is just the fucking way it is. There's nothing that either you or I can do about it."

"You know Helen, you could just turn your ass around and lobby the government, take a moral stand for God's sake. At least give clients some lead way so they can fucking eat, feed their kids. When the ministry rep first started working with our organization, bringing in this new system and the computer program that accompanied it, we were all very suspicious of your rah, rah, rah it's going to be great, speeches! Now some staff have bought into the control aspects of the legislation, squeezing the living shit out of vulnerable people AND the staff that work with them. The front line is all under phenomenal pressure to make clients successful just for stats, if we do not get the stat we don't get the funding to continue. How can you simply make social services delivery fit into a profit sector mentality? You can't and you God damn well know it!"

Navi reveled in some higher divine flow, allowing, only slightly curious as to why Helen was just sitting there allowing her to talk this way. Missing the gauntlet cue, assuming that Helen's silence was a good sign that they were on the same page, her mouth opened and on a roll, caring concern words continued to flow.

"What we really need here are support services. There is a missing piece, for those that are borderline functioning and cannot compete within the educated and marketable world in which we live. The majority of the vulnerable are so weary of trying to survive, that they just lie down and let the adversity transport truck of life run them over. They sell themselves out to the mandatory aspects of the program only to provide crappy dollar store food for their children. All staff is weary of the mandatory aspects of the program and trying to make people fit into it, so they can get another cheque for another month and feed their own kids. It's always easier to take your stress out on someone more vulnerable than you. This program is not premised in compassion, it is coercion."

Helen sat quietly, now seemed embarrassed, biting her lip then as some inner fear bug rose to the surface, spine erect, shifted back into her mission.

"Thank you Navi, for taking the opportunity to get that off your chest. It makes it easier to give you this." She pulled a file out of her brief case, slowly thumbed through and pulled out a letter then handed it across the desk.

The room swirled, eyes strained to focus. She shifted in her chair then glanced back at Helen then back at the letter and skimmed through it. ......blah, blah, blah, blah, final warning.... then Termination.

Navi, slammed out of holier than thou mode and back down into her lowly old scared self, power evaporated, gasped then looked back at Helen stiffened lips pursed who readied for rebuttal argument to come.

"We've decided to do some restructuring and your position no longer exists, effective as of five pm today. You will re-schedule your clients to Mary Fincher at HQ. Be sure to prioritize your files, leave any additional notes in a separate file, clear your client schedule then leave it at the front desk with your office keys and anything else that belongs to the organization. You are to report to HQ promptly at eight am tomorrow morning for your exit interview, unless of course, you would be interested in applying for assistant clerical desk duties in the HQ office pool. It's only, what, a two and a half hour drive for you one way?"

"What?!?"

"No, on second thought, you're not qualified for office administration and HQ would not consider a terminated employee for another position. We have a no-hire back policy. Well, your peers have other duties within the organization on top of what they are already doing, thus we are keeping them in their positions. And we figured that.., well.., since you have issues with the legislation and your co-workers ...well.., you were the logical choice. You are just not a team player. That is all. There is no negotiation. You are done here, effective as of today."

Navi meekly added "But I just got a good report and a raise. What happened?"

"It was good, but not good enough to keep you in good stead. The others fared better because they do not complain. I am tired of hearing about your inability to get along with your co-workers. Look, your dismissal severance package will get you through for a few weeks until you find something else."

Navi's mind reeled, 'like fuck it will, I'm only entitled to a couple of weeks, where am I supposed to find another job in the space of a couple of weeks?'

Helen rose and stood waiting for eye contact, "I have enjoyed working with you over the years and loved our friendship. It is too bad that you could not get with the new program. I will surely miss you. You have been a best friend to me. I hope we can still be friends outside of work."

Navi felt dizzy, head whirled, aghast.

'Friends?' mind searched for when they had ever remotely been friends outside of work, or whether she was hoping for a new kind of relationship. No, it was a token, a slight of hand, just doing her job, a lame attempt at softening the blow. Her thoughts turned to inner fear bugs .... Mortgage ... Abby ... David out of work ....

"Goodbye Navi. Give me a call sometime, we'll do a girls lunch."

Navi closed her office door behind Sold Out Bitch Betraying Boss Lady, plunk swiveled in her chair then scanned the cubicle inner sanctum; ambiance all transferred from the old satellite office of the kids, beach stones, a crow feather, inspirational quotes and funky dream goal magazine pictures hung on walls. Flyers and business cards of various community organizations strewn on bulletin boards, stacks of files lay waiting to be organized and prioritized, on one corner of the desk, computer on the other. A life defining moment, still not fully adjusting to all of the changes in home life, she wiped tears from eyes and nose. Nosey drama queen co-workers mingled around the front desk, victory giddy.

Brief case dutifully sorted of computer disks, extra pens, white out, sticky notes, business cards, staples and pens. Sifted and sorted files leaving notes on each of client status, no need for clients to suffer the staff change. Gingerly removed kid pictures off of the wall, then rummaged desk drawers twice until indignation hit. 'Oh god, what in the hell am I doing? I am not staying here another god dammed minute!' A co-worker had slid out for lunch, the other into the back washroom and she stealthily made unnoticed exit.

She drove along the lakeshore to a favourite cove and sat watching sun stream sparkles of light dance upon the lake water surface. She smoked and sat, numb from head to toe.

"What am I supposed to do now? Gran?"

She heard nothing, from Gran or anyone else in the spirit world. Separated, abandoned, banished once again and rid of. She tried to wrap her mind around a year of profound changes, of doors rudely slamming shut. Where was it exactly, that she had missed the early cues, the clues? Somewhere in work and personal life, she had inadvertently given her power away, handed it away. She took a deep breath then started the car, slowly meandered the lakeshore, for home. It was only two in the afternoon; a co-worker would have called head office ratting out her early absence. 'What are they going to do? Fire me?'

Mindlessly pulling into the general store, a takeout coffee, the local newspaper caught her attention. "Man walks away from $250,000.00 a year salary to deliver newspapers on a bicycle. Woman gives birth to Alien hybrid baby. Prophet states that Armageddon will arrive on October the eighth."

"Yup, there's a lot of weird shit going on in the world. You not working today?" the friendly and familiar middle-aged man behind the cash causally asked.

"No. I've got the afternoon off."

"Well, isn't that nice? You picked a fine one. Well, have a wonderful afternoon then."

"Good day to you", she muttered.

Then it hit. All evening, Navi hissy fit ranted and spewed about the program, Helen and the lack of support. David waited out the spew.

"Ah, I'm sorry it happened that way, but honestly? I'm glad you're out of there. It was brilliant. Don't worry about a thing, darling, we'll get by. Something will come. Things will be all right. Better than we think. I'll get rich and support you in high class."

Navi, quiet, downcast and wiping tears reeled in revulsion of platitudes that hung empty in the air. Yes, things could somehow be all right, they always did, but that did not help right now. His under-employed optimism was pissing her off.

"Look, I know things look dismal right now, neither of us have a secure income, there's abyss and a lot of unknowns right now, but you know what? I am so glad you are done. I am sooooo glad. Hey, I get scared too, but it's better to face a future with a lot of unknowns that have a world of possibilities than to stay and slowly have a place kill you. Fuck, if I had stayed, I would've either have killed someone or ended up on drugs. I think we should celebrate big time, on this last day! Blessings on your new found freedom, darling."

Her head split hurt in two, wanting to believe his optimism but the familiar solar plexus tension told a different tale. Unable to settle down, she paced then grabbed the rest of David's left over Tequila and some smokes, then headed outside.

Gentle wind fingers splayed life into office aroma hair as she drained the vile bottle and winced with disgust of foreign alcohol after taste. Unaccustomed to alcohol, a few deep breaths brought a rush of fire within.

'I'd make a lousy alcoholic. Though, I suppose you get used to it.' A beautiful fall afternoon, her face leaned into a sun stream, eyes closed and breathing in, she allowed resistance to pass.

Picking at weeds, a redundant activity so late in the season, she had never understood the corporate survival competitive game.

Weeks and months blurred incapable of taking constructive and definitive action beyond her schoolwork. Tired, she cocooned, avoiding friends and outside contact. Often wearing the same dirty garden overalls day in day out and sleeping in them. Armpit and leg nubs itched into hurt, dirty hair beginning to smell, leaving the house under a fresh waft of perfume, for errands that could not wait, or be delegated.

"God Mom! For the love of God, go take a shower!"

Navi grinned, lifted arm and blew under arm smell toward daughter. "Ah you like it, like it a lot. It is good for you, inhale deeply darling."

"God MOM!"

David masterpiece entrenched surfaced, wave holding the electric bill, his car lease, and property taxes. Seeing her wild-eyed reaction, the majority in her name, calmed in avoidance of a blowout argument "Jesus, we've already cashed in our retirement savings plans and maxed out your credit card. You've, er, I mean, we, have got to find a way to get through this."

Bizarre rage filled her eyes and clenched jaws held unbridled resentment in check, he backed away sliding the bills back into their allotted basket on the counter. "Look, I have to go and see my Mother right now. She fell in her apartment again, broke her ankle and is bruised up all over. I am so fucking sick and tired of having my balls squeezed."

Spaced out, ungrounded, Navi losing track of linear time, had taken to asking Abby every day after school, "What day is it?"

"It's Friday for God's sake. Mom?"

"Ya Abby?"

"You really need to get a life."

"Why? Don't you like having me at home?

"It's not that you're at home all of the time, but you're not at home, you're not anywhere and it bugs me."

"Well, I have a life, dear little mother child. I like where I am at."

"Bullshit!"

"I'm going to emerge a butterfly someday."

"Okay, Mom, I'll buy it. But just for a little while."

David scanned the mail, tucked one under his arm and tossed remainder aside. Ripping open the first, "Holy shit! My gallery showing is ready! Ya fuck-ho! Guess we'll have to plan a launch event."

"Way to go! I am so glad for you. Hey, did you get an advance?"

David pulls out his contract and re-reads the gallery agreement. "No. I guess maybe it's because it's my first, or maybe it's because it's a small company."

"Don't they assign you to some sort of promoter who looks after your public events?"

"Oh, I don't know. Hey, can we spare the hundred and forty bucks for the Arts Guild dues? I'd really like to do that too."

"Gees, I don't know."

"Oh God, I'm going to tour where all the who's who of the art world hang and of course do media. Yup, this time next year, I'll have you on my arm as my wife as I accept the artist of the year award!"

"Dunno about my part in all of that city vision talk." Yet, it was a new beginning, hope and promise of an exciting new life, possibilities overrode solar plexus alarm.

"From now, it's going to be galas at the Royal York, the Taj Mahal; marry me!"

"How about we stabilize first?"

"Catharine, I don't have any milk, can you manage cream."

"Only if it's clotted cream and only if you have some cookie biscuits to accompany that tea for dipping. Can you do some sort of meditation or healing for menopause and empty nest? I'm feeling all bunged up, like I am carrying blocks and resistance in my body. Shit I'm dreading getting old; I keep finding disgusting long hairs growing out of my chin and neck and so I pluck the beggars but I'm paranoid that I won't see one and it'll just be dangling away, swaying in the breeze and then it's going to reach out and touch someone."

"Ha. Hmm.., I am intrigued. You know that once upon a time, the transition from motherhood to Crone was actually honoured?"

"I didn't know that, but it does make sense. I've been putting on a brave happy front, but at night the house echoes like an empty cave. I shit you not. I miss them so much that I'm going crazy without them. How do you donate your entire life towards raising the beggars and then suddenly, you have nothing? I can't stand to be at home alone for more than a day. That's half the reason why I am in travelling mode. I'm empty nest, I should be having the time of my life, well, and I do as long as I am on the move. But as soon as I am at home for more than a day, I feel like I am going stark raving mad."

"Of course, I think I have a pretty good idea of what you are talking about. We can wing it."

Out into the bush wilderness by late afternoon the tent set and camp fire crackling, the picnic, set aside for later. Old shawl enshrouded, instantly accessing ancient universal sisterhood, Navi knew in her soul that this was not the first time to perform the sacred rite. Many lifetimes and many ceremonies, she had been born to do this and felt as natural as breathing. Old sisterhood shawl re-wrapped once around shoulders in priestly stole style, she stood barefoot then began a prayer invocation.

"I am honoured to be here with you today to share your sacred journey of change, dear friend Catharine. Make yourself comfortable, lay out flat and let go of all earthly concerns. Shift your thoughts, think of a favourite space in nature such as a field, forest, or lakeshore. Focus your connection to God and connect with Divine Sisterhood. As is above, so is below, expand this prayer to all women throughout time and to all living things."

Catharine engrossed, anticipating eyes closed, shifted legs splayed comfortable.

"Since the beginning of time, women have held the power of creation, magical and mysterious power and lifeblood waters of the Earth Mother in tune with lunar cycle tides with flowing rivers. Throughout time, women in all cultures, races and religions celebrate their biological changes. The change of life is bone DNA deep. You are cellular morphing a natural process, a new sacred space, of spirit freedom, a new wise, wild, natural, free and authentic you. This power consciously flows healing energy for family and community, all at the flash of a thought. Here personal responsibility takes on a new level of accountability as raging hormones have the power to annihilate or heal and move mountains. Abide also your soul's longings, passions, aspirations and inspirations to ripple outward benefiting all. This is how grandmothers and sisterhoods change their communities, the world.

Welcome to the ancient and timeless sisterhood, take your place and stand proud. We now affirm this heavenly bond, in the name of God, Goddess, Creator and all that is divine. Know and count on the wisdom of a grander collective grandmotherly wisdom, to future generations of a new era of global community. And so it is."

"Wow, Navi! That was amazing! Thank you, I feel wonderful. Where did that come from?"

"I don't know for sure. I suppose DNA memories of past lives with spirit world infusion."

Hope springs eternal, the best of times and the worst of times. Abby was teenage drifting, rarely home. David's new leased car was now a lawn ornament that lay dormant and unused on their front lawn.

"No, I can't fucking get out of the lease, I've tried talking to the sales guy, the manager, their corporate head office and my God Dam lawyer. The fucking lemon is not safe! I'm not sinking money into it that I don't have. Shit, I'm still paying off marriage debt."

Teenaged boredom is a drug and alcohol tsunami wave in a small rural community. Navi late night woke to bright swirling and flashing lights through the bedroom window and a pounding knock at the front door. 'Maybe the house next door is on fire.' Half sleep handicap scrambling, she groggily followed knock pounding and flashing lights out of the bedroom, down the hallway and to the front door. Heart pounding and alarm shaking, she opened the door to a dark haired heavyset middle-aged police officer.

"Pardon the intrusion ma'am. I'm Constable Bellwood of the Ontario Provincial Police."

Who had been killed in a car accident? Wonder waiting for his burning point.

"Is this your daughter?" He stood aside and pointed to a figure, standing on the step, downcast eyes. It was difficult to tell who it was in the dark, with only flashing lights behind her. She squinted then stepped out into the cold to look. "No, Abby is in bed." A girl figure moved forward as if to enter the house, as Constable motioned for her to stay back.

"May I come in for a minute ma'am?"

Navi motioned him inside and partially closed the door behind.

"May I speak candidly?"

"Ah, yes, of course", head faint swirled as she back slam braced against the wall.

"Well ma'am, you're lucky we're not picking you up to identify her body."

"...whhhaaattt....?"

"Well ma'am, your daughter and another young woman, we took her home already, were out at the beach this evening with three young fellows from Detroit. We saw the vehicle with out of province plates there at the beach in the middle of the night. We searched them all and the vehicle and well ma'am your daughter had a small plastic bag on her person of what looked like marijuana. Upon closer inspection, it was ascertained that the contents appeared to be basil or oregano. I asked her what it was and well ma'am, she refused to speak."

"...wwhhaatt..?"

"Well ma'am, if it had been marijuana or hashish or anything of such an illegal substance, it would have been in sufficient quantities that we would have held her at the station and charged her with trafficking."

"...wwhhaatt.?"

Constable Jack Arse turned and opened the door to reveal the next-door neighbours stoned daughter grinning from ear to ear.

The remainder of the dark night, Navi sat on the couch with a blank faced stoned Abby. Unhinged lunatic mother, scanning, grilling, interrogating, "You traded fake pot oregano for a bottle of wine, to strangers? You traded identification and places with the next-door neighbour? In the middle of the night? Alone? Under Age? ARE YOU OUT OF YOUR FUCKING MIND!?!?!

Okay, I don't know what else there is to say to you Abby. There is an old native saying, if the ground is not fertile and doesn't grow good food, then you have to change the soil or move to where it can grow and thrive. We are going to have to move where all three of us will thrive. This is not working, for any of us. In the meantime, the rescue ranch called looking for you. You start working back there first thing in the morning, crack of dawn, before and after school and weekends. Get some sleep now. Your life has officially changed."

Two days later, Navi hot on a solid job lead, confident the money was flowing again, bought Abby a badly neglected abused middle aged mixed breed horse who needed constant care. Within two short days, beaten weary old horse and teen torn Abby, had saved each other's lives.

Navi lucked out with the new job and first day, confidently paid bills in her mind. The program ran off an obscure pot of government money where vulnerable clients were again left unattended in dangerous conditions, putting front line staff in risky life threatening situations. Escorting one handicapped girl to the hospital in a diabetic coma was the straw that broke the camel's back; following a two day trail of dangerous incidents leaving her no other choice. The job blew up the following afternoon as Navi Jehanne of Arc, tried in vain to follow due process within the organization. The girl's elderly parents lived five hours away and did not have a phone. Frantically calling first supervisor then upper management, "Go home Navi, it's none of your business and none of our business."

"What? You've got to be kidding me?"

The young girl skirting death, exhaustion and exasperation, Navi called for outside medical and legal intervention and asked the attending doctor to file a report. Mandated to cover all aspects of care for a vulnerable sector, her new employers simply did not care. She stuck to facts, as known, handing care over, then to God and spirit world. Assured that the young girl would be fine, she drove home in a car that was also suffering neglect. Blowing black smoke covered tires, black powder and burning rubber wafted over the windshield and poured in through vents.

David's guilt whispered through an "Integrity and honour doesn't put food on the table."

Navi still livid worried after a sleepless night, called in sick. There was no immediate answer at Head Office, mustering courage, she left a message on the answering machine, "I am so for the short notice but I cannot not work for your organization another day. I will not be returning. Please call me as soon as someone gets this message so that we can clarify appropriate closure procedure."

Unknown to her, the medical report had released a juggernaut of intervention. Government men in black team arrived during the day at head office; files taken, clients re-assigned to other agencies and the entire program dismantled-un-plugged by four o'clock. In the days that followed, a letter arrived baring their letterhead; 'Dismissed with Prejudice'. There would be no entitlement to unemployment insurance or pay.

There was no time to slide into despair, it was David's grand debut. Best clothes and hanging onto hope, they could not hide desperation. Sliding easily into pretentious Artiste role, he charismatically schmoosed, new hope and seemingly unaware that aside from Catharine, Polly and herself, all were seventy. Navi had expected a media blitz, photographers, dealers, big money purchasers. Ignoring the fear bulge of falling way short of the balance sheet, of time, materials and re-allocated money to allow David his re-entry into the art world, she slid into gracious co-host, lightly chatting guests. Half listening to guests' prattle, her mind shifted to Stephen, this was his world, which typically involved not just buyers and media, but regional elite and dignitaries.

Bored Abby, polished glasses of champagne while the gallery owner hid in her office.

There was no doubt in Navi's mind and soul that David was brilliant at his craft, his works were sheer inspiration. They could simply not afford the years of stick-to-it-ness that it may require his vocation to thrive. Navi fought survival panic, rationalizing that while David's career launch audience fell far short of imaginings, there was always hope.

After a forty minute initial bustle, trays of snacks devoured and wine glasses emptied, Navi fought another panic wave realizing that while much chit chat was occurring, little procuring was happening. The food and drink tab would not balance with sales; they were in over their heads.

Out into the street to breath, smoke and plea for spirited assistance, the gallery steps swarmed with old farts, following her exit. Taking her exit as cue, they inched with walkers and canes, empty handed.

A quiet drive home, Navi drove while a soused David gently snored. To her estimation, Catharine and Polly had token purchased $40.00 pieces, his mother a $400.00 mini-series. A year of salary loss, time and effort, a year of his co-habitation, a year of his meagre money going to the former wife. They were in financial crisis, over their heads with no immediate viable way out.

Curled up in a lawn chair with a wooly sweater and blanket gathered around a campfire under brilliant stars, Navi fought depression. David, energized after a short car ride nap, downed tequila up on the roof lighting fireworks. As each noisily bang blasted into the sky the house and garden illumined in a rainbow of sparkling colour. Laughing and leaning back, he grinned in teenaged rebellious anarchy. There was still reverence for life, joy.

"Navi? Navi? Where are you Navi?"

"Hee... hee... yes, David?"

"Navi? When are you going to marry me?"

"Well, I guess when we get financially settled."

"I love you Navi. Say you will marry me now, next week, next month."

Waking drenched from head to toe, menopause sweats giving way to passion; at times a ninety-year-old achy crone, then, a sixteen year old in horny prime heat. White wiry crone hairs appeared on chin and long dangling moles appeared under arms, grey coarse horses hair sprouted brazenly on temples. Craving fruit loops with chocolate syrup for dinner, sex and tight blue jeans. The mystical veil between this side and of the spirit world, thinned before her eyes. Where once occasional spirit forms appeared, now adjusting her vision slightly, she could easily see multitudes wandering, still of an earthly existence. There were too many to stop and commune with or send off to the light of God. Electrical voltage running through skin tendrils shot through physical body, bringing forth changes in physiology. It was a full time occupation; monitoring raging, ebbing, flowing hormones, then adjusting.

David's mother rapidly accepted an invitation for a Sunday dinner that quickly turned into an overnight. At breakfast she announced, "I have a magical remedy; I would be delighted to assume mortgage on paper and deed in order to secure my old corporate mortgage and house insurance discount, if the both of you can take care of installing a granny suite renovation. I can auction off my surplus heritage furniture and that will take care of incidentals. Then in March, all titles and mortgage will revert back into Navi's name; clean, tax and debt free. I have a business background and I do have some money tucked away. I can help, I'd like to." Demurely delivered, Navi caught waves of unspoken private agenda, ignoring the sick wave of smothering darkness, she rationalized simply that the old woman did not want to spend the last days alone in longing for family companionship.

"David, it certainly sounds like a bizarre and possible brilliant solution but I don't know about just handing over ownership like that. I don't know your family history. Whatever you think is best. She is old, fragile and can't live on her own much longer and either way, you would soon have to find other arrangements for her care."

"I know that I sound like an absolute shit, but I am just starting a whole new life and honestly, I don't know if I want her here. I sure as shit don't want to look after the old bat."

Startled by the bizarre retort, Navi again ignored the warning pang, David was just feeling stressed. Not wanting to care for his mother was impossible, just stress.

A chilly north wind blew in strong off the bay, sending Canadian Geese V-lining South with elderly seasonal beach cottagers, to warm old bones destinations. The sun shone, warming the car inside, whilst a north wind threatened to move it against its will. Their little tiny beach town was becoming its annual ghost town for yet another long winter. Restaurants and cafes were winter closing with storefront windows boarded. Beach grass tumbleweeds and gusts of airborne sand flew wildly, swirling dervish upon empty streets.

Polly ambled in to the kitchen, disrobed heavy winter layers, poured a cup of coffee, comfortably settling at the table.

"Do you know why I'm here?"

"Something to do with Abby, I sense?"

"Arizona University. I have a good friend there, the Dean and I can call him when it is time. Indigenous Healing Arts program, youth counsellor, hands on. Actually integrating ancient knowledge and psychological spiritual methodologies. You can't learn this in a class room; she'd be doing hands on work with a variety of professionals and students from around the world and also class-learning the academic and theory aspects of the program."

"Thanks, I will pass it on."

"How are your spiritual courses going?"

"Good. Thanks for asking."

"I'm packing to move to Peru. I am drawn to the ancient Condor teachings and prophecies. The Andes are calling me and I am answering."

Navi, guffaw mouth gaping caught her manners, "Wow Polly. I am stunned. In awe. Actually I am really jealous, how amazing that you can just pick up and go like that." wondering if she would ever have the hutzpah to follow her own dreams. "God, I mean really aren't you scared to go off on your own like that?"

Chuckling, Polly continued "Well, I sure as shit am nervous but got to do it. You know young one, it is really a matter of how you want to be spending your time and at age, and it becomes increasingly more important. I don't know how much time I have in this lifetime, I'm already sixty." Thoughtful for a moment, Polly lovingly smiled and took Navi's hand, "Really it boils down to a simple question, and everything in life does. When you find yourself in a really shitty situation or are just bored, you ask yourself; what would I rather be doing with my time and with whom? For me right now, Going on a once in a lifetime journey is far more fun and interesting last chapter of life than spending an hour with a boring friend who wants to kill their grand kid's fucking hockey referee, or, what was on television last night, or, what fantabulous new product gets teeth whiter, bladder control, hypertension magic pharmaceutical drug and laundry cleaner."

Navi's mind swirled, adjusting to the news.

Polly bolted out of her chair looking at her watch. "Oh shit, what is the time? Damn, I must skedaddle out of here. Got places to go and things to do. I don't know if I will stay there, it is a place to start. I would say that I will keep in touch, but, better to say that God willing we do." Hesitating, she turned, grasping Navi's attention "Don't look so sad and lost my friend. Your day will come when you will walk alone with pride and confidently alive. In the meantime, love that daughter of yours until she goes off to school, this time is precious and you can never get back once it has passed. You have to walk your own journey. Besides, I am always a thought and heartfelt hug away. Good-bye my friend and know that I love you my friend."

No sooner had Polly left, then Navi bolted into the bathroom, door left open, due to urgent pee and allow a flood of abandonment tears have their way, when Catharine and a man's half knocking entered the house. Straining to pinch bursting bladder for privacy and wipe tears, she leaned forward and missing by an inch, stuck one leg out gingerly closing the door with a foot.

There would be days, weeks, months maybe even years, go by, and seemingly nothing happened out of the ordinary, then shazam; everything seemed to happen in one day.

"Coming! Make yourselves at home!"

"Halloo Navi. I'll put the tea on. Take your time."

Straining to listen to the murmur of voices coming from the kitchen, she tried to determine the man's voice. Deodorant rubbed under pits, baby powder splashed in between breasts and down undies, teeth brushed and sprits of perfume zipping up jeans. Hair tied into a knot, down hallway, turning corner, Catharine and a sixty something handsome hippie man casually chatted while pouring tea. Catching her curious gawk, Navi turned and set about serving cake, intuitively scanning, sensing, reading and trying not to stare and gawk at the smiling heavyset academic hippie in a yuppies outfit.

"I am so sorry. It's just that there is something about you, familiar. That smile, damn, you could light up a football stadium, an entire city. You smile and light pours out of you, literally."

"Ha, ha, ha. Well thank you, most candid gracious hostess."

Turning, she reviewed the quick interchange; salt and pepper pony tail, striking blue eyes, ratty old corduroys, turtle neck sweater, Birkenstock shoes and wire rimmed glasses hung at the tip of his nose.

"Ah hum."

"Come here. I would like you to meet Elijah. Elijah, Navi."

"A pleasure to meet you Navi, I've heard so much about you."

"Wonderful to meet you, would you like sugar or honey for your tea?"

"Oh stop. I want to tell you about my trip. Elijah and I met on the ship. Oh, guess what?"

"Really? What?"

"Well Elijah was the only other non-staff guest. So he quickly became my dinner and touring companion." There was a knowing secret grin and electrifying energy exchange between the two.

"Anyway, I don't want to short cut this marvelous story. Elijah is a professor at the college in Nepal. Well, I never made it to the Nile, got shanghaied to Nepal. Okay, let me start at the beginning. I got on the ship as expected, working in the kitchen washing pots and pans. Elijah was working in the laundry room for his fare. Because we were the only two guests, well working guests, we ate together and had the common room to ourselves. He used to teach at McGill University in Quebec. He went to Nepal, well, Kathmandu in ninety-four, a sort of vacation, slash research sabbatical. Anyway, he networked with the folks at the Shamanistic Studies and Research Centre there. Elijah? You tell Navi about your project."

"Well, my background is in Neuropsychology and I suppose that I have been hooked on the topic because of one special young man back in ninety-three. A teenage patient who had arrived on the ward, stating that he was missing time from his conscious memory. He exampled that he had been driving from Montreal to Vancouver and was absolutely fine until Toronto when all of a sudden he was on the Trans-Canada highway by the Manitoba border. He was so startled, that he had to pull over for an hour to get his bearings. Anyway, the staff found a small tumorous growth at the tip of his spinal column. That still did not answer the question of the time lapses, so they put him on some epileptic meds and then requested my consultation. The young man trusted me for some uncanny reason and immediately began to confide deeper experiences that he did not disclose to the other staff. When these time lapses occurred, he felt himself leaving his body. A spirit guide took him to a temple. Then poof, he would be back in his body and could not recall details or specifics of what the guide had conversed.

What added intrigue was the fact that his 'mother' had driven all of the way from Fort Nelson and apparently, he had not had contact with her since early childhood, yet somehow, she knew of his plight? One duty nurse indicated that his mother did some kind of hands on healing and then left. I did not see it or talk to her; nurses reported only that she had been and left as discreetly as she had appeared. An hour later, he refused meds and simply wanted out. Staff obviously concerned, were uncomfortable in agreeing to his discharge, but of course he was a voluntary patient without immediate signs of self-harm. He insisted that whatever it was, was gone, adamantly so. I asked if he would humour me, let me run the tests again, he agreed. There were absolutely no signs of any epilepsy or a tumour of any kind.

I could not sleep that night. I was so intrigued that I immediately set about researching shamanism and this spiritual healing business. We had touched on it in university, but it was merely from an academic point of view, functional, archaic and certainly skeptical, to the point of disregarding any validity. I tried finding this woman, his 'mother' or so she introduced herself to be, but she seemed not to exist.

I then contacted the college Dean in Nepal; the rest is history so to speak. I teach during the day and research evenings and weekends. I came home to solicit funding, form an international alumni and student, teacher exchange. It will take some time for the Review Board to fathom the validity of the project. I prefer to travel less than third class, as it makes travel an adventure and far more interesting, hence I met your lovely Catharine." Elijah admiration gazed at Catharine and tenderly reached for her hand.

"Imagine my luck or divine blessing, to have been fortunate enough to find her. What a treasure."

"Oh, I had a most wonderful time. While Elijah went about his business, I talked with students and staff, accessed the old library as well as the research department. I can't believe how open and welcoming everyone was and they all answered my incessant questions as best they could."

"Dear Catharine, of course my staff would be open to you. Our doors are always open to anyone who is a sincere seeker of the truth and fellow traveler on the spiritual development road."

"Ah, bless you Elijah. Well Navi, I've finally found my path. I couldn't articulate what I wanted to know a year ago when I began travelling but I am confident that the menopause or empty nest ceremony or prayer that you did for me helped me one hundred per cent.

Oh, my first insight is this; there are only two forces in the universe, white versus dark, and love versus fear, yin and yang and so on. If there is really only divine love, being the higher order, and fear is really just an illusion, then why does fear and darkness seem so pervasive? If indeed all of our decisions are made from the force of our emotions and thoughts, concepts and beliefs, then why do so many religions and schools of thought seemingly all seeking the same thing, divine love or at oneness with the source or god or what have you, have so much fear and evil amongst them? If one person operates from the intent of love, how can it be that another who operates out of fear and negative intent towards another and the consequences be so negative?

I figured that I had exhausted reading books and thinking about it all, I just had to go and find out for myself. It seemed that the more information I sought, the more confused I became. In trying to wrap my mind around a cultural ideal in the context of my own, I felt as if my head were going to explode. I have had the most excruciating headaches back at the top of my spine; that went up over my head and lodged into my forehead. I had sharp pains in my middle back. That is, until I met Elijah and went to Nepal." Catharine quietly gazed to Elijah, joy tears formed then trickled.

Navi ceased the interlude and returned to the bathroom, allowing them their tender moment. She sat on top of the toilet pondering Polly and Catharine's marvelous adventures.

Living life through Catharine, other aspects of the spirit world revealed themselves. Thinking and processing, washing face, hair brushing, plucking eyebrows and cleaning fingernails; she questioned. She needed time to adjust to the day's happenings. Polly was moving away and suggesting that Abby could to go to Arizona. Navi's new job gone sour and now Catharine and Elijah were moving overseas. It was a challenge, balancing day-to-day material world demands of menopause and mysterious spirit world happenings. Slumping back down on the toilet seat, she took a deep sighing breath as Gran's loving touch caressed her hair and cheek.

Back into the kitchen, Catharine hummed joyfully cooking, as Elijah's hands dove into overflowing soap suds and dishes.

"Oh hi, I hope you don't mind, you looked kind of pale, so I thought you needed to eat. Are you all right? Oh, never mind, I see that you are. Please sit and let me finish while dinner is cooking. Dinner will be ready for you, David and Abby in a jiff, all you have to do is sit, enjoy and talk about what is happening in your life. Then we'll be out of your hair."

Navi relaxed and smiled as on cue, Elijah tossed a tea towel over his shoulder and began to prattle.

"Well darling, Catharine told me a little bit of what you have been experiencing, your hidden gifts. When I strain to describe and articulate my own experiences, I have enormous difficulty in expressing my thoughts and emotions in a way that gives any sense or true explanation of the enormity of it all. I am sure that you would concur.

I remain astounded by the enormity of the research library, an unimaginable book collection. There are high tech computers and innovative software. Yet to be sorted and catalogued, are hundreds of boxes of books on every topic imaginable. There is everything from Joseph Campbell, to ancient scrolls, Egyptian glyphs, indigenous artifacts and quantum physics. You name it and they have it. I have never seen the likes, anywhere. One of the students has developed a computer program for a research group that is hot on the trail of collecting data from every culture, philosophy and religion known to humankind, both historical and current. Ancient prophecies, astrology, crop circles, ancient glyphs, current events, what NATO and the

United Nations and other elite groups are up to, looking for correlations. It is an astounding coming together of disciplines and minds working cohesively as one higher conscious mind.

Did you know that the ancient Mayan calendar system is actually more accurate than the one we use now? Archaeologists are using the Mayan calendar to track ancient civilizations. Even NASA works within this network and utilizes Unidentified Flying Object technology. Hey, did you know that Hitler had done extensive research on this? Although he was seeking omnipotent power for personal gain, he did do some amazing work. It would appear that science and spirituality is really starting to close the gap and emerge as one.

It is spiritual psychology what fascinates me in particular; one of the older staff whose own father was a renowned Shaman is a phenomenal resource. Historically there has always been a struggle between the true descendants of shamans in the school and the witches, as the old missionaries termed them. Shamans fighting with the dark ones, who continued to survive but their magic, removed. Kind of like, if you abuse it, you lose it. Yet the door to reformation is never closed. Regardless of how bad or evil that person may seem they are given opportunities to come to certain understandings on their own; yet if they are relentless, their powers are removed and they are held accountable. Shamans always preferred that they come forward of their own accord and submit to the masters for appropriate re-learning consequences. Of course, master shamans understood that these lesser folks played with the dark forces; jealous, secretly afraid of the light, or what have you. The master shamans never lost confidence in the supremacy of their own powers. Interesting that they were never afraid, merely saw the others as lesser evolved, like behaviour problematic children. Shamans were acutely aware that nothing could touch or alter the forces of the light and love and goodwill, unless fear and self-importance crept in. No one was ever judged harshly, they were simply accountable, viewed as children, learning how to make decision and choices that benefited the individual as well as the whole community, never self-serving.

You see, it is growth, learning and evolving where personas explore and arrive at the next level and the next. It seems that they have managed to frame the spiritual process of development quite well. They have been able to contextualize the cognitive development of growing up and looking beyond oneself, then into a higher state of consciousness and being.

Was there some kind of magic plant essence they ingested? Was there magic ritual or initiation? Were they genetically different from the rest of us? How did they overcome fear? How did they to connect and operate with higher powers and thoughts and behaviours? What secret magic was enabled? I concluded; every culture, every religion, every individual has the same similar tools and knowledge in some capacity or form. It is simply the OM, the quest for and usage of divine functions.

I boldly state that you are among this group of like mind, like soul. Do not be surprised when you soon peak plateau, then nose-dive into an abyss of void darkness for a time. Stay mindful that the process has many gateways, many levels. At each juncture and up-dip, there preludes a massive down dip; much like going back into the womb for a gestation period then re-birthing with new awareness. Two steps forward, one-step back. It is dark night of the soul and akin to deep dark depression, a shaman's death. I know that I am telling you much of what you already know and instinctively can sense. While you journey into the void, you may feel utterly abandoned, insane and alone, yet surrounded by a multitude of guiding spirit masters. There is no escaping the process, you signed up for it, destiny."

"Wow, huh." Navi glanced between the two of them, catching their having been there and done that, smiles.

"It is a part your mission, as you journey and move through the levels, to know that you are also doing it for many. By the way, we are moving there in short order, together."

Wow, congratulations, how wonderful!"

Grateful that Catharine and Elijah had left; she jealously slid abandoned into the sanctity of bed covers with old sisterhood shawl covering window's sunlight stream overhead.

"Jolted into a young woman's muscular body and heavily armored and surrounded in deafening ringing metallic clanging and shouting. Fingertips touch a Fleur de Lis crest engraved chest plate, conscious of triple cross dangling on a chain underneath, overlaying heart. Mist cleared slowly, standing on a battlefield amidst equestrians and foot soldiers in hand-to-hand combat of swords, armor, shields, noise, blood and chaos. Francais Freres; French brethren battle waltzing with servants of the Porc d'Anglais Chiens; English Pig Dogs, who is who? Which side is which? Navi or Jehanne could not tell. Swirling around, fighting everywhere, as far as eyes can see. It is surreal in the last of the mist; she quickly glances downward, striving to gain her bearings. Under metal blood and mud splat armor, a white robe buffered metal against unshaven leg skin, grazing under arms. A Cross symbol was engraved in the chest piece. In her right hand, she held steady a heavy sword, without a drop of blood upon it.

A woman with male energy, aware of the contrast of just how strong, sure, powerful and connected to God she felt, as opposed to ordinary life "Navi".

Consciously aware of growing weary from battles, rage, violence, hatred, greed and needless suffering, Jehanne's mind swirled dizzily. Striving to maintain strong, clear and battle engaged, her inner hearing rang silent while battle raged on, somehow enfolded in a magical luminescent bubble, divinely protected.

In the periphery of vision, one man stood out amidst the violent crowd. Jehanne's inner vision locks upon his being, knowing instantly that he is the next opponent. Eyes lock-hold to opponent, an energy field created surrounding her, a cocoon enveloping the two. Then everything blurred, fading silent surreal, as his eyes met hers. She locks him into position with a strange inner power, through her eyes, pure powerful intent. Aware of silence, one could hear a pin drop.

Jehanne's left hand extends out in front, as arm extends straight outward, two fingers point to his heart chakra. A powerful light energy comes in through her crown chakra, flows through her left arm and fingers, and extends out and into his heart. She has him totally statue locked, frozen in position, he cannot move.

Time stands still knowing that she has all of the time in the world to deal with this one man. She holds focus on the mid height rotund officer, while part of her awareness extends up and out of the top of her head, accessing divine source for information and direction. Their eyes fixed upon the other, minds communicating, without uttering a verbal word.

Jehanne silently shouts a command to lay his sword down and surrender to God. He tries to shift his body, avert eyes away to break hold, but cannot. Information imagery downloaded, seeing in an instant that he has been raping, torturing, killing women and children, stealing food caches and treasures in greed abandon. He is gluttonous with a pension for soft skin and shiny objects.

Jehanne silently shouts the command again to lay his sword down and surrender to God. Again, he tries to shift his plump body and gaze away from her hold. He wants to fight, to kill yet remains steadfastly locked into position under her pointing fingers, gaze and cocoon bubble.

Split awareness, she re-attunes with divine source and sees instantly that he was supposed to be walking the life of spirit, much like St. Francis of Assisi, protecting and loving the ones that he has stolen from then killed.

Once more, there is the command to lay down his sword and surrender to God. He resists and in the moment, imagery flashes of his path of carnage and gluttony. Her own childhood memories arise, blend and fade; "Chevauchee!" English greed knew no bounds; as warfare tactical raiding, pillaging, raping, then burning everything in sight left smoldering embers of a once thriving community. Gluttonous greed wreaking havoc, no county left untouched. Survivors forced to rise against English oppressors. Survivors who had barely recovered Black Plague devastation, a force to be reckoned, and meager material belongings in hand, they fought for honour and homeland.

Chuckling, he cunningly wills to speak, "Aha, your own superiors betray you and your God. Your own leaders exclude you from war council and strategize for acquisition's sake. They seek only your spoils of war madam. My compatriots and your superiors shall find your death in good stead. Where will your God be then, woman child?"

Stealthily, right arm and sword raises, swings up overhead, down around, then up and swiftly enters, driven into his mid-section and up inside rib cage and into his heart. Her eyes, left two fingers and heart remain locked onto him.

He crumples to his knees while remaining transfixed. Jehanne commands him to "Aller a Dieu; Go to God!" She proclaimed, "Equilibre! Il n'y aura aucune karma, pas de vengeance, aucun residu entre nous"; Balance! There shall be no karma, no vengeance, no residue left between us. In the moment, Jehanne has only unconditional divine love for this man. Sadness and grief for all whom he had ravaged including his own.

Sensing a sighing sensation, his spirit leaving body and rising upward, she declares

"Et il enest ainsi." And It Is So".

Jehanne kneels down before him, aware that her sword, in the moment was not made of metal but light, of pure light. Withdrawing her sword, she tenderly closes his eyes, a final shudder as his spirit soul taken to heavenly spheres, she lays her sword down and holding hands fisted together, gives last rites. "Je suis un avec Dieu; il est unavec Dieu!" I am at one with God; he is at one with God."

Consciously allowing time to come back into alignment, surrounding cocoon disintegrates. Remaining knees upon ground, profoundly battle weary, she lays sword down across folded knees then raises hands and eyes to the sky.

"Saint-Michael, Sainte-Catherine et Saint Margaret."

"Je demande de la mere divine, Dieu Pere, quand sera-t-elle fin?" I ask of the Divine Mother, Father God, when will it end?

"Pourquoi ne voient-ils pas?" Why do they not see?

"Je ne veux pas lutter contre tout plus!" I do not want to fight any longer!

"Je tiens a voir non plus de souffrances!" I wish to see no more suffering!

"Je voudrais temoigner pas plus!" I will not fight blow for blow nor pick up sword again!

"Je vais tenir aucune voeux, pas de vengeance." I will hold no vows, no vengeance.

"J'ai remise." I surrender.

"Je veusx vivre dans la paix!" I want to live in peace!

Into conscious awareness, eyes take in the future, or is it now, Navi wondered; the sight of what looks like space ships zipped and zig-zagged across the sky, fighting. Jehanne hung her battle-fatigued head in hands and sobbed.

"Helas, je server mon Diew et compatriot. Ainsi faire de moi digne, donne-moi la force de transmettre sur!"Alas, I serve my God and compatriot. Thus make me worthy, give me the strength to forward!

"Charles doit encore etre roi." Charles shall yet be King. *Consciously aware of Navi within, observer,* "Ma Chere soeur, j'ai ete, mais femme de treize quand j'ai entendu pour la premiere fois la voix de Dieu, Saint-Michael et plau. La crainte sous tension pour la declaration de culabilite que de visions accompagne amour divin."My Dear Sister, I was but a woman of thirteen when I first heard the voice of God, Saint Michael and more. Fear turned to conviction as visions accompanied divine love.

"Un vie est tout ce que nous avons et nous la vivons comme nous croyons en vie. Mais a sacrifier ce que vous etes et de vivre sans conviction, c'est un destin." One life is all we have and we live it as we believe in living it. Yet to sacrifice what you are and to live without belief, that is a fate more terrible than dying.

"Aller avec Dieu, soeur!" Go with God, sister!

"Etre le messager!" Be the messenger.

"A sad soul can kill quicker than a germ."
John Steinbeck

Chapter 19 ~ Tethered

David, navigating lawyers and banks, without discussion, funneled the last of his savings into a costly divorce; his ex was systematically cleaning his clock, his affair guilt-ridden conscience allowed it. His final car lease buyout consumed the remainder, "Let them all take what they want, have the whole fucking thing." Catching Navi's livid glare, he switched to "Fear not my Mermaid beloved, with my latest series out, we shall overcome and I shall keep you in style beyond your wildest imaginings. Then you shall marry me."

With only one more painting sold thus far, there was just no getting around the financial crunch. The obvious emergency option seemed to be of accepting Mother's bizarre offer while devising a better smarter long-term strategic plan. David agreed adding, "Ah, don't you worry about a thing Darling. I know she looks like a dicey deal, but I will make the addition nice. I suppose it is better than waiting for her inheritance. It will all work out good, you'll see."

Choosing to ignore the crass turned schmoozed retort, body shifted into stoic faith, the deal offer could buy time to breathe and contemplate a next move.

A whirlwind homespun renovation manifested a beautiful addition granny suite in short order.

Abby was the first to fall asleep with his mother in house, instantly complaining of eerie music and nasty children's laughter. Coy-dogs evening howled from the tree line perimeter. Dawg hovered in between feet, tail between legs, cowering, ears twitching, perked for inaudible sounds of the unknown. Career in hot pursuit, abruptly stopped by day two. He could not paint; he paced then opted for pub, meandering home schmoozed, inebriated, and crusty.

The first real hard rain flooded the living room, giving way to a never-ending sump pump running beneath the addition floor. Handy man David sober ventured out in the torrential downpour and down under, wading through mud, only to find a sea of water up splashing cottage under belly floorboards. Flashlight in hand, he traced the source to a stream entrance, three quarters of the way up the foundation that contentedly ran into the makeshift basement, forming an indoor swimming pool. Outside, he traced the stream back into the tree line; to find a massive swamp river that semi circled the house. Over the television's blare of violent murder mysteries, mother contentedly ignored the ensuing crisis. He yelled up to Navi "Jesus Christ, the house is all of a sudden turned into a fucking swamp. We are living in a swamp, for fucks sake!"

Mind searching for options and solutions came up empty. Refusing to approach his mother for money, the absolute last of Navi's savings had gone into granny suite renovations. The first signs of snow were already dancing in air; their northern tourist beach community and old Gangsta gang had closed up for winter and flew south, as did jobs.

"Guess we'll have to make the best of it for the winter, I'll go after the old prick insurance representative of yours and get him to fix some of the shit around here. Maybe I can find a freelance painting contract, or I will dig ditches to get us through the winter. The spring will look different, fine, you'll see."

Navi and Abby took to daily smudging and praying for in-house harmony and new opportunities.

Christmas Eve arrived abruptly without the traditional season's joy. Ornery mother in law had taken to bitterly complaining about the state of the house and their apparent lack of renovation skills. David threatened legal action with the insurance company. Crusty alcoholic insurance representative added another sump pump and hired a demented old man to dry wall mud over leaking ceilings and floorboards. Old geezer handy man ranted, accusing them of slamming doors too hard, making his fine artisanship rattle, further making windows break, then refused to repair the damage on principle. David tried in vain to duke it out by phone mano-a-mano while Navi scrambled to cover broken windows with heavy clear plastic sheets. A man on a mission, he researched the insurance act, her policy and emailed terse letters demanding full coverage. By late afternoon, acquiescing to interim postdated payment checks to old geezer handy man.

Winter freeze up did little to circumvent underground rivers. Navi re-packed the majority of their belongings, save the essentials, and stacked them into a storage facility. Abby, in her room alone, claimed eerie strange music preceded terrifying nightmares. Her mood dropped, blasting heavy metal gothic music, dressing in black clothes, with Edward Scissor Hands hair and makeup. David swore that he saw grey and black beings scurry out of the shadows, as eerie music preceded doors slamming. He could not sleep, eat or paint then his mood turned nasty to Abby, misdirecting buildup stress venting.

Navi, the mindful counselor, stood in between then, invocating Angelic intervention, struggling to stay in grace. Windows exploded at random, scaring the living shit out of her. "This too shall pass, this too shall pass."

David mad paced muttered, "Navi, Navi? Where are you Navi? When will you marry me Navi?" She fought tears, hairs tingling creepily; something terrible was happening to David, Abby, and their beautiful cottage sanctuary home. The gruesome household mood unnerved, not knowing what else to do, she smudged and sang old church gospel songs.

Midnight, wild with un-articulate inner torment, David ran away from home. In the dark of blizzard night tears spilling, he wandered off out to the main road where the road intersected with a black bear path crossing. Navi stayed behind, feigning last minute Christmas gift wrapping engrossed, mind racing, heart prayed for him to come home of his own clear minded accord. Unsure of how to deal with the man who had readily become a stranger, she was about to get in the car and head out into the night to find him, when he returned. Hearing a knocking on the bedroom window, Navi turned to the sounds' direction, to see a wild man lunatic image on the other side. Registering, relaxing somewhat, she rose and approached.

"Am I allowed to come in or should I sleep in the storage shed?"

Navi's heart was pounding tears, 'who is this man? This boy? This lost boy?' "What? What in the hell are you talking about? What in the hell are you doing out there?"

"Why didn't you come looking for me?"

Navi's heart pounded adrenaline stress into her stretched forehead, trying to think. "I was waiting for you to come home."

"I slowly walked out to the dirt road. I kept looking back, waiting for you to come looking for me."

"I guess I just really didn't know what to do. I was worried about you." Now that she had admitted this truth, fuming within at the building pressures and the seeming lack of the David mature professional counselor man that she needed. He curled fetal, half kneeling submissive beside her legs. Conscious of Abby down the hall, within earshot, "Shhh . . . Stand up!"

"Navi, why don't you love me?"

A straw breaking the camel's back, unbridled, she vented "What? What in the hell are you talking about? David, what am I supposed to do here. Just because I am not playing this silly game does not mean I don't love you. Give your head a shake; how old are you right now? Four?"

"I guess that means I should go and sleep in the shed. I won't bother you anymore. I'll find somewhere else to go in the morning."

"Oh for God's sake, just go to bed. I have gifts to finish wrapping and a turkey to stuff. We can talk about options tomorrow, or the day after and for the love of God, the next time you are feeling out of sorts, just come and talk to me. Don't play games, and make me guess."

By sunrise Christmas morning, inebriated David paced alone out at the fire pit, burning all of his paintings and art materials. Aware that Abby would be awake soon and ready to open gifts, she winter coat wrapped, slid on gloves, and grabbed a cup of coffee, intent on shifting the mood and getting through the festive day.

David, eyeing her approach, instantly turned on heel advancing, berating. Shocked and reeling, she fumed back into the house, slamming the door behind. Instantly livid, unbridled stressors beyond coping, he marched in her footsteps, taunting her into battle engagement. Navi retreated into the bathroom. Knock pounding to no avail, David foot slammed the door in. A wild man hand shook her, and then dropped, unclenched. Knocking her head on the vanity, she slumped onto the floor. Hands to head, holding her pounding head, curling fetal, Navi winced in painful disbelief. She did not know who this possessed man was. Tender sensitive loving David was gone.

Buying time to think, Navi played safe; sharing gift opening with Abby and then preparing the turkey, pretending all was well, anxiously contemplating their plight. Abby sensing tension, retreated to her room, stereo drowning out her shitty dysfunctional family Christmas. Mother increased her television murder mystery volume to drown out Abby's noise. The meagre amount of money saved and set aside in order to reverse the mortgage and deed had gone to old geezer handy man; who was probably having a fine Christmas, she imagined. David slid deeper into darkness, guzzling beer and watching old Christmas movies, a haunted personality change. Hope faded, as his inner battle with an evasive shadow demon extended its hateful self-outward into her.

Standing over him, Navi's epic rational reasoning ultimately fell upon deaf ears. David strained good for a brief moment, then slid back into fear, self-loathing and darkness.

The morning brought a new level of insanity. David crossed a final boundary after inebriated afternoon schmooze, groped her crotch and manhandle fondled her breasts. Navi reeled livid, backwards, out of hands reach, and stood her ground. "Don't you dare, ever, do that to me again!"

Wild man eyes instantly switched, straightening his indignant spine, chest puffed, his mouth open; ranting nonsensical. Navi was scared, rattled. Who was this dark stranger? How to disarm that dark creature inhabiting her David? She searched his eyes for the gentle loving trusted man, then retreated to the bathroom and locked the broken door, for space, to calm, think and cry. He pounded on the door, "Leave me alone!" she curled fear and grief, on the floor, she begged, "Leave me alone." Wild, he retreated outdoors, falling, splaying into a snow covered lawn chair.

His mother, oblivious, remained contentedly watching a violent murder mystery; screams and moaning loud blasted, all encompassing. Shaking off the noise, fear and sadness, she stood and called in angelic intervention, then turned to gaze out the kitchen window. Navi needed to find a way out fast, and to get them all out of there; safe and into sane objectivity.

Unprepared for the insight and imagery, she instantly saw that she was single handily amidst psychic battle with a myriad of dark grey entities that swirled around his being, each vying for control. Whispering, taunting, fuelling and feeding sensitive doubts and self-worth, his vulnerable loving nature lost. Bravely facing foes, closed her eyes and shifted awareness, aware of a black spirit sucking nasty bogie. Suddenly, scrambling backward for life as it attacked, pinned in a headlock, her neck about to snap. "No. The love of God, we shall overcome". It retreated, yet remained in the shadows.

Something drastic had to be done. Donning coats, hot mugs of coffee in hand, Navi took David by the hand and ventured outside. "I don't know what has happened, but this isn't either one of us. We have to do something, fast."

"I don't know. I don't know."

"If you can't live with your mother under the same roof, then you simply can't. This is crazy. It shouldn't be like this for either of us, or for Abby, that's for sure."

He gently touched her gloved hand and then hopelessly let it slide off. Glazed eyes focused midair, as though not seeing, or even aware of her presence. "When are you going to marry me Navi?"

Aghast, she turned hiding tears. The spirit world rang silent.

Yoga arching, a white shadow moved outside in the driveway. At first look, it appeared to be a white German shepherd. *It casually sauntered closer* to the house, looking straight into the living room window, directly into her eyes, soul. Calm, warm loving yellow eyes soul gazed. Navi was staring directly at a white wolf. "Well who are you young lady?"

Old soul yellow eyes gazed, pulsed and contracted, inner communing deep into the core of Navi's own soul and inner mind. White She Wolf turned her head, looking down and out of the driveway then back again.

"It is time to go!"

Then poof, White She Wolf disappeared. Navi stretched forward then sideways, looking out of the window, scanning the fields, then back to forest tree line, no sign of her anywhere. She plunked, leaning back into the chair and lit a smoke, glancing back to the driveway. White She Wolf stood closer, gazing in. Locking eyes, heart and soul, a communion flowed, profoundly connecting and interconnecting ethereally. It was a warm loving timeless familiarity, as though the same, as though old friends and companions.

White She Wolf spoke calmly and confidently, within inner hearing of mind and soul. "We are White Wolf Woman. Remember our teachings. She Wolf resides within all women. Our wild nature comes forth to those who allow the remembering, and are open to natural wisdom and philosophy. She comes to remind you of who you really are. Answer the call within your own soul's longing, sister.

Do not side distract over what does not belong to you for too long. Fear not, doors closing; it only means that your journey is just beginning. Your journey brings many trials and tests in short order. A day will soon come when the Dark Night of the Soul is upon you. It is only then that you will emerge, and only then that your call to teach and expand maternal female energy can blossom. Shaman's journeying, death and rebirth is your calling. Giving you a predestined conscious plan and the means to explore many paths, know that there are many paths to the divine and higher way of being. Play with your intuition and abilities. White She Wolf medicine has come to aid your own mothering instincts to open minds and awaken soul passion.

"Who are you? And why do you feel so familiar?"

"I am a guide, among many. It is time to let go of all aspects of life that no longer serve you, to turn to the higher good of all. Remember that every day is a good day to be alive, to live this earthly life. It is in being alive and aware of the unseen that you can explore two-legged human drama; all are spiritual expressions. I come to you now my friend, to ask you to go forth from this place."

'Impossible' thought Navi. There was no upsetting Abby more by adding unnecessary drama to the shitty day. There was nowhere to go, no money for a motel room, last of which were in the house and put under the Christmas tree

Within three minutes, the intrusive dark spirits began boldly manifesting out of corners and shadows. Sounds of eerie old time homespun music filled the air. Black and grey spirits zipped through her, leaving a chilly breeze that bone chilled and fog floated about the house. *'A religious person believes in hell, while a spiritual person has been there.'*

Giddy charming elegant Mother cocktail hour mingled amongst imaginary friends, long dead family and former colleagues happily milling about in a festively decorated living room. Somewhere in the span of late Christmas Eve sleep and Christmas morning waking, to evening, Mother's annoying old woman habits and quirks had taken on a completely new form. Abby opted out of dinner, packed for a surprise Dad mini vacation, avoiding all contact.

Jealous abandoned Navi shifted the immature reaction away and into an observer, calculating in take control counselor role. Gingerly served dinner as Mother Dearest sat demurely donning grotesque Hollywood make up and boldly announced, "I've had a change of mind. All verbal agreements regarding house finances were; void." Flabbergasted, Navi ignored the remark and retreated to the bathroom.

Standing at the bathroom door, waiting until Navi emerged and sure that they were alone, she block her path politely smiling. Mother Dearest quickly deteriorated into cutting remarks, enticing a catfight. "You are lower that a cockroach, at least prostitute's get paid for what they do. Since my son has nothing right now, that means that the only reason you are still here is that you are after what's mine. I am onto you, you little whore. You'll have none of it! Do you hear me, little sickly witch whore and mother to a daughter whore. And the next time you cook, I'm going to be looking right over your shoulder so that you don't feed me anymore poison."

Navi stood silent waiting for the rant to end. Unmoving, Mother closed in, back eyes narrowing, spatting on Navi's face, her old drug odourless breath hot. "Darling, I am concerned about the amount of food you are eating. It is not lost on me, what a complete lack of contribution you make to this household. I can see and smell the cancer in you. Divine retribution, I would say."

Navi gently pushed the crone aside, shaking, retreated to the upstairs bedroom. Mother gently humming a show tune, returned to her television, amplifying a horror movie.

Mind wild, Navi sat on the edge of the bed, reeling. It was the first time in her that she had looked into another's eyes and experienced pure evil. Mother Dearest Crone had swung from fully rational, coherent and shrewd businessperson just days prior, to twisted manipulative and violent evil. Navi had navigated each conversation encounter hit, until now. In official retreat out of sheer exhaustion, she searched for angelic intervention. David, exhausted, snoring, slept as the days twisted game descended into psychic warfare, leaving Navi sensitive stunned and bedridden immobile for an hour.

It had all turned horribly wrong. Grounding and accessing inner higher vision, she could see imagery of dark entities hovering over the old woman's left side, taunting. Recalling Jehenne, she imagined a cocoon of protective light, and expanded it around loved ones and house. Feeling better, catching up with after dinner mess and basement flood soiled laundry; Mother Dearest trailed nattering, scathingly venomous. Adding soap to the water-filled washtub, Navi grounded and bumped up the light while calling in Arch Angel Michael. Each recovery only served as battle fuel and dark scorpion hits. Mother Dearest, sensing non-attachment, confidently amped the assault.

"Slut! Not fit for human companionship. Get out of my house!"

Navi, instantly livid, teeth clenched, holding grace, retreated to the kitchen. David, hung over, gingerly made his way to the dinner table. Relieved to see him, assuming her back up support had arrived, she returned with fresh coffee, intent on turning the tables. David slouched with head in hand, picking at a bowl of untouched Christmas pudding.

Mother studiously eyeing him, casually repeated her earlier announcement. "I've had a change of plan, in regards to handing over deed and mortgage." David, suddenly a dutiful four year old boy, simply head nodded, acquiescing, taking the hit in submission. Arching her back empowered, Mother stood hands on hip, lips pursed, eyes narrowing insane "And just so that you are both aware, I have advised my accountant and lawyer, of the elder abuse that I am enduring here in this shithole on a daily basis. I have also notified them of my depleted accounts balance, proof as to the large sums of money that you both have stolen from me. I am onto the both of you, and it will not stand."

Livid, David lunged up out of his seat, visibly shaken. "What fucking crock of shit game are you playing here?" Mother calmly slurped a side mouth drool, grinning victorious, the engagement a raving success. "I also have changed my will; for Christmas I have given your cousin Cynthia title on all legal papers, the deed to this house, my insurance policy as well as the investments."

Over the top livid, he ranted, "Have you gone completely insane woman?"

Mother Dearest calmly retreated to her granny suite, turned on a murder mystery and maxed the volume. Reeling in exhausted disbelief, Navi retreated to bed, clothes and all.

Navi awoke to a delicious sun ray, casting warmth upon her face and within her soul. Stretching then suddenly recalling the past day's events, alert. The house was unusually quiet and calm. Gingerly venturing into the kitchen, peeking around the corner into Mother's mad space. Morning Mad Mother Dearest lovingly smiled and followed her. 'Dam it!!' Navi thought.

"Oh good morning dear! I rose early and ventured out into the community, giddily intent on spreading Christmas cheer."

"I'll bet you did" Navi closing the bathroom door behind the mad woman. That was then that the phone began to ring consistently throughout the day. Calls of consternation and concern poured into David, the busy bee old crone had gone to people's homes, advised their mechanic, pharmacist, post office staff, grocery cashier, librarian and then phoned extended family in Ottawa of her horrid elder abuse plight. Too angry to engage in conversation, they retreated to the bedroom.

"Jesus Christ, what do you think; Dementia, or demonic possession, or both? That woman is fucking possessed. You fucking see the dark entity behind her, flowing through her like she is a puppet and then there are those little grey fuckers, swirling about."

David sat at his computer desk, head hung, shaking, mumbled inaudible. Mad Mother shrieked from the bottom of the stairs; dark entity deranged.

"Jesus Christ David! Was it always like this?"

David motionless, she continued, "David, I want my house back, do something right now!"

Tears formed and spilled as he twirled a lit cigarette in fingertips. "No. I don't know. I had just forgotten how bad it was at times when we were kids."

"Jesus, how could you possibly forget something like that? We have to get her to the doctor for an assessment right now! There's got to be drugs and support care for this sort of thing."

"I don't think she'll go. Legally we can't make her. The god-dammed house is in her name. No, my cousins' name. Shit. Fuck. Now the lawyer, accountant and the entire fucking neighborhood thinks that we are abusing a poor innocent old lady. Shit. Fuck."

"We've got to figure something out, and quick. Maybe she is bluffing. She wouldn't really have transferred it all over to your cousin that fast, could she?"

He wiped a tear, face showing his soul, inner battling of old demons, falling rapidly back into Swamp Shack madness.

"Yes, I believe she has."

Navi reeled, as the front door opened, spilling forth a happily father spoiled daughter. "Hello? Mom? I'm home. Come and see all the awesome shit Dad bought me. Mom?"

"Yea darling, be right there. Better yet, just come on upstairs." She closed the computer room door, leaving him in bewildered contemplation. Hugging a city perfumed, well-fashioned happy daughter, Navi embraced.

"Jesus Mom, what the fuck is going on? You're shaking like a leaf."

"Not right now. I want to hear all about your adventure. How is your Dad, I haven't seen him in years? God you know, I am not even sure that I would recognize him."

Cautiously scanning bizarre house tension, Abby peered into her Mother's soul, intuitively searching for information. Allowing the diversion, "Ah he's doing okay. I actually realized that I am grateful they don't have any brat kids. You know, there is a chasm growing between those two, I gathered. Ha, oh by the way, he still has a picture of you in his wallet."

"No shit?"

"I shit you not, Mom."

Abby disappeared into her room, with Christmas gift inventory, and music blasting. Navi stood grateful for the breath of fresh air, or normal world happenings yet humiliated and embarrassed of their current situation. Grateful that the man had not bothered to come in for a visit. It had been fifteen years since she last saw him, and in the moment, she could not remember why exactly it was that they had parted ways; aside from obvious family lifestyle choices. Apparently, a photo of her in his wallet spoke fondly of their time together, and she hoped that he bore no ill will.

Shaking her out of the reverie, unabated Mad Mother screeched from the bottom of the stairwell "NAVI!!! I want my yogurt! Stop stealing my food or so help me, it will be the death of you, you dirty whore!

Navi, wanting to re-direct the old woman before Abby was alarmed, bounded down the stairs, opened the fridge door and turned to hand the yogurt to her. Her robe lay at her feet, free from accountability, and energized, she grabbed the yogurt out of Navi's stunned hands then wandered naked back to her suite, naked sack of wrinkles save for jewels adoring ears, neck and wrists. Re-directing and dressing the demented old woman, ear and soul piercing shrills projected. Mad Mother dressed, bent over and spoke directly into her suites heating vent, a gramophone that led to David's computer room.

"David? David, help me! Navi is taking my food and being so cruel. She hates me and contributes nothing to this family. Wake up son, that slut whore has ruined your marriage and your life. She does not deserve you, my son. She is not feeling well because she is so full of hate, anger and resentment. She has cancer eating away at her from the inside out. You can smell it on her breath and skin. Yes cancer, so pale and gaunt. Serves her right, don't you think?"

Knowing that David had heard every word clearly, she turned victorious to Navi. Navi eye rolled and went back upstairs, closing the bedroom door behind her, intent on hiding away, whilst willing a blinding third eye headache to dissipate.

"David, we have to do something, our home has turned into the Norman Bates Motel."

"I know, I know. We have to stay, with the last of our money into the house and all in her name, there's not much we can do except tough it out."

"What? God, I don't know what it is, every time I go anywhere near her, I feel like a laser beam attaches to my forehead and I can't move. Then it's almost as if my soul is being yanked right out of my body. I can't move, I can't think straight. It's taking hours to recover. I keep seeing something that looks like your Dad over her left shoulder, but it's not him. This thing is dark and nasty. We can't stay here like this!"

"Just when I think I know what I need to say and do, I'm immobile and incapable of doing anything, just acquiescing. It's weird, it makes me want to hurl."

Navi, grateful for Abby's outside world normal excursion and borrowing on it, relaxed, ready to get strategic solution orientated with her man. David abruptly turned to his dresser counting pocket change then without a word, bounded down the stairs. Assuming he would be right back, she splayed comfortable on the bed, objective and excitely ready for resolutions. The back door slammed. He had walked away, gone to find solace at the pub. Christmas means that the free first drink is free, a handful of nameless family-less bar flies, confidantes and preferred companions.

Ignoring his defeatism actions, Navi wrote out the facts and options to their current situation. By late evening rallying in a valiant effort to re-claim home and lives, she cleaned the entire house, thinking, processing mind space. A woman on a mission, the logical thing to do was to have the old woman properly assessed. With eye rolling indignant flip of hand at the suggestion of a full medical checkup, un-intimidated crone mother dearest gracefully evaded the intimation, "Oh don't be a silly-Nelly. I am perfectly fine, dandy and fit as a fiddle. Oh little slut silly-Nelly, be happy with the way things are. I am having a grand time this Christmas. Just think, as sick as you are, you will be dead soon then I will take care of my son the way he should be. Besides, my physician died years ago."

Yes, the fraud was working all right; she was going only to outpatient clinics to obtain prescription refills, thus avoiding thorough assessments and appropriate care referral. Charming and astute when she wanted to be, it was difficult to pin just how much an act, or pure unadulterated evil, it was. Possessed by some dark entity, Lunatic Mad Woman Mother Dearest brazenly opened her robe, revealing her sagging breasts, and then alluringly retied her robe.

Mind boggled and confused, Navi shared her strategy; go to the hospital and get a social worker conversation happening, enticing an inebriated David into action. "Let's go, right now and find someone who can help."

"Ah for fucks sake Navi, why? Fuck, it is humiliating enough being in this shit situation without anyone knowing our business."

"Well, someone has to do something. At the very least, you have to call her lawyer and accountant to make sure that they are not buying into her bullshit. I don't care about any inheritance, but I sure as shit care about what we have put into this house. That woman needs help, there's got to be a label and medication for whatever is wrong with her."

David paced, running stress fingers through his wild hair. "I don't know what the fuck to do! The fucking house is in her name. Shit, elder abuse, shit. It's like she's way ahead of us and without cash or bank credit to buy her out, I can't fathom what we can do about it."

Navi reeled with his seemingly inability to take action. "First thing Monday morning, you start by seeing your family doctor on your own, we need advocacy, and now."

"Ah fuck it, there's nothing I can do. We just have to tough it out."

Warrior rising within, she countered, "David, we have to. You have to! In the meantime, we at least have to give a deadline to revert the house financial and legal stuff. We have to get her assessed, and into proper treatment. Jesus, if we don't, she'll just keep picking away at us until there is nothing left. We'll all go mad."

Navi woke to a blinding headache, weak. Mad Mother confidently arrived home, from a post-Christmas breakfast, waving goodbyes to a Mercedes driving cousin Cynthia; who avoided coming in. Navi hid in the workshop, drinking coffee and downing aspirin, allowing David first crack at alpha dogging her, as Abby approached.

"Mom! What the fuck is going on here? What is with that crazy old bag in there? What has she got on you? Why is she running chaos and driving us all fucking nuts?"

"Abby! NOT NOW!" Abby, on a warrior roll, moved into her mother's face, body bossy, bully raging.

"I want to know what the fuck is going on Mom!" Navi's head reeled, as this was not her Abby. Both of them were overhearing bits of conversation from the kitchen, and David was losing ground fast. Mad Mother Dearest was clearly gaining, voice edging on shriek, and alpha-she-wolf, she was foaming mouth rabid. Ignoring his professional and positive presentation, she intentionally ranted loud; for Navi to hear.

"This is all about that wicked Navi, I know it. She is a witch, you know it and I know it. I don't know why she hates me so; I put a roof over her head and food in her bottomless pit. She steals my yogurt and tangerines. She is a nothing but a petulant useless child. Useless. I cannot fathom what it was about her that made you stray. It is not too late; you can still save your marriage. That whore ruined your perfectly good marriage."

"MOM! Just Fucking answer me!" Abby's marijuana breath wafted under Navi's nostrils, dilated eyes widened and contracted, face reddened, as tears welled and spilled.

"Abby, I don't know what you've been up to, but you picked the wrong time and the wrong approach. I just cannot do this with you right now! For the love of God, go to your room or something, and calm down! Shit, I thought marijuana was supposed to relax and chill people out. Are you on something else?"

Abby livid, undeterred, pushed further "No Mom. I want to know what the fuck is going on! What the fuck do you do all day, Mom?"

Rippling livid, straining for grace and daughters soul care, "School work, house work, renovations and job searching, damn it. You know I almost never stop. Oh shit, why am I explaining myself to a stoned kid? Abby please, just give me some space, I can't do this right now." Navi's spine erect tingled, sending stress menopause madness prickles, flushing a heat wave. A hormonal adrenaline lightening heat induced warrior rage. "Argghhhh, has everyone in this fucking house gone completely mad? Jesus, God, Angels help me now!" Stress balled and lodged in her throat. "No, I can't lose it right now. Abby, I am going to ignore that and I am telling you NOT NOW!"

Wild Abby moved in closer and clenched Navi's arm growling, "You fucking loser! Why don't you get a fucking job?"

Instantly out of mind and grace, angry scared truth humiliated reacted, Navi slapped her hard across the face then spit, "You spoiled little bitch monster!"

Reeling backward in horror of the exchange, both stood frozen in shock. Abby's hand gingerly covered an angry red cheek slap burn blotch. Navi flushed in horror and disbelief of how Abby had just spoken to her and of her own hostile reaction. "Oh my God Ab, are you okay?" Navi motioned to comfort her girl.

Hurt and offended, Abby defensively arm blocked her mother's tender touch.

"Oh my God Ab, this is not who we are."

Still hurt and angry, "Oh thanks a lot Mom! Now, I'm a bitch monster? Well, you are a fucking loser." She turned on heel, leaving Navi shaking. Then Navi followed her out and into the driveway. Shame tears filled, watching the daughter she loved so profoundly, head down the street then out of sight. Turning back towards the workshop, Mother Dearest's rant had escalated.

"Navi is getting sick because she is so full of hate! I don't know why she hates me so much! That daughter of hers is a wanton whore just like her. I see the way she looks at me. I know the way she talks about me behind my back. I may be hard of hearing, but I am not stupid! This is all her fault, the slut whore!"

Navi was fed up. Taking shots at her was one thing, but no one was going to take shots at her daughter and then live to crone chortle about it. The vengeful rage thought alarmed her. Adrenaline heart pounding rage curiously waved within. An unknown and previously un-experienced powerful emotion brought forth conjured images of holding a pillow over the sleeping nasty old crones face; then failing that, choking the living last shit breath out of her. It was odd, she felt almost taller, different somehow, as though someone else, someone equally as nasty, embodied her. Suddenly sick dizzy, she grabbed an empty bucket and projectile retched; vomited it out. Had their whole world gone completely insane?

Shaking, as she stepped out of the workshop and into the snow filled air of the driveway, thoughts turned to her girl. Abby would need to cool off before they could talk about what had happened. Her attention turned back to David and Mother. His professional voice replaced with that of a whiny boy. He had lost his ground. Livid, it was her turn now and heading for the kitchen, she built a Joan of Arc energetic cocoon, intent on giving a few quick words of her own, 'look here, I'll tell you how things are going to be'. Navi played it out in her mind, 'from here on in, you will speak to us with respect, you are going for a full medical assessment and we will assume full responsibility of the house by March first. I have the dollar figures of everything that we ourselves have put into this house and you will sign it over at that time; as we had agreed.'

Confidence evaporated as soon as she saw him. Hunched over, head bowed, soft, pliable, and utterly defeated. She could not do this alone. They had to take a stand together, it was the only way it was going to work. Hesitating, she wondered what kind of magical nasty hold the old crone had on him. What secret hook could so demoralize? She could not fathom anyone getting to him the way his mother has, for any reason. Navi shock waved, taking in the full sight of Mother. Sitting at the dining room table, directly beside him, housecoat wide open with one knee up on the chair, entire old vaginal area wide open exposed. A nineteen forty's movie star harlot, held a cigarette, alluringly Hollywood, demented and mentally ill.

"Lunatic!"

Stomach clutching vomit rose, bile filled her mouth. A Horror movie and not real life, it was Norman Bates Hotel; as if David were Norman. Navi and her daughter were hotel guests to be knifed in the shower. Mother turned, casually grinning, "Oh hi Navi, come join us for coffee before I toddle off to the grocery store. Come. Sit. We were just chatting about old times. Come. Sit. Join us, won't you dear?"

Aghast, Navi glanced at David; a captive abused boy child who had been sexually abused by this predator for years. "Jesus Christ David! Has this woman done to you, what I think she has done?"

David froze, eyes wide, sullen and submissive.

"This *is* insane!"

Her resolve evaporated, "David go upstairs and relax for a while. I will come and see you in a few minutes. I have to go and find Abby first."

"Ah, well just as well sweetheart, I've got to toddle off now before the store closes" Mother chimed, closing her robe.

David sullenly turned, heavy stepped his way up the stairs. Navi slid on a coat and boots for outside, holding her coat tight against the overcast winter chill. The old mink coated woman rammed the gas, then holding steering wheel with both hands, looked only straight ahead into snowy wind and boldly gunned the engine, reeling out into the street without regard.

'Jesus, that woman isn't safe in a house, or on the road. Thank Christ; the grocery store is only a block away. With the storm, at least there won't be any pedestrians for her to run over. I have to remember to hide her God Dammed license and car keys.'

Looking both ways, intuitively scanning the neighbourhood for loving daughter, she was nowhere to be found, not yet ready to come home. Heading back into the kitchen, she grabbed two warm cups of coffee then bounced upstairs.

"David. Are you all right?"

Slouched in his computer chair, finger swirling a cigarette, watching wincing tiny strands of smoke curls, he had just been dealt another otherworldly deathblow. "Ah shit, she has this all figured out in her tiny little demented mind. I am so sorry. Honest, I had no idea she was this bad."

Navi's spine anger erected. "If she tries that elder abuse crap officially, I swear to God I will put her in my car and haul her ass into the lockup unit for a proper psyche evaluation."

"What the fuck can I do?"

Navi's heart sank in David's defeatism. "We have to find a way to take a stand together." David nestled his head into her chest, a boy, a sad and spirit beaten boy. The front door opened, Abby boldly pounced in, face red angry scared and folded arms defensive, "I demand to know what is going on here? Do we own this house or not?"

"Abby! NOT NOW!"

David's spine went erect, instantly pissed at the righteous audacious demand.

"MOM!!! Some kind of bad shit is going on around here. I want to know whose house this is. Is this our house or hers? That crazy old crone told me that this is her house, not ours. Who is paying the bills? She says she pays for everything. Where is the money coming from? Is all that shit she's been saying true?"

Navi calmly reached her hand over to David's leg, to cue him to let her take the lead. She sensed that he was going to blow his wrath and she did not want him to repeat the riff blow done earlier. Abby would be beyond devastated.

"Abby, I will talk to you in a bit, I promise. But not right now."

Abby stood ground, scared and wildly shaking, holding her arms across her chest, defiant. David whirled silently, under clenched teeth and fists.

"How and what is none of your business. At the moment, you are way out of line and you picked the wrong day and the wrong time to do this!"

"Mom, I am not leaving this room until I have some answers. I am sick with what is going on here. I am not blind you know! That woman that demands I call her Grandma is telling me some strange shit. She is telling me how much toilet paper I can use, when I can shower and for how long. She is saying shit about how she is, and has been, paying for your lazy ass for years. Are you both stealing money from her?"

Navi anger rippled and fought for self-control. Abby was right. David shifted in his chair, body language sliding into battle mode. Before she could block him, wild eyed, he started, "Just who in the fuck do you think you are?"

Abby's face burned livid. David snickered in madness. Abby looked at her mother for support and sensing inability to take a proper stand, abruptly turned and disappeared. Sounds of banging and possessions thrown permeated the hallway and then into the computer room. David, ready to bolt after her, to continue his rant stress rage vent, inhibitions gone, hesitated as Navi firmly stood in his path. She took his hand and held it tight, tears streaming.

"Stop it! Let her be! There is weird shit going on around here that has absolutely nothing to do with her and you know it.

Sounds of Mother Dearest's car pulling into the driveway sent a ripple of stress simultaneously through them both. "I need some quiet space to think." David muttered, flopping on bed. "NO David! Get up God damn it! Some of this crazy shit might be normal to you, but it isn't to me! The whole house has gone insane! Do something, say something!"

He turned flipping a hand, dismissive "Fuck her and her crazy assed shit."

Navi sat at the computer, Dalai Lama type sounds softly chanting in the background, as occasional Mad Mother ranting waffled up to Navi's ears followed by strange prickling sensations, her forehead numbed, she was drawn and laser pulled by a dark immutable force to go down and engage in the madness; to snuff her out. Worst case scenario was a strong possibility; imagining herself asleep and waking to Mad Mother Dearest, hovering, then gracefully embedding a butcher knife deep into her chest. Mad Mother Dearest descending the stairs with butcher knife in hand, Abby already dead, with David kept as her plaything until he dies. Navi's mind turned to waiting for the old crone to fall asleep, and holding a pillow over her old face until she breathed no more.

'NO!!!!!!! You will do no more harm, old woman, you go to the light now and when ready, your husband, family and friends will greet you.'

The urge to kill was foreign to Navi. Startled, curiously contemplative, she objectively sensed and scoped the strong alien and unfamiliar urge slithering within her. Shiver shuddering, the dark and evil essence that had penetrated her mind and body, was not of her, alpha dog willed it out, off and away.

David bounced up the stairs and sat beside her. Reaching in behind the computer desk, he pulled out a beer and twisted it open, slugged hard, draining it, he burped, then lit up a smoke. Navi waited in hope.

"Okay Darling, here's the scope." Beer foam around his lips and moustache, he pulled hard on his cigarette. "Well, we went around it all again. I don't think she heard a god-dammed word that I said. Instead, went around and around about how much you hate her and how mean you are to her when I'm not around. Just so you know; I'm not buying into any of it."

Navi was livid, not because of the crazy things mother was saying, but for the possibility of doubt in David's mind.

"Well, no shit!"

"Can't you just try and get along with her for a while. It's just temporary."

"What? Are you out of your fucking mind?"

"Well Navi. Even in her madness there is an element of truth."

"What? What in the fuck are you talking about? What bizarre hold on you does she have? Have you completely lost your balls?"

"Well, it is true that you are not working right now and that she has helped us out a lot. And with the elder abuse threats and no recourse, there's not a fucking thing I can do about it right now; not until we have the money to get her out, or us out."

"David, shake it off. Shake her off for a moment. Put your social worker hat back on for a moment. Think about what you are saying!"

"Ah for fuck's sake, just what the fuck do you expect me to do about it? We are sleeping in *her* house and eating *her* groceries."

"What? Why are you saying, "Her house and her groceries"? Ah, shit! What am I doing? I am arguing shit that is not worth arguing about! Give your head a shake! What has happened to you? The David I know would not think this way! What secret does she have on you? What did she do to you?"

"Nothing. There is no secret."

"Oh yes there is!"

"Ah, don't give me that wooey woo shit. I am not in the mood for it. It's all a crock anyway. Crazy flakey assed witch shit!"

Navi felt a psychic dagger drive into her heart. David had never spoken to her that way. "Well, that's a new all-time low for you. Have I ever said that your artwork is a crock of shit? Have I ever said to give it up and go get a real job? Who are you? When is the last time you worked full time? Ah shit! She has gotten to you and now we have deteriorated into this kind of argument? Shit. What is happening to us? Just how long do you think we will last in this madness? This is insane!"

"Look, if we can tough it out with her for maybe a year or so, maybe I'll have enough money from contracts to buy her out; unless you can pull a spiritual miracle out of your ass. Maybe, just maybe, she is right and you *are* the problem. Maybe it is you."

"WOW! That is the lowest all time low!"

"Ah fuck it. I am going downstairs to get something to eat. She wants to talk to you anyway. She is waiting at the dining room table, going over the monthly budget. Are you coming down?"

Navi reeled, a blinding headache now full throttle. "Since when does she manage the budget? No! I need space. I can't think straight right now."

Dismissing the lowness of their bickering, she tried in vain to shift to social worker. There had to be a way out of this mess. Making the insane old crone have a medical and psychological assessment without legal incident requiring police intervention cannot be enforced. Navi dismissed the imagery of police in the house, lights swirling in the dark outside, hovering over a body on the floor with a white blanket over top, whose body it was, she could not ascertain.

Her attention turned to Abby, forgetting that she was so close and probably had heard their riff. Under metallic rock music, Abby, sobbing, emanated confusion and fear. Only weeks earlier, there was joy, hope and promise. Normally, there would never have been a rift or argument between either of them. David bounded up the stairs and assumed his spot with another beer and a smoke.

"I made some beans and franks. It is not much, but we need to eat. Maybe the old crone will fart so hard she will blow an aneurysm. Fuck, she'll probably out live us all, just on principal."

"This is madness."

"Ah for God's sake Navi, it's her fucking house 'cause the mortgage is in her fucking name. What am I supposed to do?"

"Nah, David, this is my house, our house. You're not seeing it. This simply is not okay. There is something dark and nasty going on here."

"Well I don't like it any more than you do. Besides, where can we go? Everything I have is here, in here."

"We have to get out of here for the night, get a room, just a bit of time to think straight and figure out what to do. You can ask your Doctor tomorrow for some advice. We need help."

"NO! I am not going to squat in a motel room. Fuck, if this were a different era, I would take out that old witch. She brings out the violent primal man in me. Don't know why I did not see it in her before. I didn't even know I had that in me, until now." David leaned back in his computer chair, breathing out a wave of fear, panic and pent up stress. He choked back tears, and then ran a hand through his beard in his thoughtful manner. "I can't even paint. I don't have any choice other than to make the best of it."

"David, this is crazy shit. If we don't do something right now, within the next day or two, things will only get worse. This is dangerous."

"Oh for fuck's sake, don't be so fucking melodramatic! I am not going anywhere. Everything is here; can't you just try and get along with her?"

"I can't believe you said that. Wake up! Jesus, we are contemplating being killed or killing another human!"

"Ah FUCK!" pacing, he lit up a smoke, then shot an eye dagger at her. It shook to the core, scaring her. He took a deep breath. "What are you saying Navi? Do you want out? Are you leaving me? If you are thinking about it, oh, you are. You are leaving me aren't you?"

Navi core shaking, leaving him had not occurred, "David, what are you doing? All I am saying is that none of this is acceptable."

Battle braced. He paced fuming, puffing on a smoke.

"Come with me to Catharine's tonight, she is away getting ready to move in with Elijah so I'm sure that we would have the place to ourselves for a bit. Let's just chill down for a minute, take a few days so that we can think straight and figure out what to do."

"I AM NOT LEAVING HERE!"

Conscious of Abby down the hall, she slid out of the computer chair and took his face into her hands then nose-to-nose firmly and lovingly whispered, "I am not leaving you. We have been fighting and we are not thinking straight. Just for a day or two. I love you."

"If you leave me now, tonight, I don't think I could ever take you back."

Rattled, scared and angry, she moved forward, held her hands on his face, turned his head and whispered firmly into his ear, "I love you. We have just had a conversation about doing someone in. I don't know what she has done to you but I know it is inhumane. She is not right of mind and this is not right. And somewhere in there is my David, my Magus."

"Please don't leave me!"

"I am not leaving *you*! Come. Just overnight. Please."

"No. I'm not going. I'm staying here."

Life force drained, she calmly whispered, "I am taking Abby and going to Catharine's. I want you to come to."

Abby tucked into the recreation room pull out, Navi curled up in front of the fireplace, quietly phone chatting with Catharine. "Stay as long as you need to." Navi plunked onto the guest room bed, alone, fell into abandoned exhausted sleep.

"Pssst! Navi Darling. Across the ethers, I sense your angst. As I sit here, I can feel you and sense your presence. A delicate light from your glowing tattoo is radiating a light of its own.

May God be with you, blessed wild woman of my soul, and know that I walk with you through this troublesome moonlit night. May you dance barefoot upon the spring grass in freedom, for you have earned it; have given so much of yourself, never asking for even the smallest things, only accepting that which comes unto you. I love you, your wholeness, your completeness, your oneness."

"How I wish you were with me now. I wish I knew who you really were. This is too hard. If you cannot come to me in person, then please spare me and leave me alone! This is too hard."

"Oh my God David, you look like shit! That's it, you're staying here."

"NO. I am not staying here! I am staying at the 'evil woman's' house with no food or money. I can't paint. I can't work. I can't sleep. I can't think."

Navi, occupied with making tea and heating leftovers, needing a moment to gather wits, to eat and become calm.

"Oh by the way, 'she' is as giddy as a magpie that you and Abby are gone. She is wearing makeup, prancing around the house nude underneath that robe of hers and treating me as though I am her husband or some sort of lover. She allows me to eat one small yogurt and an orange, share dinner on one plate. She has my day planned, like a happy couple. If I tell her no, that I am busy, she waits for a bit but then shrieks up the stairs at me like a mad woman. She buys me smokes then accuses me of smoking hers. This morning she said she was feeling a tad dizzy and needed to pick up a few things, so I took her and oh fuck; she plays the drama queen in front of the grocery store people. If that were not embarrassing enough, she put on a good show with the pharmacist and then the post office clerk. God, Navi, I know these people, they have been neighbours or clients on and off for years. Now the bank manager of mine for some twenty odd years is giving me that *look*. Shit, they are looking at me with consternation and concern about my frail old charming mother, go out and do these errands; I can't fucking believe it!"

"Come. Sit. Eat."

David sat and poked at the food in front of him, without eating. He pushed it away. "I can't eat Catharine's food."

"Eat, I bought it. Relax."

"WHY DID YOU FUCKING LEAVE ME?"

Rattled, slivers of a former David, this new one was invaded by something dark, it was not 'who he really was'.

"I didn't leave you. I left the situation. I can't help you if I am in jail or dead. I have drafted a referral for a medical assessment. We need help."

David stood, sad traumatized. "There is nothing I can do. There is nothing anyone can do." He gingerly kissed her on her forehead and then turned, picked up his beer and left.

"Well Navi sorry to hear about it all. I think you were right to take Abby and come to my house. I thought about it all last night, but then had the intuition that you both needed to work out your own ethereal shit with her. David has to work through this and find his own way."

"Oh God Catharine, how did I not see this?"

"Navi, for God's sake, he has to work it through on his own. Oh, there is something you should know. It's going to sound bloody creepy weird, so you'd better sit down."

Her spirit blood drained.

"Hmm, have you had the urge to go downstairs and put a pillow over her face while she sleeps?"

"Oh my God, how did you know that?"

"That's because you are sensing and feeling her grey spirit beings influence. They taunt you until they engage you in battle, for life, for soul. I was actually expecting your call. I have a group that I work with, who are praying for this positive outcome, among other things."

"Wow. Jedi?"

"I've had to be."

"What am I supposed to do? I have Abby."

"Just take care of yourselves. Try to focus on yourself and get on with your life, your own path without him."

In the days that followed, Navi's mind reeled from the bizarre drama. Disregarding, she focused social worker strong, by day for daughter and David, while nights brought only strange fevered nightmares. In loyal watchdog compassionate care, she remained supportive and waited his comeback. His nasty shadow boogie surfaced in livid disgust, "This is your miracle Navi? This is the best your holier than thou spiritual shit can do?"

Days turned into weeks and Abby was thriving despite turmoil. "Well, Mom, I guess it's like you always tell me, you're just supposed to walk through it with as much grace as you can and try not to let it fuck you up. Don't let someone else's shit define who you are."

"I said that?"

"Once or twice."

"What shall we do about this?"

"I just want to live my life, right now."

"Okay, you're old enough to make that determination yourself. No secrets and keep talking to me, whenever."

"Thanks Mom. Thanks for not going all ape shit over me and keeping alive all of that shit that went down at Christmas."

"Oh, don't let my calm exterior fool you. I am calm with you right now, because you are my first priority."

"Hee...heee... ya, I have days like that too, but not so much anymore."

"How did you get to be so amazing? Were you born that way?"

"Hee...hee...yup. Oh by the way Mom, David's boggy scares the shit out of me when he comes here. I can see that it all makes you sick at night, also. I do want to go back to the house and get some of my stuff though. But I don't want to be in the same room with that old witch mother of his."

"I don't know how just yet, but we'll make arrangements to go and get some stuff. It looks like this is going to take much longer than I thought. God I love you. I am so sorry that you have had to go through so much frigging crap, it's way too much for such a young precious soul."

"Ah Mom, guess I just take after you huh? You know, crap makes for the best healers and medicine women."

"Ah so wise and philosophical art thou. But you still need to be a teenager, and you deserve all good things, my darling."

"Okay, so can I have a car?"

"Get a job."

Compassion, guilt, grief, and worry, can be a dangerous trap and philosophically she knew better. He was battling Dark Night of the Soul yet within a day, David had a new plan rapidly in motion. The following week, he left for Toronto.

"What about the house?"

"Fuck it! Move on. Forget about it."

Proud that he had found a way out, on his own accord, thoughts turned to acclimatizing herself to city life and she awaited his come-hither call, while searching for a legal miracle to re-gain her cottage house investment. She prayed and waited for Divine direction.

"You must walk on alone through the desert. Parched and thirsty, you find that high stonewall, look over and jump in. See the lush garden inside? It has a deep cooling water grotto, ancient lush trees, fresh fruit baskets, a gazebo and hammock for resting. Rather than resting, jump back out of the garden, back out into the desert and wander, telling all others about the garden and how they can find it. Now you are Bodhisattva.'

"You never know how strong you are until being strong is the only choice you have."
Anon

Chapter 20 ~ Tendrils

Dear Navi;

I am settling into Toronto life of which I have so desperately needed. There are people helping me stabilize and pulling art world clique strings. Mad mother advises that the house has been sold and that there is no equity, no money for you or me. She has moved in with my cousin Cynthia. Tough luck, I desperately need money.

I think that you and I were just children of passion. Maybe we rushed. Maybe I pushed you into something you weren't ready for. I do know that I would not be painting if it weren't for you. I thank you for that; perhaps I shall dedicate my next series in honour of our time together, we shall see. I have to believe that my painting is a good thing. I had some of my most joyful beautiful life moments with you. I think we can be at peace with ourselves and with each other.

Oh, I watched a sixty five year old woman to commit suicide yesterday morning by jumping in front of subway train. She jumped and landed between the tracks, splattered by the front of the train, which ran over her. Sure screwed up rush hour on the transit train.

I have discovered a taste for Absinthe, which is a delicious redundancy that serves a higher purpose, inspiration for my work, of course.

Understand that I just can't deal with talking to you on the phone or otherwise. I have to focus on my work and anything personal just wreaks complication, a pain in the ass. Strangely, I am okay as long as I focus on my work and not you, as then God smiles upon me. So please don't call me or email me anymore.

I am happy with the simple things in a day, like having clean undies and a dammed good kick-start morning coffee. Such is life alone. Anyway, you'll be happy to know that the government artist's works in progress grant fund has paid my rent already. The bloat that shares this apartment with me is out at the moment, a bubbling madness, a phlegmatic cauldron and this is a shit living arrangement. I have no real room to work and it is hell when he is home; boiling away in madness muttering and blathering with his porn on so loud that I cannot think. He stays up all night getting stoned, pissed and more repulsive. I have to get the hell out of his shit hole.

A lady, who smokes with me out on the street, is my saving grace. She works in the kitchen of the restaurant below, brings me food and it's really nice to have female company. I have to admit that it's nice to have someone to snuggle with and to talk to.

I still love you but quite frankly, you left me there in the shit with Mad Mother. I don't trust you. I am still on enough post traumatic stress anti-depressant medication to tranquilize a monkey. I know I've fucked up two women and two families.

Yes, we had some wonderful times and some of it truly was magic. But there is life here, city life. There is so much to see and do. You can go out any time of the day or night and there is life, with people milling about. Not like back home with you at the beach, where it is dead after five o'clock at night, outside of summer tourist seasons. I have met so many interesting people in the short time that I have been here, inspiring happy people with full busy lives. Not like the same old, day after day, year after year of boring nothing new to talk about. I know that you hate the city. Scenery, trees and landscapes are nice to look at, but it does not put food on the table and it sure as shit, does not offer interesting conversation. Once you've seen it, you've seen it. I didn't realize how boring my life was, until I came here. Ah, I still get so scared at times that I can't think straight. It takes so much fucking energy just to focus on painting right now. I am surrounded by successful rich kids that blasé through the art circles.

Oh fuck, my fucking alcoholic crack head roommate pig is home now and the fucking guy watches Asian and kiddie porn. Sometimes I am hanging on to such a tiny piece of thread. If this does not work out, I don't know what I will do. I don't have anything else to fall back on. I am too old and fucked up to get a job anywhere. God, I have done things that I am not proud of, just to stay alive. I go to parties with my roommate where there are hard-core drugs, just to steal some food to eat and get blitzed.

Ah Navi, you will always be near and dear to me. I can't take care of you. I did love you and I did miss you so badly that I cried until it hurt, every day since you left. I am tired of crying. I am stabilizing in the city. Do you understand what I am saying? You left me there in the madness, the shit with that evil woman. I nearly killed myself. Fuck, I felt like I had been raped when you left. What the fuck do you expect? Ahhh FUCK!!!! I can't fucking do this right now. I've got work to do.

Goodbye. Take care. Go and find a life."

David of the city, soon to have his own crib

He was gone.

A silent void of darkness echoed emptiness and emotionally exhausted, Navi slid into it.

Lightning flashes showing gain in distancing away. Standing stern, as row man headed toward shoreline, her with babe in hand, ship sinking, deep dark water engulfing.

As the Mist cleared once again, she found herself in the dark of night, surrounded by ghostly spirit people that hung out in the upstairs area of a mid-eighteen hundreds cottage house, adjoining an upper lakeside New York community. Pacing and unable to sleep, still in her nightgown and nightcap, worn with long hair braided tucked under, bare feet pattered cold wooden floors. Gazing out the third floor window, moonlight splayed dancing sparkles across a dark water surface. Community walking trails, faded into an ancient forest, off dock's boardwalk and gazebo.

Descending narrow wooden stairs, an oil lamp in one hand, railing hand sliding with the other, she found herself entering a library. An amassed and extensive library of the world's greatest collection in antiquity, books mumble almost audibly, their findings. Historical prominent and notorious spirit world celebrities in portrait paintings and old grey scale photos, keep a watchful eye on everyone who enters. Founders and ghost inhabitants wandered the vacant apartment, library and classroom.

"Colleagues will be assembling tomorrow, in the great hall; fellow seekers of all things "spirit world". An opportunity for one lowly student such as I, Cora, in lodging normally reserved for VIP's." she said aloud.

Obviously consciously aware of Navi's presence within her, Cora began to share, giddy with the visitation. "Hello Navi, dear friend! I have a beloved sharing for you, a story of divine intervention. When I first arrived here, crowds of spirits wandered around muttering excitedly that I could see them and hear them, having much to share of the mysteries of life and other worldly things. My traditional religious mind vacillated between wondering what in on earth I was doing in such an odd otherworldly place and the anxious knowing that I must give an inspirational and moving speech in the morrow, whilst having not a clue of what I am going to say. I do like to know ahead of time, what the topic will be.

Drifting off to sleep somewhere around five am, then bolting awake promptly at seven am with a gasp, I panicked and was ready to pack up luggage and dash away. I intensely disliked the center of attention. Exhausted nervous, I would rather have high tail it out and away, if only I had a horse and carriage.

Tea and biscuits satisfied, I dressed in my Sunday best gown, warmer stockings, best bonnet, then ventured out to the great hall, to attend class. Tired, nervous, and a tad grumpy, a headache begged me to decline the speaking engagement. As my name was called, I stood ready to excuse myself, when a warm wonderful feeling washed through body. I spine straightened and my mouth opened.

What to say when at a loss for words, I nervously began. Over the years of my social and spiritual work, I have amassed a great deal of pride in being the one person in the community that everyone sought for counsel. It was a high feeling that I loved being a part of. As with all matters of confidence; life was about to test that resolve.

When my brother in law called out of the blue to confide that he had just been diagnosed with syphilis and tuberculosis, his siblings and mother were irate and disgusted. Family scuttle and gossip, knowing that the shadow other truth behind their harsh judgments lie the fact that he had once upon a time experimented and explored in some rather scandalous relations. I am to this day, embarrassed to admit that my mind vacillated between the typical chitchat and with ignorant panic of his possible contagious condition, particularly with my children.

Tea taken, biscuits finished, we strolled out to the pond and took bench, to chat in privacy. I candidly confess, I was so nervous, half listening, trying to formulate a good God loving response, while mindful that I was keeping more physical distance than normal; to the extent that I had used two very different tea cups, so as not to confuse mine with his. I am ashamed of that fact.

I awaited pause in his story, so that I could share something inspirationally strong and righteous. I had thought to myself that when he toddled back home, I could research how contagious his condition was. After his pause, I heard him say that he was on his way north, taking his small wooden skiff out onto a lake, never to return. I was to wait a good four days, before I notified authorities. He handed me the spare key to his lakeside cottage and a copy of the deed ownership, already signed into my name. Shock overrode my petty ignorant mind.

I was simply at a loss of words for anything that could remotely speak to his inner pain and anguish. I sat stupidly holding his cottage key. In short order, a wave of light, a warm wonderful feeling, washed through me and my mouth opened. I was calm and smiling; Well Darling Brother In Law, you could do what you wish and I would surely miss you. The children will miss you and I surely would love to inherit your lovely cottage, but you will not travel north and you are not going to do that which ends your earthly life. Family, like most, argue against what they do not understand. In time they will adjust as your condition improves. More importantly, your lovely soul mate woman awaits you, to marry you. So you will attend to your medical needs and pray my favorite brother in law, know that I love you and that I am here for you.

My words hung in midair, my glib speech surprising even me. He was of course, shocked and taken aback. I felt my face turn crimson in audacious embarrassment. Then ears spilled upon his cheeks. He then embraced me as though in true, soul friend, bond. He sobbed upon my shoulder, as though I was Mother and he was my child. As his tears subsided somewhat I added; Do not be mucous soiling my gown young man, and we both broke into fits of laughter.

Wait, I added, what I am I doing, may I still have your lovely cottage? We laughed until our faces cramped.

To this day, I have absolutely no idea where those calming words from, pure angelic divine intervention. It was not a time for traditional counsel, or of trite philosophy. Yet; it was what his soul needed to hear. He joined his soul mate Beth in Holy Matrimony within a fortnight.

No pastoral counseling technique in the world can prepare us as ministers for God in those life-defining moments when someone is traumatized and confronted with their own mortality. There is a gift in letting go of all notions of what is the social or professional thing to say and allowing the love and wisdom of spirit world to assume control.

I have come to confidently know that while odd at times, God and spirit knows much better than I or any man, when to interject humour, that which interrupts the stream of defeatism and trauma; wondrously and miraculously. I do not recall having this randomness of spirit communication taught in traditional religious schools, nor of the interjection of wit and humour. There are professional protocols, professional conduct and decorum, yet in allowing that source to flow through you, the transformation can be glorious. It reminds us that spirit world knows better than I we."

Navi, holding onto the essence of the journey, jumped into the car, meandering the beach, the place of their summer romance.

E-mail dumped.

Allowing waves of humiliated hurt abandon to wash within an empty darkness pervaded thoughts; mid-life without a man, job, savings, or home. 'Thank God, there is at least a home for us' gratefully she thought-hug blessed Catharine.

Ignoring the first three phone rings, Navi just wanted to sit with a coffee and align to the fact that David, finances and home were gone. All gone. She did not want to talk to anyone, not right now. Catharine giddily blurted through a crackling long distance echo, "Oh Navi, I am ever so glad you are there. I have something important to tell you that cannot wait."

Sitting down, receiver in ear, "Oh Hi Catharine, I am so glad you called, I really need to talk to you to but, you go first."

"Oh I am so tickled Navi. I love it here and I love Elijah so much. I am so glad I brazenly went on this journey. I am home now. Everything is happening so fast. My kids have adult lives of their own now so I don't need to worry about them. And guess what?"

Navi feigned happy support, stuffing jealous longing, "Ah Catharine, I am so happy for you!"

"Oh thank you dear friend. My house has been privately sold. A friend of his knows a friend who bought it out right, as is, for a price beyond my wildest imaginings. This all happened in the space of one day, Elijah proposing, his friend's visit, all over a couple of cups of coffee. Isn't life amazing?"

Flabbergasted at the irony, the dichotomy of contrasting days, hers devastating, Catharine's joy.

"Oh, I have to go now, I will get back to you about closing up the house, perhaps by the weekend. Oh, but first I want to hear your news."

Navi stumbled, didn't know where to begin, resisting sharing drama, not wanting to burden.

"Never mind. It's all good. We'll talk later. Thanks for letting me know. Congratulations."

That was that.

"Gran?"

"Yes my Chickadee. Let go of the past and strive to focus on remembering the good of who you really are. Spirit world awaits your recovery. As you heal old fears, shame and guilt, you also do so for many others in collective consciousness. This healing ripples out positively into the world, the universe. By outgrowing it all, you are positively contributing to affecting positive change for all. Not simply for yourself and your daughter in the days to come, but you will actually change lasting effects into the past and future simultaneously. Do you see? Soon you will find your balance. Worry not my darling, this too, is Abby's path to experience and learn from. One day, she too will know her own powerful medicine, able to do so because of the groundwork that you lay. Oh, is it not a fun game? To play a suffering victim separating oneself from God, the spirit world, the divine and the all that is?"

"NO! It's too hard. I want to go home, to spirit world where everything makes sense. I hate this shit life, I don't understand and I don't want to be here anymore."

"Navi, be careful of what you passionately proclaim! You must strive to find your truths. You must strive to manifest heaven on earth, not by someone else's definition, but your own, your soul's own notion of heaven on earth. In aiming to feel reverence and gratitude for life, your life, you will change both your inner and outer worlds. Go now and finish grieving if you must, do not slide too deep or far away or to long from the light of God, of the light of who you are. Find comfort in knowing that this is all, meant to be. The outcomes will surprise you."

"But what in the hell am I supposed to do now? I have no money and nowhere to go!"

Silence rang in ears. Hurt, emotional exhaustion and fear resumed. Fed up, the old haunting dark shadow nemesis pervaded her being. The spirit world failed, she had failed. Spirit friends useless in day-to-day needs. Angry, in her mind eye and with a flick of her hand, slammed the spirit world door closed, officially closed.

"FUCK RIGHT OFF! All of you! Abstract, trite spiritual new aged existential BULLSHIT!!!!"

She had to find a way to be normal and provide for Abby, normalcy and stability.

Part Three ~ Home

"But I, being poor, have only my dreams.
I have spread my dreams under your feet; tread softly,
because you tread on my dreams."
William Butler Yeats

Chapter 21 ~ Four years later

The digital clock bleated; 4:44, congruent numbers, a sign that the spirit world was making contact. A four-day fever ravaged, drifting in and out of memories, lost in timelines, ethereally searching for that one point. The juncture or defining life moment, when life at home with David and work, had turned to madness and utter shit. Memories surfaced, relived, dissipated surreal and fluid.

Awaking to the here and now, pre-sunrise crows cawed outside cabin. Navi rose soaked in fever sweat, changing nightwear, ate then found herself aching wrist soothing from constant click of Zen Solitaire, an open blank thesis hung mid computer screen. There was still time, still sick yet calculated at least a month before she would appear before the Seminary Board of trustees, to submit thesis and orate before the governing board of trustees.

The interfaith minister courses had served as cathartic healing balm over the years, mind diversion away from failed relationships, house home loss and internal drama. She knew that she was no Minister; the courses were fascinating and allowed her a bow out excuse, unable to cope in the real world of finding a job and living a normal life. All of which still evaded comprehension of just how to go about having such.

Four years cocooned in Robert's northern hunt camp cabin, nestled far north in the Algonquin National Park wilderness periphery, was also home of the First Nation's Sacred Scrolls, her hide out, sanctuary.

The closest Northern rural small town was a short forty-minute drive on a good day, two hours or more during winter storm. Getting into town for supplies, store bought coffee and a human contact fix was the easy part. Navigating back to the cabin, crossing park boundaries, an etheric wall of majestic wilderness slammed the senses. The area clearly belonged to the all that was; unadulterated wilderness, free and powerful in nature. Those who dared enter left forever changed in unimaginable ways. Those who remained resident, stayed along on the periphery, entranced. One did not want to run out of gas at night or take a wrong turn. Everything looks different at night, easy to lose track of one's way, especially in a blizzard. For all who brazen to explore its interior, thoughts turn to famed Group of Seven Artist Tom Thompsons' mysterious disappearance, some fifty years ago.

Alone in the dark of midnight, small against harsh northern snow, powerful winds constantly threatened electrical power outages. Fireplace chimney belted puffs of delicious wood smoke as high windblasts choked the roof top air vent. With computer glow and blue haunting winters' full moon illumination streaming in through the window. Wind slammed snow spatters against old cabin windows, rattling wooden doors, seeking entry. A powerful force whacked the window above her computer, rattled, and then BANGED again, startling her bones. Howling north winds blasted against the old hunt cabin, contracting her robe tighter against a cold draft. The forceful poltergeist whacked, rattled and banged on the outer side of the cabin, seeking entry. Eyes followed its sound trails, ready to take action against its unwanted intrusive demanding that her windows and doors give way. 'That's one hell of a wind.'

Déjà Vu from years ago, a defining night of change in the old country farmhouse in the midst of Matt's cancer, marriage conclusion to a masturbating Stephen. Without time to process their dissolving marriage, a love affair with once co-worker David ensued. Jobless and finances emptied, a true dark night of the soul ensued. Closing the door to Spirit world connections, the thought now brought a chuckle. They had been there all along, could not leave, giving a wide birth, making themselves consciously known and intervening only upon request.

"Good dogs, sit, stay, silent", she chuckled. "There's a good spirit", she coo mused.

With Abby away in university, just old Dawg in front of the fireplace, Robert's old cabin echoed empty but sanctuary safe. 'Maybe I should trek into town tomorrow. Maybe next week.'

Robert had owned the Algonquin park cabin out right since he was a boy, having saved his own cash; the audacious young boy boldly trekked into the land registry office with deed and real estate papers in hand. Vacation home away from all things civilization, extended family and friends for fifty years had been more of an elbow bending party-play-station, than a hunting zone.

'It is amazing what you can get used to' she thought, eyeing the ice crusted buckets of open lake water lining against the indoor fireplace wood. A refugee field mouse poked its head out of the wood, and then scampered behind a cupboard. There was once a time when the thought of a mouse in the house would entail madly disinfecting everything. Now, she could care less, his banishment simply hinged on respectfully defecating and urinating outdoors and leaving her groceries and bath soap alone. Electrical wires as ancient as the cabin, the hot water heater tank sat outside on the deck, unused and rusting. Too heavy to lift and move, it had become a patio table. On warm days, it donned a tablecloth and flowers. Rusted old bathtub, served as hygiene when it absolutely had to; buckets of water heated by the campfire, took an hour to fill, then chilled by the time a body sank into it. It was easier to walk down to the shoreline, spring, summer and fall, to eco-friendly soap cold-water bathe and leg/armpit shave.

The last of the March wintery blizzard finally dissipating, spring rain, assuming alpha over snow, brought moist musky earth odours. A seasonal scale swayed tipping crescendo, ready to break free. So close to graduating, Navi questioned whether to continue to the end goal, finish the seminary credentials with final exams and a thesis when she had yet to find balance with an inner shaman existence. Time was ticking. Avoiding blank page long enough, the introductory synopsis paragraph began with a word, deleted, new word deleted, then closed program slamming computer's power button off, hesitated, spun computer chair around and around, than began again.

HOW TO BECOME a ROGUE MINISTER,

Or, how about ...

I AIN'T NO SAINT,

Or, How I Became One Of My Welfare Bush Clients:

By; Crazy Navi

Virus fever easily exhausted, Navi rubbed weary eyes through long greying hair. Forgotten until mirror viewed, self-deprecating skewed vision showed "reach out and touch someone" wiry crone hairs, age spots and smoker's lip wrinkles.

Longing to know that she had indeed grown matured enough to repeat the same mistakes, she allowed an inner diatribe to flow. 'So what was that pinnacle choice point where everything had gone south, so far off the track? Was it falling in love with David, or perhaps just living with him too soon? Yes.

Maybe. Or is it the cowardly caring too much of what the rest of the world thinks, simply born odd, yet unable to completely conform to traditional church standards and ditch communion with spirit world? No, Gran did it, so can I. Was a critical point the inclusion of David's Mother Dearest in the sanctity of our beach cottage? Yes, an accumulation of any number of variables that rubbed an Achilles heel and original sin; that pesky dark shadow was acquired at birth, childhood, youth or young adulthood that manifested in crappy relationship choices. It is a conundrum. Oh God, Gran, spirit friends, please show me the insight; give me freedom, soul freedom.

At the end of those days there was one hero, as the final door closed to that life. One Harley driving, tattooed rogue angel mechanic years ago, saved the day.'

Robert, who in trying to save her car from the wreckers on a fateful day, was greeted by a sobbing Navi and daughter who candidly confided that they had nowhere to go and no money. Eyeing her over, his tattooed muscles flexing as he tightened a something or other under the hood of her car. Their friendship until that moment in acquaintance status, he rifled through his grease-stained coveralls then tossed two sets of keys.

"You can stay at the hunt camp cabin as long as you want. No one ever goes there anymore. I've been hanging on to the place thinking I might retire there. It's not much, but it might do if you're not too meticulous. I don't want any rent. You would be doing me a favour by being there and looking after the place. Oh, its way up north and Abby would have to transfer schools. I will see what I can do about your car but honestly, why don't you just take my Chevy truck? She's an old '72, hard on gas and a bitch in the snow, but she's reliable."

With short-term intent, Robert's northern wilderness cabin became a safe port, then a way of life. Aside from missing Matt, Polly and Catharine those melodramatic memories with Stephen had long faded along with the whole David affair.

Gingerly, un-cramping creaking aging legs, she stood, yoga stretched, then turned off the computer. Old icebox style fridge door open wide, eyes squinting resistance to painful bright inner light, reached in and guzzled down limeade straight out the container. Bachelorette prerogatives, scratched menopause itch hives under left breast, then under arm nubs. Bathroom chilly, old wooden freezing toilet seat clamped under buttock skin sending a shiver up her spine making tiny skin hairs raise and dance. Drawing old sisterhood shawl tightly in, she opened the fireplace door and tossed an all-night log onto the glowing orange flame. Old Moose head proudly hung over the field stone mantel, winking behind celebrity sunglasses that hung low over his nose under his old tilted cowboy hat. Fireplace flames shot up chimney whooshing sparks as the big log's bark caught flame, sending light shadows dancing over the walls and landing on the circa nineteen fifties stuffed Muskie displayed over Abby's make shift pull out futon bed. An old fishing rubber boot stuffed in his mouth, added fun and lightened the stark reality of a tragic death.

Navi's petite fevered lack of exercise frame creaked sliding back under layers of bedding aside old Dawg. Ears tuned into the storm, late for the season, by the weekend, spring melt would take its place, with the world alive and northern touristy cafe patios to upscale city fix bask on. She slid into a deep sleep only to standing surrounded in the familiar mist of the spirit world.

In loneliness, longing and neediness, she called in Soul Skin man.

"Soul Skin Man, I shall take you there, where the grottos cave jutties out into a greater bay. Gentle great lake waves wash in and out; echoing whispers from the ancients, its magical healing waters await our weary souls. Scaling down and into the cave, we stand on a jutting rock ledge and looking down into the cave floor is four feet of water. Look down and deep below you will see; under water surface is a large illuminated hole, light streamers splay up and outward. The illuminated hole is an entranceway, an underground tunnel that makes its way on the other side of the cave wall into the bay. In the winter, when storms rage in from open tremulous deep waters, stalactites of ice hang from the ceiling and as the waves ebb and flow and wind blows through, it is a symphonic harmony of magical tunes that vibrate within every cell. In summer, sulfur springs steam, meeting and swirling water, cleansing and magical. We float on our backs, soothed by gentle cleansing waves. Refreshed somewhat, we dive below, sun streamers lighting our way deep into caverns, communing with lake fish and misplaced corals and anemones. Soul Skin Man, you who once haunted my nighttime dreams and journeys. One day we shall meet in the physical and I shall take you there, to where the grotto's healing waves will cleanse our souls."

"Soul Skin Woman, from the land far south, summer heat and soulful music and if my heart had wings, I would fly you to my home now, this very night. I would hold you in my arms and never let you go. I would love you, for all eternity. If my heart, but had wings."

"So who are you? Are you conjured in my imagination or a real spirit or are you actually alive?"

"I am alive."

"Why do you come to me only on the etheric?"

"I suspect we live very far away from each other."

"I have to tell you that while your visits have helped through the years, it's frustrating. Your words and visits are wildly romantic, but no man I have ever met could possibly live up to that romantic ideal, all of the time."

"I would, and more my love, if destined to be so in this lifetime."

"You know, I want to meet you in person now, and find out the real day to day you."

It was a fantasy, for sure. No earthly man, no earthly relationship could be so romantically magical and real, yet she longed for some companionship manifestation, in the want of filling a David hole that remained unfulfilled.

"NO SHIT?" Loud, catching decorum composure short, rogue northern wilderness country fiftyish Pastor Rene reeled backward in her café patio chair, semi-conscious of glaringly disapproving tourist's eyes. Back straightening, consternation registered, downcast eyes falling into a tall glass of Black Fly lager ale. Bright red custom fingernails traced rivulets of hot summer cool glass sweat beads. Flicking away a mosquito that tickled skin under bangs, her fingers lingered slightly over manicured eyebrow then trailing downward, caressed shoulder length straight hair. Filtering information, with a truth stranger than fiction, she arched back. Rene authoritatively pushed celeb style sunglasses down the nose and glared at the traumatized mysterious dinner companion.

Fever fatigue chilled, Navi adjusted old Hudson Bay Company vintage shawl tighter, its blanket embrace enfolding and cozy. Conscious of its oldness, familiar comfort worn sisterhood embrace connected with ancestors, ancient spiritual sisterhoods and the spirit world.

If she had not experienced the country pastor's depth of compassion first hand and known that she was indeed an Ordained Minister, old school judgmental church upbringing may have disregarded the real life sisterhood friendship door opening at the critical point in a peculiar life. 24-7 was a motto that Rene lived by. Availability to all in crisis, mobile phone slash computer in hand, a lifeline for many. It was a lifeline that never shut up, its ringing and jingling constantly interrupting conversations and distracting driving. Most often the crisis involved the sifting and sorting of petty gossip amongst an aging congregation, akin to Navi's own childhood church life, post Gran's croaking. One would think burn out an inevitable outcome; rather it consistently kept Rene in divine flow of all that is which in turn gave hope, faith, sustenance and life to many, rippling outward in turn positively affecting families, friends and co-workers.

It was a blatant observation that Rene and Navi had begun their work and friendship as stuffed pious suits. Dubious of each other, each maintained social and professional decorum akin to wearing the holy cloth. Now, the antiquity of professional boundaries long ditched in trusting camaraderie, she openly drank beer, swore, donned blue jeans, high heels and bright red manicured nails, a new era of authentic free expression as a woman, while fulfilling a saintly vocation. Congregation here was also shrinking in antiquity, as youth opted out for city life and elders croaked into spirit world. New comers wanted new age revolution. In the moment, Navi wonder questioned their influence on the other.

Catching a soul pain flicker in Navi's watery red eyes peeking over Janis Joplin sunglasses, Rene took a smoke inhale puff and braced for more.

"I shit you not Madame!"

Madame, the term of endearment had become a playful post-menopausal way of acknowledging a sisterhood bond, playfully threatening to answer church phone calls with an enticing; 'Madame Rene Bertram's house of ill repute, how may I service you today?'

Rene intuitively scanned Navi's emotional state, and sensing anguish, consciously flowed waves of comforting divine maternal love. Intentionally enveloping those in crisis with divine love was an innate habit that instinctively passed between the two, often. Outward silent contemplation, while a universe of mind and soul communion flashed, as minds reeled; sorting out pieces of information and filling in puzzle pieces. Gazing at the long auburn greying haired woman, Rene openly wondered, "You are an enigma."

Vulnerably splaying fingers through hair shifting away a wave of tears, Navi abruptly excused herself. Understanding a need for time out to breathe and gather composure, she watched her companion gracefully navigate sardine sun tanned patio tourists huddling under beer labelled umbrellas, enjoying partial shade from mid-afternoon summer sun. Rene lit another cigarette, and then leaning back, blew curling white smoke, twirling the cig between forefinger and thumb. A swirling smoke trail drifted like a magnet to the prohibitionist yuppies beside her. Cigarette smoke was like that; it automatically drifted and hovered into the nostrils of the ones with the most aversion. Like a cat that strolls uninvited amongst a group of people and automatically annoys, molests and demands interaction with the one person who hates cats.

"If you don't like it; tough", grumbled Rene, "or you can bloody well go and sit your asses somewhere else. I am not moving."

Yuppies downed the last of their martinis, dropped a couple of fifty's on the table, lingering in hopes of catching the offending bitch smoker's eye. Failing engagement, they shared a communal disgusting glance, huffed, turned on heels, and left. Had they known whom they were dealing with, a saintly woman whose day consisted of more good deeds than they had done in a lifetime, would they have treated her intrusive cig smoke differently? Had they known from a higher perspective, that their knee jerk judgment barrier was blocking the possibility of a life altering wonderful exchange, would they have taken the time to chat, exchange business cards, and give gratitude for all that she was and did? No. The majority live life, their minds filled with day-to-day stress filled materialistic worries of physical appearance and body self-deprecation, not filled with seeing others through the eyes of God, as divine beings.

Navi had found her way to Rene's small country-wilderness church service four years prior, vulnerable, maintaining shadow discretion in a back pew, until Rene cornered her into awkward introductory conversation. Intuitive soul recognition rapidly blossomed, kindred spirits of like mind and soul, and of "Sisterhood". Flashes of a lifetimes shared, passed in an instant.

Rene caught a fleeting cynical judgment, a questionable past and dark night of the soul. It just did not fit into a sensible large picture. It was common for many to find a robed vocation following devastating life experiences, yet a piece of the puzzle spoke to mysterious pain. It was time to ferret it out into the light of day. She sighed relaxing and allowed a moment between them of modicum comfort level in sharing to pass.

Navi spine straightened, shifting into old social work mentality, "I am binding you to Pastoral Confidence Rene! You cannot tell another living soul. I have to tell someone and since I too am bound not to tell another living soul, can you do this?"

"Yes, of course I can and I will. Consider it done." Rene burned curious to know more, and so mindfully braced herself.

Stunning blonde, golden skinned, boobs on a platter, lacy black cleavage college server, clunked a decrepit dirty old ashtray onto the middle of their table, startling the conversation flow. Sharing unspoken annoyance with impatient yuppies, she made an abrupt exit prior to filling her pocket with large sums of gratuitous tips. No matter, one-day ignorant server would be seeking out one of their pastoral services for some crisis or other, to which both would lovingly oblige. Both ignoring petulant blonde boob monster, thoughts returned to each other.

Navi strained to focus, virus fever still ravaging from within, she searched for a starting point. "I want to know what happened, or how it all happened or how to sort out the residue pieces, so that I can move forward. It's almost like some old bugaboo from the past is about to explode. I want to be soul free, if you know what I mean."

Rene nodded, busying herself with checking phone messages.

Waiting, Navi fever surreal, yet determined to access some higher soul freeing insight, timeline wobbled in and out. Taking a deep sighing breath, allowing what was to come, to sort itself out naturally and comfortably. Focused, slowly mind re-creating the gist of what dramas lay behind, then unintentionally drifted off to spirit Soul Skin Tom's warm calm loving haunting and questionable presence. Straining to see an actual physical body brought a glimpse of his hand, soulful blue eyes that accompanied a soulful melodious song, almost inaudible, stirring intimacy. Singing softly, strange other world comfort, a myriad of other worldly journeys flashed in an instant; as a Jewish prisoner of war and ascending from a death pit, as she wolf running free of captivity in the dark of a cold wintry night to join her pack, as a native woman about to begin the Trail of Tears journey northward, floating in a magical healing grotto, an etheric massive bald eagle spirit visitation arose, then faded, bringing Mother Mary to timely escort her away from eminent highway death to safety, dreams of mystical people of the jade and white brotherhood surrounded, then vanished, as she fell into beach cottage homesickness.

Rene sifted through urgent messages while mindfully contemplating the strange situation at hand. "So I've only ever heard you make one verbal reference to a Rogue Guardian Angel, yet I notice that you consistently add that name to the prayer list every week."

"Well that's not a super short answer. To understand, you've got to know a bit more about the man."

Shifting comfortable, Rene relaxed as Navi searched for a memory starting point.

"I suppose his story began the afternoon Abby and I were leaving Catharine's to come here. There must have been something wildly cosmic, some lunar, or solar, or astrological, or universal alignment that day, that month, shit that whole year. We had to stay at Robert's other house for a few days in between Catharine's and coming here so that we could make arrangements.

While Abby and I hung our hats there, we were staying at Catharine's one last night, cleaning and packing. Meanwhile, unbeknownst to Robert, a midnight rescue of a teenaged girl acquaintance actually became an undercover police arranged sting operation that went terribly wrong. He had settled the girl in his own home, the other guest room for the night; while he slept, she proceeded to drug over dose; suicide. Promptly charged and convicted, it had been a bizarre sting set up by a handful of bad police officers that sought revenge from another of his heroic interventions years earlier. Many years earlier, he had then also unwittingly stumbled upon two well-dressed men kidnapping a young woman; forcing her into the backseat of a sedan. Saving that girl was the beginning of a long sordid undercover operation. He didn't know it at the time, but those well-dressed men were part of a larger group of police officers, gone bad, bad to the bone. He had interrupted a kidnapping and human trafficking foray.

I didn't know it at the time, but he had often been a Special Forces unit investigator on the sly, high tech computer work, and various other mystery contracts. This was a simple rural do good man who often bought entire skids of food, delivering anonymously to a gully tented homeless community. A seemingly biker mechanic man existence who raised and donated tens of thousands of dollars monthly to local charities and donated skids of teddy bears and toys for children's services at Christmas time. Yet, the most pivotal of his heroic acts had inadvertently caught up with him in a bizarre twist of fateful revenge. Man, you think you know that humble mechanic across town, but he is actually involved in high 007 intrigue.

Anyway, when he stumbled upon those two well-dressed men scuffling with that distraught girl, he one man massive tattooed muscles flexing machine took them both down in the dark of night. Waiting calmly, he allowed the one suit to throw the first punch. In one swift movement, he promptly took out both of their kneecaps. Suits downed, he motioned for the girl to go into the pub and get help, to call the police.

A mere hour later, confused in jail, he realized that they were actually off duty police officers. One whom had a notorious mob and drug cartel connection that networked throughout the county and beyond. This one black suited mad hornet suit let it slip that Robert had interrupted a long string of kidnapping girls, heavily drugged and prostituted out. She had apparently tried to make a sly getaway earlier that evening. Tossed into a dark alley, beaten near to death, Robert slowly crawled to a gas station; one phone call brought an ex-military Special Forces friend. Many were convicted; some took their own lives following public and familial humiliation except that one Bad Ass remained mysteriously untouched.

'Keep your friends close; keep your enemies closer', Robert once said. Had he known, he would've still answered the woman's distress call. That's just the kind of man he was. Boy, it was just a wild convergence, a multitude of forces simultaneously heading for derailment into one massive head-on collision.

I had absolutely no idea any of this was going at the time. I had just left Robert's house, picking up his cabin and truck keys that fateful night. I was in a rush, or perhaps divinely guided away in a hurry before the bad assed police officer began his wait and watch from across the road. I gather that Bad Ass Suit had waited years for sweet revenge and for Robert to let his guard down, to slip up. Apparently, Robert was hot on his trail too and close to exposing a drug, human trafficking prostitution ring, other dirty cops and a handful of prominent county officials; a hot conspirator Hollywood style movie about to go south.

Bad Ass Black Suit had coerced this particular young woman into the sting, as bait, but she had concocted a plan of her own, a way out. Once Robert was asleep, she emptied a bottle of pills into her young body; a terrible way out of a dark and sordid coerced life of drugs and prostitution. Robert was safe haven and so it was that he collided with fate. She died that night. A second girl, best friend and confidant, the only witness to the suicide plan, died before court hearings, a mysterious overdose. During interrogation she was rendered utterly useless, barely alive, soulless and lost in drugged tainted fear and could only comply under duress to dirty cop control. The truth of what really went down that fateful night, silenced.

Meanwhile, I vacillated between vomiting and running with anxiety, trying to drive but had to keep stopping. All I knew was that something bad was going down somewhere and that for some strange reason; I was sharing the experience. When I tried to sleep, I just writhed with foreboding and haunting nightmares of a drug-induced death, a mistake. It was freaking Abby out because she was also seeing and sensing a ghostly young woman clawing at her psyche. It was as though the girl realized too late, the mistake and was trying to come back to life. Spirit girl haunted us both all night with a sickly moaning begging for help. Our prayers for divine intervention did little to dissipate the horrible apparition vomiting and emotional torment. At daybreak, she finally let go, begged apology and left into the light.

It was an unconscious drive with only Polly and Catharine knowing that we were going to Algonquin Park for an extended vacation. Our old church community had pretty much long folded and faded. Looking back on all of those old doors closing, there really wasn't anyone left in our support networks. My Father died years ago. My Mother and Aunt Diane had just passed away. I do remember pleading with two church elders for support and intervention, and none knew what to say or do. God, I still remember their abhorrent facial reactions, stuck in my soul. I just felt so ashamed. You know, it wasn't someone's house burnt to the ground or a terminal illness; not an acceptable crisis.

Our Pastor was away having a hip replacement. It was the final door to life in our little beach community that had rudely slammed closed. I was so ashamed of the predicament and just didn't know what else to do or where else to go other than head for Robert's cabin. So we set out with a mere half a tank of gas, the clothes on our backs, a cooler of food and the grace of God. A new life chapter stood waiting. Looking back on it all now, being away from all of the Stephen, David and Robert drama was nothing short of a miracle and angelic intervention. God, we cocoon slept and ate for days in healing silence. I think I still am. Abby is more resilient.

Rene, the problem is that one of Robert's convictions was possession for marijuana; it was mine, wait no, sort of. It was enough to constitute trafficking but it really was not mine, my friend Catharine had sent it thinking that it might help relax me, just her home-grown back yard 'medicinal herb'. I would never have that sort of thing in my house. I completely forgot about it. I am not even sure I would recognize it in a garden. Did you know that you could get Organic Brain Disease from long-term use? I don't know if that's really true or not, David told me once that it mimics all sorts of cognitive functioning disorders. I guess the oily residue sticks to and clogs up brain neurons.

When I fessed, Robert just glibly chuckled, "No Navi, you sure as shit cannot own up to that one and Catharine must never know, it would only upset her and Abby needs you. No, what's another four months? Better me." He had said it so sternly and confidently, like there was no other option that at the time, it felt rational that I allowed myself in the moment to sway. Surely the right thing to do, would be to tell the detective and Catharine and allow us to make our own determination and do the right thing? Without a doubt, totally and utterly he adamantly, as if he knew a higher road, simply and calmly made that choice. Flipping back into my moral altruistic soul, surely there was something I could do! I could get in touch with an investigative journalist, a private detective or better yet, the media. As though reading my mind, he added, "NO!" Robert was adamant then taking a firm stance, made me swear an oath to confidence, as I make you swear Rene! I am still having one dilly of a time trying to make peace, knowing that one of those charges is because of the kindness of one of my friends.

"Jesus, Navi! Jesus, it's a good thing you weren't more involved!" Rene arched her back, thoughtfully hesitated, then added "And who in the hell is Tom?"

Startled, "I don't know any Tom, at least, not in the physical. I can't think about that now Rene."

"All right, all right, all else in good time but back up, a way up. Truthfully, I am itching to know more about your journey and you still really haven't explained how on earth you did ended up at Robert's cabin."

College blonde Playboy magazine centerfold breasted server interrupted with a bill dramatically laid on the table, then tersely motioned to a long line forming at patio entrance. Off hand, annoyed acknowledgement wave by Rene, the bosomed blonde brat monster stood solid ground. A formidable feline alpha she dog standoff.

Rene glanced upward into sun streamers that washed over massive angelic boobs. A sly grinning Rene peered over celeb sunglasses as a powerful calm yet terse professor to a delinquent student, "You just ate your tip, you know that, right?"

Blonde boob petulant princess monster's pouting face flushed red. Suppressing an inner wave of anger, she huffed, front pillow mass bobbed, then turning, followed after her. Momentarily taken in with the drama unfolding, they watched as dejected boob monster guffawed, then abruptly walked toward the line-up; switching to fake charm 'I'm your new best friend' smile upon golden made up face to the impatient patrons.

"Come on, let's go and sit at the pier for a bit. I am turning off my phone, so let me just grab a picnic blanket out of the car."

"I don't know of any other way, than to start at the beginning of the end of times with David, and with my job. It had been such a promising new beginning." Feeling better, questions answered through the sharing and content, "But, that's a story for another time. Thanks for listening Rene."

"Anytime Navi. I sense that you are on the cusp of many soul freeing changes. Give me a call soon, I am cooking up some ideas that I'd like to share with you."

It had been the first Navi had spewed and hashed it all out, freer for the intimate sharing. Despite the lingering unknown inner dark shadow, Navi slowly began to find joy and reverence for life. Simpler habits brought a sense of stability; such as it was, which brought an allowing nature's magic to show itself, to commune. Daily meandering lakeshore walks blended with growing wildlife familiarity. Snake shed its soul skin, then mated, breeding a new family under the back deck. Spring, summer and fall, the babbling creek that fed into the greater bay, danced with dragonflies. Caterpillars cocooned and emerged as glorious winged creatures. Late night starry skies displayed Northern Lights, magical green and yellow haloed wave strands of sound tones, which reverberated within her cells and senses. A large owl guarded the main road entrance, swooping up unsuspecting rabbits, squirrels and a dislocated possum. Rogue Guardian Angel car mechanic Robert's cabin had become a sanctuary.

Relationship grief and searching too hard for an unauthentic life can be a torturous, haunting, nagging, creature existence. Tethers and strands of nagging regrets, emotions, habits and intimacies shared; remain intertwined within each other's souls long after a physical relationship ceases. For some, it is simply water off a ducks back, for others it takes a lifetime, maybe lifetimes, to right the wrongs. In time, an unconscious allowing, shifts all into a new life, a natural detaching process. Attachment strands of loyalty and expectations slowly dissipate, while spiritual bonds remain beyond a lifetime.

Navi shifted and sorted, striving to allow the positive gifts of love and growth to flourish forth, while allowing all that was known, familiar and safe of her former life, to calm and adjust. While Matt, Polly, Gary and Catharine had moved on in a good way, without her, there was still lingering concern regarding the men in her life. First, there was T.J., Stephen and then, David. There was that elusive spirit Soul Skin man who freely moved backward and forward in time, seemingly at will, and often without her.

Though she recalled little memory of life without the dark haunting shadow, and strange dream journeys, conscious mind aimed gravitating to the best of what was; she had to, there was Abby; reason d'être.

Robert's warm welcome had been good medicine for the two drama weary souls. Such it is, healing begins when one door is abruptly closed, others *will* open. His words still rang within her mind, waiting for the higher truths to take hold. "I understand that you are coming out of the Dark Night of The Soul. I recognize it when I see it. Been there, and done that one. It is not your fault, shit happens to good souls all of the time, without thoughtful premonition or pre-consultation. If you can figure out what your fear, guilt and shame hooks are, you will find soul freedom. As you change within, you can also help others to do so, to live within the heart and spirit.

His parting words, "You need calm many, many relaxing drifting days. Light and love my friend, is all that there is."

"Thanks for everything Robert; I pray for you every day."

Drifting off to sleep, sliding into a heavy fog mist, she found herself walking through a park. Walking along the riverside, with the Boat Slips Marina Café still off in the distance. People milled about, children romped in the playground. Late afternoon sun filter streamed through large old trees, as a small pudgy blonde haired boy on the fringe of an adult caught her attention. The boy stood still, face blank of expression; striking navy blue eyes, staring at her, somehow, holding her. Navi stopped in her tracks smiling, adjusted herself to the boy. She glanced at the man standing behind, semi engaged in conversation, looking for a cue, a go-ahead and it's okay response from the obvious older version of the boy. With a smile and a go-ahead nod, he turned his attention back to the chat.

'Allo'. The boy stood still, expressionless, voiceless. "Well...my name is Navi. What's yours?"

Blankly, "James."

Navi's body responded with a smile, there was a familiarity with the boy.

As the thought registered into consciousness, Navi noticed the boy's eyes pulsate. Curiously gazing at them, she realized that they weren't just 'blue' they were indigo with tiny subtle flecks of magenta and shards of light that twinkled momentarily, long enough to catch her attention. In a flash, Navi saw the universe, the stars, and the cosmos with galaxies spinning, swirling and expanding, shrinking, and dissipating, then expanding all over again.

Navi smiled, and her attention withdrew back from the cosmos to the boy child in front of her. With face still expressionless, the boy held his arms up to her, for a pick up. She glanced at the father, who smiling at them, nodded a 'go ahead' then smiled at the boy. Bending with heart and arms wide, the boy reached up on his toes and in a moment embraced her with child's love. It was as though the little boy child primate became part of her, inside her own soul, their two distinct physical and individual selves melded into one being.

It had been a very long time since daughter embraced this way. It had also seemed as though only a year away, that in dream sleep, Soul Skin man had embraced her this way, two souls blending and melding as 'one'. Tears of joy welded into her eyes as he nuzzled his head into the nape of her neck, showing no signs of moving, equally content to hold the embrace, the 'oneness' of the moment.

Holding, she spun him around in a pivotal circle, his legs splaying out from the inertia as their simultaneous giggle washed through within, as one being of joy. She set him down, while grasping for and holding his hand as not to lose the connection. A podgy little hand, slid warm, soft and loving into hers. They exchanged knowing glances then turned attention to his father once again. Yet again, he returned her smile and a nod of 'go ahead'. With hand in hand, they skipped, jumped and zigzagged along the path. Spinning and swaying him as in a waltz to inner ears, as sun streamers flashed through leaves, splaying light streams upon them; as though once upon a time they had danced in a great cosmic ballroom.

Navi returned the boy to the father, the boy stood still expressionless, watching her walk away.

Continuing down the path along the riverside, she headed toward what looked like a cafeteria, hunger grumblings and full bladder stirring within. As she approached, the boy, his father and friends were already in line ahead of her. The boy turned, maintaining father handhold and stared at her yet again. 'How on earth did they get here before me?' She wondered. Inside the pavilion, through an entryway of vending machines, a washroom.

She found herself instead, sitting at a long empty table with a lone blonde haired woman on her immediate right. Scanning the room for familiar tangibles and seeing nothing but a shimmer of sunset light flashing through the window; blinding. Where was she? How had she arrived, and where had the time gone leading to 'here'? The people milling about the room looked comfortable and relaxed, as some casually chatted, while busily arranging food on a buffet table. Seeing no one remotely familiar, off balance and disorientated, she fought for mental and emotional self-control in a moment of panic. She was anxious to run, but did not know from where to where. She stifled an outcry, not wanting to draw attention.

She glanced sideways, out of the corner of her eye, to the woman sitting on her right. She wondered why the woman was sitting so close, when the room had so many empty seats. She would never have chosen to sit immediately beside a stranger, unless it was the only seat left in the room. The woman, sitting quietly, turned slightly to acknowledge her, then gently took and embraced her hand reassuringly, calming. A moment of strange anxiety and rejection flashed through her, followed by a warm wave washing; calm emotions rippled through her body and mind.

Suddenly sitting in a different pavilion room, a smaller group of people calmly milled about preparing a buffet table, some chatting, no one familiar. Yes, the room was smaller and much nicer with rough pine walls and comfortable furniture, the door opening and closing quietly as yet another person entered. Still empty seats within the room, the only other person sitting, was the dark haired woman sitting immediately to her right. Her heart thumped, eyes darting, scanning this smaller room, searching for familiarity, 'Where am I? Who are these people? How did I get here? What am I doing here? Who is this woman?' Attention turned and looking out through the window, darkness of late evening and night stars appeared. With the urge to flee again, she looked to the door, as the boy with the indigo eyes and his father entered. Still searching for familiarity and balance, she strove to regain composure and any semblance of self-control.

Indigo-eyed boy still in father's hand approached a small group of chattering people. The boy turned and stood starring directly into her soul. His father smiled in acknowledgement, then returned to his conversation. The man was obviously a leader, as he commanded an air of respect. Fighting a wave of disorientation fear, she glanced to the door again, and watched as a man calmly enters the room, door closing behind, to the dark-haired woman sitting at her side. 'Why are we sitting so close? No one else is sitting down. Who are you? Where am I? How did I get here?' The woman calmly reached and held her hand on top of Navi's, a wave of calm and caring washing through her. Without looking directly, it was as though the woman spoke in Navi's head, rather than to her.

"You are 'Mind Shifting' Navi Anna Jehanne Chickadee. And these are your people."

"Only my Gran called me that; 'Chickadee'. Mind Shifting?"

"Yes, you have been mind-shifting into different realities. All realities being similar yet differ, like trying on many shoes, yet of the same size. The common denominator is, 'you'. Is, 'us'."

Navi allowed herself a moment to wrap her mind around it all and could not, yet it all seemed strangely familiar.

"Yes, it would be familiar to you. It has just been awhile. You've been sleeping, thinking that you were 'awake'."

"These people feel strangely familiar. I do not know them, yet I feel as though I do. Familiar and friendly."

"Yes, we are a sort of family, you might say."

"I don't know who you are, but I feel as though I like you, really care for you."

"Yes, we are good friends."

"So, who are these people?"

"We, you, are a group within the Brotherhood of Light. Indigo boy is your Soul Skin boy."

Navi bolted upright in bed still fevering, sleepy eyes registering familiarity, followed by a wave of rejection. 'God, what in the hell am I still doing here at Robert's hunt camp? Dawg, under feet, roused in alarm, he stretched, yawned, circled, then settled back in a curl and dozed. Winter blizzard winds pounded the old log timbers, the massive stone boulder foundation stood solidly firm. Snow pellets wisped against rattling windows, sending goose bumps across her skin. Old stone fireplace flickered shadows were illuminating the open concept one room cabin. The Moose head lovingly named Ed, hung over the mantle, marble eyes shimmering behind sunglasses, with a straw cowboy hat; tilted. A natural propensity for naming the animal kingdom within her surroundings, it gave an extended family feel, alleviating the loneliness of rural isolation.

Beside Ed's watchful stance over the mantle rested a handmade drum. Water coloured ivy painted its taut deerskin, crow and grouse feathers adorning its trim. Drumbeating is gateway, allows altered states of consciousness, the wombs heartbeat that connects us all to mothering, and to safe journey between the physical and spiritual worlds. Adorning feathers, winged creatures carried messages from the spirit worlds. A handmade squash gourd rattle and a painted ochre clay pot rested on an old tambourine, resting, and waiting, for an occasion with Abby. Perhaps a sisterhood grounding cleansing ceremony on a warm summer's lakeside evening bonfire with Northern Lights, loons with a distant wolf howl backdrop.

The old pull out futon couch and patchwork quilt was daughter's home away from University home. The large stuffed Muskie fish boldly hung on the back bed nook wall, its blind bulging black eyes watching as she slept. Abby had named him Anemone, a rolled cigarette insinuating a marijuana joint in its formidable gapping jaw. A photocopy of Joan of Arc, holding a triple crossed sword adorned the work desk wall. A nineteen seventies record player screeched Jimi Hendrix's 'Little Wing' as Navi dance swirled with an imaginary sword in hand, Merlin, Jedi, Warrior Shaman woman and conjurer and former social services worker gone client bush wacked, happy.

A tiny kitchen off to the left, the ceiling dangled strands of dried wild chives, sweet grass, sage and roses hung upside from the rafters. Tiny drops of white mottled chicken poop remained on rafter cross beams, unreachable to clean. Grinning, Navi recalled their first night moving into the cabin, waking to find a dozen chickens had roosted in the rafters, squawking, drizzling white slimy mucous poop throughout the inside of the cabin. Like a queen bee assuming new territory, bothered by intruders, the annoyed runaways from distant neighbour's coup held firm. Mother and daughter blanketed each squawking clawing beast, setting them free outdoors, then ferociously cleaned and set up house, only to spend days afterward in battle with bats and bears.

The only uncovered year round window, in the living room, offered partial bay view, lined with cutting granite rocky shoreline and evergreens. An old fish-filleting scrubbed table now splayed stacks of ministry course textbooks, research papers, an overflowing ashtray, a spider's web, and a computer. A rubber Tyrannosaurus Rex lay atop computer screen, erotically holding its paws over primordial male parts.

Buckets of open lake water lined the indoor woodpile. Once a chipmunk had waited until midnight to announce its wood accompanied entrance, squealing and darting wildly, a lunatic Dawg barking and chasing it, cornered in the toilet room.

For the first four long years, a silent pissing battle ensued, as a young female bear insisted on enjoying the compost bin. Navi removed the bin, realizing that She-Bear would return repeatedly, knowing food bits were readily available. Ramona She-Bear had wandered in that first spring and assumed Buddha lotus style position at the bin, casually munching away on Abby's vegetarian remnants, while the girls were washing outside windows. Standing safely back, they admired her youthful clumsy bulk, black fur shimmering, spring shedding mottle drifting off into the wind, to become a winged creatures nesting material.

One week later, Ramona She-Bear arrived again, and annoyed to find compost bin empty, headed for the cabin. Windows open wide, lunch lay on the table, warm breezes carried drifting aromas to a hungry spring bear. Wondering what to do, Abby had quickly grabbed a metal trashcan lid and a stick, advancing assertively toward the bear, she banged, shouting 'HEYAW HEYAW HEYAW'. Ramona She-Bear, acquiesced and hunched in submission, then bolted, crashing deep into the forest.

The next day, the diner outpost's cook had dramatically shared that they had arrived to find the kitchen being ransacked by a sow bear. Her red neck husband, born to northern life, had just purchased a load of fireworks, still in his trunk. He aimed them, one by one, over Ramona she-bear's head and fired one after the other. Terrified, Ramona she-bear bolted into the forest. It had taken a week for the staff to repair that kitchen, claw marks embedded in the French fry making machine, the door fencing bars, easily bent under tummy grumbling bear paws. Loafs of half eaten bread discarded, shelves tossed, plastic honey tubs emptied and piled in a sticky mountain.

"Research is what I'm doing when
I don't know what I'm doing."
Werner Von Braun

Chapter 22 ~ Final Pieces

Days spent wandering the shoreline; a final thesis slowly took form. One month later, the thesis returned with an A+ and a completed transcript. Navi's history and lifestyle seemed an enigma to her superiors, waited to see where she was going with the vocation. Fully academically an inter-faith minister, it would soon be time for ordination credentials. A ministry vocation transition had yet to align, resistance continued. Simply without aspirations for all matters traditional Minister, yet not yet knowing what if anything would come of it all. Had it simply been a cathartic undertaking? Shifting the mind into higher contemplation, which slowly healed a traumatic soul?

"I still don't know what I am going to do for a living! God!!! I know that you are out there. I've got a daughter to look after still, graduating and coming home soon."

"Mind Shift."

"What? What the hell? Just how am I supposed to do that?"

"Chickadee, let go of illusions of whom you think you ought to be, and be you, out in the world. You are medicine woman, shaman, warrior, saint, sage, mystic, lifter of veils, and seer sensitive. You are all of these things and so much more. Your genetic lineage, your life's work, dictates that you will soon emerge from your cocoon, without stigma. Your authentic emerging has been pre-ordained since the dawn of eternity. You will raise many, many eyebrows, and many will gasp speechless, within your bold words. Your pen will be mightier than any sword. The masses that are ill from oppression, and the misguided norms, cloaked in 'how they ought to be' expectations, will un-cloak, and unfurl their own unique wings, and fly in soul freedom. For many, your eyes reflecting their own divine nature will see a higher-light truth, and their broken spirits will be lifted once again, and they will soar over rainbows and oceans.

As you allow illusions of expectations of the world to fall away, you will find that neither you, nor others, have ever been broken or wronged. Love thyself enough to boldly take a stand, write of the truths and insights of your journeys, and share them with those who want to hear it. Some will balk, many will ignore, yet many more will be inspired to find their own authentic nature, thus freely and creatively contributing to a better world. To love oneself though hope is a tiny seed against seeming insurmountable odds, and to love and dream despite doubt and grief, is the true path of the divine. Traits of mastery are awakening within your soul. Immortal journeys and ancient memories within others must be awakened and must be shared."

Unsure of what Gran's key point was, Navi, instead, jam-piled chunks of wood into the fireplace, sword poking at coals, squinting and bending sideways, away from rude smoke entrails. Missing Abby, Navi cloaked old shawl, curled into her patchwork quilt, and curled by the fireplace.

Bolting away, travelling through a strange light flowing wave, out into the universe, causally admiring stars and planets passing by. An abrupt landing, solid ground beneath her feet, the mist dissipated to the sound of a northern lakeshore, with calm night water gently rolling against the pebbled shoreline. Night darkness displayed expansive sky, filled with shimmering stars and a full moon. Bare foot on cold wet pebbles, as a gentle warm breeze stirred her white cotton dress and two long braids. Ankle bracelet, sinew with beads, stark native accessorized atop her white skin, contrasting indigenous affinity with spirit world, and nature against late eighteen hundreds era, and social cultural norms, for a mid-life white woman.

In hand lay a knurled wooden stick, with a tiny white crystal embedded in its tip. Vibrating slightly, catching her awareness and attention, alive and shimmering, it willed her to play. Swirling, Merlin style, dress waving outward; on tiptoes, hair braids lifted, it awaited her bidding.

The low-end tip, turning it over in hand, was a quill. An inkwell lay at her feet. Dipping in, and watching the dark blue ink drip, the wand shivered, as tiny spark lights flowed out of the tip and rose into the dark night sky, blending with the stars.

Wand-power; to awaken and see beyond the norm and into the universe, with visions of oneness and all of creation. Dare to dream a life filled with spiritual wonders, adventures, love and laughter.

Crow cawed from a distant tree. Soul Skin man morphed within Crow, his claws tight on a branch. "It is indeed a lonely path for an angel such as thee. All of the world loves a halo, better yet, one that is tarnished and advocacy battled. When walls crumble around you, voices shout out in higher truth, resisting fear, the ground beneath your feet shakes and gives way, remember then woman, that the hands of God and all of spirit world will catch you. Stray you, never again from our world of magical rainbows, sunshine, otter play, wolf howls and moonlit nights. Stay the course, walk your talk, write your words, and wait for the assurance of next step. You will know when you know."

"Hi Gran, long time no talk to. How's Mother? Father? Aunt Diane?"

"All are well. I have been waiting for you."

"I know that now. Geez, where have you been?"

"Did you see the sunset? I made that just for you."

"Yes, uh huh, sure you did. Ha."

"Welcome back, my little Chickadee."

"Thanks Gran, it's good to be back talking with you. To say that I've missed you and everyone in the spirit world would be an understatement."

"I never left you. We never left you."

"I know that, I was aware of you but I still don't understand how on earth I crashed and burned so deep."

"Those insights and more are almost upon you. What now, my Darling?"

"I have no idea."

"All in good time Chickadee."

"I love you, I love you all."

"I love you too Darling, we all love you more than you know."

Clad in bathing suits in the dark of midnight, Navi and temporary home daughter, batted away swarms of buzzing spring mosquitoes that dive-bombed ravenous for blood through open skin and eyes. Black flies snuck in under hairlines, behind ears, up nostrils and under eyelids. Smoldering cedar and pine boughs drifted out of the makeshift native lodge, held the winged creatures at bay, so it was there, that they sat. Relaxing, skin and eardrums vibrated as distant peeper frog wild spring matting frenzied.

Whilst entering the sweat lodge, a whooping crane swooped overhead, its massive brown wings spanning the breath of the camp. Its squawking sounding more pterodactyl, it scouted the lake water's surface, keeping watch for fish, frogs and other amphibious life. Clumsy Black Bear toddled nearby, crashing through the underbrush, sniffing at the two-legged stench in the air, calmly acknowledged the forest visitors, greeting-growled UMPHUMP, and then ambled off deep into bush.

A full clockwise circle to assigned sit squatting spot, sweat beaded and poured from foreheads and arm pits, eyes adjusting to darkness, smoldering cedar and steam from campfire heated rocks.

The young half-breed indigo leader; Bear Spirit Talker, assumed his position clad only in hair braids and blanket shawl. Smudging sage and cedar wafted to upside-down basket style sweat lodge, made from tree branch frame and tarp outer layers. His low confident and knowing voice, softly whispered ancient indigenous prayers in invocation, ancestors invited, in gratitude. In humid darkness, each guest respectively listened in contemplative solitude, at one with the ancestral spirit world, soul, and creation. A rattle shaken, a cup of water poured onto hissing hot rocks emitted thick strands of moist white steam, flaring nostrils, as sweat dripped from faces and under arms.

Ancient Grandfather teaching shared, stories of divine feminine, prophecies of a new world emerging out of archaic old era of victim mentality, healed, stirred and inspired. Intuitively knowing of the teachings, prophecies and spirit world communion, she drifted off into contemplation, her postgraduate thesis writing itself and validated.

In striving to find her own authentic nature and stand strong in the truth of what role she was to assume outside of church and social norms, and yet still, of the many otherworldly journeys, surfacing was a concept of oneness that was transforming her heart and soul. Though aware of a separate physical body or form and mind, there was a golden connecting fiber, tissues and strands akin to an umbilical cord, of community mind, soul and consciousness to spirit world. Hope.

Navi's thoughts drifted back to that one defining late winter night of restlessness, when life with Stephen was about to end, as otherworldly journeys amplified in intensity and meaning. It was a bold and daring higher truth, fully realizing now, that she had never been separate from anything or different in any detrimental way. Each person's path is a spiritual path, no matter their beliefs and concepts might be. All of life is evolving, despite what and how media and materialistic elites portray life to be. All of life is sacred.

Both Stephen and David offered the world marvelous creative talents, bringing fresh perspectives, insights and thought provoking gifts through their work. They were creative and sensitively challenged souls. Their pain, journey and angst, did not belong to her. Brilliant creative minds, just fuddling along life's path, like millions of others unable to cope and lost in their addictions. All of mankind was progressing through an adolescent coming of age, sifting and sorting through external pressures, trying to conform to social norms, while inner battling out of the box longings for autonomous uniqueness and recognition. For the brilliant creative souls, their minds travel to access distant realms, making day-to-day life unfathomable at times. Seeing the analogy within her life, she allowed wasteful regrets and sorrows of loves lost and drama, gently and lovingly dissipate.

When the dark night of the soul fades, finally raw and humble enough to allow higher thoughts to flow, we find our true authentic nature. None of which comes attached to religious idols, or a specific doctrine to be worshipped, but rather, with a simple knowledge of our integral part in higher divineness. Finding the flow within and without is an inarticulate knowing. What masters speak of as; faith. How does one know that wind exists? Can you see it? Touch it? How does one know that one loves another? Illogical, impractical, often immoral, always unconditionally existing, simply is; loving in nature. A mind, body and soul space, where time stops surreal in respect, awe and reverence for all of life.

It had been a long arduous journey, to this point. The years absorbed in schoolwork had served to feed mind and forge balance in the real world of insulated wilderness existence within the spirit world. Feeling freer of the shackles of conformity and gaining confidence, the shadow nemesis from the past still lingered, haunting and elusive, a memory that might explain why given all that she had learned, she still failed to thrive in the real world.

A Thanksgiving colour explosion extravaganza swirled and danced in cold northern winds, warning that precious autumn wanted to be relished. Get out and enjoy, soon the wintery snows would descend in blankets of grey and white. A long-standing arrangement with the redneck alcoholic down the road, cords of chopped wood and random snow plowings haphazardly appeared in exchange for home baked goods. The odd car repair bills and groceries were bartered for with the mechanics' aging mother, respite care provided part time, each day. Gas and other incidentals were bargained for in exchange for cooking French Fries on Thursdays and Fridays at the diner, feeding rough loggers and dusty miners.

A lifestyle far removed from the white-collar professional existence; cabin far removed from pool, expansive gardens and beach bumming. Somehow, through the drama and turmoil, Navi, Abby and Dawg had landed safely and graciously intact.

"Ah Gran, I can feel you."

"Chickadee, every circumstance that comes your way is part of a perfect plan to convert your thoughts and beliefs into having faith in a higher state of existence. Open your mind and heart, remember your words to your children; follow the path of most light, the choice of most light and love. The light will guide your way; *know* this. Feel the divine love, and practice nonattachment toward another's' pain. Consider and remember that while they may never tell you, they too do indeed miss you and your light. Stay bold and strong in this knowing. Life is a journey. Allow good, love and light. Many will come."

Attention turned to gratitude of her wilderness cabin home, where nature abounded with wild deer, moose, turkeys, eagles and grouse. Postgraduate thesis took form as the first flecks of snow danced in the grey air. The lake still alive with weekenders, the marina patio packed with snowsuit clad and noisy winter tourists. Soon the snow would be deep and lake water, a frozen highway for pickup trucks, snowmobilers and cross-country skiers. Navi, donned her shawl, poured a fresh cup of perked coffee, and settled in the lounge chair on the deck, as winter vacationing Abby and her girl pals jumped into the old pickup truck, off to a party down the lake. Looking skyward, a brilliant full moon hovered over a giant evergreen. A man renting the cabin down the road had arrived earlier in the day, and then proceeded to drink heavily, alone by his campfire, listening to blaring reggae, an odd sound in the wilderness. Old shawl donned, three pairs of woolen socks and toque against the chilly autumn breeze, she relaxed. A dozen wild turkeys mingled about the bird feeder seed carcasses scattered amongst the leaves and dying grass. Heads, chicken pecking and bobbing, brown luminescent feathers adjusting, defending feeder from invading blue jays and chickadees. The wild turkeys were the giveaway eagles who wandered cabin surroundings in droves, having escaped Thanksgiving dinners, and now anxiously awaiting Christmas dinner to pass.

Navi turned the key, firing the old truck to attention, rumbling it to life. 'Thank God', she thought, 'hopefully I'll get another winter out of it'. Barreling down the old dirt road, wild turkeys scattered. At a rising small crest around a bend, a massive bull moose stood in the middle of the road. Navi cautiously braked, slowing to a stop, intuitively reading his mood, hoping that he would not turn and ram the truck. Dark brown mottle fur and ragged massive antlers wavered, Massive Male Moose stood majestic, boldly starring, snorting, challenging.

Grabbing her video camera, she gingerly filmed as Moose drifted closer, staring, and sniffing the air for her scent. Tilting his head side to side, he circled the truck; then bored, gallivanted off into the bush.

Once back home, computer software installed and on a creative whim, she added a mixture of native drumming, loons, wolf howls and Peeper frogs. A mini movie unfolded entitled; Life Rocks', followed by added text; a thesis synopsis for a ministry text book manuscript, then left it uploading onto the Internet.

Taking her camera back outside, the late season summer'ish warmth confused dragonflies groggily danced in sun streams as a wing fluttering grouse wandered to the bottom deck step beside. Film recording, "What an amazingly calm creature with sweet cooing sounds" she whispered. "Grouse dances the spiral dance, found in aboriginal dancing for lifting spirits to higher realms; ascension. What a wonder of life is coming back; magic, hope and peace. They say that when bad things happen to good people, and yes, yes you too are good people, it's often because they will become even better teachers, guides, and helpers, to those who will one day need them to be their anchoring rock. A seasoned sage once asked; well what do you want now? I thought I knew once, with certainty. All of life is a work in progress. This is Navi, author of 'Life Rocks' an ancient new perspective on world religion and spirituality. Stay tuned for future video blogs of life in the northern wilderness. Over and Out."

Winter had brought a brief Christmas Abby visit, thesis engrossed, winter rapidly evolved into spring. A long winter quickly passed, time forgotten, immersed in research.

Shawl wrapped, scissors in one hand, dog treats, leash, a pair of pliers and bottle of 'medicinal use only tequila' in the other, Navi coaxed a limping whining meek old Dawg out onto the deck. Leashed onto a short chain, she cooed and soothingly massaged him into calm submission. Fingers dipped into Tequila, she rubbed the harsh fiery liquid around his tongue, gums and teeth. Balking, cringing and backing up, he butted against the railing and feigned a wounded howl distress. Bottle tilted, guzzled slug for self, she shivered and cringed, rejecting the bitter taste, wild fire ran through his veins. Another dip of fingers and swirl around his tongue and teeth, Dawg slumped over onto his side, content, tongue dangling, as a drool pool formed onto her foot. Pliers in hand, she braced his body against her chest, little furry head held firm in the crook of one arm. With a finger slid into his jaw side she clamp-braced his mouth wide open. Twenty-four porcupine quills surgically pulled; their tiny hook ends embedded into his jaw, gums, forehead, and neck. Scissors in hand, she then gingerly removed massive burr clusters that had bound into his fur, freeing their mini barbed thorns that dug into tender canine skin. Snuggling Dawg under, within the old shawl, cooing, she sat on the deck step, back against railing, taking in the lake view. Another pre-spring storm was brewing.

"Well, I guess we know who won that battle, huh Dawg. I'm pretty sure that your nemesis porcupine friend-enemy fared better than you, darling. You know that you are just too old for those games now."

There would be no sunset. Slush spring snow seemed even more bone chilling that normal winter snows, its heavy moisture dampened to the core. Dawg licked his lips and nose drooled, soaking up maternal attention, happily stoned and relieved that the embedded battle shrapnel was gone.

"Guess I'll get a good fire going early tonight. I'll make you a fresh bed by the fire to warm your old bones."

A chilling cold wind curled and snuck down her neck and under the old shawl. Cradling Dawg in arms, she stuck out a foot and pushed the rest of the surgical tools closer to the door, then ventured in. Stoking the fire for just the right temperature was an art form, long ago mastered. The fireplace had once been an old style open hearth; then sometime during the nineteen seventies, an insert was added, thankfully. Glass doors ajar slightly, for maximum air input large fire quick start; ripping shards of oranges and yellows consumed the kindling. Whooshing and gathering speed, she closed the door, hinged and turned down the damper. A good ten minutes to take hold, then a medium log could be added, then onto the larger, harder, all night logs, intermittently until bedtime.

Allowing slow warmth to envelope within and without lost eyes wide open into dancing flames, her mind wandered to distant campfires and of memory images of a littler Abby, Stephen, and Matt's cancer treatments, then, to the dramatic romance with David. As though viewing clips of a movie, someone else's life, images and emotions arose, then faded. Visions of childhood church doings with family, community matriarch Gran, then Father's quiet passing, which brought a changing new era with Mother, and Aunt Diane, two inseparable old gal sister pals. It had been a long wild journey of inner and outer turmoil, the drama of it all, still unbelievable. Strange otherworldly journeys and menopause made those early church expectations and truths seem cloistered now, and of tiny minds. Yes, truth is always stranger than fiction. The road ahead lay still unknown and times for new major life changes were rapidly drawing near. Navi hoped that when the time came, there would be no looking back on the past with sorrow or regret. A raven hailed outside in passing, warning of magical encounters.

"You are not the first, nor the last of the seekers to live through the dark night Navi Anna Jehanne. You cannot see, with your limited human eyes, the outcome, the goal, the inevitable evolution of your soul's journey, where you will experience profound joy in discovering your authentic, true nature."

"Who are you?" No one answered over the din of a post tequila sleep interrupted headache.

Squinting eyes, strained to focus on the misty matronly apparition before her. The tiny old gal, picking up on her thoughts, assumed a welcome invitation, and so, was slowly taking on physical form. An old multi-coloured ankle length skirt exposed an ankle bracelet of sinew and beads atop worn weathered pudgy feet. Old shawl or small woolen blanket covered her shoulders, and bare, sagging, crone breasts. A turquoise amulet stone hung proudly manicured over her heart, with a thin leather string necklace. Long greyed hair, loosely tied back and up in a bun, tendril bangs wisped and curled around her striking blue eyes and contrasting old light brown leathery skin. Bold white crone hairs waved on a wrinkly chin and under nose, danced and flowed as she struck a match and lit an old corncob pipe. Apparition smoke was puffed; thin trails spiraled upwards, carrying distinct smells of tobacco, mixed with sweet musky aromas.

"How do you do, woman child? Some called me Crazy Annie. This was my home long ago. I landed here some time ago. When the great migration, trail of tears, I got tossed into the mix, on account of my being somewhat of a medicine woman. Can't say that I was much of a medicine woman, as in knowing what plants were for what, but more so, because as a young woman, I could see and talk with the spirit world. Guess I was a bit of a misfit, even back then. Can't say for certain where the darker skin came from, didn't know my momma, or any of my family. Was raised in an orphanage, until I was old enough to go out and work housekeeping, for rich white folks. Did consulting for those that wandered by at night and through the back door of the servant's quarters. Never asked for money; knowing those that came didn't have a penny to spare. Just felt good helping out. Anyway, the woman of the house was sure I had eyes fixed on her son, so when the Indians and Blacks were being gathered up, she tossed me into the mix. Couldn't say that I was Indian and couldn't say that I wasn't. The woman of the house told the census takers that I was Choctaw, though I can't imagine where she got that. Fact was, I wasn't much like them at all. They were strong proud people, and most

of them lived far North West to where I grew up. I was just strange, and looked as though I could pass for Indian. Guess it was enough for them.

I don't know how so many of us survived that God forbidden journey. Many souls were lost to the other side, many you could just see in their eyes that their souls were lost in sorrow, when loved ones died. The first wave of us gathered on All Saints Day, November the first, we set out by wagon, but winter had other plans. Floods and snow washed out roads and broke our wagons. Food stores were scarce, but we managed to make our way to the ferry docks, where a steamboat was to take us up river, to the Arkansas post. We stayed there for weeks, doing what we could to stay alive, waiting for the frozen river to thaw and shift. Not allowing us to wander off and hunt, they gave us turnips and corn and rationed hot water.

When we finally arrived in Little Rock, the movement had already been called the Trail of Tears by some newspaper reporter, on account of just about everything that they had owned was stolen or burned down and of the many, many deaths and deep sorrow. Every day the old and weak died off from hunger, heartbroken. I spent many days wondering about the white evils of George Washington and his gang of greedy officials. In the newspaper, we were told that he said that it was an honourable cultural transformation, a relocation program, in answer to land treaties. Although, it was all invasive and intruding to civilizations in the Deep South, white people settlements were growing and simply didn't want to share the land and resources. There were Blacks thrown in too, maybe I had Negro in me, maybe, I don't know. Thousands and thousands traveled, thousands died along the way, so much death and sorrow, day after day."

Navi shifted, stretching legs gingerly out, transfixed, not wanting Crazy Annie to stop or leave. Sure that she was simply lost in thoughtful memory and staying, she reached over to the fireplace and added an all-nighter log. Dawg gently snored. Navi wrapped old shawl tighter, cold feet under Dawg's blanket, canine body heat soothing frigid toes.

"You see young woman, many a soul comes to this earthly life with challenges unimaginable. Little Rock is where old Reverend O'Neil took a liking to me. He was a self-appointed missionary of sorts who traveled many lands, openly compassionate to the Indian. He registered me as his assistant on account of the fact that I could read and write some and because I could cook and launder clothes. A kind man, a fair man, who took no liberties with my body, always made sure that I had good food and clean lodging; Most of which I readily shared with the old, and the children. After a month in Little Rock, he got papers of transfer from his church. We traveled for months northward to New York City, where his wife and two small children lived. I did not like the city, so stayed within, tending to children and family care. After a month there in their tiny cold apartment, we all set out for northern Canada. He was to set up a mission in the wilderness. His bland quiet wife and children were dutiful, never a smile shown from eyes or mouth.

We had only been here a year or so, when he took to the consumption and died. The following spring, his wife took the children back to New York. I stayed and married a handsome Algonquin Lumberjack. He too died too soon after our first-born arrived, still and cold, in death. It seemed as though I was born alone, grew up pretty much alone and lived most of my life alone. I'd likely have lost my soul to the many heart breakings, except that the spirit world kept me alive, and on the right path.

So you see, young woman, there have been many Masters, Shamans and seekers before you, who lived and encouraged the dark night, knowing on some level that it really is a re-birth. However, to the 'you' now, though you still are to heal your thoughts and emotions, know that I have been with you even though you could not see me. I have shared all of those painful emotions you have felt. I know and share those wondrous memories mixed with joy and sorrow of the love you had and lost. You still feel abandoned and traumatized as though, with Christ on the cross, as though, we have abandoned you as your loved ones have abandoned you. I assure you, all this and more have I felt and transcended. We in spirit world stand with you."

"Wow, you are such a beautiful woman and strangely familiar. I thank you."

"You may be consoled to consider this introduction as another initiation, a house cleaning prior to admittance or new relationship with the higher mind, the God Mind. The dark night was pre-ordained. You innately seek oneness with the Angelic realm, the God Mind. This is because this higher state of being is your natural state of being. This is who you really are as a spirit being. In your humanness, I know how profoundly alone you still think you are, and how still, you do not feel as though you belong anywhere, and that you do not fit in. Your faith was once strong, and will be, again. You have been a profoundly loyal companion for your loved ones. You innately understand the laws of nature and of the raising of your being into that higher power. Soon you will be moved to work it, through service to others. Yet, after all you have given of yourself, how you have learned of the magic of life and who you can be, you are still painfully left out, with no home to call your own. Now, the work in your day that inspires and expands your soul, shows that you are on the outside of the 'Other side' and outside of normal human life. I know that you are still handicapped somewhat in your longing of your old way of living, your habits and loved ones.

I know your mind. I also know your heart and soul Navi. I know that above all, you long to know stability and love again. You still battle guilt, confusion, and loss. Your light was dim amidst devastation. And Navi, all of this within an alien land. What to do? Yet, all who know you, know your potential, as you saw their divine potential, and they actually envy your light, your way of being, and yes, your path. Even now, as I speak to you in this transition time, between your old ways of life and so many new opportunities, they do not understand how you have cried when alone and how you continue to reverently pray. This time of solitude is valuable. You have always known aloneness to a certain extent Navi, and you have come to accept this as par for living the personality of you, and for the sake of your child. It will all come clear. You will simply 'know' the divine presence that comes into your space; strong, calm and softly, it will fill you. Your mind will fill with light. Your heart will 'know' and exude peace. Like a wave of warm loving light, the pain dissipates, transitioning to higher and finer frequencies throughout your physical body; flowing in from your crown, down and up your spine, your mind, your bones, your cells, your skin. All that is. As is above, so is below.

Then, in the days to follow, calm waves bringing the joy of being alive, and the inner freedom that allows you to become — transformed. Your old ideas about who you were had to be dissolved, to allow room for the new and improved state. Your suffering was magnified because you had residues of misconceptions from old experiences and yet, when you actually looked at them, you found that they did not originate from you at all, hence, do not belong to you. On and on through life, you accumulated bits of information about the world around you and who you were, from others, that blocked your growth, to varying degrees. Now you are making the transition of knowing who you actually are and what enlightenment is actually about? Do you get this?"

"Yes."

"As the energetic power of painful experiences and thoughts dissipate, you see that it is these illusions of suffering that are the root or the crux. This is the dawn of your new life. And yes, as it arises, continue to Dissolve, Dissolve, Dissolve... you know what to do. You also know that as you dissolve within, you dissolve for all. Navi, you now walk and see with new eyes, living new life, and allowing your true nature; that of continuing to intuit the divine within others, to inspire and comfort. Your dark night of the soul is over.

I part with this; acknowledge all of your wonders, love and magic of the past, it will show you the way. Do this in gratitude, even for the most seeming painful occurrences. As you practice this skill, clarity will come as well as the confidence you re-claim anew. In doing so, the Divine flow aligns again, stabilizing you for opportunities, and calm assuredness for challenges yet to come."

"I wanted to show a man of sensitive and noble character born for religion who comes to throw off the orthodoxies of his day to go out into the wilderness where all is experiment and spiritual life begins again."
Mary A. Ward

Chapter 23 ~ Going Om Home

Winter grey days abruptly turned into a wet spring morning. Daybreak mist exposed budding leaves, and the first wave of insects. Delicious fresh coffee aroma warmed a chilly morning, more than a daily ritual; it accompanied that favourite pair of blue jeans, which she had taken to wearing for days at a time. Perched on the tiny town's coffee shop old wooden deck steps, warmth of fresh spring air teased of winter-melt, exposing earthly humus dirt.

Navi tried not to gawk, as a half-breed mom scolding a gorgeous little girl. Little brown-eyed indigenous goddess pouted her lips, folding and unfolding arms under stern defiant eyes she hesitated, in hurt opposition. The standoff ended abruptly and little goddess dismissed, as mom's attention turned to answer a bleeping cell phone. Little brown-eyed goddess and angelic sun child turned on heel; hand waved shaking off her terse mother, and danced off into the nearby trees. Navi smiled. Children had the ability to spontaneously use their imagination to forget what was bothering them, and could easily be inspired by a blade of grass, tree, feather, or a bug. Hiding behind a juniper bush the brown-eyed angel nature nymph goddess girl starred, surmising intuitively that there was more behind the old white woman's causal demeanour.

A crow perched within the branches far above, fluttered shimmering black wings, tilted head from side to side, eyeing both her and nature angel girl. An early monarch butterfly flutter danced, enticing little nature goddess nymph into play.

Abby daughter memory surfaced; a sidewalk squatting toddler, tiny pudgy finger scraped an old crusted piece of bubble gum, then popped it into her mouth, before Navi could intervene. A naked nature nymph, pretending to sway with the trees in a warm summer breeze, as sunshine caressed her corn silk hair. Where did the time go? Despite adult challenges of city life and the world of academia she was now immersed in, a renewed pride of the grown-up she was turning out to be, blossomed.

The tiny town consisted of a mishmash of red necks, hippies, dislocated natives and city people seeking rural life, transient lumber labourers and miners. Though the majority of the pre-Cambrian shield quartz crystal mines had been long flooded and closed, a handful of people still eked out a meagre existence. The two lane road that passed through town held one stop sign, rarely adhered to by locals and long distance truckers, save for once weekly trains, which halted everything in town for a half of an hour. For two months each summer, city tourists descended upon the area's massive provincial campground park system and resorts, driving up already overpriced store goods to outrageous realms. Locals tried to stock up before Easter. The highway ran through town, crisscrossed by train tracks over top a raging river. Average resident population of twelve hundred shrunk indoors during summer as mosquitoes and black flies descended. Even the deer and moose retreated to deeper bush to escape the swarming madness. Tourist clad in yuppie outdoor gear and chemical sprays, ventured in and onto park trails, canoed river and lakes and hunted wildlife with expensive cameras dangling from their necks. It had been a mild winter, which meant little animal die off, meaning that the coming fall would bring local hunters a plentiful hunting bounty to feed their families.

A wild female grouse poked her head out of the juniper bush where the brown-eyed nature goddess angel nature nymph girl had been. Navi video camera filmed as the molted winged hen ventured forth, poking ground and pecking at seeds and tender grass shoots. "Knowing this out of city life still exists, gives such a lift. It's the little things given that rock a soul's healing on an otherwise dreary day."

Panning camera upward, crow fluttered his wings, tilted head, cawed, and then flew off. Little nature nymph wandered barefoot toward her, a dandelion bracelet in one hand, and her running shoes in the other. Smiling, looking to mom for okay, camera posed. A light shone forth from striking chestnut dark blue-flecked eyes, giving way the truth of her half-breed existence. Grouse casually meandered, squatting in greeting, unafraid, the light brown winged creature responded with sweet cooing sounds. Empowered by girl giggles, Grouse puffed wings, turning in spiral dance, ancient invocation for lifting spirits to higher realms in ascension. Startled by a speed barreling transport truck passing through town, Grouse flew off toward shoreline and took cover in cedar scrub brush. Scrambling startled ducks scattered then reassembled as a flock of grazing Canadian geese took flight, a chain reaction rippling outward and stirring fish below the water's surface.

Calm once again, nature child turned, camera posed smiling, then she extended her hand to Navi, gift offering the dandelion bracelet.

"What's your movie going to be called lady?"

Chuckling, Navi lovingly replied, "Life Rocks."

"Keeewwelll" she gasped. "So what's it about?"

"Hmmm, dunno yet. Maybe it's just about all the life stories of interesting people I meet, like you, and the magic of life that's all around us. I suppose it is a way of teaching or showing others who have not had the eyes to really see what is there. You know, so busy stressed with day-to-day life, that they don't see the magic that surrounds them. Hmm, sounds corny, but it is just an idea. I just wanted to share a magical moment or two with another whom might be interested, intrigued and maybe even inspired."

"Aim for their hearts. Get them with awesome! Hey, maybe someday I could see it?"

"Sure thing, If I see you and your mom and I have something to show you, I'll give a copy to your mom."

"Kewl."

'Reverence', thought Navi. "I am glad that you are in my day kiddo, have a good one!"

Lighting a smoke, pondering, Navi turned the camera back on and held it out, facing her. "This too, is you!"

Dear Abby darling daughter of mine;

It was such a trip visiting you and wow. Honestly, sweetheart, I have never seen you look better!

I am sorry for all the rough shit that life brought us thus far. But.. then.. if.. life.. happened.. the..way.. we.. wanted.. it.. to .. always..be .. and.. any.. faster.. we'd.. already.. have.. everything.. we.. ever.. wanted.. without.. learning.. to.. just 'be' where we're at and would miss out on finding out just how smart and strong we really are then we find out that life is really just about being in joy and gratitude for who we are and what we do have.

So there is the spiritual Law of Attraction and then there is 'life happens'. Oh! We were blown out to sea, tripped, fell and got hurt - really hurt. Did we give up on our dreams and aspirations? Did we waste precious time and energy blaming men or some other poor unsuspecting soul, or worse, ourselves, and each other? Did we forget life's magic? Maybe a little at first, baby woman daughter, there is the higher law of the universe, the law of love.

I have absolutely no idea what is next, where I will go or what I will do, just have to wait and see what the tide washes in, I suppose, or divine direction. And like you always say; it's all good! And oh baby daughter medicine woman, you are that in spades. I thank God for you!

So, shazam, Darling. Go forth from the world of academia with your head held high. Shake it up, rattle rafters, and roll with grace and laughter. Blow bubbles, walk bare foot in the grass, fart in elevators, eat chocolate, and know that your crazy momma loves you inside and out.

Have a contented kind of Birthday sweetheart! I wish I were with you today and can hardly wait to have you all summer vacation.

Loving you all ways,

Mom!

P.S. A Dr. Seuss quote for you; "I like nonsense. It wakes up the brain cells."

P.S.S. I am so lucky to have you as a daughter!

Navi settled into the cabin with a fresh pot of coffee on the desk and a cigarette lit, finished her final oral final exams via a three-hour conference call. Licensed and soon to be officially ordained, thoughts turned to the actualities of the vocation in service. It was an odd conundrum for one with such a powerful aversion to organized religion and doctrine, to now be considering a final call to the vocation. A haunting shadow from the distant past, skittered conscious thought.

Longing to set her spiritual psyche and soul free, confession shared with Pastor Rene.

"Well Navi, it's my experience that those in the dark night of the soul and those on the doors of death have different priorities."

"Yes, I have been contemplating that. When we take the much needed time and space to process life, we find that higher order to life. Well, most of us. We lucky ones, find out what really matters; family and loved ones. Rest assured that the former men in our lives and all of our significant others, have their own spirit guides and angels. They will too, one day, find those higher truths."

A thoughtful Navi sat in quiet contemplation, blues, oranges and yellow flames danced, casting a shadow against a magnificent magical expansive night sky backdrop. Cool breezes caressed her hair and skin, drawing her shawl tighter in. Distant emotionless objective images flashed Robert, as being the one who inadvertently rescued dislocated her and Abby. "I remember Robert's strange wisdom that he blurted after listening to my plight, "What the fuck is the matter with everyone? Are they all fucking possessed? It's like something dark entered their stupid fucking brains and they listened to that shit. Overwhelmed and devastated at the time, I had just sat there, embarrassed and ashamed; an emotional basket case. He compassionately switched his tone."

"Ah, Navi, don't be so god dammed hard on yourself. I have seen this before. It usually starts with one who needs a drinking or pot smoking companion. After a time it starts to fuck them up, as misery and alcohol and drugs do, so, they need company and initiates. Darkness loves that shit, get the unsuspecting bastards while they're partying and being social, then the next thing you know, their lives are getting all messed up beyond recognition. The loved ones love them, so keep trying and loving until either the crap really hits the fan or they just cannot take it anymore, and somebody bails. There is no pay cheque, debt is going out the roof and resentment and fear grows like wild fire. David's still fucked up. You can't save him and you can't fix this. It is just all fucked up and it's nobody's fault, so don't you get all fucked up too. You've got a kid to look after. She's getting ready for college soon and shit she's got a good mom. So just consider my door as always open, so just go, move some shit into my cabin and chill."

"I didn't think I had anywhere else to go, Abby needs some semblance of stability, so I humbly accepted your offer. Robert, you are a Rogue Angel! You know that?"

He crimson face flipped a hand, dismissing the compliment then said, "Frankly, I am surprised at David."

"Why?"

"I don't give a flying fuck about what you think you did wrong in all of this or what you think you didn't do right, it takes two as a couple to navigate life's shit storms and those men of yours choose a copout path over you and family. Guys in my circle, this is how we were raised and how we roll; a man's' women, family, house, and finances come first, over hobbies, alcohol, sex and hanging with buddies."

It had sounded harsh and contrary to a higher truth. Thinking on it now, the David situation had deeply hurt and thankfully, the sting of it was finally dissipating."

Navi's thoughts turned to the shadow haunting thoughts that still hinted and pointed toward some distant unforgivable sin, stomach churning, in unconscious distant regrets and mistakes.

Navi and daughter shifted to etheric awareness communication. Abby was sending telepathic adventurous imagery of a European vacation experience with her dad. Assured promises that she would be home soon, for summer vacation. Then the phone rang, its rarity startled.

"Navi, just thinking, I am offering you the Pastor of the church position, if you want it. I really have to chunk down my workload, and I can't think of anyone I'd rather have. There's no hurry, just let me know before summer is done. Pray for the highest good of all outcomes, and watch it magically unfold."

"Thanks Rene, I can tell you right now that I really don't think that being a Church Minister is my bag, but thanks so much for asking."

Wrapped in the arms of Soul Skin Tom, firelight flickered, as a slow passionate breathing in joyful sexual unison brought a wondrous calm wave washing through her soul. Tingling sensations of skin on skin, breath rising and falling in coupled oneness, stirring long lost intimacy soul longings, born and grown only in the love of another living soul mate. Stirring midnight satisfied awake, Navi rolled over, contemplating how life had become oddly more joyful. Unknown chapters lay ahead, alone, without solid prospects, yet strangely content in sensing the awareness of Spirit world friends hovering, and in smiling validation, had been with her all along, guiding and protecting her, bringing her to this junction in life. Gran's ghostly hand stroked Navi's hair as a wave of grandmotherly love washed and mingled with Soul Skin man's essence.

A thesis grew into a finished textbook manuscript that manifested as a published textbook. A small scholarly publisher, yet it was officially published, nonetheless. Proceeds would roll back into the school's scholarship funds, Navi's thank you gift for her own scholarship. Fulfilling a Ministers role meant shoes too small, as traditional community minds expected a missionary saint, not an otherworldly journeying misfit. There in that space of oneness with the divine and the all that is, Saint Francis of Assisi had said, "I have been all things unholy, if God can work through me, he can work through anyone."

The last insight to her soul freedom was shifting closer to conscious awareness.

Abby jumped off the small commuter bush plane, long hair dyed city red auburn, celebrity sunglasses lifting over her nose and wide grin. Many a moment of pure love glanced between the two.

In the evening following an afternoon of deck sun bathing, mosquito swatting and catch up chattering, life had come full circle. Abby's foray into the world of academia was also shifting. A cornrow haired hippie chick, inspired, was off in to the far northern wilderness with a group of her own kind, autumn harvesting and foraging for foods; foreign to Navi's' imaginings, yet leading spiritual ceremonies.

"Hey Ma?"

"Yea Abby amazing medicine woman daughter?"

"Been thinking. Have you been keeping a private journal all these years by any chance?"

"Umm, yea, why?"

"Hmm, thought so. Just thinking you ought to send that off to the textbook publisher dude and have it published, as well. Sure would make for an interestingly moving read."

"Oh, I don't know. No. Not only would I not be comfortable with my most private life aired in public, I can't imagine anyone being interested in it."

"Think about it, it's topical for your generation, finding an authentic life."

"No, journal writing long into winter nights was a last resort sanity activity. It's merely sacred space living life, in communion with the other side spirit world, while occupying a mad menopausal mind.

"Well Mom, you told me once, that story telling is the best way to teach, to show those who have the eyes to see, how life is lived in other ways, the magic of communion within spirit worlds. It has been said that the true spiritual master, the measure of a sage, that those facing object poverty, the isolation of their own mortality, are closer to God than the rest of us."

"My God, who are you old wise sage medicine woman. What have you done with my rebellious party animal daughter? No, I said, but thank you for trying to come up with ideas."

Washing dishes while Abby snuggled old Dawg, Navi thoughtfully pondered the possibilities. Images surfaced of childhood spirit communion during church, then somewhere along the line; revulsion of church doctrine. The adage 'My will, thy will' was often a confusing conundrum. She had loved her work in social services, and in retrospect, while losing that job was a grave loss; the system had changed so much that she could not have stayed.

A new understanding was emerging of how the universe worked. It was one thing to know of the spirit world, another to have spiritual morality and principles, and another to understand her role. Beyond menopause awaited authentic wisdom that brought forth strange new internal wiring, heightening the senses, as hormones and rapid firing neurons with the inability to tolerate insincerity from others, grew. Perhaps it was now knowing that time in an earthly existence was indeed short, someday she would be making her journey to the other side, joining ancestors, Mother, Father, Aunt Diane, Gran and other spirit friends.

Soul inventory still seemed more important than livelihood. Arising from that thought, she now wanted only to make amends to David's ex-wife. It was impossible to make the long drive to visit her in person, budget was one thing, and she would obviously be; unwelcome.

Navi called her in on the etheric, and spoke with her.

'I understand and I am so sorry. Please know that I had honestly thought initially that the two of you were closer to closure than what it had turned out to be. This in no way excuses my part. You know, it is funny how things turn out, call it just dessert or karma, but it may comfort you to know that in the end we too were both devastated. I think we've all suffered enough soul sister, so how about we proclaim a no more karma cease-fire? Hmmm, soul sister, I like that. We intimately loved the same man for a time and that has inadvertently given us some sort of soul bond, so yes; soul sisters. And evidently, we have both managed to survive and move forward. I wish you all good things and blessings on your journey.'

A smile slowly washed through Navi's being. All rationalizations now mute, honour and integrity life lessons inflicted along the spiritual path. 'Ah, the trap of spiritual masters; desire and the "I want what I want" conjuring, versus the natural divine flow of life unfolding in higher good and right order.'

Navi turned to her computer, a postgraduate doctorate application form appeared in e-mail inbox. Instantly inspired and jazzed, she donned her old shawl, and with coffee and smoke in hand, began.

Soul Skin, an uncommon soul journey, doctorate thesis.
Dedicated to: Abby, my Medicine Woman daughter.
From the bottom of my heart and soul, I thank God for you. Your own journey and wisdom lives on into the world. Your soul, your character, has

always been, will always be, my angel blessing. If I do not receive your postcard from some tropical coastal dream, I shall look for you with spirit eyes my love!

A cold wind blew bits of snow and icy tendrils into her neckline, swinging around and seeking entry under lower back parka and wrist cuffs. A half-moon slid in and out of cloud cover, while imagery of a thunderbird rising above the lake surface mingled with white wolf. Loon family echoed their calls, gathering to a tiny bay nest for the night. A few more weeks and Canadian Geese would be in flight, seeking southern warmth. A knock on the cabin door startled nerve endings into alarmed heart pounding shatter. Another rap registered in her brain that someone was actually knocking on her door. No one ever came to the cabin; being ashamed of the humble living space, people were never invited in. The new next-door neighbour stood with gorgeous prepubescent daughter in tow.

"Hi, I'm sorry to bother you, but my daughter wanted to ask you a question about your text book."

"Oh, sure", regaining grace at the shock of having someone at the door, then actually inquiring about her work.

"Um, just wondering how many book and video blog fans you have."

Navi chuckled, "Well, I have one member in my fan club that I know of."

Head tilting, "Who is that?"

Navi's eyes turned downward to tail wagging happy company greeting Dawg. Neighbour daughter gasped, glancing at her mother for confirmation, for clarification.

Her socially graceful mother grinned then extended a hand in formal handshake introduction. "Hi, my name if Jill, and this is my daughter Roxy, so nice to meet you."

Daughter tisk blurted, "God, how come you only have one fan?"

"I loved writing the text book and doing the video blogs, I didn't say I was any good at either."

"So Gran? What do you fine folks think of the postgraduate doctorate thesis? What would you wish me to do with it, or not?"

"Teach, Professor Navi. Shall I dictate a few thoughts to ponder?"

Smiling, Navi replied, "By all means."

"The following is a list of what we in the spirit world; meaning your dead loved ones, ancestors, guides, guardian angels and the rest of creation wish for you to wrap your mind around:

-You already are spirit – God- Creation, so own it!

- We are not dead. Physical death passage is a natural re-birthing process.

-We, who have passed into spirit, are profoundly sorry for any hardship or heart pain we may have caused you. Our passing into spirit occurred at exactly the right time. It was our time to go, but we are never completely gone, and we remain instantly handy to your wants, if needed.

-Hell is not a place, but a state of mind. When a soul is ready to go back onto to their rightful path, there are many in spirit world to aid them, having never left their side. Readiness is in allowing the light of their God being to shine, within and without.

-Physical death is shedding the physical body; a re-birthing into spirit body form as gradually a homecoming celebration ensues.

-Do not waste time and energy agonizing over regrets, mistakes, and misunderstandings, or trying to fathom the meaning of life.

-Life is simply about love; loving yourself, others and life on earth.

-The animal and plant kingdom is a part of you and your life, as are your loved ones.

-Spiritual mastery is finding out who you really are, quirks and foibles, soul longings and aspirations, then sifting through your shadows with loving compassion, and knowing what you want now, being in alignment with your soul and the all that is.

-Keep it simple; love you, love others and all of life and remember to give thanks often."

"Thanks Gran. I shall add those, and anything else you fine folks would like to add along the way."

The binging of an incoming email, startled. Dawg shifted, stretched, yawned, and then chewed at a flea. "Remind me to pick up some turbo flea chemical warfare treatment for you tomorrow, ole boy." Dawg droned a wide grin sigh, circled, in spot, three times, and then slumped curled in exactly the same sleeping position. Navi's video blog web site showed a new subscribers email.

Hey there;

Just looking for a good resource book for a friend of mine, came across your video blog and hey, check out my web site, I have already linked you in. Where can I order a copy of that spiritual textbook? Man, just looking at your blog images and just got to say this, I really feel like I know you from somewhere. I get the impression that you *are* one amazing and interesting free spirit. Anyway, I am rambling so if you can see your way to it, please email me back price and where I can order a couple of copies of your book.

Sam

Giddy for the inquiry, she promptly responded with the school's address and thanked him for the query. Sliding into the computer chair, smoke lit and clicking the inbox, Sam had already replied.

Navi:

Thank you for your quick response I surely do appreciate that. I think I will just be brave and venture forth. I am kind of a spiritual seeker myself and just have an intuition about you. Correct me if I am wrong or way off base here but, I think I know you. I know that I know you from somewhere, some place. I am sure it will come to me in time. No, I am not married and not some creepy weird predator; so don't get the wrong impression, just searching my mind to figure out this strange kindred soul connection sense I am gathering from you. Does that make any sense?

To read a fascinating mind altering good book and allow imagination to wander to the realms of the author. Your work obviously does this. To listen to unique music, transported to the place the artist is trying to paint in our minds. I aim for my work to do just that.

Hey, have you ever felt like you haven't seen someone in a really long time, and you can't wait to see them again? In my wildest guess, you believe in higher meanings, higher powers? To be journeying to far away fascinating places and spaces and that alignment causes things to happen, and as a portal closes, another opens. Do you dream of one day, awakening from a dream, to find that your life is even more blessed in reality, than in the dream? I can tell that your heart is different from anyone else I have ever met, warmly familiar. You remind me of my muse when I am song writing, this lady who journeys with me in my dreams. I had a dream about a year ago. I am convinced now, that it was about you, except that you had a little old dog. Go to my web site and download the song that I wrote and sang. Anyway, that song might have been for you.

Are you Irish? I noticed that your first name is rather ancient, meaning; prophet, visionary, seer. It matters not; just my mind wonder wandering and I sense that your nature lives up to the name.

I'm obviously from the Deep South and now I'm babbling, so I'll be quiet now and just listen, listen to your northern waves, and listen to the coyotes. Listen to the night, as mother earth sings her songs.

Sam

P.S. Sam is my stage name, my old record producer re-named me when I was a dumb ass teenager. My birth name is Tom or rather Thomas. You can call me by either. That is if you would like to stay in touch. I would be honoured and delighted to do so.

Navi lit another cigarette and re-read the e-mail then scanned through his music, familiar, blown away.

Dear Sam Tom Thomas Mystery Man;

Holy Dina, who are you? I found your web site and listened to all of your music. I feel like I know you. I am wondering if we have actually met, hmmm, strange that. Oh and I do understand what you are talking about, spirit mates, I have one too.

Thank you again for taking the time to be in contact and enjoy the read.

Navi

Giddy with the random query, she curled into bed. Dawg shifted to accommodate, his body warmth soothing chilled feet. Eyes closed, yawning, *instantly Navi zipped out of her body, and then stepping out of a log cabin, to a small farm. Pausing to see beloved husband standing looking out over a crop, maybe wheat? It stood, Golden in the sunlight, gently bowed over, and dancing lightly with a breeze. The late summer evening sun shone, streaming through trees that lined the crop field. In a state of reverence, all is good and beautiful with her world. In the reverence of watching him, husband's hair a reddish blonde, a Celt maybe. He casually lit a worn pipe, and as smoke curled and danced on the wind, tobacco aroma lightly carried, along with the smell of him. Filling nostrils, deep breath in, lungs and being filled with fresh air scents of earth and pine, mingling and caressing her hair bangs. She reached sideways, gently pulling away a hair ribbon allowing the wind to caress hair tendrils, to dance and flow. An old yellow mixed breed dog playfully chases a toad in and around his legs. A nearby creek gurgles, water dancing over the rocks. She strolled sensually toward him and then from behind, wrapped her arms around his chest.*

"I can feel you, hear your heart beat, smell your smell of earth. I close my eyes as you cover your hands over mine, then Darling, we are wondrous lost in one soul moment."

"Ah my love, my Celt in the land of heather, your hair smells of heather from the rolling in it. Have you started remembering being an Indian yet? Feel the deerskin as it silently follows every movement of your skin, your braided

hair, just like it is now but jet-black against your sun-darkened skin. A lone wolf howls into the darkness, listening for his she to respond, but all he hears, is the silence of Mother Earth as she sleeps. And so he runs along the ridge, looking for the next point, so that he can call again, his song reminding all other creatures how lucky they are to be able to share their love. We are Children of the Universe."

Navi, consciously aware of his scent, his skin touched, then blended as one soul, shifting slightly to accommodate and enfold one another, then faded.

Moist wet fog wavered.

Close by, light puffing sounds of Crazy Annie igniting her corncob pipe, followed by her distinctive tobacco herb mixture aroma.

"Hi Annie."

"Aye, good day my friend."

Late evening after heavy rainfall began to clear, Navi stood in her back yard, Crazy Annie's back yard in her time and era. Un-manicured lawn exposed an herb and vegetable garden before rugged wilderness, trees in a thousand shades of green, shimmering with new spring life and fresh rain. A gateway path entrance of two intertwined spruce, beckoned the forest beyond. A crow cawed in distant stillness. Navi turned her head upward, breathing in the fresh spring air, clean, crisp, moist and filled with smells of the earth. From behind, a gentle lapping of waves spilled and splashed against the rocky lake shoreline. From the ridge, a lone wolf's howl summoned to its mate. To the left, a campfire crackle, a metal pot slid over a rough granite table. Comforted in majestic wilderness stillness and Annie's company, Navi smiled; turned her head upward, tongue protruding outward, catching the moisture of a fine wet mist, cool and fresh. Metal pot clanged, the sizzling snap of food frying over a hot fire, followed by the flavorful aroma of fresh lake fish cooking in herbed spices.

Joining Annie aside the campfire, "May I assist you my friend?"

"This day you are my guest. Sit. We shall chat awhile, and eat in blessed company and gratitude."

"As you wish, but please, don't hesitate to ask, I am happy to help. I am happy to see you."

"Are you dreaming?"

"I think so."

"As a child, an old Choctaw woman once told me that there were four different kinds of dreams. Each has its own way of offering a teaching, or not. Some of the old most common dreams came when one slept, the ancestors and animal kingdom showing the way to provide food, make tools and acquire the necessities of sustaining earthly life. Nonsense dreams are bits and pieces that leave one feeling un-rested without insight or information that would aid daily or spiritual life. Wish dreams reflect one's desires unfulfilled. These tell you that you are wishing for, rather than living for. Wishes are always about soul and heart longings; for a soul path to go unfulfilled, and if it is about love, it goes un-requited."

Annie removed the fry pot, scooped out the fish, with a hodge-podge of root vegetables, wrapped it in a fresh wet leaf bundle and tucked inside the fire pit between rock circle enclosure and hot coals. Two weathered bone china teacups filled with fresh hot chicory coffee blend, she handed one to Navi, motioning cheers. Sitting back, lifting multi-colored skirt away from muddy worn work boots, she flicked a match and re-lit her corncob pipe, puffing, contemplative. Reaching into her skirt waist, she removed a small leather pouch and unraveled it, revealing four hand-rolled cigarettes, and handed the bundle to Navi. Smiling in gratitude, loosening her own old shawl, she picked one out, as Annie readied another match. Warmed by the fire, Annie slid her hooded shawl back onto her shoulders; revealing dark graying hair tied loosely in a bun, setting bang tendrils free and curling around ancient laser beam eyes.

"Medicine dreams, your journey dreams, are sacred. Sacred dreamtime journeys teach of the spirit world, the universe and other realities. All exist right now, as a part of the whole. Oft your spirit body wanders, looking for solutions, aiding others, touching and communing with soul mates, or traveling to distant stars.

You have been wise to keep them to yourself. Accept them as a gift, rather than a curse, for when the time is right, you will share them with the world, share them with those who have the mind to remember their own connection to the all that is. Medicine dreaming aids the receiver in his or her own growth, as an initiation process and evolving spiritual path, but more importantly, when the time is right, aids the future generations. Another gateway offered, for those who are called, will find you and through you, find, remember and open their own connection. They contain many levels of teaching, most of which will be assimilated and integrated unconsciously.

Here in dreamtime, you find many spirit soul mates, yet in your day-to-day waking earthly life, these soul mates are living out a different agenda and you may not congeal, yet you remain tethered together through eternity, in a love bond. A sacred dreamer is an old soul, a master who has held thousands of lifetimes, all on behalf of a higher agenda and greater plan. A sacred dreamer is a prophet, seer, sensitive, diviner, mystic, shaman, medicine healer, teacher, nurturer and holy woman.

Play, re-learn this skill, this is a take back re-claim your power opportunity. You can re-do a dream now in your waking time, as you are, magic, empowered and all powerful, as wizard, warrior woman, saint, witch, shaman, whatever role fits. You may ask to download into your mind, the appropriate abilities, much like downloading a file off the Internet. Ask your guides to assist. Channel those powerful emotions, guilt, regret, shame, and anger, into forces for good. Since there is 'no' time, when you do "re-do", you change its affects, which ripples back through past, now and future timelines, affecting all who need to be empowered. It makes it easier if you write it out, essentially re-writing that script. You are a "go between worlds", and now you may travel at will, invited to go beyond what is accepted as reality and possible, for the good of others, as lone seekers, yet for the whole of all."

Annie smiled, stood gazing closely into Navi's eyes and soul. Taking face into withered old warm loving hands, she used a thumb to make the sign of the holy cross on her forehead, and then gently kissed the spot, sealing the love bond in proclamation. Go now and shake off all of those times when you gave away your power!

Your cocoon is opening, so shake off the brambles and prepare to fly, daughter, sister."

Navi consciously aware of Soul Skin man, his familiar scent, skin touching then blending as one soul, shifting slightly to accommodate and enfold one another, then fading. Sensing Crazy Annie's presence, Navi shifted focus and allowed the incoming love wave to flow.

"It is time Daughter, to clear out the hunting, and Robert's family, from this place. Then we must do a blessing. You shall invoke and officiate and I shall, like a battery hold this space."

"What tradition am I to work with?"

"All are one. Go with what moves you. Shamanism is the core ancient of religious traditions, you must practice journeying at will to the other side, and within, to understand the shadow illness that has plagued this lifetime. Then, and only then, will you be free of it. Then, and only then, will you be able to navigate at will to travel into sacred dream journey for another, and call in healing, to all that suffer. As you have found, dark night of the soul, comes in levels, each cycle bringing depth to comprehension. This is the sacred scar of the wounded healer. You have been called through sacred journeying, Shamans are called by dreams and powers are often inherited via DNA."

"It is difficult to know
at what moment love begins;
it is less difficult to know
that it has begun."
Henry Wadsworth Longfellow

Chapter 24 ~ Om Home

Boldly, Navi prayed for divine assistance, to ace the College Board Post Graduate oral exams. An hour spent setting the stage for the long conference call. A fresh pot of coffee plugged into an ancient electrical outlet sent sparks flying. Hesitating, holding her breath, the garage sale percolator began to gurgle and bubble, filling the air with delicious fresh roasted beans aroma. Long accustomed to smoking reserve native contraband cigarettes with it's strange blend of American and home grown tobacco, she coughed it's rough inducing phlegm, promising that one day soon she would turn away from the addiction for good. A tacky label donned a half-naked male native warrior wearing modern dark celebrity style sunglasses, his chest puffed macho. She slid one out of its plastic pouch, twirling it around her fingers, lit it, and deep breathing; relaxed. The ancient prayer herb trailed smoky circles upward to the sky, to the Creator, ancestors and the spirit world, sending an invocation for a direct communication hotline to come in and knock their Churchly socks off.

Long gone were those early days of anal and pious church fingers pointing and huffing in indignation that had instigated a lifelong inner battle of shame and guilt of who she really was. After years of research, studying world religions and ancient philosophies, her early church teachings had become nonsensical, while higher truths of how and what the spirit world was all about, validated what she had always known.

Initial nervousness rapidly evaporated as she gracefully navigated each question, surely in the divine flow of all that is. Grateful for each enlightening thought as it arose and comfortably articulated, growing more confident, projecting masterful snippets of world renowned wisdoms into answers, then basking in their candid reactions. Three hours passed by in minutes and in the moment, she felt on par and smarter than her superiors, sure that they were impressed. As the summary gracefully fell from her lips and hung in the air, the Chairman closed the conference call.

Rather than basking in the afterglow of a job bloody well done, Navi's ego dropped into a dark cloud of self-loathing. Suddenly that old haunting shadow bugaboo that had evaded adult conscious thoughts, gut churned, leaving her feeling a fraud and unworthy of any of the credentials. 'What is that annoying shadow nemesis?' Afraid to call it out into open conscious awareness, afraid to see it, feel it, yet knowing that if she were to ever have peace of mind and soul, it had to be faced squarely, and resolved.

In the days that followed, a young spirit man shadowed the periphery of her vision. At first, keeping his distance in vague apparition form, then growing bolder, he began to interfere with her work, whispering interruptions during phone calls, and nudge waking her from deep sleep.

"Okay, enough is enough! Who are you and what do you want of me?"

Without word, he simply intimated a wave of warm familiarity. His spirit form sat upon the bed beside her, then spoke with panicked urgency, inaudibly garbled as though through water, or a metal tube.

"I can't understand you. Can you slow down, or find another way to communicate with me?"

Calming, he loving embrace snuggled into her, forming a whisper in her ear "I love you."

"Who are you?"

He stood up, turned and faced her squarely, bringing his full physical form into view. The young sandy blonde haired man was not only stunningly handsome, his piercing blue eyes radiated joy, his casual demeanour emitted waves of divine charm. She had always seen and often spoke with spirit people, but this young man was so much more real, alive and interactive. As though Abby was home and sharing one on one time, she startled at the comfortable happy go lucky, wise and fun loving approach. As though reading her mind, in affirmation of the familiarity, he did a dancing jig and boyish sidekick, which clicked from within, soul recognition. She now recalled having seen the boy off and on over the years, sensing his loving presence, and knowing him as her unborn son.

"Oh my God! Are you my unborn son, before Abby? Can I ask you some questions before we get to yours?"

With absolute full clarity he raised a hand slightly, and then turning, calmly replied, "Wait Mom, a few more minutes, please." *He turned and* resumed conference with two old men, now boldly showing themselves, in vibrant alive luminescent indigo, jade and magenta robes. Their conversation heard as murmured whispers, inaudible to her human physical ears. He returned to face her, and then causally sat back down on the bed in front of her, one leg comfortably dangling over its side.

"Hi Mom."

"Am I making this up?"

"No" he chuckled.

"Are you my child? My unborn son Thomas James Junior before Abby?

"Yes."

"What happened to the baby I lost in miscarriage, before you? I never have any sense of her other than the name Angela."

"Yes, Angela. Change in plan for you, it was meant to be, though. That one came later as Abby. Minor changes in her physical make up and personality but the same Father, T.J., and Thomas James Senior: our Father. A touch of compassion to grow in you for your work later on, was it not?"

"Yes and yes. Oh my God Thomas, I had totally forgotten all about that, unborn babies, with Abby's Father. God I have not thought about any of that in over twenty years, or of her Father, really. Tom, Thomas, your namesake. Navi sighed; shoulders slouched in grief, unrelieved. "Most of my life, before these past few years, seems as though it was not my life at all, just movie clips, or vignettes of other peoples life stories, not me, not mine, and a lot of silly bad drama. Oh my God, I had even forgotten his name at times, so long ago, I barely remember any of our time together. I wonder why I cannot remember much of that time in my life with him. I do remember Mother Mary coming to me during those hospital experiences, and feeling her comforting motherly presence. Oh, I am so sorry my love. Why do you come to me now? What do you want to tell me?"

"Thanks for asking Mom. I love you. I know how you have been suffering, and I don't want you to suffer anymore."

"Suffer? With what in particular?"

"Trying to go it all alone, all of the time. Thinking that you have failed in any way."

"How so?"

"I want you to know how much I love you. I watch over you, Abby, Dawg and Dad. There are more here that watch over you and are guiding you to the next level of your being."

"Thank you my love. I have been really feeling and sensing your presence the last few days. I have seen you; I know that you have been trying to get my attention. I did not know it was you. Sorry."

"I've been working on that, so that we can chat. No sorry necessary Mom, for anything."

"Why was it so hard to communicate with me? It's perfect right now."

"I had to wait for the right time, for you to allow it, fully."

"Oh. What did you mean when you said that you do not have much time? Are you going somewhere? Going away?"

"Yes, with the robes, brotherhood, and training mission. You will not be abandoned Mom, I know that you cannot handle much more loss. My love will always be with you. Notice how I said that? I go far above, now. Wait till you see me again soon on the other side, like blink of an eye, a breath, an in breath, but in your years from now, you will be an old woman" he chuckled. "I wait for you. Feels like I am talking through an old telephone now, yet I am sitting right in front of you, I touch your hand and flow love through your soul."

"I want you to go and be happy and grow, but I don't want you to go."

"I know Mom. Angels will take my place with you. You can call on them."

"Did it hurt you in any way? The abortion?"

"No Mom! Stop that! Stop thinking that way. It serves no purpose to hurt yourself that way. I know that you love me. You were misled, alone and scared. You were right in saying that Dad did not know how to navigate family life, he wanted a different lifestyle, but more importantly, he did not know how to help you at the time. Mom, there was a bigger plan; believe me, that I was not meant to be in the physical, this time around. Short womb time, it was a calling card you could say, a hint of life and personality bonding so that now at this time, we can openly communicate, commune. I gave you an imprint of familiarity, character and personality recognition."

"I am so sorry love, baby."

"I know Mom. I have not gone far." Navi grieve sobbed. "Ah Mom don't cry."

"Have I failed you in any way?"

"No Mom, that's what I am saying to you, you could not possibly fail, you are love incarnate, of the angel and faerie realm. You have it right, you have had it right all along, and just did not believe it. You have to share this with others who are suffering needlessly, from the hurtful ignorant words of others."

"What happened to you, after the abortion? Is your Dad okay? Is there anything I need to know about Abby? Is Gran there with you? My Mother and Father? Aunt Diane?"

"Earthly matters, matter little, Mom. Assuredly they are gloriously fine, we are all fine, and it's "all good", as Abby says. God how I love her, share this someday. I love Dad too. I have always stayed with all of you, by your side, even when you could not know it. Dad has been through hard times, he had lost his way after you, but take comfort in knowing that his crossing the bridge point is coming, I am directing him to finding you again, so that we can remind him of who he was before his downfall. That is all done, now his mission is to practice getting well and good again. Okay?

Oh, I was your father once, many lifetimes ago, and a husband once. Oh, and my soul was in good care in grandmother love, long before the physical surgery removal from your womb. Not your soul womb, a soul womb is forever and always. Womb is a good launch pad" he chuckled.

"How come you sounded all garbled the other night? How come you sounded upset?"

Laughing, he Cheshire grinned and snickered with an arm nudge into hers, "I got your attention."

"What now love? What do you want to share with me now?"

"I want you to know how I love you now, all ways Mom."

"Is that it? I know there is more that you want to share with me now. What am I supposed to do, to move forward?"

"I will show you in days to come, calling cards, sort of."

"I feel you fading love, I don't want you to go, come back" Navi sobbed, rocking baby Thomas in tender mother love, in arms over her heart, cooing.

"It's time for me to go now, Mom."

Images of billions of women grieving lost babies, comforted by ancient spirit sisterhood ebbed and flowed. As grieving mothers rock spirit babes lost in arms, sisterhood elders rock them in their own arms and beyond.

"Write this in your next book Mom, Soul Skin. I AM Soul Skin. I AM in your Soul Skin now and always, in all ways."

Navi calmed, continuing to rock lost spirit baby in her arms, a lullaby love song, mother-child love song, a song once sung to the women in the death camp showers of Auschwitz. A deeper knowing of how love bonds never cease to exist, never die, forever alive. "I am you Thomas. You are I, one love."

"Yes Mom, that's it. The warmth of love stays, only an aspect of the spirit moves forwards."

"Happy graduation. Congratulations baby love!"

"Oh Mom, such an earth Mom", he laughed.

Baby Thomas moved forward, morphing into a spirit man-child, then stood once again in front of her. Smiling stage ham joy, he gently sang a passionate Amazing Grace rendition to his mother, and then smiling, dipped into a little playful conclusion bow.

"Ah smile Mom. Divine loves you. I go to master stuff now, but I will always look out for you" he chuckled. "It's my job; somebody's got to do it. Write and teach good stuff, Mom. Write and film, loves lost and found. Laugh more, Mom. Time to grow and move on, do only the crap that is fun and that jazzes your soul. That is how you know you are on track. You know this. Life will magically align, when you let go of the past, of the people who no longer appreciate you, and of antiquated roles. Those people do not know what they really want or what is good for them anyway, as you do. Give up trying to fit into organized church ministering, give them the higher work, and make them rise up and take it, or go find an old church system elsewhere, that they can complain and gossip about. Quit futzing around with idiots and aim higher, work with higher souls, they will come, as new doors open. Maybe I will come and assist in some projects. The school beacon has already begun so research more, and then teach as you learn. Oh and Gran says Hi, and know that we all watch over you and Abby."

"You remind me of your Dad, Abby and Gran all mixed together. Do you have to go right now?"

"I have already gone, time is different here, I will explain it but I know that you already know this, and how it works. I stay with you forever; I also go to master now, go to play master games. Somebody's got to watch your ass Mom, consider it done, I am thee men on the job" he threw his head back in laughter.

"Thorns have roses, Mom. That was once your catch phrase. Watch for roses, smell the roses, glad you taught this to Abby, God I love her, she too will find her connections, soon."

"I love you sooo much my love!"

"I love you too Mom. Forever and in all ways, always."

Abby, home from university, curled in front of the fireplace quiet, lost in final school year politics, questioning why her current boyfriend is behaving like such an asshole. The apparent change in his personality and behaviour, was indicative of so many men whom, while reaching a point of maturity, opted out of their own lovely youthful nature, in favour of the tried and true traditional asshole money making machines, as did their fathers before them. This persistent lad seemed relentless in insulting her, and now Navi. It was an enigma, while boyfriend was obviously smitten with her daughter, professing love and marriage, and rather than finding it cute, she, like daughter, would like to take a round out of him, and plotted that they would, as in days of early public school pestering boys; duct tape him to a telephone pole, naked.

Shifting Abby's attention, Navi re-iterated the unborn son spirit James visits.

"Jesus, no shit Mom! I have hung with James ever since I can remember, didn't remember the part about coming into your womb for a bit before him though. Glad you didn't name me Angela again, nice name, but corny as all shit."

"Why am I surprised? You will be light years ahead of me at my age. By the way, I got a tiny inheritance from your grandmother and I just bought this place. It's our home for now, such as it is."

The late night resort rendezvous had become their meeting conference Powwow place of choice. Its deck displayed glorious coloured filled evening sunsets, and occasional Northern Lights. Loons with a side view of ancient evergreens protruding out of jagged pre-Cambrian granite, called to their mates. This night, city tourists cooed and awed at the dancing greens and yellows that splayed across the treetops against a backdrop of expansive night stars. Rene set her cell phone on mute, and then shifted her soul seeing eyes into a smile.

"I have a hunch that you will just know what you want to do, soon. Congratulations on your thesis turned textbook, by the way. All of life is a circle, bringing your youthful demeanour back anew. It seems as though you have grown through many chapters, you have lived many life times, all jam-packed into this one. Oh, by the way, I am leaving soon; I have been hired at a seminary college, stateside. I know you aren't interested in ministering my church, do you want to write me some new text books for my school?"

Navi re-iterated her spirit son Thomas's visit, words spoken, validated. Reflecting for a moment on Rene's offer, then chair shifting, "I gratefully and honourably accept your most kind and deliciously timed offer."

"Mom?"
"Yes, darling'"
"What's for dinner?"
"Road kill."

"Yummy, just like what you used to make when Matt and I were little. What kind?"

"Well, let's see what I picked up today. Hmm, it's black and white and kitty Kat kind of furry, oh and a bit stinky."

"Oh yummy skunk. How will you cook it?"

"Well first understand that you will be ingesting like mind and like soul medicine, you know how only a skunk can hang out with another skunk, only a skunk loves the smell of another skunk, well people are like that too. We need our own kind to live happy and contentedly. And judging by the way it was trampled by what appears to be a school bus, I guess I'm going to have to roll it up, tie it with a bungee cord and bake it like a pot roast."

"What are we having with it?"

"Well let's see. We have cattails, bee's knees, spider eggs, and bats ass and thistle thorns. Sound good?"

"Yummy.

Abby sprawl sat on the kitchen counter, opened the fridge with one dirty bare foot, reached in, grabbed a beer, twisted off the cap, slugged, burped, and then backhand wiped the white moustache foam.

"It used to be that we'd have these bonding moments with you splayed out in front of cartoons or on a stool helping me bake, oh gracious medicine woman."

Abby grinned, burped an "I love you".

"God girl!"

"Ah that's one of the reasons why you love me so much, I'm the real deal."

"Well that is true, a higher truth that I have learned, glad you instinctively know it daughter. I have learned many things in life, young wild woman. Like how to follow your dreams, no matter what anyone else says, no matter what anyone else thinks. Shit, if it wasn't for you, I wouldn't have a new life unfolding baby girl, this thriving no-profit text book business and video blog, oh and an old borrowed shit box pickup truck in the driveway."

"No Shit! Wow! You have done really well for yourself Mom."

"It's a code I live by."

Abby, smirking, added, "So just wondering, since I am sole heir to your vast fortune. Exactly what constitutes my entitlement?"

"My DNA, Dawg, and a pocketful of life lived less ordinary."

"Gee thanks Mom, you shouldn't have."

Abby perched, dangling one leg, turned to window gaze, as a brazen Raven rummaged the compost pile for fresh food bits. In awe, she slowly reached over to the top of the fridge, and then embraced a high-powered digital zoom camera. Eye embedded into the optics, hunched with one arm tightly wrapped around knees, as the protruding lens whined in and out. Focused on a specific point of the zoom and breathing slowly, again the lens protruded and contracted until it found its mark. "Jesus, what an amazing creature, sure wouldn't want those claws embedded in my flesh." Dawg, ignoring the outdoor garden intruder, causally looked up, as Navi tiptoe leaned forward, to see what Abby was shooting.

"Wow, did you see that Mom? That's really cool, that fisher over there on the forest fringe just snuffed a rabbit."

"Oh God" muttered Navi, turning away. "I don't want gory details Ab."

"Look at the imprint on the ground that Raven left! It almost looks like the Mayan symbol of transcendence and ascension. Huh, it looks just like your tattoo Mom."

Navi glanced back out of the window, "Huh, imagine that."

"Looks Mayan, but not, must be ancient matriarchal, Goddess."

"Ya, uh huh, that's just what I thought; Goddess."

"Look Mom, there's a Grouse. Look at his chest all puffed out, doing that circular spiral spiritual ascension dance." She slowly raised her camera with one hand, opened the window with the other, setting the tiny black knob to movie setting.

Navi quizzically raised a surprised eyebrow, "I am surprised Ab. I've never really heard you re-iterate those teachings."

"I remember everything you taught me Mom. Look, your Chickadee has come to perch too, that's our validation that Gran is with us." Abby adoringly gazed at her mother, "Mom, I teach all of those things and more to my youth groups. I could not do that without you. You made a difference in my life, you assisted me to be who I am and now, I ripple those teachings forward and the kids fucking love it."

"Thanks for saying Ab. That means more to me than you will ever know."

"So Mom, when are you going to start dating again?"

Interrupting, saved for the moment, their attention turned to Dawg as he swaggered in between Navi's legs, drunk, falling and staggering. Watching intently, intuitively understanding that something was terribly wrong, he was suddenly very sick. She gingerly picked him up, cradling his small quivering old frame. His eyes adoring, glazed over as his tiny body shook and shuddered, from head to tail. Panting, drooling, gazing far off into spirit world, Navi cooed loving comfort. Abby slid beside her mother, embracing the two, tears filling and spilling, loving and cooing both in maternal comfort. Quivers and shudders rose to a crescendo, and then slowly subsided into stillness, his loving eyes resting open on her soul. A moment of surreal solitude followed a whoosh of cool air and he was gone to the spirit world. Both glanced at each other, aware of the spiriting whoosh of his ascension. Without doubt, he was magically and deliciously happy to be re-joining his canine family, but he would also continue to make his loving presence known to them, for the rest of their days. His body lay gracefully limp in her arms. Amazed and in reverence for the journey transition, yet sad at the loss, a loyal loved one of fifteen years.

Abby gently assumed stiffing old Dawg in her arms; she tearfully cuddled and cooed his spirit journey. Laying him gently upon the dining table, she lovingly brushed away old dog tangles.

"God Dawg, I hope your breath is fresher in the spirit world. Ah little boy, I bless you and thank you for looking after Mom and me."

Without taking time to bathe away the four-day-old body perspiration, and of having worn the same blue jeans and sweatshirt, she patted baby powder under her armpits and nether regions, and then tied her hair up into an officious bun. Navi scratched at menopausal private parts itching, and knobbed legs, allowing a relief groan.

"God Mom, why don't you get something for that itching?"

"I guess. And maybe some hair dye, also. Oh and maybe something to nuke away those crone hairs that insists on showing themselves. Jesus, I go to sleep, and wake up to the damn things jangling away in the wind of my snoring. One of these days, they are going to reach out and touch someone, or scare the shit out of little kids."

"Ah, thanks for sharing that Mom."

"Ah and you are most welcome. Remember, that too, is genetic."

Old Dawg tenderly wrapped in his favourite blanket, the two women walked arm in arm outside and into the garden. Nestled into an indentation mid garden, the plant bare dirt had been worn from days of nesting and sun basking, his favourite outdoor spot.

"We are gathered together today to honour the earthly life of Dawg, our loving friend and loyal companion. Dawg, you have graced us with porcupine quill adventures, skunk stink, underwear thievery and toilet paper shredding. You will always be our angel companion, be at peace and in harmony with the all that is. Your loyal magical healing energy balm will forever live on in our hearts. You have assisted us into a higher understanding of all things spiritual, to see the world around us with your own unique curiosity and enthusiasm; to wake up happy, to greet each new day as a joyous adventure, to be randomly playful, take long zigzagging walks, to rock and roll in road kill joyful smells, and how to lounge bask in sunshine streams. We most loved that you shared our mutual disdain for being told what to do. Your motto; 'don't worry, be happy' will be our new mantra.

Life and love continues and our love connection is also the divine force that connects all of life and knows no bounds. And so it is. Amen."

"Mom, you are a good Ceremony Officiate, Shaman and Teacher. Maybe not so much as in traditional religion, but for some reason you manage to recall the old magical mysteries and you incorporate them in your work. You are real, not a crazy flake rogue and you are not torn between two opposing worlds or traditions. You *are* the new path, a bridge between old and new. That is really how things were before patriarchs ditched the feminine divine. Thanks Mom for doing this and thanks for being you. By the way, I know a lot of women who are hungry for sisterhood, my blog is growing outrageously. I think it is time Mom that we opened our doors to them."

"Abby love, you may not realize it, but you have just magically brought fifty years of polarity into balance for me. I can't thank you enough. God how I love you! Hmm, I remember Gran telling me once that to evolve; everyone must be afforded the opportunity to experience what it is like to feel as though one is not growing for a time, yet we always are. Change is inevitable. Einstein's concept of time is much like what many old masters and mystics proposed, not linear but simultaneous. Circular, but rather than full complete circle, its ends do not connect upon the other, but spirals, ever upward. Passing over an underlying circle below, another one grows over old ones in layers, visiting old similar experiences, never exactly the same, ever evolving and ascending. I see it as a sort of DNA spiraling hologram.

All of life is a circle, experiences are circular, lessons and opportunities come around repeatedly. Each time offers new opportunities to learn and grow. Consider ancient, indigenous and religious imagery and symbolology, circles are everywhere. Emotions and intents ripple outward in a circular movement, affecting past, present and future. Therefore, the universe and spirit world has a very different sense of past, present and future than what we perceive through our earthly eyes.

It is a very interesting idea and I am still playing with it. This is a clue for us; we can "thought" travel backward and forward through our timeline, and seeing the higher perspective, we can intentionally change how we feel about a situation. Effectively change its ripple effects, changing past residue, thus changing our present now moment, thus changing our future for the better.

Basking in Dawg's after ascension glow, "Want to play with it and try it out with me?"

"Wooooa, Mom, how awesome is that! That's really profound and I think I actually get it. Ya, let's play."

Both attentions turned to a Jeep slowly pulling into the old dirt driveway.

"Any idea who that is?"

Abby gigged, "It's Dad."

"Oh, were you expecting him to come and take you for a visit?"

"Yes, no Mom. He's not here for me, he's here for you, us."

Navi's heart jingle pounded alert, frozen as Abby retreated indoors. He casually emerged from a funky new Jeep and strode directly toward her; the twenty-five year distance between them disappeared. His greying beard and pony tail, wrinkles and hunched shoulders showed an adult lifetime of life hard lived and loss. His Hollywood sunglasses hovered nose ridge, stunning blue Thomas son eyes beamed a smile from inside soul outward. Knees weak buckled, heart fluttered, she self-consciously brushed away a hair strand wondering just how slovenly old she looked. Embarrass blushing, wondering looking back into the Jeep for his wife or some other eye candy woman and seeing no one, thoughts reverted to her own greying hair, lack of hygiene, aging wrinkles and postmenopausal private part ferocious itching skin. Suddenly embarrassed, her face flushed imagining the stark contrast of the shit hole cabin she lived in compared to the affluence that was his world. There might be a bit of coffee left, but the milk was sour. Abby had only one beer left, her undies were soaking in the bathroom sink; don't let Abby invite him inside. Hope to God she packs her bag quick and they go, then she can clean up the place and have a bath before he gets back, just in case she invites him inside.

Dismissing the obvious passionate adolescent attraction that she was feeling, she shifted thoughts to stoic casual friendship hostess welcome. He boldly stood boundless, his fresh cologne sent heat passionate waves through her private parts and up her spine, blinding her thoughts. Extending one arm forward to her, he offered a bouquet consisting of two red roses, tied with a yellow ribbon. Grinning and audaciously chuckling, he spoke "Even thorns have roses my Dear, except these here ones; no more thorns."

Navi backed away, self-conscious of imagined bad coffee nicotine breath and four day body odour. He stepped forward. Too intimately scared, she backed up again. He sighed, gazed at the ground, searching thoughts, for words.

Consciously aware of Abby back inside the cabin, window perched, watching the reunion unfold, Navi extended a hand and shyly gathered accepting the bouquet and introductory message. Running fingers over thorn-less stems, tears brimmed her eyelids, touched with the thoughtful, laden with a thousand transcendent meanings, gift. He had remembered the phrase, had contemplated its application, and perhaps understood the foolishness of their youthful parting. Reverent gazing, and taking in the beauty of the roses and sweet aroma, one lost lifetime of love shared, passed between the two in an instant. Their paths had naively been led astray. A forgotten teenaged love bond remembered.

In an instant, Navi now remembered the dark secret shadow, revealing itself in full emotional impact. She had indeed once sought a minister's counsel, after their first baby's miscarriage, James Thomas, and was blatantly told to walk away, to leave, to abort the evil child growing in her womb, to have the surgery that would prevent anymore hell children from being born, to repent her sins, and to leave T.J. alone. The Godly messenger was onto her, saw through her evildoer eyes, and into her sinful soul; a conjurer of magic, unworthy of God's forgiveness and may God have mercy on her soul. The other unborn fetuses could not be buried nor consecrated to sacred or holy ground, and she would have to make other arrangements, if any other clergy would have them. Any child born to her loins would inherit her sin, destined for hell and damnation.

Devastated, yet naively obedient to the ignorant long disassociated sting, she had held out for a time, birthed Abby then rebelliously refused to give up another baby. In her psyche's attempt at retaining any sense of sanity and safety, their parting rationale had translated into 'differing lifestyle choices' and T.J.'s, Tom's not readiness for family life. Initially a pet carte blanch explanation for church cronies and mother, the lie that had become a dark haunting shadowed truth, of how things really were.

In catching the shared painful memory, the same familiar confident, casual fun loving essence of their son Thomas, his hand dramatically extended to hers. Accepting, he drew her into a melting embrace, converging back into oneness.

"I've been such an asshole, for not fighting for you long ago. I've had my financial clock cleaned by my soon to be ex-wife, and my business partner" he waved an arm pointing toward the jeep, "but I've got a bit of cash left, enough for us to start somewhere."

Shock assimilating a thousand bits of information, a lifetime less lived, Navi stared into his eyes, mind swirling.

"Navi, you have always been and will always my soul mate. It's time to come home, let's go find us a home."

"Tom?"

Almost forgotten daughter, wrapped in Navi's Sisterhood Shawl, hooted and shouted from her window perch,

"Wahoo! Epic love fetch, Dad!"

Grinning, T.J. brazenly pulled her into embrace, one hand clenching a butt cheek, the other riffling upward to her breast and nipple. Pushing away, pulling back, "What in the hell are you doing?"

"Ah, that's my girl. I see that you've found your feistiness." Hand smacking her ass, "Now go have a shower, I'll take you and Ab to a decent motel, we'll check in, have lunch, you can go and get your hair done, then I'll take you shopping so you can get some decent clothes. Then we'll go back to the city, the suburbs and find a decent starter house."

"What?"

Another dismissive hand smack on her backside sent a repulsive temper ripple up her spine, "Ah, you're not the Tom that I thought you were. You're just T.J."

"Eh? What's your problem Nav'?"

Navi grinned, illuminating confidence flowing, "No T.J.! God, I can't believe I almost fell for your crap."

"Ah, come on Nav", chest puffing indignation, "What kind of slum life have you got here that beats what I am offering? I can take care of you and I don't want to be alone. I hate being alone. I want what we had before you took off with my daughter."

Navi grinned, turned dismissive then hesitated. "Doesn't matter what that asshole Minister inferred or said to either of us T.J., the bottom line is that you are a pretentious asshole right now and I am not that naive teenager that you once knew. Although, I did have it right for leaving with Ab, I just didn't know that I did do it for the right reasons but hey, thanks for validating it all for me. Actually, I feel good about the whole thing now."

T.J. frowning, slumped shoulders and downcast eyes spoke the truth of his current heart break and emptiness.

"Look T.J. I know what it is like to be ditched, financially drained and alone lost, but you are nowhere near ready for a new relationship or a re-newed relationship. There are no short cuts T.J. you have to take the time and walk the process. And yes, I like who I am now, just how I am, and I actually love my work and my life, just as it is unfolding. No, you are definitely not the Tom I thought you were a moment ago. So no thank you, but yes, thanks for trying, most illuminating. Sincerely, good luck sorting your life out. Everything will work out just fine for you, you always land on your feet."

Navi turned on heel toward her sanctuary cabin, the screen door slam bouncing behind her; side glancing, she caught T.J. leaning against his jeep, dejected yet thoughtful. An alignment had shifted into place from within, as a lifetime of Mother, Aunt Diane, Gran and spirit world teachings finally slid into its rightful place. Sighing smile, with a deep breath in, finally knowing that the dark shadow that had shadow haunted her all of those years had never belonged to her. Merely cruel words spoken by a twisted mind in the guise of a man of the cloth to a vulnerable and naïve young woman. The man was soul sick, 'May you find your peace with anyone else you may have harmed, with God and the all that is in your afterlife journey, old man. There shall be peace between us, no karma, it is done right here and right now.'

Navi beamed soul freedom, finally Om Home, in her own skin and soul. In an instant and while she had wavered, had found her alignment and claimed her power with the all that is, simply as she was. It was a quiet roar on the outside, shining in a lit smile, yet inside it bellowed within and outward across time, gathering lost and wasted energy and self-love.

Turning back to the door and holding it open to face him, "T.J., I have always loved you, will always love you but it is not for us to be together in this lifetime. Give yourself a year to get yourself sorted out, find out who you are and who you want to be, your next young woman will be there, is waiting for you."

A teary smiling grin, "Thanks Navi, I needed that, more than you know. I get it and I am sorry, for everything. I promise I will always be a phone call away if you ever need anything. In fact, I'd be happy to give you hand around here for a week, if you like. It would actually do me good."

"Thanks T.J., I do appreciate the offer, maybe you could have the hot water tank installed?"

"You don't have hot water? God woman, how do you manage to survive?" he chuckled. I'll make some calls and have someone come and take care of that. And you are welcome. And hey, before I forget, I read somewhere recently that the name Navi means Prophet, did you know that? When I first heard that, I thought it was funny but now I see that it totally suits you. You are one in a million Nav. I might be jealous of the lucky man that wins your heart."

Sensing Gran and the ancient sisterhood making their presence known, Navi was suddenly jazzed inspired, anxious to dive into writing the new text books.

Smiling, accepting the spirit world affirmation and in conscious choice making, the proclamation was made to assume the role, "Yes, I have heard that somewhere, once or twice. You take good care of yourself and my daughter, and stay in touch."

Abby tight wrapped the old Sisterhood Shawl, grinning, motioned victory hands into the air, hooted and shouted from window perch.

"Wahoo Momma! Wow, way to go!"

Both Mother and Daughter turned to the computer screen, as both eyed the incoming email dinged, inbox message from Sam/Tom now openly displaying on computer screen.

Dear Navi of the North;

I have booked a flight this coming Thursday with a car rental and accommodations, so that I will not be a burden on you. I have boldly made the decision that I am coming to see you. Please advise if you don't want me to. I hope, hope, hope that you will say yes because I can't stop thinking about you and I can't wait to see you! I know with every fiber of my being that I know you.

Please let me know if you are okay with this as I am in anxious agony awaiting your reply.

Tom

Navi beamed crimson her love life drama openly played out before her daughter."

Abby turned, smile stretched then leaned out of the window then in cutting tension, shouted "Epic love fetch; FAIL, Dad!"

Laughing, added, "You are an asshole sometimes Dad, but I love you. I'll be out in a minute; you can take *me* out for a swanky dinner, a motel and shopping."

"All religions, arts and sciences
are branches of the same tree."
Albert Einstein

Authors Note:

OM home is where the heart and soul resides; within. It is a sacred alignment with the divine, one's self, and with each other. OM, God, Creator or Allah, is that living breathing feel good divine life force that exists beyond our normal day-to-day consciousness. It is a wise, intelligent and unconditionally loving force that lives within all animate and inanimate life forms. It is a force that affirms our inherent goodness, just as we are. It unites us all, through sisterhoods and brotherhoods, and time transcends all cultures, religions, philosophies and schools of thought.

Within each of us there is a naturally evolving powerful force of self-love, honour and intuition. It is an inner wise consulting soul compass that when followed, naturally flows divine love, inspiration, passion and creativity. An individual's spiritual journey is as unique as a fingerprint and holds no ties to one faith, path, culture, modality or era. Yet, like the mysterious powerful forces and will power that is threaded throughout Navi's journey, it is our individual connection to our own soul and spirit that ultimately, when we open our minds and allow, makes us 'One' with God, and the all that is.

In spiritual growth, we come to know this divine flow as a life force and interconnectedness, where we find our own unique authentic wild nature and for many, consciously choose to forgo a traditional lifestyle, for that unchartered authentic life journey.

Each soul's existence and unique expression adds to the beautiful tapestry of the cosmos. The ancient sisterhood shawl symbolizes that divine nurturing, sense of belonging, and timeless wisdom, that allows us to walk in harmony with the all that is, just as we are, and in harmony with each other. Across the cosmos, soul mates and kindred spirits find each other.

Life is a series of defining moments, cross roads and gateways, and as each door closes, in time, new ones open. Always, all ways; follow the heartbeat of your own soul, which is the path of most light and love. Navi is the spiritual soul seeker within each of us. One woman is a tiny divine spark in a timeless sisterhood tapestry collective; all of us are Wild Women.

And so it is.

Thank you for reading this book and sharing in the journey! If you have found it useful, meaningful or positively assisted you in some way, I would love to hear about it. I would be grateful if you are so inclined, to write a short review on Amazon via my Amazon Author page or other site where you purchased this book from or frequent. If you have a moving personal story to share, I would love to hear about it via my web site contact section: InspiredSoulWorks.com. Your positive support does make a profound difference and your feedback inspires me forward! I read all reviews, reader's feedback and personal journeys with care, consideration and upon request: confidentiality.

Love and Blessings on your journey ~ Jan Porter

For Bio, more information or simply to connect online: Via blog: InspiredSoulWorks.com, GoodReads, WorldPulse, YouTube, Twitter, KindleMojo.

Other Books by; Jan Porter

~Soul Skin 1000 lifetimes, 100 journeys.
*YouTube Video: "Ode To Our Ancient Sisterhood: Soul Skin" by; author Jan Porter. This fine collection of images came together as I was writing the first draft of the novel manuscript.
A joy to view and set to all original sooth inspiring acoustic guitar by the fabulously talented musician James Buster Fykes.

~Angel Guides, love communication:
"Someone is waiting to formally meet you! Communicate and allow your Angel Guides to flow comfort, love, insights and inspiration. A wonderful life path is your birthright. Live your soul purpose in happiness, fulfillment and the inspired life you were born to live!"
Ebook and Paperback Amazon.com and wherever books are sold.

~Sacred Space, body mind soul after sexual abuse
"Your body, mind and soul are Sacred Space. Shifting wounds into wisdom and loving life, is the art of inspired transformation. The journey out of the pain of sexual abuse to wholeness is in boldly allowing insights and inspiration to bring forth authentic empowerment, fulfillment and inner peace. Sacred Space offers insights and resources from those who have been there and bounced back better than before. The power of your ancestors and the magic of the cosmos is in your DNA!"
Ebook and PaperBack: Amazon and wherever books are sold.
*YouTube inspiration Videos: 1. Sacred Space, body mind soul after sexual abuse, 2. Sacred Space, How To Forgive, 3. Inspirational quotes with all original soothing acoustic guitar of the fabulously talented James Buster Fykes.

~SHARING: our stories, ourselves, our success
Features 24 writers, a group of women from various walks of life, with different and yet very similar stories to tell. in commemoration of the National Day of Remembrance and Action on Violence Against Women. OneThousandTrees.com.

~ Life After Abuse, a practical healing guide for survivors
"Your body, mind and feelings are sacred space. The pathway out of the pain and shame of sexual abuse, molestation and assault to wholeness is in boldly walking through a soul-healing journey. Life After Abuse offers insights and resources from those who have been there and bounced back better than before. With insight and motivation, a healing journey brings authentic empowerment to the sacred space of inner peace and joy. Shifting wounds into wisdom and loving life, it is the art of inspired transformation."
Ebook or paperback via Amazon or to order wherever books are sold

~Peaceful Warrior Woman a literature fiction novella
"'Young Annish dreams of an exciting Hunter-Warrior's life rather than the traditional domestic role set out for her. A moving solo hunter's adventure odyssey unfolds bringing Spirit World visions, Ancestor guidance, powerful mysterious forces and life defining soul challenges. As the hunting expedition ends a bigger mission ensues, fulfilling an ancient prophecy. In the process, she must face hard truths of a changing world, understand her true gifts, life path and contribution to community and the world. In the moments of stillness where times stands still with heart love and hard lessons learned, Annish becomes a Peaceful Warrior Woman affecting many generations to come. One woman is a tiny divine spark in a timeless collective; all of us are Peaceful Warrior Women."
*YouTube video short: 'Peaceful Warrior, Annish's journey'.
Ebook and PaperBack via: Amazon and to order wherever books are sold.

~ Soul Calling, life purpose in a changing world
"Your soul is calling you to your inspired life purpose in our changing global community. Access the best of your Ancestors, ancient prophecy, the magic of the cosmos and practical wisdom resource tools. Hone your intuition, communicate with your Angels and Spirit Guides and navigate your path with clarity and confidence.

Your existence and unique expression adds to the tapestry of the cosmos, a journey of discovery, fulfillment and living your highest potential."
Ebook and paperback via Amazon and to order wherever books are sold.

~The Way Out, insights and perspectives on sexual abuse
As a survivor, former social services worker, career/life skills counsellor and mother, Jan was moved to write her first book, 'The Way Out', an easy-to-read grassroots self-help book for survivors and those who support them. First published by Whale Publications in 1993, the Morris Pratt Institute, Milwaukee, USA has held publishing rights for use in their Pastoral Counselling course program. Out of print, the second edition revised is entitled Life After Abuse and the latest final version entitled: Sacred Space, body mind soul after sexual abuse.

Soul Works Gifting Foundation:

Books Gifting since 1993. *Your love offerings make a difference!*

We gift donate numbers of my own book copies throughout the year to those who would not otherwise have access to my work, such as; jails, women's centres and other non-profit organizations and individuals. As an ad hoc small group of three women, we also collect hard copies for gift donations.

Most people simply discard both popular and indie innovative books and creative inspiring works, assuming that governments and organizations offer materials for those in need. We know from firsthand experience that donations are rarely gifted and always gratefully accepted. All donated materials are immediately match gift distributed where and as we are able to do so.

For more information or to contact, track us down via www.inspiredsoulworks.com.

Thank you profoundly!

Thank You!

Thank you for reading this book and if you have found it useful, meaningful or the words and love within have positively assisted you in some way, I would sincerely love to hear about it. Writers, Authors and all creative types grow on supportive feedback. As such, I would be grateful if you are so inclined, to write a short review on Amazon via my Amazon Author page or other site where you have purchased this book and or simply the social hot spot that you frequent. A share it forward movement. Your positive support does make a profound difference and your feedback inspires me forward! I read all reviews, reader's feedback and personal journeys with care, consideration and upon request: confidentiality.

Blessings on your journey!

Jan Porter

Quotes Bibliography:

www.thinkexist.com

Made in the USA
Charleston, SC
11 March 2015